HOOKED

Bobbi JG Weiss

Cover Design: Sarah Brody
@ slb-design.squarespace.com
portfolio @ behance.net/sarahbrody

Editing and Interior Design: Bobbi JG Weiss

ISBN-10: 0990360008
ISBN-13: 978-0-9903600-0-1

To
David
always

Those whom the gods wish to destroy, they first make mad.

— Euripides

The truth is that there was a something about Peter which goaded the pirate captain to frenzy.

— *Peter Pan* by J.M. Barrie

PRELUDE: SON

I never knew my dad, though I've been told that I'm a lot like him — my blond hair, my Swede blue eyes, my fascination with swords (I begged for fencing lessons way back when I was just five years old). And my temper. Oh yes, the infamous Stuart temper. Through the years I've tried to learn more than these few surface facts about my dad, but I am increasingly surprised at how little information exists.

Jonathan Edward Stuart owned a used bookstore called Excalibur Books back in the '80s in Old Pasadena, that I've learned. The building is still there, though everything around it has changed. The site is now some kind of chic boutique, barely recognizable as the cozy shop in Mom's old photo albums. Dad spent nearly every day in that store. He loved owning it and running it.

That's it. That's all I know. Dad had the bookstore. He was an accomplished swordsman. He looked a lot like me — or rather, I look a lot like him — and he loved my mother like mad.

It's infuriating to grow up knowing so little about your own father. But no matter how much I asked and asked through the years, Mom refused to tell me anything more, right up to the day she died, which was just a few months ago. Cancer. She always assured me that cancer was no longer the threat it was when she was young, thanks to modern medicine. So what did she do? She developed cancer and died. I swear it was because she worried about me so much. I would bet a year's salary that she was worrying about me up to her very last breath. And I know it's somehow because of my dad.

Thus my dilemma. Mom knew something, kept it from me because it would drastically affect me, and now I'm stuck living in worry because I have no idea what's going to so drastically affect me. I'm sure she didn't mean to leave me in this predicament, but...

Well, back to the facts. My dad led an unusual life. He must have, because one of the few things Mom ever said about him was that he died an unusual death — despite the "Natural Causes" written on his death certificate. She never showed the certificate to me, of course. I had to go searching for it myself without her knowledge.

Now, I realize that an unusual life doesn't always mean an unusual death, but I think it does in this case. I said so to Mom, and still she wouldn't talk, like it was all some big secret. I tried to find out more on my own but had no luck. Now, believe me, when the son of a woman who owns her own research company can't find information, it rings a big cherry red alarm bell, wouldn't you say? But it gets better.

Only now, after her death, have I realized that Mom did try to tell me. "I didn't want you growing up under the shadow," she confessed to me during our very last conversation. "I wanted your childhood to be a good one. But you'll need to know, son. When you get older, you'll need to know. It's all here, just read." And she gave me a fat notebook.

I didn't open it at the time. My mother was about to die, what did I care about a notebook? I presumed it was just another one of her histories on some obscure topic or another. She was always researching something and writing up notebooks and asking me to read them. She didn't seem very rational at that moment, so I took the notebook and set it aside.

The notebook became very important later on when I finally opened it up to find it filled with blank pages. What the hell?

I wish I'd have glanced through the thing while she was still alive. I could have asked her about it. But as I said, she could hardly hold a coherent conversation at the end, and I didn't want to tax her. Now I'm scared. I'm just not... I mean, I should have done something, pushed her harder for information even though she always turned into a brick wall when the subject of my dad came up. Mom was an incredibly strong woman. Even after I grew into an adult, she could put me right back into the highchair with a single look. When she clammed up about Dad, *nothing* could make her talk, not even her adult son.

Now I'm holding her notebook in my hands, and as I said, it's full of blank pages. Well, they're not blank, not quite yet, but the print is fading. Not fad*ed*, but fad*ing*, as in it's still happening. And the words actually fade faster the harder I try to read them. At this point I feel like I'm reading in the dark, like — like I know that words are there for anyone's eyes to read but mine.

See what it's doing to me? I sound like a wack job. But what am I supposed to do? I mean, how can words just fade like that on a page? In a whole notebook full of pages? And what did my mom mean by "shadow"? Why do I feel like it has something to do with my dad? Why do I sense that something horrible happened to him?

And why, *why* do I keep thinking that, whatever it was, it's going to happen to me?

HISTORY PART 1
DAD

Unhappy is he to whom the memories of childhood bring only fear and sadness.

— *The Outsider* by H.P. Lovecraft

Little Jonny dreamed of the giant...

Time to go home. He'd had a lot of fun playing with... who had it been? Oh well, it didn't matter. All of the people in this place knew him. They didn't care if he didn't know them. They didn't even seem to notice.

It wasn't daytime, it wasn't nighttime. It was no-time, and there was yellow weather outside. He loved yellow weather, like the warm expectant hush before an autumn storm. Quiet. Windless. Cloudy but not grey. Yellow. Warm and electric. Air so full of possibilities that his stomach knotted itself in anticipation without his knowing exactly why.

Everyone waved to him as he strolled down the clean suburban sidewalk. He waved back at them, watching as they resumed mowing lawns, painting garage doors, playing with pet puppies. Living their lives. He wondered who they were, these friendly faceless people. They knew him, knew all about him, and more than that, they seemed to care. Strange that he should feel separate from all of them.

And then he heard it.

Boom.

Everyone looked up.

It had been a low massive sound from far far away. The sidewalk under him shook as if thunderbolts were rumbling deep within the ground, rolling up through layers of earth, cracking a path along the crust, hitting the soles of his feet and making him jump.

Boom!

Closer now.

The peace of the neighborhood shattered. Adults, children, dogs and cats all scurried into their houses for safety. Doors slammed shut, shutters closed, locks clicked.

The street was empty. Jonny stood alone.

He ran for his house.

BOOM!

He knew that sound. Why had he left the safety of his house this morning if he'd known it would come? And he had known, somehow. It was just stupid! How could he have been so stupid?

BOOM!

He reached his home.

Home was gone. Nothing. An empty dirt lot.

But it should be there! Why were they hiding from him? Didn't they know, didn't they realize? Everybody else cared about him. Why didn't they care?

BOOM!

Jonny turned and ran down another street, running as fast as his long legs could carry him, teeth clenched in effort, lungs straining. But it was hopeless. The air turned thick as goop, a goop like cupcake icing, smooth and sickly sweet. His feet slowed, he strained, could barely move. The air became peanut butter and he fought, tried to pull free, was all but frozen, heart leaping, stomach like fire, his sneakers mired in an invisible tar pit.

He looked behind him and saw the giant coming...

CHAPTER 1

PSA Flight 702, San Francisco to Los Angeles, en route
November 12, 1989

"—drink?"

Jonathan Stuart started awake, his heart *thu-thumping* in time with a terrible booming that resounded in his ears like the rumble of a killer earthquake. He had recently been told by several highly experienced people what the growling grinding voice of the earth sounded like, and this fading dream-boom seemed about right. Of course, he had experienced several real temblors in his day — nobody lived in Los Angeles without the occasional Richter three- or four-pointer. "Did the earth move for you, too?" friends would invariably ask each other, har har wink wink make bets on the magnitude and don't let on that it nearly made you squirt your shorts. But the small quakes Stuart had experienced had made only low grumbly noises. They were nothing like the awful death-boom in his dream.

The Giant Dream. That's what he called the recurring nightmare that had plagued him as a child. Now after some thirty-odd years it was back, God alone knew why, and it was scaring him as much as it had when he'd been young. By the expression on the flight attendant's face, he had been making noises in his sleep. He hoped he hadn't done anything weird like thrash around or call for help.

"Are you all right, sir?" she asked him pleasantly. Flight attendants did everything pleasantly. Stuart wondered if they screwed their lovers pleasantly. If they went postal, would they kill their co-workers pleasantly? *Only after giving them peanuts, ha!* He ran a hand over his damp brow, disgusted at his black sense of humor. "I'm fine," he told the flight attendant. He said it pleasantly.

She indicated her beverage cart. "Would you like a drink?"

"Yeah, how about a —" He caught himself. "I mean, no. No drink. Thank you. That is, I mean, not a..." He broke eye contact, feeling an unaccustomed flash of shame. He covered it by lowering his head and gathering his yellow-blond hair back into the ponytail he normally wore. He had untied the leather string he used to bind it because he was more comfortable sleeping with his long hair loose. "Diet Coke?" he asked, not looking up.

"Certainly." The flight attendant lowered his seat tray and set down a napkin, a glass filled with ice, and a can of Diet Coke. "Anything else?"

Yes, fork over every one of those grinning little bottles of booze you've got NOW! "No. This is fine."

"Would you like a pillow?" she offered pleasantly.

"No, I don't think I'm going to sleep anymore." Stuart glanced at the seat to his right. "It's not that long a trip."

The flight attendant followed his gaze, her brown eyes full of interest as she regarded the tall package leaning against the seat like a passenger too stiff to bend. It was about four feet tall and a foot wide, cobbled together from various cardboard boxes and lots of strapping tape. Stuart knew the flight crew were dying to know what was inside. They had watched him carry it in — he wouldn't let them touch it, let alone those barbaric baggage handlers — and he had enjoyed their curiosity. "Must be breakable," their eyes had said. "Not shaped like a musical instrument, though, and way too small for furniture. Too skinny for a sculpture, too light to be dishes or electronics, too awkwardly shaped to use for clothes or souvenirs or bottles of bubbly from the Wine Country." So the Big Question remained: what could be shaped like that and be so important that a guy would purchase a first class seat for it?

No green out of my wallet, Stuart thought, gloating. *The lawyer is paying for everything.* "That's my inheritance," he decided to tell the flight attendant. It was the truth. "My uncle died, and I was supposed to inherit his house. Stuart House. It was a landmark in San Francisco."

The flight attendant caught on, as did several nearby passengers. "Oh goodness, the earthquake," she said sympathetically.

Stuart nodded. "A gas line broke during all the shaking and *whoof!*" He let his hands fly up in a whirlwind gesture. "All gone. Just ashes and this."

Nobody said anything, not the flight attendant, not the eavesdropping passengers. Nevertheless, Stuart knew what was going through their minds. They were thinking about what every Californian had been thinking about for the last three weeks, since October 17, 5:04 pm.

Seismologists had dubbed it the Loma Prieta Earthquake. It had been a seven-point-one that had lasted fifteen seconds, more than enough time to throw the San Francisco area into chaos. Television news programs across the country had broadcast live footage taken at the packed Candlestick Park as the quake struck minutes before the third game of the World Series; dramatic amateur footage of a car disappearing into a giant hole left by a fallen section of the Bay Bridge; the gruesome details of the mile-long collapsed section of the double-decker Nimitz Freeway; views of an old three-story apartment building that had, with freakish precision, folded down onto itself like an accordion, leaving what looked like a single story structure with a crooked roof in its place.

The nation had also watched helicopter footage of beautiful landmark mansions in flames on Franklin near California Street. One of them had been Stuart House. Stuart had caught the news footage on tape and had played it over and over, mesmerized by the sight of the grand old Victorian collapsing into itself like a beaten child curling inward to instinctively protect its soft belly, only to find its body nothing but a fragile hollow shell. There had been no life in Stuart House, not when his miserable grandfather Emmerich had resided within its gingerbread walls and certainly not when his curmudgeonly Uncle George had grouched around in the rooms and corridors that harkened back to horse-and-buggy days. *You're better off dead*, Stuart thought bitterly. *All of you, better off dead and rotting.*

The Stuarts were a family of hatred. Throughout his life they had bickered, threatened, yelled and thrown well-aimed fists into each others' jaws. He had thrown a number of punches himself, and had taken a hit or three.

Theodore — good old Dad — had been the nastiest of the bunch. Back somewhere around 1936 Grandpa Emmerich had succeeded in permanently alienating his two sons. Theodore had fled all the way to New York while George had stayed, gradually imploding into a bitter snipe of a man who resented his brother's success at the publishing game and blamed the world for his own failure as a human being. When the ailing Grandpa Emm had finally died, the house should have gone to Theodore. Brother George preferred to make it a point of bitter contention. He had snatched up Stuart House, all but barricaded himself in it, and then dangled the triumph in Theodore's face every chance he got.

Grandpa Emm's funeral had been a disaster. Stuart remembered it in still pictures only, silent snapshots of faces and gestures filtered through the eyes of a frightened child. As the years passed, Theodore's and Uncle George's relationship had not improved, and the brothers' attempts to fracture each other's lives from opposite ends of the country had blossomed into an art form.

In Stuart's experience, few people valued peace of mind over monetary gain. Despite this, and for all his need of money at the moment, Stuart valued peace of mind more. Dear Uncle George was good and dead from a heart attack that had killed him almost instantly the day before the earthquake. *Talk about timing,* Stuart thought. Now he himself was the sole survivor from Emmerich's branch of the family. When he died, the last vestige of Stuart family hatred would be gone forever. That could only be a good thing.

"I'm so very sorry," the flight attendant was saying to him.

"Hey fella, my daughter's house is a ruin," said a man a few rows back, as if more bad news would somehow help the situation. "I tried to bring her back to LA with me, but she won't come. Insists on rebuilding. Can you believe it?"

A woman in a crisp business suit in front of Stuart turned around to give him a tired smile. "I just went up to see my ex," she said. "He was driving on the Nimitz when it fell. He hit the gas and made it past that section just in time. He said he could see it coming down right behind him in his rearview mirror. I can't imagine..." She trailed off.

Stuart forced himself to return her smile. "But he's okay, and that's what counts."

"Well, I think he'll need therapy," the woman said. "But he's nuts anyway, so there you go."

That drew a laugh out of several passengers.

"I've been in Berkeley for a month on a special project," said one man two seats down. "JPL. Some timing I got, huh? I'm glad to be going back home."

"As long as LA doesn't get the next big one," said a big-bellied man across from Stuart.

"If it does, it'll be our fault." That from a college kid way up front. When nobody took the bait, the kid turned around and repeated, "*Fault?* Get it? Our *fault?*"

Several passengers groaned. The college kid laughed. The flight attendant shook her head and rolled her drinks trolley down the aisle.

Gallows humor, Stuart thought. *That's what keeps us sane in insane circumstances.* His own situation was certainly funny, at least to him. *Hey, Uncle George, I bet it was your shriveling hand that reached up from the bowels of Hell and broke that gas line. You must have giggled in glee to see my inheritance burn into a pile of ash.* He allowed himself a smug grin. *It pleases me no end to think that one tiny portion of your eternal torment will be the frustration of knowing that I didn't want the fucking house in the first place.* He opened the can of Coke, filled his cup and lifted it in salute. Then he came to his senses and lowered it to knee level. *To you, Georgie Porgie,* he thought at the little patch of floor beneath his feet, imaging the sizzling domain of the damned far far below. *Too bad you didn't choke on your own vomit instead of succumbing to a nice neat little heart attack. Oh well, can't have everything.* He took a long drink.

The cold liquid spread down his throat, refreshing in its own way but, *Dammit, I want a real drink!* Drinking had once been a pleasure as much as it had been a problem. These days he could only pine for the sweet tickle of a fine Chardonnay or the hot comforting burn of

Courvoisier. He missed being able to forget for a few blessed hours. He had a lot of things he wanted to forget.

He leaned back, sipping the Coke and listening to the shriek of the jet engines outside. They were taking him back to Los Angeles, back to his home, back to Melanie. He missed her.

CHAPTER 2

"Ha ha, revenge is mine!" Melanie Forrester crowed. She happily waved a twenty dollar bill in the air. "Come on, guys, my treat. Or should I say, Jon's treat. He just doesn't know it yet."

Alan Haws, perched on a stool behind the cash register at the front desk of Excalibur Books, looked up from his _Uncanny X-Men_ comic book. His eyes widened as Melanie gaily flipped the OPEN sign on the store's front door to CLOSED. "What are you doing, Miss Forrester?" he demanded as if she had just committed the most scandalous deed in history. "We can't close now!"

"Sure we can," Melanie replied. "Jon put me in charge while he's gone, so it's my call. I'm taking — _he's_ taking you to lunch." She waved the twenty again. "Petty cash."

A short buxom Hispanic girl emerged from behind the American History stacks. "What am I hearing?"

Melanie was halfway to the back office to get her purse. "Don't let anybody tell you there's no such thing as a free lunch, guys. You're about to get one."

It was sweet revenge indeed. Three days ago, only minutes away from boarding his plane to San Francisco, Jonathan Stuart had asked Melanie to watch his store while he was gone. No advance notice, no warning, nothing. Melanie had agreed to his request, but she had done so grudgingly.

It was because she was a freelancer. That meant she was open season for friends — or in this case, a presumptive boyfriend — who casually expected favors when they went out of town. "Oh, you won't have to do much," was the usual setup. "Just stop by the house every morning to feed Foo-Foo," Foo-Foo being the poodle or the parrot or the twelve-foot-long illegal killer python or whatever pet needed care. These friends — or boyfriend — never stopped to think that she might not have mornings free to feed Foo-Foo or spritz the ferns or manage entire bookstores. "But you make your own hours," was the common belief. "You can do whatever you want whenever you want, right?" Comments like that made Melanie want to scream.

She had worked hard to receive a degree in Library Science from the University of California at Northridge, only to discover during her first job at a little Burbank library that locking herself in a book-filled box five days a week wasn't her cup of tea after all. So she had packaged up her skills, mustered up her courage and thrown herself into the wild and woolly melee of Hollywood to help writers and producers hunt down obscure references and amass facts about all manner of subjects for movie scripts, documentaries, histories — whatever projects they had on the burner. Melanie was a professional researcher. She chose her own clients, and she relished being her own boss. But like anyone who had their own small business, she had to run fast and furious to keep her bills paid.

She had been nothing short of pissed off when Jon had asked her to look after the store. She had given in, though, after realizing that he would owe her big time when he came back. That kind of debt could, if properly planned, require some very enjoyable collection tactics.

"He'll kill us," Alan repeated in a whiny tone.

Poor Alan, Melanie thought. *Such a hopeless geek.* Geek or not, he was an organizational genius. Jon managed his store, but Alan was the guy who ran it from day to day. Jon had recently hired Yolanda and her overabundance of personality to intervene when Alan's geekosity level frightened the customers.

"Let's go, *amigos,*" Yolanda said, leading the way outside. "I'm starved."

Alan repeated, "He'll kill us."

"Well, he can't kill me," Melanie replied. "Then he wouldn't get laid."

Alan reddened and Yolanda burst out laughing. Five minutes later they slid into a booth at the Rose City Cafe, a pink building catty-corner from Excalibur Books. It was Jon's usual lunchtime haunt, so Alan, Yolanda and Melanie were known there as well.

"Hi, folks," said the waitress as she approached. She studied their arrangement around the table suspiciously. "Just the three of you today?"

"Yeah," Melanie replied. "Jon's out of town."

Melanie was amazed when the waitress, whose name was Rita, said, "Well," with a distinct note of relief. "Can I get anyone a drink?" she continued in a noticeably lighter tone.

"Shasta orange," said Yolanda.

"I'll, uh... I'll have what she's having," said Alan. "You know, the same thing."

Melanie ordered milk. When Yolanda and Alan both stared at her, she said, "What? I keep several industrious cows employed."

"Two SO's and a milk comin' up," said Rita, and she left.

"He's gonna throw a fit," Alan solemnly intoned once Rita was gone.

Melanie turned to the young man. "Alan, come on. Jon doesn't throw fits." Alan's silence made her add, "Does he?"

"Let me put it this way—" Alan began, but Yolanda cut in.

"Yes," she said flatly. "Sometimes he yells, when there are no customers in the store."

"You're kidding."

"I ignore him," Yolanda continued brightly. "Jon's an okay guy if you don't take him seriously."

"Easy for you to say," Alan said, speaking to her but not meeting her firm gaze. "He likes you."

"Wait wait wait," Melanie said, waving her hands for silence. "Jon *yells* at you guys? You're not joking? I don't believe this."

"He doesn't yell at us, he yells at himself," Yolanda corrected. "We stay out of the way."

Alan toyed with his fork. "I think we ought to change the subject."

"No, I want to hear this," said Melanie. Jonathan Edward Stuart was and always had been a mystery to her. If pinning him to a board with tacks and dissecting him would give her some answers, she would do it. After all, if he had the chance, he would do the same to her. She smiled disarmingly at Alan. "It's okay, Alan, I'm fully aware of Jon's charms as well as his many shortcomings. I've been dating the man for almost two years."

"You like 'em feisty, don't you?" Rita was back with their drinks.

"Excuse me?" Melanie said to her coolly.

"I'm sorry, I don't mean to offend," said Rita, "but your fella's got some attitude."

Melanie couldn't deny that, as much as she wished she could. Sometimes Jon used his mouth like a sniper used a gun. "Okay, what did he do?" she asked.

Rita didn't answer right away. She set the drinks down and then whispered, "He used some pretty fancy language in here the other day."

Melanie winced.

"It was Bitty's first day, poor thing, and in he comes for lunch. She thought he was unattached, so she flirted with him a little. Let's just say he told her to do rude things to certain of her anatomical parts." Rita pulled two straws out of her apron pocket and placed them next to the two orange sodas. "It wouldn't be a bad thing if he apologized to her."

Melanie burned with embarrassment. "I'll make sure to tell him."

"Oh. Oh, I didn't mean..." Rita flapped her hand, flustered. "I'm sorry. You're not his keeper."

No, but sometimes he needs one, Melanie thought. *He does have a definite Jekyll-Hyde thing going. But that's what makes him so interesting. Well, that and the fact that he is painfully cute.*

Rita took their orders and left for the kitchen again.

"I guess you'll just have to take my word that Jon's not an ogre," Melanie said to Yolanda and Alan afterwards.

"Of course he's not," Yolanda said. Then she grinned. "Okay, spill. I've been dying to know — how did you guys meet?"

"In a club."

"Jon goes clubbing? Get outta town!"

"No, it's just a place he used to hang out sometimes," Melanie said. "In Hollywood. A client of his had a really good rock band that played weekends. The audience was getting rowdy and Jon was sort of tipsy, and his friend called him up to the stage to sing."

Alan nearly choked on his soda. "Jon *sings?*"

"Yeah, who'd figure? He's good, too. But he doesn't sing anymore." Melanie frowned. The memory of what happened next made it flip into a smile. "He sang the funniest, most incoherent version of *Louie Louie* I've ever heard."

"I like oldies," Yolanda said, and sipped her soda. "Doesn't that song have, like, no lyrics anyway?"

"I don't think anybody knows. That's why it's so funny. Anyway, I was there with a friend, and I about fell off my chair. When he was done he tried to leave the stage, but the people in the front of the audience pushed him back up. I didn't know it then, but he sang with the band all the time. So he did another one." She giggled. "He did that Madonna song *Like a Virgin*, and he sang it just like she did. I cried, I was laughing so hard."

"Well, talk about your cosmic revelations," said Yolanda. "Wow."

"But he doesn't sing anymore," Melanie repeated quietly. She sighed. "Soon after that the band got hot and ended up touring. He stopped going to the club."

"So what did you guys do together instead?" Yolanda asked.

Melanie winked. "None of your beeswax."

They sat in silence for a moment, then Alan muttered, "They'd better hurry with the food. If he calls the store and we're not there—"

"Relax," Yolanda told him in a motherish tone. "Remember what we said — Jon is not an ogre. If he gets mad, ignore him and he'll forget all about it."

Melanie regarded Yolanda with a jaundiced eye. "Really?"

Yolanda shrugged one shoulder. "He's just got a temper. He's like a kid sometimes. Come on, you know that."

Melanie did know that. She just wished Jon might grow up a little. *Yeah, and here's where we insert that thing about pigs and wings.*

Thirty minutes later when they got back to the store, Alan eyeballed the blinking light on the answering machine behind the front desk. "I told you."

Melanie waited for him to play the message. When he made no move to do so, she huffed and hit the PLAY MESSAGES button.

Beeeeep! "Okay, where is everybody?" Jon's voice snapped. "My store had better not be closed." The answering machine dutifully replayed his aggravated sigh. "I presume you'll get this message, Melly. It's two o'clock. I missed my plane. I was at an antique dealer's shop and — well, never mind. Anyway, I got a seat on PSA Flight 702 leaving tonight at six thirty, arriving at LAX at seven forty-three. Be there. And open my store, dammit. Bye."

Alan groaned. "See, I was right. He's going to throw a fit for sure."

"Oh, don't be *un estúpido*," Yolanda said. "I told you, ignore him and he'll forget about it. Works for me."

In a fit of uncharacteristic bluntness, Alan pointed directly at her breasts. "If I had those, I'm sure it would work for me, too." He shuffled to his station behind the counter. Yolanda rolled her eyes and went back to work.

Melanie decided to take a short walk before getting back to her current research project. Rita's story kept running through her mind, about how Jon had scandalized the new café waitress. How many times did he do things like that? Never around her, thank goodness. She would never tolerate it. *Another triumph for Mr. Hyde,* she thought with a twinge of embarrassment. *Should I talk to him about it? Should I tell him to stop? Does he even know he's doing it?* That was the question that bothered her the most.

Colorado Boulevard in Pasadena was busy during the day, but that's why she liked it. Old Pasadena, where Jon's store was located, was filled with odd little shops and delis, as well as newer stores and movie theaters. The city was renovating the area so there was some construction going on, but her walk was nonetheless pleasant and she felt better when she stepped back into the store a half hour later.

Who are you trying to kid? she chided herself as she went back to work. *You knew the name of the beast when you first started dating him. His quirks are what fascinate you the most, admit it. You're twisted enough to put up with him, right? What does that say about you? Besides, nobody's perfect.* She grinned. *Thank God.*

* * * * *

Melanie hoped Yolanda's "little boy" point of view would work for her. She intended to try it on Jon when she picked him up that evening. After all, he had missed his plane. He was sure to be as cranky as a toddler with a full load.

But he surprised her. He strode briskly out the PSA doors and over to her battered little Honda, toting his suitcase and a big odd-shaped package. The sun had set, but the pick-up area was lit bright as daylight. Melanie could clearly see the big grin on his face. She didn't trust it. Sure enough, "Why was my store closed?" were the first words out of his mouth.

Melanie breezily answered, "My fault, Jon. I took Alan and Yolanda to lunch. You know, like you keep saying you'll do but never do?"

The expected hissy fit never came. Jon leaned over as if to kiss her on the lips, then playfully kissed her ear instead, making a loud smacking noise that tickled like a giant balloon squeaking inside her skull. She giggled despite herself. "Okay," he said. "Pop the trunk."

She opened the trunk and watched as he put his suitcase inside followed by the long package. "Is that it?" she asked, indicating the box. "That constitutes your grand and glorious inheritance?"

"No, there's more," Jon said, and produced a flat item from beneath the box. It was a bronze plaque about a foot square, smudged with ash and heat warped. He held it up, grinning with idiot amusement.

Melanie read, "Stuart House, Registered Landmark something something, 1905 to something... it's, uh, lovely."

"This is all that's left. Well, this, two walls and the chimney. Isn't it great? I'm going to hang it in the bathroom!"

Melanie just shook her head and got behind her Honda's wheel as other cars, anxious for her space, began to honk, their drivers making interesting gestures in her direction. Jon ducked into the passenger seat with his prize and she slowly squeezed her Honda through LAX Sunday night traffic. Several minutes passed before they made it to the onramp of the 405 Freeway heading north.

"How did it go?" Melanie asked, pressing her foot down hard on the accelerator to merge with the 70-mile-per-hour traffic. The car lurched forward.

"I'm free of that house!" Jon said with glee, tossing the warped plaque onto the back seat. "A little paperwork here, a few forms there, but I've basically crawled out from under the debris."

When he didn't continue, Melanie glanced over at him and caught a flash of mystery in his expression as he gazed out the window. "And?" she prodded.

Jon opened his mouth to answer, thought a moment, then closed it. "Later," he said. "First, the house. This is what happened. Dear stupid Uncle George went bankrupt during that mini stock market crash back in '87. Most of the family wealth was tied up in investments, and the crash wiped it right out. Well, that and the fact that George didn't have the brains God gave a balloon when it came to playing the stock market. Anyway, he had the house and some minor assets left, so he cut down expenses, insurance included, and didn't tell anybody. The man was a moron. Thank God the crash scared him into being more careful or he'd have run up enough debts to haunt *me*. As it is, his debtors are going to slap liens on the land the house sat on, and they and the lawyers can fight over that till the Second Coming as far as I'm concerned. I've come out of this mess clean as a whistle, and dear George has been reduced to a nice, quiet, permanent resident in Hell."

"Jon!"

"Sorry," he said, but Melanie noticed that his grin was still there.

"So?" she prodded further. "Do I get to know what's in the trunk or what?"

An expression of deep concentration crossed his features. Jon stroked an imaginary beard, saying in a most scholarly voice, "Vee shall see..."

"Oh, c'mon," Melanie said, "tell me."

Jon shook his head. "I'd rather show you."

"I hate it when you tease me!"

His grin grew toothy with sadistic pleasure. "I know."

More than an hour later they turned off the 110 Freeway onto California Street in Pasadena. Five minutes later they were at Jon's house.

Melanie liked his house. It was a tidy two-story, four bedroom place within walking distance of his store, and there were books everywhere. Some people put libraries into their homes — Jon had turned his home into a library. His dream abode had been funded by the death of his parents seventeen years earlier — they had both died in a car crash, leaving eighteen-year-old Jonny bereaved but well off. But to remind Jon that his home and business had been made possible because of his parents' demise invited a tirade of denial that could shatter glass, as Melanie had learned on more than one occasion.

Jon set his mysterious package on the floor of the den where classics lined the walls. Shakespeare, Hemingway, Steinbeck, Cervantes, Rabelais and the like watched as he moved the table and reclining chair over by the wall to make more room. Then he laid down on the carpet and patted the space next to him. Melanie sat down there. Jon didn't open the package, however. He didn't give it a second glance. He reached up and opened the top button of Melanie's blouse.

She shoved his hand away, but it just swung back like it was on a spring. The light touch of his fingertips along the base of her neck made her shudder. "Oh, c'mon," she said, "we just got here..."

"I know." Another button opened.

"Jon, I have a lot of work tomorrow..."

"I know." Another button.

"You're being unreasonable."

"I know." He raised himself up on one hand and brushed his lips against hers. "I missed you," he breathed, and kissed her, slowly, drawing her back down with him.

The touch of his hands on her body, one pressed into the small of her back holding her tight against him, the other luxuriating in her short brown hair, fingers gently massaging her skull, made Melanie melt. This was the basis of their sexual relationship — he would suggest, she would run, and he would chase and pounce. Some people might have seen it as a sexist arrangement, but Jon wasn't that kind of man. Melanie had discovered, to her relief, that he had been quite willing to wait for her attentions, letting her call the shots early in their courtship, letting her establish the rules. Once she had done that, however, Jon had cheerfully and systematically weaseled his way around her rules, often taking her by surprise. His idea of sex was bawdy, his nasty leer an invitation to fun and games, not sweat and domination. If she didn't want to play, he rarely pushed. If she did want to play, it became a question of *what* she wanted to play. Jon was open to anything, it seemed, so it was usually up to her.

Tonight, however, he was taking the reins. He did that every once in a while, which Melanie figured was only fair. Tonight he wanted to devour her whole body, as if he had been away from her a year rather than a couple of days. His naked hunger made her tingle with lust despite her earlier protestations. It was as if he needed to chart her body all over again, tasting every inch of her and marking his property with nips and kisses.

Melanie felt her toes curl. She wriggled her legs to catch Jon's attention. He saw her feet, gave her that nasty leer of his, and untied the leather string that held his ponytail. "Ah, the toes, the toes," he whispered into her ear. "Mmm, I love a good home *coming...*"

Melanie's toes never lied. Her clothes had already been removed, one item at a time. Jon allowed her to return the favor and, minutes later, with the lights glowing like a golden sunset, the steady rhythm of Jon's body on hers made Melanie shiver and relax in delicious alternating waves. She nestled her face into his hair and moved with him, squeezing him tight.

Funny. She rarely thought about how much she really loved this irritating man. She was usually too irritated by him to think about it. Now she realized she had missed him, realized she had worried about his safety during the short San Francisco trip, realized that she had been anxious for his return. After all, he wasn't all bad, no indeed. Her mother always badgered her, "What in the world do you see in him, Melanie? His family relationships should tell you everything you need to know. He's mixed up, honey, very mixed up. He'll mix you up, too."

So be it, she thought, clutching him passionately. *There are worse mistakes I could make.*

* * * * *

He lay on the floor watching as Melanie wriggled back into her bra. His lecherous grin was unnerving. "Stop it," she said, and turned her back, more to hide her own smile than to protect her modesty. She saw him try to peek. "G'wan, mind your own business."

"I am."

"Ha ha. Look, you gonna lay there with your bare cheeks to the ceiling all night?"

He made a pouty face, the one that for some reason made her think of Kermit the Frog. "I thought you liked my bare cheeks."

She tried not to laugh. "And I thought you had a package to show me."

"I did show you my package."

This time she did laugh. "Jon! Your inheritance?"

"Oh, *that* package." Jon shrugged innocently. "Well, it's not as fun, but if you insist. First, however..." He grabbed his shirt from under the reclining chair and pulled something out of the pocket. With as much solemnity as possible for a naked man, he handed it to her.

Melanie took the ring box. Her heart leaped. No. It couldn't be. She glanced at him. He was smiling a warm, genuine smile, but was it the smile of a man about to propose marriage? She didn't know, and it frightened her.

"Well, open it."

Trying to keep her hands from shaking, she lifted the lid. Inside was a thin gold band with a single ruby stone in it. "It's... it's beautiful," she managed to say. "But why...?"

Jon cocked his head. "What do you mean, why?" The question truly baffled him.

Melanie blushed with embarrassment. Silly her, she had actually thought he was going to propose. She had to remind herself that a gift like this meant more from Jon than from most men, but he was not the marrying type. Not yet, anyway. She had no right to feel disappointment. Still her heart ached as she slipped the ring on the third finger of her right hand. "How does it look?" and she lifted her hand for him to see.

In response, he kissed it. "You're both beautiful."

Melanie could hardly stand it. Part of her was so happy she wanted to burst, part of her had deflated, and part of her was livid with anger at him for putting her through this emotional rollercoaster. It had been two years. Why couldn't he get his act together and admit that he loved her? *Did* he love her?

"You remember my phone message when I said I missed my flight?" he was saying, oblivious to her inner turmoil.

Melanie tore herself out of her reverie. "Yeah," she said.

"Well, I missed it because I went to see an antique dealer in Japantown. That's where I found the ring, by the way." He was standing now, tugging on his jeans. After zipping them up, he ripped open the package to reveal two separate wrapped boxes, one long and rectangular and one small and square. He picked up the long box. "Here's why I went." Jon handed it to her. "Go ahead."

Melanie tore open the stiff brown paper to reveal a cardboard box, old enough that it was more age-yellow than white. She lifted the lid to reveal a wrapping of unusually thick, oversized parchment paper. Loosening that, she came to a layer of oiled cloth. She pinched one corner of it and peeled it away, then peeled back the other side. Her brows arched.

"Gorgeous, isn't it?" Jon reached into the box and lifted a gleaming saber into the light. "The antique dealer is a Japanese fellow I've known for years. He's always looking for reference on antique jewelry, but he collects swords as a hobby. He buys every book on the subject I can find. I figured he'd know something about this." Jon turned the weapon this way and that to let its straight silver blade catch the light. "He told me he's never seen one like it."

He held the saber out to Melanie, but she didn't want to touch it. Weapons were best admired through the glass of locked display cases, as far as she was concerned. "Where did it come from?" she asked.

"Well, that's the weird part." As he spoke, Jon stared at the saber as if mesmerized. "I didn't exactly tell the truth when I said that the plaque and chimney were all that was left of the house. Two firemen found a safe in the basement, a big heavy-duty brute. It was behind a wall, don't ask me why, and it survived the fire intact, so they had it delivered to George's lawyer. I got it from him." Jon tore his eyes from the saber and looked at Melanie. "Melly, George never knew the safe was there. Neither did his lawyer. It must have been put behind that wall by Grandpa Emmerich decades ago. The lawyer was trying to figure out how we could get it open when..." Jon shrugged. "Well, I was fiddling with the combination lock, you know, trying out numerical combinations that might have been significant to Grandpa Emm. I tried the name of his wife, Sylvia. It worked."

Melanie didn't follow, and her expression said as much.

Jon gave her a barely tolerant grunt. "Obviously he'd translated each letter of her name into the number corresponding to alphabetical letter order, right? So S is nineteen, Y is twenty-five, L is twelve, and so on. Add the double-digits together to make one number per letter — S becomes 10, Y becomes 7, yadda yadda. Of course, for S you have to add one and zero so that becomes just one. Anyway, then add the first two, second two and third two numbers together, and you end up with a three-number combination: eight, seven, ten. Well, then he put them backwards."

Melanie couldn't believe what she had heard. "And this just popped into your head."

"Yeah. So check it out." He raised the weapon. "Note the basket—"

"What's a basket?"

"This curvy part over the hilt. It protects my hand from my opponent's blade, see? Note that it's specifically molded to cover a left hand."

"So this is a left-handed sword," Melanie said. "I take it your grandfather was left-handed?"

"I have no idea." Jon lightly touched his thumb to the blade's edge, which looked terribly sharp to Melanie. Judging by Jon's appreciative little nod, it was. "But I'm glad this is."

Melanie noticed a thin line of intricate etchings along the blade. The strange markings composed neither words nor pictures, yet there was a symbolic feel to them as if they meant something particular. "What language is this?"

"I don't know. Neither does Masao. Maybe I'll hire you to do some research on it. I mean, those etchings are chased gold. And check out the quillions — these two wing-like parts on the hilt here. That's gold inlay and, according to Masao, those are real rubies and emeralds encrusted on the pommel, see? Oh, and the hilt itself—" He flipped the sword in the air, deftly catching it with two hands so that he could hold it out, the hilt now right in front of Melanie's nose. "That's ivory inlay between those leather braids."

Melanie didn't know whether to scream or just have a nice quiet stroke. She decided to do neither and remained motionless, hating Jon for throwing such a dangerous weapon around. He knew what he was doing, yes, but she didn't.

His fencing mania had always made her nervous. She was fully aware of his expertise in swordsmanship — she even accompanied him to practice sometimes — but she didn't like how he changed when a foil or saber was in his hand. He became belligerent and somehow dangerous. Early in their relationship she had pressed him as to why he didn't enter formal competitions anymore. He certainly had a collection of ribbons and trophies from years past. Jon's reply had come in a fleeting expression of dismay that was quickly covered by what she called his "stone face." All he would say was, "I've won enough."

Jon had no idea he had just scared her half to death. Either that or he didn't care. He continued to admire the sword, watching the blade catch the light at various angles. "This sucker's worth a bundle."

"You're going to sell it, then?" Melanie asked hopefully.

"Hell no," and Jon sank down into a fencer's stance, flicking his wrist back and forth to feel the saber's balance.

Melanie shuffled out of the way barely in time. He whipped the blade through the air so fast she couldn't follow it *fwip fwop fwip!* and then he lunged, extending so far that the silver tip dimpled a pillow on a chair halfway across the room. He slid his right foot forward and stood normally again. "I'm keeping this," he concluded firmly. "But I wish I knew what it was doing in a safe behind a wall in the basement of that house. If it's a family heirloom, why hide it?"

Melanie had seen enough of the sword. "What about the other box?" she asked, pointing to it. "Where did it come from?"

Carefully, Jon tucked the saber back in its oil cloth and picked up the other half of his inheritance. "This," he said, "was the only other thing in the safe." He unwrapped the bundle and handed the contents to her — a book. Or rather, a dog-eared bundle of crisp yellowed paper between cracked leather covers. The front cover had no official printing on it, just a crudely scratched "JH" in the bottom corner.

"Who's JH?" Melanie asked.

"Turn the page."

She cracked it open apprehensively, afraid it might crumble to dust. "'Personal Log of Jas. Hook, Capt. of the *Jolly Roger*,'" she read aloud. She laughed. "What is this, a sequel to *Peter Pan?*"

"No," Jon said slowly, "but it involves the characters. It's written as if Captain Hook retired and wrote his memoirs in the form of a log."

"So who *did* write it?"

Jon sat on the floor next to her, shaking his head. "That's what I can't figure. As far as I know there are no writers in my family. My dad was the only one involved in publishing. He was an editor at Grossett & Dunlap, mostly college textbooks. He had no talent for creating, just criticizing. And take my word, some of the stuff in that book is..." He groped for the right word, then gave up and shrugged. "Well, very unconventional. This isn't anything that got published, though I can't even say if it was written with that intention."

Carefully Melanie turned a few stiff pages. The manuscript was indeed a log, or at least, it was formatted like one — handwritten dates, times, recorded facts, one after another, entry after entry — but most of it was in the past tense, as if the writer were remembering the events of each day from a distant future point in time. The first entry began:

> Log, *Jolly Roger*, brig, March 12, 1896, about 5:30 pm.
> We were moored in Pirate's Bay, Pan's Island,
> coordinates unknown. I shall never forget the calm
> sea, the sky so blue it hurt to look at it. It was
> extremely hot and humid that day. I met my crew for
> the first time. First Mate Starkey, Second Mate Mason,

Bosun Smee and Gunner Bill Jukes all appeared able men and loyal. The ship was a beauty, a real goer the boys said, and so she was.

Melanie turned a few pages. Subsequent entries began with the next date and time, but details started to change as the log progressed. The exact date turned into the phrase "Next Day," and the exact time was left off more and more until it degenerated to "Later" or "Can't Remember When." One entry said, "After the Fading of the First Sun."

The handwriting was erratic, sometimes graceful penmanship, sometimes scribbles that she couldn't decipher. Several pages contained short scrawls in Latin and what Melanie recognized as Greek, though she couldn't translate it. On some pages, distorted drawings took the place of words altogether. She stopped at a page with nothing but a single Latin phrase on it, written over and over. "*Floreat Etona?* What does that mean?"

Jon squinted in concentration. "I took Latin in high school. Let's see, floreat... that means flowering or flourishing. *Etona... Etona...* beats me. Whatever it is, Mister Jas. Hook wants it to flower or flourish."

"Wow, big help."

"Thank you."

Melanie studied one of the drawings in the back. At first she thought it was supposed to be a dragon, but it was difficult to tell exactly, for the artist had apparently forgotten to dip his pen in the inkwell now and then. Certain lines just faded away, leaving the picture in a curious half-finished state. One detail, however, was fully sketched with some amount of skill — the dragon, or whatever it was with its great toothy mouth and long lashing tail, was eating a man. The details of the man's face were fully rendered but grossly distorted, with huge bulging eyeballs and a long tongue that lolled out one side. The artist had taken great care to show that the beast had already bitten through one leg and part of the hip. The right arm was also gone. Melanie stared with gross fascination, appalled at how hard it was to disengage herself from the bloody depiction.

"Listen to this," said Jon, and took the manuscript from her. He flipped to a particular section that he must have found earlier, for he started to read at a specific place. Melanie saw that the words there were sloppily written but still legible. "'Let it be known that the croc of which I speak measured some thirty feet in length and could pursue a ship relentlessly, up to a speed of five knots.'"

"Then that's supposed to be a crocodile," Melanie said, indicating the rendition of the sea dragon. "Oh, right. *The* crocodile from the story. Okay, I get it now."

"'Upon one occasion,'" Jon continued, "'having readied myself for the brute and armed with no less than four pistols, I chanced to hit a tooth, which loosed from its seating in the massive jaw and fell where later I could retrieve it after the wounded beast made its escape. This tooth measured eight inches from root to tip.'" Jon closed the manuscript with an odd lopsided grin and waited for Melanie's response.

It took a moment for her to formulate the words. "It's spooky," she finally said. "Who would write something like this?"

Jon studied the worn leather cover. "Somebody that Grandpa Emm knew, I guess. Gramps died in 1962, so he must have installed the safe in the basement before then. But of all the valuables he owned, and there were plenty, why would he choose to lock up an old book and a sword, and hide them behind a wall, no less? The significance of either item is beyond me unless..." He trailed off.

"Unless you contact your relatives in England," finished Melanie.

Jon set the log aside. "Which I will not do," he said, his voice as crisp as the paper upon which the mysterious Jas. Hook had written.

They sat in silence for several minutes, during which time Melanie could feel Jon's mood dip lower and lower until he was brooding. The magic of the evening was gone. *Damned Stuarts*, she thought. *One way or another, they always ruin everything.*

She stood up and scratched the top of his head, hoping to lighten the moment enough to make a comfortable exit. "I'd better be going home," she said. "It's late." He didn't respond. "Yoo-hoo."

"What?" he asked suddenly. "Oh, you know, you'd better be going home. It's late."

Melanie leaned over and kissed him. "I think it's a little later for you than for me, sweetcakes. Walk me out."

When they opened the front door, Jon's four cats all pushed in at once, bumping against their legs and complaining in a chorus of shrill whines. "Okay, okay," he said to them, "treats in a minute." They all trotted off to their food bowls in the kitchen.

"You and your treats," said Melanie. "You're a tightwad with human beings but you lavish treats on cats."

"Hey," Jon said defensively, "cats don't love. If you don't bribe them to come home, they won't come home."

"Then get a dog."

"Where's the challenge in that?"

Melanie pinched his ears and pulled him forward. "I'd say you have enough challenges in life. Goodnight," and she pecked him on the cheek.

Jon wrapped his long arms around her and squeezed. "What the hell was that? Kiss me like you mean it, woman."

She did, and she didn't leave for another ten minutes.

CHAPTER 3

Stuart gently closed the front door. He listened as Melanie started her car's engine, gunning it twice before driving away. As the steady hum of the Honda dwindled into the night, he closed his eyes and inhaled, savoring the last lingering bit of her perfume. Then he walked to the kitchen and dutifully portioned out a can of Savory Salmon Dinner for the meowing crowd.

Only three cats were there to gobble it up. "Fuzzybutt!" he called, but she didn't come. Fuzzybutt was finicky and often refused the goodies he offered. "Fine," he grumbled. "Spurn my generosity. See if I ever play string with you again."

He went back to the den where the log of the *Jolly Roger* lay on the floor. There was Fuzzybutt. The fat and very fuzzy black and white female had claimed the manuscript by stretching out across it, covering as much of its surface with her furry bulk as she could. As Stuart approached she yawned and flipped the tip of her tail once in a lazy greeting.

Stuart twitched the book out from under her, flipping the cat over onto her back. "If you don't mind."

Fuzzybutt righted herself, glared at him and relocated with great dignity to the sofa.

He sat down in the armchair and flipped pages, scanning this entry, studying that one, trying to make sense of the thing. He'd had a little time to examine it while waiting for the lawyer to finish paperwork, but something about the manuscript had seemed... inappropriate there. It was not a thing to reveal in public. Indeed, he now felt that showing it to Melanie had somehow been wrong. It belonged alone with him in a room like this, a small comfortable place with fine wood molding along the walls and leather-bound books on walnut shelves and worn, comfortable rugs on the floor. It seemed to want a fireplace as well, but Stuart couldn't accommodate in that department. Instead he got up and twisted the dimmer switch left, tipping the room further into its soft honey glow. That felt right.

When he sat back down, his big orange cat jumped onto his lap. Rebers, or properly in French, *Au Rebours*, was a typically contrary feline. He didn't want Stuart's lap. He hopped onto Stuart's shoulder and then to the armchair's high narrow back where he proceeded to groom, balancing like an acrobat while his long tail curled down under Stuart's chin like a monkey's tail holding a branch. As Stuart reopened the manuscript to read, he was aware of a fleeting sensation of rightness associated with the cat's presence there, especially the warm wiry tail.

All right, he thought, what was so special about this so-called "log" that his grandfather had found it necessary to lock it in a hidden fire-proof vault? Sentimental value? There was little sentiment to be found in these pages. Where did the thing come from? Why did Emmerich have it? If it *was* some distant family member's bizarre attempt at fiction writing, it gave a whole new dimension to the word bizarre.

"Flashed on brilliance that day," one early entry read. "Instructed Smee to fashion small pouches for each man to carry at the ready. Endeavored to collect the fairy's dust before it touched the deck. Had no plan formulated, but thought perhaps such a supply could provide the edge I needed." The next day's entry consisted of one statement in the present tense: "Methinks a butterfly net is in order."

A later entry puzzled Stuart for some time: "Lost Dimitri to a bear trap. He doubted their cunning. Damned fool." Several pages later an entry read, "I beg you, let me find the Port. I am desperate."

The ravings were the hardest to read, filled as they were with anguish and fury. That also made them the most fascinating. The handwriting of these passages was nearly illegible, the author's apparent madness struggling within the faded ink in an effort to leap up from the page. "Kill him! Kill him! Kill him!" Stuart read, and winced. "Must find weak take men cant shore boats gone build no Chief warned help find help from them Explain. Explain. Explain But they hate me cannot make them believe. Nowhere to turn."

There was one entry, approximately a third into the manuscript, that caught Stuart's attention and, in a strange haunting way, his heart as well. Aside from the odd fact that it was specifically dated — November 4, 1897 — it stood out from the other entries surrounding it, a single passage of near poetry:

> Anna, my Anna. In every cloud I see your radiant face,
> in every glint of moonlight upon the water I see your
> smile. The breeze carries the soothing caress of your
> fingertips to my cheek, and the warmth of summer
> embraces me as once your loving arms held me to your
> bosom. How your voice cries out to me in the roaring
> storm, yet I am powerless to answer. I stand in the rain
> of your tears yet cannot cry my own. Forever you
> remain with me, sweet Anna, dearest Anna, yet touch
> you I cannot, seek you I dare not. Alone must I walk
> until I die, even here, even here. And so I yearn for
> death that I may live again with you. *Au revoir*, my love.

Anna.

Stuart searched his memory, trying to recall any relatives named Anna. Two came to mind, both on the English side of the family. There was Grandpa Emmerich's first child, born sometime around 1905 or 1906 and named after Emmerich's mother. The child had died early. Then there was Emmerich's mother, wife of James. She had been a most proper woman held in high esteem in British Victorian society. If the book's author were this James, then it was he who had gone mad. Stuart had heard of no such insanity in the family. Had Anna perhaps taken a lover who had gone mad?

Aside from this single mention of Anna, the remainder of the legible entries concerned themselves with Peter Pan. Jas. Hook, pirate captain, harbored a hatred for Pan that burned beyond all rational limits. Stuart had quite a temper himself, the full expression of which no one had ever witnessed, but this fellow was obsessed. "Demon boy!" one entry screamed. "If I could kill him a thousand times I could not destroy him! He is the spawn of Hell and all its devils, and my soul is damned to battle with him until God in Heaven bestows upon His lost lamb the gift of sweet death. Let me die, dear God I beseech Thee, let me die!"

Peter Pan. Demon boy.

Strangely, in his own mind Stuart could equate those terms, though the rest of the world would never understand why. Then again, the rest of the world hadn't had Theodore Stuart as a father.

I shall always obey my parents.
I shall always obey my parents.
I shall always obey my parents.
I love my father and mother.
I love my father and mother.
I love my father and mother.
I am evil and I beg forgiveness.
I am evil and I beg forgiveness.
I am evil and I beg forgiveness.

Stuart could still see the scrawled penmanship on sheet after sheet of wide-ruled paper, the awkward block print letters getting sloppier and sloppier as the minutes wore on. He remembered how his right hand had spasmed uncontrollably after those sessions — his father had forced him to learn to write right-handed, insisting that his son's dominant left hand was evil, a sign that little Jonny was somehow less than wholesome. Sometimes Stuart had been beaten beforehand, and if he had bled, he'd had to finish the writing before being allowed to clean himself up. Invariably he'd had trouble holding the pencil on those occasions, what with the blood making it slip repeatedly through his fingers. The first twenty minutes of those sessions were an agony, the subsequent hours sheer torture that nonetheless had to be overcome.

"One hundred times each, young man," his father had said in that cold, hard, loveless tone. "One hundred times! Then off to bed with you. And I warn you — cocky boys are Hellbound boys. Anymore of your nonsense, and you may well find yourself face-to-face with a visitor tonight."

Peter Pan. Demon boy.

He came at night, his father had told him. He flew through the windows of bad little children's bedrooms and snatched them out of their beds and took them away to the Neverland. "Why is it called the Neverland, sir?" Stuart heard his child voice ask from long ago.

"Because," his father answered, "children who end up there *never* come back."

The Neverland was a place of punishment created especially for wicked children where, his father had patiently explained, "Fairies pinch you and trolls stomp on your toes and all manner of evil creatures poke you and prod you and tweak your nose and bite your arms and legs for all eternity. To go there is to go to Hell, and you, young man, have one foot across that threshold already."

Little Jonny knew of no other version of Peter Pan until he was old enough to go to school. By then he didn't believe the fairytale books or the cartoons or what Mister J.M. Barrie had written. Jonny knew the *truth*, and he was deathly afraid of it.

How strange to find similar sentiments here in this battered old manuscript. Whoever had penned these words had been insane, evidently, but Stuart nevertheless felt a certain perverse kinship with him. "No boy, no boy!" another entry shrilled. "Devil! Fiend! Creature of Hate and Loathing!"

Stuart closed the manuscript and let it slip off his lap to the floor. Images were creeping into his mind, pictures from a past he didn't want to remember. The parent-teacher conference during which his father had given his sixth grade teacher full and unconditional permission to beat him in class "when necessary." His mother saying nothing. His father taking his puppy to the pound to be put to sleep because Jonny had complained about his homework load one day and "no child who's too lazy to work hard in school deserves a pet." His mother sneaking him sips of brandy to help him sleep when the nightmares made him scream. The first time he had ever hit his father back.

A sharp pain in his stomach brought Stuart back to reality. For a moment he wondered what he might have eaten that was disagreeing with him at this hour. Then he placed the feeling. It was fear. Just thinking of his father in childlike terms had brought back the fear. And the anger.

He got up from his chair and took the saber from its box. An exquisite weapon it was, beautiful and empowering. Slowly he drew it through the air in long arcs, sweeping it this way and that, feeling its weight move with him, feeling it take hold and become one with his arm. On an impulse he brought the blade up in salute. He felt, rather than saw, an answering salute.

The den shimmered. His blade engaged air, and Stuart suddenly found himself in a black arena fighting a slow-motion duel with an unknown, elusive, invisible opponent, his saber somehow anticipating its unseen match, steel striking ghostly steel with a series of metallic clangs. His every attack was parried by nothing, his every riposte split-second quick yet slow as a nightmare. A whistle of air warned him when to duck, or a shadow, here then gone, told him when and where to lunge. But always the nothing he battled flickered just out of reach, no more than a whisper of animosity, no less than a feeling of dread. He sensed it circling him, teasing him, but it took no shape, would not commit to being.

Then something, a hand, *his father's hand*, slapped him hard across the face. Stuart's world flashed red. His body trembled as the fury of years burst free from the black dungeon of the past. It reached up like great black fingers and strangled him, jerking his perception back into real time.

With quick and furious energy he attacked anew, slashing with deadly intent, hearing his opponent laughing all around him. He hated this invisible tormentor as much as he hated his father and his uncle and his entire family, as much as he hated people and their hypocrisy and their lies and their infuriating cold hearts. He lashed out in blind rage, he the one with the edge now, he the wielder of the silver blade that was colder and sharper than the back of any hand. If only his opponent would show himself, if only Theodore or George or Emmerich would have the balls to stand before him right now, if only someone would show their ugly face for one measly second so he could—

—lunge and the blade was bound. The red haze vanished to reveal the saber's point embedded in the bulls-eye of the dartboard on his living room wall.

Stuart yanked it out and whirled around, panting. "Bastard!" he screamed. "Where are you!" But he was alone. He was *alone*. In the living room of his own house. *My God, what happened to me?*

With no thought of its value, Stuart threw the saber down. It landed with a soft thud on the carpet and he stepped away, afraid it might launch itself back into his hand.

The fingers of his left hand tingled. Red again. Everything wanted to turn red again. "No," he said firmly as the tingle flared into a burning sensation. Stuart ran to the kitchen, turned on the cold water and thrust his hand under the flow, struggling for control. "Stop it!" he yelled to himself. "*Goddamn stop it!*"

The burning tingle stopped. The red haze ceased clawing at his brain. Stuart drew in a deep breath and sank into a chair, water dripping from his hand as he stared out at his life, shuddering with the knowledge of his own violence. It was still there. As much as he had tried so hard to purge it from his soul all these years, there it was, right below the surface, the hatred and the anger and... something else.

Calm down. You're just exhausted, he told himself, pleased by his ability to grasp reason out of the frightening void. *This whole inheritance thing has rattled you more than you care to admit. You're dreaming on your feet, Jon. Go to bed.*

He walked back to the den, feeling dazed and somewhat foolish but in control. That was the most important thing. He was in control. To that end, he left the saber on the floor in the living room. He had no desire to go near the thing.

In the den, Fuzzybutt was stretched out over the manuscript as before, staking her claim in no uncertain terms. Stuart saw her there and without conscious thought kicked her off. "Get away from that."

She squealed and scrambled out the door.

"Fuzzybutt!"

He hadn't had any intention of kicking her. His foot had done it of its own accord. Stuart searched for the cat and found her hiding behind the bookcase in the hall. He would never be able to reach her back there. He tapped lightly on the case with his fingers. "Fuzzy. Hey, Fuzz, I'm sorry. I don't know why... I'm sorry..."

Confused, Stuart took a shower, made some chamomile tea and, after drinking it in the silence of the kitchen, went to bed. He lay in the dark, the covers pulled up to his chin, wishing that a dream would come and take him away, but it wasn't until the pre-dawn grey brushed the tips of the Altadena hills to the north that sleep granted his wish.

Little Jonny dreamed of the giant...

It wasn't daytime, it wasn't nighttime. It was no-time, and there was yellow weather outside. He loved yellow weather, like the warm expectant hush before an autumn storm, quiet, windless, cloudy but not grey. Yellow. Warm and electric. The air so full of possibilities that his stomach knotted itself in anticipation without his knowing exactly why.

Everyone waved to him as he walked past. He waved back at them then watched as they resumed raking leaves and waxing cars and walking dogs on the sidewalk. He wondered who they all were, why they all seemed to like him but why he felt separate from all of them. Who were they? he wondered.

And why, he wondered further, were they all carrying swords? Little swords for the kids, big swords for the adults. Even the dogs and cats had swords. How curious. He would have liked to ask what it all meant, but nobody seemed to notice they were even carrying swords, so it must not have mattered.

And then he heard it.

Boom.

Everyone looked up.

It was a low, massive sound from far far away. The sidewalk shook as if thunderbolts were rumbling deep within the ground, rolling up through layers of earth, cracking a path along the crust, hitting the soles of his feet and making him jump.

Boom!

Closer now.

The peace of the neighborhood shattered. Adults, children, dogs and cats threw down their swords and scurried into their houses for safety. Doors slammed shut, shutters closed, locks clicked, and the street was empty. Jonny stood all alone.

He ran for his house, kicking swords out of his way as he went.

Boom!

He knew that sound. Why had he left the safety of his house this morning if he'd known it would come? It always came! How could he have been so stupid?

BOOM!

He reached his home.

Home was gone. Nothing. Only an empty lot.

No, it had to be there, somewhere! They cared! They did! They must! They had to! He'd make them care!

BOOM!

Jonny turned and ran down another street, running as fast as his long legs could carry him, teeth clenched in effort, lungs gasping overtime. Everywhere lay dropped swords, big ones, little ones, long ones, short ones, but all the same one. He tripped over a few, almost fell, tried kicking them out of the way again but only succeeded in throwing himself off balance. There were too many of them!

The air was getting thick. He was slowing down. He couldn't breathe. He fought to pull free from the invisible tar pit, was all but frozen, heart leaping, stomach like fire, his sneakers mired in goop.

He looked behind him and saw the giant coming.

BOOM!

A huge black boot crashed down at the far end of the street. Concrete buckled under the great weight as the giant stepped ponderously forward, closer and closer, the thunder of its footfalls reverberating in Jonny's ribs like a cranked-up bass at a rock concert. He could hear it laughing, the velvety sonorous confident laugh of a lunatic with a loaded gun. The ground shook so badly that he could hardly stand up.

BOOM!

He tried to keep running. His house had to be here somewhere. If he could only find it, dash inside and make them care before the giant grabbed him, he would be safe!

But an enormous sword, a sword the size of a skyscraper, slashed down in front of him. Another slashed down to his left, another to his right. He could see himself reflected in cold grey metal on three sides. And he could see the reflection of the giant behind him as well, a great black figure with shining black eyes...

CHAPTER 4

Stuart banged open the door of Excalibur Books and stomped inside as two warnings flashed through his head. One, he shouldn't bang the door open. He had already broken the glass panel once that way. Two, it wasn't so good for business.

Fortunately, there was no one in the store at that particular moment but Alan, who was reading a book behind the counter. He glanced up as Stuart strode past. "Morning, Jon. Uh, you were supposed to be in about twenty minutes ago. Mister Satterlee already called and—"

"Not now." Stuart retreated to the back room and closed the door.

He was exhausted. For the sixth night in a row he had hardly slept. He hadn't eaten yet this morning, hadn't even had coffee. Stuart was no good without coffee first thing, but he had run out of beans at home and kept forgetting to go to the store for more. Same with milk, bread, eggs — actually, just about everything but soda crackers and peanut butter. Those he had in abundance, for some weird reason.

He left the sanctuary of the little room and plodded back to the front door, feeling Alan's eyes follow him. "I'm going across the street for coffee," he said, then forced himself to add, "Want anything?"

"No, thanks." Alan's answer was too quick.

Stuart stepped back out into the cool Pasadena morning and breathed a sigh of relief. The bookstore felt unusually confining today. He wanted to be in the open, with room to maneuver in case... in case...

...what?

He chuckled humorlessly and walked to the corner where he stabbed the crosswalk button and waited. What a week. He could think of no rational explanation for what was happening to him. Indeed, he could think of only one possible explanation, however ridiculous it was. He was being haunted.

During the precious two hours he had managed to sleep the previous night, Stuart had been plagued by nightmares, the same as the previous six nights. Nightmares of the giant, worse than ever before. And now the saber as well. Awful images and feelings had fanned all those old violent emotions to life, had dredged up and replayed all those ugly memories he had spent years trying to bury. He had started awake several times and felt the floor shaking with the giant's footsteps, seen the saber hovering before him, seen his terrified reflection on polished gray metal all around him until the tenacious dream-state had faded away. It was getting harder and harder to believe that the giant didn't really exist, that the saber wasn't really there, hanging over his bed at night, poised and waiting. It was impossible to ignore the strange green shadow that lingered over him in the night even after the dreams vanished.

In reality, the saber still lay on the floor in the living room where he had dropped it six nights ago. He had resorted to using salad tongs to lift the handle enough to slide the thing back into its box and push it behind the couch, but he could still feel its presence. He could no longer sit there. Just *being* in the room with it gave him the willies. For three days he had tried to move the box into the garage, but touching it, even through gloves, made his flesh crawl. Ever since the night he had first wielded the weapon, he had felt nothing but potential violence in his hands. The feeling wasn't foreign. That bothered him the most.

Peter Pan, demon boy.

Stuart did not own a copy of J.M. Barrie's famous fairytale, for obvious reasons, but he had been surprised to discover that his store shelves also failed to hold a single copy of either forms of the story, novel or play. When he had gone to the library, all copies were checked out. He'd actually had to buy the damned thing from Vroman's down on Colorado Boulevard in order to read it.

A stupid story, that's what he thought, but his stomach twisted itself into a knot as he recalled one particular passage. He had read it over and over in astonishment and had it memorized at this point, a simple description of Captain Hook: "In dress he somewhat aped the attire associated with the name of Charles II, having heard it said in some earlier period of his career that he bore a strange resemblance to the ill-fated Stuarts..."

The street light turned green. Stuart did not move. He stood there as cars flowed past him like wraiths, their growling engines a chorus of angry fiends.

Peter Pan, demon boy.

At least it was Friday. The past week had been hell to live through. Stuart had gradually come to realize that something was... well, *wrong*... with the items that he had inherited, but any attempt at explaining it, even to himself, left him feeling like a loon. He couldn't help but wonder if the old manuscript, the so-called log of the *Jolly Roger*, might not be more than fiction. Absurd? Exceedingly so.

But the saber — that was no mere speculation. That was a real object. It had an energy of its own, too, and that energy was tuned to his frequency as clearly as if his name were carved on it. He desperately wanted to get rid of it, but he couldn't. It was his. It knew his name. He could hurl it far out into the ocean and it would find its way back to his hand, he was sure of it.

The street light completed another cycle and turned green again. Stuart hastened across and entered the Rose City Cafe.

The waitresses at the cafe didn't like him. He had come to accept that fact, but he didn't understand it. It didn't seem to matter that his presence across the street for the last five years had resulted in plenty of business, and it didn't seem to matter that he recommended the place to others. They always treated him as if he were a living ice cube when he came in.

"Coffee," he told the waitress behind the counter. He knew that her name was Rita, but he refused to call her that. She wasn't friendly, so he wasn't either. She gave him coffee in a Styrofoam cup, took his money, pointed at the sugar and cream, and promptly found a spot to wipe up some distance further down the counter. "Thanks," Stuart mumbled and walked out.

He went back across the street, thinking that if he could just talk to Melanie he might be able to straighten his head out. Melanie, however, had told him she was booked day and night this week. Her research job was like that. Sometimes she had to accept impossibly short deadlines to make up for slow months. Stuart wished she would just hurry up and come talk to him. He realized with a sort of dull humor that he had no one else to talk to.

He banged the door open when he entered the store, spilled his coffee and snapped, "Shit!" before he noticed the customers three feet away, a woman with two children. The woman was polite enough to pretend she hadn't heard, but one child gave Stuart a bug-eyed look of shock and the other snickered behind his hand. Stuart hurried to the back room.

There was a note on his desk: "Satterlee phoned again. Your two-o'clock has been changed to eleven."

"Oh, great." The clock showed that it was already nine. He was supposed to go to Satterlee's office and bring the receipts for the entire year of 1987 with him. It was a doomed trip. Satterlee was the IRS auditor he had pissed off three years ago. No way was he going to get out of this alive, even if every receipt was in perfect order and every file was glittering with pristine accuracy. And now with the meeting bumped up by three hours, there was no chance for a nap. He would have to meet the dragon face-to-face with bloodshot eyes and more caffeine than blood in his veins.

Stuart went to the shelf where his tax records sat in neat rows of cardboard file boxes, each box carefully labeled and stacked in order. At least he would meet the dragon well armed for battle.

1987 wasn't there.

Stuart paused. Looked at his desk. Looked back at the shelves. Checked the floor. "Alan!" He opened the door of the little room. "Alan, get in here!"

From across the store, sitting behind the counter, Alan jumped to his feet, not so much in obedience as shock. An elderly woman put

45

down the book she had been browsing through and hobbled quickly towards the door.

"What is it?" Alan whispered after slinking past the other customers and meeting Stuart. "Geez, Jon, what are you—"

"The tax files are gone."

"What tax files?"

"The ones I need today. 1987. Where are they?"

"How should I know?"

Stuart pulled Alan in and closed the door.

Alan tugged his arm free. "Hey, man—"

"You're the only other person with a key to this room," Stuart said. "I know the files were there on the shelf. I spent a week going through them so they'd be perfectly organized. Now they're gone. What the hell did you do?"

"I didn't *the hell* do anything!" Alan squared his normally hunched shoulders and tilted his head at an angle that made Stuart think of a bull lowering its horns. His fists began to clench and relax, clench and relax with slow but definite intent. Stuart watched this display and blinked in amazement. Alan was angry. He had never seen Alan angry before. "Don't push me," Alan continued. The young college student was obviously unaccustomed to speaking his mind. It took him a moment to realize that he was yelling at his boss. But he was committed, so he plunged ahead. "I don't know what happened to the files. Yeah, I have a key, but I'd never... you know I wouldn't..." He flailed helplessly. "Why would I want your tax files? Doggone it, I've been trying to help you! I mean, geez, you've been skittery as a cat, you look like shit—" He gulped. "I mean, something's going on, right? But why blame me?" Alan paused, and Stuart knew what he was going to say before he said it. "I don't think I want to work here anymore. I'm sorry..." He fetched his coat from behind the counter and exited without looking back. Another customer, a middle-aged man, smiled insincerely at Stuart and also left.

Stuart drained his coffee cup in four gulps, ignoring how the hot liquid burned down his throat. The pain should have brought tears to his eyes, but Stuart never cried. He had to find those files.

It took a few minutes for the store to clear out. When it did, Stuart flipped the window sign to CLOSED and proceeded to search

every corner of the place. It was ridiculous, really. Alan was right —
who would steal tax files?

He went back to the shelf. Boxes in neat rows, one box gone like a
missing tooth. Stuart touched the spot. His fingers felt dust. No, not
dust. He examined his hand. Something like fine grey ash covered it.
The stuff was spongy and oddly sticky. He had to fetch his dust rag to
rub it off. He rubbed the shelf clean, too, then tossed the sticky rag in
the trash.

"Okay, Jon," he said, "you moved the box yourself. That has to be
the explanation." Still, he couldn't remember doing it. Why would he
have? It made no sense. The box belonged on the shelf, he'd always
kept it on the shelf, "Dammit, it should be right here on the shelf!"

He looked around, confused. He was behind the front counter.
He had been in the back room a second ago.

Well, there's your answer, Jon. You're having blackouts. He sat down
and tried not to panic. In the bad old days, back when he used to
drink, he had often lost snippets of time — mini blackouts, he had
called them. A flash here, a minute there, just enough to mess up
continuity in his head. He rubbed a hand over his face and took a few
deep regular breaths. Slowly his heartbeat calmed. *Face it, Jon,* he
thought, *you must have moved the files and then blacked it out.* Maybe they
were at home. He could walk there in ten minutes and find out, but
to hell with that. He would call Satterlee and cancel the meeting. Let
the IRS penalize him or whatever they wanted, he didn't care. He
needed time. He picked up the phone and dialed.

After three rings a chipper recording said, "Hi! This is Melanie
Forrester. Sorry I can't come to the phone, but if you leave a message
at the beep, I'll call you back. Thanks!" *Beep.*

"Melanie...?" He hadn't meant to dial her number. "I need to talk
to you." He wondered if his voice sounded as thick and lifeless on the
tape as it did to his own ears. "Please call me back." He hung up and
then finished quietly, "I think I'm going crazy."

CHAPTER 5

Melanie listened as Jon left his message, marveling at the fact that he was actually leaving a message instead of his usual sigh-click routine. She could have picked up the phone easily enough. The urge had made her hand twitch, but she had decided against it. She wasn't ready.

He thinks I'm working, she thought. *He thinks I'm not here.* By the time he said "Please call me back" she was reaching for the receiver, but she stopped her hand in time. No. She had to do this right, and she had only one chance.

She leaned back on the couch and put a hand on her belly. Try as she might, she felt no little life inside. She had once heard that an expecting mother could feel her baby's presence, and that notion had always intrigued her. She was making a baby right this very minute, right under her hand. What a strange feeling to think that her body was making a little person without her conscious input, all on its own. It had been busy at this task for about three months, so the doctor had told her on Tuesday. She had been devastated by the news. She still was. She didn't want a baby. It had been an accident. But there is was, whether she could feel it or not.

Jon was going to freak. She knew that as plainly as she knew day from night. He didn't like children. How she broke the news to him and when might make all the difference in the world. Until she formed a plan, she dared not see or speak to him.

Her ruby ring sparkled in the lamp light. She gazed at it, wishing things could be different. If only Jon could always be that man she glimpsed on those wonderful good days, the laughing man who peeked out every once in a while and assured her that her love was not, after all, grossly misplaced. If only he would let go of... she didn't know what. He never revealed specifics, just vague statements now and then that hinted at more unhappiness than she had ever known. She had always tried to help him face his ghosts, but he couldn't. Or wouldn't. Instead he carried the baggage around on his shoulders, unaware of the enormous burden even as he struggled to stand upright under the weight of it every day.

You're a fool, Mel. You'll never have him. He doesn't hate children as much as he's scared of them. He's scared of everything, including you. Tell him he's going to be a father and he'll run like a bunny, just watch. He'll blame you and there you'll be, a single mother with no steady job. The beginning of the end.

Melanie Forrester stared out the window at the perfect cloudless sky and wondered what on earth she should do.

CHAPTER 6

Days passed and Monday rolled around — "dark day," as they say in the theatre. Excalibur Books was closed, but Stuart was there working with the lights down dim.

He had very little energy and, he noted with sagging interest, a whole lot of work to do. He felt like that metaphorical overburdened camel — one more straw and he'd go down for good. Yolanda had done her best during the last few days to keep the store's shelves tidy and the customers happy, but she had her classes to think about. Stuart knew it was only a matter of time before she would have to cut her hours back. He wanted to hire someone to replace Alan, but with the IRS after him like a pack of hounds and the box of tax receipts gone, he had to fight to keep his concentration on the bookstore. He could hardly concentrate on anything. He was a fool for working today, considering he'd thrown up his breakfast and his skin tingled in that way it did when a fever was coming on. But he knew he would be no better off at home with his unfocused fears and overwrought imagination and that saber laying in its long box behind the couch.

He tried not to think about it, and for a while his brain was blessedly spared. But as the morning wore on he would see a glint of steel from the corner of his eye and, turning quickly, would catch sight of the saber just as it vanished. The green shadow appeared later and hovered at his shoulder, appeared again on the floor by his feet, and again high up in a corner. Once it passed right through him. The sensation was like a cold needle pushing into his chest, then pushing itself through his body and out the other side as if he was some kind of life-sized Voodoo doll. He had barely made it to the bathroom before throwing up — for the fourth time since tossing breakfast.

What was that green shadow thing? What did it want?

He stopped for a break when the tiny buzzing lights showed up. "Oh, great," he groaned, getting a can of Diet Coke from the little icebox in the back room and guzzling down half of it at once, dearly wishing it was a bottle of brandy. "Great. Now I'm seeing fireflies. Ha!" He wiped his mouth with the back of his hand and burped. That made him laugh a harsh, slightly hysterical laugh. "Buggy wuggy fireflies," he repeated weakly, watching them whirl round and round the lamp. Some flitted over his head, flaring and dimming and then winking out altogether, only to reappear back at the lamp with the others. A desire to fetch the fly swatter and smack them into oblivion crossed his mind, but Stuart was too tired. And they weren't real anyway, right? It was his imagination. If he went to sleep, they would go away.

So he sat at his desk and let his head drop down onto his arms for a nap, just like in first grade on a hot afternoon when the teacher would read them a story, a story about three bears, or a golden goose, or a knight in shining armor with a gleaming silver saber and a looming green shadow and hundreds of flitting lights and—

When someone knocked on the front door, he flailed to his feet so fast he knocked his chair over and almost fell over himself. "Wh-who is it?" he called.

"Melanie."

He picked up his chair and hurried to unlock the door. "How did you know I was here?" he asked as she stepped from beneath the cool November sunlight into the cluttered haven of the store. In her unexpected presence he suddenly felt human again. He wanted nothing more than to reach out and draw her close, but there was a prickly distance about her that checked him.

"That's a silly question, how did I know you were here," she said. Stuart hoped she might initiate a hug or a kiss, but she walked right past him. "You're *always* here." There was a sarcastic flavor to her tone. He didn't like it. "I got your phone messages," she continued. "You sounded awful."

"I haven't been feeling very well."

"Then why are you working?" She placed her palm against his forehead. He felt her fingers twitch a little. "You're pale," she said flatly. "Have you taken your temperature lately?"

Stuart sensed that her previous sarcasm had been a slip, and she was attempting to cover it with Florence Nightingale concern. He gently removed her hand from his forehead. Her fingers were cold. "Melly, what's the matter?"

She withdrew her hand. "Nothing."

"I haven't seen you for almost a week."

She laughed. "You make that sound like forever. When you're busy, I don't see you for longer than that."

Stuart tried to smile. He wasn't sure if it turned out to be a grimace or not. "If I'm so easy to find, why didn't you drop by? We could have had lunch or —"

"Don't give me that!" she suddenly exploded. "I have to pry paperwork out of your hands and drag you out the door kicking and screaming just to get your attention! I have to spend half an hour begging for two uninterrupted minutes so that I can say hi to you! Don't give me that bullshit about *dropping by* and *having lunch!* I just *dropped by* to take two lousy seconds of your precious time to tell you that I had an abortion! All right? I've said it, you've heard it! It's done! Goodbye!"

Stuart stood paralyzed, too stunned to even breathe. When Melanie pushed for the door, his arm shot out on its own, blocking her path. The action took him by surprise him as much as it did her.

Her face grew livid. "Let me go. And don't stare at me like a deer caught in the headlights. You heard what I said." She angrily blinked tears away, creating two glistening trails down her cheeks.

Stuart's arm dropped. "I... I didn't know you were..."

"Of course not!" she spat. "I didn't tell you! You're the one who hates kids, Jon, but I'm the one who got pregnant! What was I supposed to do? Let you yell at me and tell me it was all my fault and..." A sob cut her short. She threw her purse to the floor. Its contents spilled out over Stuart's feet. "...and leave me to deal with it alone?" she finished. Sobs shook her shoulders, and she turned her back on him.

This was it, Stuart realized, the last straw on a very weak camel's back. The poor animal's legs were buckling, and when it fell, he would fall with it. "Why?" he moaned. The question wasn't directed at her. "Why are you doing this to me?"

Melanie turned around slowly. "Did you just ask how *I* could do this to *you?*"

He didn't respond. He was busy trying to identify an odd sting behind his eyes, a sensation he hardly recognized. For him such a sensation never blossomed into tears, not since he had discovered the great grey wall in his mind many years ago, back when he had been a boy. He grabbed desperately at it now, slamming it down with a great interior thud, cutting off his emotions and trapping them far far away.

The stinging sensation ceased. He felt nothing. He was in control again. "Didn't you use— ?" he began evenly.

"You know I did! Look, lover," and she adopted his own sarcastic tone, "no contraceptive is one hundred percent effective." She sniffled. "I guess I was one of the lucky ones. You know, I would have been willing to keep it, but I don't want to be a single mother, not in this city. I really thought about it, though. I went over my budget and everything. But Jesus, Jon, I haven't got two spare nickels to rub together and no job security. Together we could have done it but..." She shrugged helplessly, her eyes imploring him to speak.

He said nothing.

"You shit. You're responsible for this, you know, you really are. Has it ever occurred to you that you're lucky to have a woman who loves you at all? Did that amazing thought ever flash through that thick skull of yours? Maybe my mother is right. Maybe I'm just playing social worker to a loser, but I happened to fall in love with that loser somewhere along the way and now I'm stuck." Her anger melted back into sobs. "Dammit, if you'd just ask me to marry you... even bring up the possibility..."

Stuart mechanically offered her a box of tissues. She slapped it out of his hand. All he could do was watch it fall to the floor in slow motion, bouncing through the spilled contents of the purse at his feet, scattering the items farther apart.

She was right. It was all so clear, and worse, easily solved. *She should be with someone else, someone who won't bring pain into her life like I do. I'm a mean bastard,* he admitted with a mental shrug. *She doesn't deserve that, never has.* Oh, she had learned to enjoy and had even developed some skill at the cutting repartee that constituted most of their conversations, and she had developed a remarkably thick skin to ward off his more insensitive verbal jabs. But inside she was still soft and pink, and he had always felt as though he had to tip-toe around her to keep from squishing her.

So he made a decision. He would tell her to leave and never come back. He would hurt her, one last hurt in a succession of hurts, but she would be better off for it. He opened his mouth, ready to hurt her and, worse, hurt himself by destroying the one good thing in his life. "Look, Mel—" he said, and the saber appeared and jammed itself straight through his gut.

"Jon!" Melanie cried as he doubled over, clutching his stomach, too shocked to groan. The pain was astonishing, hot yet ice cold, numbing yet so sharp he felt as if his very soul had been pierced. An impossible pain. He felt ripped down the middle.

"Have to..." was all he could say, and he stumbled for the door, banging it open so hard the glass pane shattered. He leaned, trembling, against the front display window, sucking fresh air into his lungs in long shuddering breaths.

After a moment he heard Melanie's footsteps approach. She was walking, not running. She had taken the time to gather her purse's contents off the floor. The long-strapped bag hung over her left shoulder, tidy as usual. "Are you all right?" she asked. "Let me call your doctor."

"No, I'm okay," he rasped.

In truth he felt violated, exposed, like a diary being perused by a judgmental stranger. The saber had somehow pierced his mental wall, and all the emotions he had cut off through the years were washing over him in ugly waves. The strongest was self-hatred. Instead of struggling to push it back, however, he allowed it to press down on him, to squeeze in through his pores and into his very blood, a self-made poison designed to flow straight to the heart. It hurt like hell. He deserved it.

Melanie actually laughed. It was a bitter sound. "Boy, are you a liar. You're not okay. I'm not okay. We're both really screwed up."

Stuart didn't dare speak. He had been ready to cast her out of his life. Now he was afraid to open his mouth for fear he would actually do it.

"I hate you," Melanie said. "I really hate you."

That makes two of us, toots, he thought.

"But I still don't want to watch you die, if that's what you're doing. Let me call your doctor."

"No. Go home. And I don't think—" *Wait, no!* "—you and I should—" *Stop, you idiot!* "—see each other anymore."

Perhaps in sympathy, perhaps just to torture him, Time paused long enough for Stuart to take one last look at Melanie's beautiful face, her pretty elf-bright eyes, the flawless silk of her skin, her sweet pouting lips.

Then every clock in creation resumed its ticking, and a cloud passed over her and she was made of stone. The stoplight at the corner turned green, and whatever she said so softly to him was lost in the noise of passing traffic. Before the light turned red again, she was gone.

The camel collapsed.

Little Jonny dreamed of the giant...

It wasn't daytime, it wasn't nighttime. It was no-time, and there was yellow weather outside, like the warm expectant hush before an autumn storm, quiet, windless, cloudy but not grey. Yellow. Warm and electric.

Everyone raised their swords at him in salute as he walked past. He raised his own sword back at them, then watched as they resumed clipping rose bushes and emptying trash cans and playing Jedi lightsaber with sticks. He wondered who they all were, and why they weren't using their swords to hack the rose bushes down altogether, or chop their garbage into itty bitty bits, or play lightsaber with a real blade. They weren't using their resources. They were wasting it all. Oh well, they liked him, and if he said anything they might get mad. So he said nothing, just smiled and walked on.

And then he heard it.

Boom.

Everyone looked up.

Boom.

The peace of the neighborhood shattered. Adults, children, dogs and cats scurried into their houses for safety, taking their swords with them. Doors slammed shut, shutters closed, locks clicked, and all the houses quietly turned to smoke and blew away. Jonny stood all alone on a vast empty field.

He would have run for home, but he had no idea where home was.
Boom!

He knew that sound. He'd done it again! He'd left his house! Why didn't
he ever learn? They didn't care! They really didn't care!

BOOM!

Jonny turned and ran as fast as he could, knowing that it was hopeless.
The air was already becoming thick as goop. His feet were slowing down no
matter how hard he fought to hurry. His heart pounded painfully, his stomach
burned like a fire pit, and he slowed, slowed, stopped, screaming silently,
writhing motionlessly, struggling madly to move while knowing somewhere
deep inside that he was going to die.

Finally, with effort, he turned his head and saw the giant coming.

BOOM!

A huge black boot crashed down at the far end of the street. Concrete
buckled under the great weight as the giant stepped ponderously forward, closer
and closer, the thunder of its footfalls reverberating in Jonny's ribs like the
wrath of God in an old Moses movie. He could hear it laughing, the round
resonant bone-chilling laugh of a maniac holding a lit match to a short fuse.
The ground shook so badly he could hardly stand up.

BOOM!

With a supreme effort he raised his sword. He couldn't run. His house
wasn't here. Nothing was here. They didn't care. He had nowhere to go, and
it didn't matter anyway. This time he would fight. There was no option.

But his sword shot out of his grip and flipped end-over-end until it hovered
in the air, pointing right at him. It grinned with metal teeth. Before he truly
registered that it was alive, it was flying at him. Pain ripped his gut, and he
couldn't scream.

BOOM!

A hand reached down from the clouds, a hand so incredibly huge that it
crushed him the moment those fingers gripped his little body. He did not feel it.
He knew only emptiness as he sensed his body collapsing inward, like a fragile,
hollow shell. His last thought was that there was nothing inside to leak out.

The great black figure with shining black eyes lifted him higher, higher. Its
mouth grinned open and yellow fangs flashed...

* * * * *

Jonny woke up with a start, clutching his chest and heaving. His pajamas were damp with sweat, cold terror churned in his stomach, and his heart thumped so hard that he sobbed with the fear that it would stop altogether and he would die. But the dream was over. For tonight.

He sat up. For an instant, just one swift instant, his room seemed wrong. For one thing, there was a TV across from his bed. He didn't have a TV in his bedroom. There was only one TV in the house, and it was down in the family room. And all of his models — his *Titanic*, his Sopwith-Camel fighter plane, his ferocious tyrannosaurus rex that had taken him weeks to build — they were gone. There was a telephone, a really weird-looking one with buttons instead of a dial, on his nightstand. But he didn't have his own telephone. Bewildered, he squinched his eyes shut. The strangest sensation overcame him, as if he were shrinking. Quickly he opened his eyes again, heart thumping anew.

His bedroom was back the way it was supposed to be. There were his models on the shelf, above his collection of storybooks and below his box of crayons and his stack of comics. His pogo stick was leaning against his dresser where he always kept it. His dirty school clothes were in a pile under his homework desk. Yes, everything was okay. Or it would be okay if not for the Giant Dream.

The cool Long Island breeze blowing through the window calmed him. He lay back down and reminded himself that as long as he stayed quiet and kept his arms and legs under the covers, he was safe. The giant's domain was dreamland, and the other monsters couldn't get him under the covers. Those were the rules.

Then he saw the green shadow. Jonny uttered a bark of alarm, like a startled little dog. Something was in the corner next to his baseball bat, crouching there, ready to spring!

Jonny ducked under the covers and froze. Maybe he had imagined it. If he hadn't and something really was there, maybe it would go away. He wished he could turn the light on, but the switch was way over by the door. Leaving the sanctuary of the bed was too great a risk after the Giant Dream.

A finger poked him from outside the covers, and Jonny popped right up out of bed like a slice of his favorite raisin bread from the toaster. He found himself standing on the cold floor in front of another little boy.

"Hullo!" said the boy.

"Wh... wh..."

"Did I scare ya?"

"Whh... who..."

The boy jerked a thumb at himself proudly. "I'm Peter Pan!"

Jonny screamed and stumbled backwards, putting his bed between him and the boy. Peter Pan! The demon boy who took bad children to Hell! And this wasn't a dream, which meant that his father had told the truth and children did have a special Hell and he was going there!

"Get away from me!" Jonny yelled, waving a feather pillow threateningly.

Peter floated up into the air and hovered over the bed, gazing down at Jonny and scratching his wild red head in confusion. "Wow, nobody's ever tried to attack me with a pillow before," he said.

Jonny glanced back at the door. Why wasn't his father coming to rescue him? Surely he'd heard the screams! Jonny sucked in enough air to scream again when a bright light zoomed straight at him from nowhere and something small slapped his hand. Hard. He dropped the pillow. "Wh... what...?" he tried, then stopped as Peter Pan dropped down onto the bed, bouncing and giggling. The strange boy's giggle was wonderful, a crisp fluttery sound like leaves rustling in a playful autumn wind.

"That's Tink," Peter Pan said. "She thought you were gonna hurt me with that pillow!"

The bright light that was Tinker Bell hovered over Peter. It turned crimson and shot out little sparks while a high-pitched bell tinkled and jangled. A shower of fine gold dust fluttered down as the light agitated about. Then it zoomed over into a corner and hung there.

Jonny stared. "Is that a... a fairy?"

"'Course," answered Peter. "And she says you're an ass! But don't worry, she calls everybody an ass. She has awful manners." He cocked his head, a curious glint in his eyes. "Why are you scared of me?"

Jonny gulped. "You're gonna take me to Hell."

The smile on Peter's face melted into a heart-rending look of betrayal. "Hell?" he said in disbelief, his voice cracking with genuine pain. "Who told you that?"

"My daddy."

Peter climbed off the bed and walked somberly over to the window. In the moonlight Jonny could see him better. He stood with his feet planted firmly, hands on his hips, head cocked. He was dressed in a scant green outfit made out of vines and leaves, just like the pictures Jonny had seen in storybooks, and his tangled red hair shimmered in the moon's glow. He wore two daggers, each in a leather sheath, one on his right and one on his left, his skinny boy hips crisscrossed with the double leather belts.

His face was most arresting. Peter was a beautiful boy with a classic pert nose, high cheekbones, and full cherry lips, like babies' lips. There was a feminine quality about him, but he was certainly no sissy-boy. No, Peter Pan was all teeth and claws, a real tomcat in a fight, that was plain to see by his manner. And his laugh, as Jonny had already learned, could brighten a dark room. So it was when he laughed again, whirling around to jab a finger at Jonny. "Your daddy's nuttier than a squirrel," he announced with glee, "and he's no fun!"

Tinker Bell echoed this sentiment with a single, emphatic jing.

Without making a sound, Peter leapt through the air and landed right in front of Jonny, who shuffled back. "Come with me, Jonny!"

Peter had called him by name! Jonny didn't know what to say about that. He murmured, "I don't think so..."

Peter huffed and glided gracefully up to the dresser. He picked up Jonny's comb and tried to pull it through his wild hair. It immediately snagged. Tinker Bell jingled with silvery bell laughter. "Why not?" Peter said, yanking the comb out and tossing it carelessly to the floor. "Haven't you ever heard of the Neverland?"

Of course Jonny had heard of it. He somberly recited the *truth* about that horrible fantasy world: "It's a terrible place where fairies will pinch me and trolls will stomp my toes and mean creatures will poke my nose and bite me forever. It's the children's Hell, and I'm bad because I already have one foot there already."

Peter listened with his jaw slack. He uttered a derisive snort when Jonny finished. "Man oh man! I need to straighten you out. You're definitely coming with me."

"Wait!" Jonny said, petrified. "Can you prove you're not from Hell?"

"Sure." Peter jumped down and, with one sharp clap of his hands to Tinker Bell, said, "I'll teach you how to fly. People don't fly in Hell, right?"

"I don't know."

"Well," said Peter with authority, "they don't. But you'll fly on the back of the wind when I'm done with you!"

Tinker Bell zoomed around Jonny's head, sending a sparkling shower of golden dust onto his hair and shoulders.

"Fairy dust," Peter explained. "Now think a happy thought."

Jonny had heard of this procedure before, from children who had tried to tell him the storybook version of *Peter Pan.* Jonny dutifully thought of his favorite cookies and candy, but he instantly heard his mother say, "Put that down! Bad little boys don't deserve sweets!" and thus nothing happened. He tried picturing a Christmas tree, but his father kept getting in the way, warning him to quit ogling and get to bed or Santa would never come, and the image winked out. No other happy thoughts came.

"What's wrong?" Peter asked.

Jonny said nothing.

"What about your grandfather?" Peter suggested in a sly tone.

Jonny gave a start. "What?"

"The time you phoned him. That made you happy, didn't it?"

Yes! Earlier that year, Jonny had disobeyed his father and called Grandpa Emm on the phone, all the way across the United States in San Francisco. Oh, it was forbidden to talk to anyone outside of his nuclear family because of The Argument. But Jonny's teacher had taught them about family trees that week. Every other kid had aunts and uncles and grandparents and cousins, but Jonny could contribute nothing. He didn't even know how many relatives he had or where they lived. All his father had ever told him was that his relatives were wicked, and he was never to ask about them.

And then he had stumbled across his father's old phone book and found Grandpa Emm's number. The old man had answered the phone, speaking with a strong English accent. Jonny had never heard anybody talk that way outside of the movies, and he had thought it sounded terribly exotic. But his Grandpa hadn't recognized him. And then the old man had slowly said, "Jonny? Jonathan?" And then with joy, "*Grandson?*"

All Jonny remembered after that was a sharp pain on the side of his head and his father yelling. But he had heard his grandfather's voice! Grandpa Emm hadn't sounded wicked at all. Jonny had wanted to call him again right away, but he knew his father would expect it. So he had bided his time and waited for the perfect opportunity when his father wouldn't be around. Grandpa Emm had died a mere two weeks later, before the perfect opportunity had a chance to come.

"Yeah, Grandpa Emm!" Jonny said. "He talked to me! He was glad to hear me!" Jonny floated up into the air. "Hey! Hey, look! I'm *flying!*"

"Isn't it great?" Peter said, clapping his hands with delight.

"Yeah!"

"Does this feel like Hell?"

"No!"

"Then c'mon!"

Peter sailed out the window and into the night. Without hesitation, Jonny followed.

Peter flew in a huge circle that first took them west back over Queens, over the East River and to Manhattan. From five hundred feet in the air the city at midnight was a wondrous spectacle, but Jonny was so terrified of being so high up that he ignored everything, staring only straight ahead, afraid of smashing into a high-rise or something. While Peter Pan somersaulted and spiraled and dove and performed all sorts of incredible acrobatic feats, tumbling past penthouse windows and playing leap-over-tall-buildings-in-a-single-bound, little Jonny could only hold his arms and legs out like stiff boards and fly level.

By the time they were a thousand feet up and circling Central Park, Jonny relaxed a bit. After several experiments he accepted the fact that he couldn't fall. Even when he tucked his limbs in and made a ball of his body, he simply hung in the air like a soap bubble hanging on a breeze. He really was flying! By the time they completed their circle over Manhattan, turned eastward and headed out over the Atlantic, Jonny was tumbling a bit himself, playing a silly game of tag with Tink and watching his moon shadow zip over clouds far below.

Oh, flying was everything his dreams had always tried to create, but in his dreams the wind would blow him off course, or he would get tangled in phone lines, or he would suffer from vertigo and ralph, or some great flying monster would pluck him up and eat him. Real flight was deliciously easy. You thought of something happy and off you went! Controlling your direction was as simple as wishing it.

"Up there!" Peter said, pointing into the heavens. "See it? Second to the right, and straight on till morning!"

At this height, the sky was a chaos of brilliant twinkling stars unmarred by the smog layer far below. Jonny could not fathom how Peter could possibly tell which star was which. The moon looked close enough to touch. It smiled at them as they passed by.

"Do we have to fly all night?" he asked Peter.

"Yeah, but it's not hard. Tink will keep you awake!"

Jonny thought that was a silly idea, needing a fairy to keep you awake while you flew. But after a while he started to yawn, and his eyelids fluttered, and Tink pinched him and he saw that the stars looked a little different than they had a minute ago and that Peter was so far ahead of him... or behind him... that he was out of sight. He had fallen asleep, all right. The solid earth was too far below to see anymore. He was alone, falling steadily upwards into a canopy of diamonds.

He had once read that sea gulls could sleep while flying. Now he understood why. Flying was more relaxing than lying on a water bed, better than lounging in a hot bubble bath. The warm wind feathered his cheeks, and the stars sang crystal lullabies, and he found himself again struggling to stay awake. Peter came and went, first flying by his side and then disappearing for what seemed like hours. Jonny didn't mind. Tink stayed with him, and he felt safer way up here than he ever had under the covers of his bed. He dozed.

They reached the Neverland at dawn. First they were flying among the stars, and then a bright light, brighter than Tink, brighter than the diamonds, pierced the blackness of space. A sun popped into being, Jonny wasn't sure from where, and then *another* one! After the long flight in the dark, Jonny was momentarily blinded. When his eyes adjusted, the sky all around him was blue, the clouds were cottony white, and a placid sapphire sea stretched out below in all directions. The spot of a large green island lay directly ahead.

Peter Pan crowed with delight and flew a great loop in the sky around Jonny. "We're home!" he cried. "We're home!"

Jonny was entranced. This wasn't Hell. It couldn't be. His father had been wrong, apparently about a lot of things. Jonny felt the swell of a great adventure rising in his breast, and the feeling made him want to crow with joy as Peter had done. But try as he might, he felt too self-conscious. Tink poked him as if she knew his feelings, and he heard her bell laugh. "It's beautiful," was all he could say to her. She jingled a long reply, but he had no idea what she said.

They began a slow circle over the island. Peter pointed things out as they flew. "It's mostly jungle," he said, indicating the thick green mass that covered three-quarters of the land. "We're coming up on Pirate's Bay. That rocky place over there's the Mermaid Lagoon, and up in those hills is the forest where the Indians live." They circled the tall white peak of a volcano, the tallest point on the island. "It's always covered with snow," Peter said. "I haven't gone inside yet. Gotta save some adventures for later, don't you think?"

Jonny marveled at the beauty of the island and could hardly wait to go exploring, but he wondered how on earth one dressed in a place like this. Pajamas certainly wouldn't do. Then again, he didn't want to wear leaves and vines. The rustic get-up looked good on Peter, but Jonny was sure he would only look stupid.

Peter started to lose altitude. Jonny realized he didn't know how to follow. "Wait!" he called. "Peter! How do I go down?"

Peter paused in mid-air and hung there like a helicopter for almost a full minute. Jonny was about to call him again when he finally turned around. Something about him was different, but Jonny couldn't pinpoint what had changed. "Oh, that's easy," Peter said. "Just think about your grandfather."

Grandfather? Did he mean Grandpa Emm again? "That will make me go down?"

"Oh, yes," said Peter. "Especially when I tell you that he was a lot more than just one banana short of a bunch."

Jonny felt his chest tighten. "What are you talking about?"

"He tried to hide the sword, Jonny, but you can't do that." Peter floated closer. "Your father was mad, too, didn't you know? And your Uncle George. Emmerich tried to protect them by hiding the sword in that big metal safe behind the wall, but the sword still called to them. They couldn't find it, so they went mad. Now it's found *you*, Jonny. Think about that. Just think about it, and you'll go *down* all right!"

Jonny thought about it, and suddenly he understood what had changed. It wasn't Peter Pan at all who had changed. *He* had changed. He was no longer a little boy but his grown self, hanging in the air over a make-believe island with a boy who belonged in a storybook.

Peter Pan waved happily. "Bye bye, Jonny!"

Stuart dropped like a bag of cement down, down, down for what seemed an eternity. They had been hovering over Pirate's Bay, and the last thing he felt was a ridiculous relief that at least he would land in water.

Somewhere along the way somebody changed the water into concrete.

HISTORY PART 2
DAD GOES FAR AWAY

...is this what they mean by cold chills going up and down your back? Because it is not pleasant; it starts in your stomach and goes in waves around and up and down again like something alive. Like something alive. Yes. Like something alive.

— *The Haunting of Hill House* by Shirley Jackson

CHAPTER 7

Stuart awoke to find himself lying on a stiff mattress and covered by a thick, warm, dirty quilt with frayed edges. He was on his back. A wood plank ceiling arched three feet above him. Thankfully that wasn't the height of the entire room but only the top of the alcove where his cot was located. The left side of the alcove was a wall, again of horizontal wooden planks. These bowed outward as if warped by too much weight.

He blinked, a swirling mist enveloping his thoughts, and gazed to his right.

A man was there, a thick, sturdy fellow wearing a pair of steel-rimmed spectacles and an odd droopy red wool cap. Stooped over an ornate silver tray on a little table maybe four feet away, he was busy sorting through a collection of small bottles. A ragged cloth hung over his arm. Stuart wondered if he was some kind of waiter. "Hello...?" he said. It came out as a croak.

The man whirled around and set two big brown eyes upon him. "Cap'n!" he cried.

"Where—?"

"Ah, sar, glad to see yeh've come to. I been worried sick these last two days. The crew'll be mighty cheered to see yer up an' about agin, that I can tell yeh!"

"Where—?"

The portly fellow clapped a callused meaty hand over Stuart's forehead and froze in an attitude of expectancy so intense that it made Stuart freeze as well, cutting his own question short. He waited for the portly man to say something, anything, since the fellow's mouth hung open as if words were going to spill out at any moment. They did: "No fever. Good!"

"Where—?"

"Lay back an' relax, Cap'n. I'll bring yeh some pipin' hot tea an' a nice mug o' pea soup. Yeh must be starvin', not eatin' fer two days an' all. A bit o' soup'll perk yeh up, aye?"

"God dammit, let me ask a question!" The effort to shout almost did him in. Stuart sank back onto his pillows, exhausted.

The portly man cringed, as if expecting some horrible punishment. Slowly he relaxed, his bespectacled eyes never leaving Stuart. "Beg pardon, Cap'n. Just glad to see yeh's all." His thick strong fingers adjusted the cap that perched on his long, wispy white hair. Quite frankly, he looked miffed.

Stuart cleared his throat and, with effort, tried to see past the murky film obscuring his memories. "Where am I?"

The man dipped his head to peer closely at Stuart, like a bird who has spotted a worm squirming in the earth by its foot. "Ah, fer Chrissake," he said with eerie disbelief.

Stuart registered the man's Irish accent. *I don't know anybody with a brogue, do I?* "Listen..." he tried again.

"Yeh don't know where yeh be, sar? Nothin' looks familiar like?"

"I don't recognize this place. And who are you?"

"Ah, fer Chrissake..."

Stuart shut his eyes. This was hopeless.

The man made a suggestion. "Sar, ye suffered a wallop on yer noggin, that must be it. Lemme see if there's a bump."

Stuart allowed the man to gently probe his head for injury. Within the swirling mist of his memory he did recall falling, or tripping, or something along those lines. He couldn't remember landing, though. Perhaps he had hit his head. It would explain a lot. He said this to the portly man.

"Aye, that explains it then, Cap'n."

"Why do you keep calling me Captain?"

Again the man froze, as if the worm at his foot had returned, or perhaps it had suddenly grown bigger. "Ah, fer Chrissake..."

Stuart's anger flared. Despite the quantity of energy required to feed it, he let it grow, enjoying the sensation despite its cost. "All right, enough! I've had it with *fer Chrissake* and *Aye, Cap'n!* Where the hell am I?"

With a lightening move, the man drew a cutlass and held it point-up in his right hand, as if in salute. "Right here in yer cabin, Cap'n, may Johnny Corkscrew kiss me heart if I lie!"

The cutlass appeared so fast that Stuart didn't have time to blink. Fortunately, it was clear that this fellow meant him no harm, so Stuart played his surface calm for all it was worth. He narrowed his eyes, holding the portly man's gaze. "And your name is...?"

"Why... why, I'm Smee, sar."

"Smee."

"Aye, sar."

No no no, Stuart thought, *I won't buy into this.* "Smee. Right. So how did I get... wherever this is, *Mister Smee?*"

"Two o' the boys found yer, sar — Scourie an' Biggs it was, sar, two days past."

"Found me?"

"In the bay, sar. Floatin'. Naked as a jaybird, I might add. Well, a fine puzzle it was, t'be sure. Imagine findin' a body after the battle we saw, well, we figgered the croc'd swallered yeh whole!" Smee quickly touched the brim of his cap. "If yeh pardon my bein' blunt, sar. Oh, we was plannin' a fine service fer yeh the likes o' which would ne'er be seen in Beggar's Port agin. Then up shows Scourie an' Biggs an' there yeh are! Imagine my relief when I discovered yeh wasn't dead a'tall just... well, not entirely yerself. Sar." Smee sheathed his cutlass with a slap as if to give his speech a nice punch finish.

Something knocked at Stuart's skull from the inside, calling for attention, something as small and insistent as a child's little fist. Stuart sensed it more than felt it, but the urgency behind it was too distant, too undefined to worry about. He felt emotionally drained and overwhelmed at the same time. And he was tired. Very very tired.

Nevertheless, he struggled to a sitting position, something Smee tried to keep him from doing until Stuart had to slap the man away.

Smee dodged the clumsy slap and quickly turned to the little table. He poured amber liquid from a squat bottle into what looked like a solid gold goblet and handed it to Stuart. "Here, sar. This'll clear the cobwebs."

Desperately thirsty, Stuart took the cup and gulped — and immediately spat the contents of his mouth back at Smee, who accepted it calmly on his shirt front. "What the—?" Stuart tried, but his mouth burned too much to speak. His mouth, his throat, his lips and his tongue, oh his tongue, burning as if he had licked up the wax melting down the side of a lighted candle.

"It's brandy, sar," Smee replied. "Yeh likes it better'n rum so..." He trailed off nervously.

He needn't have worried. All Stuart heard was a low buzzing of unintelligible sounds that grew louder until his temples pounded and the man before him melted into a fat bank of undulating fog. Stuart's head drooped. He would have fallen straight out of the cot had not Smee's strong arms caught him and gently laid him back on it.

The world spun sickeningly. The floor seemed to melt into twists and curves. The air in the room grew terribly cold. It wasn't until Smee was finished carefully tucking a blanket under his chin that the room became a solid thing again, firm and dependable.

Still, it did have a habit of tilting ever so slightly back and forth, back and forth. Stuart perceived the faint sound of water outside, the sparkling lap of ocean waves and an odd but pleasant creaking of wood that came from all around. Such sounds might have lulled him to calmness, but in this instant, they sent chills through his body. The little fist pounded again inside his skull, harder and with greater urgency. He thrust it back under the musty film that had once again overgrown his thoughts, like soft moss over rocks in the cool quiet woods.

Not now. Not now. He slept.

CHAPTER 8

Melanie was almost done crying. Dabbing her eyes with a length of toilet paper — she had run out of tissues an hour ago — she walked mechanically from her bedroom to the living room to the kitchen and back again, cradling the roll of toilet paper in the crook of her arm and not even noticing when she bumped into a doorway. She spotted a magazine in the rack in the bathroom, the latest issue of *Biography*. Jon had given her a subscription for her birthday.

Too bad.

She took it into the kitchen and, striking yet another match, set fire to it. She held onto it for as long as possible, thinking that she had better not forget to put the batteries back into the smoke detector later. When the burning magazine became too hot, she dropped it in the sink. Its ashes joined the ashes of several other books, magazines and photos that she had burned over the course of the evening. The books had been his. The magazines had been his. The pictures had been his. Now only ashes remained. Her landlord was going to kill her for ruining the sink.

"I hate you," she kept repeating, trying to rekindle her wrath at the man she loved. "I hate you." The litany was wearing thin. She was too tired to hate anymore. All she wanted to do was go to bed. But she knew that if sleep graciously embraced her, it would only lead to bad dreams in the end. "God, don't let this tear me apart..."

Women who lost their men and never recovered from it had always disgusted her. A woman was a whole person, fully capable of leading a healthy, happy, normal life without a male around to open stubborn mayonnaise jars and compliment her earrings or her nail polish. Melanie had always prided herself on her ability to function alone.

Then she had met Jonathan Stuart, a man who possessed none of those macho traits, a man who encouraged her to reach for independence in every phase of her life, especially her relationship with him. Without his constant prodding, Melanie doubted she ever would have had the courage to pursue a freelance career. Because of his feistiness, she had discovered a new, more confident, more adventurous woman within herself, one who rather enjoyed a good tussle, one who wasn't afraid to gamble, one who could survive a bad loss and get right back up to try again. This was what he had given her. But the price had been high. Maybe too high.

"I hate you," she whimpered, and tried to imagine how he could have said those last words. *I don't think you and I should see each other anymore.* He had sounded so mechanical, as though he didn't care.

She knew better, though. He cared. He always turned that stone face on her when he was upset, always flicked that unnerving little On-Off switch in his head that protected him from pain. There had been a time when she had admired that ability. It must be nice, she had thought, to be able to step back and deal with painful things from an objective distance. But now that she was the one being dealt with from that objective distance, she didn't think it so admirable anymore. It was cold, and it hurt.

She sat down in front of the TV, intending to lose herself in the most stupid late-night movie she could find. When the phone rang, the first thing she realized was that she was horizontal. She sleepily rolled off the couch and crawled over to the phone. "'Lo?" She had to chew the word to get it out.

"Hi, Miss Forrester," came an Hispanic female voice. "It's Yolanda, from Jon's store."

"Yolanda, whuh time's it?"

"Eleven thirty."

Melanie started. Eleven thirty? She reached over and flung the curtains up enough to see the sun high in the sky. *You jerk!* her mind cried. *You've got to meet a client in Burbank in half an hour!* "Say, Yolanda, is this incredibly important, because I've really gotta go—"

"I just wanted to ask if you knew where Jon was. He's got an appointment with his auditor here at noon, and he hasn't shown yet or—"

The words were out of Melanie's mouth before she knew it. "I don't care if he's dead, okay? I'm not his keeper!" And she slammed the receiver down. *Oh, geez. Yolanda doesn't know what happened yesterday. Damn damn damn!* Melanie quickly dialed the store back. "Yolanda? Yeah, look, I'm sorry. Um, Jon and I broke..." She couldn't get it out. "...broke up yesterday..."

"You *what?*" came Yolanda's response, a full octave higher than normal. Then she managed, "But you guys were in... I mean, I'm sorry. I'm really... *Mira*, never mind, I'll deal with this, forget I called..."

Melanie thought back to how pale Jon had looked, and the way he had suddenly run out of the store clutching his stomach in pain. "He's sick," she offered, trying to soften Yolanda's embarrassment. *I hope he's barfing his brains out,* she added to herself.

"I called his house already. If he's home, he's not answering the phone."

Melanie stood up, peeved at being inconvenienced on account of that lout. "I've got to get to work, but I'll stop by his house and see what's up, okay?" she heard herself say. She stamped her foot, angry at having committed herself to this.

"No, really, Miss Forrester, you don't have to."

"I know I don't. I'm doing it for you, not for him. I'll let you know the scoop as soon as I can."

Melanie's apartment wasn't far from Jon's house. She pulled into his driveway fifteen minutes later. His porch light was still on, and all four cats were holding vigil at the front door, hungry for breakfast and running out of patience. When Melanie's car drove up, they all turned as one and stared at her with demon eyes. Then they recognized her and, one by one, stood, stretched and mewped at her to let them in.

Melanie walked the last few steps to the door slowly to avoid stepping on the twisting, purring, bumping bodies at her feet. She rapped once with the gargoyle knocker and waited. She rapped again. "Jon!"

The cats watched her take a key from her purse.

"Hey, he gave it to me," she told them, then added, "And I'll be giving it right back in about two minutes, so there." She fit the key into the lock and opened the door. Following the feline stampede, Melanie stepped through and closed it. "Jon? It's me."

Nothing.

Melanie crossed the hall and peered up the staircase. "Hey, I'm not here because I want to be or anything. Yolanda asked me to check on you." She waited for some response, or for the sound of the shower, the toilet flushing, Jon's razor buzzing. She heard nothing. "You up there?" She shrugged and headed back for the door. "Not home. Fine." Carefully, deliberately, she placed the key in the center of the little entryway table as she passed it. "Maybe I'll see you again some day."

Then she heard a loud thud and a cry, and before she knew it she was up the stairs and through the doorway to his bedroom. She found him sprawled on the floor in his pajama bottoms, tangled in the bed sheets and feebly struggling to sit up. "Jon!" she cried, kneeling beside him. *He must have been sleeping and had that awful nightmare again,* she thought. But the minute he looked at her she knew it was more than that.

Staring at her without recognition, he cried out something unintelligible and hit her smack across the face. She fell backwards, stunned. Then his eyes focused, and he seemed to see her clearly. "...Mel... nie...?"

She scrambled to her feet. "I'm calling the doctor!"

"No!" and when he added, "Please!" there was such fear in his voice that she immediately stopped. He sat there, looking around his own bedroom like he'd never seen it before. "Where am I?" He clutched his head and gasped. "I fell..."

Melanie dropped to his side and grasped his hands in hers. "Yes," she said, "you fell out of bed."

"No... it wasn't... I can't..."

"Jon, it's okay, calm down. I'll get your robe and take you to the hosp—"

He grabbed onto her arm so tight she winced. "My head hurts," he said, and slumped to the floor, unconscious.

Melanie ran for the phone.

CHAPTER 9

The first thing he thought to do was lick his lips. Slowly, very slowly. That thick sour taste in his mouth. That dry sticky feel of his tongue…

He tried to open his eyes, but they felt puffy. No matter, his hand could tell him what he needed to know. As it had so many times in the past, it wavered up to his chin and felt stubble. He licked his lips again, noting how hard it was to get even the tiniest muscle to do what he wanted it to do.

Dear God, he'd been drinking — enough, judging by the stubble, to have lain here for hours, maybe a whole day. *No*, he thought dismally. Aloud he groaned, "Melanie…?"

She was still there, wasn't she? In his bedroom? He was sick. He had heard her words through a haze, something about calling the doctor. She would make everything all right. She always did. But when Stuart finally managed to pull his eyelids apart, he saw a man's face, that strange burly Irish fellow from some far-away nightmare, the one with the half-glasses and the weird red floppy cap. The man who called himself Smee. Stuart sat up with a start, smacked his head on the low ceiling of the sleeping alcove and dropped back on the cot with a wail of pain.

"Ah, fer Chrissake," Smee said. "Here I be awaitin' fer yeh to wake up so yeh don't wallop yerself agin, an' yeh go makin' a fool o' me by wallopin' yerself agin."

Stuart barely heard him through the kettle drum pounding in his ears. He felt a strong hand tilt his head up. Something warm and tingly poured into his mouth. "No…" Stuart tried to spit it out, to wave the glass away, but any movement made the world reel.

"Swallow," Smee ordered. Rather than choke, Stuart swallowed. It was brandy.

"No…" Stuart protested as Smee placed a cool, wet cloth on his forehead. It felt so good, combined with the inner warmth of the brandy, that Stuart's hand dropped. He could only swallow again as Smee maneuvered more of the spirit into his mouth. *Please, don't,* he thought, but his lips couldn't form the words. The brandy relaxed him, as soothing as the caress of Melanie's fingertips. Where was she…?

"There," Smee said. "Let that simmer a bit, aye? An' don't. Sit. Up," he finished as though to an imbecile.

Stuart forced his eyes open again. He saw a face. It wasn't Smee, though. It was a different face. *Melanie?* he thought. *Yes!*

Wait, no. Not Melanie. Not a woman. A boy. Stuart remembered the face of a strangely beautiful boy laughing at him. "Peter Pan," he breathed.

"Aye," Smee said with a petulant edge. "He's flown by once er twice lookin' fer yeh, the devil. But don' yeh worry, Cap'n. We ain't spoken to him, so he don't know if yer alive or not. Sure he suspects, though."

Stuart brushed the cloth off his forehead and sat up, careful this time to clear the low alcove. Before Smee could stop him, he swung his legs out, pushed and stood. And fell. Smee hauled him up and stuffed him into a hard wooden chair. "Ortter nail yeh down," the man complained, holding onto Stuart's shoulders to make sure he would remain upright.

Stuart gripped the arms of the chair, fighting for control. He was shaking, his head pounded, and waves of nausea made him grimace. But he needed control. The moment he summoned enough strength, he jerked away from Smee's grasp to communicate what his mouth could not yet say: *Don't touch me!*

Smee backed off, hands up in surrender, but his expression was one of anything but surrender. Patience, maybe. But never surrender, not this man. Stuart felt hawkish eyes watch him as he studied his surroundings.

Writing desk against the right wall; a small table with a pitcher, basin and tray on it; an armoire against the left wall with a traveling trunk at its base; a full-length oval mirror next to that; the sleeping alcove containing his cot; a low, narrow door leading... where? Beneath his bare feet a small, worn Persian rug. Two lanterns on pegs, one by the dresser, one by the desk, at opposite ends of the room. Stuart could have crossed the entire space in four strides. *I'm not in a hotel or motel, that's for sure. This doesn't look like a normal bedroom. It's so damned small! And what about the tilting and the seagulls and the sounds of water, the smell of salt? Yes, this is way too small for a house, but it's rather spacious for...*

"A ship." Stuart remembered the first time he had awakened here. Now it was so obvious. "I'm in a ship."

"Aye," said Smee, a frown tugging at one side of his mouth.

"Whose ship?" Stuart asked, but he already knew. Smee had called him Captain.

It was then that Stuart noticed the crude wooden tailor's dummy standing in the corner. Perched atop a crooked wooden pole, it was over-burdened with the riotously stereotypical outfit of an 18th-century-gone-Hollywood pirate. Stuart then noticed that he was wearing nothing but a pair of white... what would they be called? Breeches? Pajamas? Long underwear? He realized he was cold.

Smee handed Stuart a shot glass. The liquid inside was amber. "Doctor's orders," he grinned, his bushy eyebrows wiggling mischievously as if in unspoken acknowledgment of some intimate secret.

"No."

"But it's from Beggar's Port, sar," Smee wheedled, maneuvering the glass into Stuart's shaky hand. "Smiffy's private stock."

Whatever that meant. Pointedly, Stuart slapped the glass down on the table. It didn't break, but a little amber wave spilled over the side. "I said no," he repeated. It encouraged him to take a firm stand on something.

Smee slowly brought his fists up to rest on his meaty hips. The message was clear: drink voluntarily or drink involuntarily, but one way or another, you're going to drink.

Stuart flinched. Smee had thus far displayed a gentle nature, but clearly he possessed authority and used it when necessary. In his present state, Stuart was no match for the fellow, so he drew the glass back to himself, paused, and sniffed the contents. Somewhere in his memory Alexander Jergins, Stuart's sponsor at the Pasadena AA group, warned him as he had many times before: "You are an alcoholic, Jon. Never forget that. Put one foot back on that road, and you'll find yourself back in the fast lane before you know it."

The ship dipped gently as ocean waves undulated beneath. Stuart felt it, as real as he had ever felt anything in his life. The glass in his hand was solid, the aroma of the brandy sharp, and behind it, the spicy smell of salt air and the musty odor of wet wood made his nose twitch. *Alex Jergins is at home snug in his comfy bed in Glendale, Jon, while you're sailing on a pirate ship in the frickin' Twilight Zone with a Hell's Angel who believes in Peter Pan. Fuck it.* He downed the brandy, feeling his tenuous hold on sanity slip another notch. *God help me.*

Smee grinned. Except for a mouthful of yellow teeth and skin that could have been fine Cordovan leather left in sunlight for a decade, he wasn't a bad looking old salt. There was actually a rather merry gleam in his eye as he clapped his hands together in the attitude of one about to begin a much anticipated chore. "That's fine, sar! So what say yeh take a stroll on the deck, eh? Git some fresh air?"

Stuart ignored the man. He had a plan now: drink. *If I can't control the insanity, I'll make it go away,* he thought, knowing full well how irrational that tactic was. All he would accomplish would be to make himself sick. But he remembered the numbness from the bad old days, remembered it perhaps too fondly, and now seemed a real good time to feel it again. *Anyway, it's only a dream,* he told himself. *Can't hurt you in the end. It's not real.*

Stuart refilled the shot glass from the bottle on the table, tossed it back, gasped and refilled it. A strong shudder flared through every muscle at once. His body grew light. His fingertips and toes went numb. His head started to float. Everything looked about one foot farther away than he knew it really was. *Stage One. Feels good. If I've got* to be in Neverland, it might as well be a Neverland on my terms. His eye fell on the wooden dummy in the corner. "Let me guess," he said to Smee, tipping his head at the pirate get-up. "You're going to make me put that on, aren't you?" He downed the second shot in one fiery swallow and filled it yet again.

Smee calmly glanced where Stuart had indicated. "Aye." He picked up a China plate from the table and handed it over. On it was a brown biscuit. Stuart hadn't seen it there before. "Eat this an' drink yer drink while I get yer clothes laid out."

The biscuit was so hard it could have been a rock in disguise, but once it registered as *food*, Stuart's hunger growled to life. He tore into it. It was pretty disgusting, closer to a ball of packed sawdust than any kind of bread he had ever eaten. But by the time Smee had the clothes all laid out on his little cot, Stuart's stomach was content for the moment and his head had stopped pounding. He was, in fact, pleasantly tipsy. *Been off the wagon so long it doesn't take much to get a buzz on,* he thought. *Better not swig too much or I'll just geyser it right back up. Blecch.*

He let Smee dress him. Actually, he had no choice. The clothes were a total puzzle. He had no idea what to put on in what order. There was a loose white long-sleeved shirt with lacy ruffles six inches long, a blood-red cravat with gold stitching, a long red vest, tan breeches, tight white stockings, red ribbons, and a myriad of bows. The fabrics ranged from fine cottons and silks to stiff brocades with jeweled embroidery. Stuart giggled when he finally got a look at himself in the mirror. "My God!" he burbled. "Happy Halloween!"

"Sar?" Smee asked, mystified.

"Oh, Smee, you are a clever man, but there is only so much I will do, even in a dream." Stuart turned round several times, amazed by his outrageous reflection. "You know, I could work on that ride at Disneyland," he chuckled, "what's it called, that pirate thing? I forget what it's called. I hate Disneyland. Crappy kids running everywhere."

Smee sniffed. It conveyed disapproval. Stuart felt a twinge of uneasiness as the portly man said, "I'll be gettin' yer hat, sar. One moment." He left the cabin.

As much as Smee was part of the nightmare that enveloped Stuart, his presence was also a comfort. Once he was gone, Stuart felt alone and quite afraid. He regarded the brandy bottle on the table with disgust. *Jon, you asshole, what have you done?*

He wobbled a little, but steadied himself by putting his hand against the bulkhead. Hard as rock, and cold. Intrigued, he reached out, touched the wood of the little desk, worn smooth from years of fingertips and elbows. Black walnut, like his own at the bookstore. The water in the basin was icy when he dipped his fingertips into it. He shivered when he flecked drops of it into his face. *Dammit, everything seems so real! Maybe everything is real...* "Time to wakey wakey," he mumbled as Smee returned.

"Here, Cap'n." Smee held up a wig, coal black, all long ringlets that would cascade halfway down his back.

Stuart snorted. "Like hell!"

Smee got mad. The change in the man was terrifying. "Yer gonna wear what I tell yeh to wear, sar! Yer not yerself, an' it's my job to see yeh git back to normal!"

Stuart snatched the wig and plopped it on his head.

"Not like that!" Smee scolded, and pushed Stuart back down in the chair. He gathered Stuart's long hair into a tight ponytail, fitted the wig onto his head — the thing was remarkably heavy, and Stuart's skull grew warm in seconds — then approached his left ear with a gold hoop. "Why... where's yer hole?" Smee exclaimed.

As tipsy as he was, Stuart's mind zoomed in on the foulest interpretation of that question. "My *what?*" he asked darkly.

"Yer hole, sar. Fer yer earrin'. It's gone." Smee examined Stuart's earlobe front and back, bewildered, then shrugged and set the golden hoop on the table. "Later," was all he said. He made Stuart put on four rings, three of them silver and one gold, then helped him pull on a pair of black knee-high leather jack boots with wide turn-downs just below the knees. He handed Stuart a dainty white kerchief with laced edges — "Stuff it up yer sleeve there, sar." — shrugged him into a long red crushed-velvet topcoat with black velvet trim, then handed him a wide-brimmed red beaver hat with black embroidered trim, the top of it adorned with several fluffy ostrich plumes.

Stuart didn't laugh when he saw himself in the mirror this time. At first he wasn't sure why, because he certainly looked like a lunatic who had just escaped out of a billboard for Captain Morgan rum. And then it hit him. "Everything fits."

"'Course it fits," Smee said with exasperation. "It's yers, ain't it? An' here, sar, the final touch." Smee held it out.

Stuart wasn't surprised to see his grandfather's saber laying across those callused palms, tucked into a beautiful silver scabbard. "Of all things," he said with a mixture of wonder and dread, "this makes the most sense." His hand gravitated toward the hilt.

"Sense, sar?" Smee asked.

Stuart drew his hand back, slowly, with effort. The air grew heavier. "Oh, yes," he replied as Smee, ever the dutiful valet, settled a red baldric across his charge's left shoulder, the wide and heavily ornamented belt holding the scabbard at Stuart's right hip. Stuart fought down panic. His flesh was tingling with a sudden black energy, the same energy he had felt during his ghostly saber battle that night at home. How long ago had that been?

Guided once more by its own objectives, his left hand reached to his right hip and this time succeeded in drawing the saber out. He gripped it, feeling the same marvelous balance between blade and hilt, the same eerie sense of sentience. It had him. He was on *its* home turf now, and he couldn't run from it, not here. Something dark closed around him like great black jaws.

"Ah, yeh cut a fine figure, sar. The boys'll be glad to see yeh." All smiles and bounce, Smee plucked the saber from his hand and slid it back into its scabbard. He pulled out a rag hanging from his pocket, flapped it over Stuart's clothes like a butler giving his master a final dusting, then propelled Stuart towards the door. "Come on, sar!"

The doorway was small. Stuart had to stoop to avoid bashing his head. The heels of the jack boots boosted him three inches beyond his own six foot height, and the wig and the hat added another three or four inches easy. He had to remain stooped as Smee led him along a short passageway, and then he went blind as sunlight — not from one sun but two — smacked him full in the face.

His eyes may have been useless, but his nostrils flared at the intense smell of salt and sea. His ears heard vast expanses of heavy canvas flap overhead while waves rippled below. The clamor of many gruff male voices all chattering at once was interrupted as Smee cried

out, "All right, ya scurvy scugs! All hands fall in abaft the mizz'n!"
Then Smee conducted him up the starboard ladder.

Stuart could do nothing but stumble along, shading his eyes with
his hands and blinking, trying to adjust to the brilliance. As he did, he
took in more sounds from below — the pounding of bare feet running
every which way, the creak of ropes, the deep grunts and moans of the
vast wooden hull. When he could finally see, he found himself
standing on the quarterdeck of a three-masted ship, looking down
into the faces of forty or so swarthy pirates who stared back up at him,
most of their mouths hanging open to reveal an alarming absence of
teeth. Eight or nine more men up in the rigging hung like monkeys,
gaping down at him.

Stuart gaped back. It had been much easier to deal with Smee.
One man. One apparition. One entity to deny as a dream. But try as
he might, Stuart couldn't simply dismiss this motley and very real
crowd before him. If nothing else, the overwhelming stench of the
men couldn't be explained away as a dream. A pig farm smelled better
than this. He thought he could actually feel the hairs inside his
nostrils cower down and try to flatten out rather than conduct such
nauseating information to his brain.

Smee nudged him. "Say somethin'!" he whispered.

Stuart couldn't move. *Say something?*

"Call all hands from below!" came a bellow from the main deck.

Smee nodded down at the man who had spoken, a handsome
Italian pirate with a long black ponytail. "Cecco," he informed Stuart.
"Yer first mate an' a fine feller."

"I can't take this..."

"Aw, c'mon, compose yerself, sar. Fer Chrissake, this here's yer
crew!"

Stuart clutched the edge of the rail hard enough to make his
fingers cramp. "This is not my crew."

"Sar—"

"This is not my crew! I don't *have* a crew!" He glared down at
Smee, noticing how the layers of heavy clothing restricted his
movements. In order to tilt his head — Smee wasn't short so much as
Stuart was tall, especially in the jack boots — he had to strain against
his cravat. He wasn't used to anything around his neck, and it

contributed to the trapped animal feeling he already had. He struggled for control. "This isn't real. I refuse to believe this is real, and I am most certainly not—"

"Captain Hook!"

The exclamation came from a young boy no more than eight years old, dressed in a filthy white shirt and black knickers. Stuart turned toward the voice, squinting to see its owner against the dazzling suns. He saw that the boy had climbed up out of the hatch, his expression a strange mixture of relief and trepidation. Come to think of it, all the pirates wore that expression.

"'Course yeh remember Lil' Lad Jack," Smee told Stuart. "Hard worker, he is. Good learner."

"Captain Hook," Jack repeated, quieter this time. He almost sounded reverent.

"Hook?" Stuart spat out before he knew what his mouth was doing. "Hook?" He held up his hands. "I've got *two hands,* you stupid little brat! I haven't got a hook! How can I be Captain Hook if I haven't got a hook? Anybody in this loony bin got an answer for that one?"

"He's a bleedin' ghost!" someone in the crowd muttered.

At that, Cecco turned on a tall, lean pirate whose every inch of visible flesh was covered with tattoos, including his hands and bare feet. Even his face was tattooed, although it was half-hidden by a hat bespangled with coins, jewels and a potpourri of shiny baubles. "What's that you say about the Captain, Mister Jukes?" Cecco asked sharply.

Feet shuffled. Someone coughed. Jukes tried to duck behind one of his fellows, who roughly pushed him away. "Nothin'," Jukes squeaked. "I didn't say nothin'."

"Aye, nothing," Cecco repeated with satisfaction. "That man up there is no ghost, ya slackjawed jackanapes!" he boomed, and the men jumped. Stuart jumped, too — Cecco might as well have been using a bullhorn, he was so loud. "That's the only man the Sea-Cook fears! He's the only man who ever snared a siren, ate of her flesh and lived! He's the only man who outsmarted Pan, outsmarted the croc, outsmarted *death itself,* to come back and beat Pan at his own game! Now act like his crew, by thunder, or you'll feel the kiss o' the cat!"

A roar went up the likes of which Stuart hadn't heard since the last time he went to a Lakers game. They were cheering him! And not one of them, Smee included, seemed to care about his obvious lack of a hook.

"Yer turn, sar. Speak a piece," Smee encouraged him, elbowing him.

Stuart instead turned his back on the crowd and shut his eyes tight.

Cecco broke the nervous silence. "All right, back to work, the lot o' ya!"

As the crew dispersed, Smee's words filtered out of the blackness. "Y'okay, sar?"

"Get me out of here."

Stuart felt Smee take his arm. "Yer gonna be fine, sar. Let's walk a bit, eh? Yer dizzy, is all."

Smee wasn't going to let him escape, and indeed, Stuart understood with a pang in his gut that there was nowhere to escape *to*. The ship was, of course, the *Jolly Roger*. He looked up to see the black pirate flag with its white skull and crossbones waving a good hundred and fifty feet above in the wind. The vessel was moored in a quiet little bay. The shore of a small island a quarter mile away curved around it like a horseshoe, with a single mouth leading out to the open sea.

Now Stuart remembered his flight over the island. He remembered falling. The more he thought about it, the more the details came back to him, the falling and the sickening speed of it. He must have landed in this bay where the pirates found him. How had he possibly survived a fall like that? And how in the world did these maniacs think he was the captain they had lost?

Smee prodded him down a stairway and walked him slowly along the main deck as though taking him on a Sunday stroll through the park. As Stuart passed men working, many averted their eyes. Some winced or ducked as if expecting a blow. Others hurried out of his path as if afraid he might suddenly scoop them up and throw them overboard.

"They're scared of me," he noted after they had traversed the length of the ship and stood on the foredeck.

"Aye," Smee answered in a confidential tone. "Yer a stern captain, to be sure, an' yeh *have* come back from the dead, more'r less."

"Have I?" Stuart wondered. "You're not afraid of me. Why?"

Smee rubbed the grey whiskers on his chin. "Sar, there's a nasty rumor runnin' amongst the crew. They know about yer loss of, err... well, sar, yeh've forgotten a few things. Memory, I'm talkin'. When Roland an' Biggs brought yeh aboard, yeh raved like a madman. Half the crew heard yeh howlin' about not knowin' where yeh were or even *who* yeh were. Took four men to hold yeh down afore yeh passed out. I'm, uh, guessin' yeh don't remember that part."

Thankfully, Stuart did not. But he did notice Smee's obvious and abrupt change of subject. He decided to let it go. For the moment.

"Anyhow," Smee went on, "I'm sure yer memory'll return in time, sar. I mean, considerin' where we are."

"Where we are is foremost on my mind," Stuart said. "So..." He glanced over at the island. "Where are we?"

"Pirate's Bay, sar," replied Smee. "Bit obvious, ain't it?"

"No, it is not obvious!" Stuart pulled off his hat, was about to pull the wig off as well, but something about Smee's attitude told him that would be a bad idea. He scowled at the garish headgear and slapped it back on. "As for my memory, Smee ol' buddy, I report that it is as sharp as ever. You people are the ones who are confused. I've never set foot on a ship in my life. I couldn't sail a toy boat in my fucking bathtub, do you understand? I am not your captain!"

"It'll all come back, sar—"

"It can't come back! It was never there!" Stuart seized a fistful of Smee's baggy shirt and drew him close. "Listen to me, dammit. I'm from Pasadena, California. That Peter Pan thing has been terrorizing me for more than a week, and from the look of things he's brought me here to play Captain Hook for him. Well, I won't do it! Tell me how I can get back home!"

"Ah, Cecco!" Smee said jovially, and slipped free of Stuart's grasp as if there was no grasp at all, leaving Stuart clutching empty air.

Cecco gave Smee a hearty slap on the shoulder. Stuart snarled and turned away from them both, wishing he had that bottle of brandy again — though it was a toss-up as to whether he would have drunk from it or hit Smee over the head with it.

"James," said Cecco, warm and personable and quite unlike the bellowing brute he had been when addressing the crew. He spoke with an Italian accent of sorts. A bit of Cockney and what might have been a Jamaican accent were mixed in, making Cecco sound like the world traveler that he probably was. "James, my friend, you had us worried—"

Stuart shot him a dirty look over his shoulder, noting with no real interest that the Italian had a full set of impressively white teeth. "I am not your friend. I don't know who the hell you are, so fuck off."

Cecco sucked in a quick breath. "Aye aye, Captain." He saluted, turned on his heel and left.

Smee made a prissy *tsk tsk* noise. "Yer a fine one, sar."

"Oh, stuff yourself, Smee, or whoever the hell you really are."

"Aw, sar, is that any way to treat yer trusted ol' bosun? After all, I've known yeh longer than Cecco, aye? Don't ye worry, we both know not to take yer outbursts to heart. It's all part o' yer charmin' personality, heh heh." The pirate's eyes twinkled with an odd light.

Stuart couldn't stand it any longer. "That's it, I'm outta here." He pushed past Smee and headed back toward the sterncastle and his cabin, tearing off his hat and throwing it defiantly to the deck as he went. He was so frustrated he barely noticed that the pirates were opening a hasty path before him.

All except for one man, a blond Swede who stepped directly in his way. It wasn't that the fellow was tall — Stuart stood eye-to-eye with him — but he was massive, his muscles something out of a Marvel comic book, his face a cold mask of pure hatred. His skin was crisscrossed with scars that told of some appalling accident.

"Move!" Stuart thundered, desperate to be alone.

The man set in place like concrete. "*Djävul*," he spat. "*Vilddjur*. Monster from zeh deat," he finished in English, his thick accent distorting the words.

"I'm not your stinking captain!" Stuart shrilled. "Outta my way!"

The Swede raised a meaty hand and pushed with a bear's strength against Stuart's chest. Stuart heard the pirates murmur in astonishment as he stumbled backwards, flailing out and grabbing the pinrail in time to keep himself from landing unceremoniously on his backside. Nobody moved to help him as the Swede lumbered forward, holding a hand ax. Stuart hastily straightened up, wondering if the man really intended to kill him.

The Swede merely jabbed a beefy finger at him. "He say no *kapten!*" he said to his fellow pirates. "He remember noting! He valk, talk, no *minne!*" He tapped his own skull. "No *kunskap!*"

"Stow it, Sigrson," someone said, "'fore he keelhauls you again."

Sigrson's eyes burned as he repeated, "Keelhault," glaring at Stuart as if trying to kill him with the fury of his gaze.

Stuart heard Smee approaching from behind, the bosun's footfalls heavy with the intent to rescue. Stuart was in no mood to be rescued. Surprising himself with his own speed, he whipped his saber from its scabbard and aimed it at the Swede's heart, rock steady. His fingers tingled with violent possibilities. "Move," he said.

Sigrson hesitated. He considered the saber, Stuart, then the eager faces around him, some aglow with the prospect of violence, some tense with the prospect of same, every one ready for blood sport. He lowered his ax and stepped aside.

Somewhere through the red haze in his mind Stuart registered the sound of cheering, but his attention was fixed solely on the open path before him. He slammed the saber back into its scabbard, resumed his course to his cabin and ducked through the door, vaguely aware that the cacophony of monkey whoops behind him was building to a raucous crescendo.

Seconds later he was in the captain's cabin, head tipped back, brandy bottle at his lips. He guzzled amber fire until he choked and, coughing and spluttering, dropped the empty bottle. It didn't break. With an incoherent cry he scooped it back up and smashed it against the bulkhead. Several pieces of glass hit him, but they bounced off his thick clothing. He dropped the jagged-edged bottle neck. His fingers felt like ice.

His rage drained away, taking his strength with it, and he sank down onto the worn Persian carpet. The cabin started to spin. He wanted to throw up, but his stomach stubbornly held onto its roiling cargo of brandy. He wanted to cry, but his eyes had forgotten how to form tears so so long ago. He didn't care anymore if he ever understood what was happening. He just wanted it to stop. "Melanie..." he groaned.

"No, just me, sar." Strong hands hoisted him unsympathetically to his feet. "Just ol' Smee, wonderin' fer the hundredth time why yeh allow a scallywag like Vigr Sigrson to stay aboard. He's bidin' his time, y'know. One day yeh'll turn yer back an'... well."

Stuart heard himself whimper. A disgusting, embarrassing sound, like a mewling baby, but he couldn't help it. "I was ready to kill him."

"Aye, an' I'm thinkin' it mighta been better if yeh had."

"You don't understand... I drew the... I..." As Stuart spoke, his shaking hand drew the saber, as if the very words required the action. It felt disturbingly natural. "I would never kill anybody..."

"Pshaw."

"...but I... I was ready to..."

"Yer drunk."

"...to kill him..."

"Yer drunk, an' yeh'd best sleep it off."

Smee took Stuart's saber and aimed his captain at the little bed in the alcove, ready to push him into it boots, wig and all. He froze when the ship's bell rang.

"The alarm, sar!" Smee sprinted for the door.

Stuart nearly fell over. Wobbling, he corrected himself in time to catch the saber from Smee. "Yeh'll be needin' that, sar!" the bosun said. "Hurry, for pity's sake! It's Pan!"

CHAPTER 10

Pan!

With a rush of hope, Stuart shoved through the door ahead of
Smee and emerged on the quarterdeck. Squinting from the intense
sunslight, he surveyed the main deck.

Pirates were scurrying every which way, reminding Stuart of silver
balls in a pinball machine clacking wildly to and fro. But the pirates
didn't bump into each other in their frenzy, not at all. With well-
drilled precision they rushed to their posts while Cecco, a telescope
held up to one eye, called out, "Two points off the starboard bow!"
Stuart presumed this indicated some kind of firing target, but instead
of moving to the cannons, the men began backpedaling to the rails,
their sheep-like faces a study in fear. It was amazing to watch, as if an
invisible force field had shoved them all back in a circle. The culprit
was, in fact, just a light, a tiny gold spot of brilliance that zoomed at
incredible speed down from the sky and hovered over the ship.

"The fairy!" Jukes screeched from somewhere astern.

"Don't let 'er dust yeh!" another pirate warned as he took cover
behind the mizzenmast.

It was Tinker Bell. Stuart remembered her. She had helped Pan
guide him to the Neverland.

The little light flared a mischievous pink and zipped about the
deck, spitting clouds of sparkling dust everywhere. Pirates hopped and

twisted to get out of the way. "What's going on?" Stuart demanded as Smee rushed to his side.

"Whatever yeh do, sar, don't let the fairy's dust touch yeh," Smee warned him.

"But it can't hurt you—"

"I wouldn't be so sure!" came a lovely child voice, and Peter Pan appeared over their heads.

Stuart remembered Pan very well — a boy, cocky like a pup, filled with the green strength of youth, dressed in the color of trees, his two daggers crisscrossed at his hips. He grinned a cheery cherub's grin.

Stuart and Smee ducked as the boy unexpectedly dive-bombed them. "Do it, Tink!" Pan called out.

Tinker Bell streaked over to Lil' Lad Jack, the young boy who had first called Stuart by the name Captain Hook. She powdered him with dust in one twinkling poof. "Get it off me!" Jack wailed, hopping about, frantically patting the dust off his sleeves. "Get it off me!"

Instead of helping, the pirates shuffled farther away while Jack patted golden twinkles into the air. Stuart curiously watched as they all grasped the nearest stable objects at hand — lines, the capstan, belaying pins — and once they had a hold, they adopted the attitudes of those clutching onto a life raft in a storm.

"Clear your mind, Jack!" Cecco shouted, not daring to get close to the boy but obviously wanting to help him. "Don't think any happy thoughts! I'll flog your damned hide if you do! You won't get rations for a week, you hear me, boy?" He gripped the starboard pinrail and added, "Biggs, throw him a line double-quick, you bastard!"

Biggs, the closest to young Jack, started to obey, but a knife thunked into the wood by his hand and he snatched the hand back. Stuart looked up in the direction from which the knife had come and spotted another boy, much older than Pan, flitting around the portside shrouds, laughing.

"What is going on?" Stuart cried.

"Hold onter the wheel, sar!" was all Smee would say, and he clasped a spoke with both hands. Stuart did the same.

"Bye bye, Jack!" Pan sang.

The breeze that had been tugging lazily at Stuart's long black curls suddenly erupted into a gale that whisked Jack up off the deck as if he weighed little more than a feather. The ship pitched sharply to starboard as the once-calm sea threw instant waves against the port side. Everyone hung on, aware of their own plight as well as Jack's. Although the boy tried to keep hold of the rail while his feet kicked helplessly over his head, the wind buffeted him about, finally yanking him free with the crack of breaking finger bones. It hurled him toward the seaward horizon, his wails fading like the whistle of a teapot removed from a stove burner.

The wind died back down, leaving the *Jolly Roger* pitching and tossing in a mild sea. Stuart gaped out at the horizon.

"Jack!" Cecco yelled after the boy. He whirled on Pan, his sea legs holding him firmly erect as the ship gradually settled. He drew his cutlass and slashed the air in invitation. "Get down here, you devil!" Cecco said, fairly bristling with rage. "Fight a man, if you dare!"

"No!" Stuart cried out. Reluctantly, Cecco lowered his cutlass.

Peter Pan beamed with delight and dropped gracefully to the main deck. He bowed to Stuart. "Greetings, Captain Hook," he said happily. "So good to see you again." He wasn't the least concerned with the fact that he was surrounded by pirates. Rather, he acted supremely confident of his own safety.

His confidence was not misplaced. The pirates, not even Cecco, made a move against him. All eyes were on Stuart, whose alcoholic fog had cleared at the moment of Jack's death. His nerves were rock steady now, fueled by an adrenaline rush but held in check by an instinct that told him to play it cool. "Who are you?" he asked bluntly. "*What* are you?"

Children giggled from all around. Pan waved invitingly with both hands as if summoning spirits from the sky. "C'mon!" he called. "We have introductions to make!"

A troupe of wild-haired boys floated up from behind the bulwarks, down from where they had been hiding behind furled sails, even out of the crows' nest. Stuart expected to see about six — wasn't that the number of Lost Boys in the Peter Pan story? But he quickly counted at least a dozen in the air around him, ranging from maybe four to twelve years old. One of them was so chubby he looked more like a balloon than a child. Another was wearing some kind of animal skin.

There was a pair of twins who wore identical Indian-like attire, and one wore a cap of skunk's fur, tail intact, on his head.

"Wendy!" Pan said. "Captain Hook, I'd like you to meet Wendy. Wendy, this is the dark and sinister Captain Hook."

A girl of perhaps ten, dressed in a frilly white ankle-length nightgown, floated towards Stuart. She stopped just out of his reach, gazing down at him with green eyes. She clasped her dainty hands to her breast in delight and cried out, "Oh, Peter, he's just what I expected! He's marvelous!"

Stuart blinked. "I beg your pardon?"

Wendy giggled. "Oh, he's so tall and handsome, and so very polite!" She turned sharply to Pan. "Is he cruel?"

Pan nodded somberly. "Most definitely."

"Oh, he's perfect!"

"Yes, just darling," Stuart muttered, grasping for the bad pun, hoping that the wincing humor of it would make him feel better. The sound of Jack's breaking fingers still rang in his ears. *This isn't happening,* his brain stubbornly insisted, *this isn't happening...*

How Wendy heard the mutter was beyond him, but the girl clapped her hands and squealed, "He knows my name! Darling! Yes yes, I'm Wendy Darling!" She corrected herself in grown-up tones, "That is, I am Miss Wendy Moira Angela Darling. I am very pleased to make your acquaintance, Captain Hook."

Smee rolled his eyes and grunted.

"Wendy arrived last night," Pan explained. "These are her brothers John and Michael."

Two boys of perhaps eight and four floated over to join Wendy. The elder wore a black top hat, and both were dressed in striped pajamas. Their feet were bare, as were Wendy's. Stuart found himself wondering if they were cold, dressed like that. And didn't little Wendy have any sense of propriety flying around with a nightie on?

"Greetings, evil Captain Hook," John intoned with a hint of fearful respect.

Little Michael waved. "Hewwo!"

Cecco stomped forward. "Captain, are we to fight or not? Li'l Lad Jack is dead! We can't just stand here!"

The pirates gabbled their agreement, and the children gave Stuart looks filled with expectancy. Even Smee, who had remained unusually quiet these last few minutes, appeared eager for action. No one, however, seemed intent on doing a thing without Hook's orders.

Stuart felt a solemn mantle of authority settle on his shoulders. "Nobody move," he heard himself say. His voice sounded deeper than usual, filled with a confidence he did not wholly feel.

A few pirates shuffled nervously but otherwise obeyed. Smee remained silent. Wendy openly admired Stuart as she floated over the deck, oblivious of her fluttering nightgown, her smooth prepubescent features held in an expression of girlish rapture. Stuart pointedly ignored her and jabbed a finger at Pan. "You. I want to talk to you. Alone. Now."

Pan saluted smartly. "Aye aye, Captain sir!" he cried, and his lean body rose effortlessly into the air. Every pirate eye followed him.

Stuart said to Smee, "Keep it quiet," then climbed the ladder up to the poop deck where he and Pan could talk in private. It gave him the creeps to feel the boy shadow him, but Stuart recognized that authority was his aboard the *Jolly Roger* if he chose to accept it. Better to grasp it and use it than let it slip away. Control was everything. No matter that he had no idea how to run a ship. He would figure it out later, if indeed there would be a later in which to figure out anything. He strode all the way to the taffrail before turning to face Pan. "All right," he said calmly. "What do you want?"

Pan soundlessly alighted on the deck. "What do I want? Why, Captain, the game's afoot! You try to kill me, and I try to kill you. That's simple enough, isn't it?"

Stuart held his arms out. "I am not going to kill anyone. I have no intention of staying here, and I have no intention of playing games."

"Ah-ah-ah, but you have the sword," Pan said, waggling a finger at him.

Stuart had the unsettling sensation of being reprimanded by his old sixth grade teacher, the loathsome Mr. Kattenbaum, the one who used to beat him according to his father's instructions. Kattenbaum's image blotted out Pan. The old classroom tyrant curled his lip. "You can't run away from me. Face your punishment like a man!"

Kattenbaum vanished, and Peter Pan stood there. "I'm as much a man as you are," the boy said. "C'mon, I challenge you to a duel!" He unsheathed his daggers and took a defensive stance.

Stuart drew his saber — and let it fall from his hand.

"Careful, Captain," Pan warned. "You've left yourself defenseless."

"I know."

"Then you should also know that I'm only honorable in storybooks."

Stuart was amazed at how calm he felt. "That may be. I still won't fight you."

"You'd rather die?" Pan asked. He called over his shoulder, "Mister Smee! Your captain has lost his mettle! Do the men really want a leader who's afraid to fight a little boy?"

Stuart heard the pirates mutter at such a scandal. The success of Pan's blatant manipulation infuriated him. With a well-aimed kick he knocked the dagger from Pan's left hand, sending it skittering across the poop. Pan swiped with his remaining blade, but Stuart dodged aside and seized the boy by the neck. "I've had it with you, you snotty little shit!" he snarled, slamming Pan back against the taffrail. He pressed his torso into the boy, pinning his legs in case Pan had any ideas about kicking vulnerable body parts. Stuart dug his nails into the soft flesh of the boy's wrist, seeking nerve points. "Drop it, or I'll break your arm."

Pan dropped the second dagger. "You're — strong—!" he wheezed.

"And you're running out of air," Stuart answered, squeezing Pan's neck with a sneer of satisfaction.

"Cap'n, sar!" Smee said, his head poking up over the top of the stairs. "Need help?"

"Does it look like I need help?" Stuart shot back. "Just watch the other children. And," he added in a commanding tone, "no matter what happens to me, do not interfere." Stuart squeezed harder now, bringing an urgent red flush to Pan's cherub cheeks. "You have no idea how much I'd like to kill you."

"Then — do — it!"

"No. Even if I did decide to commit cold-blooded murder, I have the strangest feeling that you wouldn't stay dead. Why should I waste my time?" Stuart threw the boy to one side, hard, letting anger lend pitiless strength to his arm.

Peter Pan crashed to the deck. He lay there, dazed.

Stuart calmly picked up his saber. "Game over."

"Hardly, Captain," said Pan, and with the speed of a rabbit, he recovered one of his daggers and flew at Stuart.

Slash!

Blood flowed from Stuart's right forearm. "Jesus!" Stuart cried, more in astonishment than in pain. He spun around in time to catch Pan slashing at him again, this time ripping into his shoulder. The thick embroidery on Hook's topcoat saved him this time, but Pan wasn't finished. Growling like a tiger cub, the boy flew around him in a blur and rammed him in the shoulder.

Stuart's boots slipped on the slick deck and he fell, keeping his wits enough to flick his blade away from his body when he landed. He managed to keep hold of the hilt, but his wrist twisted painfully, and as he scrambled to his knees, cursing the thick clothes that restricted his movements, he had barely enough time to raise the saber and parry Pan's cutlass.

Wait — *cutlass?* Where did Pan get a cutlass from?

As if in answer, Pan cried out, "Thanks, Ranger!"

A lanky boy floating off the stern saluted. "I nicked it from Starkey, Peter! First his pistol, now his cutlass!" Ranger puffed with pride. "I out-pirated the pirates!"

Wendy flew into view, her eyes wide in excitement. "Oh, do watch out, Peter!" she squealed as Stuart rolled onto his back and lashed out with one foot, catching Pan square in the solar plexus. The boy whooshed out his breath and toppled backwards, but he kept grips on both the cutlass and his dagger.

"Stop!" Stuart commanded.

Pan lay there, surprised but not the least injured. "Stop?" he said, genuinely confused.

Stuart pressed his bleeding forearm to his abdomen, beginning to feel the pain. Damn, it was a deep cut. "Look," he gasped, "I don't want to do this. Why are you making me do this?"

Perhaps Pan would actually have answered the question. Stuart would never know, because a loud shot rang out. He raced to the rail and looked down on the main deck. A dreadlocked Jamaican pirate was bleeding from his thigh. Two of his fellows caught him as the wounded leg gave way.

Smee called up to him, "They got shot an' powder fer Starkey's barker, sar!"

"Huh?" was all Stuart could manage.

"His pistol!" Smee explained heatedly. "They stole it weeks ago, yeh 'member? Somehow they got hold o' shot an' gunpowder!"

Stuart scanned overhead and spotted a little Mexican boy triumphantly holding a pouch in one hand and a powder horn in the other. Hovering beside him was Ranger, the lanky older boy who had provided Pan with the cutlass. The two were busily reloading Starkey's stolen pistol, wicked smiles on their faces.

"Do we attack, sar?" Smee asked.

"But... they're children!" Stuart said helplessly.

"They're animals, sar!" Smee countered hotly.

Smee was right. These kids were animals. Stuart glanced at his cut wrist. "Fine, do whatever you want. But I want Pan!"

Smee saluted happily. "Aye aye, Cap'n!" He and Cecco started bellowing orders to the men. They scurried into action.

The Lost Boys broke their loose formation and dived away in pairs, cutlasses swinging as they targeted specific parts of the ship. First to be attacked were the mainstays, ropes tarred to rock-like density that anchored the masts to the hull. If the rigging went out of balance, the tensions between sail and ship could rip a vessel apart. Realizing the danger, pirates swarmed up the shrouds, blades clamped between their teeth.

A second pair of boys attacked at deck level, swiping at ankles with their cutlasses and using their free hands to tumble firefighting buckets of water and sand across the deck, making footing treacherous for the mostly barefooted pirate crew.

The pair of twins taunted the pirates at the bow by flying upside down over the cramped area. Slashing down with their blades, they posed a threat while keeping their inverted bodies out of harm's reach — at least for the first few minutes. Out from belowdecks a half-dozen pirates appeared, their arms filled with bows and quivers. These were quickly handed out, along with leather slings and pouches of iron grapeshot. A moaning hum rose in pitch as the slingers spun their deadly pellets.

The air was suddenly not a safe place to be. Arrows that missed the Lost Boys sped on to tear through sails and, in a few unfortunate cases, a pirate. But at least the arrows could be tracked in flight. The slings remained silent and deadly, offering only the *thwock* of impact to announce their existence. The pistols belched flame and thunder but were notoriously inaccurate beyond a few yards. More pirates were taken down during the melee than Lost Boys. To make matters worse, Tinker Bell flitted about, showering fairy dust everywhere, making the pirates jump like roaches on a hot plate to avoid it.

Stuart felt as though he had been thrown into a demented action movie. What was he supposed to do? Kill a gaggle of flying children? Sure, he had given the order, but the pirates were earnestly carrying it out!

He tore the long frill off of his shirt and tied it quickly around his cut to slow the bleeding. Overhead, one of the boys caught a pistol shot in his side and tumbled from the sky. Stuart rushed to the rail, expecting to watch the kid drown. Instead, as the boy floundered weakly in the waves, a miraculous thing happened — a porpoise swam up and, lending its dorsal fin for taxi service, waited until the boy had a good hold then towed him to shore.

"My God..." Stuart breathed as he watched.

The railing next to his hand exploded into splinters. Stuart flung himself back, rudely reminded that he was the main target onboard. Above him, Ranger brandished his stolen pistol. "Next time, Captain, just you wait!"

"Wait my ass," Stuart growled. He hurried down to the main deck and spotted a pirate armed with a bow and a quiver. "Gimme that!" Stuart said, and grabbed the bow and an arrow.

"Aye, C-C-Cap'n, sir," the pirate stammered.

Stuart wasn't as good an archer as he was a fencer, but he had the basics down. He knew enough to aim well and not poke his own eye out. He ducked down beside the starboard stairway that led up to the quarterdeck and, mentally disconnecting himself from the action around him, calmly studied the sky above.

At this point, the Lost Boys had abandoned all organization and were flitting above their foes with gleeful abandon, nettling and harassing the pirates on deck, shroud and sail. Beyond, Wendy taunted the men and egged on the boys like some spun-sugar cheerleader, flying from one fight to another and rah-rahing the combatants on. *No threat there*, Stuart decided.

And then he spotted Ranger and his tubby powderboy perched on the topsail yardarm. Just as Ranger pointed his pistol directly at him, Stuart drew his bow and let fly. The pistol's ball slammed home into the rail next to him, the flying splinters making him shield his face with his coat sleeve. A scream of pain echoed above, assuring him that his arrow had struck home. *Fuck you!* he thought of the gun-toting boy. But when he looked, it wasn't Ranger's body that was tumbling out of the sky.

It was Wendy, who must have flown by at just the wrong moment.

The melee aboard the ship stopped in eerie unison. As if tied to the same great marionette string, everyone, pirate and child alike, turned to gape at Stuart. The weight of their collective shock literally pushed him back against the portside bulwarks. His jaw hung slack in horror. He had been willing enough to hurt Ranger, who had dared to fire at him, but little Wendy? "Oh my God..."

Peter Pan slowly rose up from the starboard side of the ship and hung there, dripping with water and staring across the deck at Stuart with eyes like lasers. Panic screamed silently at the base of Stuart's skull. Had he killed Wendy? If he had, what would Pan do to him? Even if Wendy lived, what would Pan do to him?

Pan floated slowly towards him, his face flushed with such wrath that he seemed brighter than Tinker Bell, who flittered along beside him, glowing crimson and chiming soft suggestions that only Pan could understand.

Oh sweet Jesus, I'm dead, was all Stuart could think, but he forced his knees to straighten. If nothing else, he would meet Pan standing tall. Shaking, maybe, but tall.

Pan stopped before him and gently settled to the deck. He stood perhaps four feet high, weighed maybe as much as a full-grown Labrador. No matter. Physique and power weren't related in the Neverland, not in his case. "I will kill you for this," Pan promised.

Go for broke. "You're going to kill me anyway. Isn't that how the story goes?"

Pan quirked an eyebrow. "True."

Stuart had to ask. "Is she dead?"

"Why should you care? Your arrow found its mark." Pan slowly drew his dagger. "And my blade will find its mark as well."

It happened so fast that Stuart didn't feel it. In a blur of green his wounded forearm was slashed again, and then Peter Pan, Tinker Bell and the children were gone.

CHAPTER 11

He knew what had happened, and he knew that if he looked at it, he would feel it. As long as he didn't look, maybe he could convince himself that it didn't hurt. Trembling, Stuart headed for Smee, who was hastening across the deck to meet him. "Fer Chrissake hurry, sar. Yer bleedin' bad there. Lemme fix yeh up."

Stuart allowed Smee to hustle him up to the quarterdeck and into his cabin. Before the door closed, he heard Cecco shouting for the worst of the injured to be carried down to the lower deck to be tended by Cookson, who must have been the ship's doctor, or the closest thing to a doctor on this floating rat's nest. Stuart supposed that Cookson was more a traditional sawbones — little real education in medicine, just someone who could stop a bleeding wound or, if he couldn't, chop off the injured part before it turned gangrenous.

In the cool shadows of the captain's cabin, Smee guided Stuart to the chair and sat him down. He whipped a rag out of his back pocket, put it in Stuart's left hand, and made him press it down over the gaping cut. Stuart caught a glimpse. Sliced flesh. White bone. A river of red. He turned away, sucking in air through clenched teeth. *If I don't look, it won't hurt. Yeah, right.*

"Jus' hold it there, sar, while I fetch bandages," Smee said and slipped back out the door.

Stuart sat alone, splashed with his own blood, guilty of shooting a little girl, and lost in a storybook nightmare. *Block if off,* he thought, and fumbled for the great grey wall in his mind. *Block it off, make it all go away.* He slammed the wall down.

It worked, but not as well as usual. The terror and confusion would not let him go. The ugly emotions banged against the wall, determined to plague him at all costs. The pain shooting up his arm actually grew worse, burning like an ember deep in his flesh. He ground his jaws and pressed down on his forearm, rocking back and forth, back and forth.

A *thump* made him leap from his chair and reach for his saber. It was only Smee returning with a steaming kettle in one hand, bandages and a bottle in the other. "Don't yeh be lettin' go of it, sar!" the pirate admonished.

Stuart realized that he had stopped pressing on the wound in order to draw his saber. Blood was flowing freely down his intricate layers of clothing.

"Wound's not really that bad, y'know, sar," Smee assured him, opening the bottle. "If yeh don't mind," he said apologetically, and before Stuart could comprehend what the bosun had in mind, the man sloshed brandy into the raw wound. Stuart choked on a howl of agony. Smee handed him the bottle.

Without hesitation, Stuart took it and drank. The portly man was right – the wound wasn't as bad as it could have been, considering. All the same, the pain was astounding. The world swam in and out before his eyes, and Stuart knew he was about to faint. It was all too much, this whole demented scenario and worse, his preposterous role in it. He just wanted to get away, even if passing out was the only way to accomplish it.

He managed to stand the bottle up on the table before his body slipped out of the chair. The deck was cold, and as blackness rushed over him he heard Smee as if from a great distance: "Aw, fer Chrissake."

CHAPTER 12

Melanie sat in the emergency waiting room of the Glendale Memorial Hospital on Central Avenue, sniffling and wringing her hands. *He's been acting strangely,* she thought for the fiftieth time. *He's been erratic. He said his head hurt. He fell out of bed. He didn't know me.* She gasped. *A brain tumor. Oh Lord, he's got a brain tumor.*

"Miss Forrester?"

She jumped. "Oh! Oh, Yolanda, what are you doing here?"

Yolanda stood in the waiting room doorway. "Jon," she said.

Melanie stood up, feeling ridiculous. "Of course. I just meant — I didn't expect to see you, that's all."

Yolanda, as usual, was calm and collected, even within the sterile environs of a hospital emergency ward. "How is he?" she asked, motioning Melanie to sit back down with her.

Melanie wished she knew the answer to that question. She wasn't related to Jon, so at first the hospital staff were reluctant to deal with her as closest of kin, regardless of the fact that there was nobody else to deal with. She had convinced the doctor, Bernard Odet, that she was Jon's fiancée, showing him the ruby ring — an engagement ring, she had told him. Thankfully Odet chose to have mercy and treat her as next of kin. What followed was an avalanche of insurance cards, medical records, explanations — she'd had to deal with it all since Jon had been put under sedation.

When the paramedics had first arrived at his house, Jon had regained consciousness, but he still hadn't recognized her or his own house. He had become "agitated," as they put it, and eventually they'd had to sedate him.

Melanie had always harbored a perverse desire to ride in an ambulance with the sirens going full blast, running red lights and watching all the other traffic pull aside with a weird sort of reverence. Yet all she remembered about the trip were feelings of dread and near hysteria.

And Jon's behavior... something about his delirium nagged at her. She had done research for medical TV shows, and many of those shows dealt with psychological as well as physical problems. She was no expert, but something about Jon's mannerisms when she had found him on the floor of his bedroom, something about his eyes, his expression of mixed relief and desperation when he had recognized her for that one brief moment — he hadn't seemed sick or deranged so much as *scared*. No, more than scared. Terrified. But of what?

The paramedics had questioned her. The receptionist had questioned her. The doctor had questioned her. And now Yolanda. "I don't know," she said wearily. "I don't know..."

Yolanda took her hand. "He'll be all right."

"But you didn't see him," Melanie said. "You didn't hear him. He didn't know who I was. I called the paramedics and then when he woke up he went crazy and he... he started..." Melanie felt split in two as part of her tried to relate the facts rationally and another part of her shivered with sobs. "...screaming and... and..."

"Shhh." Yolanda's arms drew her into a tight hug. "Shhhhh."

Melanie thought of being a little girl when her mother used to comfort her. She let Yolanda's surprising composure quiet her sobs and allay her fear. She drifted... "Thanks," she said after a moment. "I guess I needed that."

Yolanda used a tissue to dry Melanie's tears. "Yeah, you did. So what have they said so far?"

"They" were the doctors, obviously. Melanie shrugged. "Not much. They can't find out what's wrong."

"Any fever?"

"No." Melanie suddenly registered Yolanda's presence anew. "Wait — who's at the bookstore?"

Yolanda actually laughed. "I closed it for the day. I don't think Jon cares about the store right now, do you?" She opened her purse, took out a packet of tissues and handed it over. "Blow."

Melanie plucked out a tissue and obeyed. "Look, Yolanda... what if... I mean..."

"What if he's really, like... sick?"

"Yeah," Melanie said. "Really sick." She wrung her hands. "What am I going to do?"

Yolanda took Melanie's hands in hers. "You'll deal with it, *querida*, if that's the case. But you don't know anything yet."

Doctor Odet chose that moment to enter the room, stethoscope draped around his neck and clipboard in his hand. Melanie thought he looked too much like a George Clooney wannabe. "Miss Forrester?" he asked.

Melanie shot to her feet. "Yes? Is he all right? Can I see him?"

Odet nodded. "I have a few questions for you first, if you don't mind." He eyes shifted to Yolanda.

"She's a friend, Yolanda..." Melanie realized with chagrin that she didn't know Yolanda's last name.

"Vargas," Yolanda offered quickly. "I work for Jon. I'm with him almost every day."

"Very well," Odet said. "Miss Forrester, Miss Vargas," he asked, "is Mr. Stuart an alcoholic?"

That was the last question Melanie expected to hear. From the stunned expression on Yolanda's face, she didn't know this particular fact about her employer's background. "Uh, yeah," Melanie admitted, "but he stopped drinking about a year ago. I haven't seen him touch a drop since, and he joined AA."

Odet consulted the chart on his clipboard. "Well, his bloodwork shows a very high, very dangerous amount of alcohol in his system."

Melanie's heart went cold. Jon had started drinking again, and she hadn't noticed? His extreme moods, his headaches, his temper — was it all just alcohol? All this anxiety and worry and expense over *alcohol?*

Apparently Odet could see the thoughts in her expression. "This is a serious concern, Miss Forrester. Not only is the alcohol poisoning his body, but it's complicating whatever's causing his condition."

Melanie let the breath she'd been holding escape from her mouth with a soft *whoosh*. "You mean it's not the cause?"

"We don't yet know the cause. We detect no tumors, no chemical imbalances, nothing out of the ordinary except for the alcohol. I do want to ask you about two welts on his right forearm." Odet made crisscrossing motions along his own forearm to indicate the pattern. "Do you know what they might be?"

"Burn scars?" Yolanda suggested.

"No, not burn scars or any other kind of scar tissue," Odet said. "They're not tattoos or birthmarks either. Were they there before, Miss Forrester?"

Melanie shook her head. *Welts...?* "No. I've never seen anything like that."

Odet was puzzled. "There are no breaks in the skin, but the welts are fresh, as if some sort of injury occurred recently. If you think of any accidents, or any incidents that might explain it, please let me know."

Melanie nodded.

Odet led them into the ICU ward and down a sterile corridor. He stopped in front of a door marked 207 and gently opened it. "You can see him for a few minutes."

Yolanda hung back. "Go ahead, Miss Forrester. I'll wait here."

Melanie squeezed her hand. "Thanks."

Melanie tried not to think of her sister when she walked into the room. Her sister had died in a room like this, pierced by needles, connected to tubes, a functioning body with nobody inside anymore. A hit-and-run victim, years ago. *Not the same,* she told herself firmly. *This is different.*

But Jon looked much the same as her sister had. Like a cat when it's stretched out full length, he seemed thinner than normal. His pale skin reflected the overhead light with a strange waxy gleam. The bump on his forehead, gotten when he had fallen out of bed, was covered by a white bandage. His eyes were dull, staring out at nothing, but at least they were open. His pupils narrowed when she moved closer.

Yes, there was recognition there. Thank God. "Hi," she said, and sort of hung there on that one word. She was angry with him, she couldn't help it. Alcohol! How dare he start drinking again! Worse, how dare he try to hide it from her! But her love and concern for this train wreck of a man pushed her anger aside, at least for the moment. She cleared her throat and tried once more to speak. "You look like shit." It was meant to be a joke, the kind that he might tell her if their positions were reversed.

He didn't smile. His mouth hardly moved. "You're... here..."

Melanie stepped to the edge of the bed. She wanted to take his hand and hold it tight, but the insertion points of the IV needles were bruised blue-red under strips of tape. She didn't want to hurt him. "Yes, I'm here." As she bent to kiss him, her teardrops fell on his cheek. "I love you, you jerk."

"Was... planned..." he whispered. "Help me..."

Melanie stiffened. "Planned? What do you mean?"

"... please..."

She leaned in close to him, her heart pounding. "Help you what, Jon? What's wrong?"

She could hardly hear Jon's words as they sighed through his lips. "Took... in dream..." He grimaced. "...no... sleep..." His voice gained an edge of hysteria under the sedation, and he writhed weakly, trying to sit up. "... not... hook... not...!"

Melanie yelped in surprise when a nurse appeared at her side. "He'll be fine," the woman assured Melanie, and sure enough, after the nurse fiddled with some controls on the IV drip, Jon relaxed. His eyelids fluttered. "He's going to sleep for a while," the nurse said. "You might want to get some rest yourself. You've been here a long time, ma'am."

Melanie nodded, her eyes still fixed on the man she loved. Yes, she loved him even after all this, even after she had understood that Yolanda was right — he was a child. And like most children, his behavior was extreme on both ends of the spectrum with little in-between. Why did she put up with it? She gazed down at him and wondered.

Watching him was like watching a kid trying to stay up till midnight on New Year's Eve. He fought the sedative, struggling to stay awake, his eyelids fighting to stay open. Closed. Open. Closed. Flutter. Closed.

Melanie caressed his cheek, then wiped away her own tears. "I'll be back, Jon," she promised.

CHAPTER 13

He didn't need to open his eyes. He knew where he was. His bed was gently rocking, and somewhere a seagull squawked. "No..." His head thrummed in pain. His right forearm felt like it was on fire. "No no no no noooo..."

"Aw, it's not that bad," came Smee's cheerful brogue. "Yeh've suffered worse, that's fer sure, sar. Don'tcha be grousin'—"

"NO!"

And Stuart screamed. It exploded from his lips, whether fueled by anger, fear, frustration or all three, he didn't know. But he couldn't stop. He screamed and kept screaming until his throat simply gave out. He didn't open his eyes. He didn't have to. He knew what he would see if he did, and he didn't want to see it. In that terrible moment, he would have traded all sight and sound in exchange for security. In exchange for Melanie.

She had been right there with him, right there only seconds ago. He had felt her tears splash lightly on his cheek. And then she had left him, *left him!* She didn't know what was happening to him, didn't understand, and he had been unable to tell her. And now she was gone. And he was back in Hell. He covered his head with his arms, a ridiculous attempt to hide.

"Sar," Smee began as if he saw nothing amiss, "I'm thinkin' we should weigh anchor. We need provisions an' such like. Aye, it's true we can git most o' what we need from the island, but half the time we gotta fight off the whole Injun tribe to do it, or Pan's damnable rabble." He leaned closer to add, "Cookson's watered down what's left o' the spirits, sar. Piss'd taste better. Rum's the word, aye? Heh heh!" He straightened back up. "A trip to Beggar's Port would do the trick, wouldn't yeh say? 'Sides, a bit o' Sailortown wouldn't hurt morale. Wouldn't hurt yerself neither, sar. Git more of Smiffy's brandy, eh?" When Stuart said nothing, Smee gently poked his shoulder. "Sar? Yeh listenin'? What say yeh?"

Stuart weakly waved his hand, hoping Smee would just leave and do whatever he wanted.

Smee make a happy little sound. "Aye aye, Cap'n!" he said, and hurried away, leaving Stuart alone.

Finally. Silence. Peace, of a sort. Except for the nightmarish creaking of the ship and the whispering waves that constantly reminded him that home was far far away.

From on deck, Cecco suddenly bellowed like a crazed bull. Even through the distance and the cabin's thick door, the man's volume was impressive. "All hands! Listen up, ya ruddy bilge rats! By order of the Captain, we sail for Beggar's Port with the midnight tide!"

The crew let up a cheer. Somebody started playing a fiddle, and as far as Stuart could tell by all the subsequent thumping, the men were dancing jigs of merriment. *At least somebody's happy around here*, he thought. Reluctantly he uncurled himself and, without thinking, sat up.

There was no low alcove to bang against his head.

He wasn't lying on the flat wooden cot.

He was, in fact, sitting in a long framed canvas hammock with stiff vertical sides that held in luxurious bedding. It was sort of like a canvas canoe, a snuggly nest, really, that swung gently back and forth as the ship rocked on the waves. He had to move carefully so that he didn't fall as he climbed out, and once on his feet, he almost got knocked over when the hammock swung back and smacked him. He ended up regaining his balance by grabbing the closest thing — the wooden tailor's model.

It stood wedged between two pegs that apparently were there to keep it stable when the ship moved. On it hung another lavish outfit of one Jas. Hook, Captain of the *Jolly Roger*, this one solid black linen and leather, dazzling with intricate gold embroidery and red ribbons.

Stuart pulled back from it, blinking. *Not an alcove but a hammock,* he thought. *And this model looks different.* And those two items were the only items in a tiny space that was defined by a delicate portable screen painted with a stylized Oriental landscape. Stuart's senses were anything but sharp at the moment, so he felt like an idiot when the obvious conclusion struck him: *This isn't the same cabin.*

He peeked around the Oriental screen. What met his eyes was the rest of the cabin, an enormous space the size of most of the poop deck and filled with lavish furnishings, books and artwork. Dozens of lit candles twinkled like stars, cheerfully bright even as they threw sinister shadows across every surface.

Instead of the tiny writing desk from the previous cabin, a fine walnut scroll desk with a matching cushioned chair stood to one side. The plain table that had held pitcher, basin and tray was now a jewel-encrusted marble-topped washstand with a marble basin and gold-plated ewer. The middle of the space was occupied by the finest rosewood dining table Stuart had ever seen, deep red-brown and polished like a mirror. An ornate silver chandelier hung over it, its candles illuminating the single place setting that waited before a single chair that could qualify as a throne. A harpsichord stood to the right of the scroll desk, with an ornate cabinet with a large backing mirror set against the wall behind it. A rich burgundy rug covered the center of the cabin, and a row of tall rectangular windows ran along the stern bulkhead, wrapping around to port and starboard, letting muted sunlight in through their thick rippled glass.

Here and there hung paintings and framed maps along with other curious *objêts d'art,* all of which made a striking contrast to the four grimy cannons that squatted by four closed gunports, one to port, one to starboard and two astern. A rack of cannonballs waited next to each one, along with a wooden rack holding wads, ladle, rammer and other equipment necessary for firing.

All furniture was bolted to the deck or affixed in place by chains through padeyes. Statues, Stuart noticed, were lashed down at their bases. Books were racked neatly on shelves behind wooden slats that would keep them in place regardless of the ship's movements.

Paintings, he saw after checking, weren't hung at all but nailed firmly to the bulkheads. What he guessed to be bottles of oils, perfumes and breakable toiletries were stowed in miniature glass-doored cabinets, one on the dresser and one on the washstand.

In all, the cabin was the very picture of excessive but functional clutter, a clash of good and bad taste and a strangely homey place even if, as Stuart suspected, everything in it had been stolen. What chilled him was a single unsettling but unifying theme: most every item bore at least one puncture or slash mark made by something that must have been metal and extremely sharp. *Like an iron hook*, he thought uneasily.

He pressed the heels of his hands to his eyes, struggling to make sense of the change. Had this been his cabin all along? Had Pan's magic forced him to see something different before? If not, why switch cabins? Was this a different ship? "Stop the damned mind games!" he cried, and in a fit of fury banged his fist against the bulkhead, forgetting in his rage that the arm was wounded.

The impact made him emit a short high-pitched yip of agony. "Drink!" he gasped, and in a frenzy searched the cabin for bottles or flasks. He finally found a jug of rum in the cabinet by the harpsichord. After several swallows, the pain began to subside. Or rather, he could still feel it — he just didn't care as much. *Two aspirin*, he thought, and swallowed more, slouching against the cabinet. *Better yet, a bottle of Vicodin. Is that so much to ask?*

When he looked up, he was facing his own pale, haggard visage reflected in the cabinet's mirror. The oval of crude rippled glass had been set in a carved wood motif of grape vines leafed with gold and gleaming with sapphire grapes. However, it wasn't the beauty of the mirror and its setting that transfixed Stuart. Two brief glints of gold did.

He pulled back his disheveled hair in order to see his ears. Gold flashed on each one. *Smee, you bastard! You pierced my goddam ears while I was unconscious!* He studied the sizeable stud in his right, then the hoop that Smee had first tried to put in his left. "I will *not* play this game!" he fumed, and took out the stud first.

That's when he spied something else in the mirror's reflection — a bowl of fresh fruit on the dining table. Had that been there before? He couldn't remember, but it was there now.

The last thing he had eaten had been the stale biscuit Smee had given him... how many days ago? Two? Three? More? His stomach grumbled, and instinct took over. He threw himself at the bowl and snatched up an apple, ripping his teeth into it like a madman. The first bite was the most delicious sensation, and he finished the whole thing, core and all. He tore through the rest of the fruit — a banana, two pears and a peach — then started for the cabin door, determined to find the ship's cook. Meat. He wanted meat and bread, decent food that would fill his tortured belly.

Before he reached the door, it burst open and Smee entered, carrying a tray laden with all the food Stuart craved: slices of pork, a whole roasted game bird of some kind, potatoes, a biscuit, and chunks of cheese and onion. "Thought yeh'd be a mite peckish," Smee said pleasantly. "Glad to see yer up, sar."

Stuart seized the biscuit, took a bite and followed Smee to the table, chewing. He sat down in the throne-like chair where the single setting lay waiting for use.

Smee regarded him with disapproval. "Where's yer manners, sar? Ain't yeh gonna dress first?"

Stuart swallowed the mouthful of biscuit. "No," he said, and with Neanderthal etiquette he yanked a leg off the game bird.

"Well, at least yeh oughter tie yer hair back, sar, so's it don't get in yer food. Here, let me—"

"Don't!" Stuart warned. "Don't touch me." He bit into the leg.

Smee would not give up. "Sar, at least comb it. It's all a'tangle." He reached into his vest pocket for, Stuart supposed, a comb.

That did it. As Smee rummaged in his pocket, Stuart put down the leg. He picked up his perfectly folded linen napkin and wiped his fingers. Then he took the three-tined solid silver fork by his plate and jabbed it into Smee's arm. "There! Now we're even!"

Smee squealed and staggered back, his expression more of confused betrayal than pain or anger. "Sar!" he cried, ripping the fork out and slapping a hand over the injury. "Whadya do that to ol' Smee fer?"

Stuart pointed at his ears. "Ol' Smee had better keep his frickin' hands to himself, or I'll jab that fork through your eye next time, got it?"

Smee squinted, trying to focus on Stuart's ears from a distance. His bushy grey brows drew together to make one long hairy caterpillar over his eyes. "Sar?"

"Oh, quit the act! You know perfectly well what I'm talking about!"

"Err... I do?"

"Don't ever, *ever* touch me, you got that?"

Cringing like a whipped puppy, Smee nodded. "Aye aye, Cap'n." He reached into his coat pocket, removed a bottle and gingerly set it on the table. Then he pulled the rag from his back pocket and dabbed at his injury. "I'll, uh, be goin' then, sar," he said meekly.

Guilt crept into Stuart's conscience. He fought it off, preferring anger. He understood anger. It gave him energy. It gave him focus. The last thing he needed was to start feeling sorry for the man who was, basically, holding him captive. "Fine," he snapped at Smee. "Go."

"Aye, sar. I'll be back soon."

Back? Soon? Stuart was amazed to hear himself actually growl.

"To change yer bandage, sar," Smee said hastily. "Gotta tend that wound right or yeh could lose full use o' yer sword arm. See there, sar? Yer bleedin' agin."

Smee was right. A red blotch was slowly spreading through the bandage. Smee didn't know it was Stuart's own fault for hitting the bulkhead.

"Well then, sar. If ye need me, I'll be at my sewin' machine. That is, after I tends me own arm." Smee left.

"Sewing machine?" Stuart asked the empty cabin. Then he remembered the detail from reading Barrie's novel. Smee had been described as having a sewing machine which he used quite often. Any sewing machine would be too wimpy for mending sails. Maybe he made Hook's clothes.

A rumble from his stomach reminded Stuart of his meal. He sat down to eat. The meat and bird had been prepared with nothing but salt and pepper as seasonings, but both were wonderfully fresh. The pirates must have gone hunting on the island that very morning, despite Smee's insistence that scalp-hungry "Injuns" prevented such procurement. The potatoes were cooked perfectly, the bread too hard and brown but satisfying nonetheless — at least it wasn't traditional "hard tack," which history described as being more weevil than biscuit.

The bottle that Smee had set down contained a fine muscat. Stuart downed several glasses of the sweet wine while he ate. By the time he was finished, all he wanted to do was snuggle back into the hammock and sleep for a week. He was too tired to get up from the table, though. He pushed his empty plate back, lowered his head onto his arms and closed his eyes.

* * * * *

"Sar? Cap'n, sar."

A dream image of Melanie slipped away. She had been holding his hand. He barely perceived a soft steady beeping noise and a tangy chemical smell before they drifted away as well.

"Sar, yeh oughter git dressed. We'll be under way soon."

"Five more minutes," Stuart mumbled.

"Uh, sar..." Smee hesitated. "Yeh been asleep fer three hours."

Stuart jerked his head up. "Huh?"

"Yeh oughter be on deck afore the suns go out."

Stuart was still half asleep, but he knew what he'd heard. "You mean sun."

"Suns, sar."

"*Sun*. There is *one* sun. And it *sets*, it does not *go out*."

"Err... as yeh say, sar. Just lemme change yer bandage an' get yeh dressed an' we'll be ready afore, eh... afore dark."

Stuart let the matter drop and allowed Smee to tend his arm. He decided that there had been one thing missing from his perfect meal earlier: dental floss. Toothpaste and a brush would be nice, too. *My mouth feels like sandpaper*, he thought with disgust, running his tongue over scummy teeth. Melanie called it "mung mouth" and often complained that it felt as if a cat had crawled into her mouth while she was asleep, crapped and crept back out.

Melanie. Stuart clenched his jaws, fighting down a wave of despair. Where was she? What was she doing? He wished he was home with her. He wanted to see her face, to hold her, to feel her arms holding him. All at once he wanted her so badly that he shuddered, the loss of her physically painful.

"Sorry, sar," Smee apologized, misinterpreting the shudder. He took the last bit of the old bandage off with extra care. "Well, lookit that!"

All thoughts of Melanie vanished. Stuart's eyes bugged. "It's almost healed," he said as if Smee couldn't see it himself. "It was bleeding before. The cut was huge!"

"Aye," Smee said with satisfaction. "Yer'll be hale an' hearty by tomorrow, I'm thinkin'."

"But that's impossible!"

Smee gave no reply and set to work skillfully rebandaging the wound with a fresh cloth. As he did, Stuart ripped a piece of lace frill off his napkin and used the rough fabric to scrub his teeth. The lace didn't help his mung mouth much, but it was better than nothing. He would investigate how to fashion a toothbrush and floss later.

When Smee finished with the bandage, he gave Stuart a shave using the biggest damned razor Stuart had ever seen. The man knew what he was doing, though. He didn't nick Stuart once. Then Smee urged his captain to wash his face at the washstand and take care of other physical necessities.

Using a chamber pot was not Stuart's idea of Club Med, but it was either that or the ship's head — a couple of holes off the front bow on the head rails where a man literally let loose directly into the ocean regardless of the weather. Technically quite practical, but it just seemed so... exposed. Stuart didn't consider himself a finicky man, but he wasn't ready to dangle his privates over the open seas just yet.

When he was done, he allowed Smee to dress him in Hook's elaborate attire, this time the black outfit. Smee didn't speak throughout the process, which suited Stuart just fine. After he reluctantly put the wig on and stuffed the frilly white kerchief up his right sleeve, he faced the man. "Smee—"

"Here ya go, sar," Smee interrupted, holding up a hand mirror, plainly expecting Stuart to primp.

Stuart had no desire to see himself in Hook's getup. He took the mirror and tossed it onto the padded chair at the scroll desk. "Never mind that, I have a question. Don't wonder why I'm asking and do not lie. Just tell me the truth." He paused. "Is this the same cabin I was in yesterday?"

Smee gave him a dubious squint and then peered around the cabin as if making sure it was indeed the place he thought it was. "Aye," he said carefully. "These're yer quarters, sar."

With a disappointed sigh, Stuart slapped on Hook's wide plumed hat. *So much for that.* He started for the door when Smee said, "Sar! Yer fergettin' somethin'." The bosun held out the saber in its scabbard.

Stuart's left hand twitched. He stepped back, intending to say, "No, I don't need that," but the words never passed his lips. A terrible blackness leapt up his arm and spread through his body until he felt smothered by it. It pressed in, squeezing him as if it wanted to pulverize him completely, as if his past, present and future, all of his personal existence, was distilling itself into a single terrible revelation that was trying to encompass him all at once.

"Cap'n!" Smee cried.

Stuart gagged and coughed as awful black fingers squeezed hard enough to cut through his skin and grip his very soul. His vision blurred, his heart raced, he felt as if he were being crushed in a giant hand to the point where his body would pop like a water balloon—

—and then it stopped. Stuart found himself on his knees, clutching Smee around the middle like a frightened child holding his mother's skirts. Smee was studying him warily. "Err... problem, sar?"

"...No." He stood up. "No, it was nothing." *Not nuthin', not nohow. If Smee doesn't want to make a big deal out of it, neither will I.*

But perhaps Smee hadn't seen what really happened. Stuart had already observed how the pirates simply didn't see objects and events that challenged their reality. *Captain Hook is not supposed to freak out, therefore I did not freak out.* It sounded reasonable enough. He felt perfectly fine now. Therefore, nothing had happened.

He let Smee place the baldric over his shoulder, then followed the bosun to the door, feeling unclean both physically and mentally, as tainted as if he had just lain in his own grave. He did not want to wear the cursed saber, but he knew it was useless to argue.

Smee opened the door and gestured. "After you, Cap'n."

Stuart didn't want to go out at all. "No, you first."

"Oh no, Cap'n," Smee said deferentially. "You first."

"GO!"

"Aye aye, sar!" and Smee scuttled out. Once again Stuart's eyes were assaulted by the glare of twin sunlight. He squinted, wishing dearly for his aviator sunglasses as Smee informed him, "We got about an hour o' daylight left, sar. Tide goes out at midnight, an' we'll go with it."

Stuart vaguely recalled Smee saying something about sailing somewhere. Damn, his brain was so muddled he could hardly keep his thoughts straight. "You mean we can leave the island?" he asked stupidly.

Smee chuckled. "Very funny, sar. Still got yer sense o' humor, I see." He pointed at the ocean horizon, though whether the direction was west, east, north or south, Stuart had no idea. "We kin reach Beggar's Port in eight days if the wind holds. Me an' Cecco'll take care of everythin', sar. You take it easy, git some air an' such like, a'right? Just let the men see yeh so's they know yer recoverin' fine."

Right. Great. Whatever, Stuart thought as Smee hurried down to the main deck were Cecco was supervising the crew.

Beggar's Port. To Stuart it sounded like a squalid shantytown from some pirate flick where everybody teetered around drunk and ate the same slop as the pigs. Was it within Pan's domain? His hopes soared at the thought. Maybe Pan ruled only the island. Maybe Beggar's Port was a free refuge where the pirates could let down their hair, in a manner of speaking. *I don't care, I'll eat pig slop,* he thought, *if it means I'm free of that boy.*

Daring to hope, he gazed absently off the starboard rail. Pan's island was about a quarter mile away. He could see the shore in some detail and watched as the brisk wind whipped through the palm trees. Pristine white sand sparkled on the beach, and the deep jungle lay beyond, a cloak of green that ran all the way to the base of the volcano and its surrounding mountains with their high peaks covered in glistening snow. As he studied the Neverland island, Stuart realized how beautiful it was. That struck him as terribly funny. Here he was, trapped in paradise — trapped in Hell.

Flash!

Something was out there. *Get the spyglass from the becket*, came the thought, and Stuart reached for it by the wheel. Even as he did, he wondered how he knew that a becket was a loop of rope that, in this case, secured a brass telescope to the side of the wheelhouse. He watched in fascination as his hands, as if of their own accord, slipped the spyglass free of the loop, extended it and brought it up to his eye.

Finding the spot where he had seen the flashes wasn't easy, but he finally zeroed in on it. There, beyond the palms — sure enough, Pan and Tinker Bell. It was Tinker Bell's shimmer that he had seen. *Must be hard for a fairy to keep out of sight*, he thought. *She's like a search beam with no off switch.* He couldn't spot any of the other children, but he figured they were there, well hidden. Only Pan would risk being seen. He probably *wanted* to be seen.

Sure enough, he waved merrily at Stuart. *He knows I'm looking at him!* Stuart thought, a thrill of fear racing up his spine. "Smee!" he called down to the main deck.

Smee was forward of the mizzen, talking to Cecco. He turned at the sound of his captain's voice. "Aye, Cap'n?"

"Pan!" Stuart said. "Two points abaft the starboard beam!" He hardly registered the impossible words that had left his mouth when both Smee and Cecco grinned.

"Aye aye, sir!" Cecco acknowledged. "All right, ya scum sucking sea dogs! You heard the Captain!"

"Aye aye!" the nearest crewmen acknowledged, and they started to load two cannons on the starboard bow.

"Wait!" Stuart yelled. "Wait, that's not what I meant!" The pirates continued their task, moving as if their lives depended on haste. Stuart hurried down the stairs. "Smee! Cecco! Stop them, dammit! That's an order!" He reached the main deck and started forward. The last thing he expected was to see the pirates step in his path. "Get out of my way!" he demanded as more and more blocked him, acting like puppets on strings, hindering him for no apparent reason.

Or *was* there a reason? *Trying to make me attack first, eh, Pan?* he thought angrily, and he started bullying a path through the men, knocking them down and even kicking them out of his way. For all that, he still reached the first loaded cannon too late.

"Fire one!" Cecco commanded.

BOOM!

Stuart faltered as the cannon bucked backwards from the force of the blast, its heavy breeching preventing it from flying across the deck. "Fire two!"

BOOM!

The pirates rushed to the rail, eager to see the outcome. Stuart scanned the target area as the cannonballs whizzed through the palms. A dozen children flew up from the area, scattering like leaves blown into the sky by a sudden tempest. The crew cheered until one of the children flew toward them fast, followed by a bright golden light.

"Blow me tight, we missed 'im!" Smee groused.

"Here he comes, lads," said Cecco. "Orders, Captain?" He looked expectantly at Stuart.

Stuart goggled back at him. Pan flew closer.

"Cap'n?" Smee urged.

Stuart drew his sword. He didn't mean to. It just sort of happened.

"To arms!" Cecco ordered with gusto.

"Belay that!" Stuart said. The last thing he wanted was another massacre. "I'll take care of this. No man is to show aggression unless I order attack, is that clear?"

"Aye aye, sir," Cecco acknowledged. The men reluctantly agreed.

As if the situation had played out a hundred times before — most probably it had — the pirates shuffled back, leaving Stuart in a little circle.

Pan alighted on the deck within that circle, bold as brass. Standing tall, hands on hips, he gave Stuart a cocky grin. "Two shots and still you missed, Captain. I hope you're not losing your touch." Mock concern flashed across his face. "By the way, how's the arm?"

In answer, Stuart snapped up his blade and slashed Pan's side. This time, he was the one who moved so fast that Pan didn't have time to dodge. The wound wasn't big, but it was sufficient to make Pan gasp as he stared down at a trickle of red running down into his leafy leggings.

Stuart stood ready, the black fingers deep inside squeezing his heart in a vise grip. For the first time, it didn't hurt. "Strike One," he said, and smiled.

CHAPTER 14

Blazing red with vengeance, Tinker Bell zipped over Stuart's head and showered him with fairy dust. The most elegant solution popped into his mind. He simply twirled out of the way, his long wig, topcoat, ruffles and plumes flapping so that none of the dust had a chance to settle. He stopped several feet aft, clean of the dust and pleased to hear a murmur of awe from the crew. "Next trick?" he asked Pan as if bored.

"Peter!" came a dainty cry. Wendy dived out of the sky, wearing her angelic white nightgown and apparently whole and hearty.

Stuart had completely forgotten about shooting her. "You're not dead!" he blurted.

Pan sprang into the air to join her. "That's why *you're* not dead," he intoned with menace.

"O, Peter, you're hurt!" Wendy cried, seeing blood on her hero. She glowered down at Stuart. "You'll pay for this, Captain Hook."

"He surely will!" Ranger was floating by the mainmast. "Look out below!" he cried gleefully, and with a whack of his cutlass he sent a block and tackle the size of a small man hurtling down in a long arc like Tarzan on a vine.

The pirates backpedaled out of the way while Stuart threw himself flat on the deck. The deadly missile swept over him, knocking his hat off and missing his skull by perhaps two inches. Curls danced on his head in the gust of its passing. The hardware crashed into the deck house and began to swing back, no longer a speeding missile but heavy enough to break a man's back if it struck. Stuart rolled out of its way and climbed to his feet.

"Is this what you want, boy?" he said, letting outrage cover the tremor in his voice. "Another senseless battle? Or have you come to kill one or two of us, just to round out your day? Wasn't Li'l Lad Jack enough?"

"He was a traitor, Captain," said Pan. Stuart didn't know what that was supposed to mean, and Pan didn't explain. "And no, I'm not here to kill one or two of you." He grinned. "Just you. You fired first, remember?"

"It wasn't as if I could stop them," Stuart said, indicating the crew. "You made sure of that."

"I wasn't even here."

"You didn't have to be."

Wendy placed a hand on Pan's shoulder. "Peter, two gentlemen in dispute have no alternative but to duel. Is that not the honorable way to settle this matter?"

Pan's eyes twinkled with excitement. "Yes! Let's settle it like gentlemen!" He drew a sword. "*En garde!*"

Cecco, Smee and several other pirates drew their weapons. Stuart slashed at them instead of Pan, furious that they would so much as *think* of interfering. "Stay back, you rat bastards! He's mine!"

Reluctantly they shuffled back. Along with their fellows and the children overhead, they watched as the duel began.

If there was one thing Stuart knew well, it was swordsmanship. His confidence was unshakable, even in these circumstances. The only thing that knocked him off kilter was the discovery that Pan was even better than he was and just as ferocious. The boy demonstrated flawless technique and surprising strength, and it was all Stuart could do to keep from getting cut. As if that wasn't bad enough, Pan's flying abilities outstripped his fighting abilities. He twisted, flipped and corkscrewed with ease, dodging every one of Stuart's attacks. The boy brought it to an end by darting behind his foe and kicking him hard in the back, sending Stuart sprawling on his face. The children laughed and the pirates grumbled as he climbed to his feet for a second time.

"Good form, Captain," Pan jeered, hovering out of reach.

"Come down a bit closer and I'll show you good form, boy!"

"Why bother? I've won the duel. Or did you drop your sword on purpose?"

"You've won nothing!" Stuart raged. "Where's your sense of honor? What good is victory when you have the clear advantage? You can fly!"

The pirates echoed Stuart's sentiments, shouting out accusations and insults. The Lost Boys and Wendy shouted back their own opinions on the matter. Volume grew until Stuart out-shouted them all. "SHUT UP, for God's sake!"

Pan regarded Stuart with new respect. "Captain, you make an excellent point." He alighted to the deck and sheathed his sword. "We have both drawn blood, so let us call this a draw. What do you say?"

Smee sidled up to Stuart. "Keep a weather eye, Cap'n," the bosun whispered. "He's up to somethin'."

"No shit," Stuart hissed back. "The question is, what?" He sheathed his saber as well. "A truce it is, then," he told Pan.

"No, sir, don't!" cried one of the pirates – Jukes, the man covered in tattoos and wearing the garishly decorated hat. He aimed a pistol at Pan. "Don't trust 'im!"

"Mister Jukes—" Cecco began.

Jukes fired.

Pan easily dodged the shot. His already rosy cheeks flushed to a deep crimson, and he jabbed an accusing finger at Stuart. "Truce off! Lost Boys attaaaaack!"

The Lost Boys produced knives, cutlasses, dirks and their one pilfered pistol and flew at the pirates from every direction, their young eyes bright with the adventure of battle. The pirates were always armed and ready, so they met the children steel against steel in a series of clangs and clashes.

War broke out aboard the *Jolly Roger*.

Stuart shook with rage. Not again! Not another insane battle! He fought his way over to where Jukes was dueling with Wendy's brother John, their cutlasses flashing. "You idiot!" he yelled at Jukes, and decked him with a single roundhouse punch.

"Holy moley!" John spluttered. "Thank you, Captain!"

Stuart responded by plucking John's cutlass right out of his hands. "Never play with sharp objects," he said through his teeth.

John flew away in mute terror. Stuart lobbed the cutlass overboard, then turned back to the downed Jukes and kicked the unconscious man in the gut. "Idiot!" he repeated.

"Temper temper, Captain," Pan said behind him.

Stuart whirled around in time to parry the attack. "You're one to talk, you devil!" he said, and he pressed forward, engaging Pan's blade again and again, driving him back until Pan bumped up against the main shrouds. The boy tried to escape by flying, but Stuart was expecting that and grabbed his ankle. "Gotcha!" he said, hauling Pan back down.

Pan shot up again, taking Stuart with him. "No, I've got *you!*" he laughed.

It had never occurred to Stuart that Pan could lift the weight of a grown man. If it had, he wouldn't have grabbed his ankle. He had no idea how long he could hold on with one hand. He swiped with his saber, trying to cut Pan's legs, but the boy kept kicking, knocking Stuart's aim off.

They flew out over the water. Stuart had no intention of falling into the bay, so he took his only chance — as Pan zoomed past the foreshrouds, he let go of both saber and ankle and, as he dropped, scrambled frantically for the ratlines. He managed to grasp one, but his weight and momentum prevented him from getting a firm grip. He ended up sliding down the shrouds, catching and losing ratlines like a ball bouncing down stairs one at a time. Sheer desperation gave him a firm grip before he ran out of ratlines and tumbled into the water.

"Nice save," Pan praised him, flying overhead. "But you dropped this." He had retrieved Stuart's saber. He held it out, pommel first, just out of Stuart's reach.

It was infuriating. There was his sword, but Stuart couldn't take it. There was nothing else to do but get back to the deck, no easy task while wearing Hook's tailored clothes and a pair of jack boots. He pretended not to hear Pan and Wendy giggle as he monkeyed sideways, finally swinging himself over the rail and landing safely back on the deck.

Pan offered the saber once more, within reach this time. "O, what a gentleman I am!" he boasted happily.

Stuart took the weapon, panting. "You're no gentleman. There isn't an ounce of decency in you."

At that, Pan lunged at him. Stuart parried, then chose a riposte even more unconventional than grabbing his opponent's weapon — he slugged Pan in the gut.

Pan doubled over in the air. Stuart, taking full advantage, swung his blade in a powerful arc that knocked Pan's cutlass out of his hand. It clattered to the deck. Stuart slammed a foot down on it. "Strike Two, pissant. *Now* let's call it a draw."

Peter Pan dropped to the deck at Stuart's feet, still gasping from the gut punch. Stuart couldn't believe his good fortune — the little beast was at his mercy! But Pan wasn't out of tricks yet. Barely lifting his head to aim, he jabbed a dagger through Stuart's right wrist. "Let's not!" he cried, and flew backwards to a safe distance as Wendy squealed with adoration and applauded him.

So much had happened and his adrenaline was at such a peak that, for a moment, Stuart didn't fully grasp that he had been hit. A vague stinging sensation made him look down. To his astonishment, a hilt was protruding from the bandage on his arm. The tip of a blade poked out the other side. *What a coinky-dink!* was all he could think. *Right in the same place as before!* It seemed only logical to pull the thing out. So he did.

Realization and pain hit at the same time. He grunted and dropped the blade, watching crimson ooze up through the bandage like pressurized water through a leaky pipe. "My God." The puzzle pieces suddenly fell together. "You're trying to cut off my hand!" It was like Barrie's story. He wouldn't truly be Hook until he *wore* a hook!

"Oh, that's gross," Pan said in disgust. "Captain, I have no intention of cutting off your hand."

"Then what the hell do you call this!"

"Bad aim?" Pan quipped, adding with a sly wink, "You shouldn't believe everything you read."

Stuart almost laughed. Naturally, the boy was lying. Then again, what if he wasn't?

A pistol shot rang out. A pirate fell against Stuart, almost knocking him over. He staggered back and the man crumpled, dead, an ugly hole in his chest.

"Got him!" Ranger crowed from above, brandishing the pistol. Pan gave Ranger a happy thumbs up.

The sight of the body jarred Stuart loose from his self-preoccupation. "What is happening?" he cried, at a loss to understand anything around him. "You wanted to kill me, that's what you said, but you're killing other people! Look around you! This is all your doing!"

"Aye, James Hook, it is all my doing," Pan answered brightly. "And so is *this!*" He gave a sharp whistle. Half a dozen Lost Boys swooped out of the sky and, holding a mop horizontally between them, rammed Stuart neatly off his feet and up over the rail. "I want you to meet someone!" Pan hollered after him.

Despite all his earlier efforts, Stuart ended up in Pirate's Bay after all. He clamped his jaws shut and successfully intercepted what would have been an undignified wail of surprise, only to realize in alarm that he should open his mouth at once to fill his lungs with air. Somewhere between the clamping and the realization, he slapped into the water. He sank like a stone, the weight of Hook's elaborate clothes dragging him down. Frantically he kicked for the surface, discovering in the process that jack boots were hardly designed for swimming.

That's when he heard a chilling sound, muffled but recognizable through the water: *tick, tick, tick, tick.*

No way, he thought. *Impossible!* Yet there it was, all thirty feet of it, looming out of the murky depths: the crocodile. It glided past him a mere arm's reach away, ticking as it went, one great yellow eye fixed on him.

With renewed vigor, Stuart swam upwards. The croc reappeared, gliding past him on the other side, opening its jaws wide enough for him to see way too many teeth.

His injured arm notwithstanding, Stuart's strength finally brought him to the surface. Kicking like mad to keep his head above water, he heaved in air, treading a circle in an attempt to spot the croc. He couldn't see it, but amidst the sound of battle up on the ship he distinctly heard Smee blaring down at him. A moment later the end of a rope hit the water nearby. Stuart swam for it.

The croc got it first. Open jaws rose out of the water and chomped down on the rope, giving it a sharp tug as if the beast knew there were men at the other end. Sure enough, two pirates shrieked as they were yanked overboard. The croc threw itself at the first one when he hit the water, gobbling him up in one bite. The waves made by its great body pushed Stuart back under.

He knew he would never reach the surface again without losing the fashion baggage weighing him down. Trying to forget the presence of the croc for the moment, he struggled out of Hook's beautifully embroidered topcoat, then pulled desperately at the jack boots, sinking farther and farther down every second. He finally got them off and pulled at his wig, which had miraculously stayed on his head all this time. Strangely, it wouldn't budge, so he gave up and, lungs aching, kicked for the surface.

He made it, praying that the croc wasn't waiting for him. Breathing had to come first. It was easier to stay afloat, so he trod water and panted until the terrible pain in his chest faded and his head cleared.

The croc was floating right behind him, facing the other way.

Stuart pushed down a surge of panic and quietly swam a breast stroke toward the ship. A crude slat ladder was built into the side of the hull. All he needed to do was climb up and he would be safe. That is, if his wounded arm could hold his weight. *Like you have a choice, Jon,* he told himself. *But why isn't the croc attacking? My arm is putting enough blood in the water to send any predator into a killing frenzy.*

Then he saw the body parts floating around, a foot here, part of a torso there — all that was left of the second pirate. The croc was in the middle of biting down on the man's head. The skull cracked with a weird wet popping noise. Chunks of pink and grey exploded out from between the croc's jaws. Stuart almost threw up.

"The line, sar!" Smee shouted down at him. "Git! The! Line!"

Feeling warm crimson water touch his skin, Stuart wildly eyed the line of the new rescue rope until he located the end of it. He swam for it and grabbed, holding on for dear life as the pirates hoisted him clear of the surface.

The croc turned to see its dessert rising beyond its reach. The beast leaped straight up out of the water, arcing its body with brutal grace in an attempt to bite Stuart's legs off.

"*Hurry!*" he screamed.

The pirates heaved again. Stuart flew up a good ten feet, and *snap!* the croc's jaws just missed his toes.

The pirates heaved for all they were worth. Many hands helped Stuart over the rail and back onto the deck where he collapsed, shaking and — he couldn't deny it — scared out of his wits.

The ship was quiet. "Battle's over, sar," Smee said in his ear. "Pan's leavin'."

The enemy in question flew over to Stuart. "Captain Hook, I declare you the winner," Pan said, executing a deep bow in midair.

All the children cried, "Hip hip hooray!" then broke into scornful laughter.

Stuart hardly had the strength to breathe let alone respond. Cecco helped him to a sitting position while Smee tied his work rag around Stuart's bleeding arm. Stuart merely watched as Pan joined the other children who were hovering beyond the rail, right over the croc which was now swimming a tight little circle on the surface of the water, *tick-ticking* as it went. It showed no interest in leaping up to crunch on the children's legs.

Wait, that's it! The croc! "That's why you flew me out over the water," Stuart said to Pan, unable to hide the tremor in his voice. "All this was about that... that *thing* down there."

The children pointed at him, jeering. "Mama's boy!" said Ranger. "Chicken!" said John.

"Tick tick tick!" they all chorused, adding a variety of insulting gestures.

Pan hushed them. "I think the croc likes you, Captain. I bet she'll like you even better soon, too. Real soon."

Stuart had no energy to respond, nor did he have anything to say. *You've had your fun*, he thought, wearily closing his eyes and leaning against Cecco. *Now leave me alone.*

"I wouldn't rest just yet, Captain," Pan warned gleefully. "The day isn't over!" His words were followed by an ominous crack of thunder.

"Sar!" That was Smee speaking. "Sar, yeh'd best get hold o' yerself quick like. I think a storm's comin'!"

CHAPTER 15

Stuart peeked up at the sky. Smee was right. It was growing dark, the suns fading on the horizon — yes, *fading*, not setting — so quickly they must have been trying to set a record. Steel clouds were forming way too fast. The temperature plunged, and the breeze rose to a stiff wind. Lovely sunny weather transformed into a tempest in mere seconds.

At least Pan and his brats were flying away. Stuart had never been so humiliated in his life, particularly by his reaction to the croc and the fact that the children had witnessed it.

For God's sake, he had read Barrie's story, hadn't he? He had known the croc would show up at some point, hadn't he? Most of all, he should have known that the beast wouldn't eat him, at least not this soon. He'd just arrived in the Neverland. It would do Pan no good to lose his Hook this fast. Stuart had managed only to make a fool of himself, and though the pirates weren't making a big deal out of it, his own shame more than made up for that.

His brooding was interrupted as Smee said, "Sar, storm's comin' in fast!" He rose from Stuart's side and hurried away.

"Up you go, James," Cecco said, and he manhandled Stuart to his feet with the rough insistence of a man in a hurry to tend to more important matters.

Stuart barely heard Cecco's words as he clumsily found his footing — although something did ring a distant bell. James. James Hook. Pan had called him James, too. *James...* He grabbed Cecco's arm as the man started to go. "James!" he said. "The ship's log in Emmerich's safe... Anna was his wife... Cecco, your captain was my great-grandfather!"

Cecco's handsome Italian features turned ghost white for a split second as lightning cut across the darkening sky. "What's that?" he asked, the pieces of eight he wore as earrings flashing bright gold.

"The James you knew, it wasn't me, it was..." Stuart stopped, taking in Cecco's expression. *He thinks I'm crazy. Maybe I am.* Thunder rolled over the waves and another bolt of lightning cracked the sky.

"No time," was all Cecco said, and then he was striding away, shouting, "All hands on deck! Get out here, ya mammy-milkin' dungheaps! Double-time, now, haul your fuckin' arses if ya want to see tomorrow!"

In addition to the pirates already on deck, more poured up from the holds and forecastle – the second watch, roused from sleep but ready to do their duty. Cecco began spewing orders without consulting his captain, something Stuart knew would never happen normally. It was as if Cecco knew and absurdly accepted that Stuart had no idea what to do.

"All hands make ready to wear ship!" the first mate bellowed into the rising wind. "We've got to get the wind on our nose! First watch, lay aloft, fore and aft tops'l gaskets off! Haul down the flying jib! Second watch, ready sheets and braces!"

"Biggs, Mundy, set life lines fore and aft!" ordered Foggerty, the second mate.

Some of the pirates ran to man various lines on deck while others scurried up the ratlines, working their way along the topsail yards a hundred and fifty feet above the main deck. They climbed like spider monkeys, balancing on footropes and gripping the jackstays with nothing but fingers and toes while the rising wind tried to whip them away into salty oblivion.

Stuart had no idea what they were doing. He watched, no good for anything else, with a sort of dull amazement, his emotions already burned out like overused circuits. For the first time he felt his own uselessness – here he was, captain of a ship during a crisis, and he had no inkling what to do.

An enormous swell hit the *Jolly Roger* and spilled over the bulwarks. The ship listed to starboard. Stuart clung to the nearest rope as foaming water crashed across the deck, sweeping away anything not lashed down. Tools, barrels and dropped weapons vanished. Blood from the battle washed clean. Men clung to any stable object within reach while those in the rigging held on for dear life. Washports banged and slapped, banged and slapped, draining off enough water to let the pirates burst back into action, sloshing through ankle-deep residue.

"Mind the hatches!" Smee was yelling from somewhere near the mainmast. "Thatcher, Holston, batten 'em bastards down, chop chop!"

"Gaskets off!" came a voice from aloft. High above, two squares of canvas opened like white flowers in the raging gloom, loose and flapping wildly.

"Set fore and aft tops'ls!" Cecco boomed back. Men on deck took hold of the halyards and, in unison, hauled for all they were worth. "Heave away an' wake the dead or, by devil, you'll join 'em down below!" Cecco threatened them. "Heave away like old Scratch tucked his pitchfork straight up your arse, 'cause if he doesn't do it, I will!'"

Another wave broke over the bulwarks. The men hurriedly belayed their lines and held onto the pins until they could resume hauling. Stuart watched this heave-belay-resume, heave-belay-resume sequence occur every time a monster wave leaped the bulwarks. The sheer strength and determination of the pirates astounded him, and through it all, Cecco never stopped haranguing them, eventually damning them, their parents, their families, their ancestors, their future offspring, their childhood friends, their pets, and anybody else he could think of unless they worked their bloody fingers to the bone. He produced a cat-o'-nine-tails from somewhere and whipped those pirates who needed further inspiration. "See all lines clear!" he ordered next, and waved to the man at the wheel up on the quarterdeck. "Helm up, Skylights, easy now!"

"Helm up easy!" answered Skylights, and began the turn.

Stuart closed his eyes as another squall sprayed water across the deck. A gale sent his long curls flying about his head. *See all lines clear,* he thought. *Helm up...* Somehow he knew what that meant. All the ropes — *lines* — had to be free to run because the ship, with the wind astern, was going to turn downwind — *wear* — and come round to face the storm. In any other position, the wind could knock her right over or drive her onto the beach. Her only chance was to beat her way straight into it and reach open water, clearly what Cecco was trying to do.

Stuart had seconds to wonder at this before he felt the ship begin her turn, her bow swooping to the right thanks to the raging wind and tide. At the same time yet another squall hit her in mid-maneuver. Stuart was hard pressed to keep his footing — with his boots sunk somewhere in the foaming sea below, his wet silk stockings hydroplaned over the sopping deck, making him feel like a cartoon character slipping on one long continuous banana peel. He managed to loop his good arm around a life line, envying the pirates who were hurrying around him, looking for all the world like wind-up dancers — lurching yet somehow graceful. They moved with the ship and kept upright while Stuart almost slid on his ass over the side.

"Slack away those tops'ls!" Cecco howled, waving up at the men in the rigging. "Foggerty, get the men on the windlass! We don't have much—"

That was all Stuart heard. A strange sound began filtering up to him, almost like singing, melodious and raw with emotion. It skipped gently upon the wind, the power of the storm having no effect on its progress. It reminded Stuart of the wild wail of coyotes. But this was a pleasant wail, very very pleasant indeed. Downright erotic, in fact. In the midst of the storm, the chaos and the cold blasting wind, Stuart felt a shiver of hot arousal course through his body and settle in his groin. Compelled to discover the source, he lurched to the rail and looked down.

Mermaids. There were three of them and they were beautiful, their bodies glowing softly in the angry water, their long green hair swirling in cloud-shapes around them. Like dolphins they vaulted high above the waves, smiling seductively at him, displaying their bare breasts and laughing in delight before plunging back down into the raging foam with a slap of their pearlescent fish tails. Stuart was so enchanted that he didn't notice the pirate next to him until the man spoke.

"Ain't they beootiful!" the scrawny fellow said. Stuart could not take his eyes from the mermaids, but his peripheral vision told him that the man was one of those who had been hauling on a line a moment ago. Now he was climbing up onto the rail. With a blissful smile, he jumped overboard.

Stuart jolted out of his trance. "Hey, what are you—?" he shouted, letting his query remain incomplete as he watched the man fall. Was the fellow nuts? Then he heard the scream, short and agonized as the mermaids fell on their prey, ripping him to pieces with long claws and fangs, turning the angry grey foam a gory red.

Stuart's horror gave way to an insanely wonderful idea. *I'll jump, too. Yeah, it'll be great. They're so beautiful, sooo sexy, and they'll make me feel soooo goooooood—*

Someone slapped his face. His mind cleared, and Stuart found himself in the act of climbing onto the rail. He staggered back, confused, and then he reached for the rail again.

Slap! "Fer Chrissake, don't look at 'em, sar!" Smee yelled at him.

Stuart shook his head, shock and pain bringing him fully back to himself. "What are those things?"

"Sirens, sar!" Smee hollered over the wind. "Don't look at 'em an' don't listen to 'em! We're headin' out to sea where we can weather the storm! With any luck, they won't follow!" He handed Stuart a hunk of coarse cotton. "Put a bit o' this in yer ears, sar, an' whatever yeh do, keep yer eyes away from—" He nodded at the water, averting his own eyes.

Stuart took the cotton as another pirate flung himself over the rail.

"Hurry! Pass the cotton 'round as quick as yeh can, sar!" Smee hurried off, poking his pudgy index fingers into his ears.

Stuart pulled two bits of cotton from the wad and pushed them into place. The siren's call sounded muffled now, which made it less alluring, but then it began to echo in his head, growing in volume all on its own. It sent delightful shivers up and down his spine all over again. He clenched his jaws and groaned, feeling himself grow hard, wanting more than anything in the world to hold a naked woman, to have a beautiful young thing in his arms, a budding virgin with soft pert breasts that he could suck and full luscious lips that would—

This time he managed to slap himself. *Keep sane, you idiot! Do you want to die?*

But oh, the song was dizzyingly erotic, and his mind fast-forwarded through every porn movie he had ever watched, every dirty thought he had ever had and it felt so good, all those nasty daydreams, his most obscene thoughts of what he wished he could do to Melanie, all the inventive things he had always wanted her to do to him—

He stamped down on his right foot with his left foot. The pain of his heel slamming down on his toes brought tears to his eyes. *God dammit, Jon, get ahold of yourself!*

He pulled more cotton from the wad and stuffed it in his ears, probably poking it in too hard but he would worry about that later. The song lost more potency. The maddening echo stopped. Better. He would still need to keep his wits, but better.

With flagging strength he did his best to distribute the rest of the cotton amongst the pirates, who were desperately trying to keep the ship under control as she punched her way out of the bay. He prayed that the men in the rigging were too far up to hear the sirens because somebody had to be left to man the ship after the storm. Pirates all around him were succumbing to the spell, their arms going slack, lines falling unattended. Like zombies they stood, listening to the lovely shrieking from the sea. Some were slowly shuffling towards the nearest rail, their eyes hazy with lust. The ship tossed freely, losing headway.

Stuart began to drag men back to safety, lashing them down with any rope he could find and knocking the feisty ones unconscious when necessary — one of those was Cecco. Three men leapt to their deaths before he could get to them. He had no idea how many had been lost already, nor how many might not yet be affected, but he was determined to save as many as he could. His own life depended on them.

Smee caught up with him on the foredeck. Stuart removed the cotton from one ear and Smee did the same, panting, "There's more sirens! They're singin' from the lagoon! Sar, we ain't got enough men in their right minds to man the ship! We're gonna founder on the rocks fer sure!"

So that was Pan's plan. He must have told the sirens to sing with the hopes that the pirates would steer their ship right into the rocks or, in this case, crash for lack of control. "Options?" Stuart barked. Cold heavy rain started to fall. He shivered, his frilly cotton shirt sticking to his wet skin.

"We ain't got none, Cap'n!" Smee said, the rain turning his floppy cap into a long red droop. "Last time this happened there weren't no storm, 'member? We battened down the hatches an' MacDougal played 'is bagpipes to drown 'em out. But MacDougal's dead, sar — over the side!"

Stuart wiped rain from his eyes and tried again to tug his wig off. As before, it wouldn't budge. *Dammit, what's with this fucking thing?* The long curls were driving him nuts. The illogic of the situation was doing the same. "None of this makes sense, Smee! Why kill us this way? Pan wants battle and victory, not an impersonal slaughter! We can make it through this if we can figure out what he wants!"

A tremendous bolt of lightning cracked across the sky, ending with a firecracker flash right over their heads that sent sparks showering down like fairy dust. Thunder "louder than the wrath o' God," as Smee put it, rattled Stuart to the bone. The *Jolly Roger* listed to port. Stuart and Smee tumbled to the deck, clutching each other in an attempt to not roll over the rails that tipped nearly horizontal for several seconds.

"We bin hit!" Smee wailed, managing a peek upward while shading his eyes from the weather.

The ship slowly returned to center and continued far over the other way, wind and waves giving her grief enough that she couldn't easily right herself. Over the thunder, the raging ocean and the siren's song, Stuart heard a massive groan of splitting wood. Another bolt of lightning tore its way down from the sky with simultaneous thunder. The ship flashed white and listed back to port, shuddering and moaning in protest. This time Stuart managed to grip a life line with one hand and Smee with his other as the deck tilted. From the corner of his eye he saw a man, his identity impossible to distinguish through the stinging spray, grasp for the life line, miss and disappear into the sea.

Smee pointed up into the rigging. "Another hit on the mizzen! She's comin' down!"

Squinting through wind and rain, Stuart made out that lightning had struck above and below the mizzen upper topsail yard — suspicious aim for random lightning bolts. The crippled mast held together by its rigging for the space of a breath, then the amputated topmast tilted to port. The nearly hundred-foot-long spar, with its forty-foot topgallant yard and shorter royal yard, hung suspended by rigging, swaying in a dangerous arc as the wind pounded into it, tearing the canvas sails into flailing flags.

Stuart watched, paralyzed with terrified fascination, as the whole thing came crashing down with a tremendous basso roar of destruction, dragging both standing and running rigging with it — shrouds, canvas, metal hardware, blocks and tackles, braces, and several tons of timber and rope. Some of the rigging dropped straight down. Some of it snagged on other damaged rigging and swung frantically back and forth, catching men in the swinging. The spar itself, the yards stubbornly perpendicular, plummeted over the port rail into the water and immediately dragged on the ship, causing the *Jolly Roger* to list dangerously to port and stay that way.

Taut lines snapped and became living bullwhips, slashing through the air so fast they whistled. One caught Stuart in the back and he pitched forward with a grunt, the resulting gash spraying red. Before he could regain his bearings, something hard and heavy slammed his thigh — probably a block and tackle, though he never actually saw it — and he rolled, hearing Smee's warning: "Cap'n, look out!"

Too little too late, Stuart thought, his vision going white. For a moment, he wondered stupidly if the ship had entered a fog bank. He struggled to sit up but was flattened back down again when the main shrouds landed on him. Exhaustion and the weight of the heavy canvas and ropes kept him down as another deluge washed across the deck, dumping snapped lines and loose netting into the mix until Stuart was tangled in the whole mess.

Miraculously, Smee was free and upright. He unsheathed Johnny Corkscrew and began to cut rope as fast as he could, calling out, "The Cap'n's caught! Help here!"

Gentleman Starkey and, of all people, Vigr Sigrson appeared, both bedraggled but in one piece. Stuart doubted they had heard Smee through the ungodly noise and the cotton in their ears. They must have seen the dilemma on their own.

"Cut!" Smee ordered anyhow. "Quick with it, damn yeh!"

They set to work, Smee and Starkey sawing at the heavy ropes with knives while Sigrson chopped with his hand ax. The last thing Stuart wanted to see was the big Swede wielding a blade that size over his head. He thought he caught a glint of murder in the man's eyes. But in his present circumstances there was nothing for it but to trust to Sigrson's questionable loyalty.

One leg was freed, one arm — and then the shrouds slid in a jumbled mass to port. Helpless to fight such weight, Stuart was dragged with it across bodies, timbers, tackle and debris until he smashed up against the bulwarks.

"Christ A'mighty," Smee said, hurrying over, "he's snagged to the topmast!"

You mean that big heavy thing that's sinking out there? Stuart thought wildly. He had only one hand free, so he fumbled with one of the knots that bound the other hand, already knowing it was a ridiculous effort. This wasn't like trying to undo a knotted shoelace. The big lines, some of them two inches thick or more, tar slathered with metal cables at their core — those were bad enough, but they weren't the problem. It was the smaller lines that had twisted themselves in and around and though the larger. Those were the lines that bound him willy-nilly to the bigger shrouds and the debris caught in them. One ankle was snagged anew, and the more the floundering topmast tugged, the tighter the snag became. Stuart's foot was thudding with his heartbeat from lack of circulation. Lines had wrapped around his waist, nearly cutting off his air, but Starkey was making fast work of those. Stuart gave up on his hand and was trying to bend enough to help Smee free his aching foot when the writhing mound of shrouds and lines jerked and trembled as if it were alive.

"Cut!" Smee told the men. "Cut, yeh mammy boys, 'fore he goes overboard!"

Sigrson had abandoned Stuart and was hacking at the rail, chopping off lines that still attached the foundering topmast to the ship. Smee and Starkey almost had Stuart free. Stuart climbed to his knees, readying himself for a final scramble over the tangled mass before it went over for good.

It twitched under him, a wriggly monster trying to hurtle itself into the foam below. Stuart flung his free right arm out against the bulwark for balance, praying he wouldn't get dragged up and over. Instead he screamed. He had inadvertently jammed his hand through the middle of a block and tackle caught crosswise against a scupper.

Fear gave way to dread as he realized what had to happen next. Hit by yet another wave, the incredible weight of the fallen topsail gave yet another jerk. Stuart's hand was pinched between the two heavy wooden shells of the block and tackle like a nut in a nutcracker. All he could do was scream as bones crunched. Blood gushed through the grooves in the polished wood. A wave sloshed back through the scupper, carrying two of his severed fingers with it. It drained back through the scupper and into the sea below. His wrist, sticking out from the block and tackle, swiftly turned from blue to grey to black. It was like he'd put on a glove.

Stuart gawked at it, fascinated at how fast all this destruction had occurred. It must have been, what, less than two minutes ago that the first lightning bolt had struck the mizzen? *And look at you, naughty boy, you're a frightful mess!* He wondered if he would scream again. It seemed like a good idea. He opened his mouth—

"Cut 'im free!" he heard from Starkey.

Smee was closest to the block and tackle. He was staring at it in bug-eyed realization. "I'll not cut off the Captain's hand!" came his hot reply.

Starkey winced at Stuart, his gentlemanly manners all but dissolved. Smee averted his eyes. Sigrson made no move to help Stuart and smiled slightly.

Captain, I have no intention of cutting off your hand, Pan had said. Of course! That's what he'd meant! Peter Pan demon boy was going to force Stuart to do it himself!

Where he found the energy, he did not know. How he did the deed, he did not know. All Jonathan Stuart knew was that he didn't want to die. He grabbed Sigrson's ax with his free left hand and, slamming down the grey wall in his mind, drawing that steely cold blanket around himself that numbed him from all emotions unpleasant, he sent the blade down through his own forearm.

The flesh gave way easily, no challenge at all for the ax's sharp edge. The bone fought to remain intact for a split second, sending an electric jolt up his arm that made his entire body convulse. Then it broke, letting the ax finish up the rest of the flesh underneath. The stump sprayed red. Stuart reeled back, more out of some vain attempt to get away from all that blood than to distance himself from the doomed mound of damaged rigging that had held him. He twisted in agony, dropped the ax and shrieked, the sound of it echoing over and over in the din of the storm, doubling and redoubling in his head like the song of the sirens until it overlapped itself, a cheap horror movie effect, the shrill scream of a mad scientist amidst clashing thunder and howling winds.

The sinking topmast gave its final tug. The last of the tangled debris slipped over the rail. The bloody block and tackle, with what was left of Stuart's hand squeezed inside, went with it.

Pan's voice rang in his head. "Strike Three, Captain. I'm proud of you."

HISTORY PART 3
DAD CHANGES

He was absolutely, on this occasion, a living, detestable, dangerous presence.

— *The Turn of the Screw* by Henry James

CHAPTER 16

Melanie went back to Glendale Memorial the next morning. She hadn't slept but an hour or two all night, and her nerves were shot. She had stopped by Jon's house to feed the cats and water the garden — he grew most of his own vegetables both summer and winter, a domestic aspect of his personality that, coupled with his general neatness, had added major points in his favor early in their courtship — but beyond that she had accomplished nothing. In fact, she was going to miss a big deadline tomorrow. She had been hired to do some historical research for a period film, and the client was her most prestigious to date. But the idea of caring about mere work appalled her. *Jon might be dying,* she kept thinking, *and I'm supposed to give a shit about who the ten richest men in St. Louis were in 1832?*

When Melanie entered the ICU waiting room at eight o'clock, Yolanda sprang out of her chair and hurried over. "Oh, Miss Forrester," the young girl stammered.

Melanie instantly thought the worst. "Oh God, is he...?"

"No no, he's fine," Yolanda said, "except..."

"Except what?"

Yolanda fiddled with the strap of her purse, her mouth working. Melanie wanted to slap her silly, anything to hurry her up, but she forced herself to wait. "They... he had to have..."

"What!" Melanie almost shouted.

"They amputated his hand."

Of all the expected things Yolanda could have told her, this one was not on the list. His *hand?* What in the devil did they cut his *hand* off for? Melanie was so dumbfounded she couldn't close her mouth. She knew it had dropped open in a gape of disbelief, but all she could do was let it hang there.

"I came here real early because, you know, I didn't get to see him last night," Yolanda was saying. "The nurse told me I still couldn't see him because he was in surgery, and I about freaked, you know? I thought maybe he was dying or something, so she told me that his hand... *ay Dios...*"

Melanie waited for the kicker, heart banging hard enough to make her ears thump.

"It turned black."

Melanie charged for the nurse's station. "I'm Melanie Forrester here to see Jonathan Stuart in room 207."

The nurse gave her a practiced smile. "Mr. Stuart came out of surgery a short time ago, Miss Forrester. I understand you're his fiancée?"

"Uh... yes, I am. What's all this about his hand?"

"Wait a moment, please, and I'll get the doctor."

Apparently Doctor Odet was off duty. Another doctor, an older man named Phillips, eventually showed up to inform Melanie that Jon's right hand had, for no reason that he could explain, turned black sometime between six and six fifteen that morning. "It was gangrene, no doubt about it," Phillips said, "although why it occurred and how it possibly developed that quickly... the fact is, I don't know. I've never seen anything like it."

According to Phillips there was no infection, no blockage of circulation, no injury to the tissues nor, Melanie already knew, was Jon a diabetic. One moment his hand was normal, the next it simply wasn't. "I had to amputate immediately to prevent the condition from spreading," Phillips told her. "There was no chance to save it. I am sorry." He added with sincerity, "I am also supremely baffled."

Melanie held the doctor's gaze for what felt like an hour, trying to figure out something to say. What was happening? Nothing about Jon's condition was making any sense. She was finally able to answer a few questions for Dr. Phillips, but it was clear that the good doctor was grasping at straws as much as she was. He had already consulted several colleagues, to no avail. "There is no reason, none whatsoever, for gangrene to develop in these circumstances and especially at such speed. We need to run more tests." The tone with which he said these words convinced her that he didn't expect to learn anything new and that this would go down as a complete medical mystery.

"Could it have anything to do with the high alcohol level in his blood?" Melanie asked, knowing already that alcohol and gangrene had damned little to do with each other.

"Not at all," Dr. Phillips answered.

Phillips allowed her to visit Jon for a few minutes. This time, Melanie insisted that Yolanda come, too. *I'm just plain scared,* she thought, but it was more than that. A strange tension was building up in her, strong enough to physically hurt. It was irrational, a sense of profound wrongness, of dread. She might even have described the sensation as malevolent, though she had no real basis for using such a word.

She entered the room with Yolanda. "It's okay," the girl said, leading Melanie to the bedside. "See? He's sleeping. He's fine."

Melanie looked at Jon, and all she saw was his right arm. Dr. Phillips had made the cut about two inches above the wrist. A thick bandage covered the stump. She turned away and began to cry.

She loved Jon's hands, the way he held her, the way he ran his fingers through her hair, the way he stroked her body when they made love. His hands were strong, and she felt cherished and safe when they touched her. When he kissed her, he held her face in those hands like he owned her. During those moments, she would have gladly given him a bill of sale. *It's going to be so different now,* she thought, *more for you than for me. Why did this happen to you?* Tears came, and she was reaching for a tissue on the bedside table when she noticed the bewilderment on Yolanda's face. "What?"

"Look." Yolanda pointed at Jon's head.

Melanie had avoided looking at Jon's face thus far. She didn't want to see his lively expressive features slack in drugged repose. More, she didn't want that look to remind her of her sister and how that drugged repose had gradually turned the corner into the stony mask of death.

Yolanda said, "His hair," in a thin but urgent whisper.

Melanie suddenly saw what should have been obvious. Jon's hair was different. *It's dark,* she thought, mystified. *Almost black. And... it's wavy.*

Yolanda swallowed. "*Esto es de locos.*"

Melanie said nothing, just studied his face. She jerked back, a hand to her mouth.

"What?" Yolanda demanded, frightened.

"His ears are pierced."

"They weren't before?"

Melanie shook her head.

Yolanda checked both of Jon's ears. "Maybe he got them done recently, and you didn't notice?"

"I would have noticed."

"Okay, why would the doctors pierce his ears?"

"They wouldn't."

"Then who did?"

The same person who snuck in and gave him a new 'do, Melanie wanted to say, but it would have been a sarcastic, stupid statement. Fear did that to her. It was easier to crack wise than admit that the world was going loopy. And anyway, what did hair and ears have to do with sudden gangrene in a hand? "This is nuts, Yolanda."

The girl maneuvered Melanie into a chair. "I agree, but there still has to be an explanation."

"How can anybody explain this? He was perfectly normal two days ago." Even as she spoke, Melanie knew that was a lie. Two days ago she had seen Jon double over in pain at the bookstore. Before that, he had shown signs of unusual stress and anxiety, more than could be explained by a tax audit. He had been through that before and worse. The drinking? Before she had convinced him to quit, Melanie had seen Jon drunk more times than she wanted to think about. She had seen him happily tipsy, barf-your-brains-out hung over and everything between. But drinking had never made him nervous or tense, just the opposite. Liquor tended to calm him down.

Then she remembered the Giant Dream. *Maybe he started with the brandy because of that,* she thought. But then, what had caused the Giant Dream to return? That was what she needed to find out. *High content in his bloodstream or not, he drank to escape. There's something more going on here.* The only other problem she could think of was the house in San Francisco. Her heart skipped a beat. "The house."

Yolanda turned to her. "What house?"

Something knocked at Melanie's skull from the inside, calling for attention, something as small and insistent as a child's little fist. The answer was dangling just beyond her reach, she felt it there, teasing her. Something about the house...

She stared at Jon, willing the answer to come. If there was one thing she was good at, it was tying together seemingly disparate facts to make a coherent whole. The facts were right in front of her. She just needed to recognize them and fit them together. *His hand – his right hand, gone. His hair different – from blond to black, and from straight to wavy. His ears – pierced.* She remembered the night before. *And the welts – they'd been on his right arm!* She stood. "I need to go, Yolanda. I want to check something."

Yolanda followed her to the door. "Can I help?"

Melanie was about to say yes. She had come to like Yolanda a lot, and it would be nice to have company. But if Yolanda got even the tiniest inkling of what was going through Melanie's head, the girl would think she had dived off the deep end of an empty pool. "Thanks, no. It's sort of crazy."

"We've already established that."

"Come on." Melanie opened the door. "Jon needs to sleep."

As they parted ways in the parking lot, Yolanda gave Melanie a hug. "This is sort of creepy," she said. "If you figure out anything, let me know right away, okay? I'll be at the store all day."

"You're not serious," Melanie said. "What about your classes?"

"It's his livelihood," said Yolanda. "Alan quit. I'll talk to my teachers, get a week off or something. It'll be fine."

"You're something else," Melanie told her. "Jon will appreciate this."

Yolanda managed a grin. "I'll make him give me a raise."

* * * * *

Melanie was glad she had kept her key to Jon's house after all. His trust in humanity was... well, it hardly existed, which meant that he always kept his house locked tight as a safe. She would have had to break a window or something, and that probably would have caught the attention of his nosey neighbor, old Henry Kotch, a cranky geezer who had nothing better to do than spy on everyone and, when the fancy hit him, phone the cops.

Jon's cats came trotting towards her from every direction when she unlocked the front door. They purred and bumped her ankles, complaining in no uncertain terms that the neglect they had suffered the last two days was not acceptable.

"Okay, okay," Melanie told them, putting her purse down on the entryway table. She fed them and petted them for a few minutes, then stood in the kitchen doorway, wondering. Long, dark, curly hair. Pierced ears. Missing right hand. She had recently been reminded of someone like that. She would have felt like an idiot for even thinking of that person, but she remembered when Jon had first regained consciousness at the hospital. Among his slurred ramblings, she had definitely heard him say "not hook."

"Where did you put them?" she asked the Jon in her mind, and began to search the house. She could find neither the saber nor the supposed log of Captain Hook anywhere. What she did find was a copy of J.M. Barrie's novel *Peter Pan*. It was stuffed under the cushion of Jon's reclining chair in the den. *Why did you hide it, Jon?* she wondered.

Fuzzybutt, who had shadowed her through the house with interest, jumped up on the sofa. "Good idea, Fuzz," Melanie said, sitting down with the feline. She began to read, stroking the fat cat's warm fur as she delved into the famous adventures of the boy who wouldn't grow up.

CHAPTER 17

You are beautiful.

His lover, his whore, giver of dreams and nightmares, riches and losses, joy and terror, glory and death.

My life, my heart, my very soul are yours.

He had been away too long. She hardly remembered him.

Let me serve you. Let me die in your arms.

He was ready to do anything for her, anything.

Love me. Please.

"...he's still struggling!"

"More laudanum!"

"Hold 'im down, fer Chrissake!"

"Git round there so I can—"

"Cookson, just do it!"

"Hold his arm—"

"He's slippery as a fuckin' fish!"

"Give 'im a konk on the noggin'!"

"Are you mad?"

"Sir, I can't hold him—"

"My sincere apologies, James—"

...

Crystal waves. Salt foam. Blue horizon. Grey sky.

He floated in her embrace. Silence. At last, blessed silence.

She had not forgotten him. She held him tenderly, and he drifted.

But he knew her fickle nature. She might turn on him at any moment, might cast him into the sea if he did not obey her slightest whim. Thus it was with every romance. He loved her for it. She was all he had ever wanted, all he needed. He would never leave her again.

"...careful, yeh fat baboons! Lay 'im down, that's it. Cecco, I'll be stayin' with 'im till he's fit."

"Mister Roland will take your watches."

"Aye. I'll call yeh if I have need."

"Take care of him, Smee."

"I always do..."

She was bucking and rolling on an angry sea. He easily moved with her, feeling every part of her, instinctively aware of her slightest tremble. To touch her electrified him. To command her intoxicated him.

Hush, my beauty. We shall weather this together, you and I. Never again will I fail you, I swear it...

"...yer great granddaddy... best foe Pan ever had... passion fer everythin'... refined manners one minute, devil incarnate the next..."

"...took the name Hook ... admired, almost *liked* him... rules between 'em, never spoken but always understood..."

"...downfall in the end... Anna... pleaded, cried, schemed, killed, nothin' worked... wrote letters to her, threw 'em out to sea in bottles... Pan found one once, read it back to him, just a voice in the night... poor bastard thought it was his wife... cracked... created a monster, but o' course, that's what Pan wanted... crew afraid... fiend stalked the deck nights, mumblin' an' cursin'... game wound down, Pan took pity on him, but weren't no favor takin' him home... would've been better if he *had* been swaller'd by the croc..."

"...Pan went off fer awhile. He does that, y'know. I s'pose he flew to the world to bring back more o' them Lost Boys. S'many go bad, y'see. Modern lads're difficult fer him, got minds o' their own. Lil' Lad Jack was one o' Pan's afore he decided to join with us. That's why Pan killed him. But y'know, after a time Pan come to think it was Hook he really wanted. The great foe. An' that, yeh poor devil, was the unfortunate beginnin' of *yer* venture... What's that yeh say? How many games have there been? Well, that I couldn't tell yeh. Long since lost count, y'see. Since the heyday o' pirates it's been about pirates. Afore that the game took the form of whatever children fancied..."

"...not a boy, yer right about that. He's like a god, Jon. The real thing, I swear by Johnny Corkscrew. Yer a learned man, ain't yeh? Y'heard o' Pan, right? I think it's him. An' I s'pose like any god, he wants worship. Children please him best, so there yeh be. He created a whole world fer little ones. Brings 'em here fer sport, he does, plenty o' boys but only one girl. His Wendy. She's the rudder that steers the ship..."

"...liked it so much he set up the same game agin. Found a new Wendy an' a John an' a Michael. Them sprogs today know the story, thanks to Mister Barrie's book, an' plenty want to come. The fairy was still here — they live way too long, if yeh ask me. Not sure if they die, come to think of it. Everythin' was in place 'cept fer a Hook. He searched fer yeh, Jon, an' he found yeh. He's not gonna give yeh up no matter what yeh do. Y'know what fightin' it did to yer great granddaddy, right? I 'spect yer well on yer way, too, if yeh don't keep a cool head. Now that yeh know what's really happenin', maybe yeh can make yer fate easier to bear."

"Wh... why are you telling me all this... now?"

"Well, between the trauma, rum an' laudanum, yeh'll forgit every word I'm sayin'. Over time yeh'll forgit everythin' 'cept the game. Though... well, I s'pose it's really 'cause yeh remind me o' James — yer voice, yer looks, the way yeh move. Yer eyes are the same shade o' blue, like ferget-me-nots. I couldn't help but take a shine to yeh the minute we fished yeh outta the bay. If I can, I'll spare yeh some o' the heartache that's comin'."

"...Coming...?"

"Aye."

"Like... what...?"

"The both of us'll find out as it happens, Jon."

"You... only one... knows...?"

"That this is all a game? Oh, aye, that I am. Call me gamekeeper, if yeh like. Others puzzle out the truth from time to time, but like I said, yeh forget things in the Neverland."

"Except you..."

"Aye."

"Help me... Smee..."

"I am, Jon. It's my responsibility to see that yer up an' about as fast as can be. Pan don't like to wait too long, an' I ain't one to anger him, no sar. I done all I could to bring yeh this far, an' I'll keep goin'. I know me duty. Soon enough, you'll know yers."

"Want... home..."

"Oh, enough o' this talk. I won't speak of it agin no matter how yeh might plead. I dare not. I'm as much a prisoner as you, an' if Pan got wind of our little conversation here, well... he's got his punishments, yeh'll learn that quick enough. But... I s'pose I had to tell yeh, Jon, an' this seemed the only way. Maybe yeh'll remember in dreams, enough to keep yeh from doing somethin' foolish. I'll keep helpin' yeh any way I can, too, but first yeh gotta help yerself. Play the game. Don't fight it. If yeh fight it, yeh'll truly know what Hell kin be."

CHAPTER 18

Stuart awoke in his cabin, slouched in a chair in his lounging robe, bare feet up on the rosewood table, an open book across his lap — his old dog-eared Bible. The hazy glare of the morning suns filtered softly through the thick-paned windows, supplemented by reading candles burning in the chandelier. The *Jolly Roger* was sailing steadily. Out on deck, feet stomped in unison and a song rang out:

> *Oh, my charmin' Nellie Ray,*
> *They have taken you away,*
> *You have gone to Van Diemen's cruel shore!*
> *For you've skinned so many tailors*
> *An' you've robbed too many sailors*
> *That we look for you in Peter Street no more!*

The voice belonged to MacDougal, the shantyman, whose expertise must have been needed to keep the men in rhythm as they worked the capstan. *Such a pleasant tenor he has,* Stuart thought dreamily, *and a keen knack for keeping peace in the fo'c'sul. Valuable man.*

Thirst prompted him to automatically reach to his left — a cup was indeed there. He drank, savoring the flavor. A fine burgundy with a rich bouquet, one of his favorites. *Non-alcoholic my ass,* he thought absently, finishing it off and returning the cup to its place.

Something fuzzy tickled his chin. Stuart reached back and stroked the big orange cat that lay stretched out along the top of the chair back, its long tail curled under Stuart's throat. The cat always knew the minute Stuart sat down to read — cat telepathy, he supposed — and it would appear out of nowhere to take its accustomed place behind his head, purring into his ear. The low rumble soothed Stuart's senses more than drink or a good cigar ever could. *Au Rebours,* he thought fondly, giving the cat's tail a playful tug. *My dear old Rebers.*

But it wasn't Rebers. The tip of this cat's tail kinked at the end like a permanent question mark.

He looked over his shoulder to find Dago Tom gazing at him. The burly fat-faced tabby was the ship's best mouser. Stuart remembered saving him from that skunky drunkard Bartolo in St. Mary's. The man had been about to eat the animal, for heaven's sake. Stuart wasn't above eating a cat, but only in the most dire of circumstances. Bartolo, on the other hand, would eat his own mother if that's all he could find after a long binge.

St. Mary's. Beautiful Madagascar. He leaned back and relaxed, trying to stave off the old restlessness in his soul. He hadn't seen that glorious pirate haven for years, not since coming here. *Peter Pan. Cocky boy lopped off my hand. I must have been dreaming about it. Thank God that storm didn't wreck the ship. My word, it all happened so long ago...* He frowned at his right arm. *Restlessness or no, I'll not leave this island till I've had my revenge.*

He was looking, not at his hand, but at an iron hook.

Reality slammed home.

"Fuck!" Stuart bolted up from the chair, nearly upset the table, stumbled backwards and fell on the floor. The cat hissed and ran. The Bible evidently had no intact binding because the stiff leather cover thudded to the rug amidst a snowfall of loose pages. Stuart didn't give a damn about the cat or the book or the upturned chair. He shook back the long ruffles on his sleeve and stared.

It was a hook, all right. For a moment, a fleeting moment, he thought he had worn it for a very long time. But he had never seen it before, this ugly metal abomination. It was stuck to his body like some gruesome leech. *It happened, just like in the storybook. It wasn't a dream! It really happened!* But Pan hadn't cut his hand off, had he?

No, came a dark thought. *He made you do it. He created that whole storm on purpose, to force you to do it yourself.*

Stuart looked around. *So... what am I doing here?* He remembered the terrible siren storm now. He had barely survived, had been cut and lashed and mangled by debris, and here he was lazing around in some red velvet get-up, still wearing Hook's ridiculous wig and not a scratch on him — except for the obvious missing hand, which was now a hook.

The awful thing screwed into a tapered wood base sheathed in molded silver that snugged up to the stump of his wrist, held there by a leather collar attached by rivets to three adjustable straps. Those straps then laced through a tight band below his elbow and continued up his arm beyond his sleeve. He could feel them go all the way to his armpit where they met some kind of molded leather pad that capped his shoulder. More straps from that crossed his chest and back, ducking under his left armpit and looping over the shoulder to give the crude prosthetic stability and leverage.

The whole apparatus was adjusted to fit snugly at all points. Those points had developed calluses to ward against the constant rub of leather. It was uncomfortable, to say the least, but most uncomfortable was the certain knowledge that wearing it was both alien and familiar. He had never worn the harness before, yet he had been wearing it for months. *Just like the cats,* he thought. *I remember Rebers but...*

...you also remember Dago Tom.

Up to this point in his captivity, Stuart had expected Pan to play with his head every time he awoke from sleep, but this was more than he could take. His personal history had been turned into soup this time, a simmering hodgepodge of two separate lives: his own that knew nothing of being a pirate, and that of James Hook, experienced "gentleman of fortune," remorseless murderer and, of all things, cat fancier.

Perhaps more confusing was the fact that Stuart felt no pain anywhere on his body, aside from a dull throb in the stump and the chafe of the leather harness. According to one set of memories, he had been beaten, bloodied and his hand mutilated in a storm that had occurred just before he woke up. The other part of him, however, that set of foggy parallel memories, insisted that he had lost his hand months ago when Pan had attacked the ship with his tribe of brats. The demon boy had chopped off the appendage and thrown it into the mouth of the biggest crocodile Stuart had ever seen. Stuart had almost bled to death, and the recovery had been a long and brutal process.

Stuart caught his reflection in a full-length oval stand-up mirror, a truly beautiful piece that stood on wooden claw feet. *That mirror wasn't there before,* one set of memories told him.

The other set insisted that, of course, it had been there. *It belonged to the lovely Mrs. Mary Etherton, don't you remember? Too bad she insisted on sailing with her husband to Cape Town. Dear Thomas Etherton, captain of the* Devotion. *Stupid fool had it coming, you know.* Pictures flickered across his mind — a merchant vessel sailing away, stripped of its provisions, guns and cargo; his own ship's hold stuffed with booty; his esthetics for interior decorating pushed to their limits as he meticulously incorporated the best of the Etherton's furnishings into his cabin — and all of this permeated with a sensation of pride and greedy glee.

Stuart rubbed his forehead and gazed again into the mirror. Whichever memory was true, he still had to come to grips with his reflection. He had expected to see blond stubble on his chin, maybe a scruffy beard. He couldn't recall the last time he had seen a razor. But the mirror revealed a neat pointed goatee and a stylish mustache, both as black as the perfect ringlets hanging down his shoulders. That damned wig. What was it *still* doing on his head? He yanked at it.

"Ow!"

It wasn't a wig anymore. It was his hair.

The idea was just too absurd. Stuart ran the fingers of his left hand across his head, tugging at the curls, amazed at how thick they were. The pretentious mop really was his own!

He burst into giggles. *I've got Shirley Temple hair!* His giggles slipped into hysterical laughter and he thumped to the floor, rolling around and kicking his feet and pounding the deck like a kid during a tickle attack. Somewhere in his addled brain he knew such behavior must be the product of a terror so beyond him that he couldn't face it head-on, but logic and reason held no sway over his emotions. He was wound tight as a clock spring. It all had to come out somehow.

He bolted upright, a wicked idea in his head. With a berserk, "Arrrr!" he slashed at the table with his hook, leaving a deep gash in the finish. The act of delivering such casual destruction to such a lovely object exhilarated him, and Stuart slashed a second time, his hook cutting at an angle to the previous cut and taking a little V of wood away.

What a delightful weapon! All he had to do was aim, and instead of striking with an impotent hand, he cut with an iron claw. Marvelous! He slashed at the chair. So much for upholstery. He slashed at the Oriental screen, leaving a neat slice down the main panel that cut a graceful cherry blossom tree in half. "This is great!" he cried, and whacked at one of the ship's big support beams that angled down from the ceiling.

His hook stuck. "Shit." Giggling at his own foolishness, Stuart pulled. Leather straps and sharp buckles dug into his skin. He grimaced and kept pulling. He'd really gotten the hook buried deep. He figured he could take the harness off but dropped that idea. He didn't know how to take it off. Five minutes later he was still struggling when someone knocked on the door. "What!" he barked, angry by this time.

"It's Smee, sar."

"Get in here!"

The bosun entered. His bushy grey eyebrows crawled up his forehead as he took in the scene. "What're yeh doin', sar?"

"What in damnation does it look like I'm doing?" Stuart said. "Help me free."

"Err, a'course, sar." Smee approached, but he plainly did not want to touch the hook. He tried several times to position his hands along Stuart's arm, then gingerly walked around to the other side to repeat the fumblings.

Stuart ground his teeth. "Take hold at the base, oaf."

"Uh, right, Cap'n." Smee obeyed, wincing all the while. "I suggest givin' it a tweak an' tug back," he said, turning his head aside as if the sight of the hook disturbed him. "Give it a good strong haul from the shoulder when yeh do. Don't use arm strength. One. Two. Three!"

The two of them pulled. Stuart's harness dug into his skin, but the hook popped free before the pain really got to him. Fortunately, too, none of the buckles broke. "Ah! Excellent," he said. "Thank you, Smee." He whipped the frilled kerchief from his sleeve and rubbed the hook clean, the motion automatic as if he'd done it many times before. *I've never done it before,* he thought.

Yes, you have. You stroke that hook like a lover.

Startled, Stuart threw the kerchief down. "Mister Smee, when did..." He indicated the prosthetic. "...this happen?"

It seemed to Stuart that Smee pointedly turned away and busied himself righting the fallen chair. "I'm surprised yeh need to ask that, sar. Been months. Hard to believe the croc's still followin' yeh after all this time, ain't it?"

Stuart stared. "The croc?"

"Oh, aye. It's swimmin' along with the ship this very minute, sar, if yeh want to see, though I'll be damned how the devil it moves s'fast."

The ship was sailing? Where were they going? Stuart was about to ask when the movie screen in his head flickered back to life, replaying memories of his awful plunge into the bay, his bloody introduction to the croc and his narrow escape. It then reminded him that he had once smeared chicken's blood on one of the nun buoys and tossed it to the dumb beast. The croc had instantly chomped on it, being the mindless eating machine that it was, and Stuart recalled the whole crew laughing as it had thrashed and roared in a hopeless attempt to swallow. Stuart himself had savored the sight, one of his few moments of sweet revenge. Part of him itched to do it again. There were plenty of buoys and chickens in the hold.

No. He had no desire to bait the croc. What he really wanted was for the flow of contradictory images to stop. He shut his eyes, but that hardly helped. Memories — worse than that, the feelings that went with them — continued to clash in his head until he thought he might burst.

He plopped into his chair, muttering as he had so many times before, "Cushion needs to be mended." *Dammit, I've never said that before!* He picked up his cup and held it out, hoping that wine might ward off the mental onslaught.

"I'll tend to the cushion, sar," Smee said, and filled Stuart's cup from the pitcher on the table.

There was no pitcher on the table, Stuart told himself firmly. *It was not there!*

Yes, it was, came the retort.

Fuck. Stuart gulped wine, though he could hardly hold the cup steady. Red dribbled down his chin. *You've finally gone mad, James. You tried your best but—*

Stuart dropped the cup.

He had just called himself James.

God help me, this is what insanity is!

"Cap'n?" Smee cleared his throat for attention. "Mister Cookson requests yeh check stores afore we dock."

Stuart just sat there, struggling to hold himself together, fearing that any minute he might start drooling and gibbering like a card-carrying crackpot.

"We're half a day from the Port, sar. We'll be there afore sunsss... afore dark. It's yer habit to personally inspect stores afore reachin' port." Smee waited, unaware of the delirious, foaming mayhem hidden under Stuart's calm exterior. "You've always done it, sar. Cookson's expectin' yeh."

"Stores," Stuart managed to whisper. *Foggerty,* came the thought. "Have Mister Foggerty tend to it, Smee."

"If yeh wants, Cap'n."

You'll have to record all this. "What day is it?"

"Err... day after yesterday, sar."

Stuart laughed, a short bark of manic amusement. "Of course it is. How silly of me."

The log, you buffoon. Read the log.

He blundered to his feet, wondering where the log was kept until a mental image told him it was in the drawer of the writing desk.

"Y'want me to fix yer Bible, sar?" Smee asked, grabbing the edge of the table when Stuart nearly knocked him over on his way to the writing desk. "This is the third time it's fallen apart, sar. I know it means a lot to yeh."

Stuart froze as more unbidden memories marched past his mind's eye: himself as the bosun aboard Blackbeard's ship *Queen Anne's*

Revenge; that infamous pirate giving him the Bible as a parting gift when Stuart left to assume his first command; Stuart leaving the Faith behind but still reading that Bible regularly, trying to reconcile a good Christian life with that of a thieving pirate. He hadn't yet figured that one out.

"Do it," he said curtly.

"Aye aye, sar."

Stuart found the log book in the drawer, along with a quill pen and ink.

Read the first page.

He opened to the first page. In his own handwriting it said:

Log, *Jolly Roger*, November 23, 1989: moored in
Pirate's Bay, Pan's Island, coordinates unknown. Calm
sea, no clouds, light winds. I am still recovering from
the croc attack and cannot leave my bed. First Mate
Cecco, Second Mate Foggerty and Bosun Smee a great
help. Crew in fine spirits — I am touched that all
remained loyal past hope of my recovery. No sign of
Pan or his brats.

November 23? Wasn't that the day Pan took him? Yes, it was. He had written business correspondence at the bookstore that morning, before Melanie had come to tell him that she was...

Stuart read the next entry.

Log, *Jolly Roger*, November 24, 1989: moored in
Pirate's Bay, Pan's Island, coordinates unknown. Calm
sea, fresh breeze. Heavy clouds to the east. Am feeling
better, toured the ship today. All in fine shape. Smee
sewing new flag. Old one wind-whipped beyond
recognition. Hawkins dropped MacDougal's
concertina over the side. Crew royally pissed, as am I.
Hung the idiot by his feet in the rigging till night in
vain hope he'd gain some sense. No such luck. Spotted
smoke signals over Indian forest but no trouble.

On and on it went, entries in his own handwriting of things he hadn't seen, conversations he'd never had, orders he'd never given. He turned to find Smee on his hands and knees, still gathering Bible pages. The bosun shuffled them awkwardly, trying to put them in order. "Mister Smee."

"Sar?"

"How long have I been in command of this vessel?"

Smee couldn't hide his alarm at the question. "Yeh feelin' okay, sar?"

"Answer me!"

Smee jumped. "Err, err, a really long time, sar!"

"A really... long time." Day after yesterday. A really long time. Those phrases and others just like them were going to be the only answers he would ever get to sensible questions. He had stepped off the map and was now where thar be monsters – and, apparently, no sense of time.

He flipped through the log to read more. The entry for November 25 described a terrible storm and how the ship had run for open seas to weather it out, but there was no mention of Pan or sirens or his severed hand. November 26 detailed a trip to the island during which he himself searched for the hidden home of Pan and the Lost Boys. He had found no sign of it, "as usual," the entry concluded. The next few entries detailed ship's business, and then Stuart saw what he had dreaded – the dates and times of the entries grew more and more indistinct. Phrases like "Next Day" and "Day after Yesterday" began each entry. Worse, his handwriting became shaky more often than not, suggesting that he had written in a state of great anxiety... or drunkenness. According to the number of entries, he had been in the Neverland a good six months, maybe more.

He flipped to the last page and read the top entry, the third to the last:

> Log, *Jolly Roger*, en route to Beggar's Port. The storm
> blew us far east of Pan's island. We passed Bowers
> Rock at the end of the morning watch. I have
> therefore decided to make for the Port to resupply and
> hire more men. Storm casualties have left me with a

skeleton crew. Wind NNW. Fresh breeze and squally, seas still running high. Damage to ship considerable, but she'll manage. Main hatch cover torn away, water below, men constantly at the pumps. Flooding in deck house and galley. Repairs to mizzen topsail in progress. Jukes, MacDougal, Noodler, Geo. Scourie, Skylights and Kamau still recovering from the siren spell. Lost are:

> Quartermaster Ed Teynte
> Mano Vasquez
> apprentice Tops
> Chas. Turley
> Fernando Pettengale
> Robt. Mullins
> Bosun's Mate Wolsey

Will hold services tomorrow at dawn. Bodies should be prepared by then. Damn Pan and his feral brats to the lowest circle of Hell.

So there *had* been a storm, and the sirens had wailed their deadly song. The mast had been damaged, too, just as he remembered, and many men had died. But it had apparently taken place three days ago, and whether or not the rest of the disaster's details had occurred as he remembered them, Stuart had no way to tell. What did stand out was the last line. It implied the disaster had been Pan's doing. A red roiling anger in his gut confirmed it.

He could have used the energy of that anger, but instead of helping him it plunged him into a profound depression. All this death and destruction, and for what? A stupid feud between a wild boy and a Pasadena bookstore owner? Ludicrous, that's what it was. Ludicrous and pointless. Guilt settled its ungainly weight on Stuart's shoulders, though he hadn't even known the men who had lost their lives.

On the contrary, you knew them well, came the dark thought. *They were part of your crew, and their deaths shall be added to the tally under your name. Thus is the burden of command.*

He carried the log back to the rosewood table, sat down and reached dismally for the pitcher of wine. It wasn't there. He heaved a sigh. "Brandy, Smee."

Smee scuttled past him and did something noisy at the cabinet by the harpsichord. Stuart remained seated, staring at his hook, no longer upset, just numb. Tired. Defeated.

Smee placed a goblet before him, filled with a small amount of aromatic brandy. A green bottle followed, almost full. "Here yeh go, sar. I'll just finish with the pages quick like, an' be on me way." He hurried to pick up his messy stack on the floor.

Stuart remained as he was. He couldn't move, not even to drink. Nothing mattered anymore. Pan had him. His memories were being remolded, his very flesh was no longer his own. How could he fight a power like that?

He raised his head when Smee, arms stuffed with Bible, started for the door. "Game... keeper?" he asked. The curious word had wriggled out from under the edge of his subconscious, and he wondered at it.

Smee slowly turned around. "What's that, sar?"

How strange. This was a memory that both parts of his mind seemed to share, but it was as fuzzy as it was elusive. "Gamekeeper," Stuart repeated, fumbling for the significance. "Children please him best..."

Smee dismissed the words with a shrug of one shoulder. "Dunno what yer talkin' about, sar."

Bewildered, Stuart waved him away and sat in silence, brooding.

CHAPTER 19

Melanie read and re-read *Peter Pan* that night. The next day she went out, bought a copy of the original play and read that, too. She underlined several passages regarding the enigmatic Captain Hook and read them over and over, trying to decipher an answer that she knew had to be sitting right in front of her though she could not see it. Not yet.

"His eyes were of the blue of the forget-me-not..."

"In dress he somewhat aped the attire associated with the name of Charles II, having heard it said in some earlier period of his career that he bore a strange resemblance to the ill-fated Stuarts."

"Hook was not his true name."

She also highlighted the conversation between Peter Pan and his London recruits in Chapter 4 about how Pan had lopped off Hook's right hand — Hook was a left-hander and so could still fight — and the section in Chapter 5 that described Hook's features: "In person he was cadaverous and blackavised, and his hair was dressed in long curls, which at a little distance looked like black candles, and gave a singularly threatening expression to his handsome countenance."

A creepy feeling stole over her, a back-of-the-neck prickly sensation keyed to that ancient instinct that whispers, "You're being watched." It was the same malevolent feeling she'd had at the hospital, a disquieting impression that if she made one wrong move something horrible would happen. What exactly that horrible thing might be, she didn't know.

She absently rubbed her neck, feeling stupid. "What am I doing?" she asked Jon's living room. "There is no connection between Jon and this," and she slapped the copy of *Peter Pan* down on the table. *Yeah, and Jon's hand didn't rot in fifteen impossible minutes, and his hair didn't turn dark and wavy overnight, and no little holes appeared like magic in his earlobes.*

The feeling of being watched didn't go away.

Over the next two days, Melanie delved into Jon's life, searching for clues of... she wasn't sure what. Anything. Nothing struck her as unusual at his office except for the missing 1987 tax box. He had never found it, and Yolanda swore she'd never touched it. "What about Alan?" Melanie had asked her.

"I haven't heard from him since he quit," Yolanda had said, "not that I expected to or anything. But I'm sure he didn't take the box. I mean, why would he?"

Why would he indeed? Why would anyone?

Melanie combed through Jon's house room by room, including the attic, but didn't find the tax box. She did, however, find the box the sword had been in, with its oil cloth and yellowed paper, behind the living room couch. *Where's the sword?* she wondered. *And that creepy book?* Melanie found no clues except for a trail of an odd sticky dust on the box, which she dismissed as the aged grunge of long-term storage.

She made one observation that shook her greatly. There was a gouge in the dartboard on the living room wall. She and Jon played darts every once in awhile — after making sure the cats were locked outside. Whatever had made the gouge hadn't been a dart. More like a carving knife or, she thought nervously, a saber.

Rummaging through Jon's house also produced an unexpected item, a little phonebook taped under the middle drawer of his writing desk in the den. Jon had a peculiar habit of taping things to the bottoms of drawers — letters to and from old girlfriends, photos he didn't want to lose, poetry he thought Melanie didn't know he had written, newspaper clippings. Melanie knew to look under every drawer in the house. She felt like a snoop, especially after finding and reading some steamy correspondence between first-year UCLA student Jon Stuart and "Trish" back in New York. Melanie hadn't intended to read it all the way through. It sort of just happened. At least, that's what she told herself. She put it back after her puerile curiosity was satisfied. *Finding dirty little secrets is not your aim here, Mel,* she admonished herself. *Keep to the plan.*

The phonebook contained only three names and phone numbers. No addresses. The people, she suspected, were relatives. Jon had always told her that he knew nothing about his relatives and didn't want to know. He hated his family and that was that. But if Melanie was right about these names, then some of Jon's relatives had tried to contact him over the years. Either that or they were old girlfriends like Trish. *I'll find out soon enough,* she thought, and picked up the phone and dialed.

Francine Rhodes, whoever she was, no longer had that phone number. Julia Mansir had died three years earlier. The third name yielded a living breathing person on the other end of the line. "Hello?" an old woman said. Her voice wobbled badly, leaving Melanie to suspect that she suffered from a severe palsy. Definitely not a girlfriend.

"Hello, Mrs. Lancaster? Alice Lancaster?"

Silence on the other end.

Melanie spoke quickly. "I'm not a salesman my name is Melanie Forrester and I'm a researcher please don't hang up."

That got Alice's attention. "A researcher, you say? Of what?"

The lie slipped out way too easily. "I've been hired by Mr. Jonathan Stuart to research his family tree. I understand that you're related to him."

"Well, let's see..." Alice paused. "Who did you say you were?"

The conversation went round in circles for some time. Seventy-three-year-old Alice resided in an assisted-living apartment complex in Akron, Ohio, and although she was genial enough, she had definitely stripped some screws lately. She couldn't figure out who Jonathan Stuart was, though she had obviously phoned him once. On the subject of the Stuart family in general, however, she had a clear recollection and an even clearer opinion. "My grandmother Alice — I was named after her, you know — she used to tell me about the English Stuarts. Related to royalty, my spotted behind!"

"What do you mean, Mrs. Lancaster?" Melanie asked. "Do you have any names or contact numbers?"

"Heavens no. I don't want to have anything to do with them."

"Then why does Mr. Stuart have your name—"

"Try calling my son Sylvester. I have his phone number around here somewhere." Melanie heard the *clunk* of the phone being dropped on a table, then the scrape of a chair, papers rattling, and then a scrabbling sound as the old woman picked up the phone again. "I seem to recall him being interested in the relatives at one time. Maybe he plucked up enough courage to contact one of them. I don't quite remember." She gave Melanie a phone number. "Now is that all?"

That was a dismissal if Melanie ever heard one. "Yes, Mrs. Lancaster. Thank you very much."

"I suppose." The old lady hung up.

Sylvester Lancaster's number began with the same area code as his mother's, so he lived in Akron as well. Melanie dialed. Lancaster's wife, a perky-sounding woman named Hillary, answered the phone. After Melanie explained herself, Hillary made a little sound of disgust. "Jonathan Stuart. Oh, I remember him, all right."

Melanie didn't like the sound of that.

"Sy phoned him once. Alice did, too. I'm sure you noticed that she doesn't remember things too well. She badgered my husband into helping her research for a family history that she wanted to write, oh, about five years back. She said there were secrets — that's the word she used — *secrets* that she didn't want anyone to forget. Not that she told Sy or me what they were. She insisted on writing it all down before she died. Instead, her memory began to deteriorate. It got pretty bad pretty fast. Up till then, Sy helped her write down what she could remember. He made some calls for her, too. He talked to your Mr. Stuart, but only after Alice tried first."

That's why her name is in his phonebook, Melanie thought.

"Look," said Hillary, "I don't know why your client wants to bother with a family history at this date, Miss Forrester. He didn't help Alice, and he hung up on my husband. Wouldn't tell him a thing. I won't ever forget the look on Sy's face when he told me what Mr. Stuart said. He said that the Stuarts could all go to Hell."

Good job, Jon. "Mr. Stuart does have a temper," Melanie admitted.

"The whole lot of them do, as I understand," said Hillary. "But look, I know you're just doing a job. If you want, I can ask Sy to mail you a copy of the writings he started. He gave up after awhile, and Alice forgot about it. It's sketchy, mostly names and notes, but maybe it will help."

"Anything will help, thank you."

The conversation ended pleasantly enough. Nonetheless, Melanie hung up with a sigh. The automatic thought came and went: *My boyfriend, Mr. Hyde.* She was intrigued by Mr. Hyde all the same. Jon never answered his home phone directly. He always made people leave a message on his answering machine first, and then he would decide whether to call back or not. *You might hate them,* Melanie told the Jon in her mind, *but you called them back, even if it was just to be mean to them. And you kept their numbers, too, even if you did hide them from yourself. I wonder why.*

Melanie booted Jon's Mac Plus computer in the den and opened the Z-Term modem app to log into the UCLA network. Melanie loved computers. Not many people had them yet, since they were still a new product and pretty expensive, but they were a godsend to researchers. *Francine Rhodes,* she thought as she wove her way through the college library catalog. Something about the name nagged at the back of her mind.

Geez, no wonder, she thought as she read the computer screen minutes later. Francine Rhodes was a well-known newspaper journalist in San Francisco. She also penned a weekly column about California history that was published in the San Francisco and LA editions of the *Reader* and mini-syndicated to several other alternative papers. Those articles were collected in the UCLA archives. *I've seen her name for years and never dreamed she was related to Jon!*

Getting hold of Rhodes was another job entirely. The woman did not answer her phone. *Must be a Stuart trait.* Melanie left several messages throughout the day, but Rhodes didn't phone back. She was about to leave the house to check on Yolanda at Excalibur Books when the phone rang. "Yeah?" she answered it, hoping that Rhodes was on the other end.

It was the hospital calling. They were discharging Jon that evening.

* * * * *

Jon climbed out of Melanie's Honda Civic and serenely contemplated his house. His right arm, which ended in a thick bandage at the wrist, hung in a sling and would remain that way until the soreness in his forearm eased. He stood with his good arm wrapped around the injured one, looking for all the world like he was hugging himself. His hair — it was black now, raven-black and curly — hung down over his shoulders, covering the American Booksellers Association logo on the back of his T-shirt. For some reason he had taken his shoes off in the car, so he stood in the driveway barefoot, swaying a little back and forth as if the concrete was gently tilting to and fro beneath his feet.

Melanie watched him, memorizing these details, intending to later write down everything that was happening. Events had taken a frightening turn at the hospital, and though she still hadn't quite recovered, her skills for assembling details were in full swing.

First there was the mystery of Jon's hair. Neither Dr. Odet nor Dr. Phillips nor the nurses who had dealt with Jon thought that his hair had ever been blond. Melanie had questioned every one of them, and they all claimed that his hair had always been black and curly. When she had tried to prove her point by showing them Jon's driver's license photo, she had come the closest she'd ever come to fainting — the photo ID pictured him with black curly hair.

As for the ear piercings, Dr. Odet claimed to have noticed them during Jon's initial examination. They had been fresh, and Odet had wondered in passing why Jon wore no studs to keep the new holes open.

Next was the question of the mysterious welts that the doctor had noticed on Jon's wrist, welts that Melanie now knew had eerily marked the cut line for Jon's amputation. Dr. Odet now claimed there had been no welts. And the high alcohol level in Jon's blood?

Odet told her the bloodwork had shown no high level of alcohol, either.

Melanie had nearly gone buggy trying to convince Odet that he and his staff were wrong, that Jon's driver's license photo was wrong, that something queer was going on and Jon's life depended on them finding out what it was. She had backed off when the doctor started aiming his critical physician's eye at *her*.

Then there was Jon himself. As much as having one hand less caused him difficulty, he showed no overt concern that a major part of his body had been unexpectedly removed. His one and only comment on the subject was, "Aw, shit." Melanie prayed that it was just the medications coursing through his veins, especially the Oxycontin – strong stuff. All the same, Jon seemed to have already accepted his new handicap with a sort of sad resignation, as if the whole tragedy was simply the next event on a long List of Things to Endure.

During the time that Melanie had helped him get ready to return home, he had seen himself in the hospital bathroom mirror. Not one comment about his changed hair. He acted like it had always been that way. If he had noticed his pierced ears, he hadn't commented on them either. When he did speak it was slowly, as if he were grasping for words through a thick fog. His movements were slow, too, dreamlike, as if his mind were far away. *Not all there.* A term Melanie's dad had used to describe his aging mother, a victim of Alzheimer's disease. Jon was *not all there.* Melanie watched him sway as he stood on the driveway and wondered, *What's happening to you, Jon? Where are you?*

She wanted desperately to ask him what had made him fall out of bed that first morning and what had made him scream with such terror. And the disjointed phrases he had spoken that first night in the hospital – he had mentioned something about a plan and a dream, but the topper was "not hook." She remembered those two words clear as print. He had been afraid then, too, but today he either didn't remember the episode or he was choosing to avoid it. She reluctantly agreed with her own better judgment to give him time to adjust before broaching the subject. The problem was, what if something even more bizarre happened first? That awful feeling of being watched was getting stronger. Melanie's stomach had developed an ongoing nervous twist that wasn't all that far away from the heaves. She wished that Jon wasn't so drugged. She wanted to talk to him, *really* talk.

That wasn't going to happen, not today, maybe not tomorrow. Jon should have stayed longer in the hospital, but his insurance wouldn't cover it. Being self-employed, he couldn't afford decent coverage and, being a healthy man in his prime, he had chanced buying the minimums. Despite the fact that Dr. Odet had no clue what had caused Jon's condition – he stressed that he had performed every test he could think of but they had all come up normal – he had sent Jon home with nothing more than a couple prescriptions and a, "Good luck." Melanie had tried to force the issue on Jon's behalf, but there wasn't much she could do.

Now standing in the driveway, swaying like someone mesmerized by a giant cobra, he suddenly spoke. "It's like coming home from a long vacation, y'know? You come back to your house, and it's like it belongs to somebody else."

Masking her worry with a relentless smile, Melanie dangled his keys in front of his face. "Well, it's yours, big guy. How about we go inside and feed the cats?"

Jon's head tilted down as if it were on a loose hinge. "Cats," he said, staring straight down as his four cats gathered at his ankles. They started up their whining and bumping routine. It quickly turned into an intensive sniff session.

"You smell like a hospital," Melanie pointed out.

Jon waved down at them. "Hi, purr buckets. Miss me?"

They continued sniffing his feet.

Jon gave Melanie a silly grin. "Aren't they great?" he said, and took the keys from her. After three woozy attempts to get the key in the lock, he opened the door, almost tripping over the cats who were determined to keep sniffing him whether he was walking or not.

Melanie stopped him in the entryway. "Welcome home," she said, and kissed him.

"It's good to be home," he told her. Something in his voice made Melanie's heart skip. He sounded so earnest, so uncharacteristically pathetic.

She helped him feed the cats, trying all the while not to wince at how clumsily he moved. "Sorry," he kept saying as he knocked things over and spilled cat food on the floor.

"Jon, why don't you let me do this?" she asked, wiping up the spilled food.

"Naw. Gotta learn how to cope, don't I?" He barely had the coordination to set Rebers' bowl down without falling down himself.

Melanie put the rest of the bowls down, and the cats began to eat. "Will you cut yourself some slack, Jon? You're drugged to the gills. When I had my wisdom teeth pulled, they gave me Percodan and wow — it was like being drunk."

"God, I miss that feeling," he said, and abruptly sank to the floor. Melanie thought he was passing out, but he plopped down on the kitchen tiles and petted Fuzzybutt while she ate. He turned to pet Rebers on his right and remembered, with a sort of dull dismay, that he had no hand to do it with. He lifted his left hand as if he wanted to use that, but it slowly dawned on him that it wouldn't reach unless he changed position. "This is so weird," he said.

Melanie sat down next to him. She positioned herself so that Jon could see her stroke Rebers' thick fur while he gobbled his Tasty Tuna Feast. "I want to stay here until you're better, Jon."

"Ooo, a sleepover?"

She laughed. It was the first funny — okay, barely funny — joke he had told today. His synapses were flubbery, but at least they were trying to work. "I'm talking a week or more, Jon. Maybe longer." She gave him a sly wink.

He didn't return it. His eyes were haunted. "I've missed you, Melly." He looked around the kitchen from one side to the other, studying the appliances, the drawers, the broom in the corner. Melanie noticed how his gaze lingered on the row of key hooks by the kitchen door, underneath which stood the little table where he always put his wallet and outgoing mail. His eyes finished their roving and landed on her. "I've missed you so much." His brows drew together. "Melly, about the other day—"

She knew what was coming. "Jon, you don't have to—"

"Shhh. I do. Lemme say this." He gathered his thoughts. "What I said to you at the store about... us... breaking up. I meant it. I still do."

Melanie went cold.

"But even though I'm right... you deserve somebody better than a mess like me, Mel... I want to take it back. Can I do that?"

The awful cold melted and Melanie sighed, warm again. "Of course you can. You were sick."

"I'd like to think that. Maybe it's true. All I know is that after you left that day, shit, I was more than just sick. It was like I fell into a black hole. Something happened, I dunno... I was sure I'd never see you again. For awhile there, I guess I thought I was gonna die. I don't wanna die alone..."

"Jon, we can talk about this tomorrow—"

"I love you, Melly." His words came in a slurred rush as though he was afraid he wouldn't have a chance to finish. "I don't want you to stay for a week, okay? I want you to stay with me from now on. For forever. I know I'm blitzed, but I know what I'm saying. And I know I'm not exactly the same guy I was a few days ago — couple pounds lighter, five fingers shorter—"

Melanie's laughter burst out in a surprised splutter. *Christ, Jon, how can you joke about that?* Then she realized that he had stopped talking and was looking at her with tense anticipation. "What?" she had to ask.

He was crushed. "I finally propose, and you weren't listening?"

"You..." She swallowed hard.

Wobbly but determined, Jon got on one knee and took her hand. "Listen this time," he said with an expression filled with such sincerity that she almost cried. "Melanie Forrester, will you marry me?"

Whenever Melanie read the phrase *time stood still* in a novel, she thought it was corny as hell. Talk about a tired cliché. And besides, time couldn't stand still, it only felt that way when a person was taken unawares. Well, she had been wrong. Time *could* stand still. All of Creation could pause and hold its collective breath, waiting for one single person to digest some moment of import that required more than a single measly slice of cosmic history. The universe was waiting for her at this moment, holding its universal breath. Melanie held her breath, too. Time stood still.

The events of the recent past replayed in her mind: the unexpected discovery that she was pregnant, her torturous decision to abort, Jon's reaction, their breakup, the terrible day that followed, his illness and the creepy mystery of it. What would she be getting herself into, marrying this man?

You wouldn't be getting into anything, she thought. *You're already in. Jon's wanted to marry you for a long time. It's just that he's afraid of... of himself, I think. It took massive painkillers to break down the walls enough for him to express the truth.*

She studied his face in that prolonged cosmic moment. He was different, she could see it, not just his hair and ears and his goofy drugged behavior. Under all that, a fundamental change had occurred within his very being. Her stomach gave a little twist as she recognized it, deep inside him, like a new spark of life. She didn't know what it meant. *He's changed for the better, Mel, that's what you see. He's finally opening up, maybe even growing up. An emergency sickness can do that to people. He's learned to be honest with you. It's what you've always wanted, isn't it?* Indeed it was. The prolonged moment snapped back to *now.* "Uhhuh," she said.

Jon blinked slowly. "'Zat yes or no?'"

"Yes! It's yes. Of course it's yes. Yes."

He smiled. "Thanks."

What a strange thing to say. Thanks. Melanie loved it. She loved him. She loved the whole friggin' world. "You're welcome," she said softly.

Satisfied, Jon plopped back to the floor. "Gee, that wasn't so hard. Except the kneeling part." He smacked his forehead with the palm of his hand. "I don't have a ring! Damn."

Melanie made a show of removing the ruby ring from her finger. "How about this?"

Jon gave the jewel a vague frown.

"You gave it to me last week."

"I did?" He screwed up his face in concentration. "Hot damn, you're right. How gallant of me." He took the ring. "Okay, I'm going to do this right. No no no, don't help." Awkwardly he resumed his position on one knee, bracing himself by swinging his slung elbow out enough to touch the side of the under-sink cabinet. "Okay, so like, I can't hold your hand and give you the ring at the same time, y'know?" He indicated his stump. "Sucks to be me."

Melanie was horrified and delighted, shocked and charmed all at once. Her shivers of anxiety were melting away. She was giddy with love for this goofy man who had experienced a terrible tragedy yet who was finding the strength within himself to finally follow his heart. True, he was turning the priceless moment of their engagement into a comedy act, but he had always been a funny drunk. The Oxycontin was doing the same thing to him.

"That's fine, Jon," she assured him.

"Good. Okay. Uh... Melanie Forrester, I, Jonathan Edward Stuart, am asking. Again. Will you marry my sorry ass?"

"Yes, Mr. Jonathan Edward Stuart, I, Melanie Susan Forrester, will marry your sorry ass. And the rest of you, too."

"Groovy. Gimme the finger. Ha!" He managed to slip the ring onto her correct finger, with Melanie doing most of the aiming. Then he plopped down on his butt. "Okay, it's official. I'm pooped." He did a double-take at her. "Your middle name's Susan?"

"Yes."

"Huh."

Supremely happy, happier than she ever thought a person could be, Melanie leaned her head on Jon's shoulder. She wanted to tackle him and kiss the bejeezus out of him, but that was probably a bad idea. She had never seen him this physically fragile before. *Oh, but a little rough and tumble would be nice,* she thought. The eerie truth was that long black curls sort of suited him. They gave him an old-fashioned dashing look that appealed to her. A lot. She kept reminding herself that the change was wrong, that she ought to be frightened by it, not turned on. Those thoughts were silenced by a single glance at the ruby ring happily on the third finger of her left hand.

I hope after he's better and off the drugs, he doesn't get self-conscious about his missing hand. I bet he'll be just as good in bed. She tried to keep that thought light, more like a hopeful observation instead of a fervent plea to the gods.

"Do you want to, uh, *celebrate,* future husband?" Just saying that sent a thrill down her spine.

"Uhhh..." Jon smacked his lips as if tasting the idea. "If you're suggesting what I think you're suggesting, you gotta be kidding. I'm Jello boy here."

Melanie ran her hand up the inside of his thigh. "You don't have to do a thing. I can take care of it."

Jon's head fell back, thunking against the cabinet. "Oh Lordy Lord, what a proposition... but no. Not up for it. Ha! Forgive the pun." He cupped her face with his hand. "Thanks for the offer, though."

Melanie nuzzled his palm. *Not two hands*, she thought, and was immediately angry with herself. She took his one hand in both of hers and kissed it. She kissed his fingertips, one little kiss at a time. Then she leaned forward and kissed his mouth.

He couldn't get into it. "C'mon," he said tiredly. "Let's watch TV or something. That's about all I'm good for."

She helped him up. "Maybe you should go to bed."

"Naw, not yet. I want to enjoy not being alone."

That was the second time he had mentioned not wanting to be alone. He had never spoken of it before, not even a casual reference. Melanie had always presumed that he liked being alone and quiet. For heaven's sake, he owned a bookstore. The experience in the hospital really had changed him.

She helped him upstairs to his bedroom. "We can watch TV up here," she said. "That way, when you pass out, I won't have to drag you up the stairs by your... your hair."

He took no notice of her stumble. "Good thinking, future wife."

Melanie helped him take off his clothes, a job she always enjoyed anyway, though this time it was more like trying to strip a sleepy baby — a very big sleepy baby. Jon made no effort to help at all and kept losing his balance and falling. In the end she pushed him down on the bed and ordered him to lie still. He had already been cleaned up at the hospital, so she tucked him under the covers after checking his bandage like the doctor instructed and giving him another round of medications.

He'll be zonked out in two minutes, she thought, disappointed by that but happy with the world in general. She would worry about the incongruities of life, his especially, later. She put his clothes away, stripped down to her panties and climbed into bed with him.

"Welcome home, future husband," she whispered in his ear.

Jon lay on his back, his injured arm in its sling across his chest. "Nighhh..." he murmured.

Melanie turned on her favorite old movie channel and snuggled down to watch the second half of Bogie and Bergman in *Casablanca*. *Talk about romance*, she thought, fingering her ruby ring and smiling. Beside her, Jon breathed slowly and regularly.

CHAPTER 20

The suns were fading by the time the *Jolly Roger* arrived in Beggar's Bay.

Stuart had spent hours in a terrible funk, brooding in his cabin and nodding off to sleep once in awhile. The same dream kept repeating over and over — he was back home with Melanie. Things seemed normal except that his hand was gone and he had Hook's hair. Melanie ignored those things and so did he. It was as if he had always been that way. He would finally screw up the courage to ask her to marry him — then he would wake up just as she answered. He figured she must have said yes each time, but he never actually heard the word. That bothered him.

Underneath this repeating dream was the blurry impression of standing on the quarterdeck bellowing at Cecco and the crew. *Haul up the mains'l! Square the yards! Up foresail! In fore and main t'gallants! Stream the buoy! Cast anchor!* The words held meaning but in an oddly diffused and distant way. He was wondering where he really was when—

—sound battered his ears, yells, laughter, singing, men running, wood creaking, seagulls squawking, waves slapping.

He was standing on the quarterdeck watching while his crew stampeded to starboard where half a dozen bumboats were bobbing up to the pirate ship like ducklings to their mother. They were filled mostly with eager merchants — "Black dog, white monkey! Oi, black dog, white monkey!" — holding up bottles of liquor, baskets of fresh produce and other items. One of the boats featured a gaggle of frilly women dressed in their finest which, Stuart noted with a wince, wasn't so fine. They flirted, some doing the coy act while one actually lifted her skirt and shouted, "How 'bout it, boys?" The ship listed slightly as pirates leaned over the rails and out of the gun ports, whooping and whistling and, as Smee would put it, having themselves a real hooley.

We're anchored in Beggar's Bay, Stuart realized. *This is the Port!*

Cecco barged through the boisterous crowd and joined him. "She's square by the braces, Captain. Boat crews' aft preparing to lower your gig."

It came to Stuart as if from a long distance away — he had already announced the leave schedule. Only officers would go ashore tonight. Smee had informed him that he, Cecco, Second Mate Foggerty and Gunner Alf Mason were to talk "business" in town. Starting the following morning, port and starboard watches would rotate shore leave and repair work.

The ship's bell rang in its traditional two-clang rhythm: one-two, three-four, then a final fifth clang. That meant it was six pm. The second dog watch was beginning. "Who's head of the watch?" Stuart asked Cecco.

"Majdi, sir."

"Mister Macaw!" Stuart called.

The man scurried down from the main mast top and saluted his captain. To anyone who didn't know him, Majdi Macaw came across as a frail fellow, not at all the kind who could be capable of slitting a throat or setting fire to a plundered ship. He was from Arabia, but he patterned his dress on Gentleman Starkey, whom he greatly admired. He always buttoned his shirts to the top and wore a neat cravat. Any Navy seaman would have laughed in his face, but the men aboard the *Jolly Roger* loved him, especially his riotous sense of humor. He had the guts to make fun of his own jarring countenance — he had lost the end of his nose and part of his cheek when he had riled a macaw, hence his nickname — and he would recite outlandishly rude poetry whenever requested.

"Macaw here, Captain," he reported.

"Double the watch," Stuart ordered. "Ladies and liquor may come aboard tonight, but no crew member is to leave. Any man who tries is to be shot, clear?"

"Aye aye, sir."

Stuart led his officers aft. They climbed down into the lowered gig and the men rowed steadily to shore while, behind them, the happy hooley was seriously getting under way.

The black knot deep inside Stuart rejoiced at the sight of Beggar's Island. It was very like Pan's island in the glow of the fading suns except for one very important difference: this long strip of land harbored adults only. Hook could walk as a free man, at least for a time. Stuart's heart pounded with excitement, spurred by visions of the dark pleasures that awaited.

They reached the beach, pulled the boat up onto the sand and walked until sand met the hard-packed dirt of a dockside road. "This way, lads," Smee said, taking the lead. "Business awaits!"

Stuart was not a history buff, but he had read his share. He knew of the squalor and filth of foreign ports during the great days of sail. A scattering of Hook's memories also offered some preparation for the scene to come. His parallel history claimed that he had sampled the pleasures and pitfalls of New Providence, Hispañiola, Martinique, Barbados and other Caribbean ports, while in Madagascar he had spent time in Charnock's Point, Port Dauphin, St. Augustine, Diego Suarez and lovely St. Mary's. All this was above and beyond the famous Sailortowns in Liverpool and Valparaiso, along with many other standard merchant ports. Still, this combination of book learning and "experience" could not adequately prime him for the sensory onslaught that was Beggar's Port.

For starters, the place reeked like an open latrine. Ditches had been dug down the middle of the roads for refuse and chamber pot sewage that was carelessly tossed out of the doors and out of open windows. People relieved themselves anywhere they could get away with it. Herders drove their pigs, cattle and sheep through town without a thought of what the animals left behind, and those riding horses or driving wagons couldn't have cared less when their steeds raised a tail. Stuart had gotten somewhat used to the unique fetor of his pirate crew, but at least he had found relief in the fresh ocean breeze. Beggar's Port enjoyed a breeze, true, but it wasn't enough. Stuart swore he saw the dirt streets actually *steaming.* He nearly retched while walking down the main drag and covered it by pretending to dab his nose with his frilled kerchief. His men didn't bat an eye, neither at him nor at the stink.

Stuart counted five buildings made of sturdy brick and as many of good wood. The rest were shanties cobbled together from miscellaneous wood scraps, bamboo, palm leaves, ripped sail canvas, whatever the builders could find. He made no attempt to count these — they dotted the landscape from the beach all the way up to the edge of the jungle.

To Stuart, the place was educational at best, dry land at least. To Hook and his men it was paradise — just enough civilization to relieve the loneliness of a life at sea but primitive enough to *not* draw attention to itself. No official merchantmen docked here, no one conducted legal business. That's not to say that no trading or business existed. On the contrary, the Port saw a lively trade in a great variety of goods and services. Foodstuffs, spices, rum and cargoes of plundered booty exchanged hands, deals were made, contracts of a sort were signed... or not.

And the people! Men and women of every race and color populated the place, from well-to-do Dutch merchants to chained African slaves to pirates from England, America, Holland, Poland, India, China and everyplace between. Traders were making their last deals of the day in stalls along the bumpy walks. They sold out of carts or their pockets, haggling with potential buyers in a mishmash of languages that sounded to Stuart like a kind of international music. Part of him reveled in this free-for-all chaos of blatant opportunism. The rest of him wanted to turn and run.

He could pretty much tell who the merchants were, who the pirates were, who the townsfolk were, and he definitely could tell who the whores were. He saw no sign of any legal forces, so a brawl in the street raised no alarm, and what he glimpsed going on in dark alleys raised no eyebrows but his.

The "business" that Stuart's officers had in mind was to take place at The Crimson Cock, the main tavern that occupied the lower floor of one of the few brick buildings in town. Stuart looked forward to it

— the beer casks aboard the *Jolly Roger* had run dry weeks ago. But something strange happened the moment he set foot within the town border. It made his walk to the tavern an uneasy one.

People stared at him. They gave him a wide berth. Some pointed at him, many spoke in hushed tones amongst themselves. A few ran away.

Smee had insisted that Stuart wear Hook's black-and-gold outfit, which the bosun had cleaned and repaired. Stuart knew he looked damned good in it. He was getting used to all those ruffs and frills, and now he saw that such dress stood out from any other clothing, not only on the ship but in this whole town as well. Besides being an affectation, perhaps such outlandish costuming was Hook's idea of a calling card. Everyone certainly recognized who he was.

But Stuart wasn't used to such attention. He found himself averting his eyes much like he used to when he lived in New York. "Don't make eye contact," his mother always used to warn him. "Don't give anyone reason to mug you."

No one's going to mug you, idiot, he told himself. *They're all afraid of what* you'll *do to* them! The idea delighted him. It was one thing to have the power to intimidate a ship's crew. The pirate swabs were able seamen, trained to obey their captain regardless of their pirate status. But to have that same power over an entire town?

Stuart's smile turned into an amused sneer. He started to enjoy the awe and trepidation that followed him, even as he knew that such immediate identification might pose dangers as well. *Pah! I am without doubt a better swordsman than any of these lowlifes. And maybe I can make only one fist, but I can lay a man flat with it.* That wasn't to mention the extra two loaded pistols he wore plus the dirk in his belt. All of his officers had come ashore heavily armed. As Smee had commented before they had left the ship, "Where there's a bit of decent fun, there's bound to be trouble, too."

Thus the infamous captain of the *Jolly Roger* and his men entered The Crimson Cock.

The minute Stuart stepped through the door, everyone in the place turned to look. The musicians, two fiddlers who could have been brothers, stopped playing. Voices trailed off. Someone hissed. The black knot in Stuart's soul swelled with glee, eating up the expressions of fear and especially those of hatred on the faces of the tavern patrons. Hook was known especially well here. Stuart liked that. He gave the room a snide, lopsided grin. "*Bonjour, mes amis!*" he said, and removed his hat with a flourish.

Everybody in the place reached for their weapons. Smee, Cecco, Mason and Foggerty mirrored the moves.

"Ah ah ah!" Stuart scolded his men, relishing the palpable tension in the place. "We're here to enjoy ourselves."

The pirates lowered their weapons but did not yet put them away.

"We are told you be eat by your beast," said a mean-faced Asian who was clearly disappointed by Hook's resurrection. "They say you dead."

Smee said in Stuart's ear, "Scuttlebutt gets 'round quick, don't it, sar?"

It took Stuart a moment to understand what he meant. Although he remembered haunting these waters for many years, he also remembered falling into Pirate's Bay — his arrival in the Neverland, supposedly mere months ago. *That's what this fellow is referring to. The crew still believes I miraculously survived being swallowed by the croc.* And word had traveled from the *Jolly Roger* to The Crimson Cock faster than he had walked here! *Amazing,* he thought.

The dark part of him said, *Thus is the power of rumor. Use it.*

So Stuart gave the Asian a malicious smile. "You heard the truth, my friend, although..." He paused for effect. "...the beast does not belong to me. Hunt the damned thing down with my blessing. I'm sure it'll make a fine pair of boots. Actually, more like twenty."

A wiry old geezer by the fireplace wheezed. His lips drew back, showing one lonely front tooth. Stuart guessed he was laughing.

"Now, if you don't mind, this dead man is very thirsty." He slapped the bar. "Tapman! Beer!"

The tapman set to work filling five leather jacks with beer from an oak hogshead.

Stuart boldly walked through the still-silent crowd, choosing a table in the corner. Two ruffians already sat there, but with one twitch of his hook, they gave up their seats and hurried away. "You see?" Stuart told the crowd. "We're customers looking for refreshment like anyone else."

Smee, Cecco, Mason and Foggerty exchanged looks and followed their captain. Before letting them sit down, Smee pulled his ever-present ratty cloth from his back pocket and wiped the table. "Thank you, Smee," Stuart said, and he meant it. The table looked as if it hadn't been wiped in years.

"My pleasure, Cap'n," Smee said, and the men sat down. In minutes, a big-hipped woman, her huge breasts plumped up out of her corset like mutant dumplings, brought the drinks to the table.

Stuart pulled open the drawstring pouch hanging from his belt and took out a gold coin. "*Merci, ma belle jeune fille,*" he said, and tucked the coin into her impressive cleavage.

She chortled. Her breath was like swamp gas. "You really get swallered by that big croc?" she asked him.

"He did," Smee said quickly. "Saw the whole thing meself."

"But how...?" the woman began.

With a fastidious sniff, Stuart used his hook to flick a stray strand of hair from his eyes.

The woman gave the iron attachment a respectful nod. "Thank ye, Captain, sir," she stammered, and waddled back to the bar.

Cecco leaned in. "Spoiling for trouble already, are we, James?"

Stuart hoisted his jack. "Not really," he said. "I guess I haven't felt good in a very long time, is all."

"Locked up in yer bloody cabin day an' night," said Smee. "Fer Chrissake, it'd make any man go stir." He put his hand on Stuart's arm to keep him from taking his first drink. "A minute, sar, if yeh don't mind." He stood up, raising his jack in a toast. Cecco, Mason and Foggerty did the same. "To Cap'n James Hook!" Smee said, loud enough that the whole place could hear. "Through storm an' sirens' wail, he single-handedly — an' I do mean that — rescued six men an' saved the ship. Yer officers salute yeh, sar!"

"Aye!" said the others, and they clapped their jacks against his and drank.

Stuart was dumbfounded. Had he really rescued six men and saved the ship? He did remember lashing several men down when the sirens' song had almost made them leap overboard. Is that what Smee was talking about?

He sensed the eyes of everyone in the tavern locked in his direction. He stood up. "I would like to make a toast as well," he said. "To the officers of the *Jolly Roger*. Alf Mason, as skilled a gunner as a captain could ask for — shoot what I bloody well tell you to aim at!"

Mason chuckled.

"Second Mate Foggerty — you're a donkey's ass but the craftiest whist player I know."

As if to prove the first point, Foggerty slapped his thigh and let go a laugh that sounded like a donkey's bray.

Stuart, fascinated by the unplanned and, in some cases, mysterious words coming out of his mouth, plunged on. "Bosun Smee, partner in crime — keep your damned hands off my private store of brandy!"

"Oops," Smee muttered.

"And First Mate Cecco, good friend and dependable right-hand man... so to speak. What would I do without you?"

Cecco laughed, the low wary laugh of a man who does not easily grant friendship to anyone despite his outward openness.

"I thank you, my fellow scallywags, for making life at sea something less than tedious," Stuart finished. "*Salut!*"

"Aye!" chorused his men, and they drank.

After Stuart resumed his seat, Smee tapped him on the arm and pointed. Most of the tavern patrons were still staring at him. "I hope you all took notes," Stuart told them dryly. "Please, resume your conversations. Musicians, play, for God's sake. It's like a tomb in here." He took off his diamond ring and tossed it to them. "Something cheerful."

The taller of the fiddlers caught the ring and gaped when he saw the stone. "Aye, Captain Hook, sir!" He and his partner commenced a gay tune. The noise of the tavern gradually rose back to normal.

Stuart turned back to his men while deeply inhaling the musty fug of the place: cigar and pipe smoke, dust, sweat, spirits, bad breath, an undertone of piss. "God, how I've missed a good bar."

"A what, sir?" asked Foggerty.

"Tavern," Stuart corrected himself.

Cecco took a long draught. "Ahh. This and a visit to Miss Ada, and the world will be a better place."

"Miss Ada?" Stuart asked, curious.

"Local judy," said Smee, making Cecco blush. "Y'know them Dagos, sar. Our boy here might skip from lap to lap, but at least he keeps track o' their names."

"*Ada esse la mia bella*," Cecco told Smee sternly. "I would never betray her, Smee, and you know that." He smiled despite himself. "Well..."

Foggerty slapped his knee and brayed.

"Speaking of sweethearts," Cecco went on, "what about Elsbeth, James?"

The black knot in Stuart's chest tightened, not with malice or anger but with an unexpected poignancy. "Elsbeth." He could barely say the name.

Smee nudged him with an elbow. "I know where *you'll* be tonight, eh, sar?"

Stuart riffled through the memories foisted on him by Pan, but he couldn't find anything specific about a woman named Elsbeth. Only the name itself registered, vaguely familiar. "I don't know who you're talking about," he confessed. But he did remember Melanie. Guilt washed over him at the realization that he had forgotten about her so easily.

Mason, Foggerty and Cecco exchanged worried looks. "I thought your memory was back, James," Cecco said.

"Aye, 'tis passin' queer," Smee agreed, "but a few loose ends 'er bound to show up now an' then, ain't they? When was the last time yer head got walloped by a two-ton croc, Mister Cecco?"

Cecco studied his captain until the weight of that stare sparked Stuart's anger. "She's a damned whore!" Stuart said, the words coming out without forethought. "She takes coin from any man who offers! What's that to me?"

Cecco stiffened. "Apologies, James. I just thought—"

"Well, don't!" Stuart said sharply.

The general volume in the tavern had quieted again at the sound of Hook's ire. Stuart whirled around. "Mind your own bloody business!" he roared. His mood was ruined. He considered leaving, but he had no idea where to go.

A boy approached the table. When the lad locked eyes with Stuart, his face went white. "C-C-Captain H-Hook?" he asked.

"What if I am?" Stuart retorted sourly.

The boy could barely hold out an envelope. "If y-you are, sir, th-this is f-f-for you."

Smee dipped his head and sniffed the paper. "Heh heh." He waggled his eyebrows.

Stuart caught the whiff of perfume, too, and snatched the envelope. He nodded to Smee, who gave the boy a coin. The boy pocketed his pay and ran out the door as Stuart opened the envelope and drew out a piece of parchment. Unfolding it, he read:

> *Dearest James,*
> *How dare you not come directly to me! I shall*
> *expect you immediately. No excuses. The house is*
> *yours tonight, you handsome dog.*
> *— Tawdry Audrey*

Clearly the penmanship of an educated lady. Tawdry Audrey. What a name! *If only I knew who she was,* he thought, wondering what to do.

"You must go, sir," said Mason, sounding a bit eager.

"An' ye better not go alone, for safety's sake," Foggerty added, his eyes misty.

Ah. Tawdry Audrey is a madam, Stuart realized. *I wonder if Hook treats his officers—?*

Yes, came the black answer.

Stuart knocked back the rest of his beer and stood. "Well, let's go," he said, feigning a dreary resignation. "If we must, we must."

His men followed closely as he left the tavern. "Oh, we must, sir," Mason said, and he licked his lips. "We surely must."

CHAPTER 21

The establishment run by Tawdry Audrey was the finest in the entire town of Beggar's Port, brothel or otherwise. She owned the most well-kept building, a neat three-story brick structure with merry blue paint and a riot of flowers growing along the front walk. Each window was adorned with lacy curtains that allowed alluring shadows inside to pass back and forth. *Better than neon lights*, Stuart thought.

He had never visited a brothel before. He'd rarely had trouble bringing home a lady, if that was his desire, especially during his drinking days. Now Hook's provoking notions crowded out anything remotely moral in his thinking, and he found himself picking up his pace, Hook's input directing him through the early evening light right to Tawdry Audrey's front door.

He never got the chance to knock. The door swung open, and a six-foot-three-inch tall, big-muscled bombshell cocked one hip, grinning at him. He knew her in an instant.

Audrey Miggins, erstwhile lady of London society with an unfortunate penchant for petty theft, three-time widow and now a major mover and shaker in this mess called Beggar's Port. She would have been beautiful if not for the slit nostrils — a brutal punishment for stealing, which was what had landed her here in the first place. Still, there was a genteel charm to her middle-aged features. Considering most of the faces in town, that made her a queen. Her impressive muscles somewhat ruined the effect, but she no longer entertained customers herself. No, she was her own bouncer, capable of throwing scum out on their ear, often literally. She loved her ladies like a mother loved her daughters, and she did not take kindly to abuse. That was for the cheap chowlah girls who had no madam to protect them on the streets.

"James," she cooed. "And you've brought company. How delicious. Do come in, gentlemen."

She half-lifted Stuart off his feet, throwing her beefy arm around his shoulders and sweeping him into the foyer. "You know the policy, luv."

Stuart was about to say, "What policy?" when it flashed into his head: she did not allow weapons beyond the foyer. "Of course," he acquiesced, and with the trust of years handed her his pistols, the dirk and his saber. Cecco, Smee, Foggerty and Mason did the same.

A wispy girl of no more than twelve took the copious weaponry and stuffed it all into a cupboard, which she then locked. "Safe as 'ouses," she somberly assured Stuart, and handed the key to Audrey.

The madam eyed Stuart's hook. "What about that?"

"No," he said flatly. "My policy."

She considered. "Stubborn son of a siren, that's what you are, James. Have your way, as usual, but I swear, if even one of the girls asks that you take it off—"

"Then I will *consider* doing so," Stuart answered. "Have I ever caused you trouble?"

Audrey laughed long and loud.

"I'd call that a yes," Smee said quietly.

That brought Audrey's attention upon him. "Oh, Mister Smee, you darling little goat!" she said, clapping her hands on either side of his face as if he were a beloved nephew. "Sukey is so looking forward to playing chess with you again."

Smee rubbed his gnarled hands together. "Well then, let's not keep the darlin' waitin'. If yeh don't mind, Cap'n?"

Chess? Smee came to a brothel to play *chess*? Stuart guessed that Sukey was a popular player who probably wore nothing but a grin. Just right for a dirty old man like Smee. "By all means," he told the bosun. "Knock yourself out."

Audrey gave him an odd look. "Knock himself out?"

"Never mind."

Smee allowed the red-haired girl to escort him into a side room. "Scruffy-poo!" squealed a woman from inside.

"Pumpkin!" Smee answered, and the door closed.

Audrey turned to Cecco. "Cecco, you scoundrel, how have you been? Miss Ada misses you."

Cecco gave her a polite nod. "If that is true, then I am a happy man," he said, so like a gentleman that one would never think him capable of the inventive and scathing oaths he daily hurled at the pirate crew.

Audrey fixed her appraising eyes on Foggerty and Mason. "And who might these ruffians be?"

Stuart introduced them. "Good men," he finished. "Treat them well."

"As if Tawdry Audrey would do anything else," she said. Slick as a snake, she produced a small knife and cut the purple silk coin pouch from Stuart's belt, so smoothly that he wouldn't have known but for the fact that she then shook it next to her ear, judging the jingle of coins intently. "This should be sufficient," she decided with a wink.

"How dare you, woman!" Stuart shouted. "You've ruined it!"

"I like to keep the old skills sharp, and who better to practice on than a man with a full... purse?" She laughed, gently cupping the coin-filled pouch as if it were something else entirely.

Foggerty let out a donkey bray as Stuart rumbled, "Practice on me again, Audrey, and I'll have your fingers for a necklace." He held out his hand. "Now give it back."

Audrey emptied the coins into her own pocket and moved to hand the pouch over. "Oh my, you really are vexed, aren't you? Fine, I'll have Wilhelmina mend it, shall I?" She admired the fine gold bullion woven into the silk that spelled out a large JH. "You're so charmingly ostentatious, James, I must say."

"No, I'm bloody rich," Stuart returned dryly. "I'll expect your best rum for my men, Audrey. None of that watered-down piss you foist on the locals."

"Yes yes, and brandy for yourself. It hasn't been *that* long, James."

The events that unfolded were surprising to Stuart but hardly so to the darkness within him. The ladies of Tawdry Audrey's brothel met their customers in a large comfortable parlor with a piano and plenty of couches. Drinks and snacks were served, and the girls entertained their clients with songs and dances and games that were, Stuart had to admit, really fun. The girls apparently knew him well enough that his hook did not frighten them. Not one asked him to remove it, although they gave it a wide berth and never sat to his right. Stuart felt completely comfortable, and he even allowed himself to sing a couple of nasty ditties that he didn't even know he knew, though he retained some dignity and let the other customers — several sailors and two merchants — make the bigger fools of themselves, skipping and cavorting like randy clowns while he watched with a sort of twisted fascination.

"A story!" said a brunette named Chelsea after a particularly rousing song from sailor Shanks about a shepherdess and her sheepdog. She twiddled her fingers invitingly at Stuart. "Were you really swallowed by that monster croc, Captain Hook?"

Stuart held up his namesake. "I'm here, aren't I?"

"That is no answer, sir," said a shady merchant who had given his name as Smith. "I've heard about town that you are a cursed man. What say you to that?"

Stuart phrased his reply carefully. "I say Godspeed to rumor and hearsay, and may my name never be tainted by the deadly kiss of truth."

"Here here!" chorused Cecco, Mason and Foggerty.

"I think it's all stuff and nonsense," said Rose, a brash older woman who wore beautiful bloomy knickers, stockings of the smoothest silk and a corset trimmed in lace. "Our dear James is sweet as a parson, aren't you, luv?"

"Watch your tongue, Rose, or he might cut it out for you," Audrey warned.

"Never," Stuart assured Audrey. "I'd make her do it herself."

Rose gave a hearty laugh while Chelsea sat down next to him — on his left side. "May I, Captain?" she asked breathily.

Stuart turned in his seat so that he could hold the hook out close enough for her to touch. "Careful, missy," said Mason. "It bites."

Chelsea caressed the cold iron with her fingertips, shivering in perverse delight. "Glory be, this can cut through anything, can't it?"

Stuart intended to tease her with it, maybe run it gently up her thigh or suggestively pop a button or two on her bodice with the sassy flick of his wrist. But suddenly he didn't dare move.

His missing fingers were wriggling in response to her touch.

Phantom feelings, he knew about those, a common enough phenomenon in amputees. But this was the first time it had ever happened to him. It was startling, to say the least. The ghostly sensations conjured a sense of loss and dismay that almost made it to his face. He covered it with Hook's charming leer, causing Chelsea to giggle with wicked delight.

"Oh, enough of your bumbling foreplay, Chelsea," said Rose. "Hey, Shankies, what say we go upstairs?"

Shanks bolted for the stairway. "Thought you'd never ask."

Cecco left with his adoring Miss Ada, a Spanish woman with smoldering black eyes, and in time Foggerty, Mason and the other gentlemen customers left with their chosen ladies.

Chelsea stayed with Stuart. "How about it, Captain?" she said, stroking his hook suggestively.

The phantom sensations had passed. Stuart moved to take her hand, the dark part of his soul ready to immerse in physical pleasure of any sort, of all sorts, he didn't care. He had known nothing but pain and fear for too long. The thought of a kind touch, even if he had to pay for it, filled him with a desperate desire, not simply animal lust — more a need for warmth and intimacy. He reached out for Chelsea.

Something held him back. *Melanie*, he thought. *Shit, I can't do this.* "I'm sorry." He hadn't meant to say it out loud.

Audrey noisily got up from her chair. "Chelsea, sweetheart, why don't you go get another bottle of brandy for the Captain. The good stuff."

Chelsea pouted but obeyed. The men in the Port were rarely good looking, let alone sanitary, and here was a handsome captain with cultured manners who was actually wearing perfume. She made it clear with a toss of her head that she was not pleased to lose him.

When Chelsea was gone and they were alone, Audrey sat down next to Stuart. "She's upstairs, you know."

Stuart looked at her, not comprehending.

"She told me to tell you that she'll see you, but only if you specifically ask." Audrey lowered her head and spoke confidentially. "Damn you, James, she's been no good for business ever since you first showed up in this town. She's head over heels in love with you. Now do Audrey a favor and solve this problem."

Stuart had no idea what she was talking about.

"Talk to her," Audrey went on. "Tell her it can't happen. Tell her you don't love her." She frowned. "You don't, do you?"

She's talking about Elsbeth. Stuart struggled to dredge up a mental picture of the woman in question, but as before in the tavern, nothing came. He did sense a warm glow deep inside at the thought of her, however. *No, that belongs to Melanie. My poor Melly...*

"Aw, damn all to ashes, you do love her," Audrey moaned.

"No," Stuart said quickly. "I... it's something else."

"Good." She patted his leg. "I appreciate this."

"Would you tell her I'm here?"

"Oh, she knows."

"Then..." He gestured at the staircase. "Which room?"

"You don't remember?"

He hadn't before, but he did now.

* * * * *

He knocked on her door.

"Who is it?"

At the sound of her voice, an impression of Elsbeth brushed Stuart's mind. Young, pretty elf-bright eyes, flawless skin, brown hair, trim hips, a full mouth, sexy as hell, still fresh for a woman who sold her pleasures to men. That wouldn't last much longer.

"Who is it?" she repeated testily.

"You know who it is."

No sound came from within. Then a soft click, and the door opened. Elsbeth peeked out.

Stuart stepped back, his heart suddenly banging away so hard he couldn't breathe. Elsbeth looked exactly like Melanie. *Fuck you, Pan, how far are you going to go with this?* he thought in anguish. But he already knew. Pan would go as far as necessary. Far enough to drive him mad, to force him to become someone he himself would despise. *Fuck you!* he thought again, and knew he was helpless. He pushed the door open so that he could see all of her. *Melanie...*

"Hi," he said aloud. Lame but to the point.

She put a hand to her breast. "James."

"May I come in?"

"... Please."

He entered her small room, his footfall heavier than he had intended. Thoughts of Pan had whipped up his temper, and he was showing it. Elsbeth wrung her hands as if anticipating the worst. How could she possibly know what might happen? Stuart himself didn't know what words would come out of his mouth next. Hook had taken the reins. "I had to see you," he found himself saying.

"Please say it's because..." Elsbeth seemed to gather herself. "Tell me that you love me."

She looked so much like Melanie. She *was* Melanie from head to toe, from her sweet parted lips to the awkward way she stood in tense anticipation of his answer. Oh yes, he loved her. He wanted her so badly that everything else in the world faded away, unimportant, uninspiring.

He took her in his arms, careful to keep the hook clear. "Yes," he said, and kissed her. *I love you,* he thought, shivering with the truth of it. *This will never work, but I love you. It's insane, but I love you. You're not Melanie, but I love you.*

Elsbeth pressed into him, her heat enveloping him, swallowing him up and igniting his own flame. "I adore you," he told her. "I always have, and I always will."

He laid her down on the bed, kissing her lips, her neck, her breasts in a fever of passion. Only for her would he take off the deadly hook and the harness that bit into his flesh like a constant punishment. Only for her would he chance being vulnerable in this private Hell of his. She would be his one consolation. She would pull him back from the brink, keep him sane, keep him whole. *I will not be alone here,* he thought.

CHAPTER 22

Melanie awoke in the darkness to find Jon staring at her. He lay beside her in the bed, propped up on the elbow of his good arm, the pupils of his eyes reflecting the electric gleam of a streetlight outside the window.

"Whaa!" she garbled, still half-caught in a nightmare about Stuart House. It had been aflame, and she had been locked inside a massive safe. The horror of the dream was that, although the safe was behind a brick wall in the basement, away from the fire above, she had been burning inside of it just as the house was burning, wreathed in flames, screaming and twisting, pounding on the safe's thick metal walls, kicking and pleading, choking on smoke, unable to get out.

Melanie rarely had nightmares and she bolted upright, panting like a child when waking up from one of the typical monster dreams that children often have. Her bangs stuck to her damp forehead. "Oh!" she said, seeing Jon. "Oh, thank you for waking me up. Holy cow, that was awful." She fell back onto her pillow. "I'd tell you about it, but I don't want to think about it. Whoa." When Jon said nothing, she turned to look at him.

He was watching her like a cat, his eyes weirdly silver from the streetlight.

"You okay, Jon?"

"Hm-hmm," he answered quietly, not blinking.

The orange LED of Melanie's nightstand clock read two am. "Did your meds wear off? Need more?"

"Nuh-uh." He leaned forward and kissed her.

Melanie groaned. Just that brief contact, lips to lips, a close kiss but not a long one, sent a jolt of arousal through her body. It was uncanny, like a hot blast from an over-stoked furnace, inexplicable really — it came way too fast and was way too hot. She knew what it was like to feel horny and this was definitely it, but the sensation was off kilter, not the normal way her sexual feelings progressed at all. Oh, but it was awfully nice, though. "Wow, what's gotten into you?" she murmured through another kiss.

"Other way around," he murmured back. "I want to get into you." He pushed the kiss deeper, his tongue searching for hers, caressing and probing while his gleaming eyes bore into her.

God, he was a good kisser! Melanie's eyes fluttered, and she thought she might literally melt into goo. Underneath that unusually abrupt rush of lust she felt such genuine love for this man that it nearly overwhelmed her. *And now he's mine!* she thought happily, glancing at the ruby ring on her finger as she wrapped her arms around her fiancé's neck. "You sure you're up to this?" she asked him, coming up for air after several minutes of intense liplock. "I mean, your arm—"

"I'm fine," he assured her. "In fact, I feel great."

He did sound pretty normal — well, normal for a man who was almost to the point of shivering with arousal — but Melanie couldn't help but say, "Just be careful, okay? I don't want—"

"Oh yes, you do," he said, and he rubbed against her, nuzzling her breasts, nipping at her, breathing hard. How he kept his balance with a tender wound and only one hand bewildered her, but not enough to tell him to stop. If he was comfortable, who was she to argue?

Jon drew back, gazing down at her with an almost predatory smile, black curls dangling. He really didn't look like the Jonathan Stuart she knew at all, and yet he did. Melanie decided he was the most gorgeous creature she had ever seen, even if he did seem sort of spooky now. *Must be the hair,* she decided. *Sexy but a little... animal.* "My, the wonders of modern medicine," she giggled.

"No," Jon growled playfully. "It's just you." He shifted a bit so that he was partly laying on her, his left hand caressing her cheek. "I adore you, you know that, don't you?" he asked her, his breath warm on her face. "I always have and I always will." And he resumed his assault on her mouth, kissing her with frantic want, his hunger for her so intense that Melanie's emotions, like her body, bolted from a pleasant simmer to an instant boil. The warmth from the furnace kept pounding at her until her body began to writhe, the heat between her legs deliciously unbearable. She felt her toes curl, and her hands started to wander, one gently burrowing into his hair, the other moving down his belly to regions below. As her hand moved, it brushed against something cold and sharp.

"Ow!" Something had cut her hand. She lifted the covers and peered under, wondering how Jon's bandaged stump could possibly be sharp.

There was no bandaged stump at the end of his right arm. The arm was not in a sling. There was an iron hook on the end of it.

Melanie was about to scream when a blaze of light burst into existence right at the end of her nose. It was tiny but so incredibly bright that she had the instant impression of an oncoming car with glaring halogen headlights. Her scream died in her throat, and she blinked back tears. The light was gone. No, not gone. It was zipping around like a living sparkler, dropping some kind of gold glitter all over the room, turning it into a sparkling wonderland. *It's so beautiful,* she thought, forgetting all about the cut on her hand and what had caused it.

Jon paused to watch the light, too. He grinned at it, then at her. "Love me," he whispered, and he pushed into her with a groan. Melanie curled her legs up across his back and pulled him close, clutching him tight, her body and mind lost in flames.

CHAPTER 23

The next morning Stuart awoke in a room with flowered wallpaper and lace curtains fluttering at the open window. Sounds of talking, fighting, the clomp of hooves and the rattle of wagons made him think of an old Western movie soundtrack – Clint Eastwood, The Man With No Name, spurs a-jingling as he strode down the main street of some lawless frontier town. The TV must still be on. He sleepily reached over, expecting to find the remote clutched in Melanie's hand as she slept. She did that sometimes, and he just figured this was one of those times.

Melanie wasn't beside him. He was alone. He sat up in bed, not knowing where he was. This wasn't his room. Nor, he realized after a moment, was it Hook's opulent cabin. *Last night,* he thought, catching a brief trace of loathing before it vanished in the bright light of day. He felt soiled. *Shit, what did I do?*

A red corset hung over the bed's iron headboard, and long black silk stockings were draped daintily over the back of the chair. His own clothes – Hook's voluminous layers – were scattered on the chair, the dresser, the floor, marking a trail of frantic disrobement. His boots were stuck upside down on the bedposts.

Elsbeth...

The evening's events with the Beggar's Port strumpet came back to him. Stuart flopped back on the bed. *I betrayed you, Melly,* he thought miserably. But the woman he'd held – it had been Melanie, hadn't it?

There was no such person as Elsbeth. She was just a fantasy woman in this fantasy world. Or maybe, just maybe, Elsbeth really was Melanie. He had made love to her, too, back in his own bedroom, hadn't he? It had been dreamlike, exciting and delicious, a little forceful on his part but sometimes she liked that. She certainly hadn't protested, not that he could recall. Had that been real and this the dream?

Don't you dare try to rationalize this, he scolded himself. *You fell for Pan's cruelest trick yet, you fool. You've betrayed the only real woman who ever loved you.*

Still, he couldn't deny that he felt good, at least physically. He had made love to Elsbeth — Melanie? — several times throughout the night. Amazing how much tension a body could hold without knowing it. He must have been like a clenched fist for days, months if he was to believe his own log entries. He had forgotten what it felt like to relax.

He was drifting, enjoying not having to move, when Tawdry Audrey harrumphed through the door. "Rise and shine, James." He was laying above the covers, and she gave him an appreciative wolf whistle before he had a chance to cover himself. Laughing, she threw him a robe. "One last treat before you go. Bath time, dirty boy."

Stuart gawped at her. "A real bath?" he blurted.

She made a small sound of disgust. "You've been on that barge of yours too long. Yes, a real bath. With water and soap. If you're good, I'll even give you a towel to wipe your arse dry afterwards. Now hustle. And leave the hook here. Wouldn't want it to rust."

Stuart knew she didn't want the thing in her house at all, but he would never leave it behind. He shrugged into the robe, scooped up the harness and followed Audrey, who scowled at the hook, out the door.

Stuart tipped an imaginary hat to the ladies he passed while marveling that he had gotten used to the layer of grime on his skin — almost. Memory told him that Hook did not take advantage of tropical rains like his crewmen who, like many veteran seamen, would immediately fetch soap and take well-needed showers on deck. He did wash every day, certainly, but a small cloth and a basin of tepid water could never equal the cleaning power of a hot bath or the pure carnal delight that accompanied it. He eagerly followed Audrey downstairs to a room with pink floor tiles, cheap artwork and a claw-foot bathtub filled with steaming water.

"Took me twenty minutes and every pan in the place to fill this thing," Audrey griped. "You better the hell enjoy it."

Stuart was giddy with anticipation. "Don't fret about that, my dear," he assured her. "I will." He took off the robe, tossed it and the harness on a chair and climbed in. *Oh Lord, I've found religion,* he thought, happily melting into the soothing water. The night's well-exercised muscles, already relaxed, turned to absolute jelly. He cracked his neck and stretched luxuriously, sticking his feet up out of the tub to manage it. Then he curled up so that he could fit completely underwater all the way up to his eyes. *It's afterglow all over,* he thought dreamily.

"Good morning." Elsbeth entered the room, her curves tantalizingly visible underneath a gauzy shift, a tray in her hands. "I love you," she said lustily, adding with a curl of her lip, "but you reek, my dearest."

Stuart grabbed a fistful of her hair and drew her down for a kiss. "Perfume and petticoats do not a pirate make."

She responded by pushing his head underwater. His butt slid along the bottom of the porcelain tub and hit the far end, giving his legs no choice but to surge up out of the water like two lean porpoises breaching the waves. Water splashed everywhere. Stuart slipped around in the slick tub, trying to get his head back above water. When he finally did, his face was plastered by wet curls. Only his nose stuck out. Elsbeth pointed and snorted. Stuart giggled. Within seconds they were both laughing so hard that Audrey returned. Stuart saw her peek in, cast her eyes skyward and retreat with a huff.

Elsbeth playfully set to work with soap and a scrub brush, lathering Stuart's hair and body and getting soaked in the process. The sight of her in the wet shift made the procedure all the more pleasant as far as Stuart was concerned. He let her do anything she wanted. He was happier than he'd been in days, maybe years, who the hell cared? When Audrey brought in fresh baked bread and coffee that didn't taste like mud, he warned her, "I may never leave, you know."

"Fine with me," Audrey said, "as long as you keep paying."

"Do you have to leave again, James?" Elsbeth asked him, her bright eyes sad.

"What I told you last night was the truth, and I say it again — I love you." Even as Stuart spoke, Hook's awful black fingers gripped his heart. Love dwindled under a somber cloud. "But I have my ship and my men, and I must…" He glanced at the stump of his arm. "Attend to business."

A tear fell from her eye. "I heard about the croc," she said. "What if it really gets you next time?"

"I'll feed it another clock."

"I'm serious, James!"

Stuart gently wiped away her tear. "So am I."

The rest of his time at Tawdry Audrey's was overcast with sadness, at least for Elsbeth. Stuart tried to sympathize, but the black grip of Hook was slowly squeezing out the peace he had so gratefully gained. His appetite shifted like the wind — lust for flesh became a lust for blood. Pan's blood. By the time he was dressed and ready to go, his jaw was set, his eyes hard. "The *Jolly Roger* will remain here for several days," he told Elsbeth. "I will see you again before we weigh anchor."

Elsbeth moved as if to hug him. She clumsily turned the movement into an awkward touch of his cheek. "I'll be here," she said.

"Don't get into any brawls, James," Audrey told him. "You have such fine teeth." She pulled his repaired silk pouch from her pocket and gave it to him, empty, of course. "Fill it up and come back anytime."

Stuart tipped his hat. "Ladies."

He set off for the docks and his beloved *Jolly Roger*, planning out the day as he walked, enjoying the stares that followed him. There was a lot of work to be done, repairs to oversee, and most importantly, he had to find new recruits to replace his lost crewmen. He wanted men with plenty of experience and nerves of steel. If Pan decided to throw another siren storm at them, he wanted to survive it intact this time.

He hired a local to row him out to the ship, enjoying the spectacle of her as she loomed larger and larger, his proud cannibal of the seas. He spotted Noodler sitting in a bosun's chair suspended from the bowsprit, repainting the ship's figurehead. Stuart's heart swelled at the sight of the enormous skeleton-faced mermaid holding aloft a sword, her wooden tresses flowing, her long fishtail curving beneath. Since Noodler's hands were on backwards — a bizarre disfigurement that never ceased to mystify Stuart — the little fellow wasn't useful for many tasks, but he was impressively artistic. He certainly knew how to paint. He was giving The Bloody Maid new bright red eye sockets and a blood-red sword — details that had more than once scared the pants off superstitious victims.

Stuart boarded and quickly surveyed the work crews. Smee, Cecco, Mason and Foggerty had already returned, as he had suspected, and were ready to scout the town for crew candidates. Stuart sent them off, then went to his cabin to review the ship's manifest.

What he called a manifest was certainly not the official document of a legal ship. For Hook, it was a snapshot of the *Jolly Roger* in writing. It listed the full complement of the crew; condition of the ship and rigging from bilge to crow's nest; foodstuffs, water and spirits on hand and those needed, along with a detailed draft for stowage, already provided by Foggerty as he had ordered; an inventory of arms, ship's weapons and related supplies; bosun's stores; Cookson's medical stores; the booty in the holds, divided into what was to be kept and what should be sold — *Details, details, details,* he thought, leafing through pages and jotting notes. A dull job, to be sure, but he would soon sail back to the magical unknown of Pan's cursed island, and this time, he did not intend to leave until he had exacted his revenge.

Hook's energy pushed him onward, silently explaining the meaning of ship's terms, how to respond to questions, who various people were — the voice in his head became a steady drone that Stuart came to rely on. Knowledge burst upon him like the effects of a powerful drug, an exciting input of power that he could exercise over others without being challenged. Giving orders became downright fun, especially since the men greatly feared him. More than once he brandished the hook to get what he wanted. Merely lifting it motivated quarrelsome men into action double-quick.

By two bells of the afternoon watch — one o'clock — Cecco and Smee provided him with four acceptable sailors willing to serve under his command. Mason and Foggerty arrived some time later with two good men and two drunkards who, they assured him, had plenty of sailing experience under their belts along with too much rum. "Swear to God, Captain, they came willingly," Foggerty assured him. "Everybody in the Crimson Cock'll stand witness."

Stuart used his hook to knock off the hat of the shorter of the drunks. The man fumbled to catch it and fell over. The other one sniggered at his mate. "Let them sober up in the brig, Mister Foggerty," Stuart said. "Then we shall see what they have to say."

At five bells — two o'clock — Jukes reported that the new mizzen topmast was in place, and the new yards and rigging were in progress. Noodler was finished with The Bloody Maid, and thanks to constant pumping and the efforts of ship's carpenter Jules Thatcher, water in the bilge was down from eight feet to one. *Finally, things are going my way*, Stuart thought.

Then at eight bells — three-thirty — everything changed. While standing on the quarterdeck amidst the bustle of the work crews, Stuart began to sweat almost as much as his men, thanks to the suns and his layers of heavy clothing. Out of nowhere the words *Diet Coke* popped into his head. And he had no idea what they meant.

Frightened, he retreated to his cabin and paced for some time, combing his shaky memory, searching for the meaning. When he finally hit on it, he scribbled it down in the log. An hour later he was still writing, listing names and places and things he knew — things that Jonathan Stuart knew — as fast as he could get them down.

I keep the classics in the living room, reference books in the den, mysteries along the hallway and mainstream in the bedroom, he thought, feverishly writing and sometimes forgetting to dip the quill into the ink, only remembering when the tip went dry. *I have four cats — Fuzzybutt, Clancy, Rebers and... and...* He scribbled angrily down the rest of that page and turned to a fresh page. *Okay. Okay, calm down. Think. My car. I drive a... a... Pathfinder?* He wrote the word down, but it made absolutely no sense. Was it some kind of Indian term? For that matter, what was a car? *Freeway. Hollywood.* He wrote those down, too, but they held no meaning in those forms. *Free* and *way* made sense, yes, but together? And the wood of a holly tree — what was the point? *Los Angeles.* That one he knew. He couldn't explain why he knew those Spanish words, though, and any specific significance of angels eluded him.

He fetched a bottle of brandy from Hook's personal store in the cabinet by the harpsichord — a whack with his hook on the cabinet's inner wall and a panel slid aside, revealing several bottles in a secret compartment. He opened one and gulped a stinging mouthful as a parade of terms glided across his wounded memory, teasing him with their hollowness. *Sig Alert. T-bill. Linoleum. Superstation.* What did they mean? *It's who I am, and it's slipping away. How do I stop it? What do I do?*

Let it go, came the dark thought. *You find no meaning because there is no meaning. Not here.*

Stuart downed more brandy. *Dammit, it's all because I'm drinking again. One little moment of weakness and boom, I'm right back where I was before.* Moving resolutely, he stowed the bottle back in the cabinet. *No more today, James—*

"Shit!" He fetched it right back and drank more.

The darkness chuckled. *Calm yourself. This will soon be over. Stop fighting it.*

"Get out of my head!" Stuart shouted. "My name is Jon! I'm Jon Stuart! *Jon!*"

You know who you are.

"I'm Jonathan Stuart, and I am not insane!"

Insane. He had read horror novels about insane people, hadn't he? Yes, stories about good ol' folks whose List Of Things To Do Today included a quick slice-and-dice of their spouse and kids. Or maybe they liked the taste of Lady Next Door or Ex-Wife In White Sauce. *Real* insane people, oh yes, he had read about them, too, in newspapers and magazines. They looked and acted just like everyone else until one day, seemingly out of the blue, they jumped the trolley and shot somebody, or shot a whole lot of somebodies, and they usually shot themselves afterwards. Why?

Because they were insane.

"Stop it! That's not me!"

Of course it's not. What is Diet Coke?

Stuart went for his log book. He had written it down, those words and what they meant, only a few minutes ago. There! Diet Coke, in his own handwriting. Definition?

Soda.

Stuart stepped back from the book as if it might burst into flames. *What the fuck is soda?!* Something to do with bubbles, wasn't it? Bubbles that burst and *pop!* were gone, just like his mind was going. He would hear a soft little *pop!* any second now, and the trolley would continue on down the tracks without him. He clutched his head, forgetting for a brief moment that he had a hook for a hand. He just missed poking his eye out. *An insane man would poke his eye out for shits and giggles. I would never poke my eye out. I want to see the monster in 3-D when it comes to eat me.*

Ah, but what if it *had* already eaten him? What about that? Maybe his heart wasn't pounding this hard because he was terrified. Maybe it was really *two* beats thumping in sync. Was he so oblivious that he had already let it in, so blind that he hadn't noticed it hunching down there in the inky basement, watching him, beating its heart in time with his own so that it could hide and wait for the right time to step in and take over?

No! I rode the trolley in San Francisco! I jumped on and I jumped off! On and off! I can get back on anytime I want!

Je crois que le tram à demarrer il y à longtemps, mon ami.

That was French. Impossibly, he knew what it meant: I think you missed your trolley a long time ago, my friend.

"I don't know French!" he screamed. "I don't know French!"

Mais oui!

Stuart tore at his hair, not his own hair, no, not his at all but the curly black mane of that vain psychotic interloper in the basement. Shrieking in frenzy he ripped his hook into anything within reach — furniture, paintings, maps, curtains. He knocked the rosewood table over, spilling papers and candles and his goblet and his sextant to the deck. He smashed statues and shredded a whole panel of the Oriental screen. He ended up on his hands and knees tearing at the deck itself, hammering his hook through the burgundy carpet and clawing the hard wood underneath over and over — thunk, scraaaaatch, raise the arm and thunk, scraaaaatch, raise the arm and—

—the worst of his terror passed. Crouched low, his forehead pressed against the splinters, he panted, sweat tickling under the painful straps of his harness. *God? I know I'm not much of a Christian.*

Haven't been to church in, what, ten years? But please, please, please, I'm begging you, help me...

He won't. The dark mental voice wasn't his own. *You're damned,* it said.

"Captain!" Smee barged into the cabin. "Captain, message from shore, sir—" He stopped at the sight of the wreckage before him.

Stuart didn't move. He identified Smee as the one who had spoken, but he was on another planet, somewhere in the universe of I Don't Give a Shit.

Smee knelt down and tapped his shoulder. "Sar? Yeh want to see this, sar, honest. Please, sar, look up."

Smee, afraid? Stuart thought, hearing a quiver in the bosun's voice. He raised his head.

Smee held out an envelope. "It's from Tawdry Audrey, sar. Man who delivered it said it's an emergency."

Numb, Stuart took it. He sat back on his heels and used his hook to slice the envelope open. He read:

> *James,*
>   *Elsbeth is dead. Please come.*
>   *– Audrey*

CHAPTER 24

Stuart stood on Tawdry Audrey's cozy front porch. He wasn't sure how he had gotten there. Smee and Cecco stood with him on either side like guards.

Audrey opened the door. "James," she said, her voice husky with grief. "I don't know how it happened. I didn't touch anything. She's in her room..." She moved to hug him, then thought better of it and stepped aside.

Stuart entered the house and headed for Elsbeth's room. Smee and Cecco followed, keeping a discreet distance as he strode through the foyer and into the parlor. Audrey's ladies were assembled there, some of them crying, all of them scared. They fell silent when Stuart entered and watched with teary eyes as he slowly ascended the stairs.

Moving on automatic, he pushed Elsbeth's door open. There she lay, sprawled on her bed, nude, face up, her beautiful brown hair matted with blood that had dripped down the edge of the soaked bedding and puddled on the floor. Her skull was sliced open, just behind her left ear. Her face was pearl white.

"Murder," he heard Cecco whisper.

"I swear, I don't know who did it," Audrey said. "I was here. The girls were here. No one heard anything. No one saw anything."

Stuart stepped closer. *Melanie?* he thought dully. Black fingers squeezed deep in his insides. Something within him howled in grief.

"She would take no customers last night," Audrey continued. "Poor dear, I decided to let her alone today. But after a time the girls began to wonder..."

Stuart froze. *Last night? I was with her last night! I was with her this morning!* Trying not to shake, he reached out to her right foot and actually grasped her big toe, gently trying to wiggle it. It would barely move, the muscles bound by rigor mortis.

He jerked his hand back, appalled by his own actions. What had he expected, warm supple skin and flexible joints? Rigor could last for hours, days even. When she had really died was impossible to determine, and what did it matter anyway? She was dead. And Pan had manipulated time *again* to drive the point home. Stuart had left her with the joyous expectation of seeing her again this evening — only, *this evening* had been skipped over. Pan had taken it away, made it pass by for everyone but him.

He would never see her again.

Stuart gazed into the dead woman's eyes. They were filmed over, murky like dirty water, staring out at nothing with a lingering trace of surprise. He wanted so badly to close her eyelids, but he didn't dare try in case they were too stiff to close. He didn't think he could handle that.

Smee held out a blanket that he had picked up from the floor, wordlessly suggesting that she be covered. Stuart gratefully took it and slipped it up the length of Elsbeth's body. He stopped just before it covered her left hand that lay on her chest. A memory surged up through the tangle in his mind — the ruby ring, the one he had given Melanie, the one he had purchased from Masao in Japantown during his trip to San Francisco. It was on Elsbeth's finger.

The room wobbled. Everything wanted to fizz away in a white mist. Stuart had a vague sense of unbalance, of leaning too far to the left. For some reason, he couldn't stop it. *Not now*, he thought. *Keep control!*

"Sar?" came Smee's concerned voice through the fog.

Shut it down. Yes, that would allow him to function. As he had many times in the past, Stuart slammed down the great grey wall in his mind, cutting himself off from the unpleasant, the painful, the *real.* Control returned, and with it, a chilling clarity. Feeling his face

relax into a blank mask, he looked down at Elsbeth — *Melanie!* —
resisting the urge to kiss her one last time. He wanted to, but Hook
would not allow it. Hook would never do such a thing. Instead, he
worked the ring off Elsbeth's finger and tucked it into his pocket.

Something caught his eye. He leaned closer. Dust. A smear of
dust, soft like ash, on the pillow by Elsbeth's head. More of it on the
bedding. He touched it, rubbing a bit between his fingertips. Spongy.
Sticky.

He pushed past Smee to check the window. Open. A faint smudge
of dust on the sill. *It could be anything,* he reasoned, trying to keep
himself from hyperventilating. *This town has a dozen kinds of filth that
I've never even heard of.* But another memory told him otherwise. He
had seen this kind of dust before, in the back office of his store, on
the shelf where the 1989 tax box should have been.

"Sar?" Smee prompted a second time.

Stuart growled for silence and returned to the body. The wound
in her head. It was almost neat. Her killer hadn't bashed her head in
so much as cut her skull open with something small, sharp and heavy.

"Pan?" Smee suggested quietly.

Stuart had suspected Pan, but another person now came to mind.
Someone with a grudge. Someone who wanted to destroy him from
the inside out because of it. Someone who carried an ax. "Where is
Sigrson?" he asked, turning to Cecco.

The first mate stepped back, his expression telling Stuart that the
look on his own face must have been murderous. "Aboard ship, sir,"
Cecco said. "His watch takes leave tomorrow. He couldn't have—"

Stuart started for the door.

Showing more nerve than brains, Audrey stepped in his way.
"James, are you saying that one of your own men did this?"

"Step aside, Audrey."

Cecco tilted his head, silently imploring Audrey to obey. She took
one step back, giving Stuart enough room to slip past her. He made
his way down the stairs and out into the street, Smee and Cecco at his
heels.

"But he can't've done it, sar," Smee said, hurrying along as Stuart
headed for the docks. "I mean, how—?"

Stuart stopped short and held up his still dusty fingertips. "Fairy dust," he stated flatly. "I'll wager he's been collecting it for weeks, every time he goes ashore. There are fairies everywhere in Pan's jungle, the place is rotten with them."

"But their dust only keeps its magic if it doesn't touch the ground," said Cecco.

"Plants are alive, and fairy dust falls upon the leaves," Stuart said. "That's why the jungle sparkles at night. Perhaps the dust keeps its powers if it stays wrapped in leaves."

"Sigrson is one of our best hunters," Cecco said. "He's been ashore more than most of the men."

"There you have it." Stuart resumed his brisk pace. "You said it yourself, Smee. The man's been biding his time."

"But to *fly*, sar," Smee said dubiously.

Stuart knew that somewhere in their backbrains, the superstitious pirates feared the ability to fly. Sigrson proved that any one of them might have collected fairy dust and flown at any time, but to attempt it was not only foolhardy — Pan controlled the winds — it was, in a sense, sinful. To fly crossed a line that they consciously didn't know existed but which they respected nonetheless. *Sigrson detests me greatly to do what he's done*, Stuart thought.

Smee was still trying to wrap his brain around the idea. "Yer sayin' he flew off the ship last night an'—"

"Yes yes yes, confound it! Clouds hid the moon for most of the night, aye? If he chose his time carefully, the watch wouldn't have seen him. That's also why Audrey's girls neither heard nor saw anything amiss. The floorboards of Elsbeth's room never squeaked because he never stood upon them. He never set foot on the ground or in a boat the entire time." Stuart clenched his jaws. "Revenge is a very happy thought indeed."

"Bloody brilliant," Smee mumbled.

As they rowed for the *Jolly Roger*, Cecco expressed doubts that Sigrson would be found onboard. "Why would he chance staying, unless he intends to kill you, too?"

"He does intend to kill me," Stuart replied, "but first he wants to see me grieve. That is the reason for all of this, Mister Cecco. The man is more devious than I suspected. Once we board, keep a weather eye."

"I suggest yeh do the same, sar," Smee advised. "He's a monster of a man, that one is. Don't do nothin' rash."

Stuart had no intention of acting rashly. He intended to follow a most methodical plan.

He boarded his ship to find the crew toiling away in the hot suns, shirts off and a bucket of drinking water making the rounds. The mizzen topmast and topgallant yard had already been replaced with spares kept below. Most of the men were cutting new rigging and repairing what rigging had been salvaged. On a sailing vessel nothing, not even the smallest scrap of line, went to waste. Vigr Sigrson was among those sweating up the replacement royal yard while MacDougal played his violin and led a halyard shanty. "*Oh, as I wuz a'rollin' down Paradise Street—*"

"*Timme way, hay, an' knock a man down!*" the men chorused, readying to haul on the line when MacDougal sang next.

"*A sassy flash clipper I chanced fer t' meet—*"

"*Oh, give us some time to knock a man down!*"

The pirates paused in their work at the arrival of their captain. First it was just the normal shit-he's-back-stay-out-of-his-way looks. Then they saw his eyes. MacDougal's strong tenor faltered. He stopped singing altogether. The men at the halyard froze in mid-haul. Those not hauling shuffled away from Stuart or, if their particular task prevented them from leaving their spot, they crouched or leaned as far away as possible in an absurd attempt to become invisible.

Stuart took note of all this. Good. He had their attention. "Belay that line," he told the men at the halyard. "Mister Foggerty." Foggerty hurried forward. "Please bring Mister Sigrson's sea chest to me."

Foggerty obeyed without question as men belayed the halyard line. "Mister Sigrson!"

The big Swede warily eyed his captain, but he did not verbally acknowledge the summons.

Stuart expected as much. He crooked a finger and beckoned the man over. "Empty your pockets, if you please," he ordered after the man lumbered up to face him.

Sigrson's thick brows drew together. *"Varför det?"* he demanded, adding *"kapten* sir," after a noticeable pause.

"Why?" said Cecco, stepping up to Stuart's side with his cutlass unsheathed. "Because the *kapten* told you to, you son of a bitch. Do it!" On Stuart's other side, Smee cocked his pistol.

If Sigrson was guilty of anything, he showed no evidence of it. He acted genuinely baffled as he emptied his pockets.

"Mister Mason," said Stuart.

Mason stepped forward to take the items: playing dice, a jew's harp, a chaw of tobacco, a cheap metal crucifix, a half-finished scrimshaw of a bear. Nothing of import.

"Search him."

At Cecco's nod, Jukes and the dreadlocked Jamaican named Kamau thoroughly patted Sigrson down. All they found was a small pouch under his shirt, hanging from a thin lanyard round his neck.

"Open it," Stuart told Jukes.

Jukes obeyed. Inside the pouch was a charm with a few hairs inside. *"Min moder,"* Sigrson said innocently, as if hoping Stuart would dare malign such a sacred relic as that of a loving old mother's grey hairs.

Stuart gestured for the pouch to be returned. He hadn't really expected to find what he was looking for on Sigrson's person. He was waiting for the man's sea chest. When Foggerty lugged it up from below, the Swede bared his teeth. "No right you!"

Stuart raised his hook. As if an electrical shock passed through the entire crew, every man recoiled — except Sigrson. "Say what?" Stuart asked mildly.

Sigrson's eyes were on the hook. He swallowed.

"I thought so. Open it."

Sigrson paused.

I have him, Stuart thought, but he suppressed his grin. There would be time for that afterwards.

The Swede opened his sea chest and stepped back. Stuart knelt down and pawed through the contents while Sigrson bristled. Clothes, letters, gear, mementos — Stuart carefully checked everything. *And what have we here? A box in the bottom corner!* It was small and locked. Stuart used his hook to pry the lock off. He peered inside at a moist spongy leaf that was just the right size to cover the bottom of the box and fold up to create a little pocket. In that pocket was a pile of sparkling gold dust.

Stuart stood, holding up the box for all to see. He wanted to tell the crew that the man before him had murdered an innocent woman, that he was a traitor and should be flogged to within an inch of his life and marooned with no water, no pistol, not even clothes on his scarred back. Instead, he simply upturned the box, sending a stream of sparkling dust into the wind. All eyes watched uneasily as the dust floated away, touching no one. Sigrson watched it, too, jaws clenched and his eyes a little too wide.

That nailed it.

Stuart rammed his hook into Sigrson's belly and jerked it sideways, tearing him open and spilling the Swede's intestines into his own sea chest. As Sigrson wavered, gaping down at his own guts in bewilderment, Stuart drew his saber. "If I must be damned," he snarled, "then you shall be as well." The men around him ducked as he swung his arm back, gathering the necessary momentum. Then he swung the saber in a vicious arc that took Sigrson's head clean off, spraying blood. The body toppled. No one moved.

Somehow Stuart kept himself standing steady. "Hang his head from the jibboom," he said to Cecco, wiping his blade on the dead man's shirt. "There will be no service. Throw his body overboard, along with his gear. It will not be auctioned off, is that understood? Nothing of this bastard dog is to remain aboard this ship."

Cecco saluted. "Aye aye, sir."

Stuart surveyed his crew, every one of whom stared at him in terror. "Carry on," he said, and sheathing his saber, he retreated to his cabin.

Smee had arranged for the captain's furnishings to be tidied up and, where necessary, repaired. Little evidence of Stuart's earlier outburst of violence remained. But as he closed the door behind him and locked it, Stuart could feel the lingering madness. His madness, hanging in the air like a foul stench. He felt as if he might have just closed the lid on his own coffin.

The first thing to greet him at this new level of Hell was Mary Etherton's mirror. Reflected in its oval glass were his bloody clothes,

gore dripping from his hook, his face sprinkled with red, and his eyes
— he looked closer just in time to see two bright red sparks fade from
his pupils. Words from J.M. Barrie's novel flashed through his mind:
"His eyes were of the blue of the forget-me-not, and of a profound
melancholy, save when he was plunging his hook into you, at which
time two red spots appeared in them and lit them up horribly."

Jonathan Stuart sat down at the rosewood table and cried.

CHAPTER 25

Stuart spent the next twenty-four hours in his cabin. He neither ate nor slept, but he did drink. He sat at the rosewood table in his same foul clothes, making himself sick on brandy and thinking of Melanie. A new thought had occurred to him, one more horror to heap upon the rest: what if the death of Elsbeth in this world had equaled the death of Melanie back home?

It was all because of the ruby ring. Pan must have snatched it from Melanie and put it on Elsbeth's finger. That could only mean one thing, right? That Melanie was dead just as Elsbeth was.

He had never told her how much he loved her. It had taken his disastrous abduction to the Neverland and with it, all this pain and terror and helplessness, to finally break down his emotional walls to the point where he could admit to himself just what she meant to him. She was everything. He loved her more than he'd ever loved anyone. He wouldn't hesitate to ask her to marry him now — now that it was too late. He replayed the dream he'd had before waking up in Elsbeth's bed over and over, the dream in which he had proposed. If only it were true...

So what was he left with? A most exquisite torture, a nagging question that would haunt his every waking moment and, in all probability, his dreams as well: was Melanie dead or not? If he could find a way home, would she be there to greet him? Or would he end up alone like he was now, alone and frightened and heartsick?

Smee was smart enough to leave his captain be, so Stuart sat and simmered in his own misery, his only friend a bloody reflection, his only escape a bottle. He listened to the men working on deck and in the holds below, continuing repairs and stowing provisions. The constant stream of lively shanties offered some relief, but it also reminded him of where he was — not home. Dago Tom came to his door several times, scratching and meowing to be let in. The cat would have been some comfort, but Stuart did not admit him. *I don't deserve comfort*, he thought, *even from a mangy cat.*

And the ship. He wanted so much not to care about the ship. *Let her sink*, he kept repeating to himself. *Let her take us all down and be done with it.* But fondness for the *Jolly Roger* had crept into his heart. More and more he wondered about the progress of her repairs and how long it would be before he could sail her away. Whatever allure Beggar's Port had once held, it was a dump to him now, a pile of filth with worthless human vermin crawling on it like flies. Just another of Pan's machinations to grind him down — first to give him hope, the cruelest thing of all, and in the end dash that hope and send him into an endless downward spiral.

He clutched his stomach, sure he was going to throw up again. He was in bad shape, no denying it, but he vowed not to give in to the downward spiral. He would sail the *Jolly Roger* back to Pan's island, and this time he wouldn't play the victim. It was time to turn the game to his favor.

Seven bells rang on the afternoon watch — three o'clock, almost the time that he had been informed of Elsbeth's death yesterday. Stuart staggered to the door, threw it open and yelled for Smee. The bosun appeared in the nick of time to catch his captain in a half-faint. Smee manhandled him back to his chair and then squealed, actually squealed, when he saw the condition of the cabin.

"Aw, bloody hell!" he cried. "I knew yeh been founderin' three sheets to the wind, sar, but fer Chrissake, yeh spewed all over the farkin' carpet! Dammit, after all that work to clean everythin' up after yeh... err... that is, err... I'll, uh, take care of it, sar, don' yeh worry. First, though, I think yeh need a bit o' work yerself. Hoo, an' some fresh air!"

Stuart was in no condition to assist. He had no strength and less coordination. He couldn't wash or shave himself, couldn't comb his own hair. He could hardly sit upright.

Smee's determination was unshakable and his ingenuity astounding. With much grousing and grunting, and after forcing a little soup and strong coffee down Stuart's throat, he transformed him from a deplorable wreck into some semblance of a pirate captain.

Two hours later, with the inevitable colossal hangover in full swing, Stuart wavered out onto the quarterdeck. His head throbbed with such cruelty that his eyeballs pulsed with the pressure. In his ears, the hideously steady drumbeat of pain morphed into an audible sound that was loud enough to drown out any useful thoughts he might have attempted to think. Only two words — *it hurts, it hurts, it hurts, it hurts* — looped around in his brain, literally making him dizzy.

He ducked his face into the crook of his arm, wondering if Old Scratch might ease the pain in exchange for his eternal soul. Wait a minute. Maybe he had already made that deal. That would explain why he was trapped in the Neverland in the first place. "Ohhhhhh, what the hell did I want to come out here for?" he groaned to Smee.

Cecco climbed up the starboard stairs from the main deck. "Captain! Good to see you, sir." His voice faltered. "Very good indeed," he added awkwardly.

Stuart suspected that Cecco wanted to say something soothing about Elsbeth, and he was grateful that the man apparently decided not to do so. Stuart peeked out at him through his fingers. "What... uuuh... umm... what's our status?"

"She'll be ready to sail in two days," said Cecco. "We still need to—"

"Mizzen rigged?" Stuart interrupted.

"Aye."

"Provisions stowed?"

"Almost finished, sir."

"No big holes that'll make us sink?"

Cecco half-smiled as if his captain's attempt at humor actually saddened him. "Thanks to Thatcher, she's tight as a preacher's arse, sir."

"Then we're sailing tonight with the tide."

"But, sir—"

Stuart lowered his hand and squinted at Cecco, not unkindly but with an icy overtone. "But what, Mister Cecco?"

Cecco's demeanor shifted from loyal officer to fond friend. "She'll be ready if you say so, James, you know that."

"Then see to it." Stuart stepped back into the companionway to get out of the skull-wrenching sunslight. "I want to go home."

* * * * *

At three bells of the first watch — nine o'clock that night — the tide went out. The *Jolly Roger* went with it. With his hangover easing down and the drone of Hook's voice ever in his ear, Stuart had overseen preparations to leave. Now he stood on the quarterdeck while the mates and crew jumped at his every command.

"Man the windlass!" he bellowed. In seconds he could feel the ship shudder gently as the men below began their muscular trudge around the big cylindrical machine that would hoist up the anchor.

After a time, the answering call came: "Anchor's aweigh, Captain!" The anchor was lifting off the sea bottom and on her way up.

"We'll make sail, Mister Cecco," Stuart said. "Brace the yards 'round!"

"Aye aye, Captain!"

Under Cecco's and Foggerty's supervision, the men of the port and starboard watches divided until groups equal in number were gathered at the foot of the masts, Cecco at the foremast and Foggerty at the mizzen. As dictated by tradition, first and second mates' watches would share the main mast.

Satisfied with the dispersal, Stuart called, "See all lines clear for running! Man the lee braces!"

Men began casting off lines from the brace belaying pins. Groups gathered at each line. Led by MacDougal's fiddle and his powerful tenor belting out *Pull Away Now, My Nancy O!*, the main and topsail yards were hauled into positions that would allow the sails, once unfurled and after the ship tacked, to best catch the northerly wind.

"Lay aloft, ya festering scabs!" Cecco shouted, sending men up the shrouds and out onto the yards. "Main and tops'l gaskets off and be quick about it, or I'll brand your arses with the sign of the pitchfork!"

Stuart watched, his heart swelling with pride as the tiny shadows of men in the moonlight danced across footropes a hundred feet up or more, with no support other than their own balance and a hearty desire not to die from a tremendous fall. They pulled the gaskets free, coiled them and secured them.

"Main and tops'l gaskets away!" Cecco informed Stuart.

It was time to unfurl the sails. "Slack away clewl'ns and buntl'ns!" Stuart called. "Haul away main and tops'l sheets!"

Enormous spreads of canvas fluttered down, luffing but ready to grab the wind once the ship came about on a starboard tack. The next job was to hoist the upper topsail and t'gallant yards and unfurl those sails. After that, haul the aft jib sheets on the starboard tack, fill the head yards, shiver the aft yards and get the ship before the wind.

As he accomplished each of these tasks, conducting his men like members of an orchestra, part of Stuart remained dumfounded that he knew what he was doing. Not long ago the cramped and stinky world of this twenty-eight gun frigate had been as foreign to him as another country where everything, even the language, was alien. Now he considered the ship his sanctuary.

The *Jolly Roger* finished her turn into the wind, falling off and seizing her new tack with gusto. Sails billowed with the steady blow from astern and she leaped forward, leaving Beggar's Bay behind.

"West sou'west," Stuart told Morgan Skylights, whose hour-long trick it was at the helm. "Keep a good full."

"Aye aye, Captain," said Skylights. "West sou'west, a good full."

Stuart climbed up the stairway to the poop. Alone in the wind, he faced astern, took off his hat and let his hair blow back. Balmy air cooled the sweat on his skull, and the eager but steady rise and fall of the deck settled him like the motion of a good rocking chair.

The stern lantern, big and bright on the taffrail, made it hard to distinguish the receding lights of Beggar's Port. After Stuart's eyes adjusted, he could make out the brightest dock lanterns. They slowly shrank down to pinpricks as the distance between land and ship widened.

Stuart wondered when he would see the Port again. Not that it mattered anymore. Like everything else in his life, it was over. A tear slipped down his cheek. *You have taken so much away from me, Pan*, he thought, *but you have given me one thing – the sea.*

Footsteps signaled the arrival of Cecco. By now Stuart knew the difference between Smee's shuffle and Cecco's clipped pace, as well as the footfall of many other men — Foggerty's limp, Mason's light step, Jukes' sneaky half-skip, fat Cookson's annoying thumps, and the distinctive step-clomp-step-clomp of stupid Hawkins with his peg leg. "Yes, Mister Cecco?" he asked without turning round.

"Running full and by, sir," the first mate reported. His voice softened. "How are you doing?"

"Abiding," Stuart answered. "You?"

Cecco leaned on the rail. "Vastly disappointed."

Stuart waited for him to explain.

"Well, I was looking forward to leave, sir, like everyone else."

It took Stuart a moment to comprehend the simple statement. *Oh no. Not again.* He forced himself to inhale slowly, exhale evenly. This wasn't Smee he was talking to. Cecco was a friend, but he had already questioned his captain's faculties on more than one occasion. Stuart dared not show any hint of confusion. "Aye," he managed, smooth and neutral.

Cecco waved his hand around, a universal gesture of helpless perplexity. "Well, it's the damnedest thing, isn't it, James? The confounded Port moving again? At this stage, I'm not sure we'll ever find it. I suppose it's right that we head back to Pan's land." He blew a kiss into the wind. "Goodbye, my Ada, wherever you are."

Stuart maintained a casual air as he stole a glance back at Beggar's Port. The bay and the Port along its inner shoreline were quickly slipping out of sight, lost to the curve of the horizon. He thought he saw the last dock lantern, dim and yellow over the distance, and then it was gone. Had it been there at all? *Yes, dammit, I have her ring!* He fingered the ruby ring, which he had placed on his pinky finger where it was still too tight. *This ring is real. It is fact!* "So." He tried to smile. "The bay..." He let it trail, hoping Cecco might make something of it.

The first mate shrugged. "As you said, it was worth checking. At least we know for sure the place is gone." He might as well have been talking about a missing dinner spoon.

"I'll admit it's not an easy thing to accept," Stuart said, still fishing. "I know the last few days have been hard on the men."

"Aye," Cecco said, "and you, too. Oh, you were ready to tear the town apart, you can't fool me. All I can say is I'm sure Elsbeth would have been waiting for you, just as my Ada would have been waiting for me."

Stuart squeezed his eyes shut. *None of it happened.* No tantrum this time, no panic. Just cold acceptance. All that he had experienced at the Port — hope, friendship, love, loss, revenge, murder, despair — none of it had occurred. The events lived only in his mind now, where they would fester and pollute his thoughts until all he had left was an unexplainable despair. Exquisite torture indeed. *I should have expected this.*

Cecco put a hand on Stuart's shoulder. "Forgive me, James. You honestly love her, don't you?" He sounded amazed.

Stuart opened his eyes. "No. I don't. She's just a nice dream." He ran his hand along the taffrail, admiring the smooth wood and how the fine layer of cool sea spray let his fingers slip lightly back and forth across it. *Like her skin,* he thought. *Smooth. Soft. Warm.*

He shook that memory off. *If Elsbeth never died, then maybe Melanie is alive,* he thought. Melanie, of course, might not have died in the real world in the first place, but now the possibility of it seemed less likely. He heaved a shaky sigh, feeling a bit light-headed as some of the emotional turmoil churning his guts eased. *I can't keep going like this, constantly overwrought, never knowing what's real and what's not.* He thought of his great-grandfather. *I wonder if he went though the same thing.*

Then he thought of Sigrson. If Elsbeth didn't die — "Maybe I didn't kill him!"

"James?" said Cecco, lost.

Stuart was already at the port stairs. He did a seaman's drop down to the quarterdeck and then to the main deck, sliding his hand and, by necessity, his elbow, along the stair rails, his feet never touching the steps. Men scattered as he darted and dodged down the length of the ship and raced up the stairs to the foredeck.

"Captain!" Cecco said, following him. "Smee, get over here!"

"Aye!" said Smee, emerging from a knot of men to follow Cecco.

As wary as they were regarding any action their captain made, the crew nonetheless abandoned their jobs to gather at the break of the forecastle, muttering uneasily. Stuart knew the forecastle was strictly crew territory, even on a pirate ship where naval traditions did not always apply. To see their captain rampage up to the foredeck like this was hardly standard behavior. Stuart didn't blame them for their curiosity, but he wasn't about to explain himself either.

He peered out over the rail, trying to see the end of the jibboom extending a good thirty feet beyond the end of the overlapped bowsprit, bobbing in front of the ship like the nose of a titan swordfish. *I have to be sure,* he thought, and worked his way down to the head rails where the base of the bowsprit pierced the hull, held in place by heavy gammoning. Gripping lines for support, he climbed as far as he could and leaned out over the water, bouncing as the bow reared up with each wave crest and dropped like a plunging elevator into each trough.

"Captain, what're yeh doin'?" Smee called down from the deck.

Stuart was too busy heaving a sigh of relief. Thanks to the bright moonlight, he was sure that Sigrson's severed head wasn't swinging from the jibboom like he had ordered. *Does that mean he never existed?* he wondered as he made his way back to the foredeck.

Smee and Cecco helped him climb back over the rail. "Sar?" Smee asked carefully.

Stuart met the bosun's eyes. In that instant, it all became clear. His officers, like the crew, had no bloody business knowing what he had been doing on the head rails. *Taking a crap, ha!* came the dark thought. Stuart straightened to his full height and, ignoring their confusion, asked in a crisp tone, "Does the name Vigr Sigrson mean anything to you?"

The question caught the men off guard. They had to think for a moment. Smee shook his head. Cecco answered, "No, sir."

Stuart nodded. "Excellent."

He crossed the length of the ship once again, slowly this time. No need to rush anymore. He had his answer, and for once it was a good one. So what if Beggar's Port was gone? So what if he had to take three steps back for the two he had struggled to gain? In a way, the slate was clean. He could start over, put the atrocities behind and see what he could make of the future. He crossed the main deck, strolling more that walking and fully aware for the first time that he *owned* this vessel.

No, he corrected himself, *she owns me.* The *Jolly Roger* was his mistress, a lover who demanded much but who also had much to give. If he fulfilled her demands, if he commanded her well, she would give him shelter and protection from every storm. She would love him, as he loved her. Stuart swelled with that knowledge, the raw power of it tingling just below his skin. *You are beautiful,* he thought, his eyes caressing her as he strolled along. *My life, my heart, my very soul are yours.*

Pirates shuffled aside and ducked behind each other to get out of Stuart's way, all except for one little fellow with a peg leg who bumped right into him — Hawkins, the nincompoop who had lost MacDougal's concertina. Stuart grinned as he recalled hanging the man upside-down in the rigging till nightfall. *A little blood to his brain didn't help his stupidity after all,* he thought, and he kicked Hawkins' peg leg out from under him.

The little man fell on his face. "Thank ye, Cap'n!" he cried, sounding grateful that he hadn't been skewered.

Laughing, Stuart entered his cabin and slammed the door, ready for a good night's sleep. Things were looking up after all.

CHAPTER 26

Melanie hadn't set the alarm clock, so she floated up to a wakeful state in slow stages. Usually she was up at seven sharp and out the door by eight, off to run whatever errands her work required during the morning. She usually spent her afternoons writing up her notes into report form for her clients. Late afternoon she might read a book, take a nap, or go to Jon's store to visit.

Three things crept into her mind in succession when she woke up on this morning. One: the alarm clock hadn't gone off because she wasn't planning to work today. Two: she wasn't at her own house for the alarm clock to go off anyway. Three: her body hurt. She felt used and worn out, strangely sated but achy and bruised. She sat up, consciousness swimming up from the depths of heavy sleep. The bed looked like a pack of dogs had run over it. The quilt cover was on the floor, the sheets were a rumpled mess. And Jon...

He was asleep with a frown on his face, lying on his back with his bandaged stump in its sling across his chest. The position was the same as when he had first gone to sleep, except his legs were tangled in the sheets. His hair lay spread around his head like a black halo. In startling contrast, his cheeks were the color of cream, and they were damp with perspiration. Maybe he had a fever. Maybe he was unconscious. Suddenly Melanie didn't care. The sight of him jogged her fully awake. "How dare you!" she screamed, and sprang out of bed in case he awoke and tried to attack her. "You bastard, you raped me last night! Make love, my ass! You hurt me, you goddamned..." She trailed off.

He wasn't moving.

"Jon?" She approached him carefully. "Jon, wake up."

He was so pale and still, he might have been dead. Melanie's eyes went to his chest. Yes, he was breathing, but it was shallow and slow and sounded rattly. She poked his arm. Getting no reaction, she patted his cheek, first softly and then sharply.

"Oh shit." She picked up the phone. The line was dead. "What?" she asked the handpiece stupidly, and turned back to Jon. No change. "Oh shit shit shit!" She ran out of the bedroom, down the stairs and into the kitchen to try that phone. It was working, she had no idea why the other wasn't. She dialed 911.

"911, what is the nature of your emergency?" asked a calm, almost toneless voice.

"I need medical help," Melanie babbled. "Uh, I'm Melanie Forrester at 46228 California Street in Pasadena. My, umm, boyfriend, Caucasian, 35 years old, he's delusional, something's wrong, he's—"

"Are *you* all right?"

"Me? Yeah, it's just—"

"All right, ma'am, hold on while I contact paramedics, okay?"

"Okay." Melanie bit her lip and waited while the operator contacted a Fire Department dispatcher.

"An ambulance is on the way, Miss Forrester," the dispatcher said after a few moments. He then proceeded to ask her details of Jon's condition — were drugs involved, did he suffer from any illnesses, had this ever happened before? Melanie did her best to provide answers, all the while trying not to dwell on the dead silence coming from Jon's room. It was all she could do not to throw down the phone and run upstairs.

"Hurry, please!" she finally said when the call was finished. Frankly, it had been a miracle that anybody had answered her. In Los Angeles, chances were that calling 911 got you a pleasant recording that blandly informed you that all lines were busy, please wait, so sorry if your loved one croaks in the meantime, buh-bye! But she had actually gotten a live person. *Thank God*, she thought, and ran back upstairs.

The bed was empty.

Melanie scanned the room. Jon had been nutso last night, that was for sure. Was he hiding behind the door or in the closet, ready to jump on her again? Had he gone insane and she was engaged to him and afraid of him and she would have to call it off and run away? "Jon? Where are you?" She hated how frightened she sounded.

She noticed the bed. Her eye for detail focused sharply. The sheets were in the same configuration as before, the *exact* same configuration. If Jon had gotten up, he would have moved them because his legs had been twisted up in them. But the sheets were still twisted as if his legs were still there. And his pillow — it lay with a neat dent in the middle as if his head was still there. She took a step closer, staring in horror. The mattress was pressing in on itself where his body had lain, as if his weight was still there.

She reached out. "Jon?" *Oh God, I can feel him*, she realized as her hand drew closer to where he had lain. *He's still here. I can't see him, but he's here!* Her hand reached the space where his chest would have been. She met with slight resistance, as if the air was denser in that spot. Her blood went cold as her groping hand grew warm. He was still there, somewhere, maybe just one inch to the left of reality, close enough to somehow perceive but still far out of reach.

"Jon, where are you? Wake up! Jon!"

He was fading. She could sense it as clearly as if this was something that happened every day. He *was* still in the bed, but he was leaving fast, slipping into some pocket of impossibility that she could not see or hear or touch. "Don't go!" she screamed, and she leapt on him. "Don't you dare fucking leave me!" Her entire body met that same mild resistance, and for one appalling moment it felt like skin. Then the resistance gave way, and she landed on the mattress. The warm air in that spot cooled. The presence she had always felt, the mild electric charge in the ether that had always identified Jonathan Stuart as a living being within her psychic proximity, was gone.

* * * * *

If circumstances hadn't been so preposterous, if they hadn't been so terrifyingly desperate, if she hadn't sensed Jon fade away with such eerie certainty, Melanie Forrester might have laughed at her predicament.

The ambulance came twenty-five minutes after she called. She opened the door at the sound of urgent knocking but was only able to stare at the paramedics in hysterical silence. They knew that she had suffered some sort of trauma, but her explanation, when it finally did come out, amounted to the babblings of a lunatic. Finding no one in the house other than Melanie, they took *her* to the hospital.

Now she lay on an emergency room bed, the curtains drawn, a strong sedative coursing through her veins. She wasn't surprised to be here. She remembered everything that had happened, including the fact that she had eventually started screaming, leaving the paramedics with no choice but to shoot her up with something from a syringe that had slammed her into Lalaville like a cartoon mallet to the forehead.

Everything took a new loop-the-loop when Dr. Odet came in. Melanie heard the curtains rustle and opened her eyes to find him reading her chart. "Thank God, it's you," she said, licking her dry lips. "Doctor, you sent Jon home too early, he's sick, worse than sick I don't know what it is but you have to help him—"

"Shhhh." Odet sat down on the side of her bed and took her hand. His attitude was so comforting and fatherly that Melanie fell silent. There was such understanding in his eyes! How could that be? He didn't know anything that had happened. In fact, it was his fault for discharging Jon too early and for not listening to her warnings. The signs had been there — his hair, the ear piercings, his hand, but had Odet listened to her? No. And now this. He was looking down at her with infuriating calm, as if she were a little girl who insisted she'd seen the Boogeyman.

"Miss Forrester. Melanie." Odet radiated sympathetic TV-drama-doctor vibes. "I have to insist this time that you see a counselor."

A dozen questions went spinning through her mind. They crashed together, a mental pile-up of epic proportions. "Whhhu...?"

"I know what you're going through, believe me, I do. I lost my wife five years ago. I thought my life was over. But after awhile, with help, I learned how to pick up the pieces. You're not doing that, Melanie. You're refusing to face the truth. I don't want to see you in here again like this. You need help. If not for you, for the little one." He placed his hand lightly on her abdomen.

Melanie's tongue lay like a lead brick in her mouth.

Odet took a business card out of his shirt pocket and held it out. "Doctor Kim Chan is an excellent psychiatrist. I'm not going to let you dodge this time, Melanie. I'm going to schedule you an appointment with her for tomorrow morning."

Melanie started to shiver.

Odet pulled the covers up to her chin. "You rest here for awhile. Later I'll have someone take you to a room. I want you to stay overnight. Dr. Chan will come here to see you tomorrow." He stood up. "It will get better, I promise," he told her, and he meant it. His words rang true. He really did understand something — just the wrong something.

She lay in bed for what could have been five minutes or five hours. Woozy images, half-formed thoughts, a sensation of utter madness — they swished around in her head without ever really touching her. *God bless modern chemistry*, she thought. At least, she *thought* she thought it. Hard to be sure. Had she dozed? Maybe. Now a nurse was helping her into a wheelchair. "Here you go, Miss Forrester," he said with professional cheer. "Let's take you to a real bed and let you get some real sleep."

Out of ER, into the elevator, up to the third floor, down a sterile corridor, into a sterile room. The sedative was working, all right. She could barely get into the bed. She snickered aloud because she had never experienced such a silly loss of coordination before. Her hands and feet were behaving like Jon's cats, doing the opposite of whatever they were told. Jon had always thought that was funny. "Cats is cats," was how he explained it. *Feets is feets*, she thought dizzily, and flopped down on the thin hospital pillows.

CHAPTER 27

Log, *Jolly Roger*, two days after failure to find Beggar's
Port. Returning to Pan's land, course SWbS. I pray to
God the island hasn't moved — will find out in three
more days or so. Wind NNW, cold. Seas moderate,
some high swells. Sky overcast, rain on its way. Crew
tense and unhappy on account of not finding the Port,
though I still remember time spent there — I dare not
say a word. Stranger still is the fact that the four
recruits from the Port believe they have always been
members of my crew. The rest of the crew share this
delusion. The two drunks disappeared, I think literally,
from the brig. I never learned their names. Mason and
Foggerty, who brought them to me in the first place,
do not remember ever doing so. Official entry of the
new men: Tom Farrow, Patrick O'Hea, Ahmet ha-
Sareef, Benjamin Powderham.

The *Jolly Roger* sailed gracefully through the choppy sea while
Stuart carefully monitored her progress, keeping detailed notes in his
log. It was his job to navigate the ship back to Pan's island, and the
whispers of Hook's dark voice in his head were teaching him how to
do it even as he did it.

He had found a sea chest where he swore one had not been before
and upon opening it had discovered dozens of hand-drawn maps and

charts of the Neverland. The moment he picked up the first one, he was given memories of its creation: how he had sent Cecco and a crew out in a skiff to make the initial survey of the coastline; how he had afterwards sailed the *Jolly Roger* herself around the island, using and refining Cecco's drawings; how he had been surprised to discover that the island wasn't all that big and yet it was so crammed with places, so many potential adventures that seemed to stand side-by-side like passengers on a crowded bus. Certain landmarks had radiated a palpable boisterous energy, like a child's excitement about the coming of Christmas Day.

So I drew all of these, Stuart had thought as he examined the final charts. They were neat and detailed pen drawings on stiff parchment paper. The lines had been laid with precision while the writing was embellished with little flourishes that were and were not his style — one more conundrum to toss onto the ever-growing pile.

Stuart thought it strange that he apparently hadn't yet surveyed the interior of the island. Only three features were marked: the volcano (not real difficult to figure that one out); the general spot where the Indians camped (plotted, no doubt, by watching smoke rise from their campfires); and a freshwater pool with a waterfall labeled Fairy Fall (*Where we get fresh water when our stores get low*, he thought, automatically knowing that it was the only freshwater source near enough to Pirate's Bay that his men could reach it with a decent chance of avoiding Lost Boy and Indian patrols).

There were other maps in the sea chest drawn by him, three detailing Beggar's Island and the location of the Port — or rather, where it had been. The rest of the maps detailed other islands. Stuart ruminated over them until the obvious dawned on him: the Neverland wasn't one island, it was an archipelago. Pan's island, or "Pan's land" as the pirates called it, was simply the largest, with Beggar's Island coming in second. Stuart had, his notes claimed, set foot on most of the others, though quite a few were inconsequentially small and one of them was just a low, flat, desolate oblong of sand hardly a thousand feet square that the pirates had immediately dubbed "Liverpool."

Thanks to the maps and his new knowledge, Stuart felt sure he could bring the *Jolly Roger* back to Pirate's Bay. The problem was the

weather. Heavy clouds obscured the sky and had since leaving
Beggar's Port. Stuart was granted no glimpse at all of the stars and,
under Hook's flash-fast tutelage, had only one brief opportunity to
shoot sun sights with the sextant. *Just my luck I'm in a world with two
bloody suns,* he had thought at the time, wondering if that meant
Hook's sextant was different than those used by seamen in the real
world. It had to be, didn't it? He'd made a promise to himself to learn
how to use a real sextant. *WHEN I get home,* he routinely repeated to
himself. *WHEN I get home.*

He was forced to spend a good deal of his time falling back on the
least appetizing form of navigation: dead reckoning. This involved
making regular notes on the set of the sea — the effect of the current
and wind on the ship's heading — taking into account the abilities of
the helmsmen as each took his trick at the wheel, for some men more
than others possessed the skill to keep the frigate on course according
to the compass. Men regularly streamed the taffrail log to let Stuart
know how far they had traveled in any given amount of time, and they
heaved the lead line to sound the depths, making as sure as possible
that the ship avoided shoals that could spell disaster. All these bits of
information had to be continuously weighed and calculated, giving
Stuart an ongoing approximation of where the ship actually was and
where she was actually pointed. He could then adjust her course and
pray to God he was right. At times he felt like he was playing a deadly
game of pin-the-course-on-the-sailboat.

Despite his anxiety over what the future held, and despite the fact
that his ship was basically running blind, Stuart began to like sailing.
The feel of the frigate as she plowed through the waves sent a thrill of
pride through his body the likes of which he had never experienced
before. And the freedom! Yes, he was trapped here — for the time
being — but the seemingly infinite sea gave him a sense of freedom
that pacified his anxieties. He had never much thought about sailors
or the rugged lives they had led in the heyday of tall ships. Now he
was their unexpected kin, a seaman by crazy circumstance, a bloody
captain, no less.

Not every day was tolerable, though. Ever since they had put to
sea, Hook's dark voice murmured continually in the back of his brain,
a ghostly drone that helped him run the ship, true enough. But at

other times it tried to dominate him, to twist his behavior to violence at the slightest provocation. The boogey was crawling up out of the basement, and it wanted to play in earnest now. The knowledge of it sickened Stuart, this sentient disease that was slowly infecting him, eager to fill him up with the black decay of itself.

And, God help him, it was arousing as well, like a powerful orgasm that was only a stroke away. Over the first two days of their return trip, Stuart gave in to it too many times. The blackness was ecstasy, fulfillment, a hideous joy. Each time it took him, he clawed his way back to himself, embarrassed and disappointed and at the same time immediately hungering for that sordid power again. It invigorated him, filling a void he had never known was there. Maybe that was how women felt while making love, while they were being filled up emotionally as well as physically. All Stuart knew was that he wanted more, and he hated himself for wanting it. He was afraid at how *much* he wanted it.

Sometimes the voice tricked him and withdrew altogether. At those times Stuart, unbalanced by the unexpected emptiness inside, would think he was free. He would dare to relax. He would heave a sigh of relief. And the black hand would sink its claws in all the way, giving up its dance of enticement and taking him by force, leaving him no corner in which to hide. If Stuart thought the Neverland was Hell, there was no term to describe these moments.

Hook's outward confidence and his authority over his men was one thing. Stuart reveled in it and, when things went his way, smiled more often than not. But inside? Inside was something else again. Even as he conducted the duties of a captain, Stuart would sink into melancholy reveries, pining for both Melanie and Elsbeth until he worried that his heart would burst. Most of all, he fumed over the injustice, the plain *spitefulness*, of Peter Pan.

The boy had taken his hand. Bad enough. But to throw it to a crocodile as big as a barge? The life of a pirate was fraught enough with dangers. This constant fear of hearing that ominous *tick tick tick* was too much to bear. While berthed in Pirate's Bay, i.e. ninety-five percent of the time, Stuart was effectively trapped on his own ship. He didn't dare swim in the ocean, let alone bathe in any pools on the island. He couldn't step on shore without expecting that monstrosity to come charging at him from out of nowhere. It was no ordinary beast. It could do things normal crocs could not do. It was *intelligent*. It didn't just want to eat him, it wanted to scare him to death first. And it always seemed to know where he was.

Plagued by this dire knowledge, Stuart would plunge through the hours, his actions thinly disguising the truth of his inner turmoil. Sometimes he would stare at his hook and just *hate*. No coherent thoughts, no actions, just the roaring furnace of his hatred transfixing him in a foul meditation. Woe be to the man who interrupted him during these black spells. While locked in thrall of the horror that his life had become, Stuart more and more used his hook first and considered the damage later.

During one such instance at the beginning of the afternoon watch on the third day out, Stuart paced his cabin, brooding. He had paced the length of the ship for nearly an hour, back and forth, back and forth. Randomly he had lashed out with his hook, goring a rail or a mast or a man in passing, oblivious as to which was which or why he was doing it. When he had finally raised his head above his personal storm cloud, he had found the crew tense and fearful.

They need to let off some steam, sing, dance, gamble, have at each other a bit, he had thought, totally unaware of the injuries he had caused. Under the impression that he was doing his men a benevolent favor, he relocated to the relative isolation of the poop deck to continue pacing. An hour after that he retreated to his cabin.

If someone had asked him what he was thinking so hard about, he couldn't have answered. His mind was spinning aimlessly like a pinwheel in a gale, tearing round and round and going nowhere. Smee came in to announce that he was going off watch and is there anything I can do afore I take my nap sar?

That's when the aimless spinning stopped. A ray of bright purpose broke through the murk. Why hadn't he thought of it before? "Where are the past logs?" he asked the bosun.

"Past logs, sar?" Smee said vacantly.

Stuart rapped his knuckles on his own log book lying on the writing table. "This can't be the only one. Where are the others?"

"Others," said Smee.

Stuart raised his hook. "I'm becoming irritated, Mister Smee."

"Oh, *those* logs." Smee pawed the air in a gee-how-silly-of-me gesture. "I dunno, sar."

Stuart found that hard to believe and said as much.

Smee eyed the hook and gulped. "Sar, yer the only one who knows where they are. That's how it should be." He paused. "Err... will there be anythin' else?"

"No," said Stuart, stymied.

"Aye, Cap'n."

After the bosun was gone, Stuart addressed the fiend within him. "All right, you bastard, where are they? You tell me everything else. Where are the logs?"

Are you sure you want to know?

"Don't dick with me, just show me!"

Show him, it did. A mental picture smashed into his consciousness as fast and hard as a pitcher's fast ball through a plate glass window. Stuart grabbed his head in agony and fainted dead away.

He lay unconscious for several minutes, splayed on the burgundy carpet in a swirl of frills and curls. When he came to, his first thought was that he'd drunk too much because the cabin was spinning and he thought he might vomit. He closed his eyes tight, willing the deck to pick a spot and stick with it.

A horse in mid-rear, nostrils flaring, mane flying, front hooves pawing the air. Something weird about it, an unnatural shiny quality...

The vision faded.

Stuart dragged himself to his feet. Someone was knocking at the door. Not Smee's hesitant tap-tapping. This was the first mate's loud rap.

At first Stuart couldn't respond. He sent air through his vocal chords, but only a pathetic wheeze came out. He saw a goblet on the table — had it been there before? — and sipped some of the brandy it contained. Better. "What is it, Mister Cecco?" he asked, trying to sound like he cared.

"Captain, a lad just landed on deck."

Stuart had to process that bizarre statement. *Landed.* Absurd, absolutely, but not where the Lost Boys were concerned. He fully intended to say, "Later, I'm busy," but the words that came out were, "Bring him in!"

Cecco entered, pushing a small boy ahead of him. "He came alone, sir. Banished, he says."

A fact brushed lightly across Stuart's mind: many of Hook's crew had once been Lost Boys. For various reasons they had been banished by Pan, who did not tolerate insubordination in the slightest. Hook always took them on, whether they wanted to turn pirate or not. They had little alternative. Once inducted into the crew, the boys would start to grow up, unlike the ageless mates they had left behind. The ones that didn't work out, well... Hook dealt with them.

This boy didn't look all that much different than poor Li'l Lad Jack. Same approximate age, about eight, and the same build, skinny but strong. Jack, though, had had brown hair while this boy was a beach blond. "Your name?" Stuart asked him.

"I'm Billy, Captain Hook sir," the boy said. He stuck out his bare chest like a feisty bantam cock. "I want to be a pirate!"

Stuart smiled, but it felt off, not his own smile at all. Try as he might to change it, his lips held the wry alien smirk. "Is that so?" he heard himself drawl in an oily tone that wasn't his. The words bore the hint of a cultured London accent. "What brings you from Pan's merry little band to mine?"

"I don't like him," Billy answered with such blunt honesty that Cecco snorted. Billy heard it and explained, "He always has to be in charge of everything. He always bosses us around."

"How dreadfully unfair," Stuart said, dripping sympathy. He lifted the boy's chin with his hook. "Tell me, young Billy. What makes you think you'll like taking my orders any more than Pan's, hm?"

Billy was brave, but the touch of the hook gave him the shakes.

"Your hesitation speaks volumes, lad, and none of it good."

"Y-you're a captain," Billy said quickly. "You're supposed to give orders. That's how it works."

"Aye, that is indeed how it works," Stuart agreed sagely. "An acceptable answer after all." He turned to Cecco. "Assign him a berth in the fo'c'sul. Let us keep young Billy for a few days and see what we see." If the boy could survive close quarters with the pack of troglodytes below, he would prove himself worthy of training. After that it would be a matter of how hard the ratty little mutt was willing to work. If he was the lazy type, well...

"I'm ready for anything," Billy declared, trying to regain his cockiness. "I've hunted bears, and I've been to a powwow with the Indians, and I know how to fight with a cutlass."

"My my, that is impressive." Stuart ruffled the boy's hair, all the while masking his loathing of him, of all children, with that smirk that wanted so much to be a sneer. "I daresay you've swashed a few buckles with my men, too, haven't you, Billy? Maybe sent some brave souls to Davy Jones' Locker with that mighty cutlass of yours?"

Stuart might as well have slapped him. Billy chanced a glance at the door as if calculating whether he could make it out alive or not.

Stuart laughed. "At ease, boy. I won't hold the past against you. But know that I will be watching you. Closely."

Billy nodded, his face several shades paler than it had been. "Aye aye, Captain."

"Yes, right, off with you now." Stuart shooed him out the door. "Ya little shit," he added after Cecco and the boy were gone.

The black fingers released him.

Stuart slumped, burning with embarrassment even as he fought back a grin of wicked delight. There was no denying it — scaring the pants out of that snot-nosed whelp had been awfully fun. He wanted to do it again, maybe cut the kid a little to show him who was boss.

See how easy it is? came the dark thought. *It all comes quite naturally, doesn't it?*

"Shut up!" Stuart unscrewed his hook, moving with measured, determined calm, still fighting back that hateful grin. "I will beat you," he muttered to the darkness. "I will beat you and your master. Fuck you both," and he threw the hook across the cabin. It rebounded off a bookshelf and landed at his feet. He kicked it. It stuck on the frilled edge of the burgundy rug a mere foot away. "I will not pick it up!" he snarled, and waited.

He was expecting the black fingers to squeeze and *make* him pick up the hook. They knew how to break him: by conjuring pain so bad he would do anything to make it stop, by chiseling away another chunk of his willpower, by cranking his self-loathing up another grisly notch. But nothing happened. He was truly alone, just him, Jonathan Stuart and the pitiful tatters of his conscience.

He didn't trust the wonderful silence. He knew that the second he allowed any relief to show, those fingers would pop back into existence and dig into him like razors into raw beef. The worst part would be that he would let them do it.

He spiraled back to his childhood, his real childhood, back to when the Giant Dreams had jerked him awake, screaming. First his father's hard hand, then his mother's frail attempts to calm him. She never had the ability to do it. She was more afraid than her little son. She would always resort to brandy, making him take a good swallow and often taking a swig or two herself.

Stuart picked up his goblet and gulped a mouthful. It hurt, that much of it stinging down his gullet at once, but he was getting used to it as he had been used to it a year before. Yes, it hurt. And hurting like this felt good. *I will beat you,* he thought with a shudder. *I. Will. Beat. You..*

Serene silence.

He sat down and closed his eyes. He brought the image of the rearing horse to the forefront and pondered it.

CHAPTER 28

His cunning counterpart was toying with him. The horse wasn't a real horse at all but a bronze statue. It was right in his own damned cabin on a display pedestal to the left of the door. Had it been there all along? *Does it matter?* he thought.

He was startled by the sharp pang of regret the statue evoked when he first laid eyes on the thing. A rush of parallel memories of a childhood in England explained it: *my love of horses, those strong and noble creatures; my very first riding lesson at the age of four; many happy hours working in the stables. I studied hard in school so that I could have time to ride every day, and I became an excellent horseman before I was ten years old. All too soon came my graduation from the historic and prestigious Eton College. I had done everything expected of me, learned the proper behavior of a gentleman of status, filled my brain with fine literature and poetry, the great philosophies and religions, the histories of the world. And for that my life was stolen. My father wanted rid of me and so bought an officer's commission for me aboard the HMS Lionheart. I spent years hating my fate, struggling to learn the basics of seamanship just to survive as the navy's oldest damned midshipman. How ironic – I've grown to love the sea more than my precious horses, but the King's navy? Never. I jumped ship and signed on with Ed Teach, the great pirate Blackbeard, when I was twenty-two years old. I wonder what Daddy dear would think if he learned that his ungracious efforts spurred his son to become the notorious Captain Hook?*

Something inside Stuart laughed loud and long.

His hunt for his predecessors' log books took a pause as he digested this precarious biography. He had no concrete details about his family — who they were or how they lived. But he had a distinct impression of wealth and status coupled with an overwhelming suspicion that he had never gotten along with his parents. *Big duh*, he thought with bitter amusement, not at all surprised that he had been willing to leave mum and dad behind forever once the buccaneer bug bit.

Stuart came back to himself. "Damn all, belay this nonsense!" he shouted. These weren't his memories. This wasn't his past. Grumbling, his splashed water on his face from the basin and went back to the bronze horse, focusing once more on his own concerns. He wanted the past logs of his ship. This horse was the key.

It certainly wasn't big enough to have anything inside it. Could a key be hidden in there? He tapped the horse's belly with his hook. No way to tell. He couldn't detect any seam in the statue that might suggest a hidden panel or compartment.

The horse's flailing hooves seemed to be pointing at the harpsichord. Stuart spent ten minutes going over the instrument, running his hand along the bottom of it, checking the padded bench and keyboard, propping up the lid and carefully examining inside. He concluded that it was nothing but a harpsichord.

He turned back to the statue. It had to be the statue itself, standing on its pedestal as if on a stage, waiting for him to puzzle out its frozen performance. *It's not the horse,* he suddenly realized. *It's the pedestal!*

Stuart knelt down to examine it. It was made of wood but was fashioned to look like a Roman column, with a black box-shaped base about sixteen inches square, a gold-plated plinth, a black column with alternating gold-plated fluting, and a square display top where the bronze horse reared in eternal majesty.

Stuart knocked on the base with his hook. *Tunk tunk!* Not the deep thud he would expect from solid wood. "Ha!"

Humming along with the halyard shanty *Where Am I To Go, Me Johnnies?* being sung by MacDougal on deck — Cecco had ordered the yards hauled round so the sails could catch the shifting wind — Stuart analyzed the pedestal inch by inch until he finally figured out how to open it. In one corner of the base was a crack, as if the wood had been dinged. A clever deception. The narrow tip of Stuart's hook fit into that slice exactly at a certain angle. When he pressed hard with it, it tripped a locking device inside.

There were no hinges to give the hiding place away. Stuart heard a click, and then one side of the base tilted a little, letting him take hold of the top edges. The whole side pulled away to reveal a hollow space. Stuart peeked inside and saw a box.

He took it out and opened it. The interior was lead lined to prevent water damage to the contents. The contents were neatly wrapped in oilcloth. Stuart took the bundle to the rosewood table, sat down and unwrapped it. Inside lay four books, all very old. Underneath the books, two thick folded parchments.

He decided to begin with the parchments. He gently unfolded the first, feeling like he was peeling back the dry taught skin of a corpse. A brief recollection of helping Blackbeard loot the grave of an old "friend" rudely reminded his fingertips of the real thing. *By thunder, what a day that was,* he thought absently. He got up to get two more candles from the writing desk. He brought them back to the table and lit them. *All right, let us see what marvels we have here.*

Before him lay a hand-drawn map, about two feet by two feet square, of an island. Stuart unfolded the second parchment to discover that it, too, was a map of an island. He presumed it was a different island — it certainly looked different — until he noticed the names of the landmarks along the coastline: Pirate's Bay, Mermaid Lagoon, Marooners' Rock, Moaning Cove. Those places appeared on both maps.

Heart thumping, Stuart fetched his own map of Pan's island. There they were — Pirate's Bay, Mermaid Lagoon, Marooners' Rock, Moaning Cove — but in different places on yet a different island. *Three maps of Pan's island, sharing landmarks but with different geographies. The same but not the same.*

Stuart flipped through the log books, checking the dates on each first page. The most recent one began on March 12, 1896. The next began on September 30, 1826. The next began on May 4, 1784. The oldest log began with the date October 22, 1737. All contained different handwriting. All claimed to have been penned by a pirate named Captain Jas. Hook.

He suddenly recognized the most recent volume. He had once seen a similar bundle of yellowed papers between cracked leather covers. The crudely scratched "JH" in the corner... it was the same as that on the mysterious book he had taken out of his grandfather Emmerich's safe in San Francisco what seemed a million years ago. He flipped through it. The handwriting, from what he could remember, was the same. The format and presentation of the information was the same, the *feel* of the thing was the same. This was the personal log of his great-grandfather James when he had captained the *Jolly Roger*. He must have recreated the cover when he later wrote his mad memoirs back in the real world.

"He didn't die here!" Stuart murmured. Why had it never occurred to him before? If James had been the previous Hook, how was it that he had written and left behind memoirs in the real world? *Because Pan let him go!* Was that possible? Did Pan release his players at the end of each game? *Might I be released as well?*

"Screw that!" Stuart tossed the log on the table. "I'm not going to wait, nor am I going to play any goddamn game!" He gulped a mouthful of brandy from the goblet and almost choked on it. "What!" he wheezed at the empty cabin. "I should let my brain get turned into oatmeal here, then go home and spend my retirement years sucking mush through a straw in a padded cell? Screw that, Pan! I'm not playing!"

Stop shaking, came the dark thought. *Calm yourself. And stop drinking so much.*

"Oh, go to hell!" Stuart yelled. But then he paused. For once the damned voice was right. His consumption of liquor was way out of bounds, even for him. Truth be told, he was tired of feeling sick all the time. Brandy was great to a degree, but he had tossed more cookies in the last two days than he had in the last two years. His innards were sore from heaving, and his chest burned inside as if his stomach were filled with live coals.

He opened his cabin door and tossed the rest of the brandy out of his goblet, ignoring the fact that he was throwing it right into Smee's face. The poor bosun had been about to knock on the door, probably to ask him some stupid question or another. Now the pathetic man was howling and clawing at his eyes. Stuart closed the door on him, not interested in anything but his own musings.

He composed himself and sat back down. What he needed to do was methodically study the logs and glean any useful information. With that as his goal, he flipped once more through the books, giving himself an overview.

That brought him to a dead halt. All the logs were written by Hook, right? All bore that name and no other. Stuart already knew that his great-grandfather had penned the most recent, but what of the others? He had no way of knowing the true identities of Hooks One, Two and Three.

He fingered the books, wondering. In Barrie's novel, Hook believed himself related to the long line of "ill-fated Stuarts." Were the logs here the product of his own ancestors, each one a victim of Pan's machinations? Was his branch of the family truly ill-fated, cursed in more ways than history knew? Was he simply the latest of a long line of Stuart men abducted to this hellhole, plucked from reality and tricked here to entertain a...

...a what? Not a boy, certainly. A demon? A god? *Could it be that we're being bred by Pan for this fate?* The idea frightened him so badly that he collapsed forward onto the table, hiding his face in his arms until the rush passed. *No,* he told himself afterwards. *I will not be a plaything, even for a... even for a god. I'm getting out of here before I forget the truth.*

The four Hooks before him had vowed the same thing. As Stuart flipped through their logs, he found an entry for each in which the abducted men vowed to escape Pan's clutches. There came a point at which each realized that he was part of some kind of game, and that the game was controlled by a boy — creature, fiend, devil, monster, many terms were used — who called himself Peter Pan. Each man feared that he was doomed, but each battled bravely to remain intact. Each, Stuart deduced by the writings, had eventually lost his mind.

The first Hook — October 22, 1737 — had somehow discovered the truth of his predicament early on. "Commanded mate to take cutter, coast the island, compile charts," he had written in his third entry. "Am of conviction that we are ensnared in a trap most fiendish.

I swear unto the Almighty, I shall pursue freedom or perish in the attempt." Whether he'd ever had a chance to take the survey information and draw detailed maps remained unknown. Stuart had no such materials from him.

The second Hook — Mister May 4, 1784 — had gone nuts early in his captivity. He had written very little, compared to the other Hooks, and the penmanship was sloppy enough that Stuart could make out very little of it. One page was filled with a single word, "home," written over and over again, too much ink in some places turning the word into a black blob, too little ink in other places leaving a phantasm of penmanship, dry impressions of a tortured soul's one desire.

The very last entry, however, was written as if by another man, so precise was the penmanship, so plain the message that Stuart's flesh crawled as he read: "Almighty God, save my soul." Five pages of drawings followed, very child-like drawings of people and houses and trees and a smiling sun and slavering nightmarish creatures. Anguish pulled at Stuart's heart. He could hardly make himself look at them. This poor man had lost his mind and, apparently in his impotence, had reverted to a child himself. If the low number of entries was any clue, he had met his fate with the croc — or however it happened — early on.

Hook September 30, 1826, must have been a soldier or a sailor before his abduction. He wrote with eloquent fire, never letting up, vowing to kill Pan and destroy the Neverland itself. He was the one who had drawn the first large map. According to his log, he had captured a Lost Boy and tortured him to get information about the island, the Indians and Pan. He had charted the island's shores, then mapped the interior over the course of several long and dangerous expeditions. His map was both clear and detailed and included precise nautical information such as contour lines marking sea depths, the locations and depths of shoals and atolls, the location of dangerous rocks, wave and wind patterns, and areas for good anchorage.

It bore no resemblance to the map drawn by James Stuart, Hook March 12, 1896, who had also sailed the perimeter of the island and led several survey expeditions ashore. He had drawn the second map.

Stuart dropped his forehead on the table with a painful thud. *The Neverland changes each time. I've got all this information from the past, and none of it means a damn. Pan must plan it that way. Each Hook has to exist on his own, a fresh new adversary for the little bastard to play with. And by the time we recognize the truth, we're too far gone to act on it.* Bloody brilliant, as Smee would say.

Something else occurred to him. None of the Hooks had known that the previous Hooks had existed. He was the first one to know! Was it that the other Hooks never thought to look at past log books? Or were the log books kept elsewhere and, for some reason, only he now was being given the opportunity to see them? Maybe this was a new twist to the game. "Let him discover his forebears," Pan might have decided. "Let him know the truth, and let us see what he does with it." Perhaps this was designed to create a new wrinkle in an old cloth, a vital challenge for the new Hook and, therefore, a brand new twist in the game for Pan.

So many questions, so many possibilities. No answers. Only speculations.

Stuart picked up his great-grandfather's log again. He opened to a random page and read:

> Snowfall at Christmas. Mother's hands. Children in
> the park. Little Emmerich. Riding the grey at sunrise.
> Waltzing with Anna. O, my Anna, how she floated
> across the ballroom, never touching the floor! I pray
> she still wears the pearl necklace and earrings I gave
> her on our third wedding anniversary so long ago.
> Three strings of pearls, one for each year of bliss. That
> is how I shall remember her, dressed in blue satin and
> pearls, smiling and merry as the day we met. I wonder
> what my poor Anna is doing today.

Stuart's eyes stung. *I will not cry,* he told himself angrily.

One tear did not listen to him. It coursed down his cheek, defiant and full of misery. It slid the length of his face and dropped onto his hand.

Stuart imagined his great-grandfather sitting in this very chair, penning the words he had just read nearly a hundred years before. He could almost feel the man's heartache like a lingering ghost. *I miss someone, too, Great-Grandfather. I miss her very much. And I also wonder what she's doing today.*

Many tears streamed down his face. He shut his eyes, trying to will them away. That released an overflow that spilled down onto the open log book.

With a savage grunt, Stuart knocked the book out of the line of fire with his hook and swiped at the tears with the back of his hand. "No weakness!" he growled, and reached inside to shove it down, down, down, back into the dirty depths where it belonged. He had no time for weakness. There was work to do, and not much time in which to do it.

CHAPTER 29

"Melly?"

She heard her name through a big pink wad of fluff floating between her eyes. Sleepy. Still a little drugged, then. Confused. Her dreams had been mushy and frightening. Still, Melanie recognized that voice. Before she could clearly see the young woman, she knew it was Yolanda. She thought she said, "What are you doing here?" quite clearly, but what came out was, "Wyu doohrr?"

Yolanda sat down on the chair by the bed. "Dr. Odet phoned me this morning and asked if I could come down. *Déjà vu*, huh?" She laughed nervously. "How are you doing?"

Melanie honestly didn't know. She tried to sit up in bed, failed badly and opted to let Yolanda arrange her pillows so she could slouch up with some little dignity. Whatever sedatives they had given her had left her as limp and floppy as a stalk of old celery, but at least the ball of fear in her chest was gone. *Don't be naïve, it's there. The drugs built a nice comfy wall around it to insulate you, that's all. But it's there, all right.* She put her hand on her chest. *Damn.*

Yolanda took a chocolate candy bar out of her coat pocket and tucked it into Melanie's black long-strapped purse on the bedside table. "I know what medicine you really need, huh?" She smiled. It was forced.

Melanie tried to smile back. There was something she wanted to ask Yolanda, but she couldn't for the life of her recall what it was. "Thanks."

"*Mira*, I'm supposed to remind you that Dr. Chan will be here in about an hour to see you." Yolanda's cheeks reddened. "I'm so sorry it's come to this, but I think it's what you need. Don't you?"

Melanie's head was beginning to clear. She started to say, "You idiot, it's not me, it's Jon—"

That was it! That's what she wanted to ask! Yolanda had seen the changes that morning at the hospital, his hair, his ears, his hand! Why wasn't she saying anything about it? Why was she acting so damned reserved?

No, Mel, keep your mouth shut.

She obeyed the inner impulse. Good thing. Yolanda was leaning towards her and watching her closely, as if trying to read the fine print of Melanie's thoughts.

How can I explain to her what I saw? I'm already about to see a shrink. If I claim that Jon fell through a hole in reality, they'll fit me for a nice long-sleeved jacket with buckles on the back. "What did I do last night?" It seemed a reasonable thing to ask, and she really wanted to know. What did they think happened versus what she remembered?

Yolanda bowed her head. "You lost it again."

"Again?"

Yolanda looked up, her pretty features drawn. "You don't remember last week?"

"I barely remember last night."

Yolanda shook her head. "You know, Jon would have wanted you to be strong. You've always been strong. He really loved that about you. I've been thinking about why this is happening, and I'm wondering if maybe it's his house. Maybe you shouldn't, you know... live there."

A bullet of cold terror shot through Melanie's heart. If not for the sedatives in her system, she might have gone into hysterics. *Past tense!* her brain clanged like a warning bell. *Past tense! She's using the past tense! Dr. Odet did the same thing!* "I don't get it," she said, refusing to see her terror for what it was.

Yolanda answered with more exasperation than worry. "Are you kidding me? You live in his house, you sleep in his bed, you drive his car, you run his bookstore — you're keeping yourself so close to him that you'll never be able to let him go. I mean, you haven't taken his clothes out of the closets yet. You kept his furniture and put your own in storage. You eat lunch at the Rose City Café just like he did." She picked up something small from the bedside table. It was an earring, a skull-and-crossbones design, silver and very well crafted. "*¡Dios mio,* you even wear his earring!" For a moment Yolanda looked as if she wanted to throw the little piece of jewelry across the room. But she gently set it back down and pinched the bridge of her nose. It made her look like a worried mother more than a worried college kid. "I liked him, too, y'know, despite things," she said heavily. "But he's gone. You have to come to grips with it."

The horrible subconscious secret jumped out of its box. It stared Melanie in the eyes, daring her to contradict the agonizing truth of it: Jon was dead. *He isn't, he's alive, he's NOT DEAD!* She wanted to scream it at the top of her lungs, but the sedatives stamped the urge down, allowing her a single awkward hiccup of grief, not quite a sob. It was more like a low moan that never fully formed.

Yolanda squeezed her hand. "I can't imagine what you're going through. I mean, I've had boyfriends but never anybody I'd call a soul mate. Still... I think you're letting your grief totally overwhelm you. Maybe it's not my place to say that, but we've become pretty good friends, haven't we? You'll let me tell you the hard truth if it might... save your sanity? The hard truth is that Jon didn't will you everything so that you would drown in his memory. He loved you, that's all."

Too many emotions. They raged around in her head until she had to shut her eyes, grasping Yolanda's hand to make sure she didn't blow away in the maelstrom. Jon had willed his possessions, his house, his business to her? That would mean that time had passed, a lot of time. Yolanda claimed she had wigged out once before. Odet implied she was pregnant. She was supposedly living Jon's routine as if it were her own. Could it be possible? *Have I somehow skipped through time?* "How long has it been?" she asked.

Yolanda sighed. "Why don't you rest until Dr. Chan gets here? I need to get to the store. Alan can't run it himself even if he thinks he can." She got up.

"Alan quit!" Melanie said desperately. "I remember that! Don't you dare tell me he didn't!"

Yolanda winced. "I'll check back with you after your appointment." She headed for the door.

"Wait!"

Yolanda turned halfway around, eyes searching the floor.

"Okay, maybe I sound nutso." Melanie laughed uneasily. "Maybe I *am* nutso, but I'm trying. Help me. Please, tell me... what color was Jon's hair?"

Yolanda kept her expression neutral, though Melanie saw the effort it took. The muscles of the young woman's neck stood out. "His *hair?*"

"Yeah. Please? Just answer. Don't worry why I want to know."

Yolanda opened Melanie's little black purse and took out a stiff laminated card. She mutely held it out.

It was a photo of Jon. Melanie suspected that if she asked, Yolanda would tell her that she, Melanie, had laminated it herself after Jon had died and had been carrying it around ever since. The photo showed him from the waist up. His white shirt was unbuttoned halfway, and he was flashing one of those rare brilliant smiles that always made Melanie's pulse race. Long black hair, loose and curly, fell over his shoulders, slanted by a stiff breeze. From his left ear hung the silver skull-and-crossbones earring. Looking at the photo, one thought dominated Melanie's mind: *He looks like a goddamn pirate.* It took willpower to tear her eyes away. "His hand," she said. "His right hand..."

"Oh, not that again—"

"Yes, that again. Please."

Yolanda shook her head. A tear formed in one eye and trailed down her cheek. Her mouth worked soundlessly.

"I'm sorry, Yolanda." Melanie truly was sorry, but what else could she do? "I don't want to upset you, but I need to know."

"I know, *querida.*" The muscles of Yolanda's neck softened. Her shoulders slumped. "What am I supposed to do? You don't remember anything! It's like this whole last month just," and she snapped her fingers. "Bottom line — you're scaring me, Melanie. I want you to get better—"

"And I will," Melanie said firmly. *A month? A fucking month has gone by?* "I will get better. I guess I'm weaker than anybody thought, huh? That's no crime, is it? So help me. Remind me how it happened."

It took Yolanda a moment to speak. "Years ago, before you guys met. He said he had an accident during fencing practice. He wouldn't give any details, not even to you." She turned again to go.

"One last question!" Melanie knew she was pushing, but she had to. "How did he die?"

Yolanda gave a small cry and slipped out the door.

* * * * *

The interview with Dr. Kim Chan was an awkward and laborious process. Chan was good at her job, though. Melanie liked her and appreciated her efforts. But no matter what Dr. Chan asked, Melanie increasingly resorted to silence instead of answers because she didn't have any answers to give. By the time the first fifteen minutes ticked away, she was a mental wreck. She knew Jon wasn't dead, she knew it, yet all this talk of him in the past tense created a pit of grief in her guts that became real enough to set her crying. And the letter didn't help.

Chan had come prepared. If her patient wanted to deny reality, she would have to do so while holding a copy of Jon's death certificate and his will, a two-page letter that he had written supposedly six months earlier — a letter that Melanie had supposedly read in the office of Jon's lawyer after Jon had supposedly died. It was the letter more than anything else that finally tore down the wall.

> Melly:
> Well. I guess I'm dead.
> Jesus, what a thing to have to write down. It isn't
> an event I see occurring in the near future, but one
> never knows. So much of my life seems to sneak up

and hit me from behind, I guess I'm expecting my death to come the same way. You know me well enough. It would be fitting, right?

I can imagine what you're doing right now. Either you're crying your eyes out (awful for you, but I can't help hoping that you'd miss me that much, selfish bastard that I am), or you're stunned (easier on you, so I genuinely hope this is the case). Either way, I don't think you know what's coming.

In the proverbial nutshell, everything I have is yours. I think I once said that to you, and you laughed in my face. I was serious. Here's the proof. You know I have no friends. My fault, I know how I live my life. I don't apologize for it. As for my family, well, you know that rant all too well. So it's yours, kid — house, car, bookstore, savings, stocks, the whole shebang. Do with it what you want (except I'd appreciate you keeping the cats, although if you really *really* don't want to, please make sure they end up in good homes).

Let me make two things utterly clear. 1) You are not obligated to keep the house. If you want to sell it, be my guest. 2) The same goes for Excalibur Books. Damned store doesn't bring in money to equal the effort, believe me. I run it because I want it. If you don't want it, sell it, make some bucks and go on a nice vacation or something.

I guess that's it. I'm perverse enough to sit here wondering how I died, but I guess I'll find out when it happens. Hey, hold a séance if you want to talk. I'll do my best to attend. Nobody really knows where we go, right?

I'll miss you. And please believe this — my last thought will be of you. I love you, and I apologize for leaving you. Remember me, but move on and have a wonderful life. You deserve it, and it will make me happy. I really do love you more than you know.

Jon

Melanie was grief-stricken and comforted by the letter at the same time — grief-stricken because of the horror it drove home, but comforted because Jon wrote exactly the way he spoke. She could hear him say the words in her mind, his soft baritone like a warm embrace reaching up from mere ink on paper. More, she knew that he meant every word, including the idea of the séance. Jon had no particular religious convictions, as far as she knew. He had always been highly entertained by humanity's quarrelsome collection of theological ideologies. The two of them had shared many a long hour debating the possibilities of the afterlife. *If you're where I think you are, Jon, you're way past the wildest ideas of theology.*

She tried to hide her distress at how he had supposedly died. He had been admitted to the hospital the morning of November 21, the same Tuesday morning that Melanie had found him on the floor of his bedroom. He had been delirious and had slipped into a coma. He had died the evening of Friday, November 24. The reason for the coma and his resulting death could not be determined. "Natural Causes." That's what it said on his death certificate.

Trying to digest this bizarre alternate history made Melanie's choked question, "What is today's date?" sound all too convincingly wretched.

"It's December twenty-second," Dr. Chan answered gently. "Friday. Christmas is three days away." She indicated the poinsettia pin on her sweater. "This may also be why you're suffering such heartache, Melanie. Facing the holiday season after losing someone is exceptionally difficult."

It was as if Melanie had been suffering from tunnel vision — she suddenly noticed the Christmas decorations in her room. Not much, just a sprig of mistletoe bound with red ribbon over the door and one of those little Christmas trees that's actually a rosemary plant. It squatted by the window, refreshingly green in the dull white room and covered with tiny decorations shaped like bells, elves and gaily wrapped packages. A fat red bow sat on top. She sniffed — she could smell the tangy rosemary scent. She hadn't noticed it before.

"Your mother sent that," said Dr. Chan. "Your friend that was here earlier..."

"Yolanda Vargas."

"Yes. She telephoned your mother and told her where you were."

Melanie nodded. *Poor Yolanda probably did the same thing the last time I ended up here,* she thought, adding defiantly, *even though I've never been here before!*

It was clear what was happening. As insane as it sounded to her still, there really was a being called Peter Pan. He was a glorious and magical playmate for children, whom he loved deeply, but he hated adults and was clever in how he manipulated them. He had taken Jon to — she could hardly think the name without feeling stupid — the Neverland. A parallel dimension? An isolated pocket of Time and Space? As Scrooge said in Dickens' *A Christmas Carol,* perhaps just an undigested bit of beef or a fragment of underdone potato? How was she supposed to know? All that mattered was that she knew the truth, and nobody else did. Jon was alive. He had slipped away to the left of all known reality, yes, but he was alive.

"Where's his body?" she asked.

Dr. Chan replied smoothly, "He was cremated, as per his wishes. His ashes are in your possession."

Melanie cringed. "He's in the house?"

Dr. Chan nodded. "Where did you put the urn? Relax and try to remember."

How the hell do I know? Melanie thought, and then a picture formed in her mind: a silver urn with a crossed-sword motif on the front. It was sitting on a shelf in Jon's living room all by itself, nothing else there except two white candles, one on each side. "Living room," she muttered. She watched a memory of herself placing the candles there and lighting them every evening at sunset. It was like watching a home movie that she had never made. *Those aren't his ashes! He's not dead, they're not his ashes!*

Dr. Chan was pleased. "See? When you relax, it comes back to you. I think you're going to be fine, Melanie. Time. That's all it takes." She stood up, her shiny blue pumps clacking on the tile floor. Melanie hated noisy shoes. *So did... does Jon,* she thought. *He calls women with clackity shoes Clydesdales.*

Clackity Clydesdale Dr. Chan collected her purse, her files, her coat and her scarf. She stood before Melanie's bed with her arms full and her face glowing with maternal sincerity. "You can go home tonight, but I don't want you to be alone. Do you have a family member or friend who can stay with you for awhile?"

Melanie shook her head. Her mother had moved back to Milwaukee four years ago, after her father had died of a heart attack. She had no siblings. Much to her chagrin, she had no real friends either. She had many acquaintances and a lot of business associates, but true-blue friends? Jon had been her best friend. *I always ragged him about being a recluse, and look at me.*

Yolanda was the logical choice, but Melanie would not impose on the young woman's generosity anymore. Yolanda had done too much already.

Dr. Chan must have sensed her patient's conflict because she said, "It's only a suggestion. If you want to be alone, then leave the lights in the house on all night. Keep a radio playing, or keep the TV on. Keep your environment bright. Stay connected to the world. Call your mother when you get home. Go out shopping tomorrow, or go to a movie." She handed Melanie her card, which Melanie had already obtained from Odet.

Melanie took it anyway.

"If you need me, call. Anytime, day or night. I mean it."

"Thanks," Melanie said.

"I'm prescribing forty milligram citalopram tablets for you to take, one a day," Dr. Chan added, settling a green silk scarf around her neck. "It's an antidepressant. It shouldn't make you tired, but if it does, it will probably be due to all the built-up tension you're holding. Once the drug allows you to let it go, you might sleep for a whole day, maybe longer. Keep that in mind. What's most important is that the citalopram will file the nasty edges off your emotions, give you a chance to collect yourself." Her mouth quirked up on one side. It reminded Melanie of how adults smile knowingly at children who try to pull one over on them. "Dr. Odet prescribed them to you the first time you came in. I know that you didn't fill the prescription. Promise me you'll get them this time, and that you'll take them?"

"I'll get them, I'll take them," Melanie lied.

"By the way, do you have any symptoms of morning sickness?"

Melanie moved her hand to her belly, completely unaware of the motion. *I'm fucking pregnant again!* That thought in itself almost made her heave. It had to have happened last night — or rather, a month ago, according to everyone else's reckoning — when Jon had been so strange. She remembered the weird flitting lights, her unexplained rush of lust... the hook on the end of Jon's arm. Pan had been there, she was sure of it. But why had he orchestrated the incident?

"Are you all right?"

Melanie wrenched herself away from her inner riot to find the psychiatrist staring at her with critical concern. "I'm okay," she assured Dr. Chan. "I just... was remembering the night we... it must have been that night."

Dr. Chan nodded. "Tell me. Are you happy being pregnant with his child?"

All of a sudden there was gunk in the back of her throat that wanted to choke her. Melanie swallowed. She couldn't get it down. She had to sip from the water cup on the stand next to her bed. "I don't know," she answered afterwards. "Probably." She moved to touch her engagement ring. "Hey, where is it? Where is it! It's gone, it's gone, where is it!"

Dr. Chan let her belongings tumble out of her arms. She rushed forward without trying to look rushed. "Where is what?" she asked, sitting back down on the edge of the bed. "Calm down, Melanie, and tell me what's gone."

"My ruby ring, my engagement ring! He proposed and it was my engagement ring! It was right here on my finger, where is it I have to find it!" *You're being hysterical shut up you idiot you'll end up in the psych ward!* she thought, but some pocket of hysteria had been ripped open and she couldn't stop her hand from jerking open the little drawer on the table by the bed so that her other hand could scramble frantically inside — nothing but a comb, brush, notebook, bottle of hand lotion. "It's not here!" She tossed everything in her purse on the bed and scrambled through it. *"It's not here!"*

Finally she got control. She took a deep breath. "Sorry. I'm sorry. I guess I'm a little strung out, huh?"

Dr. Chan sighed and patted her arm. "A little. Where did you have the ring last? Relax and try to remember."

I had it a fucking month ago! Melanie wanted to say. *Anything could have happened to it over that much time, especially because I wasn't around to notice!* "I'm sure I had it last night, when I was admitted here."

"I'll check with the nurses and with Dr. Odet." Dr. Chan collected her things again. "I'm sure it's here somewhere."

Melanie flopped back onto her pillows. "Let me guess. I'm not leaving tonight, am I?"

"Perhaps not. I'll stop by tomorrow morning, all right?"

"Yeah. Sure."

CHAPTER 30

While tending the ship, struggling against the darkness, and hiding his inner turmoil from Smee, Cecco and the crew, Stuart set about finding an escape from his tropical prison. He tried to keep his drinking to a minimum so that his thinking remained clear.

How can I find a way home?

He had read books on mythology from Edith Hamilton to Joseph Campbell, and he had read fantasy classics by Tolkien and Le Guin and Feist and the like. As he ruminated about mankind's persistent fascination with magical worlds and the stories told about them, whether those stories were supposed to be true or not, he recognized one similarity between them all: magical worlds hid their portals well, for places of power were not open to just anyone.

With one exception – the Neverland. Stuart already knew that the main portal to Pan's domain was located somewhere up in the sky. He had flown through it himself. Pan visited the real world and brought all his recruits back that way. But alas, Stuart couldn't fly anymore. And even if he collected fairy dust as Sigrson had, he wouldn't know *where* to fly. "Second to the right, and straight on till morning" did not qualify as Thomas Guide directions.

So he clung to the hope that there was another portal on the island itself. *Every house has a back door,* he reasoned. That back door might be in an enchanted glade or in a cave or through a magic pool of water. All he had to do was find it.

With that conviction, he considered his resources. First and foremost, he had his maps. As his own log stated, he had been here... apparently... for six months, spending much of that time surveying the environs. He already knew more in general about his Neverland than had any of the previous Hooks.

Unfortunately, he knew the least about his version of Pan's island, especially about places where a back door was most likely to be located. His map detailed the coastline, labeled the major landmarks and that was it. He needed to know more. He needed to chart every valley, every river, every mountain, every path. He needed to explore the deadly depths of the jungle to see what might be hidden there. Perhaps there were ruins up in the mountains where a secret portal existed. All of this would take time, something he didn't want to spend, but what choice did he have? It was going to take weeks to search the terrain on foot, tree by tree, rock by rock, peril by peril. Stuart could see no way around it.

Unless he could find a useful clue in his second best resource, the logs of his predecessors. Although they were more heartrending than anything else, Stuart made himself read each one from first page to last. It took all the willpower he could muster to take in each entry, each string of pleas and each mad raving as a piece of information only. *No emotions*, he kept chanting to himself. *This is input, cold data, nothing more.* He managed to convince his head but not his heart.

He made a list of their similarities.

1) The Hooks all commanded a ship named the *Jolly Roger*, each one a captured vessel, of course. The first had been a Dutch merchantman, the second a French man-of-war, and the third and fourth both brigs. Stuart added the specifics of his own ship, supplied to him by the dark voice. She was a Dutch-built frigate, which was why she had the high graceful poop and lacked the heavy ornamentation of the typical English and French fighting ships. A three-master with thirty-eight guns, she was much faster than a galleon — *anything* was faster than a galleon — but she looked enough like one that she fulfilled the expectations of most modern children's idea of what a pirate ship should look like which, for reasons known only to Hollywood, was a galleon.

2) Some of the crewmen — Cecco, Smee, Foggerty, Jukes, Mason, Noodler and Skylights, among others — were either ageless like Pan's children or their names were passed on to new men, because they were on the roster of every Hook's crew. Their ratings varied each time except for Smee, who was always bosun.

3) There was always a place called Beggar's Port within ten days' sailing of Pan's island, though its exact location and geography changed each time and whatever happened there was never committed to the logs.

4) There were always Lost Boys, though their numbers fluctuated as did their names. Stuart presumed that, although they didn't age, they were not immortal.

5) Each Hook had tried to escape the Neverland by simply sailing away. It never worked. As if Pan's domain were its own tiny globe, any travel away from the island brought the *Jolly Roger* right back to it. Changing direction made no difference — the ship always ended up back where it started.

6) Each Hook came to notice that there was but a single non-Indian female on the island. She always wore white and was part of Pan's crew. She was always called Wendy.

Stuart turned that last fact over and over, but he could find no significance other than the idea that Pan, whatever he was, felt an obligation to provide a mother figure for the rowdy Lost Boys, like in Barrie's story. Why she should be called Wendy was a mystery.

He set those notes aside and turned to his other resources — his fellow pirates. They had gone ashore lots of times to seek Pan's hidden home, supposedly with him. *Which is exactly why I can't ask them for information, not even Smee,* he realized in frustration. *I'm already supposed to know what they know.* He could chance fishing for information through vague discussion, like he had with Cecco as they left Beggar's Port, but what if somebody figured out what he was doing? He couldn't afford to lose the crew's confidence. Cecco himself had only recently put aside his concerns over his captain's loss of memory.

Stuart's only alternative was to follow the thinking of Hook September 30, 1826 — kidnap a Lost Boy and obtain information by whatever means necessary. Stuart was grateful that he didn't have to go that far. He had Billy.

That in itself made him hesitate. Billy's arrival had been awfully well timed. That put Stuart on guard. Was Billy a plant? Did Pan send the boy to trick him or turn him down the wrong road? In the end, it didn't matter. Stuart had to interrogate Billy regardless. He had nothing else to try until he regained the island.

So on the fourth day out from Beggar's Port, at the sound of the second bell of the second dog watch — 6:30 pm with clouds continuing to obscure the fading suns — Stuart ordered Billy to his cabin. *Control, control, control,* he chanted, refusing to repeat the failure of his first interview with the boy. *I will keep control. I will keep control. I will—*

The black fingers gripped him. *We must work together. You know that.*

Stuart fought back this time, stamping out the rude lust welling up in his heart. He wanted to give in, oh, how he wanted to sink into that dark embrace and give little Billy a proper interview, yes, one the whelp would never forget, an interview that got to the *point,* as it were. Instead he visualized the strangling black hands and then visualized his own hands, both of them whole and bigger and stronger than the enemy's. He grabbed at the black fingers, squeezed—

—and doubled over in agony.

Something writhed and wriggled in fury, physically inside of him, something uninvited and vile, like a snake thrashing between his organs. The pain was incredible, a silent scream that seemed to come from his very flesh. Stuart folded in his chair, clutching his stomach, afraid that he might throw up so hard that he would spew his guts right out of his mouth. Still he stubbornly maintained his visualization, squeezing for all he was worth. He had to win this time. He had to establish some line of defense. *Fucking let me go, let me go, let me go, let me—*

Billy knocked on his cabin door. The knock came soft and timid, not like the knock of any of the officers. It was the timidity of that sound against the riot in his head that caused Stuart to start. In that split second of distraction, he lost his focus and with it, the battle. The gut-twisting pain stopped. He straightened up in his chair. His breathing evened out. Interesting. He didn't really feel any different. Not really. He was just the same as before. Better, actually. Why did he always fight it so hard? "Come in, lad," he drawled in that lazy English accent.

Billy walked in. He was sporting a shackle around one ankle attached by a heavy chain to a small cannonball.

The sight made Stuart burst out laughing. *It's to prevent him from flying away! Cecco, you wily son of a bitch!*

Billy's cheeks reddened. He obviously knew why he had been chained and was determined to survive his humiliating probation with all the pride he could muster, even under his new captain's derision. He dragged the cannonball after him and, making the plosive harrumphing sound unique to children who believe they are being put out for no good reason, stood at attention. "Barricoe Billy reporting as ordered, Captain."

Stuart barely managed to quell a fresh bout of laughter. "*Barricoe* Billy, is it?"

"Aye, Captain. Mister Cecco says I need a pirate name. I heard a man at the guns say the word. If it's something to do with firing guns, I like it." Billy gave Stuart the kind of imploring look that begged for acceptance. He was too much like a puppy who bares his soft belly before the leader of the pack in hopeful submission.

It made Stuart hate the sniveling brat more than ever. He had no intention of telling him that *barricoe* was nothing more than a term for a small water cask. *It's a name to strike terror in the hearts of honest men*, he thought with a nasty interior smile. "'Tis a splendid name, m'hearty," he declared encouragingly. "Barricoe Billy it is. Now, Mister Barricoe Billy, are you a learned man of letters?"

Billy frowned. "I know the alphabet."

That made Stuart snicker. "Can you *write*?"

"Oh. Aye, sir."

"Excellent." Stuart went to his writing desk and fetched a small stack of papers that he had taken from a locked trunk earlier. These were the articles of the ship, the pirates' contract, as it were. Having been signed by every man aboard, the document — which Hook and his men had drafted in council years ago, he half-recalled — outlined the organization of the ship, distribution of wealth, crimes and punishments, and all of the democratic laws by which the pirates had, like all gentlemen of fortune, established their daring and illegal enterprise aboard the *Jolly Roger*.

Stuart knew how much things had changed over the ensuing years. Hook had become more like a king than an elected captain, especially after losing his hand. He was well-nigh a tyrant these days. Nonetheless, his crew had remained loyal because he was, in their eyes, a fair man at heart, as well as an able seaman, gifted navigator and exceptional commander. He had brought them wealth and afforded them many pleasures during their partnership, and more, his clever tactics had kept even one of them from ever getting caught and hanged.

Stuart knew that the pirates attributed their captain's black behavior to his fury at the loss of his hand and, worse, the curse of the crocodile. These were men who understood revenge. As all good Brethren of the "sweet trade," a wrong done to their captain was a wrong done to them. They were honor-bound to help Hook take his revenge on Peter Pan. Afterwards, they presumed that the cloud would lift, Hook would revert to the rowdy and daring captain he had been before, and the *Jolly Roger* would return to the world to resume her former ways.

Stuart stroked his hook over the top parchment page. *If only they knew*, he thought. *Then again, if they did, they'd mutiny... if they could organize themselves before they forgot all about it. Ha!* He set the papers on the rosewood table and held out his hook. "Swear your loyalty to me, this crew and this ship."

Billy was confused. "Don't people usually swear on a Bible or something, sir?"

"It is not the Bible that will strike you down if you should fail to uphold the articles of this ship," Stuart replied, allowing a grim note to creep into his voice. He enjoyed watching while Billy struggled to place his hand on the cruel iron.

"I s-swear loyalty to you and the crew and the ship," Billy managed.

Stuart nodded. "Now sign."

Billy took the quill, too naive to actually bother reading what he was about to sign. He carefully penned *Mister Baricko Billy* as if he were some kind of nobleman. "There, sir," he said when he finished, as if expecting applause.

Stuart set the articles back on his writing desk. "Well, Mister Barricoe Billy, congratulations. As of this moment you are a bone fide pirate, comrade of every man aboard and the sworn enemy of England — the entire civilized world, in point of fact. What do you think of that?"

Billy dared to grin. "I think it's swell, Captain."

Stuart nodded. "Good. Then it is time for me to lay a most vital question before you." He walked up to the boy and, towering over him, asked, "Why shouldn't I kill you here and now?"

Billy crumpled into himself, his whole face a terrified question.

"You see," Stuart continued, and he began to pace, "I considered taking you on as a personal apprentice, to give you the benefit of my vast knowledge and experience. You might have the makings of a pirate captain, boy. One never knows, does one?"

Billy maintained his whipped-puppy stance, but his eyes twinkled, too, at the prospect of learning the sweet trade from a master, *the* master, the man whose very name evoked hysteria in ports from the Caribbean to the eastern seas.

"Unfortunately," Stuart went on, "I find myself in something of a quandary. The fact is, from where I stand, Mister Barricoe Billy, you are a traitor."

Billy went white. "But — but — I swore!"

"True enough. As well, you signed the articles. And now that you are under my command, I require that you explain to me how you could give your loyalties to Pan, then desert him, and after all that still expect me to put my faith and trust in you." Stuart plucked his lacy kerchief from his sleeve and rubbed a smudge off his hook. Smee scrubbed and oiled the attachment every night, but daily use always left marks which annoyed Stuart's increasingly fastidious nature. "Can you see my predicament, Billy?" he asked.

Billy swallowed with an audible *glump*. "I-I'll be totally loyal to you, honest, Captain Hook! I'll prove it any way you want!"

"Ah. That is what I was hoping you'd say." Stuart tucked his kerchief back up his sleeve. "The fact is, I want to know about Peter

Pan. I want to know about his island. And I want you to give me that information."

Stuart was amazed to watch Billy's face, pale already, whiten even more. The boy's once rosy cheeks gleamed a sweaty bone ivory. "Y-you wanna know where his secret hideout is, right? So you can go there and kill him?"

Stuart wrenched enough control back from the darkness to keep to his own agenda. "Among other things," he said with effort. "But I'm quite willing to start with that."

Billy made a choking sound, as if he had swallowed a mouthful of food too fast. "I can't!" he finally blurted.

Stuart felt a terrible shadow twist his features. "What's that you say?"

"Honest, Captain! He put a curse on me!"

Stuart raised a brow. "Explain."

"Peter curses us that leave him so we can't rat on him. He makes us forget. Please don't punish me, Captain, it's his fault, I didn't want him to do it, I couldn't help it please don't kill me!"

If killing Pan had been his true agenda, Stuart would have been furious. No telling what he might have done to little Barricoe Billy. But he maintained enough control that all he did was sigh. "At ease, boy. I don't fancy what you say, but I sense it is the truth."

Billy nearly fainted with relief. Before he toppled, Stuart steered him to a chair, sat him down and made him take a sip of brandy. "Perhaps there are other things you can tell me, hm? For instance, I'm curious as to how Pan comes and goes from this world. Oh, I know about the flying. I wish to know if there are other ways out of the Neverland."

Instead of finding this an astonishing request, Billy was merely confused. It took Stuart awhile to make the boy understand what he meant by "out." Billy had forgotten all about the real world, so the concept of "out" did not exist for him anymore.

On top of that, Billy had done plenty of hard labor that day and was tired. When Smee came in to light the night candles in the great cabin — his eyes were curiously red and puffy — Stuart ordered the bosun to fetch strong coffee with real cream from the goats onboard and lots of molasses. Perhaps that would jog Billy's memory. At Stuart's urging, the boy downed three cups.

In no time at all, Billy was gabbling like a bad auctioneer, rattling off anecdotes, adventures he'd had, animals he'd hunted, tricks he'd played on his mates, and the names and personalities of all the children. Stuart took frantic notes, amazed at this breathless outpouring and frustrated that it didn't always make sense. Evidently, little Billy wasn't used to drinking coffee.

In the end, the whole exercise proved fruitless. Billy knew nothing of any secret doors or pathways that led anywhere out of the Neverland. He could give no useful information about Pan except, "Deadly with the sword, sir, and what a hunter! Best flier on the island, too, but he's all stuffed up with himself."

Concerning Wendy he said little, except to stress that she continually complained that the Lost Boys "smelled like dumpsters" and she herself was the only one to ever bathe. She had sewn a wash cloth for each of them with their very own initials on them, and she fetched water for the basin every morning, but they refused to wash unless Pan ordered them to, which wasn't often. And what Billy knew of the fairies amounted to the big "secret" that Tinker Bell had a crush on Pan.

After an hour of this, Stuart could barely refrain from slapping the boy. He dearly wanted to. His hand itched, and worse, his hook twitched, eager for blood. He finished the interrogation before the impulses grew too strong. He sent Billy off, filling the boy with empty promises and encouragements. It wouldn't hurt to have the whelp on his side. Maybe Billy would remember something later on. One thing was sure — the kid would still be awake at the first bell of the morning watch. Stuart thought of the men in the forecastle tying him down and stuffing a rag in his mouth to shut him up until the caffeine wore off.

Stuart sat at the rosewood table and filled out the jotted notes he had taken, sipping coffee after he poured a tot of brandy into it. *Puling sprog gave me damn all to work with*, he grumbled, *but I'll not presume too fast. I don't know what might prove useful later on.*

265

He had to admit that he was fascinated by the names of the Lost Boys and their personalities. He had seen them all before, but it had been during battles. He'd had no chance to view them as individuals.

The oldest was Ranger, a real soldier, the kind of kid who liked the sight of blood. He was the one who had fired Starkey's stolen pistol, and he had deadly aim. Next down the age line was Cheeks, a fat boy who always lagged behind. Younger than him was Blaster, so named because he could, glory hallelujah, fart the loudest of all the boys. Paw-Paw wore the skins of a mountain cat that the boys had killed up in the forest one time. Slade the Blade was a New York kid who knew how to give all the other kids tattoos. There were The Twins, who were British but whose parents had come from India. Their names were too difficult for the other children to pronounce so they had become simply The Twins. They dressed in identical leathers sewn for them by women of the Indian tribe, who admired their strange olive-colored skin with that dusky blue sheen. Stinky was Canadian and wore a skunk-skin cap with the tail hanging down his back. He insisted the cap didn't smell, but everybody else thought it reeked and they wouldn't let him bring it into the hideout. Flying Tiger was a Chinese kid who had studied karate, and Léon was a little Mexican boy who was trying to teach himself how to play the pennywhistle he had stolen from one of the pirates.

Then there were Wendy, John and Michael.

John was a smart boy, interested in history, Billy said, and very mannerly. Little Michael always carried his beloved Teddy bear and would pound anybody who touched it. And Wendy, well, she was a real prize — pretty, smart, and nobody's fool. She considered herself mother to all the boys, but being a modern girl, she didn't sit in her little house darning the boys' socks all day. When they went adventuring, she went with them, and woe to any boy who spoke of her as "just a girl."

A dozen Lost Boys, one simpering little minx, and Pan, Stuart thought. *Goddam ankle-biters all, and I feel like I'm waging war on Europe.*

He finished his notes and leisurely flipped through the pages, rereading them several times. All this information. It had to be worth something. Yes, it gave him a better picture of his enemies, but beyond that, was good was it really? Unless...

An idea tickled the back of his brain, maybe the beginnings of a plan. He prodded it encouragingly, but the seed wasn't ready to sprout, not yet. He let it go and decided to get some fresh air. After pacing the ship for hours in the gloom of another cold night, he retired. That signaled relaxation time for the men of the first watch, some of whom started up games of dice and cards while others sang and jigged to MacDougal's fiddle.

Stuart didn't mind the noise as he tried to go to sleep in his hammock. He knew his pacing made the crew tight as a bobstay, but so what if it did? He was captain, wasn't he? He could do what he ruddy well wanted and to hell with the reprobates on deck. They were lucky he didn't flog the lot of them, what with the rotten luck the ship had suffered lately. He had a right to damn well pace the deck. It helped him sleep. And if it didn't, he would drink. If that didn't work, he would read. And if that didn't work, he would damn well pace again. There was nothing more to do until they reached the island anyway.

If it's still there, he reminded himself yet again, and he hugged the bare stump of his arm. Sometimes, when he first put the harness on in the morning or right after he took it off at night, the stump would ache, like it was doing this very moment. He could usually ignore the dull throbbing, but sometimes a string of pain like fire would shoot up his arm, and nothing he did could soothe it. He would have to wait, helpless to help himself.

Worse were the intervals when he could feel his fingers wriggling in that other dimension beyond normal sight, sound and touch. It was bad enough when he could feel his phantom fingers at all, but sometimes he could actually make them move the way he wanted them to, as if he still possessed his hand. He could make a fist or flip the bird, all in that invisible dimension of the croc's giant stomach where his poor hand had ended up, so lonely without the rest of him.

The croc was probably somewhere nearby, swimming along with the *Jolly Roger* like it always did, licking its chops and waiting patiently for an opportunity to reunite all of Stuart in that dubious miracle of reptilian digestion. Feeling like he was falling down an enormous gullet as big as the bilge and twice as foul, Stuart dropped into an uneasy sleep.

CHAPTER 31

"Happy day, sar. There she is."

Stuart stood on the quarterdeck. He pulled his coat tighter, squinting out over the port rail, out across miles of choppy steel-grey water. The suns were just beginning to shine, ushering in a cold dawn. Freezing wind whipped his hair and made the tip of his nose sting. Tiny icicles of salt spray pelted his skin. Despite the discomfort, Stuart felt warm with relief. Pan's island lay on the horizon, a positive ID at this distance thanks to its Fuji-like volcano. There would be no repeat of the Beggar's Port fiasco. He would have his chance to find a way home.

"Would yeh like to get dressed, sar?" Smee asked, giving his captain a judgmental once-over.

Stuart had been awakened by a bellow from the crow's nest: "Oi! Pan's land fine on the port bow!" He had leaped out of his hammock and grabbed his top coat, forgetting in his haste to put on shoes. His stump was bare of its cruel hook and his toes were turning blue, but he kept his smile. He shined it on Smee. "Aye, Mister Smee, that is a fine suggestion. If you would be so kind..."

"O'course, sar," said Smee, and followed him into the great cabin.

By the time the ship neared Pirate's Bay, Stuart stood on the poop immaculately dressed, shaved, perfumed and manicured for the day. Smee had dressed him in Hook's most colorful outfit, the one with the red crushed-velvet topcoat with black velvet trim. The fluffy ostrich-plumes on his hat flailed in the wind. A small part of him felt ridiculous in the costume, but for the most part he gloried in his finery these days, knowing that it marked him as a man of taste, breeding and wealth — everything his scurvy dogs were not. *If I must mingle with vermin, I will do it on my own terms,* he thought.

He stepped down to the quarterdeck and guided the ship in, shouting commands and conducting the crew in yet another sailors' ballet. Rugged bodies, many clad in worn-out breeches and light cotton shirts despite the cold, moved to that unique choreography known only aboard tall ships, that brutal but organized scramble that did now as ever answer the fundamental demands of wind and wave.

Thanks to Hook, Stuart knew Pirate's Bay well. He needed no consultation with a nautical chart to tell him where rocks lurked just below the water or where shoals or coral beds lay high enough to threaten the keel. He knew how to manage these winds and currents, and he brought the *Jolly Roger* to safe anchorage a quarter mile offshore. The ship stopped at the same spot where she had been before and settled like a swan in protected waters, slipping her beak under her wing to doze until the next call to action.

Cecco and Foggerty took over then, ordering the men to furl sails and afterwards making sure the dozens of braces, halyards, sheets and clewlines were carefully coiled and placed on their specific belaying pins, ready for use at a moment's notice. For all their gruff and wild ways the pirates knew, being able seamen, that a single fouled line at the wrong moment could spell disaster for the ship and every life aboard her. They were a neat bunch, all considered.

Stuart watched the men for awhile, fascinated as ever by the endless variety of work shanties that issued from MacDougal and his fiddle. The shantyman's repertoire was as inexhaustible as his vocal chords. His boisterous renditions, with their hearty hitches and wild yelps between key phrases, sometimes made him sound like an ecstatic drunk. That was hardly the case. Such energy invigorated the men and maintained much needed teamwork. In a very real sense, MacDougal was the nucleus of the crew, bringing them together and keeping them in rhythm as they hauled on halyards, trudged round the capstan or muscled the heavy pumps that kept the water level down in the bilge tolerable. For Stuart, he was just plain fun to listen to.

Thoughts of the shantyman stopped. Stuart turned towards shore, head cocked. What had he just heard through the men's gruff singing? Laughter? Yes, children's laughter. He plucked the spyglass from its becket.

There, up on the rock cliffs to the north, beyond which lay the Mermaid Lagoon, two children were flying back and forth, one green, one white, and both trailed by a glittering of gold: Pan, Wendy and Tinker Bell. They were confined to an area of warm sunslight that shone down on them like a biblical ray from Heaven. Cold clung to the pirate ship like a curse, nearly turning Stuart's lips blue, but the children were warm in the sunsbeam, dressed normally and playing a game of tag. First Peter would fly after Wendy, then she would fly after him. Tink zoomed around them both just to confuse the issue.

Stuart focused his spyglass on Pan. Hate boiled up in him so strong that his ears rang and his vision went white. *You killed her, you son of a bitch. There's nothing you won't do, no one you won't hurt, all in your selfish quest to mold me into a monster. Well, I'm starting my own game, you devil, and I'm won't settle for your hand. I want your fucking head.*

He lowered the glass, panting through gritted teeth. *Wait a minute,* he thought, and subdued the pulsing black knot inside of him, struggling to calm his emotions. *Forget revenge. Just find a way out of here. That's all that matters.* He raised the glass back to his eye, the question persistent: *How?*

A flutter of white flashed past his limited field of vision. Gay girlish laughter carried on the cold northern wind. Wendy was a good flier, not as graceful as Pan but just as daring. Stuart tried to follow her as she corkscrewed a long horizontal line, then curved upwards with Tinker Bell at her toes, leaving a sparkling rocket trail in her wake.

Wendy...

The seed of the idea that had planted itself days ago in the back of Stuart's brain suddenly began to germinate as he mentally reviewed the notes he had taken from the previous Hooks' logs.

She was always called Wendy (John and Michael hadn't joined the club until Hook number three, great-grandfather James). She always wore white, usually a nightgown or dressing gown. She was always about ten years old, older than most of the Lost Boys. She rarely took action in a fight — usually she cheered and hovered in the background, watching. Peter protected her with his life, whereas the Lost Boys were on their own. Rarely was Pan seen without her and, in fact, he catered to his little lady guest. *Like when he introduced her to me,* Stuart recalled. *He made a show of presenting her, specifically, as if she were the star in a play.*

Wendy. Why did Pan have to have her around? Why was she so important?

Stuart closed his eyes. While the wind tugged at his hair and made the ruffs on his shirt and wrists dance, he calmed the hatred deep inside and focused on his memories, or what he hoped were his real memories. With careful deliberation he sifted through them, back, back to when he had first been introduced to the girl in white. What had she said then?

"O, Peter, he's just what I expected!"

Yes, those had been her words upon meeting Captain Hook. Plus she had said that he was "perfect." It had sounded weird to Stuart at the time, but he had been far too overwhelmed then to really notice it. Now he noticed it. He noticed it very much, and it disturbed him. "She's the rudder that steers the ship." He murmured the words but did not know where he had heard them. No matter.

The seed of his idea took root.

* * * * *

Stuart called Smee and Cecco into his cabin. They were openly and quite amusingly flabbergasted when their captain asked them to join him for breakfast.

On naval and merchant vessels, shared meals were traditional among the captain and his officers. Stuart, however, knew that Hook rarely invited such intimacies, even with the two men aboard that he considered friends. Smee and Cecco sat down at the rosewood table, which had been cleared to hold a fine feast, but they were not at ease.

Cookson, who had prepared and delivered the food, poured coffee all around and then left, curling a lip at Smee as he went. Even though it wasn't the normal duty of a bosun, Smee usually acted as the captain's steward and catered his meals. It amused Stuart to see the cook this miffed at a one-time change in duties.

"Gentlemen, for heaven's sake, I haven't gone mad," he assured Cecco and Smee. *Yet*, he added to himself. "It's time for breakfast, and as I also wish to speak with you both about something important, I thought to myself, why not combine the two?" He waved for them to dig in. "Please, go ahead. I'll join you in a moment."

Cecco started to reach for his coffee cup but stopped cold. He averted his eyes as Stuart began to unscrew his hook.

Stuart knew full well that Cecco had seen him put the hook on and take it off before. It was the casual execution of the operation that unsettled the first mate. As much as Cecco considered his captain a friend, he feared the hook like everyone else, and it bothered him to see it manipulated.

As for Stuart, he had been pleasantly surprised to find a box of attachments in the cabinet behind the harpsichord some days ago — a box that, like so many other things, hadn't been there before. It contained a screw-on comb, a brush, a clip for holding his hand mirror, a flat square of iron with a lip at the bottom and two adjustable prongs that would comfortably hold a book open for reading, and a fine silver table knife. It was the table knife he now screwed on in place of the hook, which he set next to his plate. It lay there like a deadly snake curled at the side of a path, waiting.

"Your coffee's getting cold," Stuart said, prompting Cecco back into action.

Smee reached for sliced pineapple. He liked fruits and vegetables as much, possibly more, than bread and meat — just one of the many oddities that marked him as an odd man, even among a crew of fierce individualists like the pirates. Fortunately for him, the pirates had access to plenty of fresh viands.

"Lemme congratulate yeh, Cap'n," he said. "Bloody fine seamanship. Clouds all the way, barely a glimpse o' blue sky, an' by thunder, yeh got us back."

"You do have a knack for navigating by the seat of your pants, James," Cecco agreed and finally sipped his coffee. "The crew was getting worried."

"Hmf. Confounded riffraff show little faith in a captain who charted the whole damned archipelago," Stuart grumbled. "I should dump the lot of them on Liverpool and let them find their own way back."

Smee snickered. "Aye, that would teach 'em."

Stuart used his knife attachment to delicately slice a chunk of breast meat from a chicken. "I want to kidnap Wendy," he announced, setting the chunk on his plate.

Smee nearly dropped his pineapple slice. "Sar?"

"You heard me. I need information, and I think she can provide it. Opinions?"

"My opinion is she ain't gonna tell you where Pan holes up, sar. Yeh know that."

Stuart caught Smee's eye and glowered into it. "What makes you so sure, Mister Smee? Have you asked her?"

"Well, sar, all's I mean is, err..." Smee exchanged a dubious look with Cecco. "No."

"And so you make my point for me."

"James," said Cecco, "what you say is true. We've never actually spoken to the girl in private. But she's devoted to Pan. What makes you think she'll betray him?"

Something black in Stuart's heart wriggled with evil glee, and he found himself saying, "Think of the possibilities should proper pressure be applied."

Smee grinned. "Torture, sar?"

"No!" Stuart snapped. "Brimstone and gall, man, what do you think I am, a barbarian?"

"No, sar," Smee spluttered. "O'course not, sar."

"On the other hand," Stuart said, "she doesn't know that. And torture... well, what does the word mean, anyway? *Persuasion* is a more conducive term."

"And it covers so many possibilities," Cecco put in with a wink.

"May I ask, sar..." Smee hesitated. "What exactly is the information yer after?"

Stuart had already pondered how to answer that inevitable question. He dared not confess his actual intentions. He planned to ask the girl — beg her, threaten her, if necessary — to reveal any way out of Pan's domain. As far as he could see, she was the closest child to Pan. If anyone would know of a back door, she would. "I want what I have always wanted," he answered Smee, his tone putting an end to that line of questioning.

Cecco nodded, chewing on a biscuit. "All right, so we kidnap her. Any ideas how? She's at Pan's side night and day."

"No, Mister Cecco, she is not." And Stuart told them his plan.

CHAPTER 32

Melanie was released from the hospital two days later, after another counseling session with Dr. Chan. The psychiatrist still didn't want her to be alone in Jon's house, so Melanie promised that she would find someone to stay with her. "At least over Christmas," she told Chan. "Today is only the twenty-third."

The truth was, Melanie had no intention of letting anyone stay with her, not even Yolanda, who offered to come even though she had a Christmas Day open house party planned. Melanie refused the kind offer. The task ahead would require all her concentration. It would require her to ruminate over materials and ideas best left to those who believed in the Neverland. *And despite the story's popularity, I bet there are damned few of us*, she thought as she got dressed on her first morning back. As Yolanda had claimed, Jon's bedroom closet and drawers were still full of his belongings exactly as he had left them. Melanie found her own clothes stuffed in her antique armoire, the sole piece of furniture she had apparently transferred from her apartment to Jon's house.

She had slept hard last night — emotional exhaustion and a prescription sedative cooperated to make that a certainty — and she hadn't expected her mind to be so clear today. She had expected to feel the logy after-effects of her hospital stay, what between the rubber-chicken food and the marshmallow-mallet drugs. *Maybe it's because I don't have much time,* she thought, hurrying downstairs to make coffee and toast while brushing her hair with Jon's brush. *I have to work fast.*

She believed Jon was alive, yes, but she did not trust that he would remain that way for long or that her chances of finding him would remain high — if there were any chances at all. She still couldn't find her ruby engagement ring. The only conclusion she could draw was that Peter Pan had taken it off her finger. When? How? She didn't know. All she knew was that it had not been found at the hospital, and it wasn't in Jon's house.

There was something sinister about the ring's disappearance. If Pan had taken it, he must surely have shown it to Jon. Why else take it? But if he wanted to show it to Jon, what did he wish to accomplish by the gesture? Was he tormenting Jon the way he was tormenting her? The idea made her shudder.

Melanie had thus far succeeded in not thinking too much about the details of Jon's dilemma. She feared that if she tried to imagine what he must be going through, the unthinkable world he had been thrown into, the depraved people he would be forced to ally himself with, his tragic and hopeless future — if she tried to imagine all that, she might lose her own grasp of reality. *I'm his only chance,* she told herself when the horrible images would come, *and I don't have much time.*

She hurried for the kitchen, still brushing her hair with Jon's brush. Her eyes flicked over to the living room. She had noticed the urn the night before. There it was on the shelf as it had been in her weird vision, a squat silver bottle-shape with a crossed-sword motif on the front. Nothing else was on that shelf except two white candles, one on each side of the urn. The candles weren't lit. She knew she only lit them at sunset.

Melanie did what she had not dared to do the previous night. She picked up the urn and opened it. There certainly were ashes inside. *Yes, but it's not Jon. For all I know it's the ashes of a pig or a large dog... or somebody's backyard barbeque, for that matter.* Grotesque, but the concept fueled her determination. *I need to figure this out. I need to find the truth!* She replaced the urn's lid and gently set it back on the shelf.

"Okay," she said to the cats gathered eagerly at the kitchen doorway for breakfast, "first thing's first. I need my notes." She went into the downstairs bedroom that Jon had used as his home office, presuming to find his copy of *Peter Pan* on the desk along with several pages of notes. To her mind, only a few days had passed since she'd read the book while Fuzzybutt had lounged on the sofa next to her. Only a few days had passed since she had searched Jon's house from top to bottom and found the little phone book taped under the middle drawer of the writing desk. Only a few days had passed since she had taken notes during her phone conversations with old Alice Lancaster and Hillary, wife of Alice's son Sylvester, along with notes covering her attempts to contact Francine Rhodes, Jon's journalist-relative.

But the surface of the desk was clear. The novel, her notes and the little phone book were gone. "He took them!" she cried, imagining Peter Pan flying in from the Neverland to snatch the materials. Whatever he was up to, the magical boy evidently didn't want Jon's fiancée to barge in and complicate things.

She scoured the house like she had the first time, but no book and no notes showed up. Her frustration built until she started throwing things around. When she came across the old yellowed box that had held the sword, she stomped on it, hollering, "Give Jon back to me, you shit!" That made her force herself to sit in Jon's armchair in the den and count slowly to fifty, to calm down.

That's when it came — the oppressive feeling of being watched. *He's here!* She hadn't forgotten about the tiny dancing gold light during her and Jon's strangely intense lovemaking. *Or maybe it's Tinker Bell.* "I don't believe in fairies!" she shouted. "I don't believe in fairies, I don't believe in fairies, so go away or I'll say it again!"

The oppressive feeling vanished.

"Shit — wait a minute!" In anger and, admittedly, some amount of fear, she had sent the fairy away... or killed her *no no don't think that!*... when instead she should have tried to communicate. Perhaps she could get Jon back through some form of negotiation.

Oh yeah, right, she thought. After reading about Peter Pan's forceful personality, Melanie doubted he was the kind to change his mind about things. He had spent considerable time and effort to set something up. The scenario was in motion. It was doubtful he would consider changing it at this stage. *But he might. I have to try.* She resolved to do so the next time the being-watched feeling returned.

She remembered to feed the cats, and then she puzzled over how to begin her researches anew. She decided to start with her home files, everything concerning her bills, finances and other personal records. She took her organizer out of her purse — the small fat volume was her daily savior — and flipped through it. She needed to piece together her activities of the missing month. It didn't take long, and the resulting picture was surprisingly clear: Jon had died; he had willed everything to her; and she had left her apartment and moved into his house, putting most of her own furnishings in storage. She hadn't quit her researching job as much as she had put it on hold. According to her organizer notes, she had spent all of December learning how to oversee Alan, who had always managed Excalibur Books under Jon's supervision. She had also expended a great deal of effort refusing to accept Jon's death.

It was all neat and clean. She didn't have to worry about money, that was for sure. She had Jon's money, her own savings, and soon enough the settlement from the Stuart House lot would come through. She could devote all her energies to finding Jon.

As for how all of her detailed notes had gotten into her organizer in her handwriting or why she couldn't remember doing the things she had recorded there or why everyone remembered events that had never happened and forgot events that had... she decided not to think about it.

Next on the agenda: create a timeline of incidents. She fetched a legal pad and a pen. After flipping through her organizer again, more slowly this time, checking notes and thinking hard, she wrote this:

- October 10: George, J's uncle, died. He'd lived in S House since Emmerich died sometime early '60s.
- October 17: SF earthquake. S House burned.
- November 9: J's appt w George's lawyer in SF. Safe behind wall in S House w sword n bk inside, only things undamaged.
- November 10: J came home w sword n bk. Only in retrospect do I see how fixated he was on sword frm

start. Relevant? Or J just being J? Strange writing on blade. We read some of bk. Freaky. I think being-watched feeling began that day. J gave me ruby ring.

- November 11-15: J hard to reach, said didn't feel gd, was busy, made up excuses, I didn't understand, do now. Pan was after him, he was scared, didn't know what was happening. Had to have involved sword n bk.
- November 16: found out pregnant.
- November 19: got abortion.
- November 20: told Jon about it. He said he was sick, looked awful. Now know he was so terrified he really *was* sick. He said we should break up. Bet he was trying to keep me safe frm Pan.
- November 21, morning: Yolanda phoned, J gone. I found him fallen out bed, delirious. He didn't know me, hysterics. Called 911, ambulance took to hospital. Yolanda there later. Dr. Odet talked about welts on J's wrist n J drinking. J mumbled "not hook." Something about a plan and a dream, too. He was terrified, not sick.
- November 22, morning: Went back to hosp, they'd amputated his hand. Hair dark n wavy, ears pierced. I came back here n read *Peter Pan.*
- November 23 and 24: Went thru J's stuff. Found phone bk, called Julia Mansir (dead, unsure of rel to J); Francine Rhodes (no contact yet); Alice Lancaster (spoke), Hillary Lancaster (wife of Alice's son Sylvester, spoke). Arranged to get Syl's partial fam history.
- November 24, night: hosp discharged Jon, I brought him home. He acted strange, hardly cared about his hand, v distant. Drs. Odet n Phillips said his hair was always black n curly n ears pierced. J settled down, proposed to me. Later that night made love but really... weird. I got preg. J not himself (I saw hook). Dancing lights – Tinker Bell?

BREAK TIL DECEMBER 21

- Woke up late morn, thought it was next day, J literally disappeared in bed. I felt him go. Ambulance took me to hosp. Odet n Yolanda both claim that:
1) J has been dead (died eve Fri, Nov 24 in hosp, "Natural Causes"), his ashes are in urn in living rm;
2) he's always had black curly hair, earring, missing R hand;
3) I've had two breakdowns over him, ending at hosp;
4) J left me everything n I have adopted much of his daily routine as my own.

She checked the timeline, frowned and scrawled one word at the bottom: BULLSHIT.

For one thing, how could Jon have been in two places at once, in reality and in the Neverland? He couldn't have had a body in both... could he? *You're talking about magic here, babe,* she thought nervously. *Who are you to say what magic can do?* She scrutinized the dates again. Maybe it was possible, magically, that Jon had been in two places at once, at least for awhile, before the Neverland completely absorbed him. That would explain his delirium. It would surely explain why he had gone off into a screaming fit. Being split in half would be... well, she didn't know, but she guessed it would be disorienting at best, mind shattering at worst. *But why the overlap?* she thought. *Why not just take him and be done with it? It's not like anybody could have stopped it from happening.* She pondered that for a long time but couldn't come up with a plausible answer.

She scrutinized the timeline, blanking her mind to let her researcher's intuition zero in on anything else. There was something... yes! Jon's dreams! She had forgotten all about them, the Giant Dreams from his childhood that had returned. He had started sleeping badly days before the earthquake, during the time he was preparing for the IRS audit. When had the dreams started? She stared at her timeline and let her mind wander, trying to pinpoint the time.

- October 10: George, J's uncle, died. He'd lived in S House since Emmerich died sometime early '60s.
- October 17: SF earthquake. S House burned.

Melanie picked up her pen and wrote a new note between those dates.

- October 10-17: J's nightmare returned. Profound effect on him.

Had George's death in some way triggered Jon's nightmare? An idea like that would never had occurred to Melanie before, but things were different now. All presumptions of how the world operated were out the window. She made a quick note of the idea and declared the timeline finished.

By one o'clock she hadn't located the notes she had taken of her Stuart family contacts, but she did find something perhaps more important — the strange book that had been in the safe behind the basement wall in Stuart House, the supposed memoirs of Captain Jas. Hook.

Back when Jon was trying to quit drinking, he had played all the games that struggling alcoholics play. He had tried to carry a concealed hip flask, he had lied about stopping by the local bar — something he had never done before — and he had tried to hide bottles of liquor, most notably in the back of his kitchen cookware cabinet. His kitchen cabinets were low and deep, which always drove him nuts. Being so tall, it meant he had to go down on his hands and knees to reach cumbersome pots and pans. He had never gone to the trouble of converting his shelves to sliding shelves, though, something Melanie knew he could afford. Eventually she had figured out why. He wanted those deep hard-to-access corners for hiding bottles, usually brandy, from her prying eyes.

Melanie was the reason Jon had quit drinking. He was never angry or resentful of her efforts on his behalf. He had thanked her for pushing him into doing what he knew was the smart thing. But that didn't mean he didn't cheat. At first it had been a game. Later it had gotten desperate. By the end, he had found the strength within himself to quit the games and sober up.

He never forgot about that hiding place, though. Melanie found the memoirs by chance — in her frustration, she took everything out of all drawers and cabinets in the house, including those in the kitchen. Jon had stuffed the old book in the very back of the deepest cabinet, behind an eight-quart stockpot that completely hid it from view.

"Damn!" she panted when she finally found it. "I forgot all about the Stashatoria!" She had given the hiding place that name when she had discovered the first forbidden bottle of brandy there, also by accident.

The cats had kept her company during her manic excavations, "helping" as Jon would have said, by sniffing every item removed from every cabinet, rubbing up against it to claim it, and in general getting in the way. Now Melanie tiptoed out the kitchen with her precious find, returning their stark feline stares with a guilty smile. "I'll clean everything up, guys, I promise. Tomorrow."

That arrangement seemed to meet with their approval. They resumed sniffing and rubbing against the crooked stacks of pots and pans on the floor. Fuzzybutt claimed a sauce pan and curled up inside of it, her furry bulk spilling over the sides so that she looked like a big mutant powder puff. Not to be outdone, Rebers curled up in the upturned lid. Fuzzy hissed at him and Rebers hissed back.

Melanie left them to their cat games and took her find into the dining room. She sat down at the table with the heavy old book with its cracked leather covers and thick parchment pages. She opened it up, not really wanting to expose herself to the insanity that lay within. "Personal Log of Jas. Hook, Capt. of the *Jolly Roger*," the first page proclaimed, the faded penmanship smooth and educated. She remembered having already read the first entry, dated March 12, 1896, "about 5:30 pm."

Melanie pondered the date. Why March 12, 1896? She flipped through the rest of the book. As she had noticed the first time, exact dates didn't last long. Entries soon began with "Next Day" and "Later" and quickly lost all specificity: "Can't Remember When," "After That," and similar. So why March 12, 1896 – "about 5:30 pm," no less?

She flipped to the very last page in the log. The author had stopped writing before then. There were about twenty blank pages at the end, but upon the very last page one thing had been written, something she had not noticed before: *Requiescat in Pace*. She had come across enough Latin in her researches to know that phrase: Rest in Peace. The neat, elegant penmanship was not that of the original writer.

Melanie reflected on this until she noticed something else about the last page — the leather cover opposite it was bulging slightly. She examined the edge and found a tight pocket on the inside back cover. Within that pocket were her missing notes and two letters.

Her hands shook as she pulled them out. It didn't take a genius to realize that her notes could not possibly be in that book. Jon had to have hidden it before he died, before he had even gone to the hospital, and he had known nothing about her initial researches at that time. She hadn't *started* her researches until he *was* in the hospital. So how had they gotten there? *Take a wild guess, Mel.*

She pushed the spooky idea aside and considered the letters. One was very old, the other postmarked December 5, 1989. She opened the old one first. Her jaw dropped as she read:

133 Gloucester Road, S.W.
January 12, 1902

Emmerich A. Stuart, Esq.
c/o Edward W. Stuart, Esq.
15 Winding Drive, Leicester

My Dear Sir:—
    I have thus far sent to you two letters (Jan 5 and May 20, 1901) regarding a very personal and important matter, that of my obtaining permissions for the use of certain names and events mentioned in the fanciful writings of your father, James Albert Stuart — those writings which I have detailed in previous correspondence re: Black Lake Cottage.
    I wish only for an answer on this matter. If you require recompense, I am at your disposal. I desire only to do what is right, as the names and events in

question interest me greatly, and I prefer that all matters pertaining to their use be legal and proper.

I implore you to respond to this, my third and final request, so that I may market my work with just and suitable enthusiasm. If I do not receive a reply by May 1 of this year, I shall conclude that I need no such permissions from you and that no monetary recompense shall be expected by you or by your immediate Stuart relations. I especially include your cousin Edward, who knows of my interests and has been kind enough to forward my correspondence to you in America.

Hoping that I am not disturbing you greatly, I am

> Yrs. very truly,
> J.M. Barrie

Melanie almost choked. Here in her hands was an unknown piece of handwritten correspondence from one of the most famous writers in all modern literature, the creator of Peter Pan!

But he *wasn't* the creator of Peter Pan, was he? Pan's existence was not confined to the pages of Barrie's wonderful story. He was real, regardless of how insane that idea sounded. "Permissions," she muttered thoughtfully. "The fanciful writings of James Albert Stuart..."

The conclusion that crept into her mind gave her a genuine hot flash. Perspiration broke out on her forehead. She wanted to run outside into cool air before she passed out, but she couldn't move. *The memoirs were written by Jon's great-grandfather! He was Captain Hook!* It took her some time to come to grips with this revelation, along with the follow-up: *Barrie somehow found the book and, thinking it to be fantasy, borrowed details for his story!*

Panting, Melanie read and reread the letter. *Did Jon ever see this?* she wondered. No way to tell. Since its writing almost a century ago, the letter had been opened very few times, and when it had, the process had been carefully done — the creases were crisp and the paper white except for a slight yellowing at the edges. *Edward Stuart, some cousin of Emmerich's, forwarded this to him in San Francisco,* she thought, *along with two previous letters.* She could find no trace of those two letters.

Mind spinning, she opened the second letter, the one postmarked December 5, 1989. It was from S. Lancaster, 28774 Raimmi Avenue, Akron, Ohio. Inside was a copy of the partially complete Stuart family history that Sylvester had created with the help of his old mother Alice. Again, how the hell had it ended up in a secret pocket of James Stuart's memoirs? Melanie was sure she had given Hillary her apartment address. She checked the envelope. "No way!" she said. "I did *not* give Jon's address!"

In the end, what did it matter? She had lost a whole month of her life, hadn't she? Compared to that, what was so incredible about a magically rerouted letter? *Guess who, Mel.*

She went outside into Jon's garden to think. Her hot flash had made her dizzy and shaky. *Okay, Peter freakin' Pan put the letters in the book that was already hidden. That means he wanted me to find them. I mean, he knows who I am. He's been watching me. He knows I'm determined to figure this all out. He must want me to figure it out.* But figure out what? What did the magical boy want her to know? She already knew that Jon was gone. She already accepted that he was in the Neverland. What more was there? For that matter, why didn't Pan just tell her? Did he enjoy watching her run around like a madwoman? *Maybe he does,* she thought. The boy was not nice to adults. Barrie's story blatantly said so and depicted Peter casually killing pirates for the sheer "adventure" of it.

She stormed back into the house. "Peter Pan! Hey, I know you exist! Show yourself, I want to talk to you!" She paused. "Oh, uh, sorry about the fairy remark earlier. Hope nobody got hurt."

She received no answer. She hadn't really expected one. She didn't feel that creepy feeling that told her she was being watched, which meant that she was truly alone. The minute it returned, though, she planned to call for the boy again. In the meantime, she studied Sylvester Lancaster's sketchy family history. It wasn't presented as a family tree but as a series of paragraphs.

- Alice Maria Hayes, daughter of Maria Susanna (Penn) and Frederick Hayes, married 1953 in San Francisco to Thomas Lancaster
  children: Sylvester, June
- Maria Susanna Penn, daughter of Alice (Brahm) and Carl Penn, married 1924 in San Francisco to Fredrick Hayes
  children: Jason, Julia, Alice, Benjamin
- Alice Brahm, sister of Emmerich Albert Stuart's wife Sylvia (Brahm) Stuart, married 1888 in San Francisco to Carl Penn
  children: Martin, Maria, Matthew

On and on it went, back in time to the mid-1700's, but the arrangement and wording of the information was very confusing. Evidently old Alice, or Sylvester her scribe, didn't care, or maybe it was perfectly clear to them. It made Melanie's head hurt trying to follow it. Moreover, it was strange that the list excluded any birth and death dates. The only dates given were marriage dates.

Melanie zeroed in on one thing right away: the name Emmerich Albert Stuart. Alice's connection to the Stuarts was through Emmerich's wife Sylvia, who was Alice Brahm's sister — and Jon's grandmother.

Melanie also noticed something else. Someone, probably old Alice Lancaster because the handwriting was shaky, had made notations in the margins: M, MS and MM. The letters were scrawled next to five names, all Stuart men: George Thomas warranted an MS; Winthrop Spencer had an MM; Albert Andrew had an MM; Phillip Edward had one M; and James Albert had an MM followed by a question mark that had been traced over and over, making it very dark on the page. After the question mark was scribbled "March 11, 1896." Melanie inferred by the date that James Albert was Jon's great-grandfather, the cursed author of the mad memoirs. So why this one specific date, March 11, 1896?

Melanie clutched her stomach, rushed to the bathroom and threw up her toast and coffee. It happened so fast that she ended up with her face resting on the cool tile floor, wondering how she had gotten there. Morning sickness? That must be it. Dr. Odet had told her she was in her fourth week of pregnancy. Most pregnant women began to experience morning sickness between the fourth and sixth weeks. That would put her right on schedule. *Lucky me.*

But March 11, 1896...

Suddenly she made the connection. She pulled herself up to a sitting position, holding her belly and making sure the heaves were over before getting up. She made it back to the dining room table and opened Hook's memoirs to the first entry: March 12, 1896. *James must have started his captain's log in the Neverland the very next day after his abduction. So naturally – or maybe unnaturally, the man ended up insane – that was the date he used to begin his memoirs of those events. Fanciful writings, poppycock! Every last nightmarish experience recounted in these pages is probably true!* She felt sick again. *Oh God, is this what's happening to Jon?*

Melanie Forrester scooped up her keys from the table and did something she'd never done before. She drove to the store and bought a bottle of brandy.

CHAPTER 33

The plan had to be carried out in the morning, after the air had had a chance to warm but not so late that the Lost Boys would be awake. The boys slept till about nine o'clock because they always stayed up too late, playing pranks by fairylight and trying to keep each other from falling asleep. At least, that's what Stuart read in the notes he'd taken from Barricoe Billy's over-caffeinated interview.

Stuart selected five men, Smee and Cecco among them, to go ashore with him at dawn. Barricoe Billy came, too, being essential to Stuart's plan. The lad had agreed to participate when Stuart assured him that Wendy would not be harmed. The boy confessed that he didn't care about Wendy as much as he feared Pan. But he dearly wanted to impress his captain. As for Stuart, he could easily have forced Billy to cooperate, but Cecco had reminded him that an enthusiastic apprentice was a gift, especially after the loss of Li'l Lad Jack.

As quietly as possible, they rowed their gig towards shore.

Stuart was armed to the teeth, as were his men. He wasn't afraid of an Indian ambush. He was afraid that the croc would show up. From the minute he stepped down into the gig his heart began to race. He, Smee and Cecco held their pistols ready, and the journey to shore was filled with gruesome anticipation as they monitored the water around the boat. Just one ripple, just the slightest discoloration under the surface, just one measly *tick* and Stuart was ready to blast away with not two but four loaded pistols.

They made it to the island with no mishaps. Stuart chose a patch of beach on the north shore by a jetty of high rocks that separated Pirate's Bay from the Mermaid Lagoon. While the men carried the boat up the sand and hid it amongst the palms, Smee used a palm frond to sweep away their tracks. If the Indians were patrolling the beach – they usually didn't, but Stuart was taking no chances – why give them any help?

Stuart turned in a wary circle, trying to look everywhere at once. The croc could pop up from anywhere, from the water, the jungle, from behind the jetty. For all he knew it had seen him coming and had buried itself in the sand like some weird beach flounder, waiting for him to step close enough to rise up and bite his leg off. Stuart's chest already hurt from the intensity of his rapid heartbeats. For a brief moment he thought of calling the whole thing off. *Get a grip!* he admonished himself. *Do you want out of this madhouse or not?* He did. By the time his men gathered around him, his expression was coolly confident. "Mister Barricoe Billy," he said to the boy. "Which path do we take?"

Billy, whose shackle and cannonball had been removed for the occasion, studied the line of palms and other foliage that marked an abrupt change from sand to jungle. The openings of several trails lay visible, all leading to different places. To walk beyond the confines of such a trail invited a myriad of dangers: getting mauled by a tiger, strangled by a python, stung by giant spiders or otherwise dispatched by a variety of nasty creatures that inhabited those shadowy depths. Not all the creatures on the island were natural, either. Some were fanciful beasts with unusual appetites. Stuart had knowledge of many of these dangers from memory, though he also knew that he had never set foot on the island before. The contradiction, as always, gave his immediate experience an illusory quality, as if he were sleepwalking into certain doom.

Billy pointed to the opening of a trail some forty yards down the beach. "That one," he said confidently, and began to lead the way.

Smee put a hand on Stuart's shoulder. "Yeh really trust the spalpeen?" he whispered. "Sar, he's gonna wait for his chance an' fly off!"

"I tink not," Kamau said. Following Stuart's orders, he had a pistol dedicated to one target: Billy. "I kill him before he get a foot off de ground."

"And I'll nail his nuts to my door," Stuart added. "I informed him of that before we left." He curtly gestured for Kamau to lead the way. "If you don't mind."

With a stoic nod to his captain, Kamau started after Billy, his long dreadlocks swaying, that uncanny gait of his making his bare feet hardly disturb the sand. He needed to stay next to the boy, but more than that, he needed to be the first of the pirates in line. Kamau's senses were unusually sharp. He heard sounds before anyone else, and he had an almost preternatural ability to sense when danger lay ahead. Naturally, he took point on most expeditions. Smee came next, then Stuart himself. Cecco brought up the rear.

Billy reached the trail head and, without pause, entered the jungle, followed by Kamau, who looked as if his brawny black body was being swallowed by a great green mouth.

Smee was about to follow him when Stuart removed his hat — he shouldn't have worn the stupid thing, it was too big to be practical on the trails — and thrust it into Smee's hands. The bosun took it obediently if not willingly. He had already been charged with carrying an eight foot length of rope which he had decided to wrap around his already wide middle so as to keep his hands free for his pistol and cutlass. Now he had a hat to carry, and not just any hat. It was the captain's hat, which meant that he would pay dearly if it got damaged. With a sigh he plodded after Kamau. Stuart, knowing full well how miffed his bosun was, snickered and followed with Cecco close behind.

Stuart did indeed feel as if he were being swallowed. Thick green walls pressed up on either side of him, the canopy abruptly blocked all sunlight, and the air became moist and heavy. Like breath. Yes, the jungle was a single gigantic being. He was inside of it, and it was breathing around him.

The sensation did not particularly bother him. He was too busy ogling everything, the bushes, the trees, the birds overhead. He recognized none of them. Yes, they *looked* like ferns, palmettos and parrots, but there was something innately wrong about them. Not unhealthy or troubling, no, just the opposite. Colors were too vivid. Birdsong was too lively. The air, moist and heavy though it was against his skin, was also fresh, too fresh. Everything sparkled, not overtly but with gentle pricks and pops of light as if the whole place was infused with an eldritch power. It was wonderful and yet disconcerting, as if the place was more beautiful than humankind was designed to handle.

This is what magic feels like, he thought, amazed at how everything appeared to be in perfect focus and at the same time softened as though viewed through gauze. If that even made sense. Yes, it made sense here. It was as if, by stepping onto the soil of the island, Stuart finally understood it, not intellectually but viscerally, in his gut where it counted. The Neverland was a magic spell in motion. It was made of the stuff of dreams. It wasn't real.

But it *was*.

He reined in his curiosity by reminding himself of his mission. He was trying to leave this place, not set up camp and conduct a field study. Still, as he walked along he noticed a pull, a yearning in his heart that hadn't been there before. He'd never felt anything like it. *If I'm here long enough, it will own me,* he thought. *It will become home, and I will come to love it even as I despise it. This place is a trap, not a paradise. Everything in it is designed to ensnare adults and give them grief, especially me. My men might as well be expendable, garnish on the plate. I'm the* pièce de résistance. *I'm what this place really wants.* That concept knocked the curiosity right out of him.

Every minute or so he glanced overhead to make sure there were no snakes or spiders ready to drop down for dinner. Memory told him that pythons were bigger in the Neverland than in reality, and spiders could be as fat as a fist. Panthers and jaguars prowled here as well as tigers, and the monkeys, even the little ones whose comical howls echoed through the greenery like Looney Tunes laughter, could be dangerous if they wanted to be.

But, oh, the beauty of the place! He couldn't help but gawk. Long tangles of liana draped through the high banyan branches like strands of giant green jungle hair. Deep green moss grew in thick pads like impeccably manicured mini-lawns. Unearthly red, green and shock-pink insects buzzed by, delicate living lanterns lit from within by magic perhaps, bigger and shinier than any June bug he had ever seen. There were flowers the size of punch bowls, ferns as tall as trees, and the sounds — chirps and caws, screeches and whoops, everything so vibrant, everything so *alive!*

For the first time, despite the horrors and the pain he had thus far endured, Stuart wished that he could have been a boy here. If only Peter Pan had come for him when he had been a child. Oh, the fun he could have had! And he would never have gone home. No, he would have stayed here, an ageless boy playing for eternity. All the beatings, the punishments, the lies — they never would have happened. Pan would have been on *his* side. If only...

Something grabbed his right arm. Stuart managed not to cry out, but the sight paralyzed him. A squatty red-green bush with whip-like foliage had literally *reached out* for him. Tendrils were rapidly enveloping his hook. More tendrils were enfolding his legs, squeezing them together with alarming strength. As he struggled for balance, a tendril from the other side of the trail snagged his left wrist. Another darted for his neck like a grotesque multi-jointed finger. If it managed to get a grip, Stuart was sure it could crack his spine. He would be dragged into the undergrowth so fast it would seem as though he'd never existed. After that... Stuart didn't want to know.

He couldn't reach his sword. He had to strain against the tendrils and pivot his right arm until the grotesque plant-fingers were pulled taut, then angle his forearm down so that his hook could slice. The stuff was as tough as rope, but Smee had sharpened Stuart's hook that morning, bless him. It took several awkward cuts to get his arm free. Stuart was shaking it wildly to get the still-clinging pieces off when the tendrils around his ankles jerked his feet out from under him. He toppled with a grunt.

As he lay on his side, stunned, he saw that Cecco behind him and Smee in front of him were in the same predicament, hacking with knife and cutlass, leaving piles of squirming green fingers at their feet.

Some of them landed on Stuart's face where they wriggled feebly, cut off from the mother-plant's bloodthirsty vigor. Stuart rolled, and they fell off even as new tendrils reached for him. Stuart would have screamed, but the last thing he wanted was for one of those ungodly digits to dart into his mouth. His guts churned at the idea of having to bite it to keep it from worming its way down his throat.

With a burst of furious energy, he surged to his knees and knocked away the tendrils that had not yet clamped themselves to him. The next thing he knew, Smee was helping him to his feet, slashing with his cutlass while at the same time pulling his captain out of the danger zone. Then Smee and Cecco stamped on the cuttings like manic flamenco dancers to make sure they were dead. Stuart joined them. Not a sound was made save hectic grunts and wheezes along with the stomping.

When they were all free, Stuart had to fight down a crazy urge to laugh. It was funny, wasn't it? The three of them silently freaking out in this perverse Eden, battling for their lives against a bunch of bushes! And what made it all the funnier was the fact that Kamau had been unable to help them. He'd had to stand there and watch because Billy was in his charge. If his captain survived but Billy got away, Kamau knew the hook would send him to Davy Jones. By God, the Neverland had a wicked sense of humor! *Even if it's aimed at me*, Stuart reminded himself.

As for Billy, this was the first time he had seen the hook in action up close. He stood transfixed with a morbid fascination made all the more intense because Captain Hook appeared to be *laughing* over the whole thing. Stuart saw the boy's fright turn to slavish adoration. The sight made him want to puke.

"Go," he snarled. The group hastened on.

By the way, that was python weed, came the dark thought. *It doesn't touch the Indians or the children. Just pirates, particularly you.*

Well, naturally, Stuart thought bitterly. *Not only does the croc want my hide, but a jungle full of discriminating plants wants to kill me, too. No wonder I don't come ashore very often.*

The animal life operates according to the same rules, the darkness added conversationally. *The children wander freely without harm. The*

Indians hunt with some danger, but they know their business. You, on the other hand—

Yes, yes, I get it, shut up!

Kamau stopped. He crouched low, raising his hand in a danger signal. Everyone followed suit, wondering what Kamau had heard. Then it came, as if Stuart's thoughts had summoned it.

Tick. Tick. Tick.

It came from their left, an incongruous sound amidst the jungle's chittering, squawking ambience. It moved toward them.

Stuart's blood became ice in his veins. This was exactly what he had dreaded, and he had walked right into the nightmare like a blind fool. That *tick-tick-ticking* monstrosity out there was going to eat him! The idea pulled the breath out of his mouth in a thin, sickly sigh. He tried in vain to remind himself that the last time the croc had seen him, it hadn't wanted to eat him. At least, no more than it wanted to eat anybody. It hadn't yet... *tasted* him. It had gone after the other two hapless pirates in the water, right? *He* had gotten away.

But were his parallel memories accurate? One set of memories insisted that he had cut off his own hand. There had been no croc involved. Maybe it didn't want him at all, at least not him personally.

Don't be ridiculous, the darkness scorned. *The story is in full play. The beast is after you and only you.*

Shut up shut up shut up! Stuart thought, a whirlwind of panic spiraling in his stomach. His mind replayed the moment of his introduction to the croc, the astonishing size of the reptile as it had glided past him that day when Pan's brats had knocked him overboard. If the beast ate him, a single gulp could do the job. It wouldn't even have to chew!

Or maybe it would chew anyway, turning Stuart's last sensations of life into unspeakable agony, pitiful pointless shrieking as the creature shook him in its jaws like a dog with a rabbit, whip-cracking his spine in a dozen places and breaking his neck with the sound of a carrot snapping in half. Awesomely sharp teeth would puncture his skin like pins through a balloon, and he would bathe in his own hot blood while he felt his flesh being ripped off his bones. Maybe, just maybe, he would be granted one last second of consciousness actually *inside* the beast as it began to digest him.

That last thought ratcheted Stuart's terror up to near hysteria. *Don't think that, don't think that, make it go away!* He grasped for the great grey wall in his mind and tried to slam it down, but he couldn't find it, not through the frenzy that passed for his thoughts. He was so close to screaming he could taste it, a ghastly metallic tang on his tongue. He hoped to God he wouldn't piss himself. He feared he might have already done it. His knees were shaking, threatening to renege their moral duty and let him drop like a disgraceful sack. He wasn't going to be able to maintain control much longer...

Tick. Tick. Tick.

Smee and Cecco, pistols in both hands, aimed them toward the sound. Kamau did the same, one hand holding his pistol and the other grasping Billy's arm. Billy, who was not allowed to carry a weapon, had picked up a big rock.

Stuart knew he should draw his pistol, too, but now he feared that four shots wouldn't stop the croc. Eight wouldn't. Ten wouldn't. The thing had a hide like steel. *And crocodiles can run on land,* he remembered from an article he had read once. Sweat broke out all over his body, hot and sticky on his skin, as the article's information welled up. *The thing can chase me. It can run. Oh, Christ, if it knows I'm here, I'm dead, that's all there is to it. I'm dead dead dead...*

Tick. Tick. Tick.

Except for following the sound with their pistols, the pirates remained motionless. The croc, somewhere beyond a thick barrier of ferns and palmetto, was moving parallel to their trail, though by intent or coincidence, Stuart couldn't guess. He did know that he was dangerously close to howling his bloody head off, especially when the croc paused for a nerve-wracking moment, its breath coming in slow deep rumbles. *It knows I'm here. It can smell me. It's going to charge at me any second with that toothy mouth grinning.* Stuart contemplated making a dash for — where could he possibly go? — when the ticking veered off, heading for the Mermaid Lagoon.

Stuart crumpled against a banyan tree, trembling so badly that even his phantom hand was twitching in its own far-away dimension, fingers spasming like cut tendrils of python weed. He knew he must look supremely foolish, but the pirates were making a point of *not* noticing that. With casual deliberateness, they turned to face any direction but his while dutifully blocking Billy's view of their pitifully unmanned leader.

"Sar?" Smee said cautiously after a full minute had passed.

Stuart nodded and attempted to stand. That was when he noticed his pinky finger. It was bare. Melanie's ruby ring was gone.

He stared, unsure what to do. He had worn the ring continuously since that fateful day in Beggar's Port. He would never have taken it off, never, and it couldn't have fallen off. It fit too tight. *The python weeds*, he thought. *They must have pulled it off during their attack. Maybe that's* why *they attacked!*

He wanted to order the men back to the battle site, but he knew he could not. His dignity and therefore his ability to command hung in the balance. This was no time to go running helter-skelter through the jungle in search of a ring, no matter its sentimental value. The pirates would think him weak and unfit if he could be so easily emasculated by the loss of a mere love token. At any other time he would challenge such a view, but not now. Begging Melanie's forgiveness, he forced himself to stand, wobbly but upright.

He was familiar with his body's terror recovery process well enough at this point — he was thrown into that state several times a day. His muscles would require a few more minutes to regain full coordination, and he would suffer from a disorienting tunnel vision for a few minutes beyond that. As for his racing heartbeat, it was already slowing down, though each individual thump hurt like a boxer's fist punching his ribcage from the inside.

Like any good alcoholic, he had brought Hook's flask with him filled with brandy. He fumbled it out of his coat pocket and took a good long pull. *Ambrosia, that's what it is, goddamn nerve-soothing ambrosia.* "I'll be fine," he started to say to Smee, and that's when he saw a dozen tendrils of python weed dart straight for Cecco's neck from both sides of the path.

Before Cecco himself saw the danger, Stuart kicked the man's feet out from under him. As the first mate fell flat, Stuart slashed at the groping tendrils with his hook, letting action transform the energy of his terror into lethal rage. In the space of a breath the tendrils were writhing feebly on the path. The wounded stalks curled back into the shadows. Smee had barely had time to draw his sword.

Stuart stood panting, surveying what he had done, stunned by the speed and accuracy with which he had done it. If he hadn't responded so quickly, one of his measly two friends in this whole wretched world might have ended up choked to death. He helped Cecco to his feet. "Sorry for kicking you."

Cecco's nod was more of an adrenaline jerk. "Any time, James, any time."

"Here." Stuart handed Cecco the flask, which he had miraculously held onto during the whole incident without spilling a drop.

Cecco took it. "As for me, I'll die at sea," he muttered, and drank. Hearing the rhyme, Stuart knew it was something that Cecco often said before taking a drink. The first mate meant it, too, especially when his feet happened to be upon Pan's land. The rhyme was the closest thing to a prayer the Italian ever uttered.

The group resumed traveling for twenty minutes more, periodically hacking at more python weed and ducking out of sight when flocks of fairies flew by. Stuart ordered his men to resist the urge to pat any dust off until the fairies were long gone. *All I need is for those overgrown gnats to alert Pan. We'd be sitting ducks with the dust already on us.* As much as they had tried to avoid it, dust sparkled on their shoulders and in their hair anyhow. The stuff stuck to them as they brushed the foliage. It was like decorative super glue.

The trail opened on a clearing where a stream bubbled out of a crevice in a rock face. "This is where she gets water every morning," Billy announced.

"Excellent," Stuart told the boy. "Continue."

"James," Cecco whispered from behind him as they resumed their trek. "If this is where the wench fetches water, Pan's hideout can't be far. Why do we need her? We can find Pan ourselves."

"Think about it," Stuart replied reasonably. "Wendy can fly. And if Tinker Bell dusts the buckets, which I'm sure she does, then they have no weight when they're full of water. Ergo, it doesn't matter how far away the water source is, Wendy can fetch it with ease. I wouldn't put it past Pan to place his hideout far from any surface water as a precaution."

Cecco patted Stuart's shoulder as if to say, "Excellent point."

It had, in fact, been pure ad lib, but Stuart nodded sagely over his shoulder as if he had spent half the night deeply pondering such things.

Ten minutes through more jungle followed by a short climb up a rocky stairway and they stood at the most lovely spot Stuart had ever seen, a small glade with a deep pool of calm crystal water. A little waterfall leaked from a crevice down into the pool, adding a soft tranquil splashing sound to the ambience. Clumps of jungle flowers, huge and bright, bordered each side of the fall. A thick wall of bamboo stood beyond, the Neverland version of a white picket fence, perhaps. Banyans leaned their branches far over the entire area, keeping it in cool shadow.

"This is it," Billy said.

Stuart checked his pocket watch. Seven forty-seven. "Go," he ordered the men, "but keep within earshot. And might I remind you that if one of you, any one, so much as glimpses her at her bath, I will rip you bow to stern, savvy?"

The pirates nodded and scattered, Kamau still in charge of Billy. Stuart decided to hide behind the bamboo. He squeezed through it and chose the rut between two massive roots of a banyan — a plant that he hoped would not try to kill him — to sit down and wait.

Billy had warned Stuart that Wendy might not show up. She didn't come to the pool every single morning. Stuart sat by the banyan, wondering if he would have to do this all over again tomorrow and perhaps the next day as well. He wished he had drunk more coffee before leaving the ship. Despite its many perils, Stuart found the jungle to be a lovely place, peaceful in a way with its lulling chorus of crickets and bird song. Every breath he took carried the intoxicating perfume of flowers and the rich smell of damp earth, a heady combination. It would be glorious to take a comfy nap in this profound greenery. It would be suicide, too.

So he spent the next thirty-five minutes closely monitoring the plants around him, wary of any sign of movement on the ground, among the leaves or overhead in the canopy. He was seriously pining for that cup of coffee when he heard it.

Humming.

CHAPTER 34

Stuart crawled over the ridge-like roots of the banyan to the bamboo. Careful not to disturb a single leaf, he peeked between the stout green poles. He had a clear but narrow view of the pool.

Wendy flew in from the south, humming what sounded like *The Merry-Go-Round Broke Down.* Her slender form alighted on the top stone stair. For a moment she stood like a statue, continuing to hum, one hand clutching an Indian weave blanket, the other a sword. She set both down after scrutinizing the area.

The little girl started to unbutton her long white nightgown, now humming the theme to *Hawaii Five-O,* much to Stuart's amusement. He averted his gaze. From the start he'd had no intention of compromising Wendy's modesty. He was no pedophilic Peeping Tom. He would wait until she was in the water, then catch her helpless, he alone. He didn't trust the others not to look.

Wendy continued to hum merrily as she undressed. Stuart waited to hear splashing. When he did, he slowly stood up. *This is damned improper!* he thought, a last ditch effort of his old morals to stay his plan. *She's taking a bath, for Chrissake!*

To hell with your morals, came the dark thought. *Do you want to get home or not? Catch the bitch!*

He crept out of hiding. Wendy was neck-deep in the water with her head under the little waterfall, one arm held out so that she could scrub it with a cloth. She heard the faint rustle of Stuart's movements and splashed forward, out from under the fall so that she could see.

In that split second during which their eyes met — the pretty brown orbs of a little girl and the forget-me-not blue lasers of an ersatz pirate — the sentient disease infecting Stuart made its move. Outwardly, he showed no change. He gazed steadily at Wendy with a sort of gentle wonder, entranced by her lovely face and sweet innocence. Inside, he swelled with black vigor, barely holding back a shudder at the sweeping pleasure of it. That small part of him that still found Hook revolting and unclean cowered in shame at the easy takeover. The rest of him, the most of him, smiled. "Shhhhh," he said to Wendy, raising a dainty index finger to his lips.

It was like casting a spell. Wendy's mouth dropped open as if to scream, but nothing came out. Her arm flopped back into the water, and she gaped at him helplessly.

Stuart turned his head a little to one side. He could keep track of her with his peripheral vision, but he deliberately made sure that he could distinguish no details through the alarmingly clear water. "How nice to see you again, Miss Darling," he drawled.

Freed from Stuart's hypnotizing stare, Wendy got hold of herself. "Captain Hook! How — how *dare* you!"

"Hush, my dear. I haven't come to peep, nor do I intend to harm you — unless, of course, you make enough of a fuss to alert the Indians. Then I promise that I shall harm you most grievously. Oh, and please do not attempt to fly away. I'd hate to have you shot."

Wendy turned a frantic circle in the water, trying to see through the wall of green around her.

"Aye, you are surrounded," Stuart said, "but I give you my word that my men are not interested in your attire or lack thereof." *I hope,* he thought.

Wendy realized that she was visible under the water. With a squeak of dismay she paddled to the edge of the pool and grabbed her nightgown. She plunged it under the surface and wrapped it around herself. "How did you know I'd be here? What do you want!"

"Quietly, please," Stuart warned her. "I only want to talk."

"Oh, right!" she spat. "You mean, nasty, evil—"

Knowing that her body was now sufficiently covered, Stuart spun around, cutting off her list of insults with his snake's stare. Holding her with it, he shouldered out of his topcoat. "Put this on, my dear. You've drenched your nightie." He held it out, averting his eyes once more.

"I will not!"

"Then I'll pull you out by your hair, and you'll come as you are."

The sound of splashing. But Wendy didn't take the coat. When Stuart turned around, she was holding her sword with one hand and holding her nightgown around her body with the other.

He laughed. "You can't be serious."

She lunged at him.

Stuart easily caught her blade with his hook, tweaked it out of her grasp and sent the weapon hurtling into the trees. He held his topcoat out again. "I did so want this to be a peaceable meeting, but if you keep this up..."

She took the coat. With an expression of repulsion at having to wear her enemy's apparel, she put it on. It dragged on the ground, a fact which annoyed Stuart — the trek back to the boat would ruin the trim — but it covered her, and that was what counted. Stuart gave a short, sharp whistle. Smee, Cecco, Kamau and Billy emerged from the foliage.

When Wendy saw Billy, her outrage doubled. "Traitor!" she shrilled.

Stuart pressed his hook to her throat. "What did I say, Miss Darling? Lower your volume, or I shall be forced to lower it for you."

She shut her mouth and pursed her lips, her cheeks flushed with restraint.

Stuart nodded to Smee, who had already unrolled the rope from around his pudgy waist. He gleefully knotted it around Wendy's waist, trapping her arms. Stuart tugged his kerchief from his sleeve. "Pucker up," he said playfully.

When Wendy opened her mouth to exclaim, "What?" he stuffed the kerchief into it.

"I do regret the need for such tactics," he told her, "but we can't have you calling for Pan, can we?" To the others he said, "Let's go."

Billy took the lead as before, sticking his tongue out at Wendy as he went past. Kamau went next. As Smee passed next, he handed the end of the rope to Stuart, who flicked it like a horse's reins. "If you would, my dear."

Wendy began to walk.

CHAPTER 35

Melanie screamed when she woke up the next morning. It was Christmas Day. There was a package lying next to her on the bed.

It was like no package she had ever seen before. Something the size and vague shape of a lemon was wrapped in rough white cloth and tied with some kind of green vine. Melanie knew damned well who must have put it there. Her mind, overwrought and depressed, suggested the worst possible contents: one of Jon's fingers, an eyeball, a piece of his scalp with a lock of hair trailing from it. *Would it be blond or black?* she wondered.

"Are you here?" she asked the room. "Is anybody here?"

Silence. That I'm-being-watched feeling was not upon her.

She picked up the bundle, curious and afraid. She had to open it. What if it was something important? Then again, Peter Pan was not above a nasty practical joke. This whole situation was one big nasty practical joke. She considered taking the easy route and throwing the thing out the window when she saw letters embroidered on the cloth.

She untied the vine ribbons and opened the cloth flat. It was a square kerchief of fine soft linen with a lace border and the letters JH embroidered in the bottom right-hand corner. It had been holding together a clam shell, the halves of which were now shifted out of alignment. Steeling herself, Melanie poked the top half off. Her ruby ring lay inside the cupped interior of the bottom shell.

"Oh God." She started to cry. "Oh God, why is this happening?" Did Peter Pan send this to her just to torment her, or could it actually be from Jon? Was he trying to communicate? Her nose twitched at a scent, faint but familiar. She sniffed the kerchief. *Jesus, it smells like him, it smells like Jon!*

The phone rang, but she couldn't move to answer it. From the downstairs machine she heard her own calm recorded voice speak briefly. Her mother's voice was much louder. "Melly, dear, Merry Christmas! I presume you've gone to church or are at a friend's house. I hope you're out having some fun with friends. You need to get out more. Oh, I wish you had decided to visit me for the holidays, but I understand. I love you, honey, and I hope you're feeling better. Call me later and let me know you're all right. Bye, sweetie. Love you."

Melanie sat on her bed for almost half an hour, holding the ruby ring in one hand and the kerchief in the other. Her mind and body were blank. No thoughts, no worries, no wants. It was as if she just shut down. The ringing of the phone again knocked her out of her stupor. This time it was Yolanda, wishing her a Merry Christmas and reminding her of her open house Christmas party. "Come anytime from two till eight tonight. I'd love you to meet some people. If you're not up for it, at least call me so I know you're okay, okay? Bye."

Melanie listened as the answering machine clicked off its recording. In that instant she knew that she would hate Christmas for the rest of her life. There was no color in the world. The day was bleak and meaningless. *No wonder suicide rates go up in December. Merry, my ass.* The happy holiday twitched like a wounded sparrow in her heart and died. It was replaced by a taffy-twisted mixture of foreboding, terror and utter despair. She knew she would feel this way on Christmas from this year onward.

She managed to get out of bed and get dressed, deciding in the process to resume wearing the ruby ring on the third finger of her left hand where it belonged. She examined it first, making sure it was indeed the same ring and that nothing strange had been done to it. Had Pan put a spell on it? How would she be able to tell? *He doesn't use magic that way,* she scolded herself. *He's just a boy. This is nothing more than a prank to him.*

That made her think. Had the boy taken something of hers to give to Jon? She checked her room carefully. Everything seemed to be there, including all her jewelry. If Pan had taken something small, she might never notice its absence.

Enough of such thoughts. She went downstairs, made coffee and toast, and resumed her researches. The only way to make all this horror stop was to unravel the mystery and get Jon back.

She turned first to old Alice Lancaster's family history. She had already studied the jumble of names and dates and had almost gone cross-eyed trying to figure it all out. Job #1: retype the information in a readable form. With a sigh, she booted the Mac Plus in the downstairs office, opened MacWrite, and began the laborious task of unraveling and carefully reweaving Alice and her son's awkward notes. Thirty minutes later, she turned on the dot matrix printer and printed out a fairly sturdy branch of the Stuart family tree that went back to the mid-1700's. It was a start.

But as she had lamented earlier, the only dates Alice provided were marriage dates, plus there were still plenty of holes with no names. Alice had also neglected to provide details about the people themselves. Except for the mysterious M, MS and MM notations, Alice's sole commentary consisted of two short notes. The first she had written next to the name of Anna (Hancock) Stuart, wife of James. She had scribbled the words "artifact 1896." By Emmerich's name she had written "America 1897." Although Melanie couldn't guess what the first notation meant, she presumed that the second referred to Emmerich's move from England to America in 1897, perhaps directly to San Francisco where he later built Stuart House.

She took the printout to the living room table. She opened James Stuart's mad memoirs and searched every line for any snippet that might augment the document. She was able to fill in a few of Alice's holes with names, but nothing made that bell in her head go *ding!*

She did find an interesting tidbit about Anna, James' wife:

> Anna, my Anna. In every cloud I see your radiant face, in every glint of moonlight upon the water I see your smile. The breeze carries the soothing caress of your fingertips to my cheek, and the warmth of summer

embraces me as once your loving arms held me to your
bosom. How your voice cries out to me in the roaring
storm, yet I am powerless to answer. I stand in the rain
of your tears yet cannot cry my own. Forever you
remain with me, sweet Anna, dearest Anna, yet touch
you I cannot, seek you I dare not. Alone must I walk
until I die, even here, even here. And so I yearn for
death that I may live again with you. *Au revoir*, my love.

This one entry, amidst dozens that began with nothing more
specific than "Next Day" or "After That," had been labeled with a
specific date: November 4, 1897. *The same year Emmerich left England,*
Melanie mused. *The entry reads like a eulogy. Might Anna have died on
that date, motivating Emmerich to flee to America to escape the sole burden
of his insane father?* It sounded plausible. She made the note and
continued paging through the memoirs.

About ten minutes later she saw it, a correlation between James'
mad ramblings and one of old Alice Lancaster's margin notes.
According to James, Albert Andrew Stuart, a staunch captain of
repute in the British Royal Navy and apparently an ancestor that
James greatly admired, had gone "inexplicably mad" on September 21,
1826. He disappeared eight days later, never to be seen again. Alice
had written MM by his name. She had written MM by James as well.

Both men had gone mad. Both men had then disappeared.
"Missing," she breathed, and dropped her pen. "Both mad and
missing."

* * * * *

Holidays are not a convenient time to conduct research. Melanie
itched to phone Alice and Sylvester but knew better than to do it. She
still hadn't heard from the elusive journalist-relative Francine Rhodes,
either, but there was no sense phoning Rhodes' work number on
Christmas Day. "I can't even go to the damned library!" she
grumbled, pacing the kitchen with a cup of catnip tea.

She had learned from Jon that catnip worked on people as well as
on cats. Ingesting it — in her case, drinking tea made from the leaves —

acted as a mild sedative. Sniffing it, on the other hand, had a stimulating effect, which she was now witnessing as all four of Jon's cats watched her, noses in the air. They started mewling for their share until Melanie couldn't stand it anymore. She stomped out into Jon's garden, which she had let fall into a sad state of neglect, although the catnip was still growing fine. "Good little weed," she cooed to it, gathering a handful of leaves and bringing them inside. "Here," she then told the cats, and sprinkled the leaves on the floor. "Now shut up."

The cats sniffed and began to eat and roll in the aromatic treat. Before Melanie finished her tea, fat Fuzzybutt was asleep on her back in the middle of a dozen green bits, all four furry paws splayed out as if she were a butterfly pinned to a board. The other three cats were rocketing around the house in a nip-induced play frenzy.

The tea did its job for her as well. Sufficiently calmed, Melanie returned to Jon's computer and logged onto her favorite research tool, the UCLA network. "Black Lake Cottage," she murmured as she typed. J.M. Barrie had mentioned it in his letter. Certainly she could find some information about it from the college collections.

She found plenty. Black Lake Cottage, still standing as a tourist site these days, was located in Surrey, England, on the left-hand side of a road going from Farnham to Tilford. Named for the nearby Black Lake, it was situated near a wild area of forest, a retreat destination for city folk who craved fresh air and escape from city noise. The house had been purchased by Barrie and his wife Mary in April of 1900. The previous owner had been Edward W. Stuart, who had purchased the house in 1897.

There's that date again, 1897. Melanie chewed it over, pushing her Researcher Brain into high gear. *Okay, Emmerich's cousin Edward, who was mentioned in Barrie's letter, owned the cottage. What is the connection? What does Edward living in the cottage have to do with Barrie reading James'* memoirs? Melanie leaned back in Jon's office chair, puzzling. Edward had bought the house in 1897, the year that Emmerich had moved to America. What if Edward had not lived in the house? What if the house was obtained to hide a family secret, a secret so socially damning that Emmerich had fled the country and come to America to avoid its taint?

James! she realized. *James lived there! The Stuarts kept him hidden away to avoid scandal! He had disappeared. He was presumed dead. MM – Mad and Missing.* The conclusion from there was obvious. If James had lived at Black Lake Cottage and written his memoirs of the Neverland there, then he must have come back from the Neverland *alive.*

Melanie popped to her feet, upsetting the memoirs which had been open on her lap. The old book fell on the floor with a thud. She didn't notice. She was totally consumed by one thought:

Pan let him go!

CHAPTER 36

When the kidnapping party arrived back on the ship, Stuart hustled Wendy into his cabin before the superstitious crew could do anything to frighten her. Having a woman onboard, even a diminutive one, would turn the ship into a "hen frigate" in some men's eyes, and the rest would see her as plain bad luck. Sailors, especially pirates, loved their women, but not aboard their vessels. In some pirates the superstition held such sway that, if given a chance, they would have tossed Wendy overboard, perhaps cutting her throat along the way.

Smee had repaired the ripped Oriental screen some time ago, so Stuart directed Wendy behind it where she could tidy herself and put her dried nightgown back on while he waited outside. He was amazed that the white garment was still in one piece. How could it have survived this long, being the single piece of clothing that Wendy wore? *Just one of those things,* he thought. So many mysteries had been shunted into that category lately. If he couldn't explain something, Stuart labeled it "just one of those things." He hadn't the stamina to worry anymore about the Neverland's endless parade of paradoxes.

He had tidied his cabin before leaving that morning, a precaution against this moment. He had put all his maps and charts away and locked his sea chests. If Wendy tried to take revenge on him by wrecking his belongings, there wasn't much she could irreparably damage.

So what was she doing, taking so damned long? Maybe she was investigating the cabin, trying to puzzle out the nefarious personality that called it home. That might prove beneficial. Stuart wanted her to know that he was just a man, an ordinary man, not some magical being like her hero Pan. If he could make her relate to him even on the most rudimentary level, he might have a chance. He paced the quarterdeck, waiting and wondering, while the men on watch tended to the ship's endless demands for maintenance.

Roland, Alf Mason, Morgan Skylights and several others were inspecting and tarring the rigging, some of them dealing with the lines within reach from the deck, others high up on the footropes with buckets and brushes. Sailmaker Francis Doff, better known as Doff Cockers, had Scourie and Noodler mending sails – though how Noodler was able to sew with his hands on backwards, Stuart could not fathom. Jukes, stupid Pegleg Hawkins and Thatcher the carpenter, along with the returned Billy complete with reattached ball and chain, laboriously crawled along the deck on their hands and knees, scrubbing the planks down with a vinegar solution in the never-ending attempt to combat the myriad diseases that commonly swept through close-quartered crews in tropical climes. Later they would fumigate below decks with pans of burning brimstone for the same reason. Both treatments stank to high heaven, but it was better than losing men to typhus, malaria or yellow fever, more commonly known to seamen as ship fever, ague and yellow jack. Somewhere in the back of his mind, Stuart knew there were better ways of combating these diseases, but he couldn't recollect what they were. Vinegar and brimstone seemed to him increasingly logical, however unpleasant.

He glanced up at the crow's nest. He had ordered Kamau to keep watch up there, fearing that Pan would show up soon, wondering where his precious Wendy had gone. Stuart was taking no chances on that front. As for Cecco and Smee, they were below with Cookson, probably drinking. Stuart gave them more leeway than the other men in that department. Unfair? Undoubtedly. Did he care? Not a whit. The rest of the riffraff were off-watch in the forecastle, spraddled in their berths snoring like buffalo.

Stuart paced, trying not to let impatience get the better of him. If Wendy knew what he hoped she knew, if she could tell him how to get out, he might be able to sneak away that very night! The prospect made him want to do a little jig of his own.

He held himself back. Gentleman Starkey was standing watch by the wheel, and he was not the type to appreciate such antics from his captain. Decorum was everything to Starkey, who punched, stabbed and even raped with a weird sort of dignity. He had, Smee had once revealed, been an usher in a public school and had never lost the good form that went with it. Normally Stuart wouldn't give a tinker's damn about Starkey's preferences, or anyone else's for that matter. But he needed the men behind him one hundred percent. Once he was gone, they would be free to think what they liked of him.

After ten minutes had passed, he straightened his long silk vest — Wendy still had his coat — ran his fingers through his hair, pinched his goatee back into its stylish point and knocked on the door of the great cabin to alert the girl before entering.

Wendy was standing prim and proper by the rosewood table, hair neatly combed, face freshly scrubbed so that her cheeks glowed an enchanting pink. She gave no other hint as to what she had been doing all this time and threw him her best haughty glare. "Captain Hook, I demand to know why I've been abducted in this manner! You know better than to be so foolish! Peter Pan will — well, he'll take your other hand for this!"

Stuart squelched the murderous spark of hatred that flamed up from his gut at the mention of Pan. "On the contrary, Miss Darling," he said, "I deeply regret the indecorous manner of your abduction. It was not the sort of scheme I would have preferred."

"Hmp!" The little girl folded her arms. "It appears that I am your prisoner. What barbaric tortures do you intend for me?"

Stuart put his hand to her chin, much the way a loving father might admire his daughter. She really was a beautiful girl. "Is that what you think, my dear?" he said softly. "I told you before, I wish only to talk."

"About Peter and his hideout!" Wendy said, pulling away from his touch.

"'Sdeath and odds fish!" Stuart grumbled. "You really do believe that's all I do with my time. Heaven forbid that Captain Hook should have a *life*. But oh noooo, I must certainly sit around all day and night brooding over Peter Pan!" He gave a growly huff of irritation. "My dear, if that was the sum total of my existence, I would end it myself. Honestly, I have no interest whatsoever as to where Master Pan sets up his messy housekeeping."

That got Wendy's attention well enough. "Then what do you want?"

Stuart feigned bewilderment. "Can't a man have a simple conversation with his neighbor?"

Wendy's lips parted. Stuart could practically see her brain take a sharp left turn. "I... I never thought of us as neighbors. I guess we are." The idea tickled her, though she tried not to show it.

She's not afraid, Stuart thought with fascination. *To her, this is all part of the game!* "Most assuredly, my dear," he agreed with her, "though our relationship thus far has been most unneighborly, don't you think?"

"You're the one who kidnapped *me!"*

"And did it ever occur to you that I am forced to behave in such a deplorable fashion because your dear Peter leaves me no choice? How could I have possibly sent you a proper invitation, hm? I can hardly step ashore without those wild boys or the Indians going after my scalp. For pity's sake, do you think I did this to myself?" Stuart held up his hook.

She recoiled at the sight of it. "You deserved it, you blaggard!"

Stuart allowed himself to scowl just enough to make her nervous. "And, pray, why do you think that? Because Pan told you I did? Tell me, were you there when he so gallantly lopped my hand off and fed it to the crocodile, leaving me to damned near bleed to death? Have you *seen* the wretched beast? Do you have any idea what it's like to have to live in its shadow day in and day out?"

"No, but—"

"That, my dear, is my predicament in a nutshell. Everything you know about me comes from Pan."

"He's not a liar!"

Stuart shrugged. "Have it your way. I chose to pluck you from your bath because I have the morals of a swine." He stepped behind the Oriental screen and emerged with his topcoat, which Wendy had thrown on the deck. As he had suspected, the trim was torn, the edges of the velvet shredded. He made a show of trying to wipe off some of the copious mud crusted all over the bottom half of the garment, then gave up with a dramatic sigh. "I suppose I chose to have this beautiful and very expensive garment ruined on your behalf because I'm a swine, too, hm?"

Wendy softened a little. "I'm sorry about that." She seemed to consider. "You... you promise you didn't peek?"

Stuart placed his hook over his heart. "I give you my word as a gentleman, Miss Darling, that your modesty remains intact." Before she could comment, he added, "And I assure you, my dear, that I *am* a gentleman when in the company of such a fine lady as yourself."

Wendy's lips quivered in what might have been a suppressed smile. It was hard to tell, though it was enchanting regardless. "Very well then, Captain. What do you wish to talk about?"

"First things first. You are my guest. May I offer you refreshment?" She had to be thirsty. The journey back to the ship had taken over an hour.

Wendy licked her lips. "Yes, please."

She's certainly polite, Stuart thought, caught by an absurd vision of being trapped at a little girl's dolly-infested tea party. He shook it off and went to the door. He called for Smee and told him what to bring. Then he turned back to find that Wendy had opened the harpsichord lid and was studying the keyboard.

"Can you play this, Captain?"

"Why else would I have it?" he answered, the words leaping out of his mouth without forethought. He knew how to play a harpsichord about as much as he knew how to castrate sheep with his teeth. He remained calm, though, fully trusting — perhaps foolishly so — the exciting black confidence pulsing within him.

Wendy pointed at his hook. "But you've only got one hand." It was the kind of point-blank statement that only a child would make to someone with a disability.

Stuart caressed the hook with that one hand. "This is more versatile than you think, my dear."

"Then prove you're a gentleman. Sing me a song." She sat down at the writing desk, challenging him with her eyes.

Giving her an agreeable nod, Stuart sat down on the harpsichord bench. Purely for show, he stretched his arms out on either side until his elbows popped. He cricked his neck first to one side then the other and made a fuss finding a comfortable position. All the while he thought of the knowledge that had come to him when he had touched the maps, the sextant, the log books. Surely it would happen again with the harpsichord?

He placed his hand on the keyboard. A breeze of information blew through his brain, a pleasant gust containing a delightfully extensive knowledge of music theory, music history and keyboard technique, along with an assortment of tunes that spanned the classics of Beethoven, Mozart and Rachmaninov to the raunchiest of tavern songs.

Feeling like a loaded gun, Stuart shot Wendy a knowing smirk. "Now who's lying, my dear? You don't really want me to be so much of a gentleman that I'll play you a pretty church hymn, do you? No no no, you want to hear the notorious pirate sing a pirate song. Allow me to oblige your curiosity."

Stuart had no idea what he was about to play. He started a jaunty intro, his left hand compensating surprisingly well for his lack of a right. The hook was able to cover more notes than he would have guessed, too, depending on how fast he toggled his wrist. This weird technique must have taken him awhile to figure out. Too bad he couldn't remember having done it.

The tune was akin to a tavern song, loose and swaggering. Lyrics jumped to his lips:

> *The bosun aboard was a hearty ol' dog*
> *Who spent watches off in a rum-induced fog*
> *But brandy, in truth, was his favorite grog*
> *So a bottle he nicked from a cabinet, ho,*
> *A pint of his captain's own.*
>
> In flagrante delicto *the thief he was caught*
> *And hung by his thumbs in the rigging to rot*
> *But lo, even dead he still lusts for a tot*
> *So his ghost it goes after the brandy, ho,*
> *An will ne'er lay at rest down below!*

Stuart finished with a glissando and grinned devilishly at his audience of one. "Like it? I wrote it for Bosun Smee. I play it for him on occasion, as a warning. The scallywag has a taste for my brandy, you see."

He had been right about Wendy. She was overcome with scandalous delight. "That was awful!" she cried, trying to maintain an air of piety and failing wonderfully.

"Yes, wasn't it?" Stuart said. He enjoyed her reaction, and he was thrilled by this sudden musical expertise. Instead of making him feel faint, this influx of knowledge left him giddy and playful. He wanted to entertain Wendy with more songs, songs that would scandalize Pan himself. What fun it would be to gently corrupt the sweet girl, introducing her to terms and ideas that would be the ruin of her one day. Such fun indeed! Too bad he had to resist the urge. He had successfully softened her up and titillated her in the process. *Keep to the agenda, James,* he told himself.

"You pirates and your liquor. And killing." Wendy shook her head, still attempting to act offended. "Why is it you talk of nothing else?"

"Why is it that your hero Pan talks of nothing but killing us pirates?"

Wendy stiffened. "He talks about other things."

Stuart leaned toward her. "Do tell."

Smee chose that moment to arrive, carrying a tray with a mug of steaming white liquid, a delicate urn filled with creamy brown paste, a large silver spoon and a tall goblet. He set the tray on one end of the rosewood table and busied himself with the items while Stuart pulled out the single extra chair at the other end. "Please, my dear. Sit."

Wendy moved from the writing desk to the proffered seat with all the grace and dignity of a proper English lady. "Thank you, Captain."

"I hope hot chocolate appeals to you, Miss Darling, though I do apologize that it must be made with goat's milk."

Wendy's pretense crumbled. "Eww!"

Stuart waved his hand in a small gesture of helplessness. "I seem to recall a time when my men had access to the Indians' cattle—"

"You mean you stole them!"

"Semantics," Stuart quipped. He did, actually, recollect something vague about trading. Hmm, maybe there *had* been a little cattle rustling, now that he thought about it. But it had happened long ago, when the pirates had first come to the island, before Pan had taken his hand and the war had begun in earnest. "In any case," he went on, "agreeable relations with the Indians are long over. Please be assured that this is the best this humble host can offer. As for myself..."

He rose from his chair, making sure that Wendy watched while he moved to the cabinet behind the harpsichord. Angling himself to allow her an unobstructed view of his activities, he opened the door, rapped once on the back of the cabinet's wall with his hook, and proceeded to remove a green bottle from the secret compartment. He could almost feel the corners of her lips raise at such ingenuity. He gave her plenty of time to regain her silly air of indignant superiority before he turned back around, holding up the bottle. "The brandy so coveted by the bosun aboard."

Smee took two nervous steps away from Stuart without pausing from his work. Stuart chuckled. He poured a generous amount of the amber liquid into the goblet on the tray and raised it. "To my guest, Wendy Darling, a most proper young lady. To her health and continued well-being," he toasted ominously, and sipped. "Mister Smee?"

"All nice an' ready, sar," said Smee. He set a cup of hot chocolate before Wendy, along with the silver spoon. "There yeh go, missy."

"Thank you."

"You may leave, Smee."

"Aye, Cap'n."

"And see to it that we're not disturbed."

"Aye aye, sar." Smee made his customary hasty shuffle out the door.

Stuart leaned back in his chair, goblet in hand. Enough cozying up, enough banter. It was time to get to the meat of the matter. He watched Wendy take a cautious sip of her chocolate and smile.

Then for no apparent reason her smile faded, replaced by an expression of confusion. Or might it have been apprehension? The candles seemed to dim. Shadows crept over the cabin. Something was changing, Wendy sensed it, but she didn't know what it could be.

Stuart knew. *He* was the one changing, and the change was affecting the very air around him. The corners of his lips were pulling down. His vision was growing sharp in the dimness, rather like a cat's, he suspected. His skin began to tingle with an exciting feverish heat. The black fingers already had him — their grasp was damned close to permanent at this point — but he was taking the risk of voluntarily letting them dig deeper than ever. He had utilized Hook's charm to capture the girl. Now he needed to tap a much more dangerous aspect of the darkness and bend it to his will. He harshly reminded himself not to enjoy it, to keep firm control, but that intention fizzled faster than a lighted match in the rain. He watched it wink out, all at once feeling the way he always did after strenuous sex — drained, content and yet buzzing inside, eager to go another round, this time with more inventive antics, baser, *nastier...*

Wendy started when at last he spoke. "Wouldn't you agree," he said in Hook's low, lazy drawl, "that there is a most unnatural appeal to the Neverland? It is rather, oh, shall we say... convenient?"

Wendy's bright eyes widened with a fear she could not name. "Convenient?"

"Why yes, my sweet. For instance, it is everything you dreamed it would be, is it not?" Stuart saw her mouth open to reply. She closed it without saying a word. "In fact," he went on, "I'd wager that if you could create a world of fancy for yourself, it would look just. Like. This. Here at your fingertips are all the elements of great adventure — a virgin island, isolated from the world, populated by enchanted boys, singing mermaids, savage Indians, magical fairies, evil pirates..." He drew out the word *evil*, watching her reaction, a slight but telling tremble of the lower lip. "That's not to mention all the ferocious beasts to hunt, costumes to wear, grand explorations to make. But most of all, here dwells a hero against whom a villain has no chance, no chance at all. Quite the storybook paradise, wouldn't you agree?"

Wendy had unconsciously pushed herself back into her chair. "What do you want?"

"Well, why don't we start with your name."

"My... name?"

"Your name," Stuart repeated, reining in an irrational urge to leap at the girl and scare her to death, just for the fun of it. "It isn't Wendy."

"But it is! I'm Wendy Moira Angela Darling!"

"And I'm Ronald fucking MacDonald!" Stuart surged to his feet, Hook's fury igniting his eyes. Wendy gasped as his hook took aim, gleaming in the yellow candle light, the shadow of its bloodthirsty curve whispering across her throat.

Stuart restrained his arm from following through. To his surprise, Wendy did not cry out. She only cringed, terrified yet aggravatingly defiant. The mention of Ronald MacDonald intrigued her, that much was clear by the little O of her mouth. Stuart himself was intrigued — he had thought his modern memories all but gone and here he had brought up, of all things, that clown-faced burgermeister.

He lowered his arm as the situation dawned on him. Wendy's eyes followed the hook as it dropped to his side. "Ahhh," he said. "It becomes clear. Quite the drama we have going here, eh, my lovely? Here stands Hook, at last on the brink of learning the truth. Alackaday! No matter what he does, no matter what he says, the fair Wendy will not reveal that longed-for truth. She remains silent, sure that Hook cannot force her to speak. And why is that? Because she is unflinchingly confident that her intrepid champion Peter Pan will save her pretty hide." He made a great show of looking around the cabin. "Funny. I don't see him."

Wendy had paled, but at the mention of Pan, her courage returned. "He won't let you hurt me!"

"O, implicit trust, the true fountain of youth!" Stuart declared. "I admire it, I really do. But let me give you a piece of advice. There will come a day, child, when trust will betray you. One day Peter Pan will not come to your rescue. You will have to stand on your own, and that, alas, will be the day you grow up."

"I'm not going to grow up!"

"Tut tut. Everyone grows up. Well, with one exception."

Wendy's bravery was both remarkable and utterly charming. She stood up, chin held high. "You do too want to know where Peter's hiding place is! You're trying to scare me so I'll tell you! Well, I won't tell you! I won't!" She flopped back into her chair. If her eyes had been daggers, Stuart would have looked more like a porcupine than a man.

He pretended to be amused by her outburst and turned away, thinking furiously. How should he proceed? If Wendy did trust in Pan so much — and how did he know for sure that her childish trust wasn't misplaced? — bullying wouldn't make her talk. Charm and tact could only go so far. *She thinks Pan will magically appear to save her if things get out of hand,* he thought. *What if that's true?* He could always nick her a little, just a pet of the hook to bring her to her senses. *No! I have to find a way to work with her.*

To do that, he had to make her feel for him, even if the only feeling he could engender was her pity. He had to show her the truth of his dilemma — *his* dilemma, the dilemma of... what was his name? His *real* name. It wasn't James, not James... Jon! That was it. Jonathan. He had to show her the truth of *Jonathan's* dilemma.

He inhaled deeply. Could he manage it? He had to try. With a determination born of desperation, he searched out the black fingers that were busily spreading a network of inky veins throughout his being, both the physical and the psychological. He visualized, not his own hands but a great gleaming vice grip. He clamped it around the root of the black finger-veins, located deep in his solar plexus, and pulled. To his amazement, the root let go easily. The veins released their dozens of tiny grips without struggle. Stuart visualized bundling the whole mess up, and he shoved it down into the basement of his very soul. He kept pushing, sending it further and further down, then visualized a thick-walled, sturdy, fire-proof safe and locked it inside for good measure.

He had expected pain, but it was more like popping the batteries out of a toy. The exciting black vitality drained away in a silent whoosh, leaving him deflated and lost. *I want it back. It's eating me alive, and God help me, I want it back!* At the same time, he felt a weary elation. He had won, for the first time, and it had been relatively easy. *Fuck you,* he thought, caught between elation and an almost paralyzing emptiness. *You don't have me yet.*

No dark voice answered him. The void allowed him to hang there, alone and helpless like a ship in the doldrums eager for a wind that would never come. *Hang time,* he thought absently. That was the term for it in cartoons, that moment when a character steps over the edge of a cliff but doesn't realize he should fall. Hang time. Yes, he was hanging in mid-air before a great fall.

But he was Jonathan Stuart again. His own weary smile defeated Hook's snide, lopsided grin, doubly baffling his young guest. "I, uh, don't know what you might have seen just now, but I apologize for it," he said. He was astounded by his voice. It wasn't that the cultured accent was gone. Well, it was, but that made little difference. The real difference was that the actual fabric of his voice lacked depth and resonance, like pitiful worn cotton that had once been luxurious velvet. Was this really his voice? Hook must have commanded his vocal chords far longer than he had realized. "I didn't mean to scare you," he went on, hating how *thin* he sounded. He laid his left hand over his hook in a sign of peace. "I've... been under a little stress lately. Allow me to introduce myself. My name is Jonathan Stuart. And you are?"

Wendy's face had gone as white as a lily in a dead man's hands. "I... I don't understand..."

"Yes, you do. If I really were Captain Hook, I wouldn't know about Ronald MacDonald, would I? Or let's see, Mickey Mouse or MTV or... " He combed his besieged memory for something else that children, especially a little girl, would know well. The real world beyond the Neverland was returning to him, perhaps because he was free of Hook's influence at the moment. Whatever the reason, he zeroed in on the image of a dolly so famous that even he knew about her. "Beach bimbo Barbie," he murmured. "Yeah... Uh, look, just believe me. I'm not Captain Hook."

He sipped some brandy, wishing for a fistful of valium. His nerves were dancing the crazy skip-trot of water droplets in hot oil. He had to pull his scattered self together and fast. He leaned back in his chair, Hook's absurd kingly throne, and sipped from his cup, trying to breathe deep and regular. He wanted to give Wendy the space she needed to regain some measure of composure. He must have done something unpleasant, maybe even bizarre, while fighting the blackness down because she was ogling him with a mixture of disbelief and horror. When he focused on such interior battles, he had no idea what his body was doing. God knows what the girl had witnessed. Facial spasms? Tetany? A psychotic fit?

"I swear to you, I am not Captain Hook," he repeated, trying to convince himself as much as her. "Just as you are not Wendy Moira Angela Darling."

Her eyes filled with thunderous disdain. "But I am!"

"Bullshit. Wendy is a fictional character from a book written almost a hundred years ago. You've been here for what, two weeks? Three? A month? Let me guess — you're from London, right? And you flew with him here, just like in the story."

Wendy bit her lip.

"You flew right out your bedroom window and followed Pan all the way here. You flew at night, because that's the only time you can see the star that's second to the right. You're a smart girl. What would you say if I told you I flew here, too?"

Wendy's eyes expanded into little saucers of wonder. "But you're a grown-up!"

Stuart thought of the cascade of black curls covering his shoulders, the riot of lace and frills along his collar and cuffs, the great ostrich plumes sticking out of the hat over there on the peg. He snorted. "So they tell me." He lifted his hook, gazing at it. "Yes, I'm a grown-up. But I was tricked here. See, I know what it's all about, why you're here, why I'm here. Pan has begun a new game, the latest one of many, I think, through the ages. You're his new Wendy. The two boys are his new John and Michael. And since it's no fun playing war without an enemy, I've been drafted to be his opponent this time round. Lucky ducky me."

"You're just trying to make me feel sorry for you. It won't work, you villain!"

"I'm not a villain!" Stuart shouted, and before he could stop himself he slammed the point of his hook into the table. Instead of lifting it out, he clawed it through the wood until it slid off the edge, leaving a raw, shallow, jagged line. He was as taken aback as Wendy by the action. It was something Hook would do, not him.

"I am not a villain," he repeated vehemently. "I'm just a nobody who believed. That's the key, girl — we both *believed!* Pan sniffed us out like a damned hound dog because we believed in him!" Stuart's trail of tragedy unfolded before his eyes, every incident a domino that had knocked down the next until they led to this very moment. "If Uncle George hadn't died, if the earthquake hadn't hit, if the house hadn't burned, if I hadn't found that stupid box of crap and brought it home, if only something had happened a little bit differently, then I wouldn't have *believed* and Pan wouldn't have found me and I wouldn't be here and I wouldn't have lost my goddam hand!"

The blackness came without words this time. Just a sensory invitation that he could translate into words: *Let me back in. You'll feel better.*

Stuart almost stuffed his fist into his mouth, a physical gesture to keep himself from mentally answering. He took another gulp of brandy as if hoping to burn the voice out. "I just want to go home, kid," he said, almost choking from the alcohol burn. "I'm no pirate, I'm a bookstore owner from Pasadena." *Not Superman, just a mild-mannered reporter...* "I like Diet Coke and watch M.A.S.H. reruns on TV..." He looked at her pleadingly, aware of the pressure just outside himself, of the blackness lightly tapping at the door like a friendly neighbor coming over for coffee. "I'm a nice guy, goddam it!" he finished in a lunatic shrill.

Wendy eyed him like a sparrow that is wary of a hungry cat on the prowl.

Stuart's arm twitched. The hook was itching for a taste of her blood. He pressed his hand down hard on the cold curved metal. "Please, whatever your name is — this Neverland is based on your fantasy, and don't try to deny it because I know, okay? I *know* it. Pan molded everything to fit your expectations. Please, show me the way out before it's too late, maybe for both of us."

"Way out?" she asked innocently.

"Yes, out! There's got to be a way out of here! If your fantasy doesn't have one, then Pan must have his own, and if he does, he'd have told you. He tells you everything, doesn't he? He likes you best of all, doesn't he?"

"See here, Captain Hook—"

"I AM NOT CAPTAIN HOOK!"

The darkness had waited long enough. It broke down the neighborly door and stormed in, latching onto Stuart, *into* him,

322

everywhere at once. Stuart wanted to scream and laugh and cry all at the same time. He was whole once more, confident, in control, damned to Hell, and very very angry.

He grabbed a hank of Wendy's hair. "Very well, my dear," he purred, pleased to hear velvet once again, resonant and rich with threat. The English accent no longer made him think of Grandpa Emmerich. He knew now that his was the same accent as his great-grandfather James, whose speech had been untainted by American influence. "I think it's time to address this problem my way." Using his grip on her hair, Stuart lifted Wendy bodily and dragged her screaming to the writing table. He threw her into the chair, his mere glance promising to kill her if she didn't shut up.

She shut up.

He opened his map chest and slapped two maps on the writing table. One was complete and detailed, the Neverland of another time, drawn painstakingly by James Stuart who had sat at that very same table, pen in his left hand, hook on his right, more than a hundred years ago. The other map was Stuart's.

Wendy was noticing the differences between the two islands. She looked back and forth from one to the other, lingering over the older one in confusion. Stuart forced her head to stay over his own map. "Finish it."

"B-but I can't!"

He thrust his hook under her nose. "My hook says you can."

Trembling, Wendy scrutinized the map while Stuart loomed over her. "No, really, I c-can't! I can't betray Peter's hiding place!"

At wit's end, Stuart cuffed her hard enough to send her sprawling on the deck. "Haven't you listened to a word I've said? I don't give a flying fuck where Peter Pan lives!"

Wendy turned an expression of such utter bewilderment on him that he wanted to crawl into a corner and hide. The shape of his hand rouged her cheek. *Shit, what have I done?*

Nothing unwarranted, nothing permanent, came the dark thought. *You see? You're a monster after all.*

"You... you really don't want to know where Peter's hiding place is," Wendy was saying, the revelation overriding her fear. "But... but you have to! You're supposed to try to hunt him down and kill him, only he's going to kill you first!"

"Because that's the way the story goes?" Stuart countered. "You *do* know, you bitch!" His words shocked him. He staggered back, appalled.

The darkness pounded at him. *Use her! She knows what you need to know! Don't be afraid, you won't kill her! After all, you're better than that.*

Stuart began to speak. As his mouth formed the words, his ears heard them as if someone else were saying them. "Don't you see, my sweet? I no longer need to hunt for Pan. I have *you.* I can make him come to me. Especially if you're in pain. Or in danger of dying, perhaps, hm?"

Wendy blanched.

"Thaaaat's better." Stuart offered her his hand. She paused, perhaps grateful that he hadn't offered his hook, and took it. He hoisted her back to her feet. "Now. Let us start from the beginning. Show me where you landed when you first arrived."

She stared at the map. "I... I don't know. In some bushes, I think. Oh, I don't know, I don't know!"

Stuart caressed her face with the hook, causing her small body to tremble in his grasp. "Is there only one Indian camp?"

"Y-yes!"

"Do they have any sacred sites, any places where they hold special ceremonies?"

"I d-don't know!"

"Are there any magic portals on the island? Doors in trees, underwater passages, anything like that?"

Wendy hesitated. Stuart pivoted the hook so that its point pushed a little dimple in the creamy flesh of her cheek. "I d-don't th-think so!" she quickly offered.

"How about tunnels under the island?"

"Yes, but I haven't seen them yet. Peter told me that's where the fairies—" The girl who claimed to be Wendy Moira Angela Darling closed her mouth.

"Ah. Go on, my dear."

"It's nothing."

"Oh, I think it's most definitely something. What about the fairies? They live underground?"

"No."

Quick as a flash, Stuart lashed out with the hook and sliced off the top of the nearest candle. Wendy screamed and tried to back away, but Stuart yanked her close. He could feel red fury burning in his eyes, and he let it burn freely. He knew she could see it. He drank in her terror, letting it fill the last of the yearning empty spaces inside. Oh, this was better than liquor, better than sex! He was truly alive, humming with power, invincible, indomitable. He shuddered with the rush of it. Wendy reacted and tried to pull away again, but Stuart put a stop to that. He ran his hook slowly down her neck, drawing a little bit of blood this time. "This is your last chance, my Darling," he crooned. "Tell me what I want to know or by all that's unholy I'll—"

"The Hollow Hill!" shrieked Wendy. "It's c-called th-the Hollow Hill!"

Success! Stuart pressed his lips to her ear. "Where is it?"

"I don't know, honest I don't!"

"What happens there?"

"P-Peter won't s-say!"

Stuart curled his fingers around her arm, squeezing too hard. "Does he go there by himself?"

"Often," Wendy answered, "b-but I don't know wh-why!" And then Wendy began to whimper, a pitiful sound of primal terror, the kind of sound that children make in the face of danger greater than their belief in magic itself.

Stuart released her, trembling. From excitement? From shame? He didn't want to know. He took out his lacy kerchief and dabbed at the sweat on his forehead. His scalp and neck were wet with it, his skin under all those layers slick with it. Had Wendy any idea of the battle he was waging inside? She would think so differently of him if he could only tell her, but who was he kidding? Who was he, period? He had been jerked back and forth so many times, he wasn't sure anymore.

Wendy was sobbing on the carpet. Stuart saw the short line of blood stippling her neck and felt sick. He knelt beside her. "Please... please accept my apologies, Miss Darling." The naked embarrassment in his voice caused the child to regard him with renewed wonder. "Come, be a brave girl. Stand up."

She tried to scuttle away, but Stuart took her arm, not forcefully this time but with a gentle strength that lifted her up and steered her to the wash stand. He poured water from the ewer into the basin and handed her a clean cloth.

He went back to his chair and stood behind it, gripping the backing with a white-knuckled hand. The Hollow Hill, eh? It was worth looking into. If it was something significant to Pan, Smee would know about it. The problem that nagged him was the fact that Smee had never mentioned it before.

After wiping her neck and fixing her hair, Wendy returned to her chair. She sat down as prim and proper as before. "I suppose you're going to make me walk the plank now," she stated grimly.

Stuart blinked. "Plank? Good Lord, no."

"But... but why not?"

He regarded her with some confusion. "Do you want to?"

"No! It's just that... I couldn't tell you what you wanted."

"True enough."

"Doesn't that make you angry?"

"Immeasurably so."

"Then what are you going to do with me?"

That was a good question, a very good question indeed. If Wendy was telling the truth about her lack of knowledge, then Stuart had no hope of finding any escape from the Neverland based on geography. The Lost Boys knew the island, yes, but they were a slippery bunch, and it would take considerable effort to get any information from them — if they could be captured at all. Billy could be a help there, but even at that, the boys would be on the lookout, what with Wendy gone.

On the other hand, if Wendy was lying, if she really did know something useful, Stuart would have to turn to torture to make her release her secrets. No doubt Cecco or Smee could offer fascinating suggestions on how to break the young girl's silence, if voluntary silence it was, but the prospect made Stuart shiver. There had to be another way. Kidnapping Wendy was one thing. Hurting her a little, well, it had been necessary. But torturing her would bring the wrath of Pan down on him so hard he would probably never know what hit him. Stuart didn't want to contemplate that scenario. He doubted he would live through it. If he did, he would probably come out of it missing yet another limb. Or maybe something smaller than a limb but oh so much more personal.

He needed time to think, so he gave Wendy a mysterious smile. "Very well, Miss Darling, I shall reveal your fate. Come with me." He opened the door and gestured for her to exit with a polite wave of his hook.

Cautiously Wendy stood. "Where are we going?"

"I am going nowhere. You are going through that door." He indicated a narrow door on the left down the short hallway that led out to the quarterdeck.

"So I'm to be your prisoner after all!" she cried.

"*Au contraire.* You are still my guest."

"Guests don't get locked up in a dirty broom cupboard!"

"Nor do they antagonize their hosts, my dear."

"They do when their hosts pull their hair!"

"Their hosts pull their hair when their guests *lie* to them."

Wendy drew herself up to her full height, incensed. "I didn't lie!"

"Didn't you?" Stuart gave her a challenging glower which made her shrink back down. Satisfied, he slipped past her and rapped his hook on the door down the hall. It was the bosun's cabin. With some trepidation he realized that he had never actually seen the interior of Smee's quarters. He hoped the man wasn't a total slob. Just because a fellow was the epitome of cleanliness when it came to his captain's effects didn't mean he treated his own the same way.

Smee opened the door, bleary-eyed. He had been off watch and sleeping. "Cap'n?"

"Out. Miss Darling will be staying in your dirty broom cupboard."

"What? The lass, sar? In my — in my *what,* sar?"

Stuart grasped the bosun's arm and hauled him out. He was relieved to see that Smee had turned in all standing. The sight of that beefy body in nothing but skivvies or less would have made poor Wendy faint. Stuart wasn't sure if he would have taken the sight well himself, for that matter. "You shall take a berth in the fo'c'sul, Mister Smee, until I say otherwise."

"In the—? But Cap'n—"

Stuart silenced him with a frown, then flicked his eyes over to check the interior of the cabin. It was very small, which was how Stuart's cabin could be so very big. There was limited space below the poop deck to go around, after all. Stuart was pleased to see that it was quite cozy, though, with its single hammock; quaint little wash stand with bowl, ewer, cup and razor; and Smee's sea chest in one corner. Lashed down in the opposite corner stood a rickety table and chair where Smee's beloved sewing machine sat ready for use. A closed gunport took up much of the outer bulkhead.

The bosun had sewn together scraps of the finer materials from Stuart's wardrobe — *He does do my sewing, ha!* — and made curtains for the window, along with wall hangings which could have been called tapestries if they had depicted actual scenes. Instead they were flag-like crazy-quilt prints that transformed the dreary whitewashed bulkheads into a colorful wonderland. Smee had even sewn himself a patchwork carpet and used layers of dried moss for padding. Stuart could see little brown tufts of it sticking out the corners.

Lord Almighty, this looks like a girl's room! Stuart thought. *All that's missing are lace doilies and a Tiffany lamp!* He clapped Smee on the back, amused and, in an odd way, touched to discover that, underneath his swarthy gruff surface, the bosun possessed a pathetically gentle nature. "I think Miss Darling will be quite at home here, Smee." He motioned Wendy inside.

Wendy looked from Stuart to Smee and back to Stuart in dismay.

Smee was busy fumbling with his fingers. "Err... right, sar, right. The fo'c'sul. No problem, I'm sure, none a'tall. Err..." He reached for his cap, felt only his wispy hair and started back inside. "Just lemme get me hat an'—"

"Later. Right now I want you to fetch Miss Darling a decent breakfast. Tell Cecco to double and arm the watch, and keep a man in the crow's nest. I expect Pan will show up shortly, and I have thinking to do before then. I don't want to be disturbed, understand? Keep the door to Miss Darling's quarters locked at all times. She is not to leave for any reason. I want two armed guards stationed here." He leaned close to Smee's ear. "And furnish her with a nicer chamber pot, eh?"

Stuart tucked Wendy's little hand into Smee's meaty paw and left them, retreating back to his cabin. He wanted to ask Smee about the Hollow Hill, but this was not the time. Later, when Wendy would not be able to hear. As he left he heard Smee babble, "Right, Miss, this way. No wait, I oughtta tidy the place up first. No, better not. Tell yeh what, missy, take yerself in an'..."

Stuart clicked his door closed.

CHAPTER 37

Melanie knew it was her the minute the woman came into view. "Ms. Rhodes?" she asked, reaching out her hand.

The woman, a business-suited blonde who wasn't old enough to need facial nips and tucks but who clearly had gone under the knife several times anyway — she had that trademark Hollywood nose — executed a model's perfect smile, revealing a set of dazzling capped teeth. She took Melanie's hand and gave it a primp squeeze. "Dusty. That's what everybody calls me. I take it you're Melanie."

Melanie listened to the introduction with humor. Dusty spoke in the round glossy tones of a news reporter, sultry enough to lure a listener's ear but countered by the crisp no-nonsense diction that defined a "voice of authority." Melanie knew Dusty had been practicing long and had recently landed her first TV gig on San Francisco's KTVU/FOX 2 News At Five: a feature entitled "On the Rhodes." Either Dusty had decided to talk like this for the rest of her life, or she was still practicing.

"Yes, I'm Melanie," Melanie told her. "Nice to meet you, Dusty. Please, sit down."

Dusty slid into the booth. The waitress handed them menus. "Can I get you ladies anything to drink?"

"Diet Coke," said Melanie.

"Margarita, Midori, no salt and a water, too," Dusty said. "Cold but no ice. With a lemon twist, please."

The waitress, used to the endless idiosyncrasies of metropolitan diners, nodded and left.

Melanie picked at a fingernail nervously. "I appreciate you agreeing to see me today, it being right after Christmas and all. This is very very important to me."

"Lucky I'm still in LA," Dusty answered. "My husband's family. If they can't have the entire clan at the old Malibu manse every twelve-twenty-five, life isn't worth living. I've learned not to fight it, but that doesn't mean I have to stay long." Dusty pushed back a lock of hair that was so stiff with hairspray it didn't need pushing back. She pushed at it anyhow, her copious gold bracelets jingling. "I know I said it last night on the phone, but I want to say it once more. I'm sorry about your fiancé."

Melanie nodded, hoping that any trace of her belief that Jon was alive didn't show on her face. "Thank you." She held up her hand to let the ruby ring catch the light. "This was my engagement ring."

"It's beautiful. You know, I understand why you want to put Jon's history together. It's the kind of thing I would do." Dusty paused. "I didn't really think I'd find you while I was down here. Every time I called your number, I got dead air. Your fax number, too. I'm glad you gave me one final try last night." She pushed again at her hair. "And I'm glad I thought to check my messages."

"Oh, about those two letters you said you sent me..." Melanie shrugged. "I looked for them last night. I didn't find them, and I still have no recollection of ever receiving them. Then again, I told you what this past month has been like." She displayed an apologetic expression for Dusty' benefit, but she knew damned well what must have happened to the letters. Same with the dead air Dusty mentioned. All this time Melanie had thought Dusty hadn't answered her phone calls when, in fact, Dusty had tried to contact her by every means possible except Pony Express. None of those attempts had succeeded. *Guess who, Melly baby!* Or maybe it really was just a quirk of the system. Melanie had moved from her apartment to Jon's house. Maybe the phone company's automatic referral hadn't functioned properly. Maybe her mail hadn't gotten delivered correctly. *Yeah, and maybe bears have beaks. Get real, Melly.*

Dusty was adjusting the lapels of her sleek business jacket. Melanie sat in her sweater and jeans and felt like a slob. Only *über urbans* — one of Jon's terms — could make her feel this frumpy. Francine "Dusty" Rhodes was without doubt an *über* urban, born in a business suit and attracted to all things smooth and shiny.

"The letters I sent don't matter anymore, Melanie," Dusty was saying. "I brought all my research with me, hoping our paths might cross. Your puzzlement over your fiancé's death is important to you, I know, but it's also important to me."

"That's what I don't understand," Melanie said. "You said you're barely related to Jon."

"True, but I grew up hearing stories about *those Stuart men*," and Dusty emphasized the words, making air quotes with her perfectly manicured red-lacquered fingernails. "My Grammy Maria talked about that branch of the family all the time. Her mother was Alice Brahm, sister to Sylvia who was the wife of Emmerich Albert Stuart who, I believe, was Jon's grandfather, correct?"

Melanie had to play connect-the-relatives in her mind to get it all straight. She vowed to make a sketch of the family tree that night so all these tangled relations could be more easily viewed. "Sounds right," she said.

"Well, Sylvia had her worries about her husband and his snooty English relatives. Emmerich never behaved irrationally, but he apparently had strange phobias and beliefs that worried her and sometimes scared her. She would confide in Alice, and like all good gossip, it passed down the line. Besides all that, I'm a reporter, Melanie, a reporter with a love of history. The two go together. And I can't resist a juicy mystery."

Melanie found herself thinking of the old Scooby-Doo cartoons, every episode another juicy mystery involving creepy old houses and moaning ghosts and walking suits of armor. *And phantom Christmas presents and fiancés who disappear into thin air and a magical boy from a magical land who steals your mail...*

The waitress returned with their drinks. "Are you ladies ready to order?" she asked them.

Dusty flashed her perfect teeth at the waitress and ordered a salad with light vinaigrette mixed separately in a cruet, no croutons, extra sliced tomatoes on the side but only if they were truly vine ripened and a cup of vegetable soup but none of those little packaged soda crackers. Melanie ordered a BLT with curly fries. After the waitress left, Dusty resumed the conversation as if there had been no interruption. "Yes, mystery," she said, almost in a whisper. "Jon's branch of the Stuart line is cursed. Now, don't say anything yet. I know I sound absurd. I know what you must be thinking."

Melanie managed not to betray what she was thinking.

"I don't believe in curses or any of that nonsense either," Dusty continued. "In this case, however, I have made an exception. I'll show you why." She paused to sip her margarita. "Do you know how many Stuart men in that one branch of the family have gone insane since the late sixteen hundreds?"

Melanie spoke without thinking. "Are you including Jon?"

"I'll leave that to you." Dusty' eyes lit up, turning her into a kind of manic Lois Lane. She plucked a paper out of her brief case. "Excluding Jon for the moment, *nine*. Nine went insane. Two of those committed suicide. Several disappeared. Here, read. Mind you, these are just the ones I've uncovered so far. The Stuarts are good at hiding scandal. They still are. But I found private letters, diaries never intended for public eyes, blah blah. Read."

Melanie took the paper and read.

JAMES CHARLES STUART, born 1666 (year London burned), went mad and committed suicide 1697 (hanged himself), age 31.

PHILLIP EDWARD STUART, born 1695, went mad 1735 at age 40 (found no records of his fate). First son of James above.

CHARLES WILLIAM STUART, Phillip's younger brother, born 1696, went mad and disappeared 1737 at 41 years old. Second son of James above.

GEORGE THOMAS STUART, born 1741, went mad 1783 at age 42, committed suicide (how??).

WINTHROP SPENCER STUART, born 1746, went mad and disappeared in 1784 at age 38.

RODRICK ANDREW STUART, 1784-1840, not mad per se but known to be extremely odd, sequestered himself in his house for the last 15 years of his life, died alone age 56.

ALBERT ANDREW STUART, born 1787 (younger brother of Rodrick above), went "violently" mad on Sept 21, 1826, disappeared 8 days later (Sept 29) at age 39. Family letter speaks of an "unholy mark" that appeared on Albert's body and caused much fear in the family. Can find no details of this.

JAMES ALBERT STUART, born 1851, went mad on March 7, 1896 at age 45. Disappeared 4 days later on March 11.

GEORGE ROBERT STUART (1915-1989). Lived secluded in Stuart House in SF, was violent to anyone who approached the house (constantly called the police until they learned to ignore him). Interviewed locals who claimed that strange sounds would come from the house, often during the full moon. Died at 74.

Melanie put the paper down. "Jonathan Edward Stuart, born 1954," she said slowly. "Began to show signs of extreme stress and agitation starting around November 11, 1989. Became physically ill November 20. Started... raving on November 21. Died November 24."

Dusty reached across the table and wrapped Melanie's hand in hers. "Are you sure you want to do this?"

"Yes," Melanie said. "I have to know."

Dusty watched her for a moment, probably to make sure that Melanie truly was all right. She pushed her margarita forward. "Drink?"

Melanie contemplated the proffered glass of frosty green. "Yeah." She reached for it, then burst out laughing. "No, I can't. It's yours, not mine. I'm being ridiculous."

"Not at all," said Dusty. "You're majorly stressed. Don't worry, I know all the symptoms. I get them all the time. Drink."

Melanie took a sip. "Ooo," she said, and smacked her lips. "I should order one of these."

"Okay," said Dusty, retrieving her glass. "You've read the paper. Talk to me."

Melanie scanned the information once more, this time engaging her Researcher Brain. "They're all in their late thirties, early forties when they go mad," she thought aloud, "except for James Charles Stuart. He was only thirty-one. And Jon. He was only thirty-five. There are two sets of brothers. In each case, the older brothers had head problems while the younger ones went mad *and* disappeared. There are two suicides in the bunch. Two shut themselves up in their houses and never came out until they died." She paused, suddenly decoding the rest of old Alice Lancaster's notations. MM she already knew meant Mad and Missing. MS *must mean Mad and Suicide,* she thought, *and M just means Mad.* Then she frowned. "How does a person go mad in a single day?"

"Bingo," Dusty said. "In each case, a year is given, if not an exact day. I'm no doctor, but I always thought genuine insanity is either a defect in the brain that a person is born with, in which case it's pretty obvious from the start, or it's a perceptible decline. Behaviors change. People see things. They gossip. Oddities get documented. But with these guys, nothing. And notice that it's only men who are afflicted. No women." She gave Melanie a truly sympathetic look. "Now, if you're sure it's okay to ask... what happened to Jon? What was going on in his life?"

Melanie had known that question would come up sooner or later. "His uncle died," she said simply. "His inheritance burned down. He had the IRS at his throat. It all happened at once."

"Not enough. I happen to know that Jon didn't want Stuart House."

"Really," Melanie said flatly, taken aback. "How would you know that?"

That Lois Lane spark flared again in Dusty' eyes. "Reporter?" she reminded Melanie. "I spoke to George's lawyer. He didn't say it outright, but I figured it out. Jon hated his uncle, and he hated Stuart House. He was glad to be rid of them both. Right?"

Melanie admitted it with a tip of her head and waited for Dusty to say more. Instead, the woman picked up her margarita and took three sips in quick succession. *Thank God George's lawyer didn't tell her about the safe,* Melanie thought. She was beginning to like Dusty — her love of her job, her curiosity about things — but she didn't want Dusty to learn about the Peter Pan angle. A story like that on the nightly news? The prospect made her feel sick. "How much interaction do you have with the family?" Melanie asked. "Did you talk to Alice Lancaster or her son? Or others? Did you see George before he died?"

"Alice Lancaster was my aunt," Dusty stated softly. "She passed away two weeks ago."

"Oh." Melanie couldn't hide her embarrassment. She should have made the connection. "Geez, I'm sorry."

"That's all right. It wasn't surprising. She'd been fading for some time." Dusty picked her list off the table, folded it and handed it to Melanie. "This is your copy. As for George, yes, I dared to knock on the door of Stuart House once, a little over a year ago. He yelled at me and tried to hit me with his cane. He was never officially declared insane, but I saw it in his eyes. He kept saying things like *you work for them* and *they'll never get me.* He sounded afraid, which makes me think he suffered from paranoia. People in the area hated him, but I felt sorry for him. The poor man was a wreck. He paid a woman an exorbitant amount of money to clean Stuart House once a week and stock his pantry. While she was in the house, he would lock himself in his study. I interviewed her, name of Flora Banners. She despised George but loved her paycheck."

"Did she say anything about George himself or about the house?" Melanie asked.

"Only that she loved being a part of the house's history. I'm sure you know it was an historic landmark. She was afraid of George, though, and was glad he chose to lock himself away whenever she was there." Dusty checked her notes. "George had a gardener, too, a Jose Hererro, but the two never met. Flora hired him for George and supervised him and his work crew."

Melanie pondered the words that Dusty had attributed to George: *you work for them, they'll never get me.* Had he merely been nutso, or might he have been haunted by Pan and his fairies as Jon must had been? If so, why hadn't he been taken to the Neverland? What made Pan take some Stuart men and not others?

"I haven't spoken with many other Stuarts in that branch," Dusty went on. "There aren't many left. Few of the men married. But I do have more information for you." She pulled a file out of her briefcase. "I'll start with the easy stuff." She held up a set of stapled papers. "This is the family line, tracing Jon and his branch directly to – get this – King Charles II of England."

Melanie's mind shot back to the day she had read *Peter Pan*. Barrie had written, "In dress he somewhat aped the attire associated with the name of Charles II, having heard it said in some earlier period of his career that he bore a strange resemblance to the ill-fated Stuarts." *Certainly that was just a fun connection to make for the sake of the story,* she thought. *Barrie was just playing with his readers.* But what if he wasn't? And if he wasn't, how had he made the connection?

Dusty, unaware of the magnitude of her work, was sliding the stapled papers over to Melanie. "I found the link by accident. I have a thing for English royalty. I subscribe to abstracts of all the major British genealogical and historical journals. A piece about Charles II caught my attention. How good are you at history?"

Melanie shrugged. "I know Charles II reigned in the second half of the seventeenth century. He fooled around a lot."

"Didn't they all. Chuck reigned from precisely 1660 to 1685 and had at least fifteen mistresses, probably more. He wasn't quiet about them, either. Most of these ladies are well documented, but recently a new name was added to the list, one Dolly Fairfax, born Gwenhwyfar Potter in Wales somewhere around 1647. In early 1666 she was a pretty up-and-coming actress, and she caught Chuckie's eye. She bore him a son, which she named James – he's on the top of the insane list I gave you. I think the whole curse thing started with him, though I can't figure out how to prove it. I don't even know what I'm trying to prove. Think what you like. You can read the details later."

Melanie took the papers and set them aside. "You really do know your history."

"I adore history," said Dusty. "It's the grand soap opera of human existence, far more outlandish than anything Hollywood can concoct. If schoolkids were taught the truth about history – that it's not all boring dates and dry facts but fascinating studies in greed, lust, ambition, passion, man's deepest beliefs about himself and the world — well, every kid would get an A, I guarantee it." She blushed. "Sorry. I can get pretty passionate about it."

"I see that."

"Bottom line, my love of history has helped my career a lot. And without it I never would have found this." She passed another paper to Melanie. On it was written:

> Bad blayde
> Hand unmayde
> So afrayde
> He gode awayde

"What is this?" Melanie asked. Blayde? Hand unmayde? *No way,* she thought, quelling the ridiculous thought before it fully formed.

Dusty was saying, "It's a sailor's rhyme that was popular around the docks of Liverpool during the early seventeen hundreds. It refers to Charles William Stuart."

Melanie glanced at the insane list, as Dusty called it. Charles William Stuart was the third Stuart to go mad and the first to disappear. "Do you know why it was written?"

Dusty nodded. "I have to backtrack a little first. Seems the relationship between King Chuck and Dolly Fairfax didn't last long. Chuckie caught sight of another pretty actress, one Nell Gwynne, and dumped Dolly. He was kind to his discards, though, and gave her a lot of money before turning his back. Dolly squandered it all and died of the pox in 1684, leaving sonny James, eighteen at the time, on his own. I don't know what he did for a living, but he had a wife and two boys by 1697, at which point he was thirty-one years old. He hung himself later that year. As you can see on the insane list, his first son Phillip Edward went mad. I don't know the details. Son number two, Charles William, subject of the rhyme and number three on the insane list, was an ordinary seaman. On..." Dusty checked her sheet. "...June 13, 1737, he was on shore leave in the Liverpool Sailortown, a place where bizarre behavior didn't particularly draw much attention. Except that Charles went beyond bizarre. He entered the Kedge-

Anchor Pub and, right there in front of the crowd, took out a sword and chopped his hand off."

"Right or left?" Melanie asked before she knew it.

Dusty seemed to take it as a matter of curiosity and not the dangerous lead it could have been. "I don't know. My information comes from a single account of the incident found in a letter of a sailor, one Benjamin Stanley, to his mother in Dorset. He was in the pub when it happened. He wrote that a doctor saved Charles' life before he bled to death, and that the news of Charles' disappearance a few days later made for gossip. What interests me is the inference in the poem that Charles was afraid of something, that he might have run away. I'm also curious about the term *bad blayde*. Stanley specifically mentioned that Charles used a *sword* to cut off his hand. Maybe that's the same *blayde* mentioned in the sailor song. Sailors were extremely superstitious. To call a blade bad..." She shrugged. "Any ideas?"

Hell yeah! Melanie thought while, in her mind's eye, she saw a long box containing an oil cloth and yellowed paper. She had to keep Dusty from going in that direction. "Why would being scared of something make a man cut his own hand off? Did you find any later mention of him? I mean, maybe he did just go nuts and run off."

"Always a possibility," Dusty said, "but I don't think so. Take a look at the insane list again. See James Albert, Jon's great-grandfather? He went nuts and disappeared, too — but he came *back*."

Melanie felt her eyes go round. *I was right! James came back! He came back from the Neverland! How did he do it?* She tried to keep from trembling. *But he came back insane. If Jon comes back, will he be the same?*

Dusty was speaking. "James disappeared from London on March 11, 1896. He reappeared on Baker Street around midnight May 3." She picked up yet another piece of paper and read notes. "He was raving and, to quote the *London Times* of the next day, howling. His hair was long and disheveled. He was dressed in rags that he couldn't account for. Most interestingly, he was missing his right hand."

"Coincidence," Melanie said, hoping she hadn't said it too quickly. "There's, what, a hundred and fifty years between these incidents? We're talking about crazy people. I've done some research in that area. Self-mutilation is not uncommon."

Dusty put her elbow on the edge of the table and parked her chin in her palm. "What I want to know is, where was he for the seven weeks he was missing? For that matter, where did any of them go? Four Stuarts vanish, and nobody has a clue where."

"James never spoke of what happened to him?"

"Well, he spoke," Dusty replied, "but what he said was nonsense. A colleague of mine in England found references in letters and one doctor's report stating that James insisted he'd spent the time as a pirate captain. He had been a captain in the Royal Navy before he disappeared — his ship was the *Divine Justice* — so I think he must have created some fantasy based on that. What's extremely odd, considering this whole thing is odd, is that James came back well fed. He was in good shape, aside from his sanity. And however he'd lost his hand, the wound was completely healed." She ran the tip of her finger along the edge of her margarita glass, round and round. "Any ideas? I'll entertain anything from alien abduction to astral travel at this point."

Melanie hid her alarm by turning her head and faking a coughing fit. *She's so close*, she thought. *So close! All the pieces are there right in front of her, but the answer is so preposterous she can't see it!*

Dusty traded Rod Serling for Lois Lane again. "You've done research, too, you said. By the look on your face I'd say you have some light to shed on this particular incident."

Quid pro quo. It was inevitable. Melanie didn't want to give Dusty anymore fuel, but it was the only way she could get her own answers. "I do indeed," she said carefully. She took some folded papers out of her purse. "I haven't been on this kick as long as you, but I did find out that James died in Surrey at a place called Black Lake Cottage, February of 1900."

"Sorry, that's incorrect," Dusty stated with all the conviction of a university scholar. "James Stuart died the year after his return, on October 1, 1897. All Souls Day, of all days. There's a notice of his death in the *London Times*."

"Well," Melanie said with as much conviction, "that notice is wrong."

Dusty's eyes glittered with interest. "How do you figure?"

Melanie had gotten the lead from J.M. Barrie's letter, but she wasn't about to mention that. "Pure dumb luck," she said. "Awhile back I did some research for a writer who wanted a history of Surrey. Black Lake and the surrounding forest has been a resort area for Londoners for a very long time, so I combed through the history and owners of Black Lake Cottage. I discovered that..." She checked her notes, acting as if the information wasn't already emblazoned on her brain. "Edward W. Stuart purchased it in late November of 1897 and sold it in April of 1900. When I started to look into Jon's family, I remembered the fact."

Dusty nodded, conceding the point. "Yes, Edward was Emmerich's cousin. Nothing strange or unusual ever happened to him, though. He led a quiet respectable life. Worked at a bank, I believe. Lived in Leicester with his wife and three kids."

"That's it exactly," said Melanie. "He lived in Leicester — but he bought a cottage in Surrey."

"Vacation home," Dusty said dismissively. "Income property."

"Not likely, if you consider the timing. James disappeared and came back in 1896, right? He came back a mental ruin. I think his wife Anna tried to care for him herself but the whole situation became too much for her. She died on November 4, just two weeks before Edward bought Black Lake Cottage *and* just three weeks before Emmerich left for America."

A grin slowly spread over Dusty' sculpted face. "Might I ask where you got this information?"

Melanie had anticipated that question and was ready for it. She had gotten the information from James Stuart's mad memoirs, but as with Barrie's letter, she wasn't about to set Dusty on that track. "I've been going through Jon's stuff. I found a box with some of his father's personal notes and correspondence. One paper mentions his parents and grandparents. Most of it doesn't pertain, but I found Anna's death date there, along with the fact of Emmerich's rather hasty move directly, I'm presuming, to San Francisco."

Dusty wanted to see those letters. Melanie saw the reference lust in her eyes. She was practically about to bust out of her slick business suit in anticipation, waiting for Melanie to make the offer.

"The rest of it's personal," Melanie assured her casually, "mostly about The Argument, as Jon called the family feud. Nothing useful to this conversation."

Dusty maintained her hard stare, clearly shooting out "Give them to me!" vibes. They didn't work, and she sighed. "Too bad."

Whew! "Well, back to what I was saying – I think the Stuarts grew tired of being gossip fodder. After Anna died, I think cousin Edward arranged for a fake death certificate along with funeral services for James. Then he hid James away in Black Lake Cottage with a nurse, I'd guess, until James died. It wasn't hard to arrange such official favors if one had connections and money. The Stuarts weren't rich but they were comfortable. Maybe the family pooled their funds. One way or another, James' death announcement ended up in the *London Times*, as you discovered, and the family resumed their lives in peace without any guilt about James and, I bet, no more gossip or harassment."

What Melanie did not add was that J.M. Barrie had then purchased Black Lake Cottage in April of 1900 and had somehow found James' mad memoirs there – probably during the extensive remodeling that Barrie's wife, Mary, had insisted upon when the house was bought. Melanie suspected that James had hidden his memoirs and Hook's sword behind a loose floorboard or something, and when he died, the Stuarts never knew the items even existed. Barrie found them, became fascinated by the memoirs, and from that scrawled laundry list of misery and torture during James' time in the Neverland was born one of the greatest children's stories of all time.

"Melanie." Dusty held out her margarita glass. "Have another sip on me. I think you may have nailed it. It fills in all the holes I've encountered about James." That hard stare flashed in her eyes again. "Did you bring a copy of your notes for me?"

"Take these," Melanie said and slid the papers over. "I've got it all on computer."

The waitress approached with their lunches. Conversation halted while she was there. Dusty took the time to tuck Melanie's papers into her file folder. Then she waited quietly for the waitress to leave.

The waitress must have sensed the conversation hanging because she smiled, with some irritation, Melanie thought, and left without asking the routine questions: would you like ketchup or mustard? more drinks? can I get you anything else?

"One more thing about James," Dusty resumed, riffling through her file. "There's more information on him than the others, not because his incident is more recent but because it caught the attention of the press. I found clips... yeah, here we go." She pulled out a paper. "The word *artifact* comes up a few times. Reporters hounded Stuart relatives for interviews. Most of them wouldn't talk, but the sister of Edward's wife, Emily Bloomburg, mentioned the word artifact. She refused to explain it afterwards, as if she'd said it by accident. Once it was out, the reporters pushed the Stuarts harder, hoping someone else would slip up. No one did and the press gave up, but the term survived within the family. I know it referred to something specific because my Aunt Alice knew what it was. I'm certain she did because she put a note about it on her family tree. Just my luck her memory was failing by the time I heard of the term and asked her about it. Have you come across it?"

Damn straight I have, Melanie thought, *and guess what? I'm not going to tell you!* She was beginning to feel guilty. Here Dusty was helping her out more than she would ever know, and thus far Melanie had reciprocated with a few facts and a slew of dodges and lies. *I'll offer to pay the bill.* The moment that idea came to mind, she felt small as well as guilty.

As for the *artifact*, she saw the word and date clearly in her mind: "artifact 1896," written next to Anna's name on old Alice's family notes. It took no effort for Melanie to decode it at this stage. *It's got to refer to the sword. Emmerich hid it in a secret safe in Stuart House. Pan started haunting Jon soon after he brought it home. The sword has something to do with Pan and the curse.* Her next thought chilled her. She had managed to quell it earlier, but it came back, determined to get her attention. *Could it be the sword from the Sailortown rhyme, the sword that Charles William used to hack off his hand? Is the sword that old? If it is, where did it originally come from? And what kind of... power... does it have?*

She tried to visualize the weapon and suddenly, clearly remembered the strange markings that had been etched into that sharp silver blade. They had been more than decoration, she had thought so then and she thought so now. They had looked like some form of writing, but in no language she or Jon had recognized. *I should have taken a rubbing of them first thing. I might have been able to learn something.*

These disturbing thoughts and plenty of others cascaded through Melanie's Researcher Brain. On the outside, she arranged her features into an expression of perplexity. "I have no idea what it might mean," she told Dusty blandly.

"Damn it and make it a double." Dusty finished her margarita, tipping her head way back so she could get the very last drop.

Despite Dusty's Hollywood nose, her studio-crisp makeup and her jangling jewelry, Melanie liked the woman. *Jon did himself a disservice by not getting to know her,* she thought. *She's smart. Feisty. Sort of dangerous. He would have liked her.*

Melanie herself, however, was of two minds. She liked Dusty, no doubt about it. The reporter would have made one hell of a research asset. This meeting could have been the beginning of a beautiful friendship. Unfortunately, Dusty knew too much, and what she knew had the power to change Melanie's life forever. Of that, Melanie was sure. So she finished her lunch with Francine "Dusty" Rhodes, letting the conversation wander as it would. Their mutual revelations about their mutual fixation had been shared. All that was left was the food.

Melanie barely touched her BLT and curly fries. What little appetite she had started with was long gone.

CHAPTER 38

"Mrow!" *Scratch scratch scratch.*

Stuart opened his cabin door. Dago Tom trotted in. "Excellent timing, Tom," Stuart told the cat. "I could use your input." Stuart sat down at the rosewood table upon which his map of Pan's island lay open, its curled edges held in place by four candles in silver candle holders. Dago Tom jumped up and sat in the middle of it. "If you want to help," Stuart said, gently forcing the cat to relocate to one side, off the map, "then stay over there, *capisce?*"

Dago Tom glared at Stuart, licked his soft grey belly fur, and deigned to accept the arrangement. He joined Stuart in scrutinizing the map, even if his point-of-view was upside-down.

"All right, this is the situation," Stuart told the cat. "While I was threatening Miss Darling awhile ago, I got an idea. A very good one, I'm sure. Problem is, I forgot it. Lots going on at the time, you know. So what we need to do is jog my memory and get the idea back. I think it involved this map, so let us focus, shall we?"

Dago Tom spotted Stuart's quill pen and batted at it.

"Tom. Please. Keep your mind on the matter at hand." Stuart moved the quill out of the cat's reach. "Now, I'm wondering if my elusive idea might have had something to do with the Hollow Hill. I've already asked Bucket-Head Billy. Stupid boy, he's never heard of it. I can't ask Smee or Cecco because, well, what if I'm already supposed to know? And oh yes, I have asked..." He tapped his skull.

345

"No help there. So, Tom my luv, what do you know about the Hollow Hill, hm?"

Dago Tom lifted a paw and licked it.

"Right." Stuart sighed. "All I've got is this map." He smoothed the parchment and slowly, thoughtfully traced every line with his long manicured index finger, following the delicate curves of the coast, trying to blank his mind so that the elusive idea might reform. What the devil had it been? Something good, he was positive of it.

The curve of Pirate's Bay seemed to grin up at him. Nothing particularly helpful here. The pirates knew this bay inside out.

Mermaid Lagoon? It was a startlingly lovely place, eerie and shadowy even by day, lush with green growing things right up to the water's edge. The mermaids — or sirens, when their dander was up — remained there for the most part in their underwater homes, but Stuart's parallel memories recalled having seen them once or twice lounging on the rocks, braiding their luxurious seaweed hair and singing, the fishy half of their bodies gleaming with rainbow scales.

On those occasions they sang as mermaids with sweet human-like voices. During those few occasions when their songs were carried by the wind all the way to the ship, the men stopped their work to listen, most of them falling into a deep melancholy that Stuart understood all too well. He had given Cecco and Foggerty standing orders not to interfere on those occasions. Mermaid and siren song both contained magic. Mermaid song held no danger, but the emotions it engendered, usually wistful and nostalgic, were strong. It was safer to let the men recover in their own time. As for a back door out of the Neverland, the mermaids might well know of one, maybe even in their lagoon. Stuart had to grudgingly discard any hope of finding it, however. The sirens would tear him apart before he got within fifty feet of their shore.

What about Marooners' Rock? It was an interesting place, to say the least, a mass tombstone, really. It was a craggy rock about a quarter mile from shore north of Mermaid Lagoon. Nothing special about it except that, during high tide, the whole thing became submerged. Some crafty fellow, probably a pirate long ago, had bolted two sets of irons into the rock. When a man was chained to them as the tide was rising, he was likely to confess to any crimes or give up any secrets asked of him. Those who refused to talk, well... their bones lay scattered below in the silt and sand.

Moaning Cove. Nothing dangerous actually happened there, as far as Stuart knew. But the sounds, good God, they could frighten a man to death! Gibbering shrieks and cackles filled the night air, sounds that could be heard only if one were close to the area. If you were fool enough to test your mettle at such times, the volume was said to be tremendous. Stuart had been told that men had lost their sanity to the ghostly onslaught, but he had never gone there at night to find out for himself. Hook was brave, not stupid.

Months ago he had taken some men to investigate and map the Cove during the course of three days, when the suns had been at their highest. His men had found nothing of interest. On the other hand, they had found every reason to never go back. Throughout the day the very water moaned like men in agony. Bubbles trailed up from the depths that suggested something lived down there, or had once lived, and wanted to emerge once more into the light if only it could find a way up. If there was a door leading back home in that place, the pirates hadn't found any sign of it.

So much for the coast. Stuart saw nothing there that triggered his idea. As for interior locations, his map showed only three: Fairy Falls, the volcano, and the Indian camp.

Fairy Falls was a waterfall, sparkling and gorgeous by both night and day. Its crystal pure water cascaded down from the top of the mountains and created a frothing pool. The pirates knew the place well — at least, the southern end of it. There, farthest from the waterfall itself, the pool gave birth to a creek from which the pirates got their fresh water. They dared not venture any closer to the pool itself because the fairies hung around the area in irritating droves. On several occasions they had slashed the pirates with their tiny swords and actually bitten them like vicious little vampires.

Stuart hated the place. The one time he had gone beyond the mouth of the creek — he had insisted on getting one good look at the pool, and that had included climbing behind the falls itself to note any caves or artifacts — he had come back with his hand, neck and face covered with red welts. Smee had, as always, tended the wounds, finagling Stuart into promising never to go beyond the creek again.

"It's a fairy domain, sar," the bosun had said. "They'll defend it to the end. No point gettin' pricked to death when the creek water's pure an' sweet." Stuart had agreed. There was nothing there. Nor did thoughts of the place rekindle his elusive idea.

What about the volcano? Stuart knew nothing about it yet. Perhaps a door existed up there, but thinking about it did not tickle his lost idea back into being.

Lastly there was the Indian camp—

"That's it!" he said triumphantly, startling Dago Tom and sending the cat scrabbling off the table with a hiss. "The Indians! Tom, don't you see? I reckoned that Wendy would know a way out of the Neverland, that she was closest to Pan and would be privy to his secrets, but I forgot all about Tiger Lily." Stuart got up and fetched the cat, plopping him back on the table. "Isn't she supposed to be close to Pan as well?"

Dago Tom refused to comment.

"Well, she is," Stuart said, sitting back down. "She is indeed. I remember now. Tiger Lily... hmm..." He tapped his finger as he mused. "Only one thing to do, I suppose. I'll have to kidnap her. How does that sound?"

Dago Tom flicked his tail.

"Oh, that's right," Stuart realized. "She'll have heard about Wendy. She'll be on her guard. Kidnapping is out then. Besides, that isn't the way one handles the Indians, is it? No no, not at all. Formality, that's what they respect." His finger continued its tapping. "I'll go to the Indian camp, how about that? I'll talk to the Chief in person. He's in charge, and he's Tiger Lily's father. What she knows, he'll know, hm?"

Dago Tom seemed to like that idea. He started to purr, at any rate.

Stuart took that as a sign of approval. "Very well. I shall present myself humbly, in my finest attire, and I will employ my finest manners. True, the Indians despise me, but they'll respect my presentation. They should admire my nerve, too, for walking straight into their camp. Ha! I like it." Stuart scratched the gruff tabby behind the ears. The cat's purring became a happy rumble. "I'll bring an entourage, of course, well armed," Stuart went on. "The savages can't expect less than that. What about a gift? Hmm... no. It might be perceived as a bribe. Not that I won't bribe if necessary. Oh, and I'll have to keep Wendy well guarded while I'm gone. Pan may—"

He suddenly leaped out of his chair as if it were on fire. "Python weed!" The two words came out like a squeak, startling Dago Tom off the table again. "Damn! The last thing I want to do is set foot in that jungle and have the damned bushes go for my throat again. Not to mention the croc." Stuart stamped his foot in frustration. "Hell and damnation!"

He plopped back into the chair with a frown. *No. Plain and simple. I am not going back there, forget it. Might as well chop my own head off and be done with it.* "And what, never set foot on land again?" he countered himself aloud. *Fine, then. Think! There must be a way around this. Bloody truth is, I can't continue to lock myself on this ship much longer anyhow or I really will go stir. My sanity's acockbill as it is. There must be some way I can go ashore with some kind of protection.*

"Wait wait wait!" He turned to the cat. "The story, Tom! Barrie's story! Didn't I... didn't Hook have some sort of vehicle?"

Dago Tom, having chosen a safer place to sit over on the writing table, offered nothing but his bright green gaze.

Something in those eyes delivered the answer. "A palanquin! Yes, Tom, that's it! In Barrie's novel, Captain Hook rides about on the island in a plush palanquin carried by four of his men!" Actually Barrie had referred to it as a "chariot," but Stuart recalled that most illustrations had shown it to be a palanquin the likes of which royalty in India were carried about.

He began to pace. "It won't protect me from the croc — nothing can, I fear — but it may make me a more difficult target for the python weed, especially if the sides are built up. And if it has a roof, I'll have some protection from overhead dangers." The idea of a tarantula the size of a coconut dropping down on him had never been Stuart's favorite. "Yes, Tom, I'm aware that the men carrying me will be vulnerable, but palanquins have legs. If a man goes down, I shouldn't tip over, right? At least, not all the way." He shrugged. "The whole damn island opposes me. Can't be picky."

He snatched up his quill, opened the ink bottle and got a fresh parchment from the drawer of his writing desk. He thought a moment and began to draw. He made rough calculations of the palanquin's dimensions and the materials that would be required to build it. *Solid wood will be too heavy for four men to lift. How about bamboo? Yes, bamboo is abundant on the island, and it's plenty strong for the job. Hm, I'll need to choose fabrics and decorations and* — he giggled — *I'll use hinges to let the seat recline!* That would take some fancy jiggering. Carpenter Thatcher would think he was daft, but Stuart knew it could work. Reclining chairs. He had heard of them before somewhere. He wanted one, if for no other reason than for show. *I have a reputation around the world, don't I? I'm a man of wealth, discrimination and ruthlessness, not to mention cleverness. Very well. I'll act like it!*

The more he sketched, the more he liked the idea of it, not just the protection aspects — those were so limited, really. It was the dignity of the thing that latched onto him most. "Let the dogs tromp through the mud, I'll not put up with that anymore," he told Dago Tom as he put a few finishing touches on the sketch. "I'm a captain, for Chrissake! Can't present myself to the Chief covered in jungle filth. What impression would that make? Riding in a carriage—" Somewhere along the way, the conveyance had taken on the term *carriage* in his mind. "—will solve that problem nicely."

His head jerked up at the clap of the ship's bell.

"Cap'n!" Smee's frantic cry came from the main deck. "Cap'n, it's Pan! He's comin' just like yeh said!"

"Ha!" Stuart dropped his quill, grabbed his baldric and headed out the door. Scourie and Jukes, pistols out, were taking up positions on either side of Wendy's door. "Lose her, you die," he muttered to them as he passed, shouldering the baldric on. They both straightened up as much as the low ceiling would allow and nervously saluted, Jukes almost knocking his ornamented hat off as he did.

Stuart stepped out into the sunlight of the quarterdeck.

"Captain Hook!" The voice was loud and angry and belonged to the boy whose hovering presence over the main deck had made all the pirates shuffle back into their customary wary circle.

Stuart stepped to the rail and flashed a fetching smile at the floating figure before him. "Well well! Master Peter Pan. To what do I owe the honor?"

"You took Wendy!" Pan accused.

Stuart thumped his fist against his breast. *"Mea culpa."*
"Give her back!"

"Well now, let me see..." Stuart delicately stroked his goatee, pretending to think about it. "No," he said.

Pan didn't think that was funny. He drew his sword and swooped at Stuart, who parried with his hook, catching Pan's blade and sending it flipping end over end over the starboard rail. Pan zipped after it and caught it by the hilt before it hit the water.

Impossible! Stuart thought, then laughed at himself. It *was* possible. For Pan, anything was possible.

Out of nowhere came the realization that, although the boy had been the focus of his life ever since coming to the Neverland — before arriving, even — they had confronted each other face to face a mere three times. Not that Pan had changed. He would always look the same, with his charmingly tousled hair, impish face and youthful green energy. Stuart recognized that energy this time. It was the same that infested the jungle and everything in it. It was magic. Pan radiated the stuff like a lighthouse beaming out across a midnight ocean. All that the Neverland was came from him, no doubt about it. *Maybe he is a god...*

Pan repeated his demand: "Give her back!"

Stuart should have prepared to defend himself. He should have drawn his sword. But at that moment, instead of thinking about his life and the fact that he might be about to lose it, he grinned, captured by a most amazing idea. *Standing before me in the guise of a cute little boy is the thing I hate the most, the thing that warped my family, turned my childhood into torture, haunted me, infected me — I hate it. I hate YOU. And despite it all, you're the one thing I can rely on in this whole frigging world.*

Strange but true. Events unfolded here in a corkscrew of causes and effects that made no sense to him. People behaved according to rules he couldn't even guess at. But right there was the one thing he understood. Peter Pan. The boy was consistent. All he wanted to do was kill Stuart. How refreshingly straightforward! Stuart hated him with a hatred beyond words, but at least he understood the score. He found this conclusion so absurdly comforting that he continued to stand there, grinning a thin-lipped grin and leaving himself wide open to attack.

Pan took advantage of it and nestled the tip of his sword against the soft flesh under Stuart's chin. "What's wrong with you?" he asked warily.

Stuart tilted his head back, easing the pointy pressure against his throat. That forced him to gaze at Pan over his nose. "Me? I'm just peachy. You?"

Pan's confusion morphed into anger. "No tricks, Captain. I could skewer you right now if I wanted to."

"How right you are," Stuart had to agree. "*Vero inter saxum et locum durum sum!*"

Pan's lithe body leaned forward in a questioning attitude. "Huh?"

"Latin, boy. Don't you know Latin? No, of course you don't, you live in a jungle. What I said was *I'm between a rock and a hard place.* True, no? Metaphorically if not physically, anyhow. If I draw my sword, you will, as you so succinctly put it, skewer me. If I raise my hook, you'll do the same. *Vero inter saxum et locum durum sum!*"

Pan did not look happy. "Have you gone nuts?"

Nuts. As in insane. As in flipped, fried, crackers, ape shit, bug fuck to the cheesy moon and back. With sugar on it. "What if I have, boy?" Stuart said, and then he did something the boy would never have expected, not from a one-handed man — he seized Pan's sword in that one bare hand. The sharp edge sliced red ruts into his fingers. He thought he probably felt pain, but it made no immediate impression.

"Isn't that what you've been working so hard to achieve?" he asked levelly. "Isn't that what happened to all the others who came before me? We're no good to you sane. Sane people don't pretend to be yo-ho-ho-and-a-bottle-of-rum pirates who chop up children for breakfast. Oh yes, I know what you're doing, boy. I'm not the puppet you think I am." He thrust the sword aside. Blood from his fingers painted his hand red. "So, am I *non compos mentis*? Am I, hm? Do I meet your specifications yet? Am I *ready*?"

Stuart thought he saw a glimmer of uncertainty in those beautiful boy eyes, but it was hard to tell. Looking into Peter Pan's eyes was like gazing into twin crystal balls. Something otherworldly resided deep within those bright orbs, and it stared out with the twinkle of stars. The impression was fleeting and unsettling.

Pan gave a sharp whistle. Stuart jumped.

Ranger and one of the other brats — he was wearing a skunk-skin hat with the tail flopping, so it must have been Stinky — had been hiding beyond the taffrail. At Pan's whistle they rose up and flew to Pan. Ranger was holding a wrapped bundle the size of a soccer ball. Stinky held something, too, but Stuart couldn't see what it was.

"Captain, watch those children!" Cecco cried, dashing up the port stairs. He stopped at the sight of blood on the deck, dripping from his captain's hand. "James—"

That's as far as he got. Stuart's eyes lasered into him. "If I want your help I'll order it! Go back to your station! No one is to interfere!"

Cecco looked as if he might disobey, then he turned and did a quick seaman's drop back down the stairs to the main deck. Stuart heard murmuring amongst the crew gathered down there which quickly subsided, probably by a gesture from Cecco.

Pan gave Stuart an appraising look. "You command your men well, Captain."

Stuart's cut fingers were starting to hurt. He pinched the edge of his kerchief and tugged it out of his sleeve. "Thank you," he said, determined not to let the pain show. "It just comes to me, you know. Funny how that happens." Unable to wrap his wounds — he had no hand to do it with — he could only squeeze the kerchief to stanch the blood flow. How stupid he'd been! He had only one hand as it was. What if he'd seriously injured it? *Pan doesn't like broken toys*, he assured himself. *I'll heal and quickly, too.* But for the moment, he was maimed, and now it hurt like hell to boot.

He tilted his head back so that he could see Ranger and Stinky floating overhead. Stinky was well out of his reach, but Ranger, no surprise, was hovering close enough that Stuart might have been able to grab his foot if he tried. Stuart was sure that Ranger wanted him to try. *Teasing bastard*, he thought. *I could plunge my hook right through your leg and gut you like a trout. But this is not the time.* "I presume you have something to show me?" he asked Pan. "Or are you all just going to flitter around up there like the bloated gadflies that you are?"

Pan nodded to Ranger. Ranger dropped the wrapped bundle at Stuart's feet. "I think this belongs to you."

Stuart didn't like the sound the bundle made when it hit the quarterdeck. It sounded like Ranger had dropped an overripe pumpkin. The thing didn't roll, it thunked down and lay there three or four inches from the toes of his boots. Stuart didn't want to touch it. He unsheathed his saber, grimacing at having to flex his sliced fingers, and used the silver tip to whip back the top cloth flap and then the one below that and the one below that. His heart stuttered when the last flap fell away. He throat constricted to the size of a straw, which was good because he would have screamed otherwise.

Vigr Sigrson was staring up at him.

The color drained out of Stuart's face. He felt himself go white as sure as he felt his gorge rise. *Oh God, I did kill him. I'm a murderer. I'm a murderer!*

The big Swede's head lay nestled in its cloth bundle like a mummified baby in rotten swaddling clothes. His skin was like soggy cardboard that had been baked to a rippling uneven crisp. His eyes had shriveled, and his blond hair stuck out like straw. His mouth was open enough that Stuart could see a hint of a black tongue behind Sigrson's grimy teeth, the gums a foul blue-grey. His neck ended in a fairly clean cut with just a couple flaps of leathery skin hanging down. He reeked like spoiled pork.

"I thought pirates were supposed to send their dead to Davy Jones," Ranger commented.

Stuart couldn't make his mouth work.

"We'll take it away if you give Wendy back," said Pan.

Stuart found his voice. "Tell you what." He dropped his sword. "Why don't you just kill me and be done with it."

Stinky gasped, turning to Pan. "Hey, he quit!" Stinky said. "He can't do that!"

Pan waved him quiet. "It's a bluff."

"No," Stuart said hollowly. "No. You might be having a good time, but this is not the life I want to live. You've got the deck so stacked you couldn't lose if I grew two new hands and a prehensile tail." He held his arms out. "Go ahead, hack away. I give up."

"Peterrrrrrr!" said Stinky the way a child does when an adult takes away a favorite toy.

Peter Pan smiled his beautiful cherub smile. "Oh, you're good, James Hook." He reached up towards Stinky who, upset as he was, handed something down to him. "Maybe this will cheer you up." Pan dangled a slim black bag on a long black strap.

Stuart didn't want to look. He didn't care. But for reasons he couldn't explain he looked up anyway, uncomprehendingly. A black bag. So what? Then his chest stiffened up as if his ribs had become stone. He took a feeble step back, thinking that he might faint. That was no ordinary bag. It was a woman's purse. He knew that purse. How could he have forgotten her for so long? "Mm... Mel..." He couldn't get past that one syllable.

"Thought you might like something to remember her by," Pan said jovially.

The emotional void in which Stuart had been floating suddenly flash-flooded with fury. The faintness left and he leaped up, hooking one of the purse straps. The purse latch gave way, and the contents spilled at his feet. *Just like in the bookstore long ago, so long ago, her purse opened and everything fell out...* Here it all was again, the same set of keys, the wallet, checkbook, lipstick, the compact, tissues, hairbrush, the little spiral researcher's notebook — everything he had seen before in the bookstore, in another world, another life, reappeared now, grossly out of context, queerly anomalous.

With his hook still wrapped around the strap, Stuart swung his arm in a quick circle. The purse snagged Pan's ankle tight. Pan started to fly, but Stuart already knew that trick. He wrapped his arm around the rail and held on.

Pan jerked to a stop in the air with an "Errk!" and fell back down. Stuart knocked him over and they rolled, Stuart's hook tangled in the purse strap along with Pan's leg. He resorted to using his body weight to hold the boy down while he reached for his fallen sword. Ranger got it first and conked Stuart in the head with the hilt. Stuart quickly found himself helplessly flat on his back with Pan sitting on his chest, blade at his throat.

"Go ahead," Stuart rasped, seeing Melanie's beautiful face in his mind, not Pan's face snarling down at him. "You killed her, didn't you, you son of a bitch!"

"Stop," Pan said softly.

And stop Stuart did. *Everything* stopped. Stuart felt as if the world and everything in it simply switched themselves off. He couldn't move. Pan leaned down to him, close enough that Stuart thought he smelled the perfume of flowers on his breath. "It was your doing all along," Pan whispered into his ear. "*You're* the monster, James Hook, not me." With a childish laugh, Pan easily twisted his ankle free and flew away with Ranger and Stinky.

Stuart remained on his back. His muscles realigned with normal Time and Space, but his emotions convulsed in confusion. What did Pan mean? That Melanie was really dead after all, and that somehow he, Stuart, had done it? *No no no, my memories are all over the map, but I would never, could never–*

Someone was calling him. "Captain! Help! Hurry!" It was coming from Smee's cabin!

Stuart wavered to his feet. "Cecco, Smee, double quick!" He stumbled to the cabin and found the door wide open. Scourie and Jukes weren't on post outside. Stuart rushed in to see the strangest sight: two legs sticking out of the open gunport, and Scourie and Jukes each holding onto one of them.

"They're trying to – pull her – out!" Scourie huffed, tugging on the left leg.

The gunport! He'd forgotten all about the goddamn gunport! All this time Pan had been stalling him, using him to keep the crew standing idly around like a bunch of cud-chewing cows while the Lost Boys had quietly opened the gunport to rescue Wendy!

Stuart angled his way between Scourie and Jukes and took hold of Wendy's nightshirt, hissing in pain when he closed his wounded fist around a wad of the soft cotton material. "Every bloody one of those runts must be hauling on her at once!" he said, putting one foot up against the bulkhead for leverage and pulling in sync with Scourie and Jukes. More and more of Wendy came back through the gunport, and then Stuart heard a loud bang.

Jukes let out a parrot-like screech. "I'm shot!" he wailed, and released Wendy's right ankle. "Yeeeeeeee! I'm shot!"

Stuart stole a glance over his shoulder to see Jukes writhing on Smee's colorful carpet, clutching his buttocks. Ranger was in the doorway with the Lost Boys' stolen pistol. "Right in the ass!" Ranger laughed. The boy made a quick withdrawal at the sound of a dozen pirates pounding up the stairs to the quarterdeck.

Wendy's nightgown slipped through Stuart's fingers. He grunted in pain and let go before realizing it.

"Sir!" Scourie said in alarm.

"I've got her," Stuart assured the man, and he caught Wendy's right ankle. It was easier to keep hold of, but he wouldn't be able to keep it up, if for no other reason than his own slippery blood.

"Let her go!" the boy John shrilled from outside. "Let my sister go!" There followed an incredibly hard pull.

"She'll split in two before I let her go!" Stuart shouted back, pulling with all his might. Wendy kicked her legs, Stuart's grip slipped, and before he could figure out how to use his hook without goring the girl, he stumbled back and tumbled over Jukes.

"Heave ho!" one of the boys yelled outside. Wendy almost disappeared through the gunport.

"Captain!" Scourie yipped, "I'm losin' her!"

Stuart snatched up a wad of cloth from Smee's sewing basket and threw it at Wendy's right ankle. He gripped that in the curve of his elbow and pulled, the thick fabric giving him a good firm grasp. Skylights, Kamau, Cookson and other pirates crammed into the tiny cabin and latched onto Stuart and Scourie to lend their strength. Stuart figured they must look like a bunch of sadists playing tug-o-war using a poor little girl instead of a rope. He had a crazy vision of Wendy popping apart at the joints and everyone ending up with a piece of her to keep as a souvenir. *I don't care if she does rip apart, she is not leaving yet!* "On three!" he instructed. "One! Two—"

The boys outside heaved first. Wendy almost disappeared out the gunport again. She screamed, not in pain, it seemed to Stuart, but in exhilaration, a wild adventurous excitement overriding her fear. Once more a sense of awe swept over him at how resilient the girl was, how damned *brave*. Then he yelled, "Three!" and the pirates heaved.

If there was one thing the pirates excelled at, it was heaving. Wendy shotgunned all the way back through the gunport. As the pirates dominoed backwards on top of each other, Stuart heard one of the most satisfying sounds he'd heard in a long time — the Lost Boys crashing into the hull outside en masse with a comical series of thumps and childish wails. There was scrabbling and arguing and swearing and hollering, and then most of them must have lost their happy thoughts because next came a series of loud splashes.

Stuart untangled himself from Skylights and Mason to find that Scourie had a firm hold on Wendy. She sat quietly in his lap where she had landed, too disappointed to struggle anymore.

"Close that goddamn gunport!" Stuart ordered. "Put the girl in irons!" Then he paused. He surveyed the fantastic scene before him. Pirates littered the floor in heaps. Jukes was still wriggling around clutching his buttocks and whining, "Ow! It hurts! Ow! Ow!" Smee's dainty decorations were ripped and scattered all over the place. It looked like the aftermath of a drunken frat party.

Stuart snickered. The pirates gave him curious looks. He began to laugh. They began to chuckle. Then they all burst out laughing, with Stuart's laughter rising to a distinct shrill. Tension, that's all it was, tension and an almost unbearable wave of relief. Stuart let it all out. He couldn't have stopped it if he'd tried. He stumbled over his crewmen to the door, his eyes tearing so badly he didn't see Cecco until he walked right into him.

Cecco put an arm around his captain's shoulders and steered him out. He started to chuckle himself.

"The gunport!" Stuart snorted between guffaws. "Forgot — and the brats — what a splash!" He fumbled to his knees, almost taking Cecco with him, laughing so hard that he ran completely out of air and almost blacked out.

Cecco got hold of himself. "Pan's gone, sir," he reported.

"And Jukes!" Stuart wheezed, pressing on with his own incoherent report. "Right in the ass!"

"James, you need to see Cookson. Your hand looks bad."

Stuart waved him off, catching his breath. "It'll be healed by tomorrow. I — I wager you five ducats I wake up with not even a scratch! No damaged goods allowed around here, oh no, ha ha!"

Cecco answered that with a dubious look as Foggerty stepped up. "Captain, sir." The second mate hesitantly tapped Stuart's shoulder, something no pirate did if he wanted to keep his guts intact. In this particular instance, Stuart just stuck an arm out at the man. He gave the other to Cecco and let the two of them hoist him up.

Stuart wiped his eyes on his sleeve, still chuckling, his hand dripping blood. The other laughing pirates exited Smee's ruined quarters. "What is it, Mister Foggerty?" Stuart managed to ask.

"You want the girl in irons in the brig, sir?"

"What? Oh. Uh, forget that. I was angry. Put her in irons, aye, but it's only decent that she remain in Smee's cabin." He took a few steps back in order to peek into the little space. "After Smee tidies it first. And make sure that confounded gunport is secured."

"Aye aye, Captain," Foggerty acknowledge, and went to fetch Smee.

"What about the head?" Cecco asked him.

For a minute Stuart thought he was referring to the ship's toilet, or what passed for it. "What about it?"

"No, James, the head that's lying on the quarterdeck. Whose is it... *was* it?"

All of Stuart's humor faded. "It's still there?"

"Aye."

Stuart regarded his wounded hand. It really was a mess. The pain of it pulsed in time with his heartbeat. His thumb and first two fingers were sliced not quite to the bone. The other fingers were okay. "Weigh it down and throw it overboard," he said.

Cecco mutely accepted the lack of details. "Aye aye, sir. And what about—"

Stuart cut him short with a sharp wave. "No more." He winced. "Just... leave me alone, I have to think." He headed for his cabin where there was soothing brandy and no severed heads. "Oh. One moment." Stuart fetched his drawing of the carriage, pinching it gingerly between his two uninjured fingers. "Give this to Thatcher," he said. "Tell him to start building immediately."

Cecco took it. "What—?"

"Don't argue with me, dammit, just do it!"

Cecco saluted. "Aye aye, Captain."

Stuart ducked back into his cabin. He felt Cecco watching as he closed the door, wanting to ask him that mysterious something, but Stuart didn't care what it was. All of a sudden he was very very tired.

CHAPTER 39

Log, *Jolly Roger*, moored in PB, the morning after my
encounter with Pan re: Wendy's capture. Have kept
her sequestered in Bosun Smee's quarters even though
Pan knows she is there. The gunport has been secured,
and I have ordered ten armed men at a time to keep
general watch, including two in bosun's chairs outside
the gunport itself. Pan has made no further attempt to
rescue her. I have not visited the girl since the first
attempt, though I have charged Smee to make sure she
is well cared for. I have provided her with several texts
and novels from my personal collection with which she
may pass her time. (I am presuming she can read.)
Regarding my carriage, Thatcher and his men
procured the necessary bamboo early this morning and
are now in the process of construction. Smee is
fashioning curtains and other ornamentations
according to my specifications. Note: My hand healed
overnight. Cecco owes me five ducats.

Stuart put down his quill and examined that mysteriously healed
hand. The wounds on his fingers weren't completely gone — red scars
still showed where the cuts had been. Stuart suspected they would be
gone by the next day. Today, though the muscles were stiff, he could

use the hand without much pain. *No broken toys,* he thought, and lifted his china coffee cup from its delicate saucer to his lips. The cup was empty.

He fetched the kettle from the tray on the rosewood table and refilled it, adding a spoonful of molasses to cut the bitterness. He did these tasks slowly, as if in a daze. He had finished breakfast just as slowly, lost in thought to the degree that he had taken forty minutes to eat four scrambled eggs and a chunk of brown bread. There were preparations to make if he was going to visit the Indians the next day. His brain was deep in the throes of scheming. At this moment, it was chewing on a particularly tough question: how could he guarantee that the Indian Chief would talk to him?

Roars Like a Bear. That was the old man's name. Stuart had found it among those first entries in his log, the ones that he had and had not written. According to those entries, the Chief had deigned to see Stuart two times in the past, one of them before Stuart had lost his hand. That had been to peaceably negotiate trade for four of the tribe's cows. After that, probably thanks to Pan's interference, the Indians had refused all communications. The second meeting had therefore taken place during a raid in which the pirates had successfully stolen two more cows. *Wendy was right,* he thought. *I'm a pirate* and *a cattle rustler. Ha!*

Still the question remained. How could he force the Chief to see him if the old man refused? Kidnapping members of the tribe and holding them ransom wouldn't work, that he knew. Roars Like a Bear and his people were warriors. Anyone captured was considered lost. So what would force their cooperation?

Stuart paced, thinking. Hook surely had a way. When circumstances were not in his favor, he turned them to his favor. He was known for getting what he wanted. In this case, how could he do it? "What do they care about?" he muttered as he paced. "What would bring them to their knees?"

His eyes landed on Hook's perfume cabinet. The size of a large jewelry box, the exquisite wood and glass container squatted on its four short legs on top of his dresser. It contained two shelves crammed with ornamental jars and bottles, each containing scents, some quite expensive, that Stuart had learned to use to combat the stink of the ship and its scabby crew. There was musk, patchouli, a spicy bay rhum that Hook concocted himself, various *eaux de parfum* that he also made from flowers on the island – lavender, rose, jasmine and others for which he knew no name.

Stuart had never been one to wear perfumes. Maybe a splash of aftershave but nothing fancy. His situation in the Neverland had changed that quick enough. He wore perfumes everyday now, applied after Smee gave him his morning shave and, if necessary, before bed. He perfumed his laced kerchief each morning, usually with jasmine scent. He liked jasmine. He also concocted a mint infusion that he used each morning and night after cleaning his teeth. Nobody else might care about bad breath, but he did. "Hmm. You have more than just perfumes, though, don't you?" he asked the darkness. A picture was forming in his mind. More little bottles. Delicate containers, works of art, really, six of them in all. "Where are they?"

The picture solidified.

Stuart hurried to his writing desk and knelt down. He felt the underside. His fingertips traced a faint square in the wood to the left of the drawer – a secret compartment. How to open it? He knocked on it with his hook. Nothing. He fetched a candle and proceeded to examine the writing desk much as he had the pillar upon which the bronze horse stood. *There must be a trigger device here somewhere,* he thought, feeling along the smooth wooden surfaces.

He finally figured it out, with no help from the black fiend within. The trigger wasn't in the desk, it was in the drawer. He pulled the drawer all the way out and examined it. He found a small hole, the size of a fingertip, cut into the bottom left edge. Stuart slid the drawer back in place and then, keeping his finger in the hole, slid the drawer back and forth. He didn't feel the tiny metal prong until he repeated his experiment, this time poking his finger further through the hole. He pressed down on the prong.

A little shelf swung down from the underside of the writing desk, carried on a cleverly designed set of metal hinges. The box sitting on the shelf was heavy, carved of black marble. Its stone lid bore a bas-relief of a skull and crossbones that struck Stuart as highly melodramatic. He lifted the lid to reveal a black velvet padded interior with six indentations molded into it. Each indentation cradled a glass vial.

None of the vials were labeled, but Stuart knew what they were. Poisons. From left to right the vials contained a strong decoction of deadly nightshade, also called belladonna; the venom of a King Cobra; a hemlock brew; arsenic powder; and bitter almond, known as potassium hydrocyanide to the modern world.

The sixth and final vial contained a deep purplish-red liquid that had no name. Stuart's parallel memories told him that he had purchased it from a Voodoo priest in Haiti many years ago when he had served as bosun aboard Blackbeard's ship in the Caribbean. The liquid was an odious combination of lethal botanicals fused with the power of the blackest of black magic. It was so concentrated that the smallest drop would kill a man in seconds. Even a light smear of the stuff on skin was fatal. The Voodoo priest had amiably demonstrated that fact by touching the wet lid to the bare arm of a village thief slated for execution. The man had gone into grotesque convulsions that had lasted about five minutes before he'd died, mouth and nose bubbling purple-red froth, eyes turned an eerie shiny grey like oversized ball bearings. The poison, the Voodoo priest had said, had no antidote. Stuart, mightily impressed, had paid an exorbitant amount for the vial.

Parallel memories also informed Stuart that he had used that poison only twice in all these years. On the first occasion, he had gathered the entire crew to stand witness as he rubbed the vial's open rim against the arm of a man who had been trying to organize a mutiny. What followed had been quite a freak show. Those who might have been in cahoots with the mutineer never followed through on their plans. On the second occasion, he had surreptitiously dispatched an ill-mannered fellow in Beggar's Port who had given Tawdry Audrey's girls trouble.

Excellent weapons, he thought, gazing at his tidy box of death, *but how can these help me tomorrow?*

The answer came delightfully fast. Stuart grinned.

It was an elegant plan and would require special preparation. First he needed two things from Cookson. He went below and obtained a small piece of sponge from the sawbones' stores, along with a cup of

sand. It was customary to carry sand onboard so that, in the event the
decks became slick with water or blood, it could be thrown down to
provide traction. Stuart took the sand and sponge back up to his
cabin and locked the door behind him.

He used his hook to tear a large patch out of one of his cotton
shirts and also out of a leather vest. He set the sand and patches aside
and dropped the sponge into a pewter cup.

He next fetched a glove from his top dresser drawer. He faced a
challenge getting the thing on. He had to resort to using his teeth. But
his plan required the use of the Voodoo poison, and he would never
dare touch that vial with his bare hand. Any residue on the glass
might absorb through his skin. If it wasn't enough to kill him, it
might make him sick enough that he would want to die.

He carefully opened the crimson vial and suddenly found himself
kneeling, faint, barely able to hold the vial upright. He managed to set
it on the table before he collapsed completely, feeling as if his muscles
had liquefied. It was hard to judge how long he lay like a dead man,
half-conscious, unable to move, his nostrils tingling as if he had
sniffed rum up his nose.

Fumes, he thought dully. Yes, he had forgotten about the fumes.
They weren't deadly, but one good whiff could knock a man out. *Case
in point,* he thought with a wry mental smile — his lips certainly
couldn't do it. His brain wobbled like a drunk. His limbs seemed to
laugh at him. All he could do was wait until the poison cleared his
system. It took about fifteen minutes. As soon as he could coordinate
well enough, he dragged himself upright and put the lid back on the
vial. The moment he trusted himself to stand with some certainty, he
opened his door and several of the levered windows to clear the air.

When he felt fully recovered, he relocked his door and returned
to the vial. What revoltingly wonderful stuff! But how to protect
himself from those damned fumes? He decided to plug his nose with
cotton — shades of his battle against the sirens' spell — and reopened
the vial. Drop by drop, he soaked the sponge in the cup until it could
hold no more liquid. *Twenty-one drops. Legal drinking age. Ha!*

He next wetted the sand with water from his wash basin and
gently molded it around the sponge until it was a hard ball. He tightly
wrapped the ball in the cotton cloth, then wrapped that in the leather

and bound it with a cord. The final product was a baseball-sized hunk of death that a man could safely carry.

Stuart tucked the vial holding the remainder of the Voodoo poison into a pouch and slipped that into the coat pocket of the outfit he planned to wear for his audience with Roars Like a Bear. If things didn't go well with the Indians, he would not be captured. He was sure they would torture him for a very long time before killing him. *I'd rather be eaten by the croc*, he thought with a shudder. One swallow of this stuff would make it all moot.

He pulled the cotton out of his nostrils and then, with some fumbling, he got the glove off. He dared not use his teeth this time, so he used his hook to carefully tear it off his hand. Using only the hook, he precariously carried the tattered glove, the used cotton, and the cup which had held the poisoned sponge outside and threw them overboard. Then he ordered some boiling water from Cookson and soaked his hook, hoping the heat would kill off whatever awful contaminants made the poison so deadly. After cooling the boiled hook and screwing it back on, he tucked the black marble box back in its hiding place and hid the poisoned ball inside the compartment under the bronze horse, there to await its journey the following day.

He was ready.

* * * * *

Early the next morning, Stuart was presented with the finished carriage.

It was everything he expected and more, ruggedly stylish, sturdy yet relative light in weight. And Thatcher had indeed managed to create a reclining chair! Along the top of the box the carpenter had fashioned gold trimmings. Two small lanterns adorned the two front posts. Smee's appointments included lovely red velvet drapes on all sides that could be closed if desired, upholstery and cushions for the chair, and a small foot rug.

"Mister Thatcher!" Stuart exclaimed happily. "A creation *par excellence*, my good man. By thunder, it's worthy to hold the ass of the no-good King himself!"

Stuart was so pleased that he gave Thatcher, the carpenter's mate, Smee and the other men who had helped build the conveyance two ducats each from his own purse. The men would, after all, share none of the benefits of their hard labor. More likely they would end up carrying the weight of their creation with their captain lounging within. A token of appreciation seemed appropriate.

Stuart also knew that such generosity was part of Hook's power over his crew. These were fellows who had gone pirate because they had been cheated and brutalized by the navies of their various countries and private merchantmen alike. They hoarded by nature. For a captain, any captain, to share his personal wealth with his crew showed unheard-of benevolence.

Stuart made the most of it. "Listen up, dogs!" he told the assembled pirates. "I will give three ducats to any man who will accompany me today on my visit to the Indian Chief. I make this offer because this journey is undertaken *proprio motu*, that is, I go for reasons of my own. It is not official ship's business. I do wish to make it clear, however, that if my audience with the savages is successful, it will spell gain for us all."

That was a bald-faced lie, of course. As with the abduction of Wendy, Stuart planned to leave the pirates high and dry if his plan succeeded. He was ready to promise the Chief anything for a way out of the Neverland. He was ready to swear never to set foot on Indian land again, to give the tribe gifts of animals and rum, to hand over weapons, anything, absolutely anything. Even give them the goddamn *Jolly Roger* if they wanted it.

No, the dark knot whispered. *Delude yourself all you like, you would not, could not, ever lose her now.*

Watch me, Stuart thought spitefully, still holding his smile for the crew. Plenty of men were raising their hands. He was amused to see Billy's hand among them. The young pirate wasn't quite jumping up and down, but he stretched his whole body as only a child can stretch in an attempt to get his hand as high as those of the adults around him.

Stuart counted out twenty men. "We'll leave in an hour," he told Cecco.

"Aye aye, Captain," said Cecco, and gathered the twenty to the break of the forecastle while the rest of the crew went back to work. Billy, slumped in defeat, started to pick up his mop when Stuart called him over.

"Yes, sir," Billy said, staring down at the deck, unable to hide his disappointment.

Stuart rolled his eyes. *Children. Disgusting creatures.* "Mister Barricoe Billy," he said, giving Billy no clue as to his true opinion of the value of his existence, "I could not help but notice that you wished to accompany the shore party."

"Aye, Captain, I do. I did. I like the Indians. They're cool."

"They are our enemy," Stuart reminded him. "That is why I did not choose you. We may have to kill a few. Are you up to that?"

Billy stared back at the deck.

"I thought not. I have no need for cowards, boy. However." Stuart waited for Billy to raise his head, as he knew he would. Billy did. "I shall give you the opportunity to prove that you are no coward. You shall stand guard over Miss Darling while I am ashore. If anything happens to her, it shall be your responsibility."

Billy did not like this idea. By the look on his face, he clearly feared that Pan would attempt another rescue while Captain Hook was gone. Stuart though otherwise. *If anything, Pan will follow me to see what I'm up to. Let the whelp stew in terror awhile. That ought to toughen him up.* "What say you, Mister Barricoe Billy?"

"Thank you, sir," Billy said desperately. "I'll do my best."

"You'll enjoy intimate relations with this if you don't," Stuart said, shaking his hook. He turned his back on the boy and, smirking, went into his cabin to dress.

He let Smee primp him for the trip. The Indians knew of Hook's obsession with his ancestor's courtly fashions, so he went out of his way to present himself well dressed and impeccably groomed. He even allowed Smee to tie his curls with small gay ribbons — appropriate for the fashions he wore even if it did make him feel like a screaming pansy.

He insisted on wearing two loaded pistols and his saber as he normally did — the Indians couldn't expect him to walk into their camp unarmed — but Smee insisted he tuck an extra pistol and knife in his belt as well. "Sneaky, them savages," Smee commented. "Can't trust 'em, sar."

Smee also pointed out a sheath on the inside of Stuart's left boot — a sheath that hadn't been there before, Stuart noted with jaded surprise. "Yeh forgit about it, eh?" Smee asked him. "What about this?" He produced a slim pearl-handled knife from one of Stuart's dresser drawers. "JH" had been expertly carved into the pearl, the letters inlaid with gold. "Yeh like this knife best, don'tcha, sar? Won it during a chess match against that scoundrel Cap'n Roberts, weren't it?" Smee wiped the blade with the rag forever hanging from his back pocket. "Yeh womped his king an' he not only gave yeh the knife, but he had yer initials carved in it. That's the mark of a gennelman in my book."

To Stuart's annoyance, Hook granted him no memory of the incident. He could only presume that Smee was telling the truth. "Never much liked chess," was all he said as he studied the pearl-handled knife. It was an excellent weapon, beautiful and well balanced. He snugged it into the boot sheath. The bulk rubbed against his calf a little, but not enough to overly bother him.

Smee gave his captain his patented once-over. "Lookin' posh yeh are, sar."

Stuart checked his pocket watch. It was almost seven thirty. "Time to go." He waved at Smee. "You go on ahead. I'll be with you in a moment."

Once Smee was gone, Stuart quickly retrieved the ball of Voodoo poison from the secret compartment beneath the bronze horse and slipped it into his pocket. He stood in front of Mary Etherton's mirror to give himself a final check. His clothes, his neatly clipped beard and mustache, his proud stance, even the gleam in his eyes... *Where am I in all this?* It was as if he were looking at someone else. He turned away from his image. *I'm running out of time...* He stomped out the door.

The twenty men who had volunteered for the trip, Smee included, were gathered down at the break of the poop, heavily armed and chattering in excitement. The pirates hated the Indians. Actually, they disliked almost every other group but their own, but the Indians were especially despised because they had sided with Pan after the incident with the cows. Since then, any opportunity to confront the tribe was always greeted with hateful enthusiasm. Stuart wondered what his men would do if they discovered their fearless captain's true intentions. As he descended the stairs to join them, he watched them cackle at each other and rub their hands in wicked anticipation.

Jukes was one of the volunteers. He limped from his wound — for all of his wailing at the time, Ranger's pistol shot had only grazed his right buttock — but he was determined to join in the fun. "We gonna wipe 'em out, Captain?" he asked, his tattooed face bright with bloodlust. "Send 'em all to that Happy Huntin' Ground they always jibberin' about?"

Stuart thrust his hook under Jukes' chin. "No, you imbecilic maggot-brained toad, we are not. And if you so much as break wind while we're in their camp, I'll take your scalp myself, savvy?"

Jukes turned into a white-faced caricature of himself, his body stiff with terror, his bugged-out eyes trying in vain to focus on the hook at his throat. "A-a-aye aye, suh-suh-suh—"

"Oh, shut up." Stuart realized he didn't like the man. Jukes had been the one to call him a ghost when he had first met the crew — a dangerous word to use around highly superstitious men like pirates. Jukes had fired his pistol and started the second battle with Pan and the Lost Brats. He had gotten himself blasted square in the butt, and he was always the first to flap his yap with some confounded stupid comment. Stuart wondered if it might not be time to shoot him someplace where it would count. *I could let him rot in the rigging and bury the pieces in that stupid hat of his.*

On the other hand, Jukes was an able seaman, a good fighter and trustworthy in his duties, if not so bright in other matters. Stuart turned his wrist a little and jerked his hook out from under the man's throat, drawing a pearl of blood. Nothing serious. Just enough to put the fool in his place. Jukes squeaked like a squirrel and scuttled back.

"Gentlemen," Stuart said to the group, "I have not called you together to attack the Indians. I intend to pursue, shall we say, a diplomatic parley."

The pirates grumbled.

"Ah ah ah," Stuart said, feeling like a teacher subduing a classroom full of rowdies. "I'm sure we'll have our fill of excitement by the end of the day. These things don't always unfold as one plans.

However, in an attempt to keep it peaceful, I have devised a means whereby Chief Roars Like a Bear will be induced to behave civilly towards us." He said to Jukes, "For those of you with the intellectual capacity of a chamber pot, that means I've figured out a way to threaten him into talking to us without killing us."

"Aye aye—"

"Shut up. Now, once in Indian territory, you are all to remain silent. Show no aggression in any form, and keep your scurvy paws off your weapons unless I command. Is that clear?" He waited until every man acknowledged the order. "The last thing I want is a massacre. What I do want is a calm discussion with the Chief." He raised his hook. "You know the consequences, hm?"

The men nodded, their wary eyes fixed on the hook gleaming in the sunslight.

"Good. Now, in the event things take a nasty turn, well, then and only then will you be ordered to apply a more vigorous form of diplomacy." At that, the pirates burst into hearty yells, brandishing their weapons. Stuart shook his head. *Animals.*

Cecco and Foggerty approached. "Captain," Cecco prompted.

"Ah. Mister Foggerty." Stuart clapped the second mate on the shoulder. "Mister Cecco will be coming with me. That means the ship is yours. I don't except Pan to attack while we're ashore, but he may. If he does, show no mercy and do not, *do not,* allow Wendy to escape. Barricoe Billy will be watching her, but I want you to watch him. Understood?"

"Very, sir," said Foggerty, looking a bit pale. Stuart knew the man was petrified of screwing up. Hook had never captured Wendy before, and if she was rescued during his watch, Foggerty knew he would feel the kiss of his captain's namesake.

"Keep liquor consumption low," Stuart added. "If Pan does attack, it'll do no good to have the crew three sheets to the wind."

"Aye aye, Captain," said Foggerty, and he saluted. He had begun to do that lately, probably following Cecco's example.

Stuart nodded in return and once more faced his motley band. "All right, men! To the boats!"

CHAPTER 40

Melanie entered the store, noticing with a pang of sadness how much the little bell that tinkled when she opened the door sounded like the one at Excalibur Books. Jon had always hated his doorbell. Hearing it every time a customer entered or left drove him nuts. But he never took it down because, "All decent bookstores have bells over the door. That's just one of many occupational hazards I have to cope with."

This place, however, wasn't a bookstore. This was a metaphysical emporium in Toluca Lake called The Mystic Rune Brewstore. Melanie knew it well. The owner, a Wiccan who went by her craft name of Raven Animata, often helped her with questions regarding history, myth and magic. Melanie didn't understand Paganism, especially modern witchcraft, except that she knew it wasn't evil and indeed never had been. "Witches *can't* worship Satan," Animata was fond of telling critics. "Satan is a Christian creation. Pagans aren't so black-and-white about things. In general we venerate the powers of Earth and Sky, so *recycle*, godsdammit!" Melanie liked Raven. The woman was a lot like Rhodes, like Melanie herself wanted to be — cool, caring and confident.

The Mystic Rune Brewstore reflected the gregarious nature of its owner. A wide variety of books neatly filled shelves on the right, while tables and spin racks in the center area of the store displayed artwork, jewelry, gems and stones, greeting cards, drums, candles and clothes. The left wall was occupied by a large glass case displaying just about every Tarot deck available on the market — hundreds of them, Melanie estimated, along with numerous oracle and meditation decks. Spell working supplies were in the back — shelves of jars filled with herbs, tinctures, incense mixes, lotions and essential oils. Here and there from the ceiling hung colorful scarves, wind chimes of every size, tie-dyed draperies, and the occasional stuffed crow or ornamental dreamcatcher. The air was thick with the mixed scents of Nag Champa incense and strong coffee — an alcove off to the left led to a small coffeehouse section offering blends with names like Ishtar's Choice and Sprite's Delight.

"Well, blessed be!" came a contralto voice with a slight Southern accent. "If it isn't the mother of all questions once again crossing my threshold." Animata, a slim woman wrapped in a beautiful multicolored sari, stepped out of the back office. Her long and rapidly graying hair was braided and decorated with a string of feathers. "Like Pavlov's pup, I am summoned by the sound of the bell. Hi, Mel."

"Hi, Anni," Melanie said. "Got any shrunken heads on sale today?"

Animata stuck out her tongue. "Har-de-har." Then she brightened. "Though now that you mention it, I do have something that you might find interesting." She knelt down to fetch something from a shelf under the cash register. When she stood back up, she held a Voodoo doll in her hands. The face had a magazine photo of Johnny Depp glued over it. "Like it? A friend of mine made it for me. She says all I have to do is stick a pin in... let's just say a most *vital place*, and Winona Ryder will dump Johnny and I'll get my chance. What do you think?"

Melanie laughed, possibly the first real unrestrained laugh she'd had since Jon's disappearance. "You wouldn't want him that way, though, would you?"

"Honey, I'll take him any way I can get him." Animata put the doll down with a sigh. "Alas, I don't practice Voodoo, and I'm too old for Johnny. Fate can be so cruel." She feigned despair, then grinned. "So how can I help you this time, O Wicked Witch of Research?"

"Pan," Melanie said flatly. "The god Pan. What do you know about him?"

"That Plutarch was way wrong."

Melanie blinked. "What?"

"Plutarch? Greek historian? Wrote the famous line supposedly from some knucklehead sailor named Thamus claiming that he heard the voice of the gods tell him, 'When you reach Palodes, take care to proclaim that the great god Pan is dead.'"

Melanie waited for some kind of further explanation, but Animata just gazed at her serenely. "Oookay. So Pan's not dead." *Too bad,* she thought. "So let's get serious here. What about him? I'll buy a hardcover book and some sage incense if you quit messing with me and talk."

"I'm not messing with you," Animata insisted. "That quote has been famous throughout the ages. But all right, all right, I'll give. Where do you want me to start?"

"All I know is that I think he was in *Fantasia*," Melanie said. "Beyond that, I have come to learn."

Animata looked at Melanie's empty hands. "I'm about to pontificate. Aren't you going to write any of this down?" She did a double-take. "Where's your notebook? Hey, where's your purse?"

Melanie didn't answer right away. When she finally did, it took some willpower to keep herself calm. "I don't know. I lost it. Spent the whole morning canceling credit cards. I came here in a cab."

"Good goddess, you paid a taxi to bring you here? We're in the middle of The Valley, Mel! You live in Pasadena!"

"I had to see you."

"Hello, the telephone has been invented! You could have bought a car for the price of such a long taxi ride!"

Melanie shrugged. "Whatever. My life has been crap for days—" *Months, you liar.* "—so it's just par for the course. Anyway, I don't need to write anything down." She took a mini tape recorder from her pocket and turned it on. "You may begin pontification."

Animata thought for a moment and began. "Okay, then. Pan. He's a very old god, older than the rest of the Greek pantheon, though his Greek incarnation is the most well known. He originated in Arcadia as a shepherd's god, hence the goat legs. Really earthy, always randy, he pretty much jumps anything female, though he likes nymphs best. Goddesses, too. There's even a statue of him found in Pompeii showing him screwing a goat."

"A real hands-on kinda guy," Melanie commented.

"Oh yeah," said Animata. "He's the god of male sexuality, but in that sense he's a good guy. He's responsible for male fertility, humans and animals alike. He watches over forests and wild places, and he's also linked with music, poetry and hunting. It's said that the ancient Arcadian hunters would whip statues of him if a hunting trip didn't result in a kill. Some stories also link him to prophecy, but I think that one's a stretch.

"Anyway, he was born on Mount Lycaeum in Arcadia, though mythology is a little mixed up about his parentage. He's either the son of Hermes or Zeus, take your pick, and his mother was either the nymph Dryope or Amalthea, a Cretan goat-goddess. Some stories mention other possible parents, too. He's not just confined to the Greek pantheon, either. As I said, that's just the most popular version of him. Almost all cultures have a god of the wildwood that often links with a god of male sexuality. The Romans, who basically stole the Greek pantheon and renamed everybody, called him Faunus. Equivalent gods are Aristaeus in Thessaly, Priapus in Asia Minor, Vajrapani in India, Min in Egypt, Nyamia in Africa — he's all over the place. In fact, he's the basis for the European prankster Puck, otherwise known as Robin Goodfellow."

"The little *A Midsummer Night's Dream* guy?" Melanie asked. "Puck wasn't a god, though, he was a sprite or imp or something, wasn't he?"

"Sprite, imp, fairy, goblin, phouka, devil — people get the terms wrong all the time. Each is a specific entity, but in Pan's case, he's a god, a supernatural creature with powers that either help or hurt humankind, depending on his mood. And his mood shifts like fog in San Francisco. You know what he traditionally looks like, right?"

Haven't met him in person yet, but when I do, I'll take a picture, Melanie wanted to say. Instead she said, "Yeah, goat legs, devil horns, Spock ears, carries that Zamfir thing."

Animata stifled a laugh. "Basically. Medieval Christians were so offended by his blatant sexuality that they adopted his image for the Devil. These days Satan's pretty much lost the goat legs, but he's still depicted with horns, which are really Pan's identification with goats and, in general, male wildlife. Oh, and the Zamfir things are called pan pipes, you cretin. He created them from reeds that used to be a nymph named Syrinx. She was in love with Artemis and spurned Pan's advances, so of course he gave chase anyway. To save her, Syrinx's father Ladon, a river god, turned her into marsh reeds. Pan made the pipes out of the reeds to remember her by."

"How romantic."

"Actually, Pan can be quite romantic, if he's in the mood. But the thing that makes him so interesting, at least to me, is that split personality act he's got going. He can be kind and generous — one myth tells of how he stopped Psyche from killing herself when she couldn't win her true love Eros. He's also a great partier. Many Pagans, ancient and modern, see him as a reveler to rival Dionysus, out for a good time at all costs."

"I'll bet," Melanie muttered.

"But he's definitely got that Dark Side of the Force thing, too," Animata went on. "Did you know the word *panic* comes from him?"

"That one I knew." Melanie had come across that fact while doing research for a linguist.

"Yeah, he likes to lie in wait in the deep woods and scare travelers for fun. *Panikon deima* is what it's called — panic fear. He can induce a state of hysteria in animals, too, also for his own entertainment. One story says that when the Persians attacked the Greeks — I guess this would be about 500 BCE, somewhere around there — Pan's war cry scared away the entire Persian army. Not surprisingly, the Greeks adopted Pan worship after that."

"Does his name mean anything specific?" asked Melanie.

"There are various theories on that. The most popular says it's supposed to mean *all* in Greek, although some think it comes from *pa-on*, the word for herdsman. Others say it comes from the Arcadian word for... uh, rustic, I think. Not sure on that one. Something like that. Pan is such an old god, it's almost impossible to pin down facts. So many stories and origins contradict each other."

"Is he a shape shifter?"

"Some myths mention him being able to turn into a goat or ram, and he isn't above wearing disguises to fool potential lovers. He wore white rams' skins to fool the moon goddess Selene, whom he loved, but she didn't love him because he was such a bad boy. There are also mentions of him being able to turn into a handsome youth."

Bingo! Now Melanie chanced a dangerous question. "Did… does… he have a thing for specific people? Like, people from certain family lines or little kids or…"

"You mean, like, for sex?"

"Ew. No. I mean in general."

Animata thought a moment. "In general, he has no favorites, not that I know of. He likes anybody who likes a good time, drunk or sober. Strictly a let's-have-fun guy, unless he's feeling mean. Then look out."

That's what I'm trying to do.

"But as I said, nymphs and goddesses are his usual romantic prey. So, shall I go on," Animata said, "or have you heard what you need? 'Cuz if you want more, I'll have to dig out a book or two." She tapped her head. "So many gods, so little room."

Melanie laughed. "Just a couple of things. Does Pan just scare people, or does he want them to go crazy?"

"You're talking technical clinical crazy?"

Melanie nodded.

"Not that I've heard. He just has a mean sense of humor."

"Is he associated with any particular weapons?"

Animata leaned across the counter, showing more curiosity than Melanie wanted to see. "Just what kind of research project are you working on?"

Melanie thought quick. "Oh, some writer who wants to do a fantasy flick about ancient gods. No matter what information I give him, he'll end up making up his own *authentic* myths anyway. I'm just doing my job and being thorough. You know me."

Animata weighed this answer and apparently decided to accept it. "Well, in the immortal words of that awful Michael Jackson song, you know, the one he did with Paul McCartney, Pan is," and she shifted her voice high and breathy like Jackson, "*a lover not a fighter.*" She laughed. "I can't believe I'm quoting that. Anyway, to answer your question, Pan is not fond of any particular weapons that I know of, just that Zamfir thing, as you so charmingly put it."

Melanie clicked off the tape recorder. "So what books do you have about him?"

"In hardback?" Animata asked, reminding Melanie of her promise. "Actually, none. But I have a couple paperbacks. Buy both of those and I'll give you the sage, as well as my lecture, for free."

"Deal."

While Animata went over to the bookcases to find the paperbacks, Melanie dug into her jeans pocket for money. She had been so freaked by the loss of her purse — she clearly remembered putting it on the couch the night before, so she knew damned well who must have taken it — that she had simply stuffed her emergency cookie jar money into her jeans pocket, grabbed her spare house key and, when the cab had arrived, hurried off to the Mystic Rune Brewstore.

Now she felt no left-over money in her pockets. What she did feel was something round and smooth with strings. While Animata searched the bookshelves, humming along with the lively Celtic music playing in the store, Melanie pulled a purple silk pouch from her pocket. It jingled with heavy coins. When she poured them into her hand, she found herself staring at ten very old, very pure pieces of eight. *Jon,* she thought with rising horror, noting the elegantly woven gold JH against the pouch's purple silkiness.

"Here you go," said Animata, returning with the two books.

Before the woman could see what was in her hand, Melanie poured the pieces of eight back into the pouch and shoved it back into her pocket. "Uh... An... Anni I... I have to go, I'm sorry, I promise I'll buy the books later but something came up and I really gotta go I'm really sorry bye!" And she ran for the door, hoping she could keep herself from screaming. She knew that Animata would try to help, so Melanie ran as fast as she could down Riverside Avenue and around a corner, knowing that Animata couldn't leave her store to follow that far even if she wanted to.

She collapsed against a palm tree in front of a trendy sushi bar, feeling an awful, very familiar gut-twisting anxiety trying to eat away what was left of her sanity. *Every time I think I've found firm ground,* she thought, unconsciously squeezing the purple pouch with all her might as if trying to crush it out of existence. *Every time I think I might be able to handle this nightmare...*

It must have been around noon because the sidewalks weren't as empty as Melanie would have liked them to be. Lunch-minded employees from the nearby Warner Bros. and Disney studios were prowling the street trying to decide which overly-expensive restaurant to patronize on this fine sunny day. A huddle of what could only have been tourists, with their eager faces and Universal Studios Tour t-shirts, approached the sushi bar followed by a woman who, like Dusty Rhodes, dressed with savage executive perfection. Melanie turned away from them all, trying to look like a local who was just hangin', having a rest in the shade. What she really did was pull out the purple pouch and examine it more closely. So, Pan had taken both her purse and Jon's and switched them. The little bastard was having far too much fun. *How long is this going to go on?* she wondered.

Animata, for all her good intentions, hadn't really provided any useful information. If Peter Pan was truly the god Pan, he was choosing to remain in the form of the Neverland's little boy, though who knew how long that would last. What powers did he really possess? When might he choose to use them? *What is my part in all of this?* she wondered miserably.

One thing was clear. She couldn't get home without money. *I need to get cash from the ATM,* she thought, then remembered she didn't have her ATM card, nor had she thought to write down her bank account number. Then again, she wouldn't be able to access her bank account anyway, even with the number, because she didn't have her ID. *But I can't go back to Anni – wait, Jumpin' Jack Stash!*

Stash was a coin dealer who also bought gold and jewelry. Melanie had visited him on several occasions when her research duties required knowledge of coins, collecting and investing — usually illegal aspects thereof. Stash was a nice enough guy and was always polite to her, but she knew his business wasn't entirely on the up-and-up. That's what made him so valuable to her. His store, Big Stash Coin and Jewelry Exchange, was about three miles west on Ventura Boulevard. Surely just one of the pieces of eight would get her more than enough cash for cab fare back home, even if he cheated her on the price, which he no doubt would. At this point, she didn't care.

Melanie got up, put the pouch of coins back into her pocket and, muttering curses at Pan, started walking.

CHAPTER 41

Stuart's journey to the island didn't take long. The three boats — two for the men and one for his carriage — soon slipped smoothly onto the sandy beach. The pirates hid them among the palms as they had when they'd come ashore to capture Wendy.

The men drew lots to decide who would carry the carriage. Starkey, Mad Mundy, Alf Mason and Doff Cockers were the lucky four. The rest of the men split up, half walking before the carriage and half following behind it. As usual, Kamau took point.

The pirates knew the way to the Indian camp, though it had been many months since they had used the trail. Stuart himself knew the path as per his map, but he had never traveled it before. Hook was providing him with no mental pictures of the trail nor what the campsite looked like. That made Stuart uneasy.

Nonetheless, he climbed into the carriage with great delight and settled into the comfortably padded seat. Kamau led them up the beach and stepped into the thick greenery, followed by the men, one by one. When it was Stuart's turn to once more voluntarily pass through the giant mouth of the jungle, he didn't feel as vulnerable as before. He was inside the carriage, floating along on the strength of four men. He felt protected, downright regal. He could hear the huffing and puffing of the men carrying him, but he was quite relaxed. *I should have Thatcher put a liquor cabinet in here,* he thought, and laughed out loud.

"What's so funny?" Cecco asked quietly, walking with Smee beside the carriage so that he could hear his captain's orders.

"Nothing," Stuart replied. "Nothing worth mentioning, anyway."

The men bore him for a good twenty minutes through the jungle until a signal from Kamau made them stop. The big Jamaican shouldered his way back to the carriage. Stuart leaned forward to hear the report. "De barrier be about five minutes from here, Captain."

Stuart nodded. "I remember," he said, which he didn't. The word *barrier* sounded unfriendly and perhaps dangerous, but he maintained his easy tone. "Lead on."

They resumed their slow trek and soon entered a small ravine filled with mist. *This must be the barrier,* Stuart thought, grateful to be in the carriage more than ever. The mist against his cheeks was cold, and something about it made his heart race. It was raw potential in physical form, preternatural energy made solid. *Magic!* he realized. *This mist... it's magic itself!*

Passing through it was intriguing, to say the least. The jungle was such a gaudy place, lush with moist mossy greenery and clamoring with a thousand animal arguments. Once in the mist, those raucous arguments rapidly dimmed, as if the jungle was speeding away from them so fast that it was a thousand miles away in a blink. All Stuart could see was swirling white living cotton that writhed and twisted in front of his eyes. The air buzzed with the persistent non-sound of utter silence. No — not silence. A low humming sound, very faint but full and rounded, like the humming of a large choir maintaining a complex chord. The humming mist seeped into the carriage and caressed the contours of his body, arousing him, igniting his lust. Power. Pure magical power, the ultimate orgasm. If only he knew how to tap it...

The mist faded away, and with it, Stuart's lust. He gripped the sides of his padded chair, blinking sweat from his eyes, relaxing the muscles of his arms, legs and back. He had gotten so worked up he felt like a big cramp letting go.

His pirate lackeys had definitely felt the effects of the mist, too. All were sweating too hard, and several were gasping. All of them resumed walking with awkward gaits for several minutes before their strides relaxed back to normal.

The group emerged into a forest, quiet, sedate, and very very old. Stuart sensed the weight of that age at once, an eerie pressure behind his eyes and a strange tingle at his fingertips. While the jungle flailed out in all directions with an excited youthful vigor, the forest grew with a solemn purpose, an ancient purpose. Pines, firs, cedars and redwoods stood majestically side-by-side, reaching high into the sky — not to cooperate in the creation of a thick canopy, but rather like individual monoliths intent on fulfilling destinies of their own. The deer, raccoons, skunks, fox, bobcats and other animals here lived furtive lives, moving like wraiths through the brush. Birds twittered cautiously to one another.

Ferns and bushes, much smaller than their brethren in the jungle, maintained space between each other, allowing loamy duff to show through, rich with decay and sprinkled with leaves and stiff brown pine needles. Here was room to walk, had the pirates wished to leave the path.

They knew better. The wider path did not demand that they walk in single file anymore, and it gave plenty of room for the carriage. But it voicelessly suggested that they keep within its boundaries. Even as Stuart wondered why, he received the answer. No python weed here, no danger of big cats attacking or snakes dropping down on them. Instead, spirits surrounded them — shades, ghosts, specters, devas, goblins — Stuart couldn't say what they were, but he could see their ageless faces peering out of stone, leaf and bark. Small round eyes blinked gold and red from within tight clumps of green mistletoe clinging to oak boughs. The soft rustle of branches in the breeze sounded more like whispers than anything else, judgmental voices engaged in secret conversation. If Stuart turned quickly enough, pine branches were arms with bony fingers, and he could just make out the curves of sensuous torsos in tree trunks before the phantoms faded. Huge twisting roots above ground seemed able to lift up as if, like feet, they could carry their tree masters after these intruders who dared disturb their slumber.

"We're not welcome here," Stuart murmured, more to himself than to his fellows.

"Now what makes you think that?" Cecco murmured back, not without sarcasm. He should have added "sir" or "Captain," but rank held no meaning in this forest, and the pirates knew it. Every man was equal here, a tiny mortal soul daring to breach the domain of the ageless. Stuart had to acknowledge that fact if he wanted them all to survive.

The path forked. Kamau stopped. He waved at Stuart, then indicated the path to the left. Stuart nodded his understanding, then beckoned to George Scourie and Morgan Skylights. They came forward. Stuart pulled the leather ball from his coat pocket and held it up.

"Take this to the end of this path," he instructed them, gesturing left. "According to Mister Barricoe Billy, the path will wind about five hundred yards through forest and end at a small lake. Hide near the shore, don't let anyone see you. Wait. If you hear the sound of pistol shots, a single shot or many, it doesn't matter which, I want you to throw this as far into the lake as you can. When that's done, return to the boats and wait for the rest of us."

"What is it?" Scourie asked, eyeing the ball in Stuart's hand.

Stuart glared at him.

"Aye aye, Captain sir," Skylights quickly cut in. "Any pistol shots, we throw it into the lake."

Stuart nodded. He wasn't happy with using a pistol shot as a signal. He wished he had another long distance option, but there were no such things as flare guns in this world. Any other signals he could think of — yells, whistles, smoke, drum — either wouldn't carry far enough or took too much time to execute. A pistol shot was quick and loud. Too bad it was also unreliable. Stuart tried not to worry about how easy it would be for any one of the men to automatically fire at a perceived threat or accidentally set his barker off for any number of reasons. A loyal bunch they were, but not the brightest lamps on the dock. "Wait for two hours," Stuart said. "If you hear no pistol shots, do nothing. Return to the boats and wait with this." He handed the ball to Skylights, who had an exceptional throwing arm. "Do not get caught."

"Aye aye, sir," Skylights said, handling the ball as if it were a grenado.

If only he knew. Stuart pointed at Roland and MacDougal. "Go with them. Station yourselves where you can observe anyone approaching the lake." Billy had said that the lake was relatively circular, and the trees along its edge grew tall but thin. Two vigilant men would be able to monitor the shoreline fairly easily. "If you see Indians, signal me with a pistol shot, but for God's sake make sure Skylights knows you're signaling me if you do. I don't want him throwing the ball into the lake on the wrong signal. Then get the hell out of there, all of you."

"Aye aye, Captain," said MacDougal.

The four men hurried up the left path. Stuart watched until they disappeared, then signaled Kamau to resume their way along the path leading to the right. As they walked, Stuart took out one of his pistols and aimed it at the sky, holding it that way while his men carried him along.

It didn't take long to find the Indians — the Indians found them. One moment the pirates were walking, the next moment they were surrounded by some ten Indian braves, bows taut and arrows aimed. "So much for sneaking up on them," Cecco muttered.

"I never intended to," Stuart retorted. "Men, put me down. The rest of you, hold your hands out, empty."

Starkey, Mundy, Mason and Cockers gently lowered the carriage and backed away, hands raised. Stuart slowly stepped out, angling his body to the right so that the last thing to exit would be his pistol-laden left hand.

At the sight of the hook, half the braves shifted their aim to Stuart. He froze. Slowly, very very slowly, he resumed moving, holding his hook out at what he hoped was a non-threatening attitude. When the braves saw the pistol emerge, one of them let loose with an arrow that struck the wood of the carriage not three inches from Stuart's ear.

He did not flinch, and for that he was proud of himself. He looked askance at the arrow with a nonchalant attitude, sniffed and stepped calmly away from the carriage, still holding the pistol aimed at the sky.

Stuart had discovered that he was a fairly courageous man. He had survived too many horrors lately to think of himself as a coward. Hell, he had just kept his cool at a moment when he might have had his ear pierced the hard way. But here was something he had never faced before. Hatred. This ring of hostile faces was making him want to grab his skirts and run. Naturally they hated him. He had known that and had prepared himself for it. But the reality was far worse than hate. These people loathed him, a loathing beyond anything he could ever have imagined. It was a murderous spark in their eyes. It made the hairs on his arms stand up.

Stuart wondered what tribe the Indians had first come from, and whether they had been brought to the Neverland willingly. Maybe they were creations of the Neverland, part of it, with no ties to the real world. Stuart knew little of American Indians or any other Indians for that matter, so he couldn't distinguish them by their physique or their fashions. All were ruggedly handsome men with dusky copper skin and black hair. All wore leather leggings, some with leather shirts, most without. Some wore their hair loose, some in braids or ponytails, all decorated with beads and feathers. All wore headbands. Most wore necklaces, too, strings of small stones, shells or other natural objects like tiny pine cones and acorns. They stood like statues, their balance perfect, their sharp flint arrows locked on target. On him. And, oh, they wanted to kill him. Their bloodlust electrified the air.

The familiar black energy, ever present within Stuart now, roiled with intent. He smiled faintly. *Yes, take me,* he thought, and gave in to it completely, no hesitation, no regret. It was a blessing. He needed Hook's overbearing ego and the unflinching confidence that came with it. He needed all the help he could get. Besides, why tremble in his boots when he could actually enjoy this encounter? *Alea jacta est, my friend,* he thought.

The die is cast, came the dark reply. *So indeed it is.*

"Good afternoon, gentlemen," he drawled, smirking at the sound of Hook's unctuous tones distorting his voice. Harrowing circumstances be damned, he felt *good!* "I have come in peace to powwow with your Chief."

"They, uh, don't speak English, sar," Smee said. "Lemme translate fer yeh."

"No! I speak!"

Only then did Stuart and his men notice the girl standing to the side, up on a rock. She stood in shadow and would have remained unnoticed if she hadn't spoken. She was perhaps sixteen years old, with long black braids and a leather headband bearing intricate beaded geometric designs.

Stuart was about to speak to her, to graciously greet her and call her Tiger Lily. It had to be her, like in the story. She was the right age, and there was an aristocratic aura about her that exuded authority. Luckily, a picture of an old Indian woman flashed before his eyes. *This was Tiger Lily shortly before she died of old age eight years ago. The girl who is presently wearing that most uncomely glower is Princess Snapdragon, her granddaughter and daughter of Chief Roars Like a Bear.*

"Princess Snapdragon," Stuart said, pouring on the charm. "I am delighted to see you again."

"Black Snake." The girl curled her lip. "You no be here. You thief. Our land. Go!"

Stuart almost laughed at her halting English. *Just like a child would expect an Indian to speak. How wonderfully stereotypical! I wonder if the Chief will greet me by saying "How"?*

He let none of this amusement show, of course. He executed a respectful courtly bow to Snapdragon, touching his hat with his hook — he couldn't take the hat off because he dared not lower the pistol. She watched the display with wary fascination. Stuart straightened back up. "Princess, I wish to speak to your father, the great Chief Roars Like a Bear."

Some of the braves made noises of protest, recognizing their Chief's name as spoken by white men. Snapdragon held up a hand, and they fell silent. She jumped down from the rock, her footsteps as light and graceful as those of a deer, and landed before Stuart, feet planted firmly, hands on her hips. The pose reminded Stuart too much of Peter Pan. "Chief no see teller of lies," she spat at him.

"Tst tst. I suggest you reconsider, my dear."

"No! You go!"

"Very well, then. Heed my words. I tell no lie when I say that if your father will not grant me an audience, I will destroy your tribe's sacred lake."

Snapdragon's brows lowered. The braves tensed. The pirates who had not known of Stuart's plan shuffled uneasily.

His threat was drastic, Stuart knew that. It was an act akin to mortal sin. The entire Neverland island was a sacred place. It had to be because Pan ruled over it. For Stuart to threaten the land itself probably crossed all lines of tolerable behavior, even for a fiend like Hook. "All I have to do is fire this pistol, and it will be done," Stuart stressed. "Your lake and everything in it will be dead. Forever." He shrugged. "You can kill me if you like, but that won't stop my finger from pulling the trigger, even if it's the last thing I do."

"Trick!" Snapdragon accused.

"Truth," Stuart countered.

The princess placed her hand to her heart. "Chief make vow."

"I don't care." Stuart raised the pistol higher — an unnecessary move, but it had its desired effect. Snapdragon drew her knife in a blur of speed and hunkered down, ready to spring at her enemy, every fiber of her being ready to tear him to pieces. The braves barely held their arrows in check. Stuart didn't like making himself such a target, but their reactions proved that they did believe his threat. That's what he needed to know.

Snapdragon locked eyes with the brave closest to her. Some sort of message passed between them.

"Do not go to the lake!" Stuart said quickly. "I will fire if a single man leaves." To the pirates he shouted, "Men, watch them!"

The brave, along with Stuart, saw Snapdragon furtively shake her head. He relaxed while his princess asked, "Why you come?"

"My business is with the Chief."

"Hmf!" Snapdragon pointed at the pirates. "You come, you no weapons."

Stuart tipped his head at the braves. "We come, *you* no weapons."

"Our land, Black Snake! Our rule!"

Stuart thought about it. "I offer a compromise. Men! Put your hands on your heads!"

"Captain, you jokin'?" Noodler asked nervously.

"Do it," Stuart said. "And keep them there until I say otherwise." To Snapdragon he added, "A gesture of good faith."

"Bah!" said the girl. "No trust."

"On either side," Stuart reminded her pleasantly.

Snapdragon wasn't done bargaining. She pointed at Stuart's pistol with her bone knife. "That go."

"Oh, no no no," Stuart chuckled, steadily holding the weapon, maintaining its skyward aim. "I keep this, my dear. No compromise."

"That go!" she said, now indicating his hook.

Stuart feigned dismay. "I deeply apologize, Princess, but I'm afraid it doesn't come off." It was a lie, but Snapdragon didn't know that. *I hope*, he thought, and waited. Snapdragon made no move. "Decide, Princess. All I wish to do is talk." He gave her Hook's most beguiling smile. "I give you my word."

One of the braves huffed at that. Stuart doubted he understood English. It was his tone that the brave reacted to, that innocent sincerity that was Hook's best bargaining tool. Hook could turn it on and off better than any snake oil salesman. Stuart's alternate memories told him it usually worked, too, but he was beginning to think the Indians were too smart for it — either that, or they had fallen for it one too many times in the past.

Snapdragon studied Stuart's raised pistol carefully. "Chief make fate," she decided. Stuart supposed that meant she would let the Chief make his own evaluation. At least she was taking him to the camp. Her, "Come, Black Snake!" suggested it, anyhow. He would soon find out one way or another.

The braves closed in on the pirates, who obediently kept their hands on their heads. Stuart knew it scared and infuriated them to do it. Too bad. Better to lose a little dignity than to die like human pin cushions.

As for Snapdragon, she made Stuart lead the group while she held her knife in his back. She used the tip to indicate which way he should go, poking him on the right or the left as necessary. Stuart knew the girl was enjoying bossing him around, so he let her do it, maintaining his smile even when she jabbed him hard under his left shoulder blade to make him veer off on another trail, a barely discernable animal path that twisted and turned through a pretty scattering of pines and oaks. It crossed a small bubbling creek, then opened onto the Indian camp nestled in a cool forest clearing.

CHAPTER 42

Snapdragon called, "Stop!" She kept the tip of her knife pushed painfully into Stuart's back.

Stuart waited, wondering what she was going to do. He counted four teepees and one wooden hut in the clearing. *Not much of a camp,* he thought until he noted how the clearing wound around a bend. The bulk of the camp had to be over there, out of his line of sight.

Snapdragon spoke sharply to her men. Six of them closed in on Stuart while more armed braves stationed themselves around the pirates. Snapdragon made a little grunt of satisfaction. She shoved Stuart hard with the heel of her hand and he stumbled forward. "You go," she commanded.

"Wait!" It was Smee. "Cap'n, yeh can't trust her translations, not when it comes to the Chief! I need to be with yeh! Fer Chrissake, sar—" He was cut short when one of the braves put a knife to his throat.

"It's all right, Mister Smee," Stuart called back. "I trust that she'll speak true." He hoped that Snapdragon believed what he said. If he wanted the Chief's help, he had to show some amount of trust himself. As much as he would have preferred Smee with him, allowing Snapdragon to translate would, he hoped, help his own cause. Besides, the question he wanted to ask the Chief was not meant for Smee's ears.

Keeping his pistol raised — his arm was getting tired — Stuart resumed walking. The six braves flanked him, three on each side, their weapons fixed on him as if he were a magnet. They rounded the bend of the clearing.

He had been right. A dozen teepees dotted the much larger clearing on this side of the bend. Two sturdy wooden huts stood at the far end next to three racks holding stretched deer skins and other hides in various stages of tanning. Three cook fires blazed, the wood crackling noisily in the forest quiet, smoke curling up in lazy curlicues like airborne filigree. People milled about, tending to daily chores. Women were cooking and weaving. Two men were making arrows, one chipping flint heads, the other fletching hand-smoothed yew arrows. One man sharpened an ax with a whetstone — an ax, Stuart noticed, much like the one that the bastard Sigrson had carried. Likely the Indians had pistols as well, then, taken from the bodies of pirates after past battles. Stuart hoped that if they did have pistols, they had never gotten the chance to steal powder and shot.

Knots of children played at the edge of the camp, scampering about in games of tag, fighting mock battles, drawing in the sand, slapping each other to see who could go the longest without crying. Typical kid games. Now they, along with their elders, stopped to stare at him. One woman uttered a small wailing sound. Several children gasped so loudly that Stuart heard their sharp intakes of breath from a distance.

Snapdragon steered Stuart into the midst of the people. "Down," she said, and kicked him behind the knees.

He went down with a grunt, grimacing as his knees hit the hard dirt. He kept the pistol up, though. "My dear Princess," he said through his teeth, "had you asked me to kneel, I would have graciously complied."

"Stay," was all Snapdragon said, as if she were ordering a dog. She ducked into one of the teepees, leaving the six guards with Stuart.

He chanced a glance behind him. His men were back beyond the bend, no doubt separated from him on purpose. All the people except the guards on that side of the camp were coming his way, curious, wary and — if Stuart was reading their eyes correctly, and he was sure that he was — filled with absolute malice. He turned forward again to see the rest of the Indians moving toward him with the same combination of emotions hardening their features. They were surrounding him.

Stuart was bombarded by hatred in palpable waves, as real as the rolling whitecaps on the open ocean, the kind that came with a freezing wind that could tear the breath out of a man's lungs. If the Indians could have, Stuart was sure they would have killed him right then and there with sheer hate. Some of them were talking to themselves, probably curses or insults.

Someone behind him threw a rock. It smacked the base of his skull. Spots danced before his eyes. Stuart didn't move, never made a sound, and he kept that pistol up. But his confidence, comfort that it was, started to slip. Getting stoned to death was not on the day's agenda.

A little boy right in front of him picked up a rock, not big, but it would do damage if it hit Stuart in the face. No one stopped the child, who took aim and let the rock fly. It hit Stuart's right collar bone and bounced off. Stuart flinched, clamping his jaws tight to keep back a yelp as white-hot pain flared down his right arm, setting his stump to throbbing.

The boy laughed. The people commented in their strange language, the meaning of their words not so much a mystery, really. He could figure it out by the heated strain in their tones more than by their words. They wanted to see him do a lot more than flinch.

He closed his eyes, maintaining dignity on the outside while inside struggling with a rising fear at what they might lob at him next. What if a rock hit him square in the face? What if they did have shot and powder? *What in God's name did I do to these people to make them hate me so much?*

God's name? came the inner reply. *Strange we should put it that way.*

If Stuart could have shrunk away from himself, he would have. *We?* Could it be that it had overtaken him completely, and he didn't even realize it? *I've been eaten alive,* he thought.

Not at all, though we did part ways with God long ago, despite your feeble attachment to that tattered Bible. See for yourself.

Hook's black memories flooded his mind, reducing Stuart to a mere spectator inside his own head. Images flashed past his eyes like bolts of lightening.

I once cut a trio of Indian scouts to pieces. Oh, I didn't just cut them, I carved them up like dinner roasts. I once orchestrated a quite clever ambush that left five out of eight of their hunters at my mercy. Release them? Please. I cut out their hearts one by one while they were still alive and stamped them into the dirt with my very own boots. I have attacked their camp and killed their bitches and brats, sent volleys of flaming arrows into that accursed hell they call a forest, booby-trapped their hunting trails–

Stuart shrank into himself, squeezing his eyes tight and ducking his face down in the hope that it might make the sickening visions stop. *Stop it! Fucking stop it! I didn't do any of that! Lies, Pan's tricks, I'd never do that–*

But we did, Black Snake. That is their name for us. All we can do is live up to it. So said the infection within him, condemning him with an icy authority that now sounded too much like his father. Theodore Stuart, an angry man, always angry, always yelling, usually at Jonny. What was it Pan had said? That his father had been insane, along with Uncle George and Grandpa Emm. That the sword had called to them, but because Emmerich had locked it in the safe, it couldn't find them. So they had gone mad, all three Stuart men, managing to live their lives with just enough functionality to pass in a crowd but always with that black buzzing in their ears like a hell fly, its bzzzz bzzzz a vindictive razor slicing away at them where no one could see. The sword couldn't have them, but it kept trying year after year, reaching out for them with a ghostly edge that chopped at them a chunk at a time. To little Jonny, his father had always looked like a normal man, but the truth came now to the adult that Jonny had become. Daddy had been a walking corpse, shredded and bleeding — not the meat on his bones but the substance of his psyche. No wonder Daddy had been such a vicious man. No wonder he and Uncle George and Grandpa Emm had become monsters.

As we are becoming a monster. That is our true inheritance.

Shut up! You're just Pan trying to tear me apart!

Sorry, m'hearty, but it's the truth of what we are. You said it yourself — sucks to be you. His inner voice giggled at that.

It was the giggle that started Stuart fearing for his life. That giggle, crazily effeminate and warped out of whack like the boards of an old house about to topple. Was he giggling out loud, or was it just the prospect of giggling that tickled his ears? And that terrible cracking sound, like a spar tearing apart in a gale — was that his mind shattering in two? Maybe that was the way Grandpa Emm's had split, and Uncle George's. Maybe his father had felt his sanity crack like this, too, like San Francisco had cracked, smooth and intact one minute and then *bammo!* gaping a fiendish crater grin with a sound like a mammoth ice cube splitting in two. *I have to get out of here, they'll scalp me, it was a mistake to come, I have to GO—*

Stuart opened his eyes, physically revving up to plow his way through the crowd, endure whatever injuries that might bring and dash like a bunny into the forest. He was in good shape. His legs were long. The Indians knew these woods, but Stuart could run like the wind when he wanted to. And he really really wanted to.

But his eyes, they weren't working right. They were open, he was positive they were, only they weren't seeing the world in front of him. Instead, more blood-soaked visions unreeled. *Dissecting them with my hook, grinding my boot heel down onto squishy red mass after squishy red mass, slashing my sword across an old man's throat and feeling hot flecks sting my face and laughing, laughing like a maniac because, because—*

His optic nerves burned with his own savagery against the Indians, every brutal image filled with gore and a hideous methodical cruelty. Picture after picture clicked by, blotting out reality. Worse, he felt it all as if he were doing it at that very moment, his real body a distant impression through a vast fog.

He reeled, thrown completely off balance, and felt something that might have been his faraway lungs expelling a burst of air — a scream? A vague sensation of hands grasping him, pounding on him. *Not a monster,* he thought with a weird distant anguish, *get off me don't want to hate not a monster!* It was getting harder and harder to believe that.

Are we the monster, James? How can that be, when these primitives follow that boy devil as if he were a god? They want to kill us, and why? Because he told them to! Who is the monster, James? Who?

Hands were tugging at his clothes and pulling his hair, dragging him somewhere but he couldn't see where, didn't know if he was up, down or sideways. All he knew were piles of carved flesh and hacked bones, trampled hearts and blood, blood everywhere, red everywhere, on the ground, on him, all over him, dripping from his hook—

"Not a monster!" he might have screamed.

The hands dropped him.

His faraway body boomeranged back to him with the force of a blow. Stuart landed on his right hip with a grunt, almost goring himself with his hook. He rolled over, fumbling for reality, his eyes wide in a frantic attempt to see the world again. The terrible slideshow of his crimes stopped. He blinked, bringing the Here and Now back into focus.

He was in a teepee.

His pistol was gone.

"Black Snake."

The voice was calm and deep, full of wisdom, brimming with authority. Stuart shuffled around on his hand and knees to find three Indians sitting on the other side of the teepee. Snapdragon sat on the left. On the right was a big man, a bodyguard by the look of him. Between them sat Chief Roars Like a Bear. It had to be the Chief. He radiated a *gravitas* that made Stuart's breath hitch. It was like meeting a king.

Snapdragon pinned Stuart with wary eyes. "Evil spirits war in you," she declared. "Why you bring your curse to us?"

Evil spirits war in you. *Bingo, baby doll, you got it in one.* Stuart wanted to say those words. For all he knew, he did say them. But wasn't he also looking down at himself in shock? Wasn't he seeing his pristine attire soiled and scuffed as if he had been in a fight for his life? His shirt was ripped, the lace on his cuffs torn and flapping. His curly hair dangled in disarray around his face, a face that must have bore a freakish reflection of his inner pandemonium. He sensed the muscles of his mouth pulled back, his teeth bared in a grin of horror. His eyes were tearing up, they were so wide, and he couldn't seem to make them relax.

What did I do? he wondered. *When the visions came, what the hell did I do?* All he remembered were the horrible pictures, the repulsive emotions surging up like deadly waterspouts, and the hands, all those groping hands, not friendly at all but hard and angry. Had he been fighting, or had the Indians been holding him down during some kind of seizure? Not knowing which stole what few ragged nerves he had left.

The bodyguard handed Stuart's pistol to Snapdragon. At a nod from Roars Like a Bear, the girl placed it before Stuart.

He tried to remember what he had brought it for. Oh yes, the lake. He had threatened to destroy the lake. Well, he never actually intended to. It was a threat, nothing more. Thank God his pistol hadn't gone off during... whatever had happened. He was sure of that much. He would have heard it, would have felt the recoil of the shot race down his arm, even across the vast distance between sanity and... wherever he had been.

He took a moment to compose himself, sucking in a slow ragged breath. He ran his hand over his face, hoping they thought he was wiping sweat off when what he was really doing was trying to massage that awful rictus away. His lips finally released their tension. His aching jaws closed with an audible pop. His tongue was so dry it lay like an autumn leaf in his mouth.

He reached out and, slowly, deliberately, pushed the pistol back toward the Chief. "I don't want to harm your lake," he said. "I thought, perhaps wrongly, that only a threat would make you talk to me."

Snapdragon must have explained the nature of the threat to the Chief, for Roars Like a Bear looked at the pistol, then at Stuart, with open disgust. He said something to his daughter. Snapdragon translated. "Black Snake clever," she said. "We no fools. This trick."

Stuart gawked at her. Then he laughed. It came out a weak wheeze, his own deranged laugh, not Hook's condescending chortle. "If this is a trick, Princess — Chief — then what am I getting out of it? Look at me!" He stood up, hoping he wasn't committing some sort of Indian *faux pas*. To hell with it if he was. "You're right, you know," he said. "I am cursed. That's why I risked coming here. I need your help." He sank back to his knees, which still ached from when he had fallen on them earlier. "I most sincerely... most humbly... *beg*... for your help. No joke." That last part slipped out before he could stop it.

Snapdragon's eyebrows shot up her forehead. She translated. Roars Like a Bear studied Stuart in silence. Then he spoke. "Black Snake want home of Pan," Snapdragon translated. "We no tell."

"Oh, for Christ's sake!" Stuart screeched in dismay. "How many times do I have to say it? I don't give a shit about Peter Pan!"

The bodyguard rose and took a step toward him, knife in one hand, ax in the other.

Stuart jerked back without checking his balance, and he almost fell over. "I'm sorry! Calm down, please! Listen, what I mean is... what I want... the only thing I want... is to leave this place." He wished the big guy would sit back down, but he remained standing, ready to leap if necessary. "I don't want to be on this island, in this world," Stuart went on, hoping he sounded sincere. "I don't belong here. I want to go back to the world I came from. To do that, to leave you and your people in peace, I need to find a way home. That's all I came to ask. Is there a way out?"

Snapdragon's haughty expression crumbled. Snorts of derision slipped out of her mouth, which she abruptly shut at a quick stern glare from her father. She composed herself and translated.

Stuart sighed, expecting the Chief to laugh at him, too. But Roars Like a Bear listened to his words with a grave expression. When he at last spoke, it was a long speech. When he was done, Snapdragon's face was filled with awe. "Chief know many things, Black Snake," she said slowly. "You see things before and things behind. You see what is not. He know this. He know you speak... truth."

Stuart's jaw dropped.

"But he no can tell. You Hook. All men have fate. This yours."

Stuart's mouth worked soundlessly. The Chief believed him! That was better than he could ever have hoped. "But why?" he asked. "Why won't you tell me? It's Pan, right? He told you not to help me, and you have to do what he says."

At the mention of Pan's name, the Chief's eyes widened. He might not have known what Stuart said, but he didn't need Snapdragon's translation to know that Stuart had it figured out.

"Ha!" Stuart cried, jabbing a finger at the Chief. "I'm right! You know I don't belong here! You know I've never done any of those things to your tribe! Christ, man, if you know the truth, why won't you help me?"

The wild look in Stuart's eye prompted the bodyguard into action again. The big man took another step, raising his ax.

Stuart backed away, hand and hook raised in a gesture of peace. "Sorry. I'm sorry. I'm just... Snapdragon, please, ask your father why he won't help me."

The bodyguard kept his ready stance while the Chief said something to Snapdragon. She nodded her understanding. "No more," she said to Stuart. "You go. No come back." That ended the audience. The bodyguard pushed Stuart out the door.

Even as he brushed past the deer hide flap of the teepee, Stuart had no intention of leaving the camp without an answer. He was too close. The Chief knew it, too. It was now or never. As he stepped into the sunlight, he reached for his saber to slash at the bodyguard. His hand clutched at the empty scabbard at his hip. Reflexively he grabbed for his pistols. No luck there either — they were gone. *Double damn the savages!* he thought. *Probably disarmed me while I was dazed. Still, I'm never unarmed while I have this!* He raised the curved death at the end of his right arm. He wound himself up for the slash that would gut the bodyguard from sternum to groin.

"Haiiiiiiiiiiiiyeeeeee!"

The screech came from across the camp, breaking Stuart's concentration. By the time he reasserted himself, the bodyguard was out of range, trotting over to the newcomer, a short round squaw who was staggering toward the Chief's teepee like a drunken zombie. Even as she tottered forward, crying and wailing, she was smearing what looked like campfire ash on her face, the stuff already gobbed all over her hands. The madness of grief surrounded her like a thundercloud.

Stuart cursed the interruption, then saw that things weren't spoiled after all. The squaw's cries were bringing Roars Like A Bear and Snapdragon out of their teepee and into the light — into his reach. At the sight of her Chief, the squaw began moaning and gasping, telling some terrible tale that sounded to Stuart like frenzied gibberish. As Roars Like a Bear listened, his aged brown cheeks paled. Snapdragon flushed with fury.

For no reason that he could name, Stuart felt that her fury had to do with him. He was right. Snapdragon turned to him, whipped out her knife and, with a scream of rage, threw herself at him, moving faster than he ever would have imagined. Only reflexes honed in countless tavern brawls allowed him to dodge aside in time, twisting around as he did so that he could catch the knife with his hook and jerk it out of the girl's hand. For one enticing moment he had a clear shot at slicing her throat with a backhand follow-through, but where he had been willing to kill before, he now felt the tides of destiny shifting. He decided to let the moment pass — and let Snapdragon live — until he knew the squaw's news. Had one of the pirates shot off a pistol, and he somehow hadn't heard? Was that it? Had the screaming woman been at the lake and seen the damage — the water turning a sickly purple, dead fish rising to the surface with eerie metal-grey eyes? He remained crouched, waiting to find out.

Roars Like a Bear yelled a curt command to his people, stopping them from falling on Stuart en masse. Then the old man asked the woman something. In response, she pointed across the clearing. Several braves were carrying a body out of the forest. When they reached Snapdragon, they gently lowered the dead man at her feet. He couldn't have been more than eighteen years of age, a perfect specimen of humanity, lithe, strong, handsome — and dead. The hilt of a knife protruded from his chest. Snapdragon, having recovered her poise, knelt down and pulled the weapon out.

It was Stuart's pearl-handled knife. "But that... that's..." Stuart groped at his boot.

The Chief's bodyguard rushed forward to restrain the move, but Roars Like a Bear said one word and the bodyguard stopped. Apparently the Chief wanted to see what Stuart would do.

Stuart checked the hidden sheath in his boot, poking his fingers deep into it even though the knife obviously wasn't there. When he looked up, feeling a twinge of raw panic in his gut, Snapdragon was holding his knife up for everyone to see. The people couldn't discern the gold JH on the handle from their distance — they couldn't read English anyway — but Snapdragon made a long speech, an impassioned accusation of murder if Stuart ever heard one. He had the dreadful impression that the dead boy had been very close to Snapdragon, perhaps her betrothed.

"I didn't do it!" he told the Indians when the princess finished. "You saw yourselves, I was here the whole time! Snapdragon, tell them!"

The bodyguard charged, along with three other braves. Stuart whipped around in a circle, hook out, ripping anyone and anything within reach. Two of the braves staggered back, horizontal lines of blood on their chests, and the third cried out, raising his hand to a spurting gash that appeared across his neck.

The big bodyguard darted far enough away to miss the danger. Then he rushed back in and swiped at Stuart with his ax. Stuart brought both arms up and caught the ax with his hook before it could split his head open. His hand latched onto the bodyguard's wrist, and he yanked the big man right up against him, not what the bodyguard expected. Stuart kneed him hard in the groin. The bodyguard folded with a gurgling sound, pushing Stuart backward into the grip of a painted brave and a tall gangly youth.

A pistol shot rang out. Two more. Stuart heard clamoring and more pistol shots. His men were fighting, too. *That means the lake...*

Guilt hit him like a sledgehammer. All that plotting and maneuvering to make the threat dangle like the pendulum over the pit, and he had done the one thing he never intended to do – go through with it. A shot had been fired after all. The beautiful fishing lake was doomed.

He had more immediate things to worry about. The brave and the youth who held him flashed vindictive smiles and shoved him forward again, right at the bodyguard who had gotten back up. The big man had lost his ax but gained a knife. Seeing the vengeful bloodlust in his eyes, Stuart tried to change his body's forced trajectory, but he couldn't do it fast enough. All he could manage was a slight turn before the bodyguard drove his knife home. The blade bit deep along his left side, just missing vital organs.

Instead of crumpling in agony, Stuart's world turned red. A furious energy jolted him upright, and he gouged into the bodyguard's belly with his hook, ripping him open like he had ripped Sigrson. Blood splashed his face. He could feel it, hot on his teeth which were exposed in a wide skeleton grimace. The bodyguard continued standing, dead on his feet. Stuart kicked him, knocking him into a heap, and spat on him — not as an insult, he just had to get the abhorrent blood out of his mouth.

Several armed tribesmen rushed forward, shouting with hate. Stuart tore the knife out of his side and again whirled in a circle, keeping them back, lunging and slashing, lunging and slashing, alternating attacks between knife and hook. Considering the odds, he was doing a fair job, but no way was he going to keep them all back. They were toying with him.

Something sharp smacked him between the shoulder blades. Another one. Rocks. Something harder bit into his shoulder, spinning him halfway around — an arrow, stuck in the shoulder pad of his hook's harness. The arrowhead pierced the hard leather, just pricking his flesh. Pain wasn't the problem here. It was the blood which made the shoulder pad slip too easily against his skin, compromising the integrity of the harness and robbing his hook of crucial leverage.

More rocks pelted him, on his chest, his thigh, his butt. One cracked dead center on his kneecap. He let out a high yipping noise, almost laughing at the kicked-puppy sound of it, and worked hard not to crumple. Another rock bounced off the side of his skull, and that did make him wobble. Someone threw a knife that buried itself in his right bicep.

It was all so stupid, so unspeakably wrong. Stuart didn't know what to do anymore. Even if his men came charging to the rescue, he would be dead by the time they got to him. Too many Indians were too close, all eager to see the Black Snake finally fall so that they could do their own job of cutting out *his* heart and stomping it into the ground. *I'm being pecked to death by birds*, he thought crazily. *A nibble here, a prick there, peck peck peck till there's not enough left to hold the pieces together and then we all fall down!*

The Indians stopped. They stopped in perfect unison as if they had all heard a whistle that Stuart had not.

He limped a slow circle, returning their hateful stares. They wanted to finish him off, that was damned clear. So why weren't they?

Why were they just standing there fingering knives and rocks but not throwing them anymore?

His fear gave way to fury. Too hyped up to feel pain anymore, he tore the arrow out of his shoulder pad and broke it in half. He pulled the knife out of his arm and threw it down. He lurched a little, panting and bleeding, but he kept his feet. The wounds weren't that bad. As Smee was fond of saying, "Yeh've had worse."

He managed a ragged laugh. "Well, whaddaya know. You can't kill me!" He let out a screechy falsetto *yee-hah!*, the triumphant cry of an hysterical man. "That's it, isn't it? You can't kill me! Golly gee, I wonder why? Could it be because Pan is supposed to have that honor? Yeah, because that's the way the story goes, right? Jesus God, you people know about the whole fucking game, and yet you're playing along like good little Indians, and to hell with me, right? I'm not worth a bag of cat shit, am I? Well, fuck you too, you goddamn puppets!"

They looked at him like he was a raving lunatic — all except for Chief Roars Like a Bear. The great man's eyes glittered with something that might have been tears.

"Oh, to hell with you," Stuart spat at the Chief. "You know everything, and still you're going to throw me to the wolves!"

Stuart looked again. The Chief's eyes... those really were tears, weren't they? The depth of turmoil in that face was unmistakable. *You're the only one who really knows! The rest of them, they don't know anything! They do what you tell them, and you do what Pan tells you. You're afraid of him, aren't you? Or could it be that you worship him? He isn't a god, you stupid fool! He's a devil!*

Stuart looked behind him. His men around the bend — *Around the bend, ha!* — weren't fighting anymore. The sounds of pistol fire, clashing knives and battle cries were morphing into wails of terror. Most of the cries faded in the opposite direction while a handful of braves came running back toward them, looking more scared than angry. They babbled a mile a minute, hands waving, eyeballs bugged. Whatever they were saying made the Indians scatter except for the Chief and Snapdragon. The Chief shouted something and four braves came back.

Roars Like a Bear spoke to them briefly. The braves nodded and took hold of Stuart.

He could have taken on two of them, maybe three, but not four, and certainly not with the wounds that were slowly bleeding the life and energy out of his body. They locked him in position between them, human vice grips with fingers that did not slip on the gore that spattered his torn clothes. One brave twisted Stuart's hook arm up and around his back, holding it there tight enough to make Stuart howl. "What are you doing?" he demanded with all the authority he had left which, granted, wasn't much. "You can't kill me!" He might as well have been whining, "C'mon, you guys, this isn't fair!"

Roars Like a Bear spoke. Snapdragon translated. "Farewell, Black Snake."

CHAPTER 43

The four braves dragged Stuart across the clearing. Stuart thrashed and struggled, exhausted but doggedly determined to avoid whatever grisly plan the Chief had for him. *Farewell.* That word had sounded neither fair nor well. It had sounded like a death sentence.

Everything had gone wrong. His plan had backfired, the lake was destroyed, the Indians had hurt and humiliated him, he had come this close to finding out the way home only to have it snatched away, a murder had been committed with his knife, and he was sure that his men had abandoned him.

"What are you going to do?" he asked the braves. Stupid thing to say. They didn't understand him. Even if they did, they wouldn't have answered. It was just one of those automatic questions, a doomed man's final attempt to understand why he has to die.

They hauled him over to two poles stuck in the ground near the edge of the tree line. The poles stood about five feet apart. Ropes had been secured near the ground and at head level on each one. Stuart saw mud-colored stains on the wood and nearby rocks that might have been bright red at one time.

"What the hell?" he cried, and struggled anew. What did they intend to do, whip him? Leave him exposed to the elements until he died? Was a bear coming, and he was on the menu?

Out of the blue he remembered the Voodoo poison in his pocket. He had forgotten all about it! He made a grab for it. The youngest of the braves muscled his arm back again while another slapped him hard enough to make his ears ring.

When his wrists and ankles were tied good and tight to the poles, the braves gave Stuart a final look of anger tinged, he thought, with what might have been pity. One held up a fist in Stuart's face with index and pinky finger pointed out at him, as if the man were warding off the Evil Eye. Then all four braves ran back to the camp. It looked as if it had been deserted, but Stuart knew that wasn't true. Everybody was holed up in their teepees for fear of...

Tick. Tick. Tick. Tick.

Stuart's knees buckled. Stark terror slammed him between the eyes.

His first instinct was to scream for help. He swallowed the urge back. One, there was nobody around to come. Two, it would make him look like a fool. If he was actually going to die, he wanted to die with dignity. The Indians were watching, peering out from behind their teepee flaps like kids sneaking a peek at lovers making out. He would not cry for help and he would not scream, no matter what. If he could manage it. He wondered if he would even notice if he succeeded or not.

The croc wasn't in sight yet. Its steady *tick tick tick* was coming from the far edge of the clearing. Stuart wondered how he could hear the sound from this distance until he realized that the forest, quiet enough normally, had gone absolutely silent. Maybe the ancient spirits who dwelled here were wary of the unnatural giant slithering along their paths. *I can't just stand here and wait for it! I should do something! I have to try something!*

He peered in the direction of the ticking through strands of damp disheveled hair. Perspiration had already cut tear-like tracks down his dirty face. He could feel how the dried salt made the delicate skin around his nose and mouth itch. His shirt clung to his sweaty chest and back. The blood made it all the worse, creating patches of warm slime. *Why is this happening to me? I don't want to die alone!*

He didn't want to die at all, but the braves had done an excellent job tying him down. Stuart pulled anyway. He tried again to reach the vial in his pocket, this time with his teeth, all the while twisting and yanking and thrashing until he made himself dizzy.

The ticking moved closer. Stuart strained to see the croc. Was that it, that shadowy mass in the tall grass at the edge of the clearing? Yes. It was looking at him, too, wasn't it? His heart became ice.

"Pssst! James!"

Stuart almost leaped out of his skin. "Cecco?" he gasped. Christ on his throne, could he be so lucky?

"Shhh. Don't move."

Stuart tilted his head enough to see Cecco's hands on his right, a knife in one. The first mate began to saw at the ropes.

Another set of hands started cutting on his left. "Smee, sar," whispered the bosun.

Who else? "Thank you, both of you—" Stuart began. He swallowed the rest as an arrow whizzed past his head. The Indians could see that someone was trying to free him, and they weren't going to stand for it. Stuart spotted several braves kneeling outside their teepees, aiming their bows. One! Two! Three! Four! Five! The arrows hissed past, one striking a pole, one missing Stuart's leg, the others making Cecco and Smee duck for cover. "Don't stop, you dogs, or—" Stuart bit back the rest as another arrow hit the pole an inch above his good left hand. *No no no, not that,* he thought, nauseated at the prospect of living with no hands at all. *I'd rather the croc chew me alive than that!*

Cecco and Smee resumed cutting. Cecco removed the last of the rope, and Stuart's hook-arm was free. Cecco knelt down and got to work on his right foot.

Stuart was about to use his hook on his other foot when the croc advanced. It came wriggling through the grass, head swinging one way while its fat abdomen swung the other. Its tail lashed back and forth behind it, flattening whatever grass was left standing after the passage of its wide heavy belly. It wasn't moving fast, but as far as Stuart was concerned, it was damned fast enough.

"Smeeeeeee," he whined, "hurrrreeeeeeee!" He began to thrash aimlessly, not helping at all. He was fast losing the ability for rational thought. It never occurred to him to cut off his fear, to trap it behind the great grey wall in his mind. His mind was too busy slipping into pandemonium.

The croc saw Stuart's movements and roared, opening its maw wide enough that Stuart saw all those teeth, each about six to eight inches long and hideously, abnormally sharp. He opened his mouth to scream, dignity be damned. No sound came out. His lungs betrayed him, or saved him, perhaps — he would need the air for better things.

The last rope fell away. He was free. "Come on!" Cecco said.

Stuart wanted to move, oh God, how he did! He took a step, another one, but that was it. Reality slipped sideways and took him with it. Time shifted from normal to nightmare, slowing everything down to that unnatural peanut-butter crawl of a child's worst dreams. Stuart's eyes sought out the two beady black orbs in the grass. He knew they were there. Against his own will, he had to find them.

There they were. He goggled at the croc, mesmerized, paralyzed. The croc, having paused, stared steadily back. More arrows from the Indians flew past, one perhaps an inch away from Stuart's head, a puff of wind caressing his ear as it whizzed by. Oblivious to it, he remained frozen, acknowledging his death before him. His *death*, leering with an intelligent reptilian grin. It was so goddamned *big*...

"He's bewitched!" Smee said from a vast distance.

Cecco slapped Stuart's face. "Come! On!"

Time slipped back to normal. The croc charged, eating up ground at a terrifying speed. Stuart whirled and ran, quickly followed by Smee and Cecco. Stuart's longer legs and singular motivation allowed him to outdistance his mates quickly and then — for the life of him, he didn't know where he got the courage or strength — he doubled back to help Smee, who was by no means a sprinter. "Climb!" he ordered, propelling Smee several feet up the trunk of a grand old oak. It was a good choice, with lots of angled branches and gnarls for foot and handholds.

Clumsy and bulky, Smee started to climb. "But you, Cap'n—!"

The croc was almost upon him. Stuart gathered to run and, pumped to his ears with adrenaline, he bounded straight up the trunk of a tall tilted sycamore. He got three steps up and launched himself out, catching a thick nearly-horizontal branch and hauling himself up along the top of it just as the croc reared like a demonic puppy begging for a treat. While its stubby front legs flailed like fat baby arms, it stretched its neck as far as it could and nipped the edge of Stuart's topcoat. It got the trim, which ripped off, sending the beast toppling flat on its back with a long strip of black velvet dangling from its jaws.

The force of that little nip was enough to spin Stuart round his branch. He suddenly found himself hanging upside-down like a kid hugging monkey bars. Now the ripped edge of his long topcoat was hanging even closer to the ground. He wished he could take the damned garment off, but that wasn't even in the ballpark of possible.

Then it came to him. *The Voodoo poison! Drop the open bottle down the beast's throat!* But how to reach the bottle and open it without spilling it, without getting it on himself, without passing out from the fumes, without losing his grip on the branch? *One thing at a time, James,* he thought, and glanced at his shirt pocket to determine how he might reach it.

His pocket was empty. He had either dropped it during his run, or it had slipped out the minute he'd gone upside-down. He tilted his head to check the ground. *Shit, there it is!* The little bottle gleamed in a shaft of sunlight next to the croc's left rear leg. As if the beast sensed it, it moved that leg in a casual kicking motion, sending the bottle flying into the brush. Stuart heard a strange rhythmic rumble and had the most hideous impression that the croc was laughing at him.

There was nothing to do now but hang on as the croc reared up again. Stuart felt the jolt as the beast clamped its jaws firmly into his dangling topcoat. It pulled in earnest.

"James!" cried Cecco, safely high up in another tree.

"Cap'n!" squealed Smee, precariously keeping his own balance within the branches of the gnarled oak.

Stuart hugged his branch tight, his entire body pressed close to it, arms and legs curled around it as much as human limbs could curl. The weight of the croc on his topcoat came like the strike of a hammer. He was pulled downward with such force that for a sickening moment he thought he would lose his grip or the branch would break.

Neither happened. As if the whole scenario was part of some sadistic kiddie cartoon, the already damaged topcoat started to rip at the seams. Stuart could hear the sound of individual threads breaking. As each one did, the coat became a tiny bit looser. The croc paused in its work as if evaluating the minute sounds, giving Stuart a fraction of a second to adjust his grip on the branch.

The croc tugged again. Stuart yelped and held on, stark animal terror keeping that branch in his grasp as his body bowed in the middle under the croc's weight. *Rrrrip!* The seams around his armpits gave way. *Rrrrip!* across the shoulders. *Rrrrrrrip!* along the main back seam. Stuart's straining muscles were about to give way when the bulk of the coat ripped free, leaving him with nothing but the sleeves on. The incredible weight of the croc fell away.

He renewed his grasp on the branch, babbling incoherent prayers as the croc, once again on its back, flipped itself over. Stuart felt rather than saw the beast gaze up at him, formulating new strategies while it audibly munched on his coat like a bad boy chomping bubble gum.

"Cap'n!" Smee called.

"James?" said Cecco. "Say something!"

Words. Echoing down a long tunnel. They were too far away from Stuart's dilemma to matter. Smee and Cecco were safe. He, on the other hand, was on the front lines. He was the one the croc wanted. He deleted his crewmen's voices from conscious input and focused on a curious scrabbling sound coming from below. Shaking so hard that his breath was coming in herky-jerky hiccups, he bent his head back. That way he could see the scene below him, albeit upside-down.

The croc, having swallowed his coat, was trying a new tactic to get the rest of him. It was stretching itself up along the side of the sycamore's tilted trunk, pulling its bulk vertical by scrabbling with its chubby front legs and their murderously long claws. Its powerful tail lay flat along the ground as a counterbalance. Seen upside-down, the croc looked like it was trying to dig a hole in the sky. That would have been easier to believe than the truth. *It can't do that!* Stuart thought in wild amazement. *Crocodiles can't climb straight up a tree!* Then came the kicker: *Minus the tail, its body must be twenty feet long!*

The branch Stuart clung to was less than twenty feet up.

If the beast managed to reach high enough to nip the fabric of his shirt or — the mere idea made him whimper — a hank of his long dangling *hair*, it would be able to pull him right down, no questions asked. Stuart was sure he wouldn't be able to hold on during another tugging session, not like before. His wounds were bleeding fire, his overwrought muscles were shivering with exertion, and he was crying now, his control gone to hell, his eyes spilling hot tears mixed with blood that made the impossibly climbing croc look like a blurry red dragon.

An idea came to him. It was beyond insane, but what did that mean anymore? If the croc could do the unthinkable in this unthinkable world, maybe he could, too. After all, he had already run up the side of the tree, hadn't he? He looked down again, blinking tears out of his eyes. *Do it do it there's no choice James move or die!*

Carefully but quickly he wormed his way around the branch so that he was once again lying across the top of it. Gathering his nerve and not for one second looking down, he unfolded until he stood upright. Then he leaped straight up.

Days later both Cecco and Smee would tell him they'd never seen anything like it. "Like a bloomin' acrobat yeh were, sar," Smee would tell him. "I couldn't believe me eyes!"

"I swear you had wings," Cecco would add in astonishment.

Stuart really didn't know what he was doing. Some primal instinct was conducting his body movements, and that was fine by him. He knew he had jumped. He knew he was aiming for a branch eight feet above his head. He knew when he got a grip on it.

His hand slipped. He was going to fall. He rammed his hook into the wood. His harness protested by digging into his flesh while the blood-slicked shoulder pad threatened to slip dangerously askew. Too scared to pray for heavenly intervention this time, Stuart just hung there stupidly, the iron blasphemy that wasn't his hand saving him from a hard fall and an agonizing death.

The croc roared, straining and scrabbling, trying in vain to nip his toes off.

Stuart regained a handhold. Cursing furious encouragements to his quivering muscles, he climbed up onto the higher branch. It was nice and thick, a big sturdy arm of wood that would hold his weight as long as he might want it to. That was good, because Stuart had no intention of leaving. Nothing was going to make him move from this spot until the croc gave up and was long gone. That wouldn't be for quite awhile. The beast was trying to climb up again, growling and *tick-tick-ticking* like an angry bomb.

Unlike a man with an ego, the croc didn't care that it looked completely absurd with its bulk precariously balanced at an angle not meant for the species. Stuart watched it numbly, his fear spent, his wounds dripping warm red onto the maddened beast and making it slaver with hunger. It snarled and snapped at him, its breath wafting up in hot blasts that stank like garbage in the sun. It lost its balance and fell. Again it tried to climb. Again it fell. Again it tried to climb. It would keep trying until it had utterly exhausted itself. Stuart knew that as well as he knew that he would stay in that tree as long as it took for the croc to get that exhausted.

"Sar! Cap'n, sar! Y'okay?"

"James, for God's sake, answer! How badly are you hurt?"

Stuart still made no reply. He couldn't have formed words if he wanted to. He had found the croc's eyes, and he was drowning in them. It was trying to hypnotize him like it had before.

"Fer Chrissake, don't look at it, sar!" Smee advised urgently.

Somehow that got through. Stuart flicked his eyes the other way, breaking the connection. The croc roared furiously. Stuart shuddered. *Hold on, James*, he thought. *Hold on. Hold on. Hold on. Hold on...*

CHAPTER 44

It came to her during the cab ride back home from Big Stash Coin and Jewelry Exchange. It came to her out of the blue, a connection, an answer that must have been simmering just below her level of consciousness for some time. When it finally surfaced, it hit her like a zap of electricity, a sudden pulse of realization that touched the very marrow of her bones.

What is my part in all of this? she had asked herself while sitting under the palm tree in front of the trendy sushi bar twenty minutes earlier. *I'm Pan's insurance that his twisted game will continue! I'm pregnant with Jon's child! It will be a boy, it'll have to be, and he'll become the next Hook!*

This one conclusion allowed many of the disparate facts in her Researcher Brain to finally come together. Jon had seemed not all there ever since falling out of bed. Why? Because he really hadn't been all there. He indeed had been suspended between two worlds. She had wracked her brain for a reason why Pan should do such a thing, and now she knew: Pan had to keep enough of Jon in the real world long enough for him to get her pregnant. Jon had disappeared for good after their night of what she now recognized as magically induced passion.

And the sword — Jon's great-grandfather James had been the last Stuart to be abducted by Pan. When he was released from the Neverland, he had come back with the sword. The sword, along with his mad memoirs, ended up in Emmerich's possession, which meant that J.M. Barrie, one way or another, had returned both items to the family. Somehow Emmerich had resisted the pull of the sword, had managed to lock it up in the safe behind the walls of Stuart House, and thus Pan had never come for him. The sword had remained hidden throughout Theodore's and George's lives, so they were spared abduction as well.

Pan must not be able to find his targets without the sword. But the sword must still have pulled at them, and that's why they weren't sane. That's why all the Stuart men in that branch of the family are unstable. Even if the sword doesn't take them, they're still affected by the very fact that it exists. It must be, I don't know... tuned to them. Perhaps that's the reason for the violence and abuse in the family, too.

When the Loma Prieta earthquake had happened, the safe had been revealed, and Jon had taken the sword. Now Melanie understood why, the night he'd returned from San Francisco, he had been so mesmerized by the weapon. It had already taken hold of him. *So what do I do now?* she wondered.

She had an idea, but she didn't like it, not one bit.

* * * * *

Over the next few days, in an effort to avoid contemplating what she knew she would have to do, Melanie probed farther into the Stuart family, hoping to find answers to the rest of the mystery. Where did the sword originally come from? How did Emmerich get it from Barrie, and why was he able to resist it? Why did he hide the book and sword in a safe and not simply destroy them?

The first person she called was a contact she had at the Yale University Beinecke Rare Book and Manuscript Library. She got up early to call so that Theresa Baker would just be settling down for work. Melanie had learned that it was always best to catch Theresa before she got going full tilt and her day's duties caused her to let her answering machine take all calls.

The conversation was short, as it usually was. Melanie had found out on the internet that the Beinecke Rare Book and Manuscript Library owned the copyright to J.M. Barrie's will, amongst other papers of his in The J.M. Barrie Collection. Melanie wanted Theresa to fax her a copy of the will. Theresa said she would do so as quickly as possible.

Later that morning Melanie called Masao, Jon's jewelry dealer friend in Japantown, San Francisco. Masao was the only one besides Jon and Melanie to have seen the sword. She found his phone number in Jon's computer address book.

She dialed and waited as the phone rang. A gruff male voice answered, "Moshi moshi. Herro. Masao Jewelers." His Japanese accent was so thick that Melanie had a hard time understanding him, although his grammatical knowledge of English was pretty good.

"Is this Masao speaking?" Melanie asked him.

"Hai. How may I serve?"

"I'm Melanie Forrester, Jonathan Stuart's... well, fiancée, but..."

"Ah," said Masao kindly. "Very very sorry what happened. Good man. I share grief."

"Thank you. I was curious about the sword he inherited from his uncle. He told me that you examined it."

Masao barely hesitated. "Yes, indeed! Beautiful weapon! Tried to buy, but he would not sell. Too bad for me."

Melanie smiled. "Can you tell me about it? How much do you remember?"

"Will never forget, Missa Forrester. Single-hand saber, thirty inch blade, jewel encrusted pommel. Was worked in Oriental fashion, is to say, folded and hammered so blade is composed of thousands layers. Called Damascened steel in West. Gives much strength and flexibility."

"Did you notice anything unusual about it?"

Masao had to think for a moment. "Remember dragon lines — tempering process make length-wise lines, waves like ripples in sand on beach. Show where metal shift from soft iron in center to carbon steel at edge. Fine fine weapon, very deadly." He paused. "Remember etchings on blade. Curious."

"I saw them, too. Do you have any idea what language they were in?"

"Not sure a language. Maybe only decoration."

"You didn't by any chance copy them down or do a rubbing of them, did you?"

"No, sorry."

"Can you tell me anything else that you remember about it, anything at all?"

"Very sorry, no," said Masao. "Except will buy if for sale!"

Melanie could hear the hope in his voice. "Sorry, I don't have it anymore," she told him. "It was... stolen."

"Ah!" Masao practically wailed with dismay. "Very bad! Terrible! You will try to find?"

"Of course, but it doesn't look good."

"If I can help, please call."

"Thank you, Masao. Good bye."

"Sayonara, Missa Forrester."

Melanie hung up just in time to hear Jon's fax machine, on a separate phone line, ring. The machine answered and began slowly spitting out its weirdly slick thermal papers. The first page read:

> Section IV. J.M. Barrie's Will dated 1937
> A28 WILL (photocopy)
> 1937 Jun 14, London
>
> 91. 33cm.
> Extracted from the Principal Registry of the
> Probate Divorce and Admiralty
> Division of the High Court of Justice
> and signed by the Registrar.

Melanie dived in and began to read.

Ten minutes later she found what she was looking for. Barrie had specified that "the contents" of a certain box marked with a star, which was sealed and not to be opened, be mailed immediately upon his death to one Emmerich Stuart at Stuart House in San Francisco. Since Barrie had died in 1937, that meant Emmerich received the sword when he was far too old to take up the role of Captain Hook. A quick glance at the Stuart family tree revealed that Emmerich would have been sixty-two. *So it found him and turned him more nutso than ever, but he was able to function well enough to recognize the threat and deal with it.* But not efficiently. Old Emmerich had not gotten rid of the hellish item but had only hidden it away, along with his father's mad memoirs, in the safe behind the basement wall.

There was one last angle Melanie wanted to pursue before she faced the horrible deed that lay ahead of her. She checked the notes provided her by Dusty Rhodes to find a name: Flora Banners, the housekeeper who worked for Jon's uncle George while he had lived in Stuart House. To Melanie's relief, the woman still lived at the same address in San Francisco's Sunset district. Melanie tracked down her phone number and punched it in.

"Banner wesdence," said a cute childish voice, muffled by heavy breathing as the child held the phone too close to his/her mouth.

"Hi, there," said Melanie brightly. "I'm looking for Flora Banners. Is she there?"

A loud thunk indicated that the child simply dropped the phone. "Gwamaaaaaah!" the kid screamed.

Melanie had to chuckle as the child abandoned the phone, his/her little feet thumping away into the distance as he/she continued to scream for Grandma. A moment later the phone was picked up and a mature Hispanic voice said, "Yes, who is this, please?"

"Mrs. Banners? My name is Melanie Forr—"

The woman's tone became harsh. "Is this a sales call?"

"No, no, I'm calling about Stuart House," Melanie said quickly.

The woman paused. "What about it?"

"I'm Melanie Forrester, a professional researcher. I was also the fiancée of the late Jonathan Stuart, who would have inherited Stuart House."

"You were going to marry into *that* family?" the woman blurted, unable to hold back her incredulity.

No matter how many times she had endured such responses from people, the harsh words made Melanie flinch, especially now that Jon was truly gone. The woman on the other end of the line seemed to suddenly process Melanie's use of the term *late.* "Oh! Oh, I'm sorry, that was uncalled for. Yes, I'm Flora Banners. How can I help you?"

Melanie recovered herself. "I've been told that you worked for George Stuart and that you know a lot about the house."

"Oh, I certainly do. At one time — a long time ago, mind you, before George took over — I was hired to give weekend tours by Mr. Emmerich. His wife had passed away nearly twenty years earlier and he had no children, not living in the house, anyway. He valued his privacy and always said he did it for the mad money, as he put it, but I think deep down he wanted company."

"May I ask what Emmerich was like? I mean, personality-wise?"

"A decent man, but what a temper! I did not stay around the house much, though I wanted to. It was the most beautiful house I have ever seen. I cry just thinking of it... nothing now but ashes. Your fiancé must have been devastated."

A thought occurred to Melanie. "Were there weapons on display in the house? You know, family heirlooms like swords or knives?"

"Let me think," said Flora. "Mr. Emmerich had a family crest over the fireplace in the parlor... lots of artwork and paintings, some quite valuable... but no, I don't recall any swords. I have plenty of photos, though, if you would like to see them. Maybe they would help. I loved that house, but my memory..." She trailed off, the "it ain't what it used to be" left unsaid.

"That's not necessary, Mrs. Banners. Just one more question, if I may. Do you know anything about a safe being in the house, specifically behind a wall in the basement?"

"A safe? Not in the basement. Mr. Emmerich kept valuables in a safe in his office, and there was a wall safe behind a portrait of his wife in the parlor." She lowered her voice to a whisper. "He didn't know I knew about that one. I saw him open it one day and ducked out of the room before he could see me. I don't snoop into what isn't my business, so I don't know what he kept in there. Couldn't have been much. It looked like it was pretty small."

"Well, he was a rich man, everybody knows that," Melanie said. "I'm not surprised he kept a safe or two. But you say there wasn't one behind a basement wall?"

"I've never heard a thing about that. I can tell you that Mr. Emmerich did remodel his wine cellar in... when was it... 1937, I think it was. He became quite the connoisseur. He began to buy wines from around the world. Drank wine with dinner every night after that

416

until the day he died. Perhaps he put a safe down there at the same time. You know those Stuarts. They're paranoid, and that's a fact."

Melanie was busy putting two and two together. Talk about a perfect dovetail! "Well, that's it then," she said, knowing that she sounded a bit absent, but she couldn't help it. "Thank you, Mrs. Banners, very very much."

"You're welcome," Mrs. Banners said, and she hung up.

Melanie dropped her phone into its cradle with a triumphant yet pained grin. *Remodeled your wine cellar in 1937, eh?* she thought. *And Barrie just happened to die that same year and send you a package? You must not have liked that package very much, Emmerich. You hid it away awfully fast.* The fact that he had become a wine enthusiast after that made Melanie laugh darkly. *It started getting to you right away, didn't it? I bet drinking helped. You're not the only one who tried that.*

Melanie left Jon's office and crossed the living room, trying to ignore the silver urn on its shelf flanked by two white candles. She couldn't do it. She had to look at it, even if only for a second. She didn't know anymore if she could ever get Jon back. She had no plans on giving up, but there was a task to perform first, a horrible task that nonetheless would ensure that no one else fell into Pan's trap ever again. She lifted the phone book off the living room table and went into the kitchen.

Neverland, she thought as she flipped through the white pages, looking for the name of the abortion clinic she had visited not that long ago. *No matter what the cost to me, Peter Pan, you are never going to take another Stuart there again, never, never, never!*

CHAPTER 45

He came back to the world while sitting at the rosewood table.

I'm alive. His first thought.

It didn't get me. Second thought.

Brandy. Third thought.

He sipped from the cup in his hand.

How long have I been back?

A long time, long enough that his wounds were healed. His back was stiff, his neck and shoulders like lead, as if he had been sitting in this chair for hours and hours. His bones creaked when he adjusted his position, making him think of some old gummer in a squeaky rocking chair on the porch at sunset. *Addie May, yeh lazy woman, where's mah mint julep!*

Ah yes, the ever-present alcohol. But the brandy seemed to be working backwards for some reason. It was sending Stuart into a deep drunk in reverse, which made no sense at all. The blurred edges of the table, which had been a thousand miles away a minute ago, were rushing back at him, slipping into focus. His feet, stuck in his boots for God only knew how long, were pin-tingling their way back to functionality as if they had been deprived of circulation and now it was all rushing back in. His sluggy brain was trying to turn the cranks. He could hear the groans of mental gears as they reluctantly pulled the gaudy actuality of Hook's great cabin back into his consciousness. The events of the last twenty-four hours were shuffling around in his head and had been for some time, he realized, trying to pull themselves out of a mucky mire and sort themselves into coherent order.

Ooo, are the photos ready? Can I see 'em, huh? Can I, can I?

With abnormal eagerness — he shouldn't have wanted to have anything to do with the last twenty-four hours — he opened the photo album of Memory and stepped back to the Indian forest and the sycamore tree. The fear returned, a pulsing knot in his chest. Part of him didn't want to go back there after all.

Too late, too late! Don't be afraid! Come one, come all, walk right up and see the 'fraidy monkey in the tree, ook ook!

He had stayed up in that tree for hours, three, maybe four. More than that? Possibly. Tenacious was a good word to describe the croc's disposition, but even a hardened predator has its limits. Possessing a cold-blooded metabolism, it had to spend the cool Neverland nights in water. When the suns had started to go out, the croc had reluctantly slithered away, grumbling to itself as it *tick-tick-ticked* through the twilight forest, through the misty barrier, back into the night-cooling jungle and out to the sea.

Enter Smee and Cecco, my personal Dynamic Duo. Bless their ruddy hearts, what would I have done without them? Oh that's right, I would have died! Ha!

How long had his devoted duo called to him, beckoning and urging, begging him to climb down? Another hour after that? Two? His muscles had locked into position. Fatigue finally did what reason could not. He had gradually lost both balance and grip, exiting the tree in a sort of slow-motion Raggedy Andy plummet. He hadn't broken any bones thanks to Smee, who had heroically tried to catch him. The bosun had missed, but he *had* cushioned Stuart's fall quite nicely. Stuart recalled hearing a loud "Oof!" that hadn't been his own.

O, what loyalty! It would break me 'eart, if I had one left. What about the trip back to the boat then? Hmm and hmm, this part makes no sense, Sherlock, no sense at all...

He had been half-conscious at best, feverish in the aftermath of such prolonged terror and depleted of all energy reserves. He remembered the fumblings of hands on his body as bosun and first mate had struggled to carry their captain over the long trek. They had dropped him a couple of times, not that he had complained. Stuart didn't think he had been in his body during the journey anyhow. He had watched it all from the side, as if he had been walking along next to himself, disappointed by the miserable scenario playing out. Talk about a botched job. Talk about your basic colossal bungle. The whole day had been a pathetic disaster, punctuated by the fact that he hadn't even been able to make his exit like a man. No brave limping of a wounded hero, not even the grim determined crawl of a defeated but still proud warrior. No, he had been hauled away like a jumbo sack of chicken feed.

The Indians had not pursued them, thank God. Either Roars Like a Bear had believed Captain Hook dead, or the Chief had granted him freedom by virtue of his having survived the croc's attack. There was always the possibility that the Chief had never intended to kill him. Maybe the old fart had arranged nothing more than an entertaining revenge scenario. Stuart wondered if it might not have been better if a dozen braves *had* pursued and chopped him into confetti then and there.

Probably save a lot of grief down the line, he thought. *If something this bad doesn't happen again, something worse will. Tst tst, don't be so negative, old fellow! Bad form, very bad form.*

Once they had reached the beach, Smee's first words had been, "Ah, fer Chrissake! The barnacle-brained idjits wrote us off!" The boats had both been gone, along with all the other pirates. Smee and Cecco had fired their pistols, alerting the first dog watch out on the ship. A very humble Foggerty had sent a boat to fetch them.

Stuart's perception of events after that were blearier than a bug smear. *Chop chop, let the heartwarming story continue!* he urged his memory, not really wanting to go on with the dismal replay *But what the hell, right? Failure is the only thing a man can truly call his own, and I have soooo many new memories to cherish, oh, I've collected the whole set! If screwing up was gold, I'd be richer than Almighty God!*

The bug smear of memory slowly began to clarify into images, like single freeze-frames from a particularly depressing film. Each frame came to life, one by one, to tell its story.

It was more than Stuart could stand. He buried his face in his arms, trying to hide from the flash impressions of his crew once he had returned: how they'd had to sway him up from the boat to the ship like a Guernsey in a sling; how they had gawped with combinations of awe, embarrassment and shame; how they had whispered after he had been carried into his cabin. More images, these of Smee once more tending his pathetic raggedy captain, peeling off his ripped and bloodied clothes, bathing him, binding his wounds, coaxing a little broth down his throat. Stuart had been as helpless as a babe.

I might as well have been in diapies sucking on a binky! Did da big bad piwate captain take a nappy-poo afterwards?

Stuart figured he might have slept but not in bed. If anything, he must have nodded off right where he was sitting. At some point someone – Scourie? Skylights? one of them, maybe both – had made a report concerning the poisoned lake. Stuart couldn't remember much of it except the phrases "boiled like lava" and "dead fish came floatin' to the surface." That was enough.

So here I am, King of the Cosmic Assholes, back on my throne so that I can get unceremoniously booted off it all over again. It'll happen when I least expect it, probably when I think I've got a really good scheme going. Stuart thunked his forehead down on the table with each word: "I. Have. To. Get. Out. Ow!"

Well, that was stupid.

He rubbed his head and giggled. "The beastie under the bed almost got me, yo ho ho and a bucket o' suds! Must be more clever than that, Jimmy ol' boy, clever clever clee-ehh-verrrr. Only that will save our precious hide. Must be smart and beat the bad guy. *'Forsan et haec olim meminisse juvabit'*!" Latin, a quote from Virgil's classic Æneid. It translated as, "*Maybe we'll laugh about this one day.*" Stuart was finding it increasingly delightful to plumb the impressive depths of James Hook's education. He raised his glass. "Alas, poor Æneas, I didn't know you well, but I know how you felt. Tossed about by an uncaring sea with no port to call home. At least you weren't followed by a psychopathic crocodile."

Smee's hard knuckles rapped on the door. "Sar. Yeh awake? Cookson made his specialty, sar. Helluva fine salmagundi. Got a plate of it here fer yeh, if yer up to eatin', that is."

Food! Aye, hungry! He was mucho very hungry! Stuart banged on the table. "Aye, bring it in, Mister Smee!"

The bosun entered, bright and cheery as if he had spent a week basking lazily in the tropical suns instead of fighting Indians and running from giant crocodiles. "Yer soundin' better, sar. Fer awhile there, I was afraid yeh'd lost yer rudder."

"My rudder is intact and fully functional, thank you," Stuart replied. He was surprised to note that he did all of a sudden feel extremely well. So what if his plan had gone spinning down the toilet? *Seats of ease,* he corrected himself. He still had his life, his ship and his crew, right? *Try again, try again, that's what I'll do,* he thought, feeling a grin that was a little too wide spreading over his face. *So what if I fail again? Try again, fail again, what's the big deal really? It's not all bad here. Just have to keep a weather eye, is all. A weather eye and a handful of bona fide miracles, and I ought to come through all this just ducky.*

He inhaled the spicy aroma of the salmagundi, allowing Smee to perform the service of setting the steaming plate before him. The bosun placed a spoon next to the plate and a goblet to Stuart's left. "What would yeh like to drink, sar?" Smee asked while flicking a linen napkin open and laying it across his captain's lap.

"Coffee. Oh, and fetch wine. And some bread." *Hell,* he thought, *why not a psychotherapist while you're at it, wot wot? I feel good, and there's not one damned reason why I should! What cheer ho, James m'boy, why worry? You have the rest of your life to do that, heh heh!*

"Cookson didn't make bread today, sar," Smee was saying. "All we got is hard tack. A might weevily."

"Never mind then."

Stuart scooped up a spoonful of Cookson's specialty. Salmagundi was a traditional seaman's dish, a sloppy cross between salad and stew. It could be made with any kind of meat: mutton, pork, fish, chicken, turtle meat, even a couple of seagulls if stores were down and the cook was creative. The meat was marinated in spiced wine then roasted and combined with anchovies, egg, cabbage, olives, pickled vegetables of any sort, whatever was on hand. The whole mess was then spiced to the sky — at least, that was the way Cookson handled it. Generous salt, enough pepper to make a man's tongue swell, enough garlic to make his breath tarnish silver, all lubricated with vinegar and oil.

This particular batch featured turtle meat and something that was as hot as habanero pepper. Stuart chewed a spoonful and started coughing. He barely managed to swallow before blowing the mouthful everywhere. "Obesity and bunions!" he choked, wiping his eyes. "What the bloody hell's in this? It could damned well bring a man back from the grave!"

Smee had fetched a bottle of merlot from Hook's cabinet. As he poured he said, "Injuns call it *makcha*, sar. Some kind of herb on the island. Cookson found out about it from Barricoe Billy." Smee chuckled at the boy's name. "The pup's a worker, sar, that's fer sure. Might just turn into a fine addition to the crew."

"If he doesn't over-spice us to death first," Stuart said hoarsely.

"Too much, sar? I can get Cookson to—"

"No no, it's fine. Took me unawares is all. Give my compliments to Mister Cookson." Stuart rubbed his forehead with the flat of his hook, aware on some level that he already equated that cold touch of iron to the living fingers he'd once had. "My word, it does clear the cobwebs, doesn't it?"

"I'll get yer coffee, sar," said Smee, and started for the door.

Stuart spoke softly. "Wait a moment, Smee."

"Sar?" The bosun's expectant expression told Stuart that he already knew what his captain was going to say.

"About what happened ashore... I owe you my life. You and Cecco."

Smee tried to shrug it away. "Yeh saved my life as well, sar, pushin' me arse up into that tree, fer Chrissake."

"Yes yes, I know," Stuart said dismissively. "But you came *back* for me. We both know you didn't have to, hm?"

It had never occurred to Stuart to punish those pirates who had abandoned him on the island. Lord knows, he should have. The bastards had left their captain to die. Any other captain would have screwed them up by their thumbs in the rigging. But when it came to the croc, normal pirate laws and loyalties did not apply. When it came to the croc, Captain Hook was on his own. Stuart didn't know why he knew that. He just did. And he knew that was the way it had always been. "I won't forget your loyalty," he told Smee.

An embarrassed but pleased blush rose on Smee's bristly cheeks. "Sar—"

Stuart waved his hand at the man before he had a chance to blurt out some cockamamie gush. "I want to ask you a question, and I want you to answer honestly."

"Always, sar."

"What went wrong?"

That caught Smee off guard. "Wrong, sar? Y'mean, with yer plan? Err... I ain't one to harp on about I-told-yeh-sos, but, well, sar... I told yeh so. Yeh've never had luck with the Injuns, y'know that."

"Or the... that... *thing*," Stuart added, thinking of the croc.

Smee nodded knowingly. He didn't comment, though. Neither, however, did he leave. It seemed as if he wanted to say something, maybe something comforting, but couldn't quite manage it.

Stuart poked at the salmagundi with his spoon. "Do I have luck with anything, Smee? I mean, have I ever had a plan that went *right?*"

Smee rubbed his neck. "Mighty queer thing to ask, sar. A man don't command his own ship an' turn a profit fer hisself an' his crew without cunning an' the mettle to match. Yeh come up with some mighty clever ideas, sar, dangerous ones, too, an' yeh've got the sand to see 'em through. But if I might say, sar, lately yeh've been fightin' the devil himself, an' when a man does that, well... he can't win."

Stuart caught the bosun's eye. "Devil?" he asked quietly.

"Oh, well, it's just, err..." Smee cleared his throat. "This string o' bad luck, sar. From the devil hisself, says I. Wouldn't yeh agree?"

Stuart wanted to say that luck had nothing to do with it, that luck was something that didn't exist in this world, at least not for Captain Hook. Ah well, what would be the point? He held his tongue and gestured for Smee to leave. He could actually feel his good mood slinking away into a corner, leaving as quickly as it had come, easily bullied by a growing gloom that wanted to stomp flat every positive cheerful thought he might ever have for the rest of his life. Just another of Hook's melancholy moods. This time, though, it hadn't announced itself by a stranglehold of the black fingers on his insides. It had tip-toed into him like a thief, stealthy and slow. It had gently dug its fangs into his neck and sucked him dry before he had even been aware of it.

He ate in silence, drinking plenty of wine to cool the hot but delicious food. Smee brought his coffee, but they didn't exchange any more words except for Smee's deferential, "Sar," as he set the china cup down in its delicate saucer.

When Stuart finished eating, he called for boiling water and made a cup of strong tea, using dried mint from the personal herb stores he had found in the liquor cabinet. Hook knew, and so he knew, quite a bit about herbs and their uses the same as he did perfumes and poisons. He had an impressive assortment for basic ailments and remedies, some that Cookson hadn't even heard of. After Stuart drank the tea, grateful that it would ease the heartburn already flaring in his chest, he removed his coat and laid down in his hammock.

He wasn't tired enough to sleep, but he felt drained. He dozed, listening to the footsteps on deck and MacDougal singing some ditty or another. Not a work song. The suns had faded an hour ago. The first watch had little to do but chat and play cards by lamplight. Many of them had been ashore for the tragic Indian encounter, and all they wanted tonight was peace and quiet. MacDougal's tenor was sweet and soothing, a lullaby for men at the end of a strenuous day.

Stuart couldn't stop thinking about the croc. "My death, my death," he kept repeating, a gruesome personal mantra. The truth was that it *would* be his death if he couldn't find a way home. That ticking was a puzzler, though. The beast had swallowed a clock, yes, but weren't all clocks in the era of the Neverland wind-ups? Which meant that sooner or later the clock would run down. It should have run down long ago. When it finally did — it would have to, wouldn't it? — he wouldn't hear the beast coming. *That will be the day I die.* Then again, maybe it was a magic clock that would keep going forever. *It doesn't matter, James, you won't be here that long.*

A string of words popped into his head: *Takes a licking and keeps on ticking!* He laughed out loud, comforted by the unexpected warmth that came from the dim memory of hearing those words spoken on... what was it? Something called a... a... well, some kind of box with pictures in it. *Soon that vague recollection will be gone, too,* he thought, *gone, gone, far far away, la la-la! No more picture boxes, just blank faces swimming in the ether, lookee lookee, here I am but you can't see me, I'm right in front of you but you can't reach me, neener neener!*

He hugged his pillow. So many things he used to know, gone. People, places, hopes, dreams. Gone. He was alone in a warehouse of empty shelves. Boxes were supposed to be stacked high on those shelves in neat rows, each one clearly labeled. But they weren't there anymore. New boxes had been delivered and were sitting patiently on the loading dock, waiting to be carried in. No labels. All the strapping tape still intact. There were shapeless bags, too, and piles of stuff he couldn't identify. Soon those things would get stacked on the shelves. More stuff would come and be tossed up on the shelves until the warehouse was packed anew. Then he would be locked inside with it and left on his own to make sense of it all. To eventually accept it. To eventually come to believe that it had all been his own from the start.

I'm not really James, am I? Trouble is, I don't know who I am. Was. Gotta call myself something, don't I? But James? I don't think so. Whoever I am is almost gone, and... he's taking over.

He unscrewed his hook and tossed it down. It clattered on the deck.

He isn't a ghost or a person, you know, came his inner voice with that unnerving accent. *And he is most definitely not Peter Pan. He belongs to us, James. He is we. He has always lived behind the wall, didn't you know? You've spent your life trying to cut him off, but he always comes back. He is we, James. You can't cut him off. He is we.*

Stuart whimpered.

On deck, MacDougal was starting a capstan shanty, slowly and with unaccustomed feeling, transforming the gruff lyrics into a strange nautical love song. Without realizing it, Stuart started to sing along with him, his voice no more than a whisper.

> *Sheet home yer big tops'ls, haul aft yer jib sheets,*
> *Sheet home fore 'n' aft, boys, ye'll git no darn sleep;*
> *Come aft now, God damn yeh, come aft one an' all,*
> *For over yer heads flies the bonnie Blackball.*
> *O, bound away! Bound away! Through ice, sleet an' snow,*
> *She's a Liverpool packet, Good God, let us go.*

A knock on the door, loud but respectful. Stuart recognized the knock as Foggerty's.

"Captain! You awake?" Yup. Foggerty.

Stuart grumbled and swung out of the hammock. "I am now," he growled to the second mate after opening the door.

Foggerty gulped and pushed on. "Captain, Pan just flew by. Dropped this on the deck, sir. It's yours, isn't it?" He held out a saber. *The* saber.

Stuart had completely forgotten about it. The Indians had taken it from him, and he hadn't given a thought about it since. Other things had been on his mind. "Aye, it's mine," he said simply.

The black voice inside commented, *No, it isn't yours and never has been. You know who really owns it.*

Shut up! Stuart thought back as he took the weapon. There was a tight green bundle tied to the hilt. He lifted it with the bare wooden blunt of his arm. "What's this?"

Foggerty, like all the men, tried hard not to notice the absence of the hook, which meant that he couldn't stop staring at the empty spot at the end of his captain's arm. "I... I don't know, sir. I figured you ought to be the one to—"

"Right, thank you." Stuart shut the door.

The green bulk was a package made of large leaves tied tight with stringy python weed. Feeling a horrible dread settle on him, Stuart retrieved his hook from under his hammock and used it to slice the tough weed free. He tore the leaf wrappings off.

Inside was his pearl-handled knife and a note, written in the scrawl of a child: "Give her back, you codfish. P.S. This throws real nice!"

Stuart dropped the weapon. *Pan killed that Indian kid with my knife! He murdered an innocent just to mark me!* He staggered to his chair and fell into it, appalled. *He was watching the whole time. He knows I'm trying to get out. Jesus, what is he going to do next...*

That's when he saw the bag on his writing desk. Not really a bag. A purse. A woman's black purse with long straps. It hadn't been there seconds ago.

"Melly." Stuart took the bag and hugged it. The strength left his legs, and he folded to the deck. *I forgot about you. I did, I forgot, I forgot you again!* He wanted to go to the writing table and log her name. He wanted to write out a description of what she looked like, how she talked — what he could still remember, anyhow. *I can't forget again! I can't lose you, Melly!*

He tried to make it to the table, had to make it there before she was gone, but it was too far out of reach. Everything started to spin away from him as if he were some kind of hellborn repellent that drove away anything inherently good. Melanie began to dissolve away even as he fought to cement her picture in his mind. Arms that had enfolded her countless times forgot the curves of her hips and breasts. His hand, the one lousy hand he had left, with fingers that had touched her skin, given pleasure to her and taken pleasure from her, lost all sense memory of her warmth. What did her voice sound like? The memory crumbled. The smell of her hair, the tingling warm wetness of her tongue, her eyes, her laugh, her tears, her silly giggle, her lips, her sigh, her self. Going. Going. Gone.

He wept, forgetting along with everything else that long-ago time when he had been incapable of shedding a single tear. He had thought himself such a hard man then. He had lived his life in a shell of his own making, all the while convinced that he was weathered and invincible, strong enough to ward off any harsh blows.

Now he lay on the burgundy carpet, moaning and sniffling, too lost, too enervated to pluck his kerchief from his sleeve. His eyes spilled their tears while his nose ran freely. Soon the sobs came so hard that tears mixed with snot and spittle, and he didn't care. He curled around the black bag, knowing that it meant something important but unable to remember what that might be. All he knew for certain was that he would lay here all night and cry. Because tomorrow he had to think of another plan. He couldn't do it tonight, but he would do it tomorrow, after the melancholy passed. He had to get out of here. He had to get out. He would think of another plan tomorrow. As for tonight? Nothing but misery.

Little Jonny no longer dreamed of giants...

*Time to go home. He'd had a lot of fun playing with... who had it been?
Funny, he couldn't remember the boy's name. No, wait. It had been a little
girl, not a boy. Yes, and she had been very pretty. What was her name...
Mandy? Sandy? Mindy? Oh well, it didn't matter. She knew him. Everybody
here knew him. They didn't care if he didn't know them. They didn't even
seem to notice.*

    *It wasn't daytime, it wasn't nighttime. It was no-time, because the caves
had their own special glow. Not yellow weather, like before an autumn storm.
More like silver weather, all sparkly and magical.*

    *Yes. Magic. That wonderful silver power that hummed in rock and water,
in the very molecules of air that he breathed. It was so full of possibilities that
his stomach knotted itself in anticipation without his knowing exactly why.*

    *He started for home. But right away he had to stop. He didn't know
where home was. How had he gotten into these caves in the first place? He
looked around. The chamber in which he stood was small and heavily pierced
by sparkling stalactites and stalagmites. He could hear water, a light playful
trickle of it from somewhere nearby and a much larger, much grander roar of it
somewhere far away. He couldn't tell which direction either was coming from.
Three openings yawned in the glittering stone walls. Any of them might lead to*

the sounds, or to somewhere else. One of them had to lead home, didn't it? Which one was it?

And then he heard it.

Bssssss!

What a strange sound. Like a swarm of flies very far away. Or bees maybe. The sound leaked into the cavern from everywhere, a living kettle hiss that began to echo so that it was impossible for him to determine which tunnel the sound came from.

BSSSSSS!

He didn't like that sound. He picked a tunnel at random and ran as fast as he could. Already he knew it was hopeless. The silver magic glowed feebly here, making him stumble in the murk. Smooth water-worn rocks glistening with moisture tripped him or disappeared out from under his feet altogether, forcing him to jump over bottomless chasms without knowing if there was another side to land on. He eventually stopped before a line of tall stalagmites that had formed perfectly vertically, each one the same height as the one next to it so that they stood like a jumbo-sized picket fence from an quintessential American front yard. He wondered if they were there to keep him from getting out or to keep something outside from getting in.

BSSSSSS!

The pretty little girl appeared behind him. She ran past him, leaped high into the air and flew over the stalagmite barrier. "It's mine!" she shouted as she landed on the other side. "You can't have it!"

"I need to get in!" he told her.

"No! Stay away!"

"Please!" he said. "They're coming! Can't you hear them?"

BSSSSSS!

The girl stood on tiptoe, gazing through a gap in the fence and past him. "They're going to kill you, Jon."

"I know that!" he cried. "Let me in!"

The girl reached for him between the stalagmites. "All right, give me your hand."

He reached through. Her gentle fingers wrapped around his wrist. They tightened too hard. "Hey!" he said. "That hurts!"

Her grip tightened further until he felt as if his wrist were caught in a vice. She pulled harder, smiling all the while. What was wrong with her? No way could she have that kind of strength! "Stop it!" he shouted, his own efforts to pull his hand back causing even more pain. She giggled and kept her grip and pulled until he was smashed up against the picket-fence stalagmites, too big to pass between the narrow gap between them. The tendons along his arm began to ring with pain, and his fingers tingled from lack of blood. "Stop it!" he screamed. "You're going to pull my hand off!"

That's exactly what she did.

HISTORY PART 4
DAD'S LAST STAND

"…I thought there was a something in his voice that came familiarly to my ears, and yet I don't know him…."

— *Varney the Vampire or, The Feast of Blood*
by James Malcolm Rymer, 1847

CHAPTER 46

Melanie didn't really wake up because she hadn't really fallen asleep. She had been hanging on the edge of consciousness, aware of sound but not sight, and she was tired, oh, so very tired. She had never known exhaustion like this ever in her life. Her muscles hurt, her bones ached — she was sure that if the tips of her hair could scream, the air would be filled with tiny wails of pain. Her hair was certainly damp. Sweat, all sweat. Her whole body was slick with it. She may as well have just run an all-uphill marathon or scaled Half Dome Peak using nothing but toothpicks and dental floss.

So much effort. So much sweat. She was thirsty.

As if she had spoken aloud, a kind voice said, "Here, Melanie," and a straw was placed in her mouth. She sucked up as much cool water as she could as fast as she could. "No, not too much at once," the voice said, and the wonderful straw was pulled away. Melanie wanted to ask for it again, but the voice continued, "You're doing fine, Melanie. Let's just adjust your bed a little, because we have a surprise for you."

Surprise? Melanie blinked her eyes rapidly to clear them. "Hey, I've been here before," she croaked.

"Well, you've been here awhile," said the voice. It belonged to a nurse. Her face was as kind as her voice, with healthy pink cheeks and a wide smile. She had a peculiar twinkle in her eyes. "You know, I've worked here for eight years, and I still feel giddy at this moment every single time. Get ready."

Get ready for what? The biggest surprise Melanie could see was that she was in the damned hospital again. *Oh great, what happened this time? Did I wig out during the abortion? Did I wig out on the way to the clinic? Did one of those right-to-lifers beat me up?*

"Here we are!" Kind Nurse said as another nurse entered the room.

"Take him carefully, like this," said the second nurse, and she placed a warm wriggly bundle into Melanie's arms.

Melanie stared into the baby's forget-me-not blue eyes. "Oh, shit," she said.

The two nurses exchanged surprised grins. "I've heard new mothers say a lot of things, but never that," said Kind Nurse.

Melanie lay in the hospital bed and held her baby son. *What the fuck is happening?!*

The answer came. Oh, it came, all right. Dozens, hundreds, thousands of memories stampeded into her brain, exactly eight month's worth. *I never went to have the abortion. I straightened up my act and never had another breakdown over Jon. I put some of my own furniture in the house, sold Excalibur Books and went back to my research job. I read every baby book on the market and made sure I got the best prenatal care money could buy. I wanted this baby more than anything.* She squeezed her eyes shut, feeling faint. *Oh God, Pan did it again!*

Kind Nurse immediately moved to grab the baby in case Melanie dropped him. "Are you all right?" she asked.

Hell no, I'm not all right! "Yeah," Melanie whispered. "Yeah, just... it's just... so much..."

"I know the feeling," Second Nurse said. "When I had my first, a baby girl, I felt so giddy I thought I was drunk."

I wish I was. And with that thought, Melanie shoved her baby son into Kind Nurse's waiting arms and abruptly threw up all over herself.

Kind Nurse held the now crying baby away from the mess while Second Nurse rushed forward. "Hang on, let me get that." She bundled up the ruined blanket and set it aside. "I'll call the doctor—"

"No," said Melanie. "No, I'm just..." *Spinning out of control through Time like a damned leaf in a cyclone!* "...I'm okay now."

"You're sure?"

Melanie wanted to slug Second Nurse, but she didn't have the energy. "Like I said, it's just... overwhelming."

The two nurses watched her for a moment, caught each other's eyes, and then Second Nurse went to get a clean blanket for Melanie's bed.

"Can I have him?" Melanie asked Kind Nurse.

Kind Nurse handed the crying baby over. "What are you going to name him?" she asked.

Melanie cooed to the baby and gently bounced him in her arms. He settled down, gazing up at her face with those big blue eyes that seemed to physically grab her own and hold on for dear life. The mother-child connection was complete. "Jon," Melanie said softly. "His name is Jon."

CHAPTER 47

Morning at last. The suns ignited their furnace fires and warmed the island. Birds twittered. Seagulls wheeled. Flowers unfurled their petals, and a thousand creatures began their day.

Stuart had his plan.

He rap-tapped his hook on Smee's cabin door. "Miss Darling?" How he loved his voice this morning! Smooth and resonant and, if he did say so himself, commanding. He had wondered, upon singing as he dressed, that his English accent was thicker than it had been only the day before. That was ridiculous, of course, and he had dismissed the notion. "Miss Darling?" he repeated, sing-songy, and rapped again. "I know you're in there, my dear. Please be so kind as to respond."

"Why?" She sounded bored.

"I would like to invite you to breakfast. Would you do me the honor?"

Silence.

"It has been four days, Miss Darling. Surely you'd appreciate a bit of fresh air, hm?"

Pause. "Only if you do something for me."

"And what might that be?"

"Make pancakes."

How cute! Through trial and suffering, all the little tot wanted was a plate of flapjacks. "I believe that can be arranged, Miss Darling.

Shall we say eight o'clock?" Stuart opened his pocket watch. "It is now seven twenty-five. What say you, my dear?"

Pause. "Okay."

"Excellent. Till then."

Stuart stepped out onto the sunny quarterdeck and observed his crew. Smee had them scrubbing and cleaning already, shiny with sweat and grunting with effort. Stuart stretched luxuriously and ascended the stairs to the poop deck. He liked it up there. It was captain's territory. He could be alone with the wind.

He gazed out at the island shore, thinking of Wendy's timid "okay" to his breakfast invitation. Her pretentious womanly airs were gone, it seemed, drained away by four lonely days in a small musty cabin. Stuart felt bad about that. She had been so spunky and so very entertaining. Had she been broken that easily?

Codswallop, he decided. *She's tired, angry, spiteful, any number of things. But defeated? Her? Never. She knows that Pan hasn't abandoned her. Anything but. She knows he's biding his time, that's all, so she is doing the same. The question is, what might Pan be waiting for?*

As much as that question nagged at him, there was no answering it, so Stuart turned his attention to the coming meal. He descended belowdecks and saw to it that burly old Cookson concocted the flapjack batter as daintily as possible. "No no, not so much salt!" he admonished the cook, slapping the man's gnarly hand. "Brimstone and gall, she's not one of the mates who works in the hot suns day in and day out. She's a little girl!"

"She's bad luck, yer ask me," Cookson muttered, stirring the batter in a big bowl with a wooden spoon.

"I did not ask you," Stuart snipped at him. He headed back to the weather deck, adding over his shoulder, "Cook them slowly so they get fluffy!"

"Yeah yeah — sir," Cookson grumbled.

This kind of snarly banter was the usual mode of communication with Cookson. Stuart didn't particularly like the man, but Cookson was inventive with food and had thus far managed not to poison anybody, accidentally or otherwise. He would make the pancakes as well as they could possibly be made.

Stuart decorated the rosewood table himself, setting out a vase of jungle flowers, fine linen napkins, and his personal china and silver. A plate of fresh fruit finished the settings, along with a mug of hot chocolate for Wendy and coffee with milk for himself and Smee. *Ah yes, Mister Smee. He doesn't yet know he's coming!* He ordered Foggerty to fetch the bosun.

"What, breakfast agin?" Smee asked him, scratching his head. Little white flakes fluttered down from his scalp. "Yeh got another plan up yer sleeve, eh, sar?"

"Just be on time," Stuart answered. "And wash your hair, or what's left of it. You're snowing."

"Sar?" Smee scratched his head harder. More flakes danced. He shrugged. "I s'pose yeh'll be wanting Mister Cecco then, too."

"No, just you."

At that, Smee gave him a curious look. Stuart detected a hint of apprehension in those bloodshot eyes. The captain rarely invited his two friends to dine. He had never ever invited only one of them. *Smee has every reason to wonder,* Stuart thought with a mischievous grin.

At eight o'clock sharp he pushed his key into the lock and opened Smee's cabin door. He hadn't yet seen how well the bosun had tidied the place since the crazy gunport tug-o-war. It had been patched together quite well. Wendy, as always in her white nightie with her feet bare and her long brown hair draped over her shoulders, looked as fresh as a jungle bloom among the bright fabric-covered bulkheads. She greeted Stuart by saying, "I read the book about Greek mythology." She held up one of the books that Stuart had lent her.

This was hardly the greeting Stuart expected. "Really?" he said. "What do you think?"

"Your mother must have been a Gorgon."

Stuart laughed. "You flatter me, Miss Darling. Actually, my mother was a pussycat compared to my father."

"Was he a pirate?"

Stuart gave her a grave look. "No, Miss Darling, he was far worse. He was a married man."

A great splutter of laughter slipped out of Wendy's mouth, something which she obviously did not expect, judging by the odd mixture of amusement and confusion on her face. Stuart enjoyed the sight. If things went according to plan, this would be the last time he'd see her so gay. He escorted her down the narrow corridor to his cabin where they found Smee waiting, cleaned up — as much as the bosun ever cleaned up, anyway — and with wet hair. *Good*, Stuart thought. *At least he won't shed in the coffee.*

As before when Smee had been among those sitting at the table, Cookson served the meal. And as before, Cookson made it clear with a glare at the bosun that he did not appreciate this annoying shift of duties. When at last the huffy cook left, Stuart harrumphed. "Well. That was a dubious start to what I'd hoped would be a pleasant repast."

Smee picked up a roasted breadfruit. "Sar, if I may ask..." He hesitated. "What's on yer mind?"

Stuart held out the dish of flapjacks so that Wendy could take some. She smiled shyly as she took two between her knife and fork. Apparently she found them acceptable, at least visually. Stuart set the plate back down. If Smee wanted any, he could get them himself. "Do I look like I have something on my mind, Smee?" he asked.

"Yeh got that spark in yer eye, sar."

"Is that so." He offered Wendy the silver butter plate. She took it, caught between sniffing the butter suspiciously — she must have suspected, and rightly so, that it was made from "ewww!" goat's milk — and listening to the exchange. "Aye, Smee, I suppose I do have something on my mind. You see, I have stumbled upon a most perplexing dilemma. I wish to discuss it with the two of you."

Wendy put the butter dish down so abruptly that it almost tipped over. "With *me?*"

"It pertains to you directly, my dear." Stuart sipped his coffee. "So. Here it is. I am delighted to report that I finally know what I have to do."

Smee swallowed a mouthful of his breadfruit. "In terms o' what, sar?"

Stuart detected a forced joviality in the bosun's tone. Interesting. "Well, to begin with, what I am about to tell you must be kept secret. Can you do that?"

"O' course, sar. I obey yer orders."

"Then I so order. What about you, Miss Darling?"

Wendy's eyes went hard. "I don't make promises to pirate captains."

Stuart shrugged. "Doesn't matter, really. I doubt you'll live through it anyway."

Wendy's fork clattered to her plate.

Stuart paid her no heed. He rose smoothly from his chair and walked around the table. "I want the both of you to know that I finally accept my situation. I do not accept the fate attached to it, but that is another matter. Suffice it to say, I accept that I am indeed trapped in a game, a very special and, I believe, very old game." He reached the cabin door, drew a key from his pocket and locked the lock with a sharp click. "You two know this as well as I do, hm?"

"Sar—"

"Shut up, Smee. Just listen." Stuart stepped back to his chair and sank into it with the grace of an aristocrat. "I am supposed to battle Peter Pan. That's what this," and he gestured airily at their surroundings, "is all about. But, silly uncooperative me, I don't want to play along. Now, I've tried several times to find a means of escape, but my plans never work. I've a feeling they never will. That's part of the game, too." He gave Smee a knowing look. "Isn't it?" Smee started to speak but Stuart waved him quiet. "Well, the answer came to me last night in a dream — I'm fighting the wrong foe! It's not Pan who controls the game at all. It's *you*." He faced Wendy. "It's your fantasy, your construct. Pan created it, but he created it according to your desires. Alas, there is no back door." He sighed at that. It had been such a good idea. "But then I thought, what do I need a door for when I can simply destroy the place?"

"Whuh?" Smee blurted, his mouth full.

"You sound a mite too concerned, Mister Smee. Any particular reason?"

"Well, err, that is..." Smee struggled to swallow. "Sar, yeh'd be messin' with powers yeh don't understand."

"And you do?"

"'Course not, sar. But I swear by Johnny Corkscrew that this island has a power about it that shouldn't be disturbed. Ask any o' the men, sar, they'll say the same."

"I'm sure they will. They're all constructs like you. But I am real, and I want my life back. So. If I take *you* out of the picture," and he pointed once more at Wendy, "the Neverland will have no reason to exist. It will dissolve, and I will be returned to where I belong."

"Sar..." Smee wrung his hands. "Sar, yer talkin' mad."

"Mad, am I?" Stuart slapped the bosun's face. The move was so quick that Smee never saw it coming. "Aye, I'm mad all right, and with just cause, so shut up and do as I say!" He grabbed a coiled rope off the harpsichord bench, a rope he had placed there earlier, and threw it at Smee. "Tie up the girl and gag her."

Wendy ran for the door. Stuart watched her impassively, keeping Smee in his peripheral vision. While Wendy tried in vain to open the locked door, pounding and kicking it and crying for help, Smee fumbled with the rope as if he didn't know what it was.

"Obey me, Smee."

The bosun saw a flash of the hook and moved to obey.

"No no!" Wendy screamed as Smee captured her flailing arms. "Peter won't let you do this!"

"We're going to see what Master Pan can and cannot do very soon, my dear. In the meantime..." Stuart pulled his lace kerchief from his sleeve. "Smee?"

Even as he overpowered her, Smee remained gentle, an expression of dismay on his hard face. He bound Wendy's hands and hobbled her feet. As he deposited her back in her chair, Stuart waved the kerchief in her face. "Open up."

Wendy pursed her lips together. "Mm-mm!"

Stuart poised his hook over her ear. "You'll still be able to hear, I think, but matching earrings will be out of the question."

She opened her mouth with a squeal of alarm. Stuart stuffed the kerchief in, muffling the sound until Wendy ran out of air. Then he faced Smee. "Hand over your pistols."

"Say what, sar?"

"I won't ask again."

Smee pulled his pistols from his belt but did not hand them to his captain. He stood, a pistol gripped in each hand, and studied Stuart like he might study the clouds in the sky to see what weather lay ahead. The promise of suns from scattered puffs of fluffy cumulus?

The hint of a mild drizzle from slowly-building stratus? The threat of storm-foreboding wind-whipped cirrus?

"Are you contemplating shooting me, Mister Smee?" Stuart spread his arms. "Go ahead. I won't die, not by your hand anyway. I'm actually getting used to pain, too, so please, do what you have to do. Makes no difference to me. This scenario will play out one way or another because I'm not going to give up. Ever."

"Sar," Smee began. He made small helpless circles with the pistols in his hands, like he was trying to stir the air. "Please don't."

"Don't what?" Stuart asked, easily relieving Smee of one pistol, which he stuffed into his belt, then the other, which he held casually as if it were a spoon or a bit of bread. "How do you know what I'm going to do?"

"Yer thinkin' o' killin' the girl!"

"Why would it matter to you if I did?"

"It matters to Pan, sar, an' that means trouble fer all of us."

Stuart laughed. "What Pan does to you is your problem." He aimed the pistol at Smee. "There's another coil of rope behind you on the dresser. Please bind your legs with it."

Smee got angry. "Cap'n, fer Chrissake—!"

He got no farther. Stuart brought the pistol muzzle to his grizzled throat. "How peculiar that only yesterday I told you I would never forget your loyalty. You and Cecco did save me from the crocodile, putting yourselves at risk to do so. That makes it doubly difficult for me to treat you this way. I want you to know that." He reached into his pocket with his hook and tugged out a red scarf. "But then, you've been lying to me, Mister Smee. You've been lying to me since the day you fished me out of the bay."

Smee's eyes went wide.

"Ah! You remember that day, too, I see. It was the day I arrived here. But dear me, how could you possibly know about that? Technically, it never happened, hm? I've always been captain of the *Jolly Roger*, isn't that right?" Smee hadn't yet tied his legs. Stuart, keeping the pistol at the man's throat, brought up his hook and aimed it at Smee's eye. "How would you like to wear a patch?"

Smee sat down and began to tie his legs. "Sar, please, yer not well—"

442

"Damn straight I'm not." Stuart backed away, flapping the red scarf with a series of slaps as if the very air deserved punishment. "You're going to tie your own gag with this, but first you're going to answer a question for me. Where is the Hollow Hill?"

Smee froze.

"Ha! I knew it! Oh, dear Smee, you aren't quite as clever as you think you are." Stuart leaned back against the rosewood table, keeping the pistol aimed. "Want to hear something else? I know my name. It's Jon. Not James, like everyone keeps calling me. Jon. I don't remember much about him, but he was me. Thanks to Wendy, I had a dream about him last night. And about the Hollow Hill. Strangest of all, when I woke up, you were speaking my name. You weren't there, of course. It was a memory... I think. But it was quite clear. You were calling me Jon as if you knew who I really was. How could that be, I wonder?"

"Sar—"

"Don't answer, fool, it was a rhetorical question. You see, a number of singular aspects of our relationship came together in my head last night." Stuart began to pace, waving the pistol around for emphasis as he spoke. "For instance, why would a bosun be his captain's valet? A bosun has plenty of duties on his own. Also, why would a bosun tend my wounds when it should be Cookson's duty? I began to ponder these oddities, so I went through my log. True, I have no memory of writing all those entries, but they are in my handwriting, no doubt about that, so... well, there you are. What I found was a series of curious notations I'd never connected before. For example, it was your idea to go to Beggar's Port. In fact, you harped on about it until I gave in. And look what happened that very night. The sirens attacked the ship and... I don't know... something bad happened to me, something very very bad. For some reason, I think you let it happen."

"Sar—"

"Later when we reached the Port, I lost the only woman I have ever loved. I had to kill one of my own men for it. Again, I don't know why, but I'm sure it's all because of you."

"Sar, yer ravin'. The men wanted off the damned ship, is all. We'd been at sea fer months."

"We were moored right here at Pan's island! The men had all the bloody shore leave they could want!"

"Sar, it ain't safe here!"

Stuart shrugged. "Having sampled the amenities of the Port, I find it difficult to see much of a difference. But I'm not finished. What about the meeting with Chief Roars Like a Bear? That is a fine puzzle, to be sure, Mister Smee. You wanted too much to translate for me when it was clear that Princess Snapdragon could do so."

"What's odd about that?" Smee said. "I don't trust them savages, an' you don't either. Why yeh used her, I dinno. If yeh ask me, things mighta turned out better if yeh'd listened to me."

"Perhaps," Stuart admitted. "But what really bothers me is how you know their language to begin with. No one else does."

"Yeh know me background, sar. I've been all over the islands fer half me life. I learned the native tongues an' plenty o' variations."

"Uh-huh." Stuart ambled over to Wendy in her chair. He checked the knots on her ropes and gave her gag another poke to make sure she couldn't work it out of her mouth. "I could mention other things. How you never fail to hand me a drink, for instance. Easier to manage a drunk, I suppose. Or how you tried to keep me from finding the past log books. Or how you said only yesterday that I was fighting the devil himself. Not the most unusual of statements under the circumstances, I grant you. It was how you said it." Stuart stopped pacing and aimed the pistol at Smee's forehead. That familiar weathered face seemed so different, so fascinatingly small, when viewed down the barrel of a gun. "What really clinched it for me, though," he said dreamily, imagining Smee's forehead with a hole in it, "was something you said about the Fairy Falls. Remember when we mapped the area? Actually, I don't remember much... it's like I wasn't really there... but I do recall something you said. You referred to the place as a fairy domain. You said the fairies would defend it to the end. I didn't make much of it at the time, but now it strikes me as a peculiar thing for you to say. Why would the fairies fight to the end for a waterfall, Mister Smee? They have the whole island to play in. Plenty of other waterfalls to claim." Stuart lowered the pistol. "What's so special about that one?" He went to the liquor cabinet and rapped on the panel with his hook. The move created a dilemma — which item to carry, pistol or bottle? Not much of a choice, really. Stuart set the pistol down, opened the bottle and drank. "Unless that's where the Hollow Hill is," he finished, wiping his mouth on his sleeve.

Smee was tying the last knot on his legs. "Sar, I don't know what yeh've got in mind, but please listen to me. Yer not well. Yer talkin' crazy like. I know yesterday was an awful ordeal, but why take it out on yer ol' Smee? Fer Chrissake, yeh've got me tyin' meself up like a pig at a roast!"

Stuart nodded. "That's because you're going to stay here, Mister Smee. I don't think you'll like what I have in mind. I think you might try to turn the men against me."

"Never!" Smee declared.

"I appreciate your enthusiasm. I don't believe it, but I appreciate it." The red scarf was still dangling from his hook. Stuart tossed it to Smee. "Gag yourself, if you please."

"Sar, there's no such place as the Hollow Hill!"

"Don't make me kick you."

"I'm beggin' yeh, sar! Don't go there!"

Stuart snorted. "Ha, so it *does* exist! It's a poor liar who can't keep his story straight, Smee."

There was no indication of guilt or embarrassment on Smee's face. He radiated a sense of urgency that almost broke through the madness of Stuart's scheme. Almost. "It's dangerous, sar," the bosun said. "Please listen to me. I'm yer friend! The only one yeh've really got."

"The fact that you're so eager for me to stay away serves to confirm my suspicions," Stuart responded lightly. "The Hollow Hill does exist. It is located somewhere near the Fairy Falls. And inside lies the secret to Pan's power."

Smee did nothing, made no reaction, no words, no sounds at all. But his ruddy cheeks went pale.

"Good! Ha ha, I'm right again! I'm right, I'm right!" Stuart did a little jig and drank from his bottle. "What happened was, you see, Wendy let slip that Pan goes there often, although he never lets her join him, the chauvinistic piglet. Whether or not the second point is true, I believe the first one is true, and it is vital to my escape. Whereas Wendy is the rudder that steers this foul ship—"

Smee let out what sounded like a sob and bowed his head.

Stuart couldn't figure out why he would do that. He stopped, genuinely concerned. "What's this about?"

Smee shook his head, eyes downcast.

"Smee, Smee, I thought you'd be pleased with my brilliant deductions. I had a headache by the time I had it all figured, you know. I'm a pretty smart man, but these days thinking hard for a long time sort of... hurts." Stuart drank from the bottle. "Anyway, I concluded that since Pan rules the fairies — I believe I'm correct in that, he orders Tinker Bell around enough — the fairies must worship him. All gods need worship, eh? And Pan is a god... or something akin to a god. Is he human? Maybe. But there's more there besides. Bottom line, I'm going to get rid of him by getting rid of whatever's in that hill along with our little virgin in white here. Bye-bye Peter Pan, bye-bye Neverland, hello freedom for Captain Hook." He waved at the red scarf that had landed in Smee's lap. "Tie the gag, Smee. I won't ask again." He watched while his bosun tied a gag over his own mouth. "Tighter," he said, seeing slack. Smee grunted something unintelligible and tugged the scarf tighter. "Good. Knot it." Smee obeyed.

"'Ow uht?" Smee asked, his eyes gleaming with apprehension.

Stuart walked over to him, wary of the bosun's strong hands. They were not tied. Even so, Smee showed no desire to fight his captain. Stuart decided not to give him an opportunity to change his mind. He cracked the brandy bottle over the bosun's head and watched as Smee slumped to the floor, awash in amber liquor. Stuart giggled. "You know I'd only whack you senseless with a bottle of Smiffy's private stock, right? You know that, dear Smee. Enjoy!"

He heard a gasp and turned around. Tears were streaming down Wendy's face. "Ohhh." Stuart strode over to her and gently wiped the tears away. "There there, Miss Darling, don't worry about Smee." Stuart rapped his own skull with his knuckles. "Very hard head. He'll come 'round in no time. Please, don't cry."

Smee had tied her up well. Wendy could hardly move. Still, she tried to shy away from Stuart's touch, howling incoherently behind the kerchief in her mouth.

"Now now," Stuart cooed, "don't thrash around. There's nothing to be afraid of." He grinned. "Yet."

CHAPTER 48

"Mister Barricoe Billy, do come in."

Billy entered Bosun Smee's cabin. "Captain," he asked, "why are you in here?"

Stuart was standing by Smee's sewing machine with his hands behind his back, an innocent smile on his face. At his feet was an open trunk which he had emptied of Smee's fabric scraps beforehand. "I have a special favor to ask of you, son," he said. "Come here."

At the word "son," Billy practically exploded with pride. He hurried over to his captain, eager to serve. "Aye, sir?"

Stuart was holding a wooden spoon behind his back. In the spoon lay a small wad of cotton. He held it out. "Smell this and tell me what you think. Don't touch it, just sniff it."

Baffled and blindly obedient, Billy sniffed the cotton. He passed out.

Stuart laughed. "Sorry, Billy." He set the spoon down and picked Billy up off the deck. It was a simple ruse, really. Billy could foil his plan and therefore had to be dealt with. Tying him up would not suffice — Stuart had to be sure the boy would not awaken until his plan was complete. So he stuffed Billy into the trunk, along with the wad of Voodoo-poisoned cotton. *Thank you for that, at least, Master Pan,* he thought, remembering how delighted he'd been to find the vial of deadly liquid back among his poison supplies. Either Pan had retrieved it from where Stuart had dropped it during the crocodile attack, or the demon boy had the power to recreate it as needed. It didn't matter to Stuart either way, just so long as he still had the stuff to use.

The vapor shouldn't hurt Bucket Boy permanently, he decided as he closed the lid of the trunk, propping it open a crack with a fold of fabric so the kid wouldn't suffocate. *I put barely a drop on the cotton. It should keep him unconscious as long as the lid is closed this much. And if he does die, well... too bad.*

Stuart exited the cabin and snugged the door closed. Then he locked it and moved to the next phase of his plan.

* * * * *

Up on the poop deck, Stuart waited for Cecco to arrive.

The first mate climbed up the stairs and saluted. "The crew is waiting, Captain."

"Thank you, Mister Cecco."

Stuart had instructed the first mate to gather the crew abaft the mizzen, the usual place for special announcements. He headed for the stairs, giving his hat a jaunty adjustment. He was in full raiment for the occasion, including several new rings on his fingers and an ivory broach at his throat. The broach was carved into the shape of a skull and crossbones, which Stuart had found hysterical when he saw it in his jewelry case. There seemed to be no end to Hook's use of the Banner of King Death.

Funny, though. The moment he'd pinned the broach on, he had stopped laughing. A strange, darkly pleasurable grimness had washed over him. Aye, it was the dismal truth that all his schemes had failed thus far, but this one, ah, this one would be different. He wasn't going to bother fighting Pan or anyone else anymore. He was going to blast his way out of the Neverland and leave nothing behind. *Damn them all,* he thought.

"Sir, where is Mister Smee?" Cecco asked as they both descended the stairs to the quarterdeck.

"I will explain shortly," Stuart replied. "Join the men."

Cecco saluted. "Aye aye, sir."

Stuart stood a pace from the rail for a moment, gathering himself. The men on the main deck could not yet see him, but he could hear them. Casual conversation, a few yells as bickering broke out. *Where two or more are gathered on my deck, there shall be quarreling*, he thought with a snicker. *Just wait, my laddies, just you wait.* He stepped forward and gazed down over the rail.

"Silence, dogs!" Cecco shouted.

The crew quieted. Every eye fixed on the captain.

"I have unfortunate news," Stuart declared. He paused, making them wait for it. "There is a traitor among us!"

Murmurs began.

"The man in question," Stuart continued, "has been in cahoots with Peter Pan for some time. Although I have not thus far discovered how he entered into his heinous agreement with the boy, it appears that Mister Smee—"

The murmurs exploded into gasps and cries of disbelief. Cecco should have ordered silence, but he was as flabbergasted as the rest.

"Aye, our own Mister Smee," Stuart repeated after a distraught wave for silence. "I have suspected his behavior for some time and took it upon myself to uncover his plans. I invited him to breakfast this morning and forced the truth from him. He is presently tied and gagged in my cabin."

"What's he done?" Noodler asked.

"From what I understand, Pan has a store of hidden treasures on the island. These treasures he has plundered from passing ships. From this we must conclude that he and his Lost Brats intended all along to take the booty from the *Jolly Roger* when the time was right. In any case, Smee learned of this hidden trove and struck a deal with Pan. He was to arrange for our cargo to be easily available to the Lost Boys, probably during one of our expeditions ashore. For his troubles, Pan was to grant him a percentage and deliver him straightaway to Beggar's Port where he could then find passage out of the Neverland and so escape our wrath."

"But de Port, she move," Kamau reminded them all. "Nobody know where she is."

"This is Pan we're talking about, Mister Kamau. Do you honestly believe that he does not know where the Port is?"

Kamau nodded as if to say, "Good point."

"Let me assure you, gentlemen, this is as much of a shock to me as it is to you. Mister Smee has been a great friend to me. I find this discovery..." Stuart paused as if unable to go on. "Most dispiriting." He suddenly pointed down at the men accusingly. "I do not believe that Smee had an accomplice, but I warn you all — if any one of you is found to be in on this most contemptible plot, you shall die horribly, I promise you!" He drew a deep breath, pretending to regain control. "We have been for many years a brotherhood bound by blood. It saddens me to announce this treachery. Worse, it hurts me to have to expose one among us so accomplished and admired." Stuart ended his speech by turning away as if emotionally overcome. The men would believe such a move. Hook was known both for his murderous temper and his disposition toward the more tender sentiments. Bowing his head, he listened to the reactions below.

"It isn't true. I don't believe it." That from Starkey, who had always admired Smee's handiwork on the sewing machine. A strange occupation for a pirate, perhaps, but Starkey recognized and appreciated fine skills when he saw them, and he judged men accordingly.

"He always seemed a mite fancy to me." That snipe came from Cookson. "I think he's been meanin' to get his gain from us and leave fer a long time. A plotter, that one is."

"An ol' pisser like him?" That had to be Mad Mundy. "He got the brain, aye, but what—"

"If anybody could pull the wool over the Cap'n's eyes, it'd be Smee." This was Skylights. "He knows the Cap'n best. He'd know how to hide it from him."

"From all of us," Holston put in.

"But he were always nice t' me!" That from Hawkins, who would defend anyone onboard who treated him with respect. Smee was the only one who ever did.

Stuart faced the men once more, wearing a calculated mask of determination mixed with just a touch of bitter grief. "As required by the ship's articles, we must call a Council to decide this matter. I was forced to render Smee unconscious but—"

"Wait, Captain!" MacDougal waved for attention. "Sir, what about that treasure you mentioned?"

Stuart pressed his hand to his chest and let his jaw go slack, pretending to be appalled by the mention of mere worldly goods at such a mournful moment.

"Yeah!" Jukes chimed in. "If Pan's got a treasure, we oughts'ta find it. Take it for ourselves an' leave before he tries to take ours!"

Several more men chimed in, waving their arms and gabbling like turkeys. Stuart motioned for silence. "Let me get this straight. You're suggesting that we further insert ourselves into this calamitous entanglement?"

It took a good ten seconds for the men to unravel such lofty words. "Ehh... why not?" Roland finally said. "We're pirates, ain't we?"

"Did Smee tell you where the treasure is?" Cecco asked.

Stuart quelled a smile. Even Cecco was going for the bait. *You are pirates indeed, you slithering rat-assed bastards*, he thought happily. "He did not tell me outright," he said aloud, "but I deduced its location."

"Where?" several men asked.

"Equal shares in everything," cried Jukes, "includin' the whereabouts o' booty!"

"Aye!" more men chorused.

Stuart waved his hand at them. The largest of his new rings, a sapphire that hadn't been in his jewel box before... *quell surprise...* glittered beautifully in the sunlight. The men settled down. "Before I tell you anything, I must address one important matter — that of my revenge against Peter Pan. After all, is it not revenge that binds us to this island?" He raised his hook. "Each and every man jack of you has supported me in this regard. I say now, that under these circumstances, I am more than willing to release you from that aspect of your loyalty to me."

The men shouted at once, a barrage of earnestness that summarized their desire to see that Pan pay for the taking of their captain's hand. Stuart humbly waved for silence yet again. "Gentlemen, gentlemen! I am deeply touched, truly I am. But let us be honest. Do you desire petty revenge," and he bellowed out the rest, *"or the plunder of kings?"*

A roar issued from the men.

"Aye, that's what I thought!" Stuart hollered over them. "Prepare to go ashore!" Raising his hook in salute, he ducked into his cabin.

He found Smee still inert upon the floor in a scatter of broken glass and spilled brandy. Stuart watched him for a moment. Good, he was alive and breathing. Stuart gently patted the man's brandy-moistened head. "Poor Smee. You don't deserve this. Or maybe you do. Either way, one thing is for certain." Stuart fetched his extra pistol and began to load it. "I don't deserve any of it."

When his pistol was loaded and tucked neatly in his belt with the other two, he hoisted Wendy to her feet. "Soon comes your most glorious hour," he said softly in her ear, running his fingers through her hair. Soft and shiny, like the silken strands of a siren's mane. He should know. He was the only man to ever have touched one and lived.

He had spotted her in the waves, venturing too far beyond the Lagoon, and he had shot her with a pistol. He'd had to haul her up to the deck by himself — the men were too afraid to have anything to do with her — and he had sliced off a chunk of her with his hook. He had cooked what was approximately her left thigh and eaten it, throwing the rest of her back into the sea.

Tasted like tuna, he recalled, and would have burst out laughing, but the blank mask on Wendy's face quelled it. She was staring at him, just staring. He could not guess at what she might be thinking. He placed his fingers on her neck so that he could feel her pulse. A gentle *thump thump thump,* just like the siren before she had died, flopping on the deck like a human salmon, shrieking so loud the crew had fled belowdecks. Only Stuart had remained above, bearing her screams by sheer willpower so that he could watch her die. *Thump thump thump. Th-thump. Thmp.* She had made a lovely corpse.

Wendy, on the other hand, was very much alive. Her rosy blood was pulsing through her little girl veins, source of life, symbol of death, a cocktail that could go either way. Life. Death. It just depended on circumstance, didn't it?

This girl is no demon fish, he thought. *She is a doll, a perfect porcelain doll, unique, exquisite, beautiful. And breakable.*

* * * * *

The *Jolly Roger* bustled with activity. While Cecco and Foggerty chose men for the shore party, Stuart attended to his own preparations. The men believed they were going for treasure. *Muttonheads*, he thought as he descended the companionway to the gun deck. They'd even forgotten that he had never divulged the all-important whereabouts of the alleged treasures. *Dangle a shiny bob in their faces, and their greed blanks everything else out. God bless 'em.*

He found gunner Alf Mason at the end of the row of cannons on the port side. Squatting like an ape-man behind the long row of black iron hulks, Mason whistled gaily as he poked through a crate of ammunition: cans of case shot, chain shot, bags of grape shot, grenadoes, and other crude but effective projectiles, all designed to wreak maximum mayhem upon an enemy target.

Mason saw his captain approach and stood up, tilting his head precisely enough to keep from smacking his skull on a lantern. He knew the gun deck *better* than the back of his own hand. "Sir?" he said attentively.

"Mister Mason, I require your expertise. Our success on this venture may necessitate the use of force."

That got Mason's attention. "Where exactly are we going, sir?"

One muttonhead emerges from the fog! "Pan's treasure is in a cave, a place on the island known as the Hollow Hill." Stuart watched for the man's reaction.

Mason acted as if he had never heard of it. "Is it in Indian territory? You think we'll be attacked?"

"It lies near the Fairy Falls. Hardly Indian land, but they might have an interest in it for sacred reasons. I want to be prepared for all eventualities."

Mason was nodding. "Understood, sir. You got any ideas how to keep the fairies from attacking?"

"I think I do, Mister Mason. I doubt we'll have trouble on that score."

Mason gave him a nod of acknowledgement. "Aye aye, Captain."

Swept up in his acting role, Stuart gave the gunner a hearty clap on the shoulder. "If Pan has even half the swag Smee claims, we are going to be very rich men, Mister Mason."

That brought a deliciously ghoulish grin to Mason's face. "I like the sound of that, sir!"

Stuart laughed. "Then get to it."

He next visited Rajeev, the bosun's mate, who was assuming the duties of bosun in Smee's absence. He found the man forward, readying the boats. "Mister Rajeev."

"Aye, Captain sir," the man said, bringing his hand up to his turban in salute. He was one of the pirates who loved Hook *because* Hook was a tyrant. He was the type who would only accept orders from someone who commanded absolute authority.

"I want you to prepare a dozen pans of brimstone," Stuart told him. "Our destination is the Fairy Falls, and I'm thinking that the stink of the stuff might be enough to keep the damned gnats away. Surprising that I never thought of it before. An obvious solution, really. What do you think?"

Captain Hook had never asked Rajeev for his opinion on anything before. Stuart watched the man blink his eyes furiously as if thinking and blinking were connected functions. "I am thinking it might work well," he said with a slowly growing smile. "Yes, yes, a very bad stink up their tiny noses!" He nodded enthusiastically. "We leave pans burning all 'round, correct?"

Stuart nodded back. "Exactly. See to it, Rajeev."

"Aye aye, Captain sir!"

Stuart headed back to his cabin. Burning sulfur was a clever idea, true enough, but he couldn't help thinking there was an easier way to combat the fairies. He had a vague recollection that maybe there was a phrase that one could say to them, or some kind of spell one could cast. Certain words could kill them, he knew that somehow, but ponder as he might, Stuart couldn't remember what the words were. *Stow it. Brimstone will do the trick.*

Jules Thatcher caught up with Stuart as he reached the stairs leading up to the quarterdeck. "Captain, will ya be wanting your carriage ashore?"

Stuart thought it over. "No, Mister Thatcher. I suspect that if we don't have to fight out way in, we'll have to fight out way out. Pan won't let us take his, uh... treasure easily. I shall walk with the rest."

"Aye, sir."

"Oh, and Thatcher. Tell Mister Cecco that all members of the shore party are to bring coats or blankets, something to cover their clothes with. Hats as well." At Thatcher's blank look, he explained, "In case the fairies dust us."

"Oh!" Thatcher's round face brightened. "Clever, Captain."

"Let us hope so, Mister Thatcher. Let us hope so."

Stuart returned to his cabin to find Smee still unconscious. Once more he fingered Wendy's silken hair. "What a shame," he said, and took a swig of brandy from a new bottle.

Wendy shouted something from behind her gag.

"Oh, do be quiet. Thanks to you I'm short a valet. Have to do everything myself." He unscrewed his hook from its base, Wendy staring in rapt horror all the while, and screwed on the hair brush. "Peter Pan, the deuce you say," he sneered, and began to brush his curls. When he was done, he unscrewed the brush and threw it at Smee. It hit the bosun's big belly and rebounded to the carpet. Smee didn't twitch.

Stuart abruptly turned and pointed his right arm at Wendy, the silver-capped base of his harness naked. He felt his phantom fingers ghostily reaching for her. "I know what he's doing!" he snarled in sudden rage. "He's waiting! He could rescue you at any time, I'm not so stupid as to believe he couldn't. He could burn this bloody ship to cinders, if nothing else, maroon all of us and leave us for the Indians. I'm no fool, Miss Darling! I know what I'm up against!"

Wendy, her eyes huge with fear, made no sound.

Stuart screwed his hook back on. He took his hat off the tailor's dummy and settled it on his head. Primping in the mirror, he said, "You're to blame as well, little Darling. I am not responsible for what is to come. You decided your fate when you decided to lie to me."

Wendy's expression turned to one of great confusion.

Stuart regarded her in the mirror. "Don't play innocent. You know where the Hollow Hill is and would not tell me. You'll suffer for that, I promise you."

"Mm mmm!"

Stuart turned, daintily putting his hand to his ear. "What ho? She attempts to speak! What might she have to say, I wonder?"

"Mmm mmmm!"

He ambled over to her, slapping his hook in the palm of his hand with each step. "Do I detect a change of heart?" He pulled the kerchief out of her mouth.

Wendy coughed and flapped her tongue, trying to form enough spittle to make it work.

Stuart fetched her a glass of water and held it to her lips so that she could drink. "Now," he said when she was finished. He let the word hang.

"Behind the waterfall."

Three simple words. Behind the waterfall. "That's it?" Stuart asked.

Wendy nodded, miserable with guilt and embarrassment.

Stuart stuffed the kerchief back into her mouth before she had a chance to close it. "Shame on you, Miss Darling. We explored that area. There is no cave behind the waterfall. Nice try."

Wendy briskly nodded her head. "Mm! Mm!"

Stuart leaned close to her. "What could you possibly have to tell me? You said you've never been there. Peter won't let you."

She shook her head. "Mmmm mm mmmmm m mm mmm mm mmmm!"

He pulled out the kerchief again. "Last chance," he warned her.

"Believe it's there," Wendy said meekly. "Believe it's there, and it will be there."

Stuart tried not to show his astonishment. How gloriously obvious! How many cockamamie times was he to look magic square in the eye and not see it? It was the curse of the adult mind, he supposed. *Believing is too easy a solution to problems that become increasingly more complex as one goes through life,* he thought. *Adulthood is a series of terrible faith-bursting noes. No, this idea is ridiculous. No, that could never happen. No, this plan will never work. No, you're being foolish. Yet even the Bible says that a man may move a mountain if he believes he can. The entrance to the Hollow Hill might be right here in my own cabin, if I truly believed it.*

He patted Wendy's cheek. He wanted to say something to her, assure her that she had done good, that he wouldn't hurt her after all. She wanted to hear him say it, too, he could see it in her eyes. She had corrected her mistake. She had told him what he wanted to know. She wanted her just reward.

She would never get it.

Stuart hoisted her to her feet, laughing. "You like adventures," he said to her. "I guarantee this will be an awfully big one."

CHAPTER 49

Two boats brought thirteen pirates, one little girl and two heavy sacks of grenadoes to shore. Stuart was anxious to get to the task ahead, but he cautioned himself not to be foolhardy. He ordered four men to watch the water during the trip, pistols ready, and he ordered silence for all so that any telltale ticking could be heard.

The croc, if it was nearby, chose not to attack. The boats made it safely to shore at the southern end of Pirate's Bay. A ten minute walk from that point would bring them to the creek. The falls and the pool were a small hike from there.

Stuart did encounter one problem from the start, something he expected but was nonetheless irritated when it came about. "What's *she* need to come for?" Jukes asked, indicating Wendy with a wave of his blunderbuss. "She'll slow us down."

Not as much as you will if I chop your bloody leg off, Stuart thought, holding his hook back with effort. Jukes. It was always Jukes. "Pan's treasure is inside a cave," he said tightly. "Mister Smee would reveal no more than that. Miss Darling, however, can take us right to it."

Wendy huffed and puffed behind her gag. It made Jukes laugh. "Yer might as well rip out her tongue, Captain. She ain't gonna say a word!"

"I suggest you follow her example," Stuart told the man. Then he leaned close to Wendy's ear. "Stay quiet, my dear. From here on it is I who must protect *you* from *them*," and he indicated the pirates.

459

As he had during her initial capture, Stuart held a rope tied to Wendy's middle like a leash on a dog. Wendy's hands were still bound, but her hobbles had been taken off so she could walk. Even gagged, she could have made noise enough to cause trouble – Stuart had expected her to try to tell the pirates that the whole story about Pan having treasure was a lie – but she was choosing silence, at least for the moment. *Saving your breath for a better opportunity?* Stuart thought. He didn't anticipate she would get one, but as ever, he was fascinated by her bravery.

He signaled Kamau. The Jamaican took point, and the party slipped into the jungle.

This trail was wider than the others Stuart had traveled. Not surprising. Pirates stamped their way up and down it every day, fetching fresh water for the ship. Long ago they had leveled the trail as best they could, along with slashing all python weed to the ground. The stuff always tried to grow back, which meant that weedlings were uprooted daily. Stuart spotted a few weaving up through the grass, trying to flourish behind other plants. He could almost hear them whispering to each other: *Shhh! Grow quietly! They won't see us if we hide!*

He pulled them up. One writhed in his hand, the tender shoots trying to wrap themselves around his fingers before the detestable plant expired. He threw it down in disgust and crushed it under his boot.

He saw Wendy's eyes gleam with grim satisfaction. A terrible moment passed, one of the few in which Stuart genuinely wanted to hurt her. She knew what was coming, she had to. *She knows, and she'd rather die than tell me.* He fought down the urge to crack her pretty skull open and read the future written on her brains, his future, there in her head, penned in neat crimson letters, most likely with hearts instead of dots over the i's. All little girls seemed to go through that phase. Hearts instead of dots over the i's. He hated that. And bows in their hair. Little girls and their damned bows in their hair. At least Wendy didn't wear a bow in her hair. He would have torn it off and made her eat it if she had.

Mason, ahead of him, stopped walking. They had reached the creek. At the head of the line, Kamau waved.

It was time to don cloaks and hats. The pirates shrugged on a variety of tattered apparel while Stuart waited, content to keep his apparel as it was. *Let the fairies try dusting me. I'll catch one and bite its head off.* Per his orders, Skylights had brought a cloak for Wendy. He set it upon her shoulders and drew the hood over her head, covering her completely.

When the jostlings were over, Stuart gestured to Rajeev. Pans and chunks of yellow brimstone were passed around. The men frowned at the sight of the stuff, but they knew the strategy. Tinder was laid in the pans. Flint and steel birthed feeble flames that grew as fuel was added until each pan glowed with fiery coals. Carefully, the brimstone was crumbled and scattered into the pans.

Noxious yellow smoke soon clouded the air. The rotten egg stink was so bad that the lucky men chosen to carry the pans lifted them high over their hats in a desperate attempt to escape the foul fog. Some men tied neckerchiefs over their noses and pulled their hats and blankets over their heads. Wendy actually whimpered. Noodler had brought two corks, and now he shoved them up his nostrils, grunting with pain but apparently determined to save his olfactories at any cost.

Stuart would have laughed if the stink wasn't so awful. He had brought a perfumed scarf, which he now tied over the lower half of his face. He took a deep breath — through his mouth and with the protection of perfume, and still he could smell the stink — and caressed one of his pistols. The smooth contours of the weapon calmed him.

The stench of the brimstone grew to nauseating proportions in a very short time, but it did the trick. As the pirate band neared the falls, a swarm of fairies flew at them from the north. Stuart heard the soft buzz of a hundred tiny wings and saw pinpricks of light zigging and zagging through the trees, hurtling towards them like pint-sized firebolts. Chipmunk voices gave out shrill war cries, and there came a sudden sensation of being bombarded by a herd of flying toothpicks. His face, neck and hands were pricked and slashed for several seconds before the fairies started looping crazily backwards, screaming out in their wee bell language, coughing and cursing. They regrouped and attacked again, but the expanding yellow miasma again drove them back. Another swarm approached from the east, and another from the west. The same thing happened.

"We gots 'em, Captain!" Mad Mundy said with a husky laugh.

"Hush, fool!" Mason whispered.

"Our presence is known," Stuart told Mason. "The gnats are already on their way to inform Pan, which means we have to hurry." He called to Kamau, "Find the path that goes behind the waterfall!"

Kamau lowered his ridge-like brows. "Captain, dere's no way to get behind de waterfall. We look already."

"We missed it last time," Stuart assured him. "Show some skill, for God's sake."

As Kamau systematically poked and prodded amidst the foliage, Stuart untied his perfumed kerchief and tucked it back into his pocket. The stink of the sulfur wasn't as bad here by the freshwater spray, and he would gladly endure a little discomfort to maintain his illusion of superiority. As he expected, several of the pirates saw what he did and proceeded to remove their own various devices of olfactory armament. Even Noodler pulled out the corks in his nostrils, but he quickly stuffed them back in. "Still stinks," he whined. "Don'tcha smell it, Captain?"

Stuart ignored him.

Four long minutes passed before, to his own obvious puzzlement, Kamau found the path. He insisted to Stuart that it had not been there before — Stuart waved him on with an impatient, "Yes, yes, I'm sure it wasn't." — and quickly led the pirate band along.

The remaining fairies, meanwhile, changed their tactics and began a second attack. They bravely flew into the choking fog just long enough to shower down fairy dust. The pirates maintained their pace. If a sudden wind rose, they would simply discard their outerwear and keep going. After awhile the fairies, realizing the tactic, gave up and waited for Pan. They hovered at a distance in angry red grumbling bunches, surrounding the pirates in a wide circle like guard dogs held in check by short leashes.

The path narrowed as the pirates rounded the Elysian pool of crystal blue with its fringe of green-red bushes, their glossy leaves big enough to cover an entire man. It then rose to a steep climb, bringing them up behind the thundering waterfall. It shrank to a chancy ledge

462

that continued along the cliff behind the falls. The ledge widened to a shelf halfway across and stopped. Beyond that, there was nowhere to go.

The pirates bunched up on the shelf, all of them wanting to get off the narrow ledge. "Notting's here, Captain!" Kamau yelled over the din of the cascading water. "De path stop!"

Stuart held up his hand for silence. He handed the end of Wendy's leash to Cecco and faced the cliff, bringing his hand and hook up so that they rested at head-level against the cold wet rock. He touched his forehead to the rough surface. *This is not rock*, he thought, trying to mentally project his will into the rock itself. *There is a cave here. I believe there is a cave here. The opening is here. I believe this to be true. There is a cave here. I believe it. I believe it with all my heart. I believe it, in fact I know it's here, it must be here, it has to be here because if it isn't here I'm screwed and I refuse to believe that!*

The next thing Stuart knew, he was falling forward with a, "Shiiiiiiiit—!"

* * * * *

He came to in darkness, the kind of darkness without shadow, a darkness so complete that he could detect no significant difference between having his eyes open or closed. He could see neither hook nor hand in front of his face. The ground beneath him trembled as if a herd of horses was galloping past. The air thrummed with a continuous, muffled roar.

He tried to sit up. His hand slipped on a patch of something moist and soft, and he fell back with a grunt. The sounds of his scrabbling, pebbles rolling, his own sharp breathing — none of them created an echo. Every sound, even the tiniest, came wrapped in a thick cottony ball. *Like hiding in the closet when I was little*, he thought vaguely.

"Captain?" It came from high above. Cecco. "Captain!"

The roar... *It must be the waterfall. That's what it is. All that water is crashing down on the rocks above me.*

"Captain, are you all right?"

Stuart climbed wearily to his feet. "No broken bones," he answered, dusting himself off.

"What in blazes happened, sir? What did you do?"

"What does it look like?" Stuart said. "I found a way in."

"But there wasn't—"

"Stow it, Mister Cecco. Throw me down a torch, I can't see a thing down here." He shuffled backwards, hoping he was moving away from the spot where the torch would land. Once he had gotten up, all directional sense had scrambled.

A lightning bolt of orange broke the darkness as a lighted torch dropped at his feet. Stuart stepped back before his boots got singed, then picked the torch up by its long wood handle and held it high, turning in a circle. Rock floor patched with sickly yellow lichen — *That's what my hand slipped on,* he thought. Dull rock walls. A jagged ceiling too high to see. He was in a cave about the size of his cabin aboard the *Jolly Roger.* Unimpressive.

About ten feet up one wall a roundish hole gaped in the rock, like the end of a sewer tunnel. It was just big enough for a man to fit through. After hopping up and down several times, Stuart got a good look into it. It had an unusually smooth surface and was maybe twenty-five feet long. He could see a shaft of light at the far end. *I must have fallen down a hole, hit this tunnel, slid along it and fallen out into the cavern.* No wonder he felt bruised.

The wall opposite the hole — Stuart could now calculate that direction to be north — was split, only barely, by a fissure that ran from floor to ceiling. Stuart held the torch up to it, revealing a narrow passageway. *That must be our path,* he thought, not liking at all how precariously balanced it appeared, as if the walls were going to slam together at any moment. The pirates would have to walk sideways, too, but hopefully not for long.

Well, there was nothing for it. "Oi!" he called to his men. "Are you scugs coming or not? Get the bloody hell down here, or Pan will be all over us before we even find the treasure!"

While he patted more dust from his clothes and retrieved his fallen hat, he heard a soft flopping noise — a coil of rope falling — heavy scrabbling — someone was on their way down. Stuart hopped like a bunny again and caught sight of Mad Mundy crawling his way down the tunnel, using the rope so he wouldn't slide out of control as his captain had. Stuart held up his torch to light the man's way. Mundy managed to drop down without landing on his head.

"I done lived in worse places as this," Mundy concluded after a quick glance around.

Stuart whistled up the tunnel. "The girl next! Untie her so she can crawl! And tell her if she removes her gag, I will shoot her!"

After a moment, Wendy peeked out from the tunnel, obediently gagged. Stuart handed his torch to Mundy and held out his arms. "Jump. I'll catch you."

Wendy did not want to do that.

"Jump, Miss Darling, or I'll tell the man behind you to light your bottom on fire."

Wendy jumped, thrashing when Stuart's arms curled around her. "Mmm mmm mmmm!" she demanded.

"Hold on, hold on." Stuart deposited her on her feet with a gracious smile. In truth, she had boxed him square in the jaw. It hurt. "You're welcome," he said pointedly. "Next time I'll let you fall on your ass, shall I?" He expected another stream of *mmmms*, but Wendy just glared up at him, trying to be her old defiant self. *Difficult to do with naked fear in your eyes, girl.* He had finally crushed her confidence. She was truly afraid of him. *Good. She should be.*

He snatched up the end of the rope still tied around the girl's waist and checked the knot at the small of her back. It was tight. Her hands might be free now, but she would never be able to get free of the rope. "Hotfoot it, Cecco!" he called. "I'm growing old down here!"

One by one the pirates joined their captain. Mason gently pushed the bags of grenadoes in front of him as he crawled, handing them down to Stuart before he dropped down himself. Skylights dragged two bundles of picks and shovels after him, which were then distributed to make the burden even among them. All the men left their fairy-dusted coats and hats behind.

"Noodler is stationed up top at the entrance," Cecco reported after arriving last. "Majdi is with him. They'll keep the brimstone burning so no fairies come in after us."

"They will signal us when Pan shows up?" Stuart asked.

"Aye, one pistol shot if it's Pan, two if the brats are with him. Sir, you do know we may not be able to hear those shots if the cave goes very deep."

"It is a risk we must accept. Let's be off." Stuart indicated the narrow passageway in the north wall. "I presume we go this way," he said to Wendy.

She put her nose in the air without any real disdain to back it up and shrugged as if to say, "How should I know?"

"Ah yes, you've never been here," Stuart drawled. "My mistake." He motioned for Kamau to lead the way.

The fissure mercifully opened into a wider tunnel that twisted and turned, sloping downwards at a good thirty degree grade. Bathing it section by section in flickering orange torchlight, the pirates and their captive followed it for what Stuart calculated to be about five minutes, making their way carefully over the rocky floor, slipping often and cursing when they did.

"Rocks is gettin' slimy," Doff Cockers declared when Wendy, after a couple of close calls, finally fell down with a muffled yelp. She rubbed her hip and held a hand up to Stuart, expecting him to offer her help. He hoisted her up by the rope instead, which got her up but threw off her balance, making her have to fumble for footing all over again.

The pirates laughed. Cecco did not. "James?" he asked quietly.

Stuart gave his first mate a sidelong frown, as much as to say, "Be quiet." He knew how surprised Cecco was to see Hook act with such discourtesy. Stuart was surprised himself. *You don't know what I'm going to have to do,* he tried to tell Cecco with his eyes. *You have no idea what's really going on.*

Jukes resumed the conversation as Wendy reestablished her balance. "The rocks is slimy 'cuz they's wet, toadbrain," he told Cockers. "See 'em shinin' in the torchlight?"

"It's gettin' cold, too," Cockers noted blandly.

"How can the rocks be wet?" asked Scourie. "There's no water down here."

"Cap'n," said Skylights, "if the treasure's heavy, we're gonna have us the devil's own time haulin' it outta here."

"What if it's big?" Mad Mundy asked. "Y'know, like them gold statues what we stole from the gov'nor o' Hispañiola?"

"Martinique," Cecco corrected him.

"Whatever," Mundy said.

Scourie made a greedy guttural sound. "Damn difficult to carry, but what a fortune!"

"'Zactly," said Mundy. "How'll we get somethin' big like that outta skinny tunnels like that one behind us what we just been through?"

"One step at a time, gentlemen," Stuart soothed them, flicking Wendy's leash. "Let us find the treasure first."

"Captain!" It was Kamau from the front of the line.

Stuart picked his way down to the man, tugging Wendy after him.

"What you make o' dat?" Kamau was staring at something about thirty feet ahead.

Stuart took the Jamaican's torch and held it high. "I don't know," he said. It might have been a dead end, or the opening to a large cavern, or maybe it was a cliff at the edge of a black abyss. Whatever it was, the torchlight could not penetrate it. Stuart moved forward with Kamau at his side and Wendy behind. Step by step they progressed, and still the torchlight did not illuminate the dark patch. They reached it. Stuart lifted his hand. Gingerly he pressed his fingertips against it.

It was like touching a wall of wispy cotton candy. Some form of matter existed here, but it was nothing the pirates had ever encountered before. It gave way around Stuart's fingertips, parting like a school of fish divides around an obstacle in its path. His fingers grew fainter the farther he pushed them into... whatever it was.

He pulled them out. The stuff closed in to remake the solid wall. His fingers were dry. The tips tingled as if a whore had just sucked on them. "It's a magical barrier," he told Kamau. "Like in the forest." He turned to Wendy. "What's behind it?"

"Mm mm!" Wendy said.

Kamau scowled at her. "Mon, you a nasty one, girl."

"Captain, the forest barrier is a fog, nothing like this," Cecco said, joining them. "And it's white, not black."

"Den dis is something else," Kamau concluded. "A portal?"

Stuart scratched his nose with his hook. Was this the secret doorway he had been hoping for, a doorway leading out of the Neverland? *It could be anything, James. Don't be hasty.* "I suggest we throw something through," he said.

"Her," said Kamau with a nod to Wendy.

"Mmmmmm!"

Stuart shook a warning finger in Kamau's face. "Control yourself, heathen, or I'll throw you in head first." He gave Wendy's leash to Cecco, freeing his hand, and took out his sulfur-abused kerchief. "Let us begin with this." He tossed the lacy cloth into the barrier. It penetrated partway and hung there in midair, halfway in and halfway out.

Both Cecco and Kamau took a wary step back. Wendy took a step forward in fascination. As for Stuart, he moved in until his nose was almost touching the edge of black. "Cloth must be too light to penetrate all the way," he said, noting how the inserted half of his kerchief appeared faded like his fingers had, as if it was far away while still being within his grasp. He tugged the little cloth out and examined it. Undamaged. "Cecco, fetch something heavier."

All the pirates had shuffled closer to see the strange spectacle. Cecco had only to reach out to seize Jukes' bedizened hat. "Hey!" Jukes said. "You can't just—"

"Aye, you talking turd, I can," Cecco responded. He passed the hat to Stuart.

Stuart was astounded at how heavy the thing was. No wonder Jukes was so stupid. He'd spent years weighing his brain down with magpie booty. Stuart curled his wrist and with a snap sent the hat twirling through the barrier. It vanished.

"That was my hat!" Jukes cried.

"Shhhhhh!" someone hissed at him.

Through the noise, Stuart was pretty sure he heard the hat land on a firm surface beyond. "Sounds like there's ground on the other side."

"I say we push Jukes through," Kamau suggested. "If he scream, we know not to follow."

"I heard that, ya snake-haired savage," Jukes snapped.

Stuart seriously considered Kamau's idea, if for no other reason than it would be extremely funny. *But what if that's not just a barrier?* "No, Mister Kamau," he said. "I shall go through first." He tucked his kerchief back up his sleeve. "Wait and listen. Hopefully we'll be able to hear each other." *And if it's a doorway out, you can all stand here waiting till Hell freezes over as far as I care!*

"What if we can't hear you?" Cecco asked.

The man the pirates called Captain Hook flashed a cheerless toothy grin. "What's life without a little adventure, hm?"

Cecco was not amused. "Be careful, James."

"Oh, I'm not going alone." Stuart retrieved Wendy's leash from Cecco and grabbed the nearest torch. Mad Mundy didn't expect it, and he gave a startled *eep!* as it was plucked from his hand. Then Stuart squared his shoulders and stepped into the barrier, pulling Wendy in after him.

His torch immediately sputtered and winked out. The light of the torches behind him went dim and disappeared altogether, plunging him into an inky void. He tried to speak to Wendy and found he could not. His lips could form words, but his breath carried no sound. The leash was still in his hand. She was behind him, then, wasn't she? He tried to turn around to look, but his body would not turn. Nor could he step backwards. This was nothing at all like the white barrier in the Indian forest. This void somehow propelled him forwards, step by step, while giving him no hint as to his destination.

Three steps in and the temperature plunged. His skin seemed to clamp closer to his bones, making him feel squeezed inside of himself like an overfilled sausage. Invisible spiderweb wisps gently snagged at his clothes and hair. His breath exited his mouth in frosty plumes.

A fifth step, and he heard a noise, though nothing like the singing produced by the white barrier in the forest. This was more like breathing, a strange steady thread of air flowing rhythmically in and out. In and out of what, he had no idea, nor did he want to know. He took another step and another, wondering if he might be damned to walk in this stringy nothingness forever, wondering if the barrier was ever going to end—

—and then he emerged into the most beautiful place he had ever seen. If his torch had still been burning, he wouldn't have needed it.

He had entered a world of kaleidoscopic light, sparkles and shimmers of a kind that could only come from thick blankets of live fairy dust. "Fairyland," he breathed in awe.

There was no way to know how big the cave was. To Stuart it seemed that a path wound forever through a vast labyrinth of variegated rock. Dozens of great lumpy stalagmites rose up from an uneven limestone floor, some looking like giant droopy half-melted ice cream cones, others like segmented poles. Many met icicle-like stalactites reaching down from the tall ceiling to create solid columns of slurring reds, browns and crusty whites. Some of the columns sprouted unlikely arms of strange dripping green, making them look like stone trees.

Directly over his head a series of ancient calcite drips had created long rippling curtains of red, green, and honey gold that reminded Stuart of the great Northern Lights. Crystalline dripstone had frozen in a cascade over a crumble of rocks like too much vanilla frosting over cinnamon rolls. Walls were spotted with what looked like cauliflower heads — quartz that had taken thousands of years to ooze through cracks far enough to amass into clusters of bumpy white knobs.

Everything sparkled with dust.

Stuart stared in astonishment at the glittering fantasy surrounding him, forgetting about Wendy, forgetting what he was even there for. The air was warm and filled with the scent of flowers. *How can that be? I'm underground!* No matter. He had entered a realm where magic didn't just exist, it *breathed*. It enticed life from solid rock in the form of moss, lichen and delicate ferns that huddled in cracks and crevasses, defying logic and growing despite the lack of soil and adequate light. Magic allowed red, blue, orange and purple butterflies to flitter amongst the totem-pole-like columns and alight on squat palms and jungle flowers that had no business growing in limestone. Birdsong, the last thing Stuart expected to hear in this place, twittered cheerfully, though where the birds were remained a mystery. He saw none, though he did hear the flutter of wings despite the river flowing noisily below the rough stone bridge upon which he stood.

"Mm mmmmmm..."

Stuart whirled around. Wendy. It was only Wendy, making some fuzzy comment about the fantastic scene. He had forgotten about her. His mission came back to him. "Do you know where we are?"

Wendy shook her head.

Stuart turned back to the barrier. "Cecco, can you hear me? Kamau! Foggerty!" No answers came. He touched the black wall.

Solid.

"Bugger all!" With a sudden and rather irrational idea of breaking the thing, Stuart swung his hook at it. It struck and immediately rebounded with a rubbery boinging sound, sending a jolt of pain up his arm. "Goddamn motherfucking *ouch!*"

Wendy laughed.

"You think this is funny, do you?" Stuart spat at her. "Did it ever occur to you, Miss Darling, that if I am trapped, you're trapped as well?"

"Mmm mm mm mm!" Wendy said.

Stuart debated briefly with himself, then untied her gag. If the pirates couldn't hear him through the wall, then they wouldn't hear Wendy, either. She couldn't blow his ruse.

"Peter will find me," she said defiantly, however cottony, once the gag was removed. With her tongue dry, her pronunciation was thick.

"Pan doesn't know where you are," Stuart said.

"I'm back on the island. Peter knows everything that happens here."

As if to prove her point, a voice cried out, "Halloooo!"

Wendy hopped up and down, waving her arms. "Peter! Here I am!"

CHAPTER 50

Stuart tried to look everywhere at once. A futile effort. The cavern was so full of hiding places that he could have spent a year checking them all. Damn, the boy bastard had been waiting for him! *He knows my plan! How?* Stuart clenched his jaw. *No, he does not know my plan. He only knows I want out. That would be enough to put him on the alert.*

"Pan!" he called. "Show yourself, you devil!"

"Halloooo!" Pan answered. The word bounced gaily back and forth through the stone space, making it impossible to determine whether its speaker was near or far, up or down. "Hallooo!" This time the voice was a little deeper, with a crisp London accent. "Hallooo!" Deeper still. Stuart could have sworn it was his own voice. "Hallooo!" It *was* his own voice, Hook's voice. "Mister Cecco! Mister Foggerty! Can you hear me?" Pan bellowed, imitating Stuart perfectly.

"Aye!" came Cecco's muffled reply through the barrier. "We were getting worried, Captain!"

"Cecco, that's not me!" Stuart exclaimed. Beside him, Wendy giggled. Her courage was back full force, thanks to Pan's presence.

"Is de barrier safe for us to pass tru?" asked Kamau.

"No, confound it! Stay right where you—"

"Aye, come through!" Pan told the pirates jovially. "I've found the treasure!"

Happy whoops and cheers filtered through the barrier. Stuart saw the faint images of the first pirates penetrating the void. "Cecco, stay back! It's a trick! Cecco, you bloody fool, listen to me!"

Wendy was laughing now. Hidden behind one of hundreds of stalactites and stalagmites, Peter Pan giggled mischievously.

"Pan!" Stuart shouted, incensed. "Come out where I can see you!"

"Red Rover, Red Rover, let Cecco come over!" Pan sang as Cecco emerged first through the barrier.

He came through transparent. Flabbergasted, Stuart reached out. His hand passed through Cecco's body as if his first mate were a ghost. "Captain? James!" Cecco looked right through Stuart. "Where are you?"

"I'm bloody right here in front of you!" Stuart cried, poking and waving at the insubstantial figure.

Wendy clutched her stomach and howled with laughter. Furious, Stuart moved to slap her. He stopped himself just in time and, converting his fury into words, addressed the cavern. "Pan! Come out and face me or prove yourself a yellowbellied pantywaist son of a bitch coward!"

The only reply he got was a piggy snort of mirth.

Transparent pirates were passing through the barrier in twos now, confused by their captain's apparent absence. "Where is he?" Mason asked.

"Where's *he*? Where's *we*?" Mad Mundy whispered.

"My hat!" Jukes spotted his hat, a see-through bundle of sparkles slouching on a weird mushroom-like rock. He happily picked it up and fitted it on his see-through head.

"Captain," called Scourie, "are you hiding? Is this some kind of joke?"

"No joke at all, Mister Scourie," Pan answered for Stuart. "I'm down this way! Follow the trail!"

Stuart whirled to his left. Pan's last comment had come from that direction, he was sure of it. But there was no trail leading that way. After some thirty-five feet in that direction the floor lifted and squeezed itself into an ever-narrowing path that melted right into a solid wall. The wall was decorated with so many bulging cascades of fairy-dusted white and red flowstone it couldn't have been missed by a blindfolded man. The pirates, however, led by Cecco, were obeying their "captain" and walking straight for it, along some phantom trail that only they could see.

"Stop, you idiots!" Stuart shouted, even though he knew they couldn't hear him. How could he stop them? He needed them! He especially needed the grenadoes carried by Mason and Skylights, who struggled under their weight even though Stuart could see right through the bags.

With a furious growl, he pulled out a pistol. "Pan, let them go!" He fired at the cave ceiling. The shot shattered a stalactite, spraying rocks. Some scattered over the bumpy floor, some plopped heavily into the river. Stuart watched dumbly as some passed through the bodies of the pirates without any effect. They kept moving along their phantom trail, gabbling happily and slapping each other on the back.

"Captain, I wouldn't do that again if I were you," Pan said in warning.

Stuart promptly drew a second pistol from his belt and fired that. It broke a hole through a striated column that must have taken thousands of years to form. "Or what?" he cried. "You'll feed me to the crocodile? That threat is getting old, boy! What can you really do to me that's worse than what you've already done?" As soon as he asked that question, Stuart knew it was a mistake. He tensed, expecting Pan to streak out from somewhere and slash him.

Pan, however, let the fairies answer for him. Swarms of them came buzzing from every direction, out from behind rock formations, from deep within the curled petals of flowers, from behind trees and up from beneath the bridge over the river. *I can see them!* Stuart thought, shocked.

Thus far, the Neverland fairies had just been lights in the sky that zipped around like sentient sparklers. These fairies were visible people-shapes about as tall as his hand. Not only were they armed but they were armored from head to foot, dozens of tiny soldiers in a formal, however miniature, army. *Probably cross-bred with cockroaches,* Stuart thought as they fell on him.

Their swords sliced deeper than those of the jungle fairies. They buried long spears in whatever flesh they could reach. Wincing as a spear plunged into his neck, Stuart had a sudden vision of hypodermic needles. The fairy spears were like needles jabbing into him, but instead of injecting medicine they were injecting poison. He could feel his flesh grow numb where they struck, costing him coordination and maneuverability.

He shook himself like a dog to get them off and lunged for the line of pirates. Oblivious to the dilemma of their captain, they were marching with blind anticipation *through* the solid wall with its bulging cascades of white and red flowstone.

Stuart joined their march, hurrying past them and through them, heading for the wall, too, and hauling Wendy after him. "Stop it!" she said, gripping the rope and trying to keep her bare feet from slipping. "Slow down!"

He ignored her protests. *There is a passageway ahead,* he was thinking with as much conviction as he could summon. *I believe there is a passageway ahead. If my men can go through it, I can, too. There is a passage, there is a passageway, I believe it with all my heart and soul and I will follow my men through it—*

He smacked face-first into extremely solid rock. Wendy skidded to a stop before she smacked into him. When she found herself standing *inside* Jukes, she shrieked and leaped aside. Jukes didn't pause a wink, just kept on marching up to the wall, through his stunned captain and into whatever illusion Pan was creating for him and his mates on the other side.

The fairy army had paused to see what Stuart intended to do, charging at the wall like he had. Now, watching him hold his bruised nose while howling and stamping his feet in pain, they shrieked with bell laughter, along with Wendy and Pan.

Stuart calmed himself in time to see the last of his crew walk through him and disappear. "Where are you taking them, Pan?" he called, letting go of his throbbing nose and straightening up. He had to regain some dignity even though he really just wanted to bawl in agony. His poor nose felt as big as a weather balloon. "Did you hear me, Pan? If you dare harm them—"

"I'm not the one with grenadoes," Pan pointed out.

Stuart's heart sank. The boy knew his plan, after all. *But he can't know all of it,* he assured himself. *He might know what's in the bags, but he can't read my mind. I still have a chance. I still have her.* He glowered at Wendy, feeling his eyes go hot red with purpose.

She saw it and screamed. The fairies renewed their attack.

Stuart bulled his way straight through the swarm, keeping his head down and letting his hat shield his face. A few fairies managed to thrust spears through the base of the hat and into his skull, a particularly painful sensation made all the worse when the poison took effect. It made him groggy much faster than any of the prickings on his arms, legs and back. He let out a roar-like scream, as much to vent anger and pain as to shock himself awake, and wound Wendy's rope round and round his fist, reeling her in like a fish. When he reached the bridge, he yanked her close. "Take a deep breath," he advised her, and picked her up.

"Hey!" she cried, struggling.

From the corner of his eye, he saw a streak of green heading for him. *Too late, boy!* he thought and, hugging Wendy tight, he leaped into the river.

He knew the risks. For God's sake, they were underground. Not only was the river as cold as snow, it might at any time duck under the surface of the cavern floor and flow through rock for yards, for miles, forever. He might drown, thrashing uselessly in some giant vein of the earth, eventually getting coughed up on an isolated cavern shore where his flesh would rot and his bones would remain, unseen and unknown, forever in the dark.

On the other hand, Stuart was guessing that fairies could not enter water. That, coupled with the fact that he had seen no other exit from the cavern, prompted him to accept the risk of the river.

The minute he and Wendy hit the water, the current sucked them under. Stuart kept a tight hold of his captive, betting that Pan wouldn't allow her to drown despite her predicament. Oh, Pan had allowed her to be kidnapped, probably because, deep down, she'd wanted to be. No doubt he had allowed her to be maneuvered into the caves with the pirates for the same reason. Wendy was the spunkiest little brat Stuart had ever encountered. She savored danger like some people savored fine wine. So Pan, ever the good host to children, was giving it to her. When the time was right, he would play the storybook hero and save her, Stuart was positive of that.

Then again...

Through the bubbling water he saw a very big, very dark maw rushing straight at him. A tunnel. The river was indeed heading under the rocks! Stuart kicked up to the surface for air, bringing Wendy with him so she could do the same. He hoped she had a chance to get a lungful because he had to pull her down again when Pan dived for her. Pan got some of her hair and some of Stuart's, too, but then the river ducked underground and he lost his grasp, tearing hair out in the process. Stuart was so numb from the cold water that all he felt was a mild tug on his scalp. Then Pan was gone. Everything was gone. He and Wendy were gobbled up by stone.

As luck would have it, they didn't remain rock-bound for long. The river rushed them through icy nothingness long enough for Stuart to begin to worry, then all at once he and Wendy had all the air they could want. They were dropping over the edge of a waterfall.

CHAPTER 51

Stuart never lost consciousness. The waterfall jostled him with a few gut-wrenching rolls and belched him out into shallow water. He dragged himself up, laboring to breathe, trying not to puke. This was the second head whack in one day. That was bad enough, but coupled with the fairy poison, he was not at all feeling good.

When the tension of the rope in his hand went slack, an alarm rang somewhere in his jangled brain. He looked up blearily.

Splash splash splash!

Not an outrageous sound in a place like this. The waterfall, which fortunately for him hadn't been very large, had dumped him into another cavern, this one covered wall-to-wall with several inches of water so pristine he could see every detail of the limestone beneath. Anything moving would make a splash in this place, of course it would.

Splash splash splash!

Yes, like that. Stuart sat up, trying to think why this sound should be particularly important. He looked at the rope in his hand. He eyeballed it all the way to the other end. The other end, freshly cut, was laying on a flat rock next to his soaked hat and his pearl-handled knife.

A rope... a knife... a girl... *She cut herself free!* He snatched up the knife and staggered after the splashing, which was sounding far away and getting farther.

It didn't occur to him till then that he could see. This cavern wasn't mantled in live fairy dust, but fairies must have used the place recently. There were enough old patches of dust to give off a faint glow, casting everything in shadowy gold.

Compared to the cavern above, this one had a relatively open floor. The ceiling was low, though, and crowded with stalactites of every length and thickness, dangling down like flowstone fringes on a vast limestone chandelier. Stuart had to crouch as he ran to make sure he didn't whack his head yet again.

"You can't get away, girl!" he called gruffly, following the splashing while having to veer around dripping columns and jutting rocks. His boots were full of water and he was chilled to the bone, but he thought his coordination might be returning. Perhaps he had lain half-conscious long enough for the fairy poison to wear off. *Either that or this is another stage of its progress,* he thought with perverse humor. *A burst of lunatic vitality before an excruciating death, how about that?*

"Shut up," he growled to himself, and moved faster. He couldn't run too fast — the bottom of the pool was slippery — but he thought he might be catching up. The splashing ahead seemed to be getting closer, didn't it? Not quite so echoey. More defined, a bit frantic, created by delicate bare feet that were no doubt numb and blue by now. Yes, a very telling sound, wasn't it, that *splash splash splash!*

A lot like *boom boom boom!*

He stopped dead. It had been a low, massive sound from far, far away. He knew that sound. Why had he left the safety of his ship this morning if he had known? It was so stupid! It didn't make sense!

BOOM!

Stuart resumed running, going as fast as his long legs could carry him, teeth clenched in effort, lungs straining. But it was hopeless. The air turned thick as goop, a goop like cupcake icing, smooth and sickly sweet. His feet slowed, he strained, could barely move. The air became peanut butter and he fought, tried to pull free, was all but frozen, heart leaping, stomach like fire, his boots mired in an invisible tar pit.

Behind him, the giant was coming.

No! he realized. *There is no giant! There's nothing behind me, nothing behind me!* Far ahead he caught sight of a flutter of white before it disappeared around the bend. Yes, ahead. The focus was ahead, not behind. He was the one chasing now. He was the giant. He had always been the giant.

BOOM!

His foot crashed down. Water fountained up around him as he pushed forward, eating up the distance between himself and his quarry in white, the watery smash of his wooden heels reverberating in the cave like muted jungle drums. He could hear breathing all around him, a great dragon growl. It urged him forward, piercing his muddled mind and giving him one clear objective. He didn't need to waste time thinking. He *knew* what he had to do.

BOOM!

"I seeeee yoooou!" His scabbard slapped his thigh as he ran. Wet curls flapped around his head. "I'm going to gehhhht yoooou!" He vaulted over a pile of rock debris, drenching himself with freezing spray when he landed on the other side. The chancy maneuver saved him the few extra seconds it would have taken to go around.

He turned a bend and spotted Wendy before she darted away with a squeal. *Without Pan by your side, you're just a scared little whelp after all,* he thought. "Come back, little Darling!" The ceiling rose higher in this section of the cavern. Stuart put on more speed. "You can't escape me!"

The cavern contracted into a narrow alley of murky wet brown. Wendy's splashing footfalls were very clear now. She was just up ahead where the fairy dust was thinning out, making it difficult for Stuart to see her. Oh, but those footfalls were all he needed. He fancied he could hear the girl huffing and puffing as well, making little blubbering sounds of terror between each girlish gasp. "I'm catching up!" He broke out in a maniac's grin. "Boogah boogah!"

He reached the spot where the fairy dust diminished. Only a few thin patches clung to the walls, providing less light than a single match. Before him the alley split two ways, both completely lacking fairy dust, turning them into long snake mouths that could lead anywhere and he wouldn't know until it was too late.

Stuart stopped, wishing he hadn't discarded his torch. He strained his senses. Yes, the splashing was clear enough, but from which direction? Right? Or left? He stepped into the right tunnel and felt the wall. Dry. He backed up, stepped into the left tunnel and felt the wall. It was wet from the splashing of a frightened little girl.

He went left.

"Yeeeiiiiii—!"

Wendy's scream rolled back to him through the cramped space, a high-pitched steam whistle of distress. It came from up ahead and, for all the world, sounded like it was going downward. Something bad was in the darkness in front of him. Stuart tried to put on the brakes. His boots slipped. He fell, landed on his back and instead of stopping swiftly gained momentum, caught in a curving halfpipe of rock worn slick as a water slide and bending almost straight down.

He landed in yet another deeper chamber lit by torches along the walls. For the moment he accepted that unlikely fact. He had a bigger problem to solve first. He had landed in a pile of something that felt like ashes.

He coughed out a mouthful, gagging and spitting. The damned stuff was so annoyingly light and fluffy and... wait. Where was the water? He looked back up but couldn't see a thing, not the rock slide nor any indication of all the water he'd just been splashing through. He could hear it, though, the soft burble of a stream somewhere overhead. How could that much water be up there and not penetrate this cavern, which as far as he could tell was dry as a desert?

He examined his powder-encrusted hand. The stuff felt sort of spongy. Sticky, too. Any kind of regular dirt or silt would cling to his wet body, naturally, but this stuff stuck like glue. *Dead fairy dust,* he realized. He spat again and got up, disgusted to feel it plastered to his clothes, his skin, his hair, the inside of his mouth and ears and nostrils. He took out his kerchief to blow his nose. The kerchief was powdered in grey as well. He discarded it and just blew air out of his nostrils in hard angry bull snorts, not caring what else came out as long as the awful dust went with it. He shook his head and flapped his coat, feeling like a pork chop dredged in maggoty flour.

A small noise made him freeze. Close by, a girl-sized jumble of grey was moving.

Aversion to the dead fairy dust fell away. The mystery of the lit torches was set aside. Stuart enjoyed a surge of triumph. "There you are, my dear." He had her. Regardless of what might come, he had her. He would not let her go this time. Everything was going to be all right.

Jostling off puffs of dust with every move, Stuart made his way over to Wendy. She lifted her head. She, too, wore a layer of dead dust. The edges of her mouth, eyes and nose were crusted with it, her beautifully smooth hair limp with it. She coughed hard with the grinding hack of a chest cold.

"Easy," Stuart told her. "Catch your breath. You must be tired, hm?"

Wendy glared at him. "Get away from me! Peter Pan is—"

"Not here," Stuart finished. "You ran from me, Miss Darling, to no avail. Pan could not follow. He let you go. Didn't you feel it?" He rubbed his head. "I certainly did."

Wendy scooted backwards, away from the hand Stuart offered. Her movements sent dead dust flying. "Leave me alone!"

"I will do no such thing. This is the end of the trolley, I'm afraid." Whatever the hell that meant. Stuart raised his pearl-handled knife, which he had held onto during the chase. *No no no, not that. The hook. The hook!* Yes, that would be more appropriate. He casually threw the knife over his shoulder as if playing darts backwards.

It clanged against something big, something metal. *Metal? Down here?* Stuart turned around. A brass bell hung from a worn and pitted belfrey — a ship's bell, sitting there on a rock, far from its proper home upon the sea.

Up to this point, he had been so single-minded that he hadn't bothered to look around. He had presumed, not unreasonably, that he was in yet another cave, nothing fancy, just another fat air pocket in the guts of the island. *With lighted torches,* he reminded himself apprehensively.

Part of this cave was a pit of gritty dirt smattered with piles of soft dead fairy dust like the one he and Wendy had fallen into. Stuart guessed that the flying vermin regularly congregated here, dropping their disgusting bodily gunk as they hovered in swarms. The other part of the cave began where the floor rose steeply up to what he thought was a flat area, but it was too high for him to see to be sure.

On the verge of that rise were two ship's bells, one on each side, both hanging from what appeared to be their original belfries. For some reason they reminded Stuart of pictures he had seen of the mysterious stone lions at the entrances of ancient Chinese buildings. Like the lions, these bells were alien things, baffling and otherworldly in this subterranean maze, as foreboding as twin tombstones.

"Who lit the torches?" Wendy asked.

Stuart gave no answer. He had already dismissed her, zeroing all his attention on the bells. With care he climbed partway up the rocky rise so that he could see the left one more closely. Its belfry was a simple flat wooden arch that, judging by the metal mounts on top, had most likely hung from under the foredeck rail. A decorative filigree had been cast in the brass around the bell's bottom edge, interspersed twice, front and back, with two words: *Jolly Roger*.

Stuart moved to the bell on the right. Much older, this one, with an ornate four-poster belfry indicative of the sixteenth century when everything, including ships of war, boasted ostentatious decoration. In contrast to its design, the condition of the wood hinted that a good knuckle knock would bring the whole thing down in a rotted crumble. The bell itself bore an ugly crack and, like the other one, two words: *Jolly Roger*.

Slowly, dreading what he might see, Stuart finished the climb up the rise so that he could see beyond.

There indeed lay a large flat area of rock. Seven great stalagmites sectioned off a wide circle not unlike a miniature Stonehenge. Torches on columns threw twitching eldritch shadows of orange and red that licked a crude stone table within the circle. The table was flanked by two towering pillars that were not, Stuart realized uneasily, stone at all but frozen humanoid shapes. Their slender, irrationally elongated bodies were similar to the spirit-figures he had seen within the trees of the Indian forest. But these were bigger, much bigger. The one on the left had a female face, disturbing in its overly-stretched loveliness, with thin knives of hair falling a good twenty feet straight down. The left figure mirrored the right but it was a male, handsome and stern-faced. Stuart looked up into their eyes and felt the jolt of sentience. They were looking back.

Eerie as this was, it did not particularly frighten him. The looming shadows and the dead silent air did not frighten him. What frightened Stuart were the objects on the table. No, not table. It was an altar. There were five objects, erected on a row of five stone slabs, each one propped up so that the bloody torchlight could caress their delicate forms from every angle, making their shapes, even from this distance, impossible to miss.

"Holy God..." Stuart pinched his eyes closed. Opened them again. He had found what he was looking for. It really did exist. This was the seat of Pan's power. An altar, deep in the bowels of the Neverland. He sensed the energy now, a high, weirdly ticklish vibration not meant to be easily identified by human senses, flowing along some plane of reality where fairies, spirits, gods and their ancient magic had roamed freely since, perhaps, the dawn of all Time.

The five objects on the altar were not sacred in and of themselves. Stuart knew that because of what they were. They were just symbols, but powerful symbols because they each had been abysmally tuned to Pan. The little god's objects of power were hands. The severed hands of the Hooks.

Stuart stumbled into the circle, not caring a whit about the spirit guards on either side. Part of him wished they would spring to life and crush him with one blow. That would be a blessing. Because now that he was here, he didn't want to be here at all, didn't want to do what he had planned to do.

It must be done. There is no other course of action.

"Shut up! Shut up! Shut up!"

The spirit guards exchanged soft, high-pitched hums at Stuart's outburst. It seemed to him they were enjoying his plunge into enlightenment.

Have to see, have to know, he thought madly. *Have to make sure...* But that was silly, wasn't it? He had no need to make sure. He was sure.

He looked anyhow.

The oldest hand was on the left end of the line. Not entirely skeletal, still hanging on to strips of thin, shriveled, papery skin, it had been impaled wrist-down on an iron spike ages ago. With its flesh rotted away, it should have fallen down yet here it was, impossibly upright all the same as if the spike were still holding it. An engraved stone strip below it read: ≈Charles William Stuart, 1737≈.

Stiff and moving on automatic, Stuart stepped to the next hand, also on a spike and also impossibly still upright: ≈Winthrop Spencer Stuart, 1784≈. The next hand had more skin left, some of it clinging in patches to the dry white bones beneath, some of it dangling in dead grey confetti strips: ≈Albert Andrew Stuart, 1826≈. The fourth hand was shriveled, mummy-like but mostly intact, with a twinkling diamond ring on the third finger: ≈James Albert Stuart, 1896≈.

Great-grandfather, Stuart thought in unbearable horror, and the horror kept on growing worse like a cancer inside, growing worse with every breath and pulsing in time with his laboring heart. *James! I am James! No, I am... I am...*

He didn't want to look at the fifth hand. He did anyway. Greyish-white skin, intact, covering shrunken flesh. Long slender fingers, withered a bit but maintaining their graceful contours. Fuzzy green and brown marred the skin, confined within the fine wrinkles of the knuckles, but it would spread. Otherwise the hand could have still been attached to his wrist. No mutilation. No smashed bones. No rips from a block and tackle. Just a clean cut a couple of inches above the wrist, a cut that must have been made by, say, a good sharp sword.

≈Jonathan Edward Stuart, 1989≈.

He should have screamed. He had the right and certainly enough reason. Seeing his hand like this — at such a distance, detached from home base, as it were — it terrified him and, perhaps moreso, puzzled him. *Am I really so special?* he wondered. *What did my ancestors do to warrant such monstrous attention over so many years?* Was it bad luck? Random destiny? He might never know, and moreover, the knowledge was irrelevant now. *All that matters is that it ends with me*, he thought. *It ends with me, here. Today.*

He wasn't surprised to find Wendy behind him when he turned around. He expected her to be there. Willfulness and Curiosity were her middle names, not Moira Angela. She wanted to see.

He wanted her to see. If he could make her recognize Pan as the monster he really was, then she would die in terror of him. What potent blood that would make! Spilling it here before this wretched altar should surely unravel the spell of the Neverland.

"What do you think of your hero now?" he asked her with a smirk. "Still think he's a boy?" A brilliant revelation came to him.

"He's the crocodile, you know." He moved towards her. "And you, my sweet, are nothing but food to sate his eternal fiendish appetite. He soaks up your adoration of him, you and all the puking brats that love him so much, and he positively gobbles up my misery like candy. Then he shits out magic as bait to bring in more kiddies and thus keeps the cycle going. What do you think of that?"

Wendy regarded him with disgust. "You're gross!"

"I'm gross? What do you call that?" Stuart jabbed a finger back at the stone altar. "What do you call this?" He waved his hook in her face.

Wendy turned to run. Stuart's hand whipped out, snagging her wrist and jerking her back to his side. Stupid girl, where did she think she could go? "I'm sorry I have to do this," he said, and poised his hook so that its sharp inner edge would slice her throat. "Truly I am."

He intended to kill her, he really did. Enough of his sanity had jumped the track that his trolley car was holding onto the straight and narrow with little more than good intentions. Not that he cared anymore. He had found Pan's true heart. All he needed to do was cut into it, and he would be free. If anything were to stop him at this stage of the game — *Game, ha!* — it would have to be Pan. Pan was the local hero. No one else had the right.

Except that they did. A thin finger of stone, preposterously long, stabbed itself between Stuart and his victim and flicked Stuart back as a fussy diner might flick a speck of dust from the tablecloth. Wendy remained unharmed while Stuart spilled across the hard floor in his unique jumble of frills and curls. By the time he righted himself, the hand of the female stone guard had retracted. He saw it slide neatly back into the position it had held before, gracefully hanging parallel to the folds of her long stone gown. There it froze, daring any sane mind to even consider the possibility that it had moved. The lady-thing's eyes sparked with life, as did those of her protracted mate, watching him with cold humor.

So big, and it didn't make a sound when it moved! Stuart suddenly felt small. What was he doing here anyway? What was he trying to prove? That he could maneuver himself into a situation that would lead to a death more gruesome than that of crocodilian consumption? That he might incur the wrath of this living island and cause it to swallow him alive, digesting him over eons while stalagmites and stalactites drip-by-dripped a cold stone tomb around him?

Never happen. It's not how the story goes.

I could rewrite it.

But it's no fun that way. I'm supposed to be—

"Having fun, Captain?" Pan popped up from behind the altar. "How do you like my collection?"

"Peter!" Wendy practically screamed the word. "Oh Peter, you're here! I was so scared—"

Act now last chance! Stuart thought. Before Wendy finished her sentence, he pulled her to him and slashed with his hook, aiming for her throat, praying that the hot spray of blood that would burst from such a deep slice might not bring the wrath of magic upon him but might quash that magic forever and set him free.

Wendy shrieked as the hook jolted to a dead stop inches from her neck.

Pan hovered at Stuart's ear, holding the hook back. "You know what, Captain?" the boy said, grinning as he strained to stop the cut while Stuart strained to complete it. "I think you're ready."

CHAPTER 52

That was all it took. Four words. Four little words, and Stuart crumbled.

He looked perfectly fine on the outside. A little crazed, maybe. To the casual observer, intact. Inside, though, the foundation of his psyche was cracking with the sound of a cathedral window collapsing. *Maybe that's all I am inside. Glass. And I thought I was so tough.*

Pan easily knocked the threatening hook away and lifted Wendy up until the two of them were hovering safely out of reach. Stuart, meanwhile, stood before the altar of hands and quietly fell apart.

"He's mad!" Wendy gabbled at Pan. "He was saying awful things about you and magic and, and he's scary and he's making no sense at all! Look at him! Look at him!"

"It's okay," Pan soothed her. "I fear the good Captain has suffered too many bumps on the head today. He needs to go to bed early. What do you say, Captain?"

Stuart trembled. Slowly his arms wrapped around his middle, and he hugged himself as if he had just emerged from a cold bath, head down, teeth clenched against chattering. No coherent thought, just sensation. He was spreading out like spilled sand, his connections becoming disconnected, his attachments becoming unattached. He was water flowing from a jug, splashing hickity-pickity every which way. He was feathers in the wind, dissipating fog, segments, pieces, holes, old scars tearing open afresh.

Out. Out. Desperation crept into the tippy-top corner of his consciousness and managed to patch together a few of the scattering fragments, enough to do the job. *Want out.* A complete thought. Another one squished that one aside: *Still a way.* He could have used that way at any time, too. Why hadn't he thought of it before?

Hectic energy boiled up from the depths of his being and Stuart bolted for the altar, preparing to gouge his hated hook into his own throat this time. If Wendy's blood would work, his should work even better. He would drench the altar in crimson and end his imprisonment one way or the other.

But the altar wasn't there. The only objects before him were seven crate-sized calcite formations that resembled, if anything, giant cakes dripping with thick cream frosting. They encircled a wide lump of limestone with a top surface weirdly veined and melted, like the scarred skin of a burn victim.

"Where did it go?" He spoke from the bottom of a well, his vision narrowed to a circle framed in coal. "There was... of... they were right... it ..." He pulled at his hair, trying to tug the memory out through his skull. *It just happened, for fuck's sake! They were just there!*

What was just there? What had it been? Something important, vital to his survival...

I'm hallucinating.

"Where am I?"

He was in the glittering fairy cavern, that's where he was, standing next to the black cotton-candy-like barrier. He was clean of dead fairy dust, and he was holding Wendy's leash, the other end of which lay like a hempen snake on the floor. No Wendy.

"I'll tell you where you are," Pan said cheerfully. "You're here!"

The green devil was standing right next to him! Stuart leaped aside, much like Wendy had when she'd found herself standing in the middle of Jukes.

The sight of a grown man jumping like a girl made Pan giggle. What a lovely sound amidst the rigid tapestry of primordial stone! "I sent Wendy on ahead," Pan said, ascending like a happy bubble into the air, flapping his feet purely for effect. "She's smart, so I don't want her to hear this. It's just between you and me, Jon."

That name. Something about that name. "Wh...whaaat..." Stuart struggled to hold onto the simple question, to get it out of his mouth. Most everything behind his eyes had dissolved, for some odd reason, making everything blurry. It was very hard to think. "... what did you say?"

Peter Pan grabbed his toes and turned lazy summersaults over the icy cold river. "You're great, Jon. Totally. None of the others got this far. But wowie zowie, you are mule stubborn! Took you all this time to come 'round!" He uncurled and took a position standing upside-down, wagging a finger at Stuart like a schoolmaster while his wild hair hung straight down — or straight up, Stuart supposed, from the boy's point of view.

"Lesson One," Pan said. "You're never getting out, so forget it. Lesson Two: you can't poison the island. I won't allow it, so stop trying. Lesson Three: you had better be nicer to Wendy from now on. If you so much as poke her hard, you'll never find Beggar's Port again, got it? Lesson Four: have fun! I mean, it's just a game."

"To you," Stuart managed to say.

"It's your game, too. Play! Or fight it and don't have any fun at all, I promise you. Your choice."

That choice sounded familiar. Somebody had given him that choice before. He couldn't remember who, though. He could not maintain eye contact as he asked, "When will it end?"

"Sort of up to you. See, Wendy isn't going back." That made Stuart raise his head. "Hates her parents. They abuse her. I won't tolerate that, so she's staying here. Oh, don't worry about how much she's seen or heard in the last few days. She's already forgotten everything but the game, just like you will real soon. As for the Lost Boys, they come and go all the time. No big deal." Pan darted down to pat Stuart gaily on the head, zooming back up before Stuart could react, not that he was in any mind to. "We are gonna have sooooo much fun for a looonnnnng time, aren't we, Jon?"

For the first time, Stuart seriously mulled it over. If there was no way back... back to... wherever... then why *not* play the game? That's all it was. A kid's game. Maybe it could be entertaining, if he threw himself into it. There was plenty to eat and drink, men who practically worshipped him, his own ship, booty up to his earlobes, ready and willing ladies at the Port when he wanted — *flash* — the ship's hold — *flash* — two goats in their tight stalls, flanked by sheep and a stack of tiny cramped chicken coops — *flash* — milking the goats every day, taking from them as long as they could give — *flash* — butchering them when they were used up, taking all that was left of them, flesh, skin, bones, without so much as a thank you for all their years of forced productive service.

He drew his sword. "I'm not a fucking goat!" *Or am I?* he thought miserably.

Pan flew at him feet-first and kicked him through the barrier.

WHAT HAPPENED NEXT

Hook shot through the barrier like a bullet. The strange blackness sucked him in and spat him back out in the space of a breath, leaving him blinded by sudden sunslight.

Though he could not yet see, he could hear sounds of battle raging around him — pirates yelling and cursing, children screaming and laughing, pistol shots cracking the air, swords *swooshing* like the wings of giant bats. He recognized John's boyish war whoops, little Michael's squeals of excitement and Wendy's gay laughter. Through it all, the tinkling scree of fairy voices weaved in and out of the tumult like the audible stitching of a chaotic war fabric.

A blurred figure windmilled toward him. Cecco's voice shouted from it. "Captain, we've got them this time, The Lost Boys and the wench, too!" Cecco's face came into focus as Hook's vision cleared. "But the fairies are armored, and I think Pan is coming!"

"Pan is here!" came a merry shout from on high.

Hook whirled. That voice! That nettling, loathsome, exasperating voice! He blinked furiously against the suns, drawing his saber and searching the skies for that damnable green figure.

He had been thrown out onto a beach. Already the twisting caves and all that had transpired within them were fading into a lost world. As his eyes adjusted to the brilliant tropical light, his broken mind adjusted to a lonely interior dark. His origins and the life that belonged to them fell away, irrelevant now. Feelings of fear and rebellion vanished beneath a swelling tide of overwhelming rage. Hate was a living ball of fire in his gut. He was at war, a celebration of blood that might finally grant him the ultimate revenge that would set him free.

"Where are you, Peter Pan!" he shrieked at the sky.

"Present and accounted for, Captain!" said the boy, cannonballing with the sunslight at his back, blinding Hook all over again. "Tag, you're it!" Pan cried, and slapped the light-dazzled Hook on the left shoulder.

Hook leapt upward, swinging his saber at the retreating imp. If not for Pan's speed, the boy would have lost his feet. "Always flying!" Hook railed. "Always cheating!"

Pan stopped dead in the air. The Lost Boys and the pirates, noticing this and sensing a great significance in it, paused in the midst of their own battles to watch.

"Cheating?" Pan called down, truly offended.

"Aye, *cheating*, you swaggering buffoon!" Hook pointed his saber at his enemy. "All talk and no walk, as I've heard you put it! I tire of your cowardice! Stand your ground – the real ground – if you want to fight!"

Pan alighted in the sand with such grace that he barely disturbed a grain. "That I will do," he said solemnly. His lips curved into a cruel smile. "And more besides."

Hook slowly circled him. "It's you or me this time, boy."

Pan cocked his head "Isn't that my line, Captain?"

Hook leered. "Is it? Then here is your chance to school your better, if you can." The pirate poised both saber and hook. Pinpricks of red ignited in each of his pupils. "Proud and insolent youth, prepare to meet thy doom."

Pan grinned. "Dark and sinister man, have at thee!"

They met in a clash of steel on steel.

In the long and varied annals of the ever-changing Neverland, many battles have been waged. This one outstripped them all for sheer ferocity and savage animal bloodlust. As Hook and Pan engaged, Hook roared commands to his mangy horde, who renewed their attacks. Countering, Pan ordered the Lost Boys and the fairies to meet them. The beach erupted into desperate hand-to-hand clashes, attackers and defenders bobbing and weaving in a tuneless dance of death.

Hook fought furiously, feeling all the while that he must have, for some unfathomable reason, held back before. Had he never truly intended to kill Peter Pan, just *injure* him enough to teach him a lesson? Codswallop! The wretched boy who had taken his hand was going to spill every drop of his life's blood on the sand today. Hook was tired of playing games.

He maneuvered with both saber and hook, coordinating his movements so that one or the other was always before him, parrying or slashing with edge or point. Pan could hardly parry fast enough to block the rain of blows. The pirate captain's smile gleamed as his foe was driven back, back until Pan was nearing the mouth of the jungle where he would be hard-pressed to fly and escape should he choose to abandon the fair fight and flee.

Then Hook heard a terrible *jing jing!* Golden dust flittered down upon him, and a tiny hand yanked his earring hard enough to almost tear it out. With a startled cry he batted Tinker Bell away, vigorously shaking his head where most of the dust had landed. Pan saw the opening and lunged, ducking low and scoring a deep cut across Hook's right thigh.

Hook roared like a mad bull and slashed his saber in a killing arc, missing Pan by a hair. "After you're dead I'm going to catch that tiny wench," he huffed, "and when I do, I'll pickle her in a jar and keep her as a centerpiece on my dining table!"

"The day you capture Tinker Bell will be the day *three* suns shine in the sky!" Pan answered.

"Always a possibility," said Hook. He lunged, thrusting his saber straight at Pan's unprotected belly. Pan would have died in that instant, but Hook's wounded leg gave way beneath him. Pan beat the blade down, scuttling aside crabwise. By the time Hook recovered, the boy had already dodged around him and run back onto the open beach, but not before grabbing a lock of his enemy's hair and slicing it off as a final insult.

Hook took the opportunity to quickly view the rest of the battle. As always, the others had left him and Pan to their private duel. His men were holding their own pretty well, considering the confounded fairies were involved. Smee, Foggerty and Thatcher were armed not with pistol and cutlass but with great palm fronds which they were waving to and fro like giant flyswatters, knocking what fairies they could to the ground and stomping them into the sand. Hook had never thought of that strategy before and was pleased to see that it was effective.

As for the flying children, they were darting around like angry crows, slashing and kicking while the pirates slashed back and fired pistols. Mad Mundy, Rajeev and Skylights had brought leather slings and were whipping rocks into the sky with good aim. For the few seconds that he dared watch the fight, Hook saw a rock bounce off Ranger's skull, toppling the vicious brat to the sand. Hook hoped he was dead. Of all the Lost Boys, Ranger always posed the greatest threat.

Hook snapped his attention back to Pan, who was slowly approaching, gallantly keeping his feet on the ground as per their agreement. The sight made Hook snarl. The snarl made Pan grin. He charged, kicking up sand and waving his sword over his head.

Hook thought for one horrifying moment that the magical boy was going to *throw* the sword at him. He raised saber and hook in a crossed high guard, ready to dodge to one side if need be. But instead of throwing his sword, Pan jammed it into the sand and used it like a pole to vault himself feet-first at his foe. He slammed into Hook's chest and knocked the pirate backwards. The breath *whooshed* from Hook's lungs, and his saber flew out of his hand. He nearly lost consciousness as his head smashed into the sand.

Pan stood upon his prey, one foot on Hook's chest, the other holding down his left wrist. The boy thumped his breast and crowed his triumph. "You're beaten, Captain! All I have to do is thwicky-thwak," and he slashed his sword back and forth, "and I could chop off your other hand!" He brought his blade to a stop over the threatened target.

This was the one scenario Hook dreaded more than any other, even death by the croc. To be eaten by the croc would be excruciating beyond imagining, but the agony would at least come to an end. To live with no hands at all — he could not conceive of such prolonged torture.

"Do it!" he snarled, baring his teeth like a cornered dog who shows anger to hide the terror behind it. "Do it and have your victory and then for Hell's sake shut up about it!"

Peter Pan crowed again. The Lost Boys cheered. Wendy, John and Michael laughed and clapped their delight, especially Wendy, whose admiration for Pan was so great she could not possibly have conceived of what was about to happen next.

Hook's men stood silent, an amazing variety of expressions on their faces that nonetheless all amounted to the same thing — they were not going to leave the field victorious. Their captain was about to be maimed, if not slain outright. They were going to be the losers.

Yet even with the strain it was under, Hook's great brain was not paralyzed as everyone believed. He was hatching a plan. It matured within seconds, and he knew exactly what to do. The plan was simple, and he executed it with a grace that almost rivaled that of his ethereal foe. Even as his face maintained its expression of doom, he jerked up one leg and kneed Pan between the legs from behind.

Pan, careless in his glee, couldn't dodge the blow. Green-faced, he toppled forward. As he did, Hook rolled aside. Quick as a flash he was holding down Peter Pan instead of the other way around.

"'Sdeath and odds fish, I'm surprised you fell for that," the pirate captain sneered. "I guess you don't know everything after all, hm?"

"Peter!" Wendy cried, and she flew to her hero's rescue. Ranger, Cheeks and Stinky followed.

"Back!" Hook thundered. "Stay back, or I'll slice his throat from ear to ear!"

Cecco had started forward to aid his captain and immediately stopped. John and Michael, ready to fly to Peter's aid, froze where they were in midair. Roland, Starkey, Kamau, Smee and the rest of the pirates grinned at their captain admiringly. Everyone eagerly waited to see how the situation would play out.

"You know," Hook said amiably, "for just a moment — a wee moment, mind you — I considered slicing off *your* hands." The idea put a wide and thoroughly wicked smile on his handsome countenance. "It would certainly qualify as a fitting revenge, wouldn't you agree?"

"Aye, that it would," Pan said gravely.

The red pinpricks in Hook's eyes grew brighter. "But I have decided to opt for a more permanent resolution to our tumultuous relationship. Farewell, Peter Pan. I send you to *le grand peut-être*." His hook arm drew back, the point of the hook aiming for that slender throat—

—and suddenly Pan wasn't under him anymore. The boy hadn't even wriggled! Against all odds, against all possibility, he had just zipped out from under his captor like a snake through a greased hole.

Hook looked up, utterly baffled. He saw a flash of dazzling silver, felt a line of heat draw across his right cheek, and suddenly the right side of his face was warm and wet.

"It's not time to say out farewells just yet, Captain," Pan said. The boy was hovering high above the beach with his adoring Wendy by his side. "We'll meet again, I'm sure!" And he flew away with John, Michael and all the Lost Boys, including the wounded but very much still alive Ranger. The fairies followed in a sparkling cloud of gold.

Hook put his hand to his face. His fingers came away red. "You cut my face!" he shrieked after Pan. "You cut my face, you devil!" He was so mad he hopped up and down, shaking his fist as the flock of children disappeared beyond the palms. "Damn you, boy! This is going to leave a bloody *scar!*"

Smee shuffled over to his captain. With a firm manner that only he could impose on his superior, he pulled Hook down into a lean so that he could examine the wound. "Oh, sar, it don't look that bad. Let's get yeh back t' the ship an' I'll git yeh all cleaned up."

"But he's scarred me, Smee. I'll be scarred for life!" The red in Hook's pupils faded away, leaving forget-me-not blue blazes of fury. "First my hand, now my face. My *face*, for God's sake!"

While Hook continued to wail and whine, Smee steered him to the boats on the shore. The rest of the pirates picked the beach clean of weapons and any other valuables that had been dropped during the battle. There were no bodies to bury. Neither side had suffered a fatality, though most everyone had been injured.

Except for Pan and Wendy. More often than not, that was the case. It irritated the pirates no end, but there was nothing for it but to plan another battle and hope for the best — or in the case of Pan and Wendy, the worst.

Hook waded out to the captain's gig. Before he boarded, he turned back to the island with its rumpled white beach spotted with crimson. His injured face was twisted by a terrible frown as he drew a breath in and exhaled it in a long, deep, quavering sigh. "I will have my revenge," he said as if making a vow to the universe. "I am going to kill Peter Pan if it's the last thing I ever do."

FINALE: SON

Jonny Jr. dreamed of the giant...

...and I write about it in my journal every time I do. The dreams
started two months ago, and they're unlike any other dreams I've ever
had. And I've had some doozies. The weirdest thing is how real they
seem.

They always start out in a big empty room paneled in dark
rosewood and lit by torches, like the kind in the old *Indiana Jones*
adventure movies. In the dreams I always accept this weird locale as
the USC New Lyon Center where I am, in fact, the new Fencing
Team captain and saber coach, *Go Trojans!*

But the dreams... they make no sense. I'll be coaching somebody,
and all of a sudden a wall of the Center building comes crashing
down in a single gigantic piece, just missing me but squishing my poor
student. A man comes charging at me, armed with a sword. We fight,
real down and dirty stuff, all rules off. This guy, who never has a face,
always displays exceptional skills, but I'm no slouch either. I've
trained since I was a kid. Competition fencing is my life. But though I
hold my own against this stranger, it takes all my strength and
cunning to do it.

Up to this point the dreams are always that — just dreams. And I
know they're dreams even while I'm in them. But somewhere during
the fight it all changes. The faceless man begins to grow. He gets taller

and taller until he's the size of a tyrannosaurus rex. Still we continue to fight, even though the guy's sword grows right along with his body until it's as big as a tree trunk. I always think how absurd it is that I'm still a match for this giant, but I always hold my own. I have to. If I make a single mistake, one wrong move, I'll die. I know it at that point. The dream become a nightmare, and the nightmare is just too real.

It always ends with the faceless giant throwing away his sword and reaching down to pick me up. The first few times I had the dream, I woke up at this point, panting and terrified, but I recovered quickly and even laughed. Talk about too much fencing. Maybe I need to take up ping pong or something.

But the last time I had the dream — just last night — I bolted awake with this impossible hot sticky feel of giant fingers curled around my body, squeezing. I actually screamed and scared the snot out of myself. I had to take a shower. I had to get the feeling off of me. It wouldn't go away. It was *physical.* That can't happen, right? So what does it mean? What's happening to me?

Right now I'm sitting at my computer, trying to make sense of it. It must have something to do with Mom's death. I took it hard. Mom was all I had of my past, my origins. She held the secret to who I AM. Sure, I could research the family tree, but every time I look — on the net, in libraries, in government files — nothing is there. It's like the Stuart family has been erased. I have an apartment, car, career, girlfriend, but I feel like I'm alone someplace, trapped, and I can't reach them, I can't connect anymore.

And now, to top it all off, this damned box arrived this morning. There's no address or return address, so it can't have come through the mail. It's just a plain cardboard box with a left-handed saber in it. Deb, my girlfriend, found it on the back doorstep. She thinks it's a gift from one of my students who wanted to remain anonymous. Could be. I'm pretty close to my students. I like them, and I've gotten to know them well. I've gotten birthday gifts and such from them, but never anything like this.

No, this can't be a gift. It's old, for one thing, and by the look of it, expensive. Nobody just gives away an antique. And the feel of it in my hand... I keep picking it up because I can't believe the feeling. It's like it was made for me. It fits my hand in a way I can't describe. It's as if it's always been mine. I like the way it makes my fingers tingle.

END

ABOUT THE AUTHOR

Bobbi JG Weiss made her world debut one Christmas morning *cough-mutter-mutter* years ago, and as long as she can remember, she's wanted to be a writer. Why? She has no idea. Probably a birth defect.

After several normal jobs, her writing wishes came true — she and her husband/writing partner David Cody Weiss began to make their living as full-time freelance writers, focusing on Hollywood tie-in merchandise like movie/TV novel adaptations, comics, and other related and often ridiculous products. After 20+ years of this, the "WeissGuys" decided to enter the wild world of self-publishing.

You can find more information about Bobbi, her books and her weird life at bobbijgweiss.com. She also posts on Twitter, Facebook, tumblr, Pinterest, Goodreads, and she writes a blog called *The Writer's "I"* that posts every 2nd and 4th Wednesday of the month on her site.

Oh, and Bobbi loves reviews. She looooves reviews! She encourages you to write a review for *Hooked* at your favorite retailer. And tell your friends. And family. And people you don't even know. And shout it from the rooftops! And scrawl it all over... no, scratch that. Just leave a review.

Thank you!

Other Books by
BOBBI JG WEISS

WRITING IS ACTING:
How To Improve the Writer's Onpage Performance

Writers are Actors.

I know that for a fact because I've been both. And over the years I've realized how much the two arts overlap. Writers are onpage actors. The skills necessary for the page parallel those necessary for the stage. So I've turned my training as an actor into a handy little bag of writing Tools, Techniques and Tricks that I still use to this day. Come discover a whole new, hands-on, and if I do say so myself, *fun* way to develop characters, plot solid stories, and just plain energize your prose!

Writing Is Acting was originally published by Heinemann in paperback, and it's coming soon as an ebook! Check out my website for more info.

And now for an excerpt —

1

• WRITING IS ACTING •

INTRODUCTION

This book is the answer to a question I first asked myself years ago when I was in a bookstore checking out the newest "how to write" books. I was a published author at that point, but I've always maintained that a writer can never know enough. So there I was, searching for a new pearl of wisdom to strengthen my craft.

I went away disappointed, and later it occurred to me why. "How to write" books always approach the subject the same way — from the point of view of a successful writer sharing hard-earned wisdom. Well, that's logical, right? Yet these successful writers urge their students to do things like "let your imagination run wild" or "think about how you would feel if" or "visualize the scene."

My question: how does a person actually *do* stuff like that? In other words, if I'm a writer who needs to hone such intangible conceptual skills, how can those skills possibly be taught to me? What does it really mean to "let my imagination run wild"? How can I *learn* to do that?

I've never found a writing book that effectively answers those questions.

Now that I'm a successful writer with fifteen years of full-time freelance credits behind me, I realize that the answers don't lie in the art of writing. They lie in the art of *acting*. You see, before I was a writer, I was an actor, and only recently did it occur to me that *acting* exercises taught me how to visualize, how to let my imagination run free, how to feel what another person might feel, and many other such intangible conceptual skills. More importantly, acting exercises taught me how to express the results in a controlled, reliable and entertaining fashion. Unlike writing exercises, acting exercises force you to access your gut, that base level of personality and instinct that holds the ultimate spark of creative power. Acting exercises teach conceptual skills from the bottom up. They teach you how to *do* it.

This approach works so well that I've decided to write the book that I always looked for but never found. *Writing Is Acting* offers a unique point of view to a well-worn subject, as well as a completely fresh set of tools that writers can use to improve their craft — and themselves.

When I began to develop the *Writing Is Acting* concept, I had to ask myself some questions — questions that you're probably going to ask as well.

Why compare writing to acting? They're two different things!

As writers of fiction, our job is to tell stories about fictitious characters and fictitious events. In order to make a reader believe in our characters and relate to them and their circumstances, we must become the characters on the page — that is, we must see through their eyes, hear through their ears, touch with their fingertips, feel with their hearts. Then we must convey all that juicy subjective data in such a way that the reader will feel the same things that our characters are feeling, thus making the reader care about the characters and become concerned about their circumstances. Guess what?

That's acting.

But I'm Not an Actor… Am I?

Yes, in fact you are. Everybody is. We humans are goal oriented creatures. We want food, we want shelter, we want love. In order to achieve these and many other goals, we "act" in ways that will bring us the best results. Acting to achieve goals is a natural strategy for success.

So If All People Are Actors, Are All People Writers, Too?

Bingo!

The process of acting towards a goal — a salesman trying to make a sale, kids acting cool within their peer group, two friends meeting to mend a rift in their relationship — often involve prepared speeches. We think about what we're going to say ahead of time. Sometimes we even write speeches down or practice them out loud before a mirror, as in the case of job interviews, first dates or that moment when you ask your boss for a raise. We compose text in our heads, revise it and edit it, shaping it just right so that it communicates exactly what we want to say at just the right moment.

That's writing.

How can acting techniques help writers?

Acting techniques can help us discover facets of our personalities of which we might not be aware. Acting techniques can help our day-to-day interactions, thus making our efforts more successful. Many people take basic acting classes with no desire to enter the profession — they just want to use the techniques to enrich their lives and relationships.

Those same techniques can help the writer's ability to "act on paper," making our creative efforts all that much more believable and effective. Some acting techniques can help us to understand our characters better. After all, just as we real people "act" to obtain goals, so too should fictional characters "act" to obtain their goals. Some acting techniques can improve our prose, dialogue and ability to plot stories. Some techniques can help us brainstorm ideas. There are even aspects of acting that can help us during the revision and polishing stages of a manuscript. By thinking about story and character as an actor would, we suddenly have a whole new bag of tricks that can help us approach our stories and characters from a fresh perspective.

Well, I think that's a pretty good lead-in to this whole *Writing Is Acting* gig. It's time to get this show on the road. Okay, places, everybody! Cue the next page and — *action!*

CONTENTS

CHAPTER 1

What Is an Actor? What Is a Writer?

An actor is a physical instrument that plays itself before a live audience. An actor is a conduit between a world that is real and a world that is not real. An actor is a medium, calling into reality the spirit and personality of someone non-real so that spectators can see, hear, smell, touch, sometimes taste — even interact — with that non-real being. An actor is a walking, talking puzzle whose carefully-shaped pieces fit together to bring imagination to life, to make fantasy reality, and to entertain and enlighten.

A writer is exactly the same thing. A writer's performance is not live and onstage, however, but live and onpage, a print performance forever ready for that moment when the paper curtain rises.

Welcome to the Psych Ward

The greatest challenge facing both actor and writer is to be both the player and the instrument being played. In other words, actors and writers are professional split personalities.

The basic function of the actor is to perform two jobs simultaneously: objectively bring an imaginary character to life, and subjectively maintain a sense of self as the artist who controls the physical performance. The actor's mind has to share two points of view at the same time and keep them focused, interactive and yet carefully separate and balanced. The actor inwardly draws on all the learned techniques of performance while outwardly displaying only those tangible qualities that support the character.

The job of the writer is that and more. We writers not only have to maintain our sense of artistic self, but we have to do so while *literally* performing every single character in our story. Plus we have to perform all the tasks of the director, producer, casting director, set designer, lighting designer, stage manager, prop master, make-up designer, costumer — and in the case of film and television, we're camera operators, grips, gaffers, script supervisors, Foley artists, location scouts, musical directors, stuntmen, coffee gophers — yeegads, we writers have to do it all!

Yet even with this insane burden, writers have one great advantage over actors — we are spared the pressures of delivering our final product before a live audience. True, we eventually face that Moment of Truth when our carefully crafted words meet the eyes of a reader, but we're usually not present at the time.

If we're lucky.

Artistic Intent

J.D. Salinger once said, "You were a reader before you were a writer." I think it's safe to say that all writers and actors these days were audience members (probably TV watchers) before becoming writers and actors.

Artists of all kinds first *appreciate* art before they attempt to create it themselves. Appreciation usually motivates those first attempts. So both writers and actors know what their audiences expect: entertainment, enlightenment, an experience that will in some way move them or change them, or at the very least, divert them for a few hours.

Both the writer and actor practice their craft with artistic intent — that is, we create because we have some final goal in mind. For the writer, the goal is to tell a story. For the actor, the goal is to bring a character to life in order that a story may be told. Either way, we both have the audience in mind. They are the ones who will receive our efforts. It is for the audience that we practice our crafts in the first place.

There is one important difference to bear in mind here, however. The actor is, in the simplest of terms, an interpreter. Artistic intent for the actor must mesh with that of the playwright. As well, the actor's artistic intent has to mesh with those of his fellow actors (unless he's undertaking a one-man *Hamlet* or something). Even then, the actor still depends on some kind of lighting crew, stage manager, costumers, etc. The key to acting, then, is *interacting.*

Writers, on the other hand, write alone. And we control everything. Our artistic intent is whatever we want it to be. Ah, but as Uncle Ben said to young Spiderman, "With great power comes great responsibility." And a lot of hard brain work. If the key to acting is interacting, the key to writing is *intra-acting.*

We writers do not stand among our characters, we *are* the characters, all of them all at once. We exist inside of them, motivating them across their story stage, as well as outside of them, moving them across the printed page. We writers have to make a constant stream of creative decisions that can tax our imaginations to their limits.

Tools, Techniques and Tricks

Fortunately a wide variety of methods have been developed to aid the creative process. Both the writing and acting art forms have a long history, and in many ways, a shared history. Each form has undergone countless metamorphoses as its practitioners constantly respond to changing society and look for new ways to improve their art.

In this book I am using the terms *Tools, Techniques* and *Tricks* to describe those methods. A *Tool* is an acting point of view, attitude, skill or exercise that can help a writer develop himself in order to better understand himself and thus better understand human nature. Tools help a writer become an artist.

A *Technique* is an acting point of view, attitude, skill or exercise that can help a writer develop plot and characters, block scenes, and compose text and dialogue.

Tricks are the instruments of revision and fine-tuning — acting points of view, attitudes, skills and exercises that focus on critical analysis of the completed work. Tricks help a writer to analyze her work, identify problems and, hopefully, fix them.

Writing + Acting = Playtime

Armed with our new Tools, Techniques and Tricks, the job of writing will become a little easier. But writing should be a joy as well as a job. Like the professional actor, the professional writer (or the writer-in-training and even the *dilettante*) needs to see the craft as a form of play. Cavorting around in Wonderland is one of the reasons why we artists enter the creative arts in the first place, isn't it?

So if there's one prerequisite for this book, it's this: *ya gotta be willing to play.* Actors play all the time. General acting classes hone general skills that focus on both the body and the mind, ridding the actor of inhibitions and freeing his creative spirit. The rehearsal process involves improvisations and other games that lead to personal insights, character insights, and a clearer understanding of how to communicate the plot in question. The purpose of this book is to borrow a variety of those acting philosophies and exercises and present them for the benefit of writers.

Some of the exercises offered are strictly mental: things to think about, objects to study, techniques of inner and outer observation — in other words, things to do while sitting down quietly alone, with a partner or in groups. Other exercises will involve physical play, activities to be done in the privacy of the home as well as some that are best done in public alone, with a partner or in groups. The degree of physicality required varies.

You'll find four kinds of exercises within these pages:

- — traditional beginner exercises I've borrowed from acting without major modifications;
- — traditional exercises I've borrowed and modified to better meet the needs of writers;
- — exercises I've made up that parallel the spirit of the acting profession yet appeal to the more solitary, shy writer-types out there;
- — exercises that I've made up for my own use and now share with you.

There are exercises in this book to suit everybody, as long as you're willing to play. I mean, think about it — why are children so creative? Because they *play.*

C'mon! Let's go make mud pies!

end of sample

For purchasing options, visit BobbiJGWeiss.com.